NOTHING BUT!

NOTHING BUT!

BOOK TWO:

THE LONG ROAD TO FREEDOM

Brigadier Samir Bhattacharya

PARTRIDGE
A Penguin Random House Company

ISBN:	Hardcover	978-1-4828-1475-0
	Softcover	978-1-4828-1476-7
	Ebook	978-1-4828-1474-3

To order additional copies of this book, contact
Partridge India
000 800 10062 62
www.partridgepublishing.com/india
orders.india@partridgepublishing.com

CONTENTS

Dedication

This book is dedicated to my late father Narendranath Bhattacharya and my mother Sova Rani Bhattacharya because it was entirely through their sacrifices, spirit and guidance is what I am today.

Family Trees of the Eight Families

(Principal Characters Only)

1 Sikandar Khan—Muslim Family from Kashmir
First Generation—Sikandar Khan—Wife Zainab Khan—Brother Sarfaraz Khan
Second Generation-Curzon Sikandar Khan—Wife Nusrat Shezadi
Third Generation—Ismail Sikandar Khan3
Fourth Generation—Shiraz Ismail Khan(Adopted Son of Ismail Sikandar Khan)

2 Harbhajan Singh Bajwa—Sikh Family from Kashmir
First Generation—Harbhajan Singh
Second Generation—Gurcharan Singh Bajwa—Wife Harbir Kaur
Third Generation—Daler Singh Bajwa—wife Simran Kaur
Fourth Generation—Montek Singh Bajwa

3 Sonjoy Sen-Bengali Hindu Family from Calcutta
First Generation—Sonjoy Sen
Second Generation—Naren Sen—Wife Shobha Sen
Third Generation—Samir Sen—Ronen Sen—Purnima Sen

4 Apurva Ghosh—Bengali Hindu Family from Chittagong
First Generation—Apurva Ghosh
Second Generation—Debu Ghosh—Wife Hena Ghosh
Third Generation—Arup Ghosh—Swarup Ghosh—Anup Ghosh—Mona Ghosh

5 Haji Abdul Rehman—Afridi Pathan Muslim Family from Peshawar
First Generation—Haji Abdul Rehman
Second Generation—Attiqur Rehman—Wife Nafisa Rehman
Third Generation—Gul Rehman—Aftab Rehman—Arif Rehman—Shenaz Rehman
Fourth Generation—Aslam Rehman—Fazal Rehman—Mehmooda Rehman—

6 Shaukat Hussein—Muslim Family from Calcutta
First Generation—Shaukat Hussein
Second Generation—Dr Ghulam Hussein—Wife Suraiya Hussein
Third generation—Nawaz Hussein—wife Shenaz Hussein
Fourth Generation—Imran Hussein(Shiraz Ismail Khan)

7 Edwin Pugsley—Anglo Indian Family from Calcutta
First Generation—Richard Pugsley
Second Generation—Edwin Pugsley—wife Laila Pugsley
Third Generation—Shaun Pugsley—Debra Pugsley—Sandra Pugsley—Richard Pugsley-Veronica Pugsley

8 Colonel Ronald Edwards—Only son of Roland and Gloria Edwards—British Family from England—First Generation

Chapter-1

The Homecoming

It was in late January 1920, when Lieutenant Colonel Reginald Edwards received his orders to proceed back to India and he was simply delighted and he took the first boat out on 13th February from Tilbury. It was the SS Macedonia, one of the largest troop carriers in the British Fleet and on board was a full battalion of the Manchester Regiment with their officers and families. They were going to India on their tour of duty and many amongst them were young soldiers who had never before set foot outside the British Isles. The next day 14th of February happened to be Saint Valentine's Day and the Captain of the ship considering it to be auspicious, decided to sail out only after midnight. That evening, while Reggie was strolling on the deck, he was pleasantly greeted by two Indian doctors from the Indian Medical Service. They were also returning to India after the Great War.

"Good evening Sir. You remember me. I am Captain DR Thapar. I was the doctor who was generally on duty at the hospital for the wounded Indian soldiers in Brighton and this is my colleague Dr Khan Sahib," said an excited Captain Thapar as he introduced the handsome Pathan from the North West Frontier Province of India to Reggie.

"Well of course I remember you and how could I ever forget. You were the only Indian doctor who had besides treating the patients also had this awful additional duty of cremating and burying the dead," said Reggie as he warmly shook hands with both of them. Both Thapar and Khan Sahib were also delighted. They had found atleast one known good Englishman for company on board the ship for their long return journey back to India.

"But Sir.if I am not mistaken, I think I was told by Captain Attiqur Rehman that because of your war time injury you had been delisted from service, but what makes you return to India," asked Captain Thapar.

"That is absolutely right and my voyage back to India this time is for two very good reasons. The first one is for a noble cause and that is to raise funds and find employment opportunities for our brave Indian soldiers who like me have been invalided out of service and it is also my duty now to try and rehabilitate them. The second reason is somewhat personal, but I might as well share it with you. You all must have heard about late Naik Curzon Sikandar Khan, VC from the gallant Punjabees. Unfortunately, my courageous and old faithful Jeeves from Gilgit is no more. We lost that gallant soldier during the Battle of Loos in September 1915 and once I get to India and as soon as spring is over, I will make my journey back to Gilgit across the high mountain passes to personally hand over the Victoria Cross Medal to his only surviving son Ismail Sikandar Khan. And it will also give me the opportunity to offer my heartfelt condolences to Sarfaraz Khan, the old faithful agency cook and late Curzon Sikandar Khan's uncle and father-in-law and who is now the only other surviving member of his family," said Reggie.

"But what about the boy's mother and I hope atleast she is alive," asked Captain Thapar.

"That is another tragic story because she also died while giving birth to a second child and the second child, a girl did not survive either. And mind you both these tragic events happened during the summer of 1915 when we were fighting the Germans with our back against the wall on the battlefields of France," added Reggie as he took out the Maltese Cross and the gold medallion that was presented by Lord Curzon to the little boy on his birth. When he showed them to both the doctors and told them the old history of the medallion, both Captain Thapar and Dr Khan Sahib were visibly moved.

"I wish I could keep you company during your trip to Gilgit Sir. I believe the vale of Kashmir is very beautiful during spring, but I do not think that will be possible, atleast not till the end of summer because of the demobilization that is still in progress. And moreover having been away from home for so long, I need to spend some time with my family, my friends and my old parents.Nevertheless the journey to Gilgit I believe is very tough and time consuming and with your physical handicap you should be careful not to over exert yourself Sir. After all Gilgit is not some place next door which can be visited anytime of the year." said Captain Thapar as Dr Khan Sahib dug into his pockets. There was pin drop silence for a while till Dr Khan Sahib broke the ice and said.

"By the way Sir do you play cards? I mean do you play Bridge."

"Yes ofcourse I do and I would love to and it would be a good pastime during the long voyage too," said Reggie.

"Well that makes three of us and all we need is to find a fourth player to start the first rubber," said Dr Khan Sahib as he in all enthusiasm took out a deck of cards from his pocket and shuffled it with a flourish. However, finding a decent fourth on board the ship proved somewhat abortive since the only gentleman that they found was a complete novice.But that did not dampen Dr Khan Sahib's spirit.

"Never mind in that case we will play cut-throat Bridge," said the handsome Pathan while inviting Reggie and Captain Thapar to his cabin.

"That sounds great and with today being Valentine's Day, we could all play for love too," added Captain Thapar in good humour.

"No please not just for love, because that will not be proper bridge and it will only lead to gambling. Therefore just for kicks we could keep the stakes low and we could settle for five pence a point," said Dr Khan Sahib who was a keen and avid bridge player.

"Agreed," said Reggie as they all sat down to cut for the deal. Over a few pegs of gin and tonic water or over a glass of chilled beer before lunch the three of them enjoyed a few hours of their cut throat bridge practically everyday. To them it was a good pastime and Dr Khan Sahib who was an expert player himself meticulously maintained the running score at the end of the day in his small pocket diary.

Throughout the long voyage the three of them had found good company in each other and they would often discuss about the consequences of the war and the rapidly changing political situation in India. At times they were also joined by some other British Officers, but once the ship entered the Suez Canal and sailed nearer to the shores of India, the friendship and camaraderie that existed on board between the British Officers and their families with the two Indian doctors kept on diminishing progressively. And once the ship entered the Arabian Sea, the colonial and imperialistic attitude of the Britishers became all the more evident. Finally, when the 'SS Macedonia' finally docked at the Ballard Pier in Bombay on the 7th of March, the two Indian doctors had practically once again become strangers to most of them. The only exception was of course Reggie.

Noticing the change in the attitude of the British officers and their families, an angry Dr Khan Sahib who had spent many years studying and serving as a qualified doctor in England was quite vocal about it as he came down the ladder with Reggie and Captain Thapar. Speaking to no one in particular but to everyone in general he loudly said.

"You know it is indeed a pity and rather sad too that after all that we have contributed and sacrificed in the battlefields of Flanders, Mesopotamia and Palestine, even today we Indians are being treated like dirt in our very own country. Instead of repaying us with love, honour and gratitude, we are still being discriminated and subjugated with draconian laws like those of the recently proclaimed Rowlatt Acts. In fact we are now being treated as if we were criminals and the powers that be have no moral, legal or social justification to thrust such harsh laws upon us."

His impromptu remarks did raise a few eyebrows amongst those Englishmen who were disembarking with them but Dr Khan Sahib was not the least bothered.Reggie was in full sympathy with the two Indian doctors. He hated the colour bar and to compensate for it, he even cancelled his room booking at the Royal Bombay Yacht Club. The RBYC was an exclusive residential club, but it was only for the privileged whites and it did not even include the British boxwallas. Reggie had often stayed there but today he wanted to be with his Indian friends.

"Come on let us all stay the night at the Taj Mahal hotel and since it will be our last night together, we should make the best of it. From tomorrow we will all be on our way to our separate destinations and God knows when we willl meet again," said Reggie as he called out to the coolies to help with the luggage.

"In that case the drinks tonight will be on me. After all I did make a little more than five pounds as my bridge winnings on the voyage," said Dr Khan Sahib.

"Well then that settles it," said Captain Thapar as they piled into the two phaetons with their luggage and made their way to the Apollo Bunder. The magnificent Taj Mahal Hotel on the waterfront built by a noble hearted Parsi was the best hotel not only in India but in the whole of the east.

It was in the 7th Century AD after the crescent and the sword of the Muslims swept through Persia, when the small community of Zorastrians, the devotees of Ahura Mazda from the province of Pars on being threateaned to either convert to Islam or die by the sword together with their holy book of Zevesta sailed out from their native town of Sari and landed at the small fishing village of Nagmandal on the Gujrat coast of India. On being welcomed by the locals to the land of snakes by which the village of Nagmandal was known, they soon established themselves and called it Navsari or their New Sari. Quickly adjusting themselves in their new country, they soon became a community to reckon with. Thus it was in 1863, when Jamshetji Tata's father Nusserwanji Tata and whose forefathers had landed from Sari realized the potential of the real estate business in Bombay. With Mr Premchand Roychand as his partner, Mr Nusserwanji

Tata had registered the Backbay Reclamation Company. Slowly and steadily the acres and acres of land which ran into hectares and hectares from Colaba Point to Malabar Point and which was once an unsavoury rubbish heap was now being transformed by them into prime habitable areas. While the land was being reclaimed, a fifth of the total area as per the contract was being progressively handed over to the Government.

In 1898, after the 10,000 square yard plot on the Apollo Bunder was taken on 99 years lease by the Tata's with an option for renewal for another 99 years, the foundation stone for the construction of their first luxury hotel was laid. On the two and a quarter acres of land with a forty feet deep foundation, Mr Jamshetji Tata with a Hindu draughtsman hired by him as his architect started the construction. Insisting with his architect that the building must be outwardly in Eastern style, Mr Jamshetji Tata also gave him his own ideas. Soon with domes flanking each corner and with the largest one in the centre, it became a landmark for the international traveller. With the technical help from a German firm at a cost of two annas per unit, the hotel was electrified. A laundry with electric irons for ironing clothes was installed. The kitchens and the cellars were fitted with the latest type of cooking equipment. In order to have the best modern day sanitation, Mr Tata provided the visitors to his hotel with luxury Turkish baths. And not only that, he soon had a post office, a resident doctor and a chemist shop functioning from within the premises of his great hotel. Concurrently, the Wellington mews occupying nearly 12000 square yards on the Wodehouse Bridge Road was constructed. For India the Taj Mahal Hotel was a new ornament on the Bombay waterfront and for Asia a new era in the hospitality industry. When Reggie with Dr Khan Sahib and Captain Thapar walked in through the big door of the hotel they were given a thumping salute by the tall well turned out smart doorman. While the three of them were busy entering their particulars in the hotel register, they were pleasantly greeted by Mr Dorab Tata and his pretty wife Meherbai. Both of them were immaculately dressed. Dorab Tata was in a three piece Saville suit with a matching tie and handerkerchief, while Meherbai wore a pink coloured gold embroidered saree in typical Parsee style.

"Welcome to our hotel," said Mr Dorab Tata as he shook hands with all three visitors.

"Good Lord and don't tell me it is you the owner himself. Remember me. We once met, but that was a very long time ago and to be precise I think it was sometime in early 1903. That was when the construction of the hotel was nearing completion and you Mr Tata very graciously had invited me to come for the opening which unfortunately I had to miss due to exigencies of service. Nevertheless, I am delighted to be here today with my two good friends," said Reggie while introducing the two Indian doctors to the elegant couple.

"But tell me how is the magnificent hotel doing," asked Reggie as he complimented the couple on the beautiful décor of the lobby.

"Well touch wood and by the grace of God it did fairly well during the war and now it is doing even better thanks to officers like you who won the war for us. But to be honest during the early teething years we did have some problems soliciting customers to patronize the place. So much so that even on the day of its opening and though we had some hundreds of people gathered outside the gate of the hotel at sunset to watch the spectacle of Bombay's first public building to be lit by electric lamps, the total number of invitees inside who had accepted our invitation and who had turned up as our guests numbered only 17 and that was rather demoralizing," said Mr Dorab Tata.

"Yes it must have been terrible and I can well imagine what you must have gone through, but now the credit must go to you and Mrs Dorab Tata," added Dr Khan Sahib.

"Well in that case and to reciprocate the complement may I invite all of you for a cup of coffee before going to your rooms," said Meherbai as they all sat on the cushioned wicker easy chairs that were neatly laid out in the vast courtyard and enjoyed the hot coffee and Dr Khan Sahib added.

"I must say Mr Dorab Tata that your father was a great visionary and I frankly learnt a lot about him while I was doing my medicine in England. But it is rather unfortunate that he died a year after the hotel was constructed. I also believe he was the first one in Bombay to have his horse drawn carriage fitted with rubber tyres and it amazed the pedestrians on the cobbled road as he silently road by."

"And not only that, in 1901 your father I believe was the first Indian to have a motor car in Bombay and I was told he insisted that his number one stagecoach driver must learn to drive the vehicle himself. And when he was told by an Englishman that the Indian would ruin the car, I believe your father very firmly but politely ticked the man off by replying and I quote 'Please Sir let the Indians learn to do things for themselves'said Captain Thapar.

"Well then let me tell you something more about the great man which I was personally witness too.In October 1899, Mr J N Tata was invited to Simla by no less a person than the Viceroy. Lord Curzon had heard so much about the man's character, public spirit and generosity that he immediately agreed to Mr Tata's proposal of opening an Institute of Science in India and Bangalore was selected as the place. Then during the Great Delhi Darbar celebrations on that New Year's day of 1903, and just two days after Mr Tata' return from the United States of America where he had gone to visit the then foremost Iron and Steel works at Pittsburg Pennsylvania, when I saw him sitting in the arena of the amphitheatre clad in his simple white Parsee dress, I was amazed by the man's simplicity. And mind you though he was by then one of the most prominent Indians, but he had come all the way as a private visitor to the royal durbar. Actually a man like him should have been officially invited, but someone somewhwere down the line had goofed up it seems," added Reggie.

"I must say I am very impressed by your knowledge about the great man and like all of you I too am very proud of my dynamic, enterprising and resourceful father-in-law. For had it not been for him, we would have neither had our first iron and steel works at Jamshedpur, nor the Tata Hydro Electric Company that today provides us with electricity that comes all the way from the waters of the man made lakes at Lonavala and then through the giant pipes under the Duke's nose at Khandala," said Meherbai.

"Yes and that is not all. Let let me tell you something more about the remarkable man. In 1899, when Mr J.N.Tata came to Simla, Major R H Mahon who was an artillery officer and the Superintendent of the Government Ordnance Factory at Cossipore near Calcutta submitted his memorable feasibility report regarding the prospect of manufacturing iron and steel in India. After this was discussed, with Mr Tata, the Viceroy Lord Curzon immediately gave it the desired impetus by making changes in the old stringent rules of mining," said Reggie.

"No wonder the small village of Sakchi in Bihar that is situated on the banks of the Rriver Subernarekha and which literally also means the river with a golden streak has really struck it rich for the enterprising late Mr J N Tata and his equally enterprising family," said Captain Thapar.

"Yes and strangely enough, though the foundation stone for the iron and steel plant was laid in May 1909, but the first iron rod manufactured by the plant rolled out only on 2nd December 1911 while the King and the Queen were on their way to India. And thanks to Mr J.N Tata's vision, what better a gift could they have given to His Majesty on that historic occasion than the good quality iron and steel that was produced at Tatanagar and which subsequently also played a vital roll during the Great War," added Dr Khan Sahib.

"Well now that all of you have spoken so very highly about my dear old late father, I thing it is time that I too said a few good words about him. I can see the oldman smiling at me and putting up his collar in heaven, and he will be very upset if I didn't. Don't you think so Meher," said Mr Dorab Tata in good humour.

"You bet he will darling and it better be something interesting and real nice," added his wife Meherbai as she put some more black coffee into Reggie's cup.

"Alright, let me then relate to you a very interesting incident, and which happened on the day I was to get married to this beautiful better half of mine. It was in 1898, and I was not young either. I was 38 and my wife was only 18. It was also the year of the worst bubonic plague in Bombay and in order to ensure that everyone irrespective of whether he or she was from the girls' side or the boys' side was well protected from the dreaded disease, my father insisted that everybody, male and female, young and old must get themselves inoculated by a Russian doctor."

"That morning when the Russian doctor set up his shop in our Esplanade house, Mr Bhabha, my father-in-law to be and the father of the bride at first would have none it. He did not seem very happy with the idea of being injected by a Russian doctor, but there was no way that he could get away from it either. The Russian doctor who was more popularly known as Professor Haffkine had only recently introduced the system of inoculation against cholers in India, but Mr Bhabha thought that everyone was being made a scapegoat by him. Till some one wittily remarked."

"Oh Bhavaji. It is better to be a scapegoat and remain alive rather than be a dead goat and give a feast to the vultures. And when that remark brought in a round of laughter from those around, the gallant Mr Bhabha promptly presented himself before the Russian doctor," said Mr Dorab Tata with a big smile on his face.Hearing the anecdote Meherbai also wittingly remarked. "'My God had my father refused that inoculation we may have not got married at all and poor Dorab would have probably remained a bachelor the rest of his life."

"Yes maybe and like I am still today," said Reggie as all of them took leave of their gracious host and hostess and went up to their rooms.

It was sometime in early May 1920, that Reggie with the Victoria Cross and the old medallion finally arrived at Gilgit. There was not much of a change to that place ever since Reggie had left that small sleepy townt in 1905 and a heart broken Sarfaraz Khan on seeing Reggie completely broke down.

"This is all that I have been left with Sahib," said the faithful old cook as he pointed towards the six year old Ismail Sikandar Khan who was busy playing with some of his friends outside the Agency Gate.

"Oh my God, he looks a carbon copy of his brave father," exclaimed Reggie as Sarfaraz Khan called out to the boy to come and meet the Englishman. The six year old lad with expressive blue eyes and a sharp nose had till then only heard stories about his father and the kind Englishman, but when Reggie gave him a smile, the little boy promptly did a courteous salaam and came and sat near Reggie's feet. While Reggie patted the boy, he could not hide his emotions and said.

"Don't worry Sarfaraz Khan and do please remember that this boy Ismail Sikandar Khan is not a son of an ordinary man. He is the son of a war hero who was personally decorated with the highest gallantry award of the Victoria Cross by His Majesty the King himself and therefore not only my regiment and I, but the whole British Indian Army is indeed very proud of Curzon Sikandar Khan. And the Punjab Regiment in general and my Battalion in particular have therefore decided to do all that they can to give the unfortunate lad the best of education and opportunity in life. And even Maharaja Pratap Singh and the C-in-C State Forces, Raja Hari Singh with whom I have already had a word on this account are fully in agreement with me. They have also promised to help in whatever way they can," emphasised Reggie as he took out the Maltese cross and the old Victorian medallion, the gift from Lord Curzon and put both of them around the boy's neck. For a second Sarfaraz Khan just stood there in total silence. The memory of the old medallion had brought tears into his eyes. Wiping them away he said.

"That is indeed very kind of all of you, but what will I do if you take him away Sahib. I have nobody else."

"But I am not just taking him, I am also taking you along with him too," said Reggie.'

"But where to Sahib," asked Sarfaraz Khan looking rather confused.

"Well that has all been worked out and you will not be without a job either. Initially we will all go to Srinagar where you will become part of the team that looks after the Maharaja's kitchen in the palace and there you will work as a special cook. You will also be given an independent quarter and while you will be kept fully busy in the kitchen, young Ismail Sikandar Khan will go to school. And it will not be just an ordinary school or a madrassa, but the one that is being run by Mr Tyndale Biscoe and he has promised to take special interest in the boy's initial education and upbringing. And once the boy grows up, he will then be sent to one of the better day school's or to one of the best boarding schools in India and God willing thereafter to college for higher education.And you will not have to worry the least about his expenses, because the regiment and I have promised to take care of everything. Thereafter it will be all in the hands of the lad as to what he wants to become in life. Considering the fact that the Government is now giving commission to Indian Officers on completion of their training at Daly College Indore, it is quite possible that in the near future they may even be sent for training to Sandhurst Military College in England and return home as King's commissioned officers and that is what I will pray for," said Reggie as he affectionately hugged the little boy.

The very next morning, all three of them were on their way to Srinagar. Enroute they did not halt even for a minute at the village of Kanzalwan though it had been rebuilt to some extent. Neither Reggie nor Sarfaraz wanted to bring back the memories of the tragic past to the young boy who in any case had never been there before, though he had heard about the place. On reaching Srinagar, Reggie met Mr Tyndale Biscoe.

"Do not worry Colonel Edwards; I will see to it that little Ismail Sikandar Khan is given all the necessary attention and as far as his education is concerned I will also ensure that he not only excels in his academic subjects, but excels in games and other curricular activities too, and the Biscoe School is indeed proud to get a son of a decorated war hero. Unfortunately he is not a blue blood from a princely family or else after a few years I would have recommended him for admission to the Mayo College at Ajmer," said Mr Biscoe as he smiled at the shy young lad.

"Thank you very much for those kind words and even though the boy is not from a royal lineage, but that does not matter. The boy is now from the lineage of my proud regiment, the Punjabees and we will see to it that he becomes something big in life when he grows up. And if he does well in your school in Srinagar, may be the Regiment will continue to give him additional scholarship for his higher education in England," added Reggie.

"That indeed will be wonderful," said Mr GEC Wakefield, the newly appointed Chief Private Secretary to Raja Hari Singh, the heir apparent to the Kashmir throne. Mr Wakefield had accompanied Reggie to the school that morning and barely had he finished completing the sentence when, Mr Biscoe said.

"Mr Wakefield, please if you do not mind, can I ask you something in strict confidence."

"Yes do please go ahead but I may not have the answer to it right away, therefore do not be disappointed," said Mr Wakefield. Reggie thought that probably Mr Biscoe was going to ask for some additional financial grants from the Maharaja for improving the facilities in his school and was quite surprised when Mr Biscoe in all seriousness said.

"You know Mr Wakefield of late there have been some awkward rumours which of course may not be hundred percent true, but it seems that the old Maharaja is not too very fond of his only nephew Hari Singh. Is that right?'"

That question no doubt took Mr Wakefield with complete surprise and for a moment or two he pondered on how to answer it. Then having realised that both the gentlemen were of pure English blood, he very confidentially told them the truth.

"Yes there is some friction between the two, but nothing to be alarmed about. It is a sort of a love hate relationship between the Uncle and the nephew which at times becomes quite evident at the weekly council meetings. Sometimes with the monologue by his Uncle, the young Prince gets a little restless and he scribbles a note in English on a piece of paper which is primarily meant for my eyes only and then rolls it down the table for me to read. Invariably the message reads 'Have a headache and must leave.'

"Is this a fall out from the 'Mr A' episode in France,'" asked Reggie.

"Now what episode is that," asked Mr Biscoe looking rather surprised.

"Never mind Reverend Brother that may be too much for you to digest," said Wakefield.

"Yes and let us not get involved with the Maharaja's internal palace intrigues and problems," added Reggie as both of them took leave of the clergyman.

While on his way back to the Maharaja's guest house, Reggie decided to call on Colonel D'Arcy Bannerman, the British Resident in Kashmir. While walking along the bund he was pleasantly surprised to meet Arthur Cunningham Lothian, a not too senior officer from the Bengal cadre of the Indian Civil Service.

"What the dickens are you doing up here Arthur and do you remember me?" said Reggie. The two of them had last met sometime in December 1913, when young Lothian with just two years of service was Sub Divisional Officer of Munshiganj in Dhaka district. The place was more popularly known as Bikrampur and it was Reggie who had assisted young Lothian in conducting the flag marches through the streets of Dhaka which was then the Headquarters of the revolutionary Dhaka Anushilan Samiti. The Samithi was a well organized and active group of young Bengali revolutionaries who were determined to throw the Britishers out of Bengal, if not India.As they shook hands Arthur Lothian who was now on deputation as the First Assistant to the British Resident in Kashmir said.

"Of course I very well remember you Sir. I was then just a greenhorn and you also worked as an interpreter in Urdu with the Black Watch Regiment which did most of those flag marches in Dhaka those days."

That evening after a drink or two, Colonel Bannerman then said.

"Arthur tell me with your experience in Bengal, do you really think that those hot headed educated young Bengalees will ever give up violence and submit to the advice of peaceful sathyagraha as is no being spelt out by Mr Mohandas Karamchand Gandhi. And sometimes I really wonder where these hot headed people originated from?"

"Well Sir, as per one of the renowned pundits of Dhaka city and which most believe is true is that sometime in 900 AD, when King Adishwara of Gaur was ruling over Bengal, he brought to Dhaka five high caste Brahmin priests from Kanauj a small town in the United Provinces and requested them to perform certain Pujas or religious ceremonies for the prosperity of his kingdom. These five priests having completed their Pujas married the local women and settled on the eastern side of the mighty river that flows through Dhaka. They had children and they called themselves Barendra Brahmins. And as time went by and after the Moghuls conquered Bengal, some of them converted or rather were forced to convert to Islam. Thus the spoken and written language whether you are a Hindu or a Muslim in that part of the world still remains Bengalee," said Lothian.

"That sounds somewhat convincing, but that could not be the reason for the Bengalis to be so hot headed,"' said Colonel Bannerman as he poured another round of scotch to his guests and sought Reggie's opinion about Mr Mohanchand Karamdas Gandhi.

"Now Reggie I believe you are on your way to Bombay with the specific purpose of meeting this Mr Gandhi who I believe has come all the way from South Africa, and if that is true then may I know the reason why are you so keen on meeting him."

"But that is not abslutely correct Colonel, and I am also going to Bombay to primarily meet some influential and prosperous business people and who could help in contributing funds to the forthcoming Poppy Day which is due in a few months time on the 11th of November. And since I am going to be there in that city for sometime, I have therefore expressed my desire to meet the gentleman who had caused such a hue and cry in SouthAfrica and is now doing the same over here. And Gandhi I am told does wield a fair amount of influence with the business community and I feel that he could be of great help to this good and noble cause. After all the funds to be generated on Poppy Day will be utilized hopefully in India for the benefit of not only those Indian soldiers who sacrificed their lives for the King and Emperor, but also for those who survived the war and sacrificed their limbs and health for the integrity and survival of our Indian Empire,' added Reggie.

On the 16th of July 1920, a retired Colonel Reginald Edwards, called on the frail Indian at Mani Bhawan, a house that was located near the famous Chowpatty beach in Bombay. Sitting with him that day was Subhas Chandra Bose who had only arrived that very morning from England and was on his way to Calcutta. Having stood fourth in the Indian Civil Service open examination that was held in London, Subhas had decided to resign from service and join the movement for Swaraj (Freedom) instead. It was a movement to get total independence for India from the British Raj. Like Reggie, Subhas Bose was also meeting Mr Gandhi for the first time. Dressed in his simple white cotton self made half dhoti, the man who had finally returned to India in January 1915 for good did the traditional Namaste with folded hands as Reggie entered the room, and Reggie having reciprocated in a similar fashion apologised in his good Urdu by saying.

'Please do pardon me Mr Gandhi and I am sorry to have barged in without taking any prior appointment.

'But you do not have to render an apology. In this humble abode everyone is welcome at anytime and I am personally delighted in meeting a British Colonel. But now tell me what brings you here and what can I do for you,' said Gandhi.

The simple man who had humbled General Smuts in South Africa, and who during the war in August 1914 had raised the Indian Ambulance Corps in England, and who in 1917 had gone all the way to Champaran in distant Bihar to fight for the cause of the exploited and poor Indian indigo workers, and who later gave the call for total satyagraha against the imposition of the Rowlatt Acts that had made India come to a grinding halt on the 6th of April 1919 was now India's hope for the future. That afternoon the same very man who was now an apostle of peace and was determined to win India her freedom sat patiently and listened to Reggie as he explained the purpose for celebrating the Poppy Day in India.

"It is indeed a very noble idea Colonel but do make sure that the brave Indian soldier who sacrificed so much on the fields of Flanders and elsewhere during the Great War gets his just rewards, and you must also ensure that the collections made in India are not repatriated for those who are not Indians. Like the colour of the poppy which is red, so is the colour of blood in all human beings and it is irrespective of the fact whether he is an Indian, an Irish, a Scot, a Welsh or a British. My only submission therefore Colonel is that there should be no discrimination just because superficially our colour that of the Indian is generally brown and at times also black. Though I guess a person with a surname like Brown or Black, whether he is residing in India or for that matter anywhere else in the mighty British Empire and if he happens to be that of a white man like you, then he will always be addressed and respected as Mr Brown or Mr Black.But strange is the English language isn't it Colonel. However, do be rest assured that I will pass the message around to the Indian business community and hopefully something good will come out of it for all our brave war veterans," said Gandhi.

"And let me also assure you Mr Gandhi that we are indeed very proud of our Indian soldiers and more so in the army and in my regiment the Punjabees in particular and which is the oldest, and, we do not consider the colour of a soldier's skin. To us who are in military uniform it is therefore of no consequence of whether he is black, brown or white or whether he is a Muslim, Hindu, Sikh or a Christian. To us soldiers they are all the same," said Reggie as he did the traditional Indian namaste with folded hands and took leave of the saintly figure and of the man who was now determined and destined to show India her path to freedom.

When Reggie left the room, Gandhi once more read the letter that Sarojini Naidu had written to him from Duke's Hotel, St James Place London. Though the nightingale and poetess from India was in bad health and specialists thought that her heart disease was in an advanced stage, but Sarojini Naidu didn't mince words while castigating the British.

Addressing Gandhi as 'My dear Friend,' she deplored the stand taken by the British Government on the Punjab debate that was held in the British House of Commons. To her Mr Montague had proved to be nothing but a broken reed. Using her command over the English language, the lady who was an ardent admirer of Joan of Arc and who at the age of 11 made her first speech on that very subject wrote.

'It is in vain to expect justice from a race so blind and drunk with arrogance of power, the bitter prejudice of race and creed and colour, and betraying such an abysmal lack of knowledge about India and her aspirations. And as for you my friend, you have in you all the seeds of true greatness: be great my little child fulfill yourself nobly in accordance with all the profound and beautiful impulses and ideals of your nature-but always remember that you are the symbol of India.' Putting the letter into his pocket, Gandhi wondered whether he would be worthy and capable for the task ahead.

Meanwhile in London, the 11th of November 1920 was indeed a memorable day. It was the second anniversary of the Armistice. Debu Ghosh and Naren Sen standing in the crowd near the Westminister Abbey saw the grand solemn spectacle, when six black horses of the special carriage that carried the Unknown Soldier arrived at its final destination. On the way to the Abbey the carriage had stopped for a while at The Mall, Whitehall where the King unveiled the Cenotaph. From there the Monarch with his three sons, all members of the Royal family, and with his Council of Ministers followed the coffin through the streets till it arrived at the North entrance of Westminster Abbey. Passing through an honour guard that consisted of a 100 recipients of the Victoria Cross, and to the strains of the hymn 'Lead Kindly Light' the coffin made its way to its final resting place. When the coffin reached the west end of the Nave, the King took a handful of the special soil that had been brought from the battlefields of Ypres. Then he stood to attention, saluted and sprinkled it on the coffin. Six barrels of that special earth had been brought so that the coffin of the Unknown British Soldier might lie on the soil where so many of his gallant comrades had laid down their lives for the honour and defence of the Empire.

To the singing of the hymn 'Abide with Me' the coffin was finally lowered to its hallowed place in history. Thereafter, the entire congregation sang Rudyard Kipling's Recessional 'God of Our Fathers.'Finally the Reveille and the Last Post were sounded and the grave was covered by a silk funeral pall and with the Padre's flag above it. Thus came to an end the touching ceremony honouring and glorifying all those nameless soldiers who had sacrificed their lives for the honour and integrity of the Empire. When the massed brass band struck the notes of God save the King, everbody including Naren and Debu stood to attention in the cold outside and sang the national anthem in chorus with the others. It was a touching scene as mothers, fathers, sisters and brothers of those loved ones whom they had lost sobbed and cried. For all of them it was as if the man in that coffin was one of their own kith and kin and he was now being honoured by none other than their grateful King and all his subjects.

The history of the Unknown Soldier began in 1916, when Reverend David Railton whilst serving as a chaplain to the forward British troops in France came across a makeshift grave in a garden at Armentieres. Though it was marked only by a crude rough wooden cross, but on it was written 'An

Unknown British Soldier.' The good reverend priest Railton who had never lost sight of that scene wrote a letter four years later to Mr Ryle, the Dean of Westminster to convey his remembrance of that scene. The Dean recognized the message spoken by that grave in France and this resulted in the Tomb of the Unknown Soldier of Great Britain.

The search for the selection of the soldier who was destined for burial in the Nave at Westminster Abbey began in France. On the night off 7th of November, 1920 the bodies of four unknown British war casualties that were exhumed from the battle fields of Aisne, Somme, Arras and Ypres arrived at St Pol in Northern France. There as they lay in the chapel at St Pol each covered with the Union Jack, Brigadier General L.J. Wyatt the Commander of all British Troops still in France and Flanders selected one at random. The one selected by the Brigadier General became the Unknown Soldier of the Great War, as two officers placed the body in a plain coffin and sealed it, while the remaining three bodies were reinterred in a nearby military cemetery. On the next day the 9th of November, the plain coffin was placed inside the new coffin that was made of oak wood. The coffin had arrived from Hampton Court in England and into the bands that secured the new coffin was inserted a 16th century crusaders sword that was selected from the Tower of London collection. Finally a plate on the coffin was put and inscribed on the plate were the words 'A British Warrior who fell in the Great war 1914-1918 for King and Country.' The coffin was then ceremoniously put on HMS Verdun and escorted by six warships made its way across the straights of Dover to its final resting place in England.When it arrived at Dover, the coffin was greeted with a 19 gun salute. Then six warrant officers from the Royal Army, Royal Navy, Royal Air Force and the Royal Marines bearing the coffin as pall bearers bore the coffin home to its sacred British soil. It was put on a special train and taken to the Victoria Station in London and from there to the Westminster Abbey. For seven days thereafter the Tomb of the Unknown Soldier lay under the watchful eye of a military ceremonial guard, while thousands of mourners filed past to pay their last respects. On 18th November a plaque inscribed with the words 'Greater Love Hath No Man Than This.' was added to the coffin. Thus the body of the man selected by Brigadier Wyatt gave that Unknown Soldier a place of eternal rest in the hearts of mankind.

Chapter-2

India—The Roaring Twenties

While the Unknown Soldier was being laid to rest as an eternal hero in England, in India as the Year 1920 came to a close, the largest number of delegates in the history of the Indian National Congress arrived at Nagpur for their annual meeting.There they gave the clarion call for "Swaraj" and the famous resolution on Article 1 of their constitution read. 'The object of the Indian National Congress is the attainment of Swarajya by the people of India by all legitimate and peaceful means.' When the details of the resolution together with Mr Gandhi's comment that Swaraj would be obtained within a year and more specifically by 31st December 1921 was published as headlines in all the leading dailies of Calcutta, Sonjoy Sen ran with his copy of the Statesman to Shaukat Hussein's house.

"Now you don't have to get all that excited about it, and do please read between the lines too. The Congress has only demanded Swaraj which only means self rule. They have not asked for 'Purna Swaraj' or complete independence, and Gandhi is no fool for he knows that complete independence is rightnow a far cry"

"But I wonder if it is ever going to be possible even to get Gandhiji's version of Swaraj so easily with peaceful means and that too in such a short period of time," said Ghulam Hussein as he brought the two cups of tea with some glucose biscuits on a tray.

"Nothing like Chai biscoot on a sunny winter morning," said Sonjoy Sen while smacking his lips like a child and before taking the first sip.

"And I think Ghulam does have a point in what he has just said because if Gandhiji is planning to achieve it with another round of Satyagraha and that to of the peaceful type that is being preached by him through non cooperation with the British, then the Congress will have to work out an implement an effective control mechanism by which to keep the Indian masses under control, and it should not snowball into a free for all mob violence like it did after Gandhi gave his first call for Satyagraha to protest against the passing of the Rowlatt Bills," said Shaukat Hussein.

"Well I think we will talk politics later and now let me exchange a few notes with your son Ghulam Hussein, our good doctor," said Sonjoy Sen as he dipped a part of his second biscuit into the strong flavoured rich Darjeeling tea.

Well then Dr Ghulam Hussein now tell us what is the latest news from your two lawyer friends in England? I hope they regularly keep in touch with you, or have they also forgotten you as they have forgotten us," added Sonjoy Sen somewhat sarcastically.

"Well Uncle it seems that they are both very busy preparing for their final exams and therefore they may not be getting adequate time to write long letters home,.however, they do send me picture postcards once in a while with a few lines scribbled on it. But more often than not the pictures are either that of the Tower of London or that of a Coldstream Guard in his ceremonial red dress with a huge bearskin cap over his head standing like a statue on duty at the Buckingham Palace," said Ghulam Hussein as his two year old son Nawaz Hussein came crying from inside the room looking for his father. Nawaz was Ghulam Hussein's and Suriaya's first born child and Shaukat Hussein's first grandson. The boy incidently was born in the early hours of the morning of 11th November 1918 and that was a day of thanksgiving and rejoicing in the entire world because his birth coincided with the Germans signing the Armistice agreement in the forest of Compeigne in France that ended the Great War., Sonjoy Sen had therefore promptly nick named him 'Vijay' meaning Victory, and seeing little boy's bad mood, Sonjoy Sen quickly gave him a biscuit and the little boy was soon all smiles again.

"What a damn rogue," said Shaukat Hussein as he took the little boy in arms and kissed his rosy cheeks.

"Now there comes my two young rogues to also keep us company," exclaimed Sonjoy Sen when he saw his two grandchildren Lalloo and Ronen duly escorted by their faithful Oriya servant Dhoni Ram approaching. Lalloo's real name was Samir, but since he was born on the 7th of November which coincided with the birth of The Russian Revolution and was a Red letter day for the proletariat, Shaukat Hussein had aptly nicknamed him Lalloo meaning Red. Naren's second son Ronen was only eleven months younger to his brother Lalloo, but his grandfather Sonjoy Sen always lovingly addressed him as Botcka Babu.

"Come to think of it the two boys have hardly seen their father ever since they were born, so don't be surprised, when their father Naren return's from England and the boys address him as uncle," said Shaukat Hussein jestingly as he called for one more plateful of biscuits for the kids.

While the two grandfathers were busy with their grandchildren, the two young mothers, Suraiya and Shobha each with a pencil and a small notebook in their hands seriously took notes as Hussein Begum Sahiba from inside the kitchen spelt out the recipe for the delicious mutton biryani and then followed it up with a a live demonstration of how it should be cooked in typical frontier style.

"We call this 'Dum Ghost' cooked in rice, but in Calcutta it is called mutton biryani," said Begum Hussein as the men folk got ready to sit down and have a taste of Begum Sahiba's cooking skills.

"Well whatever one may call it, but it simply is delicious and mouth watering," said Sonjoy Sen while complimenting the Begum Sahiba and thanking her for educating his wife Shobha on the finer points of frontier cooking.

While the two young wives, Shobha and Suraiya were busy learning the finer points of frontier food, there was something bigger cooking in the minds of the Congress leaders. After the success of the Nagpur Congress of 1920, the non cooperation movement was now at its peak. And though Tilak was no more, but the momentum for freedom had been maintained. To raise funds, Seth Jamnalal Bajaj donated Rupees one lac to the Tilak Swaraj Fund and the Congress party decided to enlist one crore members and targeted a collection of a similar sum in Rupees for its fund raising. By July 1921, the fund was over subscribed by Rupees 15 lacs and both Naren Sen and Debu Ghosh having recently returned from England as barristers also contributed handsomely towards it.

In early 1921, while Gandhi was working out his strategy for a gradual and controlled movement of non-cooperation with the British masters, the Viceroy Lord Reading with the Vicerene was planning his forthcoming visit to the vale of Kashmir.

What a pity all of us will be going with the viceregal train right upto Rawalpindi and maybe a little beyond, but we will not be allowed to visit Kashmir which I believe is not very far from the rail head," said a dejected Edwin Pugsley as he joined his friends Sonjoy Sen and Shaukat Hussein inside the railway yard for a cup of tea.

'Do not worry. Our time to visit the beautiful valley will also come and that day is not very far since the Congress and the people of India have whole heartedly joined Gandhi's non cooperation movement to get rid of the British," said Sonjoy Sen.

"My bloody foot and do you think the British are bloody fools? You think they will simply keep quiet and give away the fat goose that lays their golden eggs for them so bloody easily? Do you think they are bloody nuts? And do you think the Maharajas and Princes of India and particularly the Maharaja of Kashmir whose princely state is so strategically located will tow the Congress line And if that is your reasoning then you have high hopes man," said Pugsley looking somewhat surprised at Sonjoy Sen's remark.

"Alright we can debate this some other time," said Shaukat Hussein as he diplomatically changed the subject to that of cricket which by then had become very popular in Calcutta.

"Well talking about Kashmir do you remember the first match that was played between the Bengal Gymkhana Club and the Maharaja of Kashmir's team in 1911," asked Shaukat Hussein.

"Of course we all remember.The Bengal Gymkhana Club had only recently been founded thanks to a generous donation of Rs 10,000 that was given by Maharaja Nripendra Narayan of Cooch Bihar, and who by virtue of his contribution was also made the Club's first founder President and the match was also played on the Maharaja's Woodlands cricket ground in Alipur," said Sonjoy Sen.

"Oh yes and I also remember that day particularly well too because I had a bloody ball drinking away that afternoon though the match was more of a bloody tamasha if you ask me," said Pugsley.

"But why do you say that," asked Sonjoy Sen.

"Because during the match not only did I manage to wangle out a few bottles of good chilled English beer at the reduced price of 4 annas a bottle from the Maharaja of Kashmir's make shift bar which otherwise would have cost me 6 annas in the market, but I also went and sat in the VIP enclosure," said Pugsley.

"But how the hell did you manage to do that," asked Shaukat Hussein who was fully aware of Pugsley pulling a fast one.

"Well you see the bar was under an awning and it was just behind the Maharaja of Kashmir's royal pavilion shamiana," said Pugsley as he laughed away remembering the incident.

"Now stop laughing and tell us the truth so that we can all laugh together," said Shaukat Hussein.

"Well you see it was nearing lunch break and with both of you having left for home, I decided to scout around a bit. Looking at the VIP crowd sitting leisurely under the specially erected shamianas, watching the match and enjoying their drinks, I was also tempted and could not resist joining them. Though a chee chee by birth but a whiteskin otherwise, I managed to sneak in. Initially I confidently stood near the bar, and when the big turbaned Maharaja of Kashmir decided it was time for him to go out and bat I quietly took a seat inside the big shamiana.You see it hardly mattered to the Maharaja which team was batting. That was his privilege and he could bat at anytime for any team that he wanted. So while two of the Maharaja's faithful aides padded him up and another two adjusted his batting gloves and a third aide waited to carry his bat, I confidently ordered a beer from the bar. That was the right moment to strike because everyone's attention was focused on the Maharaja's entry into the field. When the Maharaja all gloved and padded and with that huge turban on his small head started walking up to the batting crease, and the band started playing the Kashmir State national anthem, I got my chance. Because by then everyone's attention had been diverted and as the Maharaja while waving out to the crowd made his royal entry into the cricket field, I struck the deal with the barman. And when everyone stood up to cheer His Royal Highness, I quietly smuggled out the four chilled bottles of good English beer and that was that," added Edwin Pugsley feeling mighty proud about the whole affair.

"But how did you manage to hide those big bottles and get away so very easily," asked Sonjoy Sen.

"That was even simpler and all I did was to take off my big coat, put those bottles inside it and like a washerman's load on my back I confidently walked out."

"Trust you and only you could have done a thing like that," said Shaukat Hussein.

"Yes but I paid for them too and in hard cash and it was not just 'muffat ka mal'(gratis)," said Pugsley looking a bit annoyed with Shaukat's comment.

"I am sorry and it was not implied, but tell us how you did like the Maharaja of Kashmir's batting," asked Sonjoy Sen.

"'It was nothing short of hilarious if you ask me and you should have been there man," said Pugsley.

"What do you mean by hilarious," asked Shaukat Hussein.

"Well if both of you are that interested then let me tell you what actually happened. Firstly when His Highness took his guard from the umpire, he was greeted with a spate of salaams by all present both on and off the field. Secondly when Prince Victor Narayan the younger son of the Maharaja of Cooch Bihar who was also captaining the Bengal Gymkhana got ready to bowl the first ball to the Maharaja, the wise umpire cautioned him to bowl only slow deliveries. Thirdly any ball that was delivered with a few lobs outside the off stump and could not be connected by the Maharaja was promptly declared a no ball. Fourthly, whenever the Maharaja managed to connect the ball with his bat, he was greeted with great applause and the umpire immediately signalled a four to the scorers. Fifthly it was only after the tired Maharaja's own individual score on the big black board read 25 runs with six fours and one single to his credit that the gracious Maharaja was persuaded to finally retire not out. Sixtly, when His Highness started his walk back to the pavilion, and the band again played the State's national anthem everybody like dummies again stood up. And finally all this side show only ended when the Maharaja sat down in his special tent to enjoy the smoke from his long water pipe. Now if this was not a tamasha of cricket than what was it," said Pugsley.

"True, but it was not 'gulli-danda' either and maybe because the man was the Maharaja of Kashmir which is so many more times bigger than Cooch Bihar that the royal family of Cooch Bihar felt that they must be show some extra courtesy on the cricket field to him," added Sonjoy Sen.

"Oh come on tell me another one my friend and that certainly was not good crixket," said Pugsley as he lit his tenth cigarette for the day and then walked along the railway track towards the Howrah railway station to buy himself a new packet of his favourite Cavenders navy cut cigarette.That evening over a meal at Sonjoy Sen's house, both friends renewed the debate on Gandhi's non cooperation movement.

"I am afraid that the four stages of non cooperation as spelt out by Gandhiji is fine, but it is not working as planned," said Sonjoy Sen as both Shaukat and he sat down to enjoy the mutton biryani that had been cooked by his daughter-in-law Shobha.

"But what makes you say so uncle," said Ghulam Hussein while appreciating Shobha's maiden attempt at cooking moghlai biryani.

"Well the first stage, which was a call to all the students to boycott all government controlled schools and colleges and for the lawyers to boycott their practices in courts and which is about to be over on 31st March, that I am afraid till now has hardly had any impact on the masses," said Sonjoy Sen.

"But one thing has been definitely improved and that is the spinning of the chakras in the villages and I did some spinning myself, when I went home a week ago," said Sonjoy's wife very enthusiastically from inside the kitchen.

"But I believe in the second stage they are preparing to boycott all British goods and foreign cloth in particular and the plan it seems is to make bonfires of them in public," said Shaukat Hussein.

"But I only hope and pray it does not lead to goondaisn, looting and arson which is very much a possibility unless proper control and restraint is exercised by our so called leaders on the general public," said Shaukat's wife who disapproved of the idea entirely.

"There are also indications that the All India Congress Committee is also very much against the proposed visit to India by the Prince of Wales which is scheduled for the coming winter, and if the Prince does arrive then they intend boycotting him too, and this I have heard from a very reliable source who is also a young active Congressman and a good friend of Subhas Chandra Bose," added Ghulam Hussein.

"All right no more politics please and finish your food first," commanded Sonjoy's wife rather sternly as Shobha came in with another tray full of hot steaming biryani.

"Just one small more ladel full Bouma,(dear daughter-in-law)" said Shaukat Hussein as he complimented Shobha on her cooking and the compliment was loud enough also to be heard by Sonjoy Sen's wife who graciously acknowledged it by saying.

"Please eat to your hearts content Bhai Sahib and there is plenty more inside the kitchen for all of us."

It was in August 1921, that Viceroy Reading with the Vicerene crossed the frontier check post at Domel and entered the Maharaja's kingdom in Kashmir.

"I must say the scenic beauty of this place is simply out of this world," said the Vicerene as she got out of the car and went for a short walk to the nearby pine forest. Seeing a group of young children playing there, she walked upto them, fondled their rosy cheeks and gave them an anna each. All the children were thrilled except for one who simply refused to accept that bakshish.

"What is your name son and why are you shy of accepting it. It is only an anna," said the Vicerene. The young Sikh boy with long hair was about 10 years old and he seemed to be the eldest in the group, but he simply stood there and did not answer.

"Please do pardon my little son," said Gurcharan Singh rather apologetically as Daler Singh hid himself behind his father.

"That is perfectly alright but I hope he is not handicapped in any manner with his speech," said the Vicerene.

"No, not at all Your Excelleny. He was my late father's favourite grandchild, but eversince the boy came to know about the tragic circumstances under which his grandfather died at Jalianwalawa Bagh, he has not reconciled to the tragedy," said Gurcharan Singh.

"I can well understand that," said the Vicerene as she got into the car with her husband and the aide beckoned the driver to resume the journey to Srinagar. It was by chance that Gurcharan Singh Bajwa that day was fortunate enough to meet the Viceroy of India and his wife at Domel. He had come to the border customs check post that morning to collect his weekly demands of rations and stores that had arrived from Rawalpindi. After the death of his father, Gurcharan Singh had also set up a small tea shop near the custom post at Domel for his younger brother Devinder Singh.

Meanwhile at Srinagar, Maharaja Pratap Singh was getting a bit impatient waiting for the Viceroy to arrive as he beckoned the British Resident, Colonel Windham to come a little closer and in his mixture of Hindi, Dogri and broken English jokingly remarked.

"Colonel Sahib please do tell me as to why is the British Government trying to establish a Yehudi or rather a Jewish rule in India?" Colonel Windham taken aback and looking a bit confused at the remark made by the Maharaja simply asked.

"But what makes you say that Your Highness."

"Why it is so simple. First of all the new Viceroy Reading is a Jew. Mr Montagu the Secretary of State and who holds the key to India is a Jew. And now even Mr William Myers the High Commissioner I am told is also a Jew," said the Maharaja as he took another big dose of his favourite opium.

On arrival at Srinagar, when Lord Reading was apprised of the Maharaja's subtle remark about the Jews ruling India, he gripped the Maharaja's small palm firmly and having pumped it vigorously for a couple of times congratulated him for his keen observation. But at the same time he also told him not to comment about this to the Prince of Wales when he arrives in the state during the coming winter season.

On 26th October 1921, at sunset with the massed military band playing the 'Auld Lang Syne,' the battleship cruiser 'Renown' with the Prince of Wales on board sailed from Portsmouth for its long voyage to India and the Far East. While the Prince surveyed the send off from the saluting platform above the bridge, a pretty 20 year old young lady fondly waved out to her sweetheart.

"Well Dicky I wish we could have taken her along too," said the Prince to his handsome and tall naval ADC.

"Not to worry Sir, because she will be joining us in a few months time," said Lieutenant Louis Mountbatten.

Born on 28th November 1901, the pretty lady had only recently met the young handsome naval officer of royal blood while they were both on a cruise on the Vanderbilt yacht. It all started at Ostend in Belgium, when the two went for a long walk on the beach and which was followed by tea at the 'Omar Khyyam', the little seaside café, and a bit of dancing thereafter. Edwina had come to see off Dicky at the docks, and before the ship sailed he reminded her to keep an eye on the time by looking at the little watch that he had presented her with.

Meanwhile at Bombay heeding to Mr Gandhi's call to the people to boycott the visit of the Prince of Wales, even the women of that city decided to show their full solidarity to the movement. On the 16th of November, a day prior to the arrival of the royal visitor, a large number of high born, cultured and educated Indian ladies from all communities congregated at the Marwari Vidyalaya Hall in Bombay. And while the 'Renown' with its distinguished visitor neared the shores of the Empire's jewel in the crown, another Indian jewel in the form of a fiery lady exhorted the gathering of Indian ladies under the auspices of 'The Rashtriya Stree Sabha'(The Peoples Women League) to show their dissent to the royal visitor. Speaking to the ladies inside the Marwari Vidyalaya she not only told the ladies to whole heartedly boycott the entire visit, but she also severely criticized the programme of welcome to the Prince of Wales that was being organized by the Bombay Municipal Corporation on the next day. Presiding over the function, Sarojini Naidu castigated the Bombay Municipal Corporation for their decision to honour the royal guest with an address of welcome at the Apollo Bunder. Later that afternoon, when the meeting was over and the ladies in the audience, most of whom were wearing either homespun Khaddar or Swadeshi clothes with flags in hand slowly marched in procession through the streets of the city, it was an unusual spectacle. And on arrival at the Madhav Bagh Temple, when all the ladies irrespective of their caste, creed or religion offered their prayers for India's attainment of Swaraj, it showed that women power through solidarity in India had also become a force to reckon with.

That very morning, Edwin Pugsley with Shaukat Hussein and Sonjoy Sen had also arrived with the royal train from Calcutta and while they stood watching the strange form of protest by the leading ladies of Bombay, Pugsley very casually remarked.

Say what you may'man, but India does have really beautiful women and today it is like a beauty parade with all of them dressed in white and with no make up at all. In fact they all look simply glamorous without it and therefore it is no wonder that not only the Chee Chees like me, but even the heaven born white skin rulers and the boxwallahs from England are not at all keen to leave India," said Edwin Pugsley.

"That indeed is a very nice complement to the Indian women coming from you Mr Pugsley, but do also remember that under the present circumstances these beautiful Indian ladies with a natural tan also have hot Indian blood in them and which at the moment seems to be at a boil and don't you therefore dare pass any more of your casual witty remarks at them," said Sonjoy Sen.

"Dont be bloody stupid man and how can I ever think of doing that. I do not want chappals and shoes raining on me. But the fact still remains that some of them are simply stunning," added Pugsley as he took out his hip flask to raise a toast to the patriotic Indian women.

'Well then here is to Indian womanhood," said Pugsley as he took a large swig of the neat triple xxx Indian rum from the house of Meakins.

"But since when, and why have you come down from regular Scotch whisky to Indian rum," asked Shaukat Hussein who was not feeling too happy about Pugsley's drinking in public.

"The comedown to tell you the truth has been since the day I produced the fourth child and now the fifth one is also on the way," added Pugsley while having another swig.

"Well if it carries on like this and you keep producing more and more then I am afraid Mr Pugsley you will have to soon switch to the local brew that is commonly known as Tharra," said Sonjoy Sen.

"Yes I guess you are damn well right and my wife Laila too I think now requires a little break and rest because five kids I think is more than enough," added a smiling Edwin Pugsley as he took another quick swig from his handy hip flask.

It was early in the morning of 17th November, when the Prince of Wales came out from his suite of cabins that were normally reserved for Admirals and other VIP's and standing on the deck had his first glimpse of Bombay.

"Well here is to India the jewel in our crown," said the Prince as he lit his cigarette and raised a toast with the glass of juice that he was holding in his hand. The city of Bombay seemed unusually quiet that morning as the battleship 'Renown' approached the serene Bombay harbour. Then at sunrise the British East Indies Squadron and French Cruiser D'Este broke the morning silence as their guns boomed in salute to the royal visitor. At 10 that morning, when the barge carrying the young Prince swung alongside the Apollo Bunder where the Viceroy of India received him with full honours he was giving a rousing applause. Passing through the imposing and historic Gateway of India, a lofty unfinished arch on the waterfront, the Prince finally came and stood on the gold carpet under the silken canopy that was facing the not to large assemblage. While his ADC, Lieutenant Mountbatten stood by his side, the Prince of Wales began his short speech by saying. "I want to grasp your difficulties and to understand your aspirations. I want to know you and I want you to know me."

Though the Prince did not hear any discordant note while his state procession escorted by the scarlet cavalry carried him through the five miles of the flagged streets from the modern European quarter to the Government House at the end of Malabar Hill, but elsewhere in the Indian quarter of the city there was rioting. Although Gandhi was himself in the city that day and had called for a peaceful hartal, but it seems once again that things had gone out of hand. In the evening while the Prince visited the University, the Seamen's Institute and the Royal Yacht Club, armoured cars and armed troops patrolled the old city. That evening on the big maidan as he presented colours to the 7th Rajputs and even witnessed a cricket match between the Presidency and the Parsees, little did he know of the turmoil inside the city?He even made a one day visit to Poona, the city of Bal Gangadhar Tilak and laid the foundation stone first to a memorial at Shanwar Wada for those gallant Mahrattas who fell in the Great War and then to the memory of Shivaji, the founder of the last Great Mahratta Empire and the hero of all Mahrattas. Jeweled and painted elephants saluted the Prince as his State barouche passed with an escort of Gwalior Lancers from the site of one memorial to the other. When the Prince laid the foundation stone with mortar spread from a gold basin for the great Shivaji, the multitude of crowd shouted "Prince ki Jai" and the two Maharajas of Scindia and Kolhapur respectively saluted in obeisance.

And while the ceremonies were in progress, somewhere in the crowd stood Vinayak Godse a peon in the Indian postal service with his 11 year old son Nathuram. And both of them also cheered and clapped as the Prince waved out to the large crowd. In the afternoon the Prince himself a keen sportsman enjoyed watching the horse races at the Western India Turf Club at Poona where he presented cups to the winners and throwing all protocol and formalities to the wind walked among the crowd like any other commoner. Later that very evening the Prince boarded his special train and returned to Bombay.

While the Crown Prince and the future King was busy visiting various parts of India by the royal train, at Bardoli, a place not far from Surat where the British had first landed to establish trade links with India, Mohanlal Karamchand Gandhi now more popularly known as the 'Mahatma' or the Apostle of Peace, sat on a mat and drafted his final ultimatum to the Viceroy of India. The name Mahatma was given to the unassuming little man by the great Indian poet Rabindranath Tagore. With the pressure mounting from the more militant group in the Congress, Gandhi had finally agreed to undertake a mass civilian disobedience movement. In his letter to Viceroy Reading dated 1st of February 1922 he wrote, "Unless the Government's repressive policies were not changed within a week, we will be constrained to start the new disobedience movement with a no tax campaign in the Bardoli taluka of Surat District." was soon after the Ahmedabad Congress of December 1921, that Gandhi had formulated his two pronged strategy for the non cooperation movement. It was a master stroke of both constructive and destructive measures and with both acting in tandem. The constructive measures included, establishment of national educational institutions, village panchayats and courts, abolition of untouchability, fostering of better Hindu-Muslim unity, the promotion of swadeshi and the mass spinning and weaving of cloth in all homes in India. The destructive ones included the boycott of councils, courts, foreign goods, all government aided schools and colleges, bonfires of foreign cloth, renunciation of all titles, decorations and honours bestowed by the British on Indians and disassociation from all official functions. Even though the members of the émigré Communist party of India led by Mr MN Roy from Tashkent had sent their good wishes advocating that the poor workers and peasants of India were hungry and that they should be led on to fight for the betterment of their conditions, Gandhi was not impressed. For Gandhi had made it very clear that the entire movement was to be guided only by the policy of truth and his principle of non violence. He wanted the Khalifat and the non cooperation movement to also move hand in hand, but when the government through its policy of repression declared both the Khalifat movement and the Congress as unlawful bodies and banned all public meetings and processions, the battle lines were drawn and Gandhi began his movement by returning to the Viceroy the title of Kaiser-i-Hind which he had received for his war services. He had now decided to strike back at the British and with all the forces that he could command.Meanwhile in Calcutta on the morning of Christmas Eve, Subhas Bose too had called for a complete hartal and for the boycott of all British goods. It was in protest of the Prince of Wales visit to the Empire's second city, and Debu Ghosh had also joined him.

"Let the young blue blooded Prince of Wales realize that we mean business," said Debu Ghosh as he tried to persuade his friends Naren Sen and Ghulam Hussein to join the movement.

"I think we should wait and see. After all, the young Prince cannot be blamed for the immature actions of the Viceroy and his Council," said Naren.

"I agree, but we should not be just mute spectators either, while the Prince enjoys his damn Christmas week parties in Calcutta," said Debu Ghosh feeling somewhat disappointed at the poor response from his two bosom friends. Though a young practicing barrister, Debu Ghosh had by now come under the strong influence of Gandhi and his call for civil disobedience. He had also become an active member of the Congress party and a strong ally of the young firebrand from Bengal, Subhas Chander Bose.

"Well the decision is entirely yours, but on the 27th of December I am definitely going to be with my friend Subhash and his mentor CR Das and if required we will peacefully court voluntary arrest," said Debu as Edwin Pugsley the royal train driver walked in with a Christmas cake.

"Well folks it is party time again and I have specially come to invite all of you my dear friends for a Christmas Eve cum house warming party at my newly acquired two bedroom flat on Kyd Street which is off Chowringee and. I expect all of you to be there with your wives at 7 PM sharp tomorrow, and I am sorry for the short notice," said Edwin as he handed over the freshly baked plum cake to young Naren Sen

"Thank you for the cake, but I am sure that could not be the only reason for the party?" said Sonjoy.

"Yes you are right and another reason is that I was one amongst the very few with whom the young Prince shook hands with when we arrived at Calcutta from Patna," said Pugsley very proudly.

"And pray what is he like?" asked Ghulam Hussein.

"Well the guy is quite a chick and like me he loves to smoke too," said Edwin as he lit one of his own Cavenders navy-cut cigarette.

"But what does he look like? I mean is he tall and handsome like most of the princes that children read about in story books," asked Naren rather enthusiastically.

"Though every inch a royal prince, but he certainly is not tall and the total number of inches from head to toe is nothing much to rave about either, but he is handsome alright and he is full of charm too and absolutely informal in his ways. So much so that he even invited me for the races this coming weekend," said Edwin with his usual confidence of mixing fact with fiction and while reminding all of them to come for the house warming the next day.

'Thank you for the invitation and I cannot vouch for the others but I am definitely going to be there minus my better half though to guzzle your good whisky," said Debu Ghosh.

The small but comfortable flat on Kyd Street was elegantly decorated with a colourful christmas tree, a small manger with Mother Mary and the infant Jesus inside it, and it was well lit with candlesticks. There were colourful paper buntings all along the newly painted walls as Edwin with his beautiful wife Laila, their eldest son the 10 year old handsome Sean, their two lovely four year old twin daughters Sandra and Debbie and one year old Richard in his mother's arms stood at the door to welcome their guests.

Debu Ghosh was the first to arrive and was elegantly dressed in a three peice suit, a black bow tie and with a dunhill pipe in his mouth, and that evening he looked every inch a Brown Sahib. Being the first guest, Debu also took great pleasure in presenting the Christmas gifts that he had so thoughtfully brought for each member of the Pugsley family.

"But why did you have to spend so much money. Just one small gift for the entire family on this holy night would have been more than sufficient," said Laila while appreciating the beautiful filigree work on the silver broach as Pugsley fixed for Debu and for himself a real large scotch with ice and soda.

"Cheers to our friendship and a merry Christmas to follow," said Pugsley as the two clinked glasses. A few minutes later and before the other guests had arrived, Pugsley quietly took Debu to a distant corner and softly whispered to him.

"I am not going to discourage you Debu, but a dear friend of mine from the special branch of the Police at 14, Elysium Road who is primarily responsible for monitoring political dissent has categorically mentioned to me today at the races that they will leave no stoned unturned if Mr Subhas Bose goes ahead with his political hartal against the Royal visit. And that as you can see could mean a couple of month's atleast inside the Alipur jail for him and maybe for the others too," said Pugsley.

"Thank you for the early warning, but knowing Mr Bose's resolve, the young tiger from Bengal will never ever give in," replied Debu very confidently as he walked across to the makeshift bar and added a little more soda to his already stiff double scotch whisky.

On the 27th of December, 1921 Subhas Bose stuck to his resolve. He courted arrest and was taken to the Lal Bazaar Police Station and was sentenced to six months imprisonment. At Alipur jail he was put in a cell next to his guru and mentor, Mr CR Das. Maybe because of Pugsleys influence on his police friend from 14, Elysium Road that Debu Ghosh was not booked that day.

The last week of December in Calcutta was a very hectic and enjoyable one for the young Prince of Wales. With great pride he opened the beautiful Victoria Memorial that was named after his great grandmother. He also presented the Viceroy's Cup to Mr Goculdas whose horse 'Roubaix' had won the main event. He also witnessed an open air historical pageant that was staged by the Hindus and Muslim communities of Calcutta and saw the poor of Calcutta being fed on the great Maidan. He also unveiled the imposing war memorial, and in addition attended the customary dinner and dance parties at the Government House in Calcutta, while young Subhas Bose languished in the Alipur jail.

"Where are you off to now," said Sonjoy Sen as Debu all dressed up in a spotless white khadi kurta pyjama, with a wollen jacket tied around his waist, a white Gandhi cap on his head and a small suitcase and bedding in his hand came to say goodbye to his in-laws.

"I am off to Bardoli in Gujarat," said Debu very proudly showing off the invitation that he had received from Vallabhai Patel, another aspiring lawyer who had also now whole heartedly joined Gandhi's movement.

"Do remember you have a wife and children," said Naren's mother as Debu touched her feet to do the traditional Hindu pranam and took leave.

It was on the morning of the 5th of February 1922, when Debu arrived at Bardoli. The place was a beehive of activity as Gandhi and his followers waited for the reply to the ultimatum that Gandhi had sent to the Viceroy on the 1st of that month. Then suddenly everything changed that night, when unconfirmed information started trickling in about a massacre of some Indian policemen at a place called Chawri Chaura in the United Provinces.

"Where the hell is that place and why it did have to happen now," said a visibly angry Vallabhai Patel while asking for more authentic information regarding the circumstances of that terrible tragedy. A few days later Gandhi too was furious when he came to know the real truth.It seems that on the morning of the 5th of February at Chawri Chaura, a small village in the Gorakhpur District of United Provinces and not far from the Nepal border, Bhagwan Amit a pensioner had led a well organized body of volunteers and marched through the village picquetting and protesting against the sale of liquor and the rise in food prices. Bhagwan Amit was only following Gandhiji's call for non cooperation in a peaceful manner, when the local police on orders from their superiors arrested him. He was picked up and taken to the police station. There inside the police station while he was being beaten up, the crowd standing outside steadily grew in numbers and demanded his immediate release. Soon the entire village had surrounded the police station and when despite their persistent demands to let their man free fell on deaf ears, the angry villagers threatened violent action against the entire police force that were inside the chowkey. When the police force saw the huge menacing crowd demanding the release of Bhagwan Amit, they panicked and opened fire on the hapless unarmed villagers. When the angry mob saw their own kith and kin being shot at, they burnt down the police station, roasting alive all the 22 police personnel who were trapped inside. Shocked by the incident that Indian policemen were burnt alive by his very own people, Gandhi addressed the Congress leaders who had assembled at Bardoli with a heavy heart. There was pin drop silence as Debu Ghosh sitting in one far corner of the room heard what Gandhi had to say.

"Gentlemen let me remind you that only a few months ago my strictures were violated in front of my very own eyes when on 17th November, the Prince of Wales landed in Bombay. That day I had called for only a peaceful hartal, and a boycott of British goods, and would have been glad if our people were arrested and taken to prison like lambs to the slaughter house. But they rioted, the police resorted to firing and precious lives of our very own people were lost. I personally resorted to three days of fasting to atone for it. That day 'Swarajya' stunk in my nostrils and today because of Chawki Chaura it stinks even more. I am therefore proposing and requesting that as members of the Congress Working Committee we pass a resolution strongly condemning the inhuman conduct of the mob at Chauki Chaura and suspend all mass disobedience movement forthwith."

There was a buzz in the air when Gandhi the man who at the Nagpur Congress promised to free India in 12 months spoke those last few words of discontinuing with the movement. On the 12th of February, after the resolution was passed, a sense of demoralization started creeping into the Congress. When Debu Ghosh returned to Calcutta he looked every bit a dejected man.

"But tell me why are you all the time sulking," asked his wife Hena as Debu with his two sons Arup aged 5 and Swarup aged 3 years sat down quietly for his first home meal after a gap of more than a fortnight.

"It is nothing very serious, but all the same I am not in agreement with Gandhji's decision to call off or suspend the entire mass civil disobedience movement which had picked up such good momentum. But now everything will be back to zero," said Debu as Hena brought some more of the freshly cooked hot fish fries from the kitchen for him and her children.

"If you ask me frankly I think you should simply quit all this tamasha of politics and Swarajya and concentrate more on your profession seriously.Because tomorrow if they also lock you up like they have done to Subhashda, who will bring up the children?" added Hena sounding rather agitated.

"Do not worry about that because the British will have to think twice before putting me inside. After all I am a lawyer and I know how to play the game too," said Debu Ghosh very confidently.

"And if they do lock you up my dear brother-in-law, it may not be in the luxury ambience of the Alipur jail, but more likely at the Cellular one in the Andamans,' said Naren as he walked in with a bowl full of prawn curry that was specially prepared by his mother for Debu's home coming.

"Now why do you always have to come up with such awful comments," said Hena while admonishing Naren Babu for his lack of concern for her and her children.

"I am sorry, but I was only joking," said Naren as he lovingly fondled the cheeks of the two little boys and helped himself to a fish fry.

Gandhi's decision to suspend the mass civil disobedience movement did have its effect on some of the more important leaders and their followers and Debu was no exception. The British seemed very happy as reports of Gandhi's influence in the party started waning.

"I think the people of India have now started losing confidence in the man for abandoning the civil disobedience movement," said the Viceroy confidentially to some selected British members of his Council in order to seek their opinion. And strangely enough on the 10th of February 1922, two days before the Congress resolution was passed at Bardoli, in Delhi, Dickie the handsome young naval lieutenant and an ADC to the visiting Prince of Wales proposed to his lady love.

The beautiful Edwina had landed in Bombay in January where she was received by Lieutenant Colonel and Mrs Carey Evans, the Viceroy's personal physician. After a quick cup of tea at the Royal Bombay Yacht Club and escorted by the Carey's she took the evening train to Delhi. Edwina was a personal guest of the Viceroy and while Dickie was busy accompanying the Prince, young Edwina sat in the sun enjoying Delhi's winter and played the only gramophone that was in the Prince's room. Some times she even danced by herself while listening to her favourite Kalhua Blues. The very next day after her engagement and accompanied by her fiancé, the young handsome Louis Mountbatten, she joined the Prince's party for the foundation stone laying ceremony of the India Gate. The massive stone structure when completed would be a fitting memorial to those Indian Army personnel who were killed in the First World War. Standing a few paces away and on special duty as the medical officer for the Indian contingent at the ceremony was Captain Attiqur Rehman, and a few paces behind the Prince's party, stood retired Lieutenant Colonel Reginald Edwards.Because of his proficiency in the Urdu and Hindi languages, Reggie had been selected as a standbye intrepreter to accompany the Prince of Wales for his forthcoming visits to Peshawar, Jammu and Dehradun. Once the ceremony was over, Reggie took Attiqur to one side and remarked that one day when it will be fully ready the name of Naik Curzon Sikandar Khan, VC would also shine in eternal glory on this beautiful monument. Meanwhile as soon as Mr Edwin Lutyens the chief architect got busy showing Edwina his final master plan for New Delhi, Attiqur Rehman introducing himself to both of them proudly said.

"Sir you may not aware, but there are already seven Delhi's that were made and ruled by previous Kings and rulers of India and most of them came from outside. Now let us hope that atleast this eighth Delhi or New Delhi as it will now be called brings hope, happiness and freedom to all those who belong to this sacred land." And having said those words, Attiqur Rehman closed his eyes and offered a prayer to Allah.

That is indeed is a good patriotic thought Captain and I will also pray that in the not too distant a future the Empire's jewel in the crown should atleast be given dominion status, if not full independence," said Edwina.

That was indeed very kind of you to say so Madam and let us hope that it is done peacefully and not through violence," said Captain Attiqur Rehman as he smartly saluted the pretty and charming young Edwina and escorted her to the waiting carriage.

"See you on the 19th, Sunday at the colour presentation ceremony and which will be followed with the finals of the Ratlam Cup," said Reggie as he waved out to Attiqur Rehman.

On Sunday morning, the Prince of Wales after presenting the colours to the 16th Rajputs surprised the entire audience and the parade participants by giving his first maiden speech in Urdu.

"Hats off to the charming sporting Prince," said Reggie while leading the applause and a few minutes later, Reggie with Attiqur Rehman were on their way to the Polo ground.

"Whom are you cheering today?" asked Reggie as they looked for their seats in the shamiana.

"Well I think this is going to be a real touch and go affair because both the teams have the same goal handicap and are equally well matched too. However, I will put my money on the Rajputs of Jodhpur," said Attiqur confidently.

'Well good luck to you my friend, but my hunch is that the Sikhs from Patiala will bag the Gold Cup this time," added Reggie as they both took their seats under the colourful shamiana.

The Ratlam Cup was the ultimate in polo in India and today's match was going to be the most prestigious polo match that would be played in the presence of the Prince of Wales who was himself a very good polo player and the chief guest for the occasion. It was not just between the Sikhs and the Rajputs, but between the two princely states of Jodhpur and Patiala, and more aptly between Sir Pratap Singh of Jodhpur and Maharaja Bhupinder Singh of Patiala. Attired in their princely best, with shining swords in emerald studded scabbards by their sides, some fifty Princes from various States of India waited for the game to begin. From the moment the bugle sounded, the thundering of hoofs shook the polo field as the rival teams played the game at a blistering pace. It was a game of five chukkers, but by the end of the third the Patiala team was leading by 3-0. At this point a desperate Sir Pratap of Jodhpur went up to his team and gave them some sound advice and some pep talk too it seems. Because as soon as the fourth chukker started, the Jodhpurians having put on the heat they scored a few goals thereby reducing the margin. By the time the fifth and final chukker was about to end the score stood level at 5 goals each. There were still three minutes for the final whistle and by now everybody was on his feet, including those in the grandstand. Everybody, including the Prince of Wales and the Viceroy were bouncing on their seats and senior officers from the Indian Civil Service, British Governors from the various Provinces, elderly Judges from the judiciary, the royal Indian princes were all shouting and yelling like school children as the two teams fought it out sportingly. Probably the tension was too much for Sir Pratap Singh who was the only one who kept sitting quietly on his chair. And then with only seconds to go for the final whistle, when the Jodhpur team scored the winning goal, Sir Pratap's face lit up in sheer ecstasy, while the hugely built Maharaja Bhupinder Singh shook his head in disbelief. When the Prince of Wales looking smart but school boyish in his riding kit with a scarf round his neck and a sporting a golf cap over his head got up to give away the prizes, a round of applause greeted him. When he finally handed over the coveted Ratlam Gold Cup to the Captain of the winning Jodhpur team, the huge crowd of spectators cheered and clapped and Sir Partap nearly collapsed with joy.

Immediately after the Polo match was over, Reggie took the train to Lahore. He had to oversee the military pensioner's camp and the camp for the war veterans that was being organized in connection with the Prince of Wales visit. On arrival at the pensioner's camp Reggie was pleasantly surprised to find young Captain D R Thapar from the Indian Medical Service on duty there. Captain Thapar had been detailed as the medical officer in charge of the pensioners' camp and he had gone about the task very meticulously indeed.

"You are looking rather smart today Captain," said Reggie as he complimented Thapar on his newly acquired ceremonial uniform that the young doctor had specially got made in honour of the royal visit.

"Yes Sir, but this including the sword has cost me a bloody fortune and I am still learning how to salute with it," said Captain Thapar in good humour.

"Well just for dress rehearsal let's have you saluting me with it right now," said Reggie as they heartily shook hands.

The camp held nearly 3000 miltary pensioners and they were mostly from the Punjab and the North West Frontier Province. They were the guests of the Government and for them not only a proper reception centre and living areas were established, but there was also an adhoc equipment department that had been set up for them. The department's responsibility was to properly and correctly equip and kit all those pensioners who were in need of uniforms and other accessories and it also included a medal issuing section. Some of the pensioners and medal winners of the Great War from Reggie's own Punjab Regiment were delighted to see their veteran Commanding Officer and that evening with Reggie as their chief guest when they gathered around a bonfire and over a few tots of rum talked and joked about their exploits in France, it was like good old times.

The Prince of Wales who always had a soft corner for the Indian soldier was delighted to meet the pensioners and the war veterans. A few of them were now well into their eighties and nineties, but they all stood erect and saluted the Royal Prince. Each one of them it seems had some interesting story to tell, and the Prince listened to them most patiently. One had only a half medal of the China war which he said was given to him by his good commanding officer in appreciation of the good work that was done by him as a non combatant, because in those days non combatants were not entitled to any medals. An old bearded man very proudly also displayed the sword which was presented to him by none other than Lord Roberts, the first Commander-in-Chief of the British Indian Army. Another displayed a piece of paper on which his dying company commander had signed his name with the blood oozing out of his wounds. The Prince shook hands with all the Viceroy Commissioned Officers, some of whom were Honorary Lieutenants and Honorary Captains. He also took intense pride in kissing the sword that was presented to the veteran Indian sepoy by Lord Roberts and requested for a photograph of the letter written in blood. When the Prince of Wales bid his final farewell to all of them, one could see the compassion and gratitude in his face. He was indeed very deeply touched.

While the Prince of Wales was busy visiting Lahore, Reggie arrived at Jammu as part of the advance party. The Maharaja of Kashmir, Maharaja Pratap Singh had initially started the construction of a new building at Jammu which would have housed the Prince of Wales, but the project fell through at the last moment when plague broke out in the city two months before the Prince's arrival.To show the Prince and his entourage the true worth of Indian hospitality and grandeur, the Maharaja had therefore constructed a city of tents on the plains of Satwari, four miles from what was now the 'Forbidden City.' It was complete with modern sanitation, electric lighting, telephones and even paved roadways ornamented with beds of flowers.For the formal banquet a lofty building of brick had been especially erected, but the Maharaja did not like it and had it brought down at the last moment. Instead, two spacious and luxurious tents, lined with silk carpets were combined together as a drawing room and a dining room for the royal guest. Though the visit would be just for 27 hours, the lavish setting of the place only confirmed to Reggie the desire of the Indian rulers to entertain the Crown Prince and the heir to the British throne regardless of the expenses being incurred. That was not all. In order to exhibit to the Prince and his entourage the craft and culture of his Kingdom, a mini market for a day was set up to display carpets, shatoosh shawls, woodwork and carvings on walnut wood, papier mache from the valley. There were also little shops with silver and devil charms, necklaces of jade and other precious stones, and jewellery in silver and gold from the far reaches of Leh and Ladakh. It was like a mini bazaar and there was even a large contingent of Tibetan monks who were brought especially from the lamasery at Hemis near Leh to perform the traditional Lama dance that only they can perform while wearing those curious masks and dancing to the sounding of the gongs. Though the Prince's apartment in a wooded park adjoining the tented camp was in a plain modern building, but it was lavishly furnished. The carved walnut wood furniture in all the rooms was specially made for him by the best craftsmen of Srinagar. The Maharaja's own camp which was a mile from the temporary tented city of Satwari was no less in luxury. From the durbar tent hung age old precious shawls, the roof was supported on pillars of inlaid silver and on the low canopied dais were placed two silver thrones with arm rests of gold in the form of crouching lions.

On the very day of his arrival at Jammu, Reggie formally called on the Maharaja who was delighted to see him and he quickly fired off a few interesting questions.

"Now just tell me honestly Colonel Reginald Edwards. What is the young handsome Prince of Wales like? I mean is he friendly and easy to get along with or otherwise? What are his preferences for food and wines? Does he like cricket and outdoor sports like shikar and cross country riding?"

"To tell you the truth your Highness, the Prince is a very informal and an absolutely unassuming person and he will eat and drink whatever you give him. He is also an all round sportsman and would have loved to play cricket with you, but there is unfortunately no time for such luxuries," said Reggie.

"Then in that case he will definitely make a very good King," said the Maharaja as he helped himself to another doze of opium. And as he was about to put it in his mouth, Prince Hari Singh his nephew who was now the Commander-in-Chief of the Kashmir State Forces and heir apparent to the Kashmir throne entered the royal tent and smartly saluted. He was in full ceremonial uniform having come back after the full parade dress rehearsal.

"The review parade for the Prince of Wales rehearsal has gone off very well your Highness and now that Colonel Reginald Edwards is also here with us, I would strongly recommend that once the parade is over, young Ismail Sikandar Khan, son of late sepoy Curzon Sikandar Khan, VC should also be presented to the Prince of Wales," said the young heir apparent.

"Yes and why not after all he is the son of the only Victoria Cross winner from your Kingdom and I am sure the Prince will be delighted, and as the future King and Emperor he must also be made aware of.your contribution of soldiers in the the Great War. And though the late Curzon Sikandar Khan was not from the State Forces, but nevertheless he was your loyal subject from Gilgit," added Reggie.

"Alright so shall it be but how do we get him here from Gilgit at such short notice," said the Maharaja.

"But he is very much here with his uncle and the boy is now 12 years old and goes to the Biscoe School in Srinagar. And since the school is now closed for the winter vacations, the young lad is presently helping his uncle Sarfaraz Khan in the royal kitchen, and thanks to Colonel Reginald Edwards, Sarfaraz Khan is a great cook and an expert on all Kashmiri dishes, both vegetarian and non vegetarian," said Prince Hari Singh.

"Then where is the problem. Let the young lad be presented after the parade, but do see to it that he is presentable too," said Maharaja Pratap Singh as he adjusted his turban and took another small doze of opium.

On the morning of the 2nd of March, 1922, the viceregal train carrying the royal visitor from England steamed into the Satwari railway station and as soon as he stepped out from his saloon, 31 guns boomed in royal salute. Welcomed by the Maharaja, the Prince inspected the Guard of Honour that was presented smartly by the contingent from the Maharajas 3rd Kashmir Rifles, which was also known as the Raghunath battalion. Thereafter, the Prince of Wales escorted by the Maharaja's Bodyguard Cavalry in their colourful red ceremonial uniforms drove to his apartment. Later in the evening, when he drove to the Maharaja's camp, all the State elephants with their colourful howdas were lined up all along the route. After the formal banquet, the Prince witnessed the fireworks and was entertained with the folk dances of Kashmir which also included the Tibetan devil dance.For the return journey to his apartment, the Prince of Wales rode on the largest elephant and for a while he found it be great fun till he noticed a stupid junior police officer half drunk dancing and singing away local Dogri songs in front of his mount. The Prince was not in the least amused and disgusted with the man's antics he looked at his ADC and said "What does that bloody fool want?" When Reggie heard that, he immediately moved across and quietly pushed the man aside and made sure that the culprit did not surface again.

Early next morning, the Prince of Wales reviewed the parade of the Maharaja of Kashmir's elite forces. Commanded by their own

Commander-in-Chief, the young Prince Hari Singh, and the troops gave a superb display of arms drill. This was followed by the presentation of medals to serving and retired World War veterans. When the presentation of medals was over, Reggie sought special permission from the Maharaja to present young Ismail Sikandar Khan to the royal guest. It seems that the Maharaja's protocol department had once again conveniently forgotten to include it in the programme.

"But it is never too late and moreover the boy's father was a Victoria Cross holder from the King's Indian Army and I am sure the Prince will be delightedto meet the young lad," pleaded Reggie.

"Well then go ahead and have it done fast," said the Maharaja.

Young Ismail Sikandar Khan smartly dressed in a new white shirt, a grey woolen pant, and a new blue blazer with a tie to go with it stood motionless for a while with his head down till the Prince of Wales lovingly put his arm around the boy and asked him in simple Urdu.

"Now tell me son do you go to school?"'

Feeling nervous in front of so many distinguished people, Ismail Sikandar Khan kept quiet and did not answer.

"Yes Sir, he does and he goes to the Biscoe School that has been founded and run by the Reverend Mr Tyndale Biscoe in Srinagaer," said Reggie as he introduced the veteran missionary to the Prince.

"That is very good indeed and incidentally I was there on that day in France when my father, the King Emperor pinned the Victoria Cross on the gallant soldier. We were on the ambulance train that was carrying my father who had been badly injured after he fell off from his mount. And though Curzon Khan probably knew that he had no hope of survival, the gallant sepoy looked so very happy and contented when he received that honour, and he actually smiled at all of us in appreciation, but unfortunately the doctors could not save him. To honour the sacrifice made by the young sepoy, I would therefore like to make a humble request to the Maharaja and to Colonel Reginald Edwards. I have also been told that the regiment to which he belonged, the gallant Punjabees has voluntarily and willingly committed themselves to do all they can for the good upbringing and education of the young lad and that is also very laudable. As you are aware in a few days from now I shall have the honour of opening India's first military school for young boys at Dehradun and it is going to be an institution par excellence and it will be called The PWRIMC, the Prince of Wales Royal Indian Military College and I will personally be more than delighted if a seat is kept reserved for the son of that gallant soldier provided he qualifies for admission to it when eligible. Therefore in order to give him a fair chance may I request Reverend Mr Biscoe to do his very best and prepare the lad accordingly please?'

Though a Prince by birth, one could feel the sincerity and compassion in the man's heart as he saluted the Victoria Cross that was around the boy's neck. And while the others cheered there were tears of joy in Sarfaraz's eyes as the charming Prince of Wales the beloved Edward to his family got into his saloon at the Satwari railway station for the next leg of his journey to the North West Frontier Province.The very fact that the future King and Emperor of India had expressed his wishes and desire that Ismail Sikandar Khan should be admitted to the very military school that would soon bear his royal title was something that he had never even dreamt of. And while the young Prince of Wales looked forward to his visit to one of the most sensitive and dangerous areas of the British Empire, there were rumours in the bazaars of Peshawar that he might be killed. Therefore in the very early hours on the morning of the 4th of March and while it was still dark, Haji Abdul Rehman on a tip off from a reliable source rushed to the local CID office at Peshawar. He had heard from another source too about the plot to assassinate the Prince of Wales.

" Huzoor it will be a shame if it happens and the Pathan's code of conduct of hospitality must not be allowed to be violated," said an agitated and visibly moved Haji.

"But how authentic is your source?" asked the Deputy Superintendent of Police somewhat angrily, and not feeling to damn happy about the information at that unearthly hour of the morning.

"Allah Kasam Sahib. It is very authentic and I have no any reason to lie. The fact remains that the royal train will steam into Peshawar station a few hours from now and we cannot afford to argue or waste time. It seems that someone has been paid a sum Rupees one thousand to do the job and the Prince's life is in real danger."

On hearing those words, the Deputy Superintendent immediately sat up on his chair.

"Well in that case we simply cannot take any chances and I must report the matter immediately to my superiors," said the Deputy Superintendent as he thanked Haji for the tip off and rang up e his immediate boss.

"Yes I agree we cannot take any chances, but at the same time we must also step up the security and the vigilance, both at the railway station and along the selected route of the Prince's entry into the city," said Mr John

Maffey, the Chief Commissioner of the North West Frontier Province to the Senior Superindent of Police.

"But that may not be good enough Sir and it will be better if we change the route," said one of the senior staff members from the Chief Commissioner's secretariat.

"That is no doubt a practical solution, but it must be kept a closely guarded secret till the procession with the Prince arrives safely at my bungalow," said John Maffey.

While the well armed selected police vigilance squads in civilian clothes scouted for their prey along the original route through which the procession was to pass, Chief Commissioner Maffey with the Prince and his entourage safely made it back to the Commissioner's bungalow through the back streets of Peshawar. And once the Prince was safely ensconced within the four walls of his bungalow, Mr John Maffey felt very proud and relieved indeed. But during lunch when the Prince came to know the real story he was not one bit pleased or impressed.

"You mean to say I am only worth Rupees one thousand in this country and that the assassin was to be paid only that measly sum to throw a bomb at me, and had I been told about this earlier, I would have gladly accepted the challenge," said the charming Prince as he looked through the four day programme that would now take him to the Khyber and the Malakand Passes during his stay in the North West Frontier.

Next morning after attending service at the St John's Church, the Prince motored across the plain to the Jamrud Fort, which guarded the southern exit of the gorge. It was a beautiful bright morning with not a speck of cloud in the sky, and while the piercing cold wind swept down the narrow valley, Haji Abdul Rehman with other Afridis from the nearby mountain villages squatted for hours on the road waiting to have a glimpse of the royal Prince. Finally when the Prince's convoy with his armed escorts passed by on their way to the Khyber Pass, Haji Abdul Rehman stood up and did a traditional salaam. He was happy that the Pathans code of conduct to honour a guest had not been violated. Atleast till not yet.And while the Prince of Wales was enjoying his visit to the Frontier, the British authorities in India with the blessings of the Viceroy were finalizing their plans to arrest Mr Gandhi.

'This to my mind is the right time to arrest that man and charge him with sedition. His popularity as a leader of the Indian masses after his withdrawal of the Satyagraha movement following the heinous crimes at Chauri Chaura is on the wane and it is time to act now," said the Viceroy to his Council members. And while the firm date for Gandhi's arrest was still being debated and finalized, the Prince of Wales enjoyed his visit to the Malakand Pass and later as the personal guest of the Commander-in-Chief India, General Rawlinson at Rawalpindi, when he also met another contingent of the First World War veterans he was more than delighted.

On the 10th of March, Gandhi was arrested at Ahmedabad and his arrest as correctly visualized by the Viceroy did not evoke much response from the Indian masses. However, in Calcutta on the next day, a visibly upset Debu Ghose while sitting with his friends Ghulam Mohammed and Naren Sen over a cup of coffee at the College Street Coffee House discussed the pros and cons of the Viceroy's action.

"This has no doubt made the Britishers smile, but let me see for how long they will keep smiling. This is nothing but their game plan to sideline our great leader so that he languishes for a longer period in jail and his disobedience and Satyagraha movements dies a slow natural death. But my young colleagues and I in the Congress will never let the Mahatma down," said Debu Ghosh as he lit one more of his current favourite brand of 'Passing Show' cigarette.

"But strangely there has been no protest movement worth the namee against his arrest," said Naren.

"That is true no doubt and come what may I am off to Ahmedabad and if the Mahatma's trial is held there then believe you me it will be a very sensational one, and I would'nt like to miss it," said Debu Ghosh.

But what are the charges and are they so damn serious to warrant a trial?" asked Dr Ghulam Hussein whose knowledge about law understandingly was not all that good.

"Well if you are really keen to know about the gravity of the charges then let me give you the full background to it. You see while at Ahmedabad Mr Gandhi had been writing regular articles in 'Young India.'It is a magazine published by his good friend Shankerlal Banker and in which he has been castigating the British rule in India left right and centre. To the British, three such leading articles during the past six months were found to be highly provocative, and they now feel that if the trend is allowed to continue then the very existence of the British administration in India could be at stake. The first article "Tampering with Loyalty" appeared on 29th September last year. This was followed by "The Puzzle and its Solution" which was published in the issue dated 15th December and then came "Shaking the Manes "which appeared recently on the 23rd of February, just over a fortnight ago. And this last one it seems has really shaken the British authorities also. As per their interpretation, all three articles were bringing or attempting to excite disaffection towards His Majesty's government established by law in British India and this according to the Englishman was a very serious offence punishable under Section 124A of the Indian Penal Code," said Debu while ordering for another round of that special freshly ground aromatic coffee that only this particular coffee house could produce.

"In other words Ghulambhai the man is being charged with sedition," said Naren.

"So if he is found guilty how many years can he get?"' asked Dr Ghulam Hussein.

"Well it could be anything upto 6 years rigorous imprisonment," said Debu Ghose.

"Will they send him to the Andamans? asked Ghulam Hussein.

"I do not know, but with the Prince of Wales still around, I do not think they will be that foolish to even think about it," said Naren.

On the 13th of March, Debu Ghosh arrived at Gandhi's ashram in Ahmedabad and offered his services as a junior lawyer for the trial that was now scheduled for hearing on the 18th of March.

"That is indeed very kind of you young man but I don't think I will need a lawyer at all," said Gandhi as he put an arm around Debu's shoulder and thanked him for the offer. None the less, Debu stayed back at Ahmedabad to witness the historic trial.

On the day Debu Ghosh arrived at the Sabarmati Ashram, the same afternoon of that historic day of 13th of March 1922, the young Prince of Wales arrived at Dehradun to open The Prince of Wales Royal Indian Military College. The place chosen was the old Princely Rajwada where not very many years ago stood the Imperial Cadet College for the Princes of India. Now it was a military educational institution for only a few selected boys with the main criteria being that the boy must not only have the right level of education and aptitude, but his parents too must be diehard British loyalists. By the time it was formally declared open by the Prince of Wales, the college was already functional. Just ten days earlier on 3rd March, the Prince of Wales had laid the foundation stone of another military school at Jhelum. This was a brainchild of Major OH Radford of the 13th Frontier Force Rifles who was the first Commandant of the Army School of Education, when it was established in Belgaum in 1921. Major Radford strongly felt that good schools were also required for the sons of serving, retired and deceased ex servicemen not only as a means of recognizing the services of these veterans, but also to give to their young boys a military oriented education in order to make them a good source of quality manpower in the ranks. Thus with the solid backing and supporting funds that were made available by King George the Vth, the ruling King, two such schools were established in Punjab. One was for Muslim boys at Jhelum and the other for the Hindus and Sikhs at Jullunder. Since the King himself had issued the warrant for their establishment, they were therefore named King George's Royal Indian Military School.

Edwin Pugsley the royal train driver stood quietly in one far corner as the Prince of Wales escorted by Colonel J L Houghton, the tall six foot three handsome Commandant from the 11th Sikhs made his way to inspect the cadets who were standing in line.

"I think they should have atleast given the Prince a pair of stilts under his trousers or a specially made pair of high heeled boots or else they could have had someone of his own height and built escorting him for the inspection. Because whatever you say on such a historic occasion like this, the combination of the very tall with the not so tall at all does look a bit funny and it reminds me of those pictures from Gulliver's travels which is the only book that my mother sometimes read to me," said Pugsley.

"May I suggest that you please keep your comments to yourself because the Prince of Wales is not someone to be joked about and moreover he is a royal guest in our country and must be given due respect," said Shaukat Hussein somewhat angrily.

"I am sorry I did not mean any disrespect to our future King, but the fact remains that he is not a guest at all. Afterall India is part of the British Empire and the Prince is officially visiting the jewel in the empire's crown and one day he will rule over us too," added Pugsley.

"All right we get the point," said Sonjoy Sen as he with Shaukat Hussein very diplomatically took Pugsley to one side. Both of them were afraid that Pugsley with his crude sense of humour may drop another brick and it could be detrimental to their own careers, As it is all three of them were now on the verge of retirement and it could affect their gratuity and pension.

Sergeant Major Gorman from the Durham Light Infantry, a beefy figure with waxed moustaches had for the past couple of days drilled his cadets well. But during the inspection, when Cadet Thimayya from Rawlinson Section who was very much taller than the Prince lowered his eyes to have a good look at the royal visitor, Pugsley felt pity for the boy. And then when he saw the anger in the Sergeant Major Gorman's eyes he remarked.

"After God Save the King today lets hope God saves the boy too!"

For the second part of the programme, Edwin Pugsley felt indeed very proud of himself and his old school as he kept clapping and shouting hip hip hooray when the gracious Prince presented the King's colours to The Lawrence Royal Military School, Sanawar. It was in recognition for the service rendered by the boys of the school who fought in the Great War, and it was the first such school outside England to receive such a grand royal patronage.

That very evening the Prince as the guest of Sir Harcourt Butler, the Governor of the United Provinces arrived at Gajraula to witness the semi finals and finals of the prestigious Kadir Cup. The cup was the blue riband of pig sticking competition in India and it was being held in a camp that was not far away from Meerut where in 1857 the Indian sepoys had led the mutiny against the British Raj.

Colonel Reginald Edwards who was also very fond of this sport after having visited the old bungalow in Meerut where he was born also arrived at the camp next morning. At the old bungalow in Meerut he did not find anyone from the old guard and felt sorry when he was told that the old faithful gardener Hariram and his entire family had drowned in the River Jamuna when their boat capsized midstream in a thunderstorm a few years ago. They were on the way for Hariram's eldest grand daughter's wedding.

That morning in the camp Reggie felt miserable thinking about the tragic accident. However, in the afternoon while waiting for the Hog Hunter's Cup to begin, and in which the Prince of Wales himself was taking part on 'Bombay Duck,' a horse that belonged to Capt West of the Royal Horse Artillery, the cheering and shouting by a small group of spectatators led by an elderly man who looked more like an Englishman attracted his attention. The man was acting as a bookie and was taking bets from all and sundry but only on 'Bombay Duck' and he was giving odds at five to one for the horse to lose.and he seemed so very confident that Reggie too decided to place his small bet on that same very horse.

'Bombay Duck is good for a meal any day, but it is not going to be Bombay Duck's day today," kept shouting the bookkeeper as Reggie took out a one rupee silver coin from his purse and as he was about to hand it over to the bookie, he found that the bookie was non other than the Anglo-Indian engine driver.

"My God I just cannot believe that it is you Mr Pugsley who has been crying himself hoarse, but what makes you so confident that 'Bombay Duck' will lose,' said Reggie as he handed over the money to him. Seeing the smile on Reggie's face, Pugsley immediately shouted for Sonjoy Sen and Shaukat

Hussein and both of them were delighted to meet the retired British officer who was now working for the welfare of the Indian soldiers. The last time they all had met was on 23rd December 1912 at Delhi, when a bomb was thrown at Viceroy Hardinge during the formal handing over of India's new capital at Delhi and that was nearly a decade ago.

"But tell me what makes you so damn cocksure that 'Bombay Duck' will lose," asked Reggie once again.

"For the simple reason Sir that the rider of that horse is none other than the future King and Emperor of India and being young and a great horseman, he just cannot lose," said Pugsley very confidently while accepting the wager.

"But stupid man with the odds that you are offering you will surely end up as a pauper if Bombay Duck really loses," said Shaukat Hussein who had no idea whatsoever on what the Hog Hunter's Cup was all about.

A while later, when the sound of a bugle was heard and which heralded the start of the race everybody was excited. And a few minutes later as all the horses galloped towards the victory stand, Pugsley seeing the excitement just could not control himself anymore.

"Come on Bombay Duck give the rest of the pack the royal bloody fuck," shouted Pugsley as the Prince galloped away in style and finished lengths ahead of all the others and Pugsley nearly fainted with joy. He just could not believe his eyes and when the Prince was presented with the cup, a delighted Pugsley with all the winnings in his pocket aptly remarked.

"Well I guess gentleman it always pays to be patriotic." And he was not very wrong because most of the punters given the odds of five to one by him had put their bets on Bombay Duck to lose and it won. But at the same time in Ahmedabad the frail man and a lawyer by profession who was now known as the 'Mahatma' was also gearing up to tell the British what patriotism was all about.

At 6 pm on 17th March, 1922 after the Prince of Wales unveiled the Baluch War Memorial at Karachi, the 'Renown' set course for the Far East. The very next day on the 18th of March the great trial of Gandhiji at Ahmedabad began and within a few hours it was all over, and by evening the learned judge had also pronounced the sentence. Sitting under the dim lantern light in his dingy room at the Sabarmati Ashram, Debu Ghosh wrote a detailed account of the historic trial to Barrister Naren Sen, his dear childhood friend and brother-in-law.

"Dear Naren,

What I write today may well take quite a few long pages and it will definitely take another day atleast for me to do full justice to it and finish it. Therefore, before my thoughts desert me, let me narrate to you what Gandhi had to say at his own trial. And all I can say is that the man is simply a genius."

"It was exactly at the dot of twelve in the afternoon today the 18th of March 1922, when Mr CN Broomfield of the Indian Civil Service and the District and Sessions Judge entered the courtroom and took his seat, and I was fortunate to find myself sitting behind a galaxy of India's freedom fighters, both men and women. There was Kasturbhaji, the wife of the prime accused with the ever smiling and witty Mrs Sarojini Naidu seated next to her. A few chairs away were another two charming ladies, Mrs Anasuyaben Sarabhai and Mrs JB Petit and with the learned Mr Madan Mohan Malviya and a few others keeping them good company.".

"There was absolute pin drop silence, when Judge Broomfield entered the courtroom. When Mr Gandhi's name was called out and he entered the court room, the learned judge himself rose in respect from his seat. Seeing his example all the others followed suit. It was indeed a rare courtesy shown to the Mahatma by the distinguished judge and that to an Englishman from the heaven born service."

When Mr Broomfield read out the charges against the Mahatma and asked. 'Mr Gandhi do you plead guilty or do you claim to be tried.' Without batting an eyelid Mr Gandhi looking frail in his homespun khadi loin cloth simply smiled and said. "I plead guilty your honour."

For a few seconds there was a din in the courtroom as we all waited for the Judge to give his verdict, but Mr. JT Strangman, the Advocate General together with Rao Bahadur Girdharilal, the Public Prosecutor for the Crown insisted that the full procedure should be followed. They wanted the honourable Judge to take into account the circumstances for the occurrences of rioting and killing that had occurred in Bombay, Chauri Chaura and at other places before passing the sentence and to this the Judge readily agreed."

"Thereafter the learned Judge respectfully asked Mr Gandhi if he would like to make a statement before he announced the judgment. Gandhi was not even defending himself and there was a twinkle in his eye as he thanked the Judge for the privilege. Then began his historic statement punched with facts and at times laced with sarcasm and bold honesty that shook not only the courtroom that afternoon, but one that might well also soon shake the mighty British Empire and this is what he said, and I have tried to put it down in verbatim in as much that I could remember and from whatever notes that I could take down in my limited short hand during the trial," wrote Debu Ghose while continuing with his letter of what Gandhi had to say.

"Milord, let me first endorse the learned Advocate General's remarks. For what he has said is absolutely true. I have no desire to conceal from this court the fact that to preach disaffection towards the existing system of government has become almost a passion with me. He is even more right by stating that my preaching of disaffection did not commence with my connection and with the publication of my articles in Young India, but that it commenced much earlier and it is my painful duty to admit before this court that yes it did commence much earlier."(You should have seen the face of the learned Judge and the Advocate General when he concluded that last sentence. They were simply stupefied. Now to continue further)

"Milord it is thus a painful duty which I have to discharge knowing the responsibility that rests on my shoulders. I therefore wish to endorse all the blame that the learned Advocate General has thrown on my shoulders in connection with the occurrences at Bombay, at Malabar and at Chauri Chaura. Thinking over these things deeply and sleeping over them night after night, it is impossible for me to disassociate myself from the diabolical crimes of Chauri Chaura or the mad outrages of Bombay. The Advocate General is also quite right in saying that as a man of responsibility, and a man having received a fair share of education and having had a fair share of experience of this world, I should have known the consequences of my acts. I know them. I know that I was playing with fire. I ran the risk and if I was set free I would still do the same. I have felt it this morning that I would have failed in my duty, if I did not say what I said here just now" (Once again you should have seen the faces of Judge Broomfield and the Advocate General Mr Strangman when Gandhi concluded that last sentence. Whereas the judge was an embodiment of calmness like that of a true heaven born, Strangman's face was like that of a hangman.)

You have to excuse me now my friend and I will continue later with the letter after I complete my routine evening duty at the ashram. The duty is in the common kitchen and the dining hall and it is nothing strenuous. I have only to help the others to serve the evening meal to the men in the ashram and then clean up the kitchen." It was around 10 at night, when Debu Ghose got back to the unfinished long letter and he continued from where he had left of.

"Though there is a ban on smoking here, but I am having one like a thief in my small little room. This is primarily to get back to my thoughts on today's sensational trial. Therefore, coming back to where I left off, here is what the great Mahatma had to say further and I quote."

"Milord, I wanted to avoid violence because that is the first article of my faith, but it is also the last article of my creed. But I had to make my choice. I had either to submit to a system which I considered had done an irreparable damage to my country, or incur the risk of the mad fury of my people bursting forth when they understood the truth from my lips. I know that sometimes my people have gone mad and I am deeply sorry for it. I am therefore here to submit not to a light penalty, but to the highest penalty. I do not ask for mercy. I do not plead any extenuating act. I am here therefore, to invite and cheerfully submit to the highest penalty that can be inflicted upon me for what in law is a deliberate crime, and what appears to me to be the highest duty of a citizen. The only course open to you as the Judge is, either for you to resign your post, or inflict on me the severest penalty if you believe that the system and the law you are assisting to administer are good for my people. I do not accept that kind of conversion. But by the time I have finished with my statement you will have had a glimpse of what is raging within my breast to run this maddest risk which a sane man can run. I owe it perhaps to the Indian public and also to the public in England, to placate, which this prosecution is mainly taken up, that I should explain why from a staunch loyalist and cooperator, I have become a non compromising disaffectionist and non cooperator. To this court I should say why I plead guilty to the charge of promoting disaffection to the Government established by law in India.'

"It is now getting fairly late. Moreover there is hardly any oil left in the hurricane lamp. The flame is quivering like the British rule in India and hopefully like this lamp that will also soon be extinguished for good. I will continue with the letter at the break of dawn with the hope that there will be a better tomorrow for all of us. Till then a very good night to you," wrote Debu Ghose as he lit one last cigarette for the day and went to bed.

That night Debu Ghose hardly slept. His thoughts were torn between what would happen to India if Gandhi was kept behind bars for a full six years and who would lead the mantle to free India from the British yoke. He remembered that as a young student he had sided with the extremists like Bal Gangadhar Tilak, Aurobindo Ghose, his brother Barindra and such other like minded people and now wondered if that was the real answer to freedom.

Early next morning Debu went for his routine early morning walk on the banks of the Sabarmati River. Sitting by the riverside he did his morning meditation and having invoked the blessings of the rising sun as it came up on the horizon, he sat under a tree to finish the long letter.

"Dear Naren,

This is the second part of my long letter to you regarding the sensational trial. Today is 19th of March and just a day before the trial commenced I believe that the Prince of Wales sailed away from Karachi on his battleship 'Renown.'. It seems rather ironical that while the future King and Emperor of India is sailing away further east and in royal style on the battleship 'Renown,' a frail Indian in loin cloth is languishing in a jail. Maybe he is probably thinking about his next move to give battle to the British peacefully whereby he will be more renowned I guess in the not to distant future. Now let me continue with the court proceedings. Mr Gandhi then gave a flashback to his life and this is what he said and I quote."

"Milord, the man whose public life began in troubled weather in South Africa in 1893 and who as a man there discovered that he has no rights because he was an Indian. The very man who when the Empire was threatened by the Boer challenge, had voluntarily raised an Ambulance Company for the British Army and who had served in several actions that took place in the relief of Ladysmith. The man who in 1905 and 1906 at the time of the Zulu revolt had raised a stretcher bearer unity and served in it till the end of the rebellion, and for which he was awarded medals, and was even mentioned in dispatches for gallantry. The same man in 1914, when the war broke out against Germany raised a volunteer Indian Ambulance Corps in London consisting chiefly of resident Indian doctors, Indian students, and whose contribution was valued by the authorities? The man who appealed to the Indians to become soldiers and fight for the British Empire and who was awarded the Kaiser-e-Hind gold medal. And that very same man today is being accused of sedition and of waging war against the King and Emperor? The same man who in spite of the forebodings and grave warnings of friendship with his own colleagues and friends at the meeting of the Amritsar Congress in late 1919 and despite what happened at Jalianwala fought for cooperation and support of the Montagu-Chelmsford reforms with the hope that the British authorities and the British Prime Minister in England would redeem his promise to the Indian Muslims and heal the wounds caused to the Punjab is being tried for being unpatriotic. In all these efforts at service,

I was actuated by the belief that it was possible by such service to gain a status of full equality in the Empire for my countrymen. But now all that hope was shattered. The Khalifat promise was not redeemed. The Punjab crime was whitewashed. Most of the culprits were not even punished. Some were even rewarded. The man now realized that those reforms were only a method of further sucking India of her wealth and of prolonging her slavery. Let me have the honour to tell this honourable court that Section 124 'A' under which I am happily charged is perhaps the prince among the political sections of the Indian Penal Code designed to suppress the liberty of the citizen."

"Milord, affection cannot be manufactured or regulated by law. If one has no affection for a person or a system, one should be free to give the fullest expression to his disaffection, so long as he does not contemplate, promote, or incite violence. But if mere promotion of disaffection is a crime then I consider it a privilege to be charged under that section. I have therefore endeavoured to give in the briefest the reasons for my disaffection. I have no personal ill-will or disaffection against any administrator and much less against the King Emperor, but I hold it to be a virtue to be disaffected towards a Government which in its totality has done more harm to India then any previous system. India is less manly under the British rule than she ever was before. Holding such a belief, I consider it to be a sin to have affection for the system. And it has been a precious privilege for me to be able to write what I have in the various articles tendered in evidence against me. In fact, I believe that I have rendered a service to India and England by showing in non-cooperation the way out of the unnatural state in which both are living. In my opinion, non-co-operation with evil is as much a duty as is co-operation with good. I am here, therefore to invite and submit cheerfully to the highest penalty that can be inflicted upon me for what in law is deliberate crime, and what appears to me to be the highest duty of a citizen. The only course open to you, as the Honourable Judge and the assessors, is either to resign your posts and thus dissociate yourselves from evil, if you feel that the law you called upon to administer is an evil and that in reality I am innocent. Or to inflict on me the severest penalty, if you believe that the system and the law you are assisting to administer are good for the people of this country, and that my activity is, therefore, injurious to the weal."

"When the Mahatma ended his long submission or rather statement with that last hard hitting sentence of British injustice versus fairplay as quoted above, Judge Broomfield looked at Gandhi with admiration and then after a little pause the learned judge in all humility and probably even in pain said and I quote."

"It is impossible for me to ignore that you are in a different category than any other person I have tried or likely to try. Nevertheless it is my duty to sentence you to six years of imprisionment. If however, his majesty's government should at some later date see fit to reduce the term, no one will be better pleased than I."

"The learned Judge was probably caught in a catch 22 situation, but all the same we all appreciated his magnanimous gesture. With the trial having ended with a six years sentence in jail for the Mahatma, I guess we will now have to wait for his next calculated move. I am sure that even from behind the high walls of the British jail, the Mahatma will have the British administration soon running in more circles. I intend leaving for Calcutta in a couple of days from now and therefore more of this and other news when I return home. It is Sunday today and all post offices are closed. However, I intend posting this at the railway mail office with the hope that you will receive it before I arrive," concluded Debu Ghosh as he made his way to the railway station.

During the first week of April, while the Prince of Wales with his ADC, Lieutenant Mountbatten and party were on the high seas for their visit to the Far East, Edwina as the guest of Viceroy Reading and the Commander-in-Chief India, General Rawlinson visited Kashmir, the North West Frontier including the Khyber Pass. For her return journey to Bombay, Edwina boarded the Frontier Mail at Rawalpindi. The train was commonly called by the Britishers during the long hot summer months in India as the heat stroke express and as she was about to get into her first class reserved compartment, she was surprised to see Captain Attiqur Rehman standing with his family on the platform.

"Don't tell me all these lovely boys are all part of your family," said Edwina as she smiled at them and took the youngest Arif in her arms.

'They sure are maam but what we desire now is a little girl," said Attiqur Rehman while introducing his wife Nafisa to the young and beautiful Edwina.

"On that score I must say that you are absolutely right because without a girl no family is really complete," replied Edwina.

Since the other two boys, Gul Rehman and Aftab Rehman who were in school had their summer holidays, the family had therefore decided to spend it in Mussorie, a lovely hill station near Dehradun. And in the bargain this would also give Captain Attiqur Rehman and Nafisa the opportunity of visiting the newly opened PWRIMC. Attiqur was keen that all his sons when eligible should try for admission into it. When the train stopped for a long halt at Lahore, Nafisa joined Edwina in her compartment to keep her company for a while. Edwina was feeling so very hot that she had removed her dress and was sitting inside the big ice tub that had been placed in her reserved compartment and she only had her petticoat on.

The heat must be terrible for you I know but what you need to be really careful about is the hot breeze blowing outside which we in the local language strangely call it the 'loo' and that is what gives a person the dreaded heatstroke and it could be fatal if proper precautions are not taken in time. Therefore do not open the windows at all and keeping drinking lots of water." said Nafisa. Little did Nafisa know then that the beautiful Edwina would one day come back to India as Vicerene and with her husband Dicky would preside over the partition of the country?

The non cooperation movement and his strong resolve to get India her independence at all costs but without violence had now brought Gandhi to the forefront of the national struggle. The Gandhian era had now started in right earnest in India's political history and he was now the leading light to get India her much desired freedom. The lawyer, who at the bidding of his political guru Gopal Krishan Gokhale had returned to his motherland had from the very first day when he landed in Bombay on 9th January 1915, resolved that India must free herself from her bondage and poverty. With the passing of the Rowlatt Act, the once war time recruiting sergeant of the British Empire had now turned into a rebel. After Lokmaniya Tilak's death in July 1920, Gandhi had become the most dominant leader of the Congress, but with Gandhi now in jail and the non-cooperation movement withdrawn after the horrific Chauri Chaura incident, the wave of nationalism had started also waning. This also created differences between the Congress leaders compelling men like Motilal Nehru and CR Das to breakaway and form their own Swaraj Party.

Born on 23rd July 1856, Bal Gangadhar Tilak had been described by the British as 'The Father of Indian Unrest' and quite rightly so. Swadeshi, Swaraj (Self Rule), Boycott and National Education, these were the four sacred words preached by Tilak and 'Kesari' the paper edited by him had become his mouthpiece. In 1897, the British imprisoned him for more than a year on charges of instigating the people to rise against the British Government through his columns in the 'Kesari,' but on being released Tilak the teacher and lawyer by profession had become Tilak the politician and as he stepped out of the Yerwada jail on Deepawali day in 1898, he was taken in procession through the streets of Poona and it was he who in 1906 had first formulated the non cooperation movement against the British masters. Addressing the Indian National Congress in 1907, Tilak charged the alien government of befooling the public and for ruining the country. He called for the boycott of British goods and resistance to British rule which he termed was the most powerful political weapon for the Indians. He did not want the Indians to become clerks and remain so as willing instruments of our own oppression in the hands of an alien government. For writing the article titled 'The Country's Misfortune' which condemned the attitude of the British towards the young Indian revolutionaries and the cruel treatment that was being meted out to them in the various jails, Tilak was charged with treason. He was arrested on 24th January 1908 and on being sentenced to six years imprisonment was exiled to a prison in Mandalay, Burma. Though the man who thundered that 'Swaraj is my birthright' and whose very slogan had inspired millions of Indians had passed away on 1st December 1920, time had once again come for young revolutionaries to surface on the lines of what Tilak had preached.

"Yes Swaraj is our birthright and we shall have it any cost," said Sachindranath Sanyal soon after Tilak's death as he spelt out his ideas for a new revolutionary party to a handful of his colleagues during a secret conclave that was held somewhere in Northern India. But by the time he could muster the required volunteers there was trouble for the British in the North West Frontier.

In 1923, while the country lay rudderless with Gandhi in prison, Afridi outlaws in the North Western Frontier Province became active against their British masters and a spate of kidnappings and killings of British families and officers were now on the rise. Attiqur Rehman who had only recently been promoted as a brevet major was on duty at the military hospital in Kohat when in the early hours of the morning of 14th April, the dead body of Mrs Ellis the wife of Major A J Ellis, the officer on General Staff at Kohat District Headquarters was brought in for postmortem. She had been brutally murdered by a gang of Afridis, while her husband Major Ellis was away on temporary duty. At around two o'clock early that morning five Afridis had daringly broken into the bungalow which was next door to the Flagstaff house and in the heart of Kohat Cantonment. Mrs Ellis and her 17 year old daughter Molly were asleep in their respective bedrooms when the Afridis armed with knives entered the house. It seemed that they had initially planned to kidnap Mrs. Ellis, but she being a light sleeper on hearing the unusual noise in her room had woken up. Her daughter Molly who had

had several rides on her favourite pony 'Brandy' the previous evening was fast asleep in her bedroom. It was not till Molly heard her mother's repeated cries for help that she finally got up and in her pyjamas ran to her mother's rescue. When Molly entered the room she found her mother struggling and fighting the Afridis. One of the Afridis then got hold of Molly and he soon held her hands and legs in a vice like grip. Molly also struggled and in the bargain broke the lantern lamp that the gang had brought with them. One Afridi then held a dagger to Molly's throat and threatened her with death. Molly ceased to struggle and tried to persuade her mother to do the same too, but Mrs. Ellis was a brave and courageous woman. She kept fighting till one of the Afridis slashed her throat and taking Molly as hostage the Afridis left the bungalow. Then for three days and nights the kidnappers with Molly as their prized catch made their way through the mountains to the Afghan border, hiding and resting by day and moving only by night. A barefooted Molly wearing only her pyjama suit and a cotton coat which the kidnappers had given her fearlessly stood the ordeal. At times when she felt exhausted and dead tired, the kidnappers took turns to carry her on their backs. On learning about the murder of Mrs. Ellis and abduction of young Molly, the entire military garrison at Kohat was immediately alerted. Though strong armed columns and patrols locally known as 'Ghashts' were instantly sent out in all directions to apprehend the culprits, but they all returned empty handed.

On 18th April, and nearly five days after the abduction the old Haji Abdul Rehman's intelligence network at Peshawar indicated that the abductors were in Khamki Valley in the Tirah mountains. The intelligence reports also indicated that it was the same notorious gang led by Ajab and his brother Shahzada from the Kohat Pass Afridis who were responsible for Molly's abduction. It seems the brothers had planned the abduction partly out of revenge for the reprisal against their own Bosti Khel section of Afrides which was conducted by the 3rd Sikhs.

The 3rd Sikh was a crack Piffer unit who a month earlier in response to the theft of 46 police rifles from the Kohat Police Thana had not only recovered the rifles, but had also used harsh repressive measures against the Bosti Khel Afridies. The theft of the rifles by cutting a hole in the roof of the police armoury was also master minded by the two brothers. During the raid not only the stolen rifles, but also other stolen property including the clothes of Colonel Foulkes, an officer from the Royal Army Medical Corps who with his wife were murdered at Kohat in 1921 was also recovered. Later that same evening one of Haji's reliable informers also came back with the good news that Miss Molly Ellis was not only alive, but she was in good health too. On getting this information, Mr John Maffey, the Chief Commissioner of the North West Frontier Province at Peshawar requested help from Mrs Lillian Starr, a medical missionary and the matron of The Peshawar Missionary Hospital.

Lillian Starr, the wife of Dr Vernon Starr had come to Peshawar in 1913. Inspite of her husband being killed by a hot headed Afridi in 1917 she had stayed on to do her missionary work at Peshawar. Her husband the good Doctor was stabbed and killed in front of her very own eyes when he answered a late night call at the front door. She was the daughter of Reverend Wade and as a young girl had spent a number of years with her family in the Kashmir valley where her father with Reverend Tyndale Biscoe had set up the Biscoe School. In the early hours of that 20th of April[1] and unannounced to the world, the young and pretty matron risking her own life and accompanied by Risaldar Major Moghul Baz Khan, the Political Assistant to the Chief Commissioner and Khan Bahadur Quli Khan, the Assistant Political Officer Kurram Region made their way via Kohat, Hangu and Shinwari to the Khamki valley. Immediately on reaching the appointed place for the rendezvous, hard and tough negotiations followed. Finally the kidnappers handed over Molly to Mehmood Akhunzada, the influential Muslim Mulla from the Orakzai Pathan tribe. On 24th April, 1923 a triumphant Lillian Starr with a visibly shaken but brave Molly Ellis arrived back safely at Peshawar, while the gang escaped across the Durand Line into Afghanistan. Apparently the kidnappers had treated Molly well. John Maffey the Chief Commissioner was simply delighted and so was Molly's dear friend at Kohat, Miss Barbara Edge. The very next day while as a guest of the Chief Commissioner in his bungalow, Molly played a few sets of tennis in order to forget her agonizing ordeal and a day later on 26th April on the grand occasion of the King's second son Prince Albert's marriage to Lady Elizabeth Bowes Lyon, the charming daughter of the 14th Earl of Strathmore, there were more celebrations to follow.

It was on that very evening, while Haji Abdul Rehman stood outside the office of the Chief Commissioner waiting for his turn to offer his congratulations for the royal wedding that he first saw Molly Ellis. She was on her way for a game of tennis and as she passed by, the old Pathan smiled and gave her the traditional long salaam and Molly Ellis too returned the courtesy by waving out her tennis racket to the smiling Haji.

'Thank Allah that she has been brought back hail and hearty by you and your team," said Haji Abdul Rehman while inviting Riasaldar Major

Moghul Baz Khan for a meal to his house that evening. They were not only celebrating the royal wedding but also the safe return of Molly Ellis. A few months later and on the 7th of November, the same gang again struck at Parachinar. This time they wanted to kidnap Mrs. Watts, wife of Captain Watts from the 1st Battalion of the12 Frontier Force Rifles who had been recently seconded to the Kurram Militia. When both the husband and the wife put up stiff resistance, the kidnappers mercilessly killed both of them.

It was in 1892, when the Kurram Agency in the North West Frontier was created and the Kurram Militia was raised. Lieutenant George Roos Keppel was the son of a English father and a Danish mother and he had been seconded from his own regiment, The Royal Scots Fuziliers to serve in the Kurram Militia. Keppel had now become a famous frontier administrator and a Pashtu lexicographer. He was also the first adjutant of the Kurram Militia, while his Commanding Officer the then Captain Ernest Maconchy was the one who selected Parachinar as the future cantonment. On the brutal murder of Captain Watts and his wife, when Major Attiqur Rehman was detailed to proceed on long temporary duty to the Kurram Militia, he decided to send his family back to Peshawar.

The very next evening taking a spot of casual leave, Major Attiqur Rehman with his six month old pregnant wife Nafisa and their three sons, Gul Rehman, Aftab Rehman, and Arif Rehman aged 9, 7, and 4 years respectively arrived at Peshawar. With the Frontier not being safe even for an Afridi born Indian Army Medical officer, Attiqur Rehman had finally decided to shift his family from Kohat to Peshawar for good. He knew that his parents would be delighted to have the grandchildren with them and there was no doubt that they would all be well looked after and would stay in greater comfort in the big house that their aging grandfather had built for them. For his services to the British, Haji Abdul Rehman had been recently conferred the title of Khan Bahadur and in order to match his new found status, he had constructed a new palatial house just on the outskirts of the Peshawar Cantonment. Attiqur Rehman's three boys were now growing up and he wanted them to go to his old alma mater, The Saint Edwardes Missionary School in Peshawar. Moreover his wife Nafisa was also due for delivery in early February and they were hoping for a girl this time.

"Yes I want a grand daughter this time and don't you disappoint us," said a smiling Khan Bahadur Haji Abdul Rehman as Nafisa brought in a plateful of delicious sheek kebabs for her father-in-law.

"Yes you are right Abbajan because as it is these three little devils are more than a handful for all of us put together and getting a fourth will be simply suicidal," said Attiqur Rehman as he gave a mischievous smile to his wife. Poor Nafisa feeling somewhat embarrassed simply blushed and ran back into the kitchen.

On 5th February 1924, Gandhi was released from prison and the same very morning Nafisa also produced a beautiful daughter.

"Congratulations Major Rehman and though we had to do a Caesarean, but your wife and the child are both well and there is nothing to fear," said Lillian Starr the pretty young matron as she came out from the operation theatre to give the good news to the family. The old Haji was thrilled as he warmly embraced his son. Then he took out two small boxes covered with red velvet casings from his pocket and gave it to Mrs. Starr and said.

"Will you be kind enough to give the big one with the gold necklace inside to my dear daughter-in-law because that is my gift to her for having kept her promise of producing a girl," said the Haji.

"And to whom do I give the second box to?" asked the smiling matron.

"Oh it is only a tiny gold bracelet and that is for my first dear grand daughter and it also has her name Shenaz meaning pride in the Persian script inscribed on it and that is what we will be calling her from today. After all that was my late mother's name too," said the proud Haji.

Chapter-3

Revolutionaries Reborn

While the Rehman family at Peshawar was celebrating the birth of little Shenaz, and while Gandhi was recovering from his appendicitis operation at the Sassoon Hospital in Poona, a group of young revolutionaries from the United Provinces and Punjab, under their leader Sachindranath Sanyal met clandestinely to plan their future strategy. They were all members of the newly formed HRA, the Hindustan Republican Association. It was a revolutionary organization who felt that the Mahatma's doctrine of non violence was a non starter and that the only way to get rid of the British Raj was through organized armed revolution.

"Gentlemen, let me remind you of what the great Lokmaniya Tilak said way back in 1902 and I quote. 'We will not achieve any success in our labours if we just croak once a year like a frog. We must therefore act now and act decisively too,' said Sachindranath Sanyal.

"That's all very well said, but how do we do that. We have no money and neither do we have weapons," said Ashafqualla Khan, the young six foot tall handsome Pathan from Shahjahanpur.

"We know that and therefore we will have to get that money and those weapons even if we have to loot a bank, a government treasury or even a police armoury if need be," said Ram Prased Bismil who also hailed from the Pathan's native town of Shahjahanpur.

"Yes that is right, but before we do that, we must first educate and motivate our own youth to join us in this armed struggle," added Sachindranath Sanyal as he spelt out the salient points from 'Krantikari,'the HRA's proposed manifesto. The meeting finally ended with a consensus that something dramatic had to be done and done quickly in order to inspire the young Indian youth to join in the nationwide revolt that would shake the Brtish authorities from its very roots and give them the Indians their much needed momentum towards achieving freedom. But the question was what should be done and how it could be done.

It was not long, before Ram Prasad Bismil found the answer. The youngman from Shahjehanpur whose ancestors belonged to the Thomarghar area in the Chambal region of the Gwalior State where dacoity was a way of life soon made his mark. In order to generate the necessary funds for the procurement of weapons, Ram Prasad Bismil with his gang of young revolutionaries resorted to armed dacoities, but that too was not good enough. Then one day lady luck smiled on him. While traveling by the 8 down train from Shahjehanpur to Lucknow he noticed something strange happening. At the very first station where the train stopped, Ramprasad had alighted on the platform to have a cup of tea and when he was about to have his first sip from the cup, he found the station master with a bag of money in his hand getting into the railway guard's compartment. A few minutes later he also saw him coming out with an empty bag. Thereafter at each and every station, when the train stopped, Ramprasad noticed that the same drill was being followed meticulously. At one railway station he went and sat in the compartment next to the Guard's van to find out where all the money was being stacked. By a stroke of luck when the slow passenger train stopped at the next station and the guard alighted and came down to have a cup of tea on the platform, Ramprasad seized the opportunity and managed to peep inside the Guard's van.When he noticed a big iron safe inside that was completely unprotected, he knew he had found his answer. When he alighted at Lucknow's Charbagh railway station there was a big smile on Ram Prasad Bismil's face when he saw the iron safe full of railway cash being wheeled away on a trolley.

Meanwhile in Calcutta on 12th June, Gopinath Shah a young revolutionary's solo attempt to assassinate Charles Teggart, the dreaded Police Commissioner of Bengal misfired and instead Mr Ernest Day an Englishman was killed. Gopinath Shah was caught and sentenced to death. The resurgence of revolutionary activities in Bengal had now also begun in right earnest and it was steadily on the increase. From early October 1924, the special branch of the police operating from 14 Elysium Road, later named Lord Sinha Road kept the house at 38/2 Elgin Road under total surveillance. This was Subhas Chandra Bose's father's house and Subhas too was now a marked man.

With Charles Teggart keeping a close watch on Subhas Bose in Calcutta, Viceroy Reading accompanied by the Vicerene was once again on their way to the beautiful vale of Kashmir as the honoured guests of Maharaja Pratap

Singh. As they motored down in their Caddilac from Rawalpindi to the valley, they were warmly greeted along the way by their Indian subjects. At Domel custom check post after they had crossed into the Maharaja's kingdom, they were welcomed with a cup of hot tea and biscuits by the Maharaja's special reception team. This was to be followed with a welcome song in English that was to be given by a small group of boys from the high school at Muzzafarabad and it was to be led by the 13 year old tall handsome young Sikh, Daler Singh Bajwa son of Gurcharan Singh Bajwa. But at the last moment young Daler Singh Bajwa conveniently feigned sickness and complained of severe stomach ache. It seems he could not reconcile to the fact that he should sing a song of welcome to those who had killed his beloved and loving grandfather Harbhajan Singh Bajwa and other innocent people who were massacred at Jalianwala Bagh. The young boy's English teacher, a Kashmiri Pandit who had rehearsed his ward so very well was in jitters, but no amount of coaxing and cajoling could get Daler Singh to the makeshift small stage and as a result of which two days later Daler Singh Bajwa's name was struck off from the rolls of the school. It was in fact a blessing in disguise. His father then took him to Srinagar and got him enrolled into the Biscoe School. Though Daler Singh Bajwa was a little senior in age to Ismail Sikandar Khan, but they were both in the same class and they soon became very good friends.

Having stayed a night in the picturesque valley of Uri in the Maharaja's well furnished rest house on the banks of the roaring Jhelum River, the Viceroy and his party did the last leg of their journey from Baramulla to Srinagar in the Maharaja's royal barge. At the quayside at Shaletang they were greeted by Hari Singh, the Crown Prince and Commander-in-Chief of the Kashmir State Forces. The Prince was in crutches. He had broken his leg while toboganning. Seeing his condition, someone among the Viceroy's staff jokingly remarked. "I only pray Mr 'A' is not back to mischief again.".

"Well even if he is, it will be a difficult task for him to perform with just one leg," remarked another. The joke did arouse some laughter, but luckily it did not reach the ears of their gracious royal host. And while the Viceroy of India was enjoying his holidays in Kashmir, there was trouble for him once again in Bengal.

In March 1923, Charles Teggart had taken over the duties of Police Commissioner, Calcutta from Mr Reginald Clarke and from that very day Teggart with Mr Corbett his Chief Police Intelligence Officer systematically and methodically followed all activities of the rising son of Bengal. By now the 'Swarajists'under their leader CR Das was the largest single party in the

Bengal Council. Moreover, the elections under the 1923 Act had given them complete control of the wealthy Calcutta Corporation too. Deshbandhu CR Das was elected the Mayor of Calcutta and he had appointed his young trusted political associate, Subhas Chandra Bose as his Chief Executive Officer.

On the early hours of 25th of October 1924, the police raided the house on Elgin Road and the entire Bose family and their household staff was taken completely by surprise. The police party searched every room and even ransacked a few in order to gather some hard evidence. Finally they seized some papers which to them were seditious in nature and the police promptly arrested the 27 year old Subhash. By the time the news of his arrest reached Debu Ghosh, Subhash Bose had been whisked off to jail. Just a day before the arrest, Lytton, the Governor of Bengal who was the son of a former Viceroy with his Police Commissioner Charles Teggart had finalized the list of the people who were to be arrested under the Bengal Criminal Law Amendment Ordinance. Later on that very day, the Governor quietly slipped away to an idyllic retreat in the sylvan surroundings of the Teesta valley leaving Charles Teggart to do the dirty job. Meanwhile in England a new Conservative government with Stanley Baldwin as the Prime Minister and Lord Birkenhead as the Secretary of State for India had only just been sworn in.

Strangely enough while the witch hunt was being conducted in Bengal, the acting Commander-in-Chief of India and the Colonel designate of the 13th Frontier Force Rifles, General Birdwood, who was himself a Piffer was busy unveiling the new Frontier Force War Memorial at Kohat to honour all those Piffers who sacrificed their lives during the Great War of 1914-1918. Standing beside the new lofty 30 feet high obelisk stone that rested on a plinth, he spoke to the gathering both in English and in perfect Urdu.

"Gentlemen as the senior most Piffer today I will be failing in my duty if I do not recognize the valour and courage of our gallant Indian soldiers who today are no longer with us. But let us not forget that had it not been for their bravery, courage and devotion to duty, we would not be standing here today to honour them. The Frontier Force has fought in every theatre during the Great War and that itself is a great honour. Our Piffers while fighting in France, Mesopotamia, Palestine, Gallipolli, Egypt, East Africa or in the Frontier itself showed to the world the stuff they are made off. In these battles no less than 171 Indian officers, 121 NCOs and 3425 Piffers all hailing from India had laid down there precious lives and led us to ultimate victory. Therefore let us all today salute them with the pride and honour that they so richly deserve."

As the sound of the bugles echoed around the hills of Kohat, there were tears in the eyes of some of the British Officers. For Major Attiqur Rehman it was indeed a very touching and poignant moment as the entire congregation saluted the fallen heroes. This was followed by a special church service for those British Officers from the gallant Frontier Force Regiment who had also laid down their lives for the honour of the Union Jack. It was another tearful moment for the British Officers and their families who were stationed in Kohat. Some had lost their erstwhile brothers and comrade in arms, while others their near and dear ones.When the acting C-in-C entered the St Augustine's Church to unveil the names of those gallant British Officers who had laid down their lives for the honour of the British Empire, there was hushed silence. As the names were read out, some of the ladies in the congregation sobbed inconsolably, while a few completely broke down. Colonel Reginald Edwards though retired and not a Piffer himself was visiting Kohat as a guest of Major Attiqur Rehman and as he knelt on the pew listening to the names being read out, there were tears in his eyes too. Some of them were his dear friends and colleagues from Sandhurst.

On 1st December, Queen Alexandra widow of the late Emperor Edward the VII celebrated her 80th birthday at Sadringham. Surrounded by all her loving children and grandchildren it still wasn't a very happy occassion for her. The recent death of Sir Deighton Probyn her devoted comptroller of household at the age of 91 years was a great loss to her. Ever since the death of her dear beloved husband, Sir Deighton Probyn from the famed cavalry regiment of The Probyn's Horse which was named after him and a winner of the Victoria Cross during the 1857 uprising in India had been her constant companion and friend. While in London the King congratulated his mother and wished her a long life, at the Sabarmati Ashram in Ahmedabad, Gandhi having undergone his 21 days of fast for Hindu-Muslim unity, sat everyday in right earnest jotting down notes for his book 'My Experiments with Truth.'

Meanwhile and towards the end of 1924, Sachindranath Sanyal had completed the draft for the Constitution of the Hindustan Republican Association. It was written on yellow paper and he had spelt out clearly the aim and objective of the organization. "The object of the Association shall be to establish a Federal Republic of the United States of India by an organized and armed revolution," he wrote.

On New Year's Day 1925, while Gandhi contemplated his next non violent movement, the Hindustan Republican Association (HRA) circulated its first manifesto throughout Northern India calling for an armed revolution. They offered justice to everyone free of cost and also equal opportunities to them, be they high or low, rich or poor.

On 25th January 1925, Subhas Bose was brought from Alipur Jail to the lock up at the Police Headquarters at Lal Bazaar.

"You will spend the night here and tomorrow we will get rid of you. You will be deported to a place from where neither you nor your writ and nor your mischief will work," said the police officer while doubly ensuring that the cell had been properly secured with a double lock.With Subhas Bose in the lock up, Calcutta was agog with strange rumours. Some said that Subhas Bose would be eliminated for good, while others thought that he would be quarantined for ever in one of the many islands of the Andamans, never to be to seen or heard off again.

"But I think that this is sheer bullshit. The British will never dare to do such a thing. Subhash is no ordinary criminal. He is a national leader and though young he is respected and revered by all. At the most they will probably deport him to the Mandalay jail in Burma like they did to the great Lokmaniya," said Debu Ghosh and how right he was. That night Debu Ghose with some of his colleagues kept a constant vigil on the Lal Bazzar Police headquarters. Early next morning on the 26th of January and as planned, Debu Ghosh with Naren Sen and Dr Ghulam Hussein went for an early morning walk to Babu Ghat on the Strand Road. When the police van with Subhash Bose inside raced towards the jetty on the River Hoogly, Debu Ghosh indignantly remarked.

"I am afraid this blatant and unwise move by the British will someday prove very costly to the Gora Sahibs. By deporting the Chief Executive of the Calcutta Corporation who was duly elected and branding him as a common criminal just because the man loves his own motherland is going to backfire on them someday. The British have once again grossly erred in their judgment and believe you me someday our very Subhash Bose, the tiger of Bengal will make them pay very heavily for it."

As the ship with its prized catch and escorted by the port pilot sailed away towards the Diamond Harbour, Charles Teggart the Police Commissioner breathed a sigh of relief.

On 16th June 1925, the man with a law degree from England who as a young barrister and with his powerful handling of the Alipore bomb conspiracy case had not only saved Aurobindo Ghosh from the gallows, but who was also responsible for having him acquitted met an untimely death. The whole nation mourned the passing away of the 55 year old Deshbandhu CR Das. For Subhas Chandra Bose who was still languishing in Mandalay Jail it was not only a tragic loss, but an irreplaceable one too.

"I wonder who will lead us now," said a grief stricken Debu Ghosh as he with his friends Naren Sen and Ghulam Hussein joined the multitude of people both Hindus and Muslims to pay their last respects to another great son of Bengal.

While the Indians were mourning the loss of their great leader, at Landhikotal in the Officer's Mess far away in the North West Frontier, the British were celebrating the completion of the Khyber railway project. It was indeed a spectacular feat of railway engineering for military purposes by the British. This was the second such strategic railway line to be built in order to secure India's borders against any invasion from the North and North West and conversely to support any future military expedition for the expansion of the British Empire into Afghanistan, Central Asia and the oil rich Middle East. The first such railway was built from Sibi to Quetta via Harnai in 1887 by General Buster Browne. As Colonel Gordon Hearn, the Chief Engineer and the main architect of the Khyber project clinked glasses with Mr Victor Bailey, his senior engineer in charge of the actual construction, Major Attiqur Rehman stood quietly in a corner sipping his glass of fresh fruit juice. He was in no mood to celebrate.

It was only after the Third Afghan War in 1919 that Colonel Hearn was given the task of extending the railway line from Peshawar-Jamrud to the Afghan border at Thorkham and he had completed it in a record time. Armed with 30 years of railway experience, the veteran of the Tirah Campaign, the Second Afghan War and the war of 1914-1918 where he was mentioned in dispatches not just once or twice but a record four times and which were signed personally by Mr Winston Churchill, the Colonel felt indeed proud of his team of railway officers and staff. The construction of a railway line through such narrow confines and over such formidable obstacles and in such a hostile environment was by no means an easy task.

On the 25th of July 1925, Whilliam Birdwood the C-in-C designate India and Colonel Commandant 13th Frontier Force Rifles while returning from home leave unveiled at a cathedral in Orleans, France the memorial erected in honour of the Indian soldiers killed in France during the First World War. Reading the long list of fatal casualties and the sacrifice made by the Indian troops, he was deeply touched. The name of Curzon Sikandar Khan, VC from the Punjab Regiment was on that list too. When he boarded the ship 'Narkhanda' at Marseilles he was delighted to find the Viceroy and his wife Lady Reading on it too and it was they who gave him the good news about Colonel Hearn's great achievement in connecting the strategic Khyber Pass to the Indian Railway network.

In early August 1925, while the British were still celebrating the successful completion of the Khyber railway, Naren Sen arrived at Shahjehanpur, a small district town in the United Provinces. He was there to defend a young Bengali lad from Calcutta who had been falsely charged with theft by the in-laws of his own sister. The boy's family it seems was demanding more dowry and was constantly harassing the young bride who was not even 14 years old. When the girl's brother being the eldest in the family came to plead with her in-laws to give them some more time, the greedy in-laws instead filed a false case of theft of a gold necklace against the lad. The trial however did not last even a week and thanks to Naren Sen's spirited defence as the boy's counsel, the jury on 9th August had pronounced the lad not guilty.Having got the boy honourably acquitted, Naren Sen took the first train to Lucknow. It was the same 8 Down. Naren had decided to spend a few days in Lucknow with some of his relations before returning to Calcutta. Till now he had only heard stories about the great Nawabs of Oudh, their palaces, their sophisticated life styles, their culture, their magnanimous hospitality and their various types of kebabs and he.was now keen to taste atleast some of them. For a while he kept day dreaming about the place and soon fell asleep.Then suddenly while it was approaching sun down, the train came to a screeching halt in the middle of nowhere. It seemed someone had pulled the chain.

"Which is the next station and how far are we from Lucknow?" asked Naren from one of his fellow passengers in the second class compartment.

"Next is Kakori station which is only a few minutes run from here and we will soon be in Lucknow," said the co-passenger.

Hardly had the man completed the sentence, when Naren found three young men jumping out of the neighbouring compartment and with revolvers and pistols in their hands they pounced upon the train guard. The guard had come to check as to who had pulled the chain and for what reason. It was the handsome tall Pathan Ashfaqulla Khan who had pulled the chain and who with the help of his two colleagues Sachindra Bakshi and Rajendra Lahiri from the Hindustan Republican Association had quickly pinned the guard face down on to the railway track.

"Do not look up or shout for help or else we will shoot you," warned one of the revolutionaries as the Guard pleaded for mercy.

At first Naren thought that probably some dacoit gang had attacked the train. Then he heard two shots being fired and an announcement also being made. Someone from amongst the young revolutionaries was seen running along the track and he kept shouting. '

"Dear travelers and fellow countrymen do not be afraid. We are revolutionaries fighting for our country's freedom. Your lives, money and honour will be safe if you keep calm and do not come out of the train or peep outside. Just stay where you are. We are on a mission and as soon as we accomplish it we will let the train resume its journey. We do not want any bloodshed."

Initially Naren was a bit scared, but he soon gathered a little courage and looked out of the window. He was only trying to see as to what exactly was happening outside. As he put his head out, one of the revolutionaries pointed the revolver at him. Naren was terrified. However, he intuitively nodded his head and gave him a big smile which probably indicated Naren's approval of their action. Immediately the man lowered his revolver and Naren without batting another eyelid withdrew his head and went and sat quietly in one corner. He was dumbfounded for he realized that they were the same three people whom he had seen at the Shahjehanpur railway station. Infact he had even offered to pay for their tea to the tea vendor because the train was about to start and the tea vendor did not have the requisite change for the eight anna coin that was being offered to him by one of them. Closing his eyes Naren prayed to Goddess Durga.

A few minutes later in the silence of the wilderness and with the sun going down, Naren heard sounds of loud banging. It seemed that someone with a big iron hammer was trying to break open something. With his own compartment not being far away from the Guards van, Naren could hear the loud noise quite distinctly. A group of revolutionaries had successfully pushed the big iron safe out of the guard van and were now desperately trying to force it open as they kept hammering on it. The safe had a big strong lock, but neither the driver nor the guard had the keys to it. It did have a narrow slit through which the money was dropped, but it was not large enough for a hand to go inside and take the money out. Even the strong Pathan's mighty blows with the iron hammer were making no impact on that heavy iron safe.To make matters even worse the long whistle of a train coming from Lucknow in the opposite direction was heard. The revolutionaries were now in a state of panic. The very thought of a moving train coming from the opposite direction and colliding with the 8 down which could result in a catastrophe unnerved Bismil, but there was nothing that he or anyone else could do. None the less, Bismil halted all the activities lest it aroused suspicion from the engine driver and the guard of the on coming train. Luckily for them and the passengers on the 8 Down, the chain had been pulled at a place not far from Kakori station where there were two lines. As the on coming train from Lucknow got on to the second track, Ram Prasad Bismil heaved a huge sigh of relief. He had only a few minutes earlier thought of aborting his plan, when he told Ashfaquallah to stop using the hammer, but when the train from Lucknow passed by hooting away and got out of sight, the revolutionaries were back into business again as they went literally hammer and tong against the strong iron safe to force it open.

It was nearing dusk, when a newly married young man in Naren's compartment stuck his head out from the door. A shot was heard and the man was instantly killed. His poor young wife traveling in the women's compartment with the rest of the ladies did not realize till later that she was already a widow. A while later the metallic sound of the hammer blows on the safe which echoed in the distance also suddenly stopped. Naren took courage and peeped out. He no doubt felt sorry for the newly wedded bride, but he also felt proud of the young revolutionaries when he spotted them with bundles of the looted railway cash on their heads fading away into the far distance. On reaching Lucknow and though being an eye witness to the dacoity he wisely kept the story to himself. The police had already cast there net far and wide and were even offering high rewards to those who could give them a clue for their capture, but for Naren it was a closed chapter. took the police more than a month to get their act together and on the morning of 26th September, 1925 Ramprasad Bismil was arrested. But before they could get to Ashfaqualla, the Pathan had escaped into the sugarcane fields a good half a mile from his own house at Shahjehanpur. For days he hid there while his friends brought him food in the dead of night. But one night they also brought the bad news of the arrests of all the other members of the group. It was now only he and Chandreshekar Azad who had managed so far to escape the police dragnet.

Finding it unsafe to remain in the sugarcane field for long, Ashfaqulla Khan with some money from home managed to first reach Benaras and where for a while he stayed with some of his friends who were studying in the Benaras Hindu University. Then with the help of the same group he sneaked into Bihar and got a clerical job in an engineering company at Daltongang in the Palamau District. With a flair for writing Urdu poetry in couplets, he soon became quite popular with the owner of the firm who shared the same taste and and took great delight in hearing him at the various 'Mushairas,', a recital of Urdu couplets by poets who adored and loved the rich Urdu language. Daltonganj also had a fairly large population of Bengalis and the Pathan with his flare for languages was soon singing in Bengali too. By this time a new young revolutionary poet and writer by the name of Kazi Nazrul Islam with the nickname of 'Dhuku Mia' or the sorrowful one had emerged in Bengal.

Born on 24th May 1899, in the village of Churulia in the Burdwan District of Bengal, Nazrul was now a rage and had become a poet of the masses. Having lost his father at a very early age Nazrul was brought up in penury by his devoted mother Zahida Khatun. And to earn a living he even worked as a young boy in a bakery and at a tea shop at Asansol in order to have two square meals a day. As a young lad not only did Nazrul serve as the Imam of a local mosque, but he also served during the First World War in the 49th Bengal Regiment and rose to the rank of a Battalion Quarter Master Havildar. Even as a soldier he continued his literary activities and published his first book 'The Autobiography of a Delinquent' and that was in 1919 when he was still in uniform and was posted in Karachi cantonment. After the war, when the 49th Bengal Regiment was disbanded, Nazrul returned to Calcutta to begin his journalistic and literary life. To express his own patriotic fervour and support for Gandhi's non cooperation movement, Kazi Nazrul the 22 year old young poet in 1921 composed some of his greatest songs and poems of which 'Bidrohi,','The Rebel.' had made him an overnight sensation. In 1922, Nazrul published a volume of short stories titled 'The Gift of Sorrow.' The publication of an anti British political poem by Nazrul in the bi-weekly Bengali magazine 'Dhumketu' (The Comet) led to the young poet's arrest. He was sentenced to one year's rigorous imprisonment. While undergoing his sentence at Howrah jail, Nazrul began a fast to protest against the maltreatment of prisoners by the British jail authorities. Gurudev Rabindranath Tagore who had dedicated his musical play 'Basanta' to the budding poet immediately sent a telegram to him saying. "Give up hunger strike. Our literature claims you." On his release from prison in December 1923, Nazrul once again went back to his literary pursuits. While working at Daltonganj, Ashfaquallah Khan had also become fond of Nazrul's poems and writings.

While the Police were still hunting for the rest of the revolutionaries involved in the daring Kakori train dacoity case, in Kashmir with the death of Maharaja Pratap Singh on 25th September 1925, Prince Hari Singh, the heir to the Kashmir gaddi was proclaimed as the new Maharaja. Both the younger brothers of Maharaja Pratap Singh, Raja Ram Singh and

Raja Amar Singh had pre deceased him. The only male heir and claimant to the Kashmir throne was the thirty year old Prince Hari Singh, the one and only son of Raja Amar Singh. On completion of his education in 1915 from the prestigious Mayo College in Ajmer, Prince Hari Singh was sent for military training to the Imperial Cadet Corps at Dehradun and thereafter on completion of his training was attached for a year in 1919 with the 18th Lancers. In 1920, with the honorary rank of Captain in the British Army he was appointed as the Commander-in-Chief of The Kashmir State Forces.

During the period of mourning for the late Maharaja, Colonel Reginald Edwards called on the new Maharaja Hari Singh to offer his condolences. One morning as a guest of the British Resident in Kashmir while browsing through old official documents that were lying in the records of the British Residency, Reggie was pleasantly surprised to come across some authentic letters not only about the kind of court intrigues that surfaced during and after the death of each successive ruler, but also of the tremendous powers that was wielded by the Viceroy of India and that of the British Resident in Kashmir in selecting and proclaiming who should be the next to sit on the 'Gaddi.'(Throne)

By the Treaty of Amritsar of 16th March, 1846 the Article 1 read 'The British Government transfers and makes over for ever in independent possession to Maharaja Gulab Singh and the heirs male of his body all the hilly or mountainous country with its dependencies situated to the eastward of the River Indus and the westward of the River Ravi including Chamba and excluding Lahul, being part of the territories ceded to the British government by the Lahore State according to the provisions of Article iv of the Treaty of Lahore, dated 9th March, 1846.'

Article 3 of the same treaty read. 'In consideration of the transfer made to him and his heirs, Maharaja Gulab Singh will pay to the British Government the sum of Rupees seventy five lakhs, fifty lakhs to be paid on or before the the 1st of the current year, AD,1846. ' The entire treaty comprised of ten articles and Reggie went through each one of them one by one with a fine tooth comb. He found the last Article Number 10 to be the most interesting and he could not but help in a jocular vein ask Mr Evelyn Howell from the Indian Civil Service who was the British Resident in Kashmir whether he had received one horse, twelve shawl goats of the approved breed, six male and six female, and the three pairs of Kashmiri shawls from the late Maharaja before he died. For a moment Mr Howell was quite foxed with the query till Sir Albion Banerjee, the Prime Minister of the State asked, 'But what for?'

"Well that was I guess part of the Treaty of Amritsar which states in writing that Maharaja Gulab Singh acknowledges the supremacy of the British Government and will in token of such supremacy present annually to the British government the items that I have just mentioned and all this is given in black and white," said Reggie as he handed over the document to the Prime Minister of Kashmir for his perusal.

"Yes the Colonel is very right and we better check our own records if we are still honouring it Sir. Moreover, the treaty has been signed by no less a person than Governor General Harding, Mr Frederick Curries and Brevet Major Henry Montgomery Lawrence on behalf of the King Emperor and by Maharaja Gulab Singh himself on that very day and we should not default on it," said Albion Banerjee.

"Yes and I suggest we collect the booty yearly or else we will be losing a lot of revenue too Mr Prime Minister," said Reggie laughing away to himself.

The next day Reggie found still more interesting correspondence on the subject. On the 7th of April, 1884, apprehending the death of Maharaja Ranbir Singh who had been suffering for a long time, the letter from the Government of India to the Secretary of State for India stated the following facts.

"Firstly that the ruling Maharaja Ranbir was very sick and he could die very soon. Secondly, that the administration of the State had completely broken down and thirdly that the heir apparent, namely Maharaja Pratap Singh was unsuited in character and habits to govern the State.The letter also stated that the ruling Maharaja Ranbir Singh had also entertained the idea of setting Pratap Singh aside and appointing his youngest son Raja Amar Singh to the throne. However, the letter also mentioned that despite the failings of Raja Pratap Singh as reported from some quarters, the Government of India was not in a position to take cognizance of the vices attributed to Mian Pratap Singh and he being the eldest son, should be proclaimed at once on the death of the present Maharaja. The letter also adds that in the general interest of peace and good order among the Native States, no encouragement must be given to the idea that an eldest son can be set aside at the wishes of his father. The letter further mentions that The Government of India is entirely opposed to permitting any partition of the Kashmir State, by will or otherwise among the three sons of the present ruler as desired by the ailing Maharaja."

'Thus in anticipation of the above, instructions for necessary guidance of Lieutenant Colonel Sir Oliver St John, the British Officer on special duty in Kashmir has already been issued states the same letter. And lastly the letter also proposed that on the death of the present Maharaja, a Resident Political Officer will be appointed who will exercise a general supervision over the affairs of the Kashmir State."

"Imagine how things might have changed if Raja Ranbir Singh had his way and had divided his kingdom between his three sons," thought Reggie as he took out Legal Document No 8. This was a letter from the Secretary of State to The Government of India and it stated very uneqivocally that in case of the death of Maharaja Ranbir Singh, his eldest son, Mian Partap Singh, will succeed to the undivided Chiefship of the State and the new Maharaja will be called upon to introduce such reforms as may seem necessary and that henceforth a Resident Political Officer will be stationed in Kashmir. The document also stated that as long as Maharaja Ranbir Singh was alive, the Government of India will not propose to make any changes to the existing policy, and if His Highness still refers to the subject of executing any testament on the partition of his territories, he should be quietly dissuaded from doing so. Finally in case of death of the present Maharaja, the Viceroy will immediately recognize the succession of Mian Pratap Singh and formally install him on the gaddi of Jammu and Kashmir."

Oh so that is how finally on 12th September 1885 on the death of his father Maharaja Ranbir Singh, Mian Partap Singh was proclaimed to the gaddi," said Reggie to Mr Howell while asking for one more cup of fresh hot tea.

"But you must read this particular document also," said the Resident as he handed over a report on the affairs of the State of Jammu and Kashmir to Reggie that was written by the then Resident on 5th March, 1888 to the Government of India. It was like a bombshell to Reggie as he read through the contents. In his letter the Resident minced no words and he wrote very specifically.

"I think that the Government of India should be under no illusion as regards Maharaja Pratap Singh. From first to last I have failed to discover in him any sustained capacity for governing his country, or any genuine desire to ameliorate its conditions, or to introduce those reforms which he has acknowledged to be necessary. More than two and a half years have passed since his accession, but not only has he achieved nothing, but he has opposed beneficial measures proposed by others. I do therefore earnestly advice that the Maharaja be made plainly to understand that he has had his chance, and that he will not be allowed any longer to stand in the way. He may reign but not govern. As to the form of Government—one option is to appoint Raja Amar Singh as Prime Minister, but I have grave doubts if he can also be trusted. I do not think it will be safe to employ him. He has not forgotten his father's intentions on his behalf, and the object he is working for is to become the Maharaja of Kashmir. Once he gets power in his hands he will use it without any scruples to attain his end. At present the Maharaja is friendly to Raja Amar Singh, because he wishes to break the bond which unites the two younger brothers and the present Prime Minister Dewan Lachman Dass But there is no genuine affection or confidence between them and the well known fact that the late Maharaja would have liked to supercede Partap Singh in favour of his youngest brother is a special cause of jealously in the royal family."

'My God if all this is true, it is nothing less than plain cut throatism' said Reggie as he called for another cup of the fresh Darjeeling tea.

'Well if you would like to read something even more interesting then just go through this one,' said the Resident as he handed over another document to Reggie. This was a letter written by Maharaja Partap Singh to his younger brother Raja Amar Singh on 8th March, 1889, and it was an edict of his abdication.

'But how did all this come about?' asked Reggie.

'Well this was as a sequel of the 34 confidential letters allegedly treasonable in nature which it was believed was written by Maharaja Pratap Singh in his own hand. Those somehow came in possession of Colonel Nesbit who was then the Resident in Kashmir. Colonel Nesbit promptly took them to Calcutta and handed them over to the Government. On the strength of these documents, Maharaja Partap Singh was deposed and thereafter the State was run by a council of ministers which included his two younger brothers and a few others who worked under the close supervision of the British Resident and this continued for the next 16 years. But of course we did restore his gaddi back to him in 1905, when Lord Curzon who had only previously had the privilege of installing some ruling Indian Princes to their gaddhis had now set a unique record by installing a deposed Maharaja back to his own seat. That indeed did make history, but let me also tell you confidentially that history would have probably repeated itself in some other manner if Maharaja Pratap Singh had his way too," added Reggie.

"How do you say that it would have repeated itself," said Howell as he fixed Reggie a drink.

"Well we all know that the relationship between the Uncle and the Nephew was never ever cordial. Infact there were strong rumours at once stage that he even wanted to disinherit Hari Singh. This he had confidentially sounded to Viceroy Minto when he visited the State and even sought his permission to adopt the second son of the Raja of Poonch as the next heir to the throne. Initially Viceroy Minto verbally agreed to the proposal, but later on the advice of his principal staff officers he had second thoughts and did not give his written approval. The Viceroy feared and rightly so that a decision like that could set a very wrong precedent to the other Princely States which were so very many in India. In order not to displease the Maharaja, the Viceroy however agreed that the adoption could be permitted, but only for the purposes of the incumbent to perform the Maharaja's last funeral rites, but he would have no claim to the gaddi."

"Then I must say our so called Mr A has been really very lucky and it was because the Uncle was issueless that he became the Maharaja," said Reggie as he put a cube of ice into his whisky.

But strangely enough the present Maharaja Hari Singh too despite his three marriages has yet to produce an heir. So far he has produced neither a boy nor a girl. His first marriage to the niece of the Thakur Sahib of Rajkot in 1913 was a tragedy when she died in 1915. Then the second marriage in that very year to the daughter of the Raja of Chamba also met the same fate. She also died issueless in 1920. And now with the third bride who happens to be the daughter of the Maharana of Dharampur let us hope atleast from her one male issue will surface," said Mr Evelyn Howell.

"Well till then let us keep our fingers crossed and hope that the young Maharaja Hari Singh will not create further hereditary problems for us," said Reggie somewhat jokingly as he raised a toast to the new young ruler of Jammu and Kashmir in absentia.

Mr Evelyn Howell had just about finished pouring a second peg of whisky into Reggie's glass, when the wine waiter announced that there was an elderly Kashmiri by the name of Sarfaraz Khan with a young boy standing at the gate waiting to meet Colonel Reginald Edwards.

"Please show them right in," said an excited Reggie as he made his way to the portico.

"Well well it seems we are not getting any younger and I am also limping like you," said Reggie as he embraced the faithful old cook, while the young teenager Ismail Sikandar Khan, tall and handsome for his age and with a tremendous resemblance to his late father stood quietly behind his grandfather. When Reggie went behind and embraced him also, the boy was really touched. '

"My God he is a carbon copy of his father," said Reggie as he put his arm around the boy's shoulders. Seeing that friendly gesture, Sarfaraz Khan could not control his feelings either and in a voice choking with emotion said.

"Sahib I am getting old too and so are you and who will look after this only grandson of mine when we are both gone. Presently he is studying in the Biscoe English School and is a fairly good student also, but after he finishes from there what then? Will someone help him to become at least a soldier in the Indian Army like his father was? Or give him some clerical job after he completes his schooling?" added the old agency cook as he looked expectantly at Reggie for an answer. Seeing the sadness in Sarfaraz Khan's face, Reggie too was moved.

"Do not worry, and if I have my way I will make sure that he does not become a mere soldier or an ordinary pen pusher but something bigger in life. God willing maybe some day he will become an officer and pass out from the prestigious Sandhurst Military Academy like I did. But in order to achieve that the boy will have to put in a concerted effort for admission first to the Prince of Wales Royal Military College at Dehradun and for that we have still another two to three years in our hands. Though the minimum qualifying age for admission there is fifteen and a half but he being the son of a VC, we can always ask for a relaxation in age if desired. After all if he does qualify then Ismail Sikandar Khan will be the first son of a VC to study there and I am sure the PWRIMC will only be highly honoured to have him as a student, provided of course he qualifies both academically and in the interview that is conducted for the selection to the premier institution. The institution today is the cradle for producing some of India's finest young military officers, some of whom incidentally are already serving in the British Indian Army, and maybe someday when India becomes a free country these very officers will become her military brains and leaders," said Reggie.

"May your golden words someday come true Sahib and may Allah give you a long and happy life and may you and I live to see that great day," said Sarfaraz Khan as he clutched Reggie's hand and kissed it.

That day as he lay in bed, Reggie thought about his lovely days at Gilgit and of late Sikandar Khan's family who were so very close to him. But on that very evening there was some bad news when the Resident announced that Queen Alexandra, the King's mother had died. It was the 25th of November, 1925 and on that day the King Emperor experienced the stark moment of abandonment like Reggie did some 22 years ago when he too realized that he was no longer a son.

A few days later in December 1925 a tall handsome and fair young Parsi gentleman born of a Parsi father and a French mother briskly walked up the stairs of the Bombay House that was located in the commercial Fort area of the port city. Bombay House was the nerve centre of the Tata Empire and had been designed by Mr John Wittet, the architect who created the beautiful Gateway of India at Appollo Bunder.Born in Paris, France on 29th July 1904, the young handsome gentleman who was always thrilled everytime he saw a flying machine in the sky was reporting that morning to sign his name on the rolls of Tata Sons as an unpaid apprentice. The young man who as a French Citizen in 1923 had even done his spell of compulsory military service with Le Sipahi, an Algerian regiment located at Vienne, a small district town South of Lyon was thrilled that day since his father had presented him with a blue Bugatti motor car.

Driving his blue Bugatti, the young dashing JRD was on his way home to Soonita, the beautiful bunglow on top of Malabar Hill which was built by his father and named after his dear mother Sooni. As the mud guard less and windscreen less Bugatti got into second gear to take on the last steep climb leading to the Ridge Road, he was stopped by the handsome Pathan army doctor.

"Please do pardon me for stopping you. I am Major Attiqur Rehman from the Indian Medical Service and I will be indeed very grateful if I could get a lift upto Mount Pleasant Road since I am already late for the tea appointment with Mr Mohammed Ali Jinnah and taxis here are difficult to find," said Attiqur.

"Sure hop in Major and that will also give me some more time to drive this beauty of mine around," said a smiling JRD as he introduced himself. But as soon as the car came on to the Ridge Road, it was flagged down by a police sergeant.

"Sorry you cannot go beyond this point Sir, atleast not till we complete our investigation of the murder," said the police sergeant.

"Good Lord but who has been murdered or killed or was it a road accident," asked Attiqur Rehman as he produced his military identity card for the sergeant to examine.

"It is plain murder Sir, but who is the other gentlemen in the car who is driving?" asked the Sargeant while pointing to the young driver who was at the wheel.

"He is Mr JRD Tata and this is his car and he lives in a bunglow not far from here," said Attiqur Rehman.

"Then in that case maybe one of you could help us in identifying the dead body of the victim," said the police sergeant as both Attiqur Rehman and JRD got down from the car and followed the police sergeant to the spot where the blood stained body of the victim was lying on the roadside and a young beautiful lady was moaning over it.

"Sorry but we have no idea who the poor unlucky man is and whoever committed the crime and that to in broad daylight and on Malabar Hill must have planned it very thoroughly," said Attiqur as he and JRD walked back to the car.

It later transpired that the dead body was that of one Mr Bawla, a wealthy businessman, and the lady in moaning was the bewitching and glamorous Mumtaz Begum. She was a ravishing Muslim dancing girl from Indore and allegedly the ex mistress of Tukoji Holkar, the Maharaja of that state. She had run away to Bombay to become Mr Bawla's mistress, but when the Maharaja came to know about it he decided to teach both the lovers a lesson.He had therefore sent his own henchmen from his palace guards to get rid of the man. And as far as the woman was concerned they were ordered to cut off her bloody nose. The henchmen accordingly had killed Mr Bawla alright but they could only manage to slash the face of the young dancing girl.

A few months later not wishing that the incident should become a scandal, the British gave the Maharaja two options. It was either to appear before a commission of enquiry to prove his innocence or to gracefully abdicate. Fearing the terrible damage that it would do to his own reputation and that of the members of his royal family in case he was proved guilty, the Maharaja abdicated and gave his gaddi to his son Yeshwant Rao Holkar.

And while there was turmoil in the Holkar royal family at Indore, in Jammu it was time to celebrate and anoint the new Maharaja. In February 1926, Maharaja Hari Singh bedecked in gold trimmed finery with jewels, medals and pearls glinting from head to toe sat in the ornamental coach. Driven by four magnificent horses he made his way from Jammu to Akhnur for his coronation ceremony. Situated some 20 miles from Jammu on the banks of the Chenab River, Akhnur was a small town of religious significance to the Dogra rulers of Jammu and Kashmir and the Raj Tilak ceremony of the young handsome Maharaja was to be performed there. As the royal coach carrying the Maharaja made its way from Jammu, all along the route, his subjects, men, women and children dressed up in their best of clothes and with folded hands cheered and paid obeseiance to their new ruler. On arrival at Akhnur the young Maharaja sat in a golden howdah of the big royal elephant 'Jamna Dass.'Escorted by the large retinue of royals from other Princely States of India, the spectacular procession proceeded for the Raj Tilak ceremony. When the ceremony was over, His Highness

Raj Rajeshwar Maharaj Adhiraj, Maharaja Hari Singh, the great grandson of Maharaja Gulab Singh, the first Dogra ruler of Jammu and Kashmir in all humility declared. 'It has pleased providence to place me in the position I now occupy. As a ruler I have no religion and my duty is to look after everyone with equality.'

For Colonel Reginald Edwards it was a momentous occasion too for this was the first time that he was attending the crowning of an Indian Prince. Surprisingly Lord Reading the Viceroy of India was missing. He it seemed had sent his apologies on the plea that he was soon to relinquish his appointment as the Viceroy of India and was busy packing to go home.

While the festivities on the crowning of the new Maharaja continued unabated in the state of Jammu and Kashmir, at the Mandalay jail in Burma on 18th February 1926, Subhash Bose accused the British authorities of the ruthless and inhuman treatment that was being meted out to the prisoners and he went on a hunger strike. A few weeks later he developed tuberculosis. TB as the disease was known worldwide had no known cure then. A month or two later his condition became rather serious. Fearing that the death of the young son of Bengal in custody at the Mandalay jail may spark a backlash in India, the British authorities released Subhash Bose. On his arrival in Calcutta on 16th May he was once again greeted as a hero. Debu Ghosh with a huge garland of marigold flowers and a bouquet of fresh white tube roses stood patiently at the Khidderpur dock to welcome the rising son of Bengal.

"You must get absolutely well first for the country needs you very badly," said a jubilant Debu Ghosh as he garlanded his old friend.

"Do not worry this disease TB will not kill me. Atleast not till we throw the British out from India," said a smiling Subhash.

A couple of months later, on the occasion of the Bengali New Year's day celebrations in April 1926, the Bengalee community at Daltonganj had invited Ashfaquallah Khan to sing a few Bengali songs and Ashafaqualla Khan felt highly honoured.That evening, when he came up on stage and started with a song from poet Nazrul's composition, Naren Sen was shocked to see the familiar face. He had recognized the handsome Pathan with the bearded face. Though there was admiration for the young man, but there was also a sense of fear in Naren Sen's eyes. However, he decided to keep his mouth shut. Naren Sen with his brother-in-law Debu Ghosh together with their families had come to Daltonganj to spend the Bengali New Year with some of their cousins who had settled there. Though the police were still offering a rich reward for the capture of Ashfaqualla Khan in the Kakori train dacoity case, Naren Sen was not going to be lured into it.

Ashafullah Khan as a clerk had worked for nearly a whole year at Daltonganj and would have remained free all his life had he remained there for good, but fate decided otherwise. He went to Delhi to find out how he could go abroad and continue with his studies. In Delhi he met a Pathan friend who had been his classmate at school in Shahjahanpur. For the sake of a monetary reward the friend betrayed him. Now with the exception of Chandrashekar Azad, all participants in the sensational Kakori dacoity case had been apprehended.The court case went on for more than a year and a half, and though eminent Indian leaders and lawyers like Jawaharlal Nehru, Govind Ballabh Pant, Acharya Narendra Deva and others formed a committee under the chairmanship of Pandit Motilal Nehru to defend the revolutionaries, it proved abortive. Four of the main accused, Ramprasad Bismil, Ashfaquallah Khan, Roshan Singh and Rajendra Lahiri were sentenced to death and the rest were given life sentences.

While all those in the Kakori Rail dacoity case were languishing in various prisons waiting to go to the gallows, on the 8th of February 1927, the Viceroy opened the magnificent new Council Chamber in New Delhi. The beautiful circular structure built by architect Sir Herbert Baker and located off the Kingsway and close to the Viceregal Palace did add to the splendour of the new capital, but to the members of the Hindustan Socialist Revolutionary Association it was nothing more than one more edifice of British imperialism.

The month of December 1927 was also a month of sorrow for Naren Sen, Debu Ghosh and Ghulam Hussein. On the 18th of December, Rajendra Lahiri was hanged. The very next day at the Gorakhpur jail Ramprasad Bismil kept smiling and shouting "Vande Mataram and Bharat mata ki Jai' while being led to the gallows. The same very day at the Faizabad jail, the handsome Ashafaquallah Khan smiled and kissed the noose. When the hood was put over his head in clear ringing tones he prayed aloud "La ilahi il Allah, Mohammed Ur Rasool Allah" (None has the right to be worshipped but Allah, and Mohammed is the messenger of Allah.) And finally on the 20th of December, when Roshan Singh was executed, Debu could take it no more.

'These bloody Englishmen are too **damn imperialistic, power** hungry and pig headed in their attitude and one day they will have to pay for it heavily mind you. And it all started in 1599, when the Dutch traders who controlled the Indian spice trade raised their prices. Feeling the pinch, a group of London Merchants formed the East India Trading Company and just three months later Queen Elizabeth signed the royal charter granting them exclusive trading rights with all countries beyond the Cape of Good Hope. These Redcoats who had come to do business soon became our masters after Colonel Clive of the East India Company at the Battle of Plassey in1757 defeated Sirajudaullah Khan the ruler of Bengal and thereafter they kept gobbling away our sacred land. There was however a whiff of revolt in 1857 to throw off the slavery, but it all ended with a whimper till Queen Victoria by a royal decree in 1858 dissolved the 'John Company' and today we are back to square one as they keep throttling our young blood by sending them to the gallows or to the dreaded Andamans," said a visibly moved Debu Ghosh as he tore to pieces the copy of the Calcutta Statesman which had reported the deaths of the four young Indian revolutionaries.

Meanwhile in Punjab, another young man was boiling with rage as he lectured to the young crowd and said.

' I know we are all feeling very sorry for the four great young Indian martyrs, but don't worry if the British do not heed to our aspirations of giving us our freedom, then there will many more such martyrs in the years to come. The young educated Sikh was trying to convince his friends to join the Punjab Nawjawan Bharat Sabha, an organization of young men whose main political objective was to inspire the youth of India to challenge the hegemony of the British Raj and fight for the freedom of the country.

Born on the 27th of September 1907 at Banga, a small village in the Lyallpur District of Punjab, Bhagat Singh was the second son of Kishan Singh and Vidyavati. As a young boy on the 14th of April 1919, on hearing about the massacre of innocents at Jalianwala he had taken a train to Amritsar and had visited the place. Seeing the bloodstains of those killed and the atrocities that were committed by the British on innocent people, he stood there in complete silence for a few minutes. Then he picked up some earth from the soil and rubbed it on his forehead. Returning to his village the 12 year old boy refused to have his food that night. A few years later the young lad came under the influence of Sachindranath Nath Sanyal, a man with a strong revolutionary zeal. With a letter of introduction from him, the 15 year old Bhagat Singh left for Kanpur to join Sanyal's revolutionary movement. At Kanpur under the assumed name of Balwant Singh he worked in a press that produced revolutionary pamplets and literature. Here he met Bhatukeshwar Dutt from whom he even learnt Bengali. Soon the young Bhagat Singh was heard reciting Kazi Nazrul Islam's famous poem 'Bidrohi'(The Rebel).

When Gandhi called for the boycott of all Government and Government aided educational institutions, Bhagat Singh joined the National College which had recently been founded by Lala Lajpat Rai, Bhai Parmanand and Sufi Amba Prasad. In March 1926, the 19 year old youth was appointed Secretary of the Punjab Nawjawan Bharat Sabha. At Lahore on the 11th death anniversary of Kartar Singh Sarabha, the revolutionary from Punjab, the man who was his childhood hero and whose photograph he always carried in his pocket, Bhagat Singh stood before the life size portrait of the departed soul and payed homage to him. At the condolence meeting that day he urged the young men and women of not only Punjab but of the entire country to join the Sabha and to fight for India's freedom. Standing silently in one corner, Professor Bhagwati Charan Vohra with his wife Durgawati and Sister Sushila Devi watched the solemn event. They were all members of the Hindustan Republican Association and felt very proud of the young Bhagat Singh.

CHAPTER-4

Time To Rub The Salt In

In November 1927, the British Government had appointed the Simon commission to investigate into India's constitutional problems and make recommendations to the Government on the future constitution of India. It was a sequel to the Government of India Act 1919 which was based on the Montague-Chelmsford reforms and whereby a statutory commission was to be appointed at the end of 10 years to determine the next stage in the realization of self rule in India. The Commission consisting of six Englishmen, all of them Members of the British Parliament and led by Sir John Simon, who were to decide the future fate of India surprisingly did not have even one single Indian as a member, and therefore both the Congress and the Jinnah faction of the Muslim League decided to boycott the commission. The Simon Commission was soon to arrive in India, but the Indian leaders were in no mood to welcome them.

"What right does the British Parliament have to frame a constitution for India without having a single Indian on the commission? It concerns India and we Indians alone have the right to decide about our own future,' thundered Lala Lajpat Rai, the Lion of Punjab while moving a resolution in the Central Legislative Assembly in February 1928.

Born on 28th January 1865, in the small village of Dudhika in the Ferozepur District of Punjab, Lala Lajpat Rai was a lawyer by profession. A very staunch nationalist he had earlier joined the extremist wing of the Congress led by Bal Ganghadar Tilak and had been deported in 1907 to Mandalay for his strong resistance against the Punjab Colonization Bill. The bill seriously affected the interests of people of the canal colonies in Punjab and he was in no mood to compromise on it. In 1920, after the Great War when the ban on him was lifted, he returned to India. With the spark of extremism still in him he secretly kept in close contact with members of the Punjabi Naujawan Sabha and the Hindustan Republican Association and naturally the young revolutionaries like Bhagat Singh, Sukhdev, Chandrashekar and others, they all simply revered him.

While Indian leaders debated and protested against the visit of the forthcoming Simon Commission, the first contingent from India ever to take part in the Olympics had already set sail on the ship Kaiser-e-Hind from the Ballard Pier in Bombay. It was the British Indian hockey team which was soon to create history, but there were only three people to see them off and that included the President and Vice President of the Indian Hockey Association and a lone journalist. All hopes were on the shoulders of a young sepoy from the Punjab Regiment whose father Sameshwar Dutt was a Subedar and the elder brother a Havildar in the British Indian Army. The boy who started playing hockey as a young boy using a branch of the date palm as a stick and with old rags of cloth as a ball had only completed his sixth class, when a British Officer seeing the potential and enthusiasm in the boy recruited him into the boy's platoon of the Punjab Regiment.

Born on 29th August 1905 at Allahabad, the dark complexioned young boy in 1922 was enrolled into the army as a sepoy. Though his actual name was Dhyan Singh, but because he practiced the game alone and all by himself even under moon light, his British mentor had named him Dhyan Chand since the word 'Chand' was the Hindi equivalent of the word for moon. In 1925, at Jhelum, Reggie with Major Attiqur Rehman had watched him play in the finals of the Punjab Indian Infantry tournament and both of them were highly impressed by the magic of his stick work. Dhyan Chand's team was already two goals down, but with his magic stick work when the lad scored a fantastic hatrick during the dying minutes of the game, Reggie and others among the spectators promptly christened him as the wizard of hockey. When Reggie heard about Dhyan Chand's selection for the Olympic squad, he promptly sent a congratulatory telegram to him and to his unit, the 14th Punjab Regiment. When the team arrived in England to play some practice matches and they won every one of them, Reggie was thrilled and he now prayed for India's win in the Olympics.

The 31st of January 1928, however was a sad day for Reggie. The news had arrived early that morning that Field Marshall Haig, the man who led England to victory in the First World War and who had appointed Reggie to his Poppy Flag Day Committee had died peacefully on the previous night. Reggie on that day was in Calcutta and attended the special condolence meeting that was held at the St Peter's Anglican Church located in the centre of the star shaped Fort Whilliam. Completed in 1824 from a design conceived to resemble the chapel of Trinity Hall of Cambridge, Reggie kept admiring the memorable monument inside the church that depicted the last supper of Lord Jesus. Throughout the entire church service he kept thinking not only about the gallant Field Marshall but also about his own parents who were married in that same very church very many years ago.

From Calcutta, Reggie visited some of the tea gardens in Upper Assam where his late mother as a young girl had spent a few years with her uncle and aunt who had brought her up. At Panitola near Dibrugarh he visited the graves of his maternal grandfather and grandmother. And while Reggie was enjoying his stay at the Panitola Tea Gardens as a guest of the Manager, in Calcutta, Debu Ghosh was busy trying to muster support from his friends to agitate against the proposed visit of the Simon Commission to India. One day sitting at the coffee house on College Street he waited for Naren Sen and Dr Ghulam Hussein to join him. It was routine and customary for the three of them to meet there on every Saturday after the day's work was over. And as soon as the two arrived, Debu Ghose ordered the special aromatic south Indian coffee for them and took out a copy of the manifesto of the Punjab Naujawan Bharat Sabha. The manifesto was written by Bhagwati Charan Vohra on 6th April 1928, but was received by Debu clandestinely sometime in the last week of May.

"Read every word of it and this is what I call true patriotic spirit and I admire Mr Vohra's style of putting it across to those who are waiting to welcome the Simon Commission," said Debu somewhat tauntingly. Thereafter holding the manifesto in his hand, Debu Ghosh in whispered tones read out a few key sentences from the manifesto as Naren and Dr Ghulam Hussein listened attentively.

"Does it require any revelation now to make us realize that we are enslaved and must be free? Shall we wait for an uncertain sage to make us feel that we are an oppressed people? Shall we expectantly wait for divine help or some miracle to deliver us from bondage? Do we not know the fundamental principles of liberty?"

Having completed the last quote from the manifesto, Debu Ghosh then said.

"So what do you both have to say to all this. Don't you think that the man is right?"

"Well come to think of it, there is a lot of sense in what the writer is trying to put across, but do we as Indians have the inclination or the will to join such a radical movement," said Naren Sen.

"I guess the majority of us who are a little more educated do not have the guts because we are quite happy with the typical Babu mentality of a 10 to 5 job," said Dr Ghulam Sen.

"Yes. I guess you have correctly hit the nail on the head, but I wish there were more men like Bhagwati Charan Vohra and Subhash Chandra Bose who are not only highly educated, but also are staunch nationalists to the core," said Debu Ghosh when he noticed the elderly Edwin Pugsley walking in.

"Bearer ek garam coffee hamare liye bhi jaldi lao man (Bring me a hot coffee too and do it fast) ordered the jovial and aging engine driver in his typical anglicized Hindi, while joining his young friends on the table. Noticing the seriousness on their faces, Edwin Pugsley as usual wittingly remarked.

"Well folks, what is the matter with all of you today. It seems all of you neither had a good breakfast or a decent snack. All of you look so bloody shagged out and downcast that it is time t all of you gave up drinking coffee and switched over to beer or whisky instead. Come on let all cheer up friends for we have every reason to celebrate," said Pugsley as he ordered three more cups of hot coffee and two plates of chicken sandwiches.

"Good Lord but for heaven's sake atleast do first tell us what are we celebrating and for whom, and moreover who is going to foot the big bill," said Naren Sen with a look of total surprise on his face.

"Well there you are Babu Moshai. You are always thinking about your pocket first and everything else thereafter. But you need not worry. Atleast not this time because the treat is on me today and I have just won a big bet and the loser happens to be another chee chee colleague of mine. That guy was backing the Dutch team all the way but they lost. And for your information the news has just arrived through the ticker tape that the Indian hockey team has won the Olympic gold at Amsterdam by beating the Dutch 3-0 and that to in front of a partisan crowd of 50,000 spectators. Now isn't that a good enough reason enough to celebrate," said a delighted Pugsley as he quietly took out his hip flask and had a large swig from it.

"And gentlemen that is not all. The blackie human eel Dhyan Chand from India who is probably today the world's greatest centre forward took the field inspite of his running a high temperature and he scored two of those three goals. And my dear friend Richard Allen the Indian goal keeper had the unique distinction of not even conceding a single goal during the entire tournament," added Pugsley as he helped himself to another quick one from the flask.

Well in that case we have created history because that medal is the first ever won by an Asian country and therefore only sandwiches and coffee will simply not do. Therefore let us cancel the last order and go to some nice cozy joint in nearby China Town for a wholesome Chinese meal with a drink or two thrown in for good measure. But pray don't please refer to him as a Blackie," said Debu Ghosh.

"I am sorry for that but this what is really called true real team spirit and cheers to that," said Pugsley as he winked at the waiter and cancelled the order.

During the summer of 1928, Colonel Reginald Edwards together with young Ismail Sikandar Khan arrived at the Prince of Wales Royal Indian Military College, Dehradun. Thanks to Tyndale Biscoe, Ismail Sikandar Khan had on his own merit qualified for a seat there. Standing in front of the building which was once the Rajwada for the military training of the Princes of India, Reggie felt proud of his Punjab Regiment who had whole heartedly agreed to bear all the expenses for the boy's education. And while he waited for his turn to deposit the fees, Reggie noticed a familiar face.

"My my look who the devil is here, and pray what the dickens are you doing here?" said Reggie as he walked up and embraced Major Attiqur Rehman.

"Well Sir, I am simply trying to convince my eldest son Gul Rehman who is playing outside that since he has qualified for admission to join this royal college, he must not miss this golden opportunity. And now if I may ask Sir, what is the bachelor and an old retired Colonel of the Indian Army doing in a place like this,?" said Major Attiqur Rehman as the two warmly shook hands.

"Well like you I am also getting someone admitted here in the same institution, and the only difference is that the boy happens to be not my son but that of my Regiment, the Punjabees," said Reggie very proudly.

"Well that is indeed very thoughtful and good of you, but where is the boy." asked Attiqur Rehman.

"There he is sitting quietly on the bench in front of the main office," said Reggie very proudly as he called out to Ismail Sikandar Khan. And as soon as the boy was introduced and shook hands with Attiqur Rehman, the good Doctor was simply delighted. He immediately shouted for his son Gul Rehman who was playing outside to come and meet the son of the Victoria Cross winner.

This is my eldest son Gul Rehman,' said Major Attiqur as Reggie vigourously shook the boy's hand and then introduced him to Ismail.

"This indeed is a welcome reunion and now that your son Gul is also here I have nothing to fear at all and even if I go back to my roots in good old Blighty, I know that you will take care of young Ismail too," said Reggie.

"You bet I will Sir," said Major Attiqur Rehman as he lifted Ismail Sikandar Khan in his big arms and having kissed him on both cheeks said.

Well as of now you are like my son too and therefore from this very moment whenever you feel like you will be more than welcome to come and stay with us."

On hearing those words, Reggie was undoubtedly very touched and he warmly embraced Attiqur and thanked him for his spontaneous friendly gesture.

"You do not have to thank me at all Sir. I consider this as a sacred duty towards the late Curzon Sikandar Khan," said Attiqur as he saluted Reggie.

"In fact it is I who should thank you Doc for all the assurance and I too am getting on in years. And I sincerely hope and pray that both the boys grow up as brothers and bring glory to India and to their families," said Reggie as they both once again embraced each other.

And while the admission for the new batch to the PWRIMC was being conducted, more young revolutionaries were also being enrolled into the HRA. Though the Kakori case was a major set back for the young revolutionaries, but that did not deter their spirit. On 9th and 10th of September 1928, 60 young men and 5 women revolutionaries from the Hindustan Republican Association secretly met at the Firozeshah Kotla ground in Delhi to adopt a new programme. By adding the word Socialist it had now become the HSRA, '.The Hindustan Socialist Republican Association', an army of Indian revolutionaries with a young man as its first Commander-in-Chief. Plans were made to open bomb factories at Lahore, Calcutta, Agra and Saharanpur. With the British intelligence sniffing around, they had shifted their base to Agra for a while and where they held their secret meetings at the Nai ki Mandi. It was therefore now time for them to call for the total boycott of the Simon commission too.

"Over our dead bodies, we will not allow them to enter Lahore, and if they do we will call for a total hartal and greet them with black flags," said an agitated Bhagat Singh as the meeting concluded for the day.

On the 30th of October, 1928 the Simon Commission arrived at Lahore. Though prohibitory orders were enforced, a huge crowd of men, women and children led by Lala Lajpat Rai greeted them with a sea of black flags at the railway station and shouted at the top of their voices 'Simon Commission, go back!' The crowd was unprecedented and it was the thickest on the route along which the members of the commission was to pass. Soon the security arrangements made by the police crumbled, and J.A. Scott the Superintendent of Police, Lahore ordered a lathi charge. The order was immediately complied with force and as the police with their stout staves, truncheons and lathis came charging towards the ring leaders, the small dedicated band of young revolutionaries like Bhagat Singh. Sukhdev, Yashpal, and Bhagwati Charan surrounded their leader and stood there like solid rocks. Then Scott shouted to his young deputy J P Saunders and said.

"Come on young man what the hell are you waiting for. I want action and I want you and your policemen to get after those damn idiots."

Without wasting anymore time, Saunders himself vindictively led the charge. The first blow of the lathi fell on Lala Lajpat Rai's umbrella, the second on his shoulder and the third on his head. Then Scott himself took the lathi and kept beating the Lala mercilessly. Bhagat was about to attack Scott, but the Lala restrained him from doing so. Though he was sick, Lala Lajpat Rai had led the procession that day and was now badly injured. But despite the injuries, he did not relent and held a public meeting. Addressing the huge gathering that evening he publicly roared. "I declare that the blows hurled at me today would be the last nails in the coffin of the British rule in India."

Immediately after the meeting was over he was removed to a hospital, but 18 days later on 17th November he succumbed to his injuries and died. Bhagat Singh was in tears.That evening after the cremation of his leader he went home and sat quietly by himself. His thoughts went back to his young days when as a boy he proudly read the clarion call of the Ghadar Party. Like a well orchestrated advertising campaign to fight the British, the Ghadar Party's propaganda machine motivated the young to take up arms and become martyrs if necessary. Posters and leaflets with captions like.

'Wanted Enthusiastic and Heroic Soldiers for organizing Ghadar (Revolution) in Hindustan and with death as remuneration and martyrdom as reward,'had attracted his attention, but Bhagat Singh was very young those days to take up arms. After returning from the cremation, Bhagat did not have his meal and he remembered the golden words of Kartar Singh Sarabha his mentor who told the judge during his trial that. "It matters little to me if I get life imprisonment or capital punishment. But I will prefer the latter so that after rebirth I may again be prepared for the struggle of India's freedom. I will die again and again till India becomes free and this is my last and final wish."

On the 4th of December, some members from the HSRA had committed the Punjab Bank dacoity at Lahore and on the night of 10th December a secret meeting of the HSRA was convened. It was attended by a selected few which included Bhagat Singh, Chandrashekar Azad, Rajguru, Sukhdev, Jai Gopal and Durga Devi.

"In order to avenge Lala Lajpat Rai's death we must finish off Scott," urged Durga Devi and the rest unanimously agreed.

"In that case please let me have the honour and the privilege to execute it," pleaded Bhagat Singh promptly while offering himself for the task.

"We will grant you that but you will not be alone in its execution. It will be a team work and we will all assist in whatever way we can, The death of our leader was a national insult and even the demands of a judicial enquiry on our leader's death has been rejected by the British authorities," said a visibly angry Durga Devi.

"Therefore there is all the more reason that the great Lala's death must be avenged," vowed the rest of them. Now Lajpat Rai dead was even more dangerous than Lajpat Rai alive as the leading members of the HSRA decided to unleash their wrath on the British.

For the next whole week, Bhagat Singh and his group studied the entire movements of Mr Scott, the Police Superintendent of Lahore. On being convinced that the operation would be a total success provided complete secrecy was maintained, they finally selected the date and time for the act. The evening of 17th December 1928 was now selected as Scott's day of reckoning and they decided to shoot him dead as soon as Scott completed his day's work and stepped out of his office. They were convinced that Scott would be on his way home from the secretariat and that would be the ideal time to get him. The plotters also took into account that being winter, darkness would fall early and this would therefore enable all of them to make a quick and safe gateaway. Led by Bhagat Singh the five member hit team were now allotted their tasks. Jai Gopal was tasked to be the look out man and was made responsible to give the early warning signal as soon as Scott came out on the road from the secretariat. Once out off the gate, Bhagat Singh and Rajguru with their loaded pistols would fire at their target, while Chandrashekar Azad armed with his revolver would cover the two hit men and keep a watch on the area around Once Scott was dead they would all take different routes and escape. The plan was simple no doubt but by a fate of luck it did not turn out the way they wanted it to be.

It was 4.15 pm, when instead of Mr JA Scott, his deputy the young Mr J P Saunders came out of the District police Office. A few minutes later, when

Saunders on his motorcycle came towards the gate, Head Constable Charan Singh was seen shouting and running after him. Saunders therefore stopped and waited for the head constable to catch up with him. It seems that Saunders had forgotten his keys in his office and Charan Singh managed in time to hand it over to him. With the keys safely in his pocket, Saunders restarted his motor cycle and as he got out of the gate, Jai Gopal without checking the correct identification of the rider gave the go ahead signal and ran. As soon as Saunders got on to the main road, Bhagat and Rajguru who were waiting in ambush fired on him. Rajguru's bullet it seems got Saunders first and on being hit the motorcycle skidded and Saunders was now seen lying on the ground. To make doubly sure that the victim was dead, Bhagat Singh then ran forward and pumped four more bullets into the man. With the deed done, though on the wrong Englishman, Bhagat Singh, Rajguru and Chandrashekar Azad ran through the Court Street towards the DAV college compound. Having heard the shots and seeing the trio fleeing, Head Constable Charan Singh gave chase. As he approached the DAV College, Chandrashekar Azad warned him to retrace his steps and to go back, but Charan Singh refused and Chandrashekar Azad had no other option but to shoot him too and one bullet was enough. While Charan Singh lay in a pool of blood, Bhagat Singh and Sukhdev with the help of friends hid inside the college premises. Late that evening having shaved off their big growth of beard, they all got into borrowed warm western clothes and waited for nightfall. After a few hours they made their next move. Dressed in proper western suits and hats they quietly slipped out from the College premises.

It was around 11 o'clock that night, when they knocked on the door of their friend Sohan Singh Josh's house at Bara Ghara Islamabad, Lahore. Luckily Josh's family had gone away to their village near Amritsar, but Josh was surprised to see his two friends all dressed up in western clothes and that too in that late winter night. Having heard the entire story and knowing that the two of them were hungry, Josh quickly offered them a few chappatis and some vegetables from what ever left over food there was in the house and rounded of the frugal meal with two glasses of milk for his two friends.

"Remember we must get to Bhabhi Durgavati's house before it is dawn," said Bhagat Singh as the two tried to snatch some sleep.

Early next morning, when they knocked on Durga Bhabhi's door, the lady of the house who was also the wife of Bhagwati Charan was not in the least surprised. She was alone with her little son as her husband was in Calcutta attending the Annual Session of the All India Congress. After a sumptuous breakfast prepared by the graceful lady, the getaway plans from

Lahore were given the final touches. With the rupees five hundred that was handsomely contributed by Durgawati all of them decided to catch the next mail train to Calcutta. It was decided Bhagat Singh with Durgavati would pose as man and wife and with her young child would complete the family, while Rajguru would accompany them as a servant/attendant. Taking on a new identity Bhagat Singh and his family posing as westernised Indians had therefore decided to travel first class while Rajguru posing as their servant would travel in the attendant's compartment adjacent to their first class coach. While Chandrashekar Azad in his make up of a devoted sadhu dressed in saffron clothes would be traveling in a nearby third class compartment. For their own self defence they all decided that they would all carry their loaded pistols with them.

In the evening, when the phaeton carrying Bhagat Singh and his newly acquired family reached the Lahore railway station, the place was teeming with policemen and plainclothesmen. They were checking for suspicious characters and for the killers of Saunders and Charan Singh. A shaven Bhagat Singh having partially covered his face with a military type overcoat over his big shoulders, a felt hat covering his head and with the baby in his arms confidently walked past them, while Durgawati along with their servant Rajguru following closely behind with the luggage, they too boldly got through the police cordon. Flashing the first class tickets to the ticket inspector they coolly got into their reserved compartment and what surprised them was that neither he nor his party were stopped, searched or asked any questions. And when the train finally steamed out of the platform, all of them breathed a sigh of great relief. It was nothing short of a miracle that they all managed to get away from Lahore without being questioned, but it was also probably the lack of good intelligence by the British that had saved them.

Traveling in the same train, but in the Interclass compartment was Debu Ghosh. The Inter class was neither a first nor a second class but something in between. For a middle class Indian it was a comfortable and cheap way of rail travel. Debu Ghosh was on his way back to Calcutta after attending a preliminary meeting for the preparation of the Lahore Congress which was scheduled to be held next year. The killing of British Police Officer Saunders with such boldness in broad day light had no doubt impressed him about the capabilities of the young HSRA revolutionaries, but what impressed him still more was the audacity with which the organization publicized the deed. Somehow or the other Debu had managed to get copies of a few hand written leaflets that had mysteriously found their way into the heart of the ancient Moghul city. These had been pasted at prominent places by the HSRA activists on the dead of night after the deed was done. It seems they wanted that by the very next morning of the 19th that the writing for the British to quit India should be on the walls and literary they were there. One of the leaflets read.

"JP Saunders is dead. Lala Lajpat Rai is avenged.'" Another declared. 'Beware, Ye Tyrants; Beware. Do not injure the feelings of a downtrodden and oppressed country. Think twice before perpetrating such diabolical deeds." And a third read "Long Live the Revolution" and "Inquilab Zindabad." Most of them were written in bold dark capital letters and one poster even said "Sorry for the death of a man. But in this man has died the representative of an institution which is so cruel and so biased that it must be abolished."

That night while traveling in the train, Debu Ghosh wondered where the wanted men could be hiding and while he prayed for their well being and safety, he did not realize that the three most wanted men were on the same train. Next day, when the Calcutta Mail made a long halt at Lucknow railway station, Bhagat Singh boldly got out of his compartment and came out to have a cup of tea on the platform. It was all prearranged to check if all of them were safe. Seeing Bhagat Singh with a cup of coffee in his hand, Rajguru acting as the servant went to fetch some milk for the baby, while Chandrashekhar Azad chanting and singing hymns about the famous Indian sage Tulsidas went to the railway tap to drink some water. All three then exchanged glances signaling that everything so far was alright.

In the meantime, while the train was being watered, Debu too went to buy a newspaper from the stall of AH Wheeler and Co and was pleasantly surprised to find a young Indian lady with a baby in her arms and a gentleman in a felt hat getting into the first class compartment.

"They must be from some rich family to travel in such luxury," thought Debu as he waved out to the little child and who in turn waved back at him.

"Intelligent kid I must say," thought Debu to himself as he read the headlines.

"British Police Officer and one Head Constable brutally killed at Lahore by so called revolutionaries. Government announces heavy reward for the capture of the culprits." Putting the paper under his arm Debu Ghosh returned to his compartment. Meanwhile Durgawati from the railway mail office had managed to dispatch an urgent telegram to her husband in Calcutta. It read. "Reaching Howrah by the Mail tomorrow evening along with brother and child. Do receive us at railway station."

It was Congress week in Calcutta and the Howrah railway station was full of Congress workers waiting to welcome the delegates and amongst them was Bhagwati Charan with her sister Sushila. As soon as Bhagat Singh with Durgawati and the child alighted, they were whisked away to a secret destination. Keeping a low profile, Bhagat Singh with Durgavati and her son Shachi stayed on the topmost storey of Sir Chajju Ram's three storey house that was in the heart of the city and it was all arranged by Sushila Devi.

The venue selected for the historical Calcutta Congress meet to be held from 25th December to 31st of December was the Park Circus Maidan. It was in an area surrounded by a steaming Muslim Ghetto. Subhas Chandra Bose was made in charge of the ceremonials and he decided to do it in perfect military style including a ceremonial guard of honour to Motilal Nehru who had been elected as the Congress President for that year. To keep order and discipline, Subhas Bose had given it a complete military touch. To the 2000 odd Congress volunteers half of them in uniform he had even given them a short training in military drill. The officers in the volunteer force even had specially designed steel chain epaulettes shining from their shoulders to go with their uniforms. Bose himself had his complete military uniform made from the British tailoring firm of 'Harmans' in Calcutta. Looking smart in his stylish new uniform and with a side cap covering his head, Subhas Bose looked every inch a General Officer Commanding that he had designated himself to be for the great occasion.

When Mahatma Gandhi arrived, the ghetto resounded with 'Mahatma Gandhi Ki Jai'. As the volunteers marched past and gave their salutes, a proud Subhas Bose stood erect at attention next to Motilal Nehru. Seated among the many spectatators dressed in a typical Bengali style of dhoti, kurta and with a shawal around his broad shoulders was Bhagat Singh. This was his first visit to the second city of the British Empire, but he was there on that day primarily to have a glimpse of the Mahatma. The Mahatma was 59 years old and he was just 21.

"My God I just cannot believe it," said Debu Ghosh to his friends Naren and Ghulam Hussein when he noticed the man with the broad shoulders sitting among the spectators. Because only a week ago while traveling in the train he had seen the same gentleman dressed in a fashionable western attire with even a felt hat over his head and had thought him to be an anglophile who enjoyed aping the British. But seeing the same person today in a typical Bengali dress, Debu Ghose got a bit worried and while pointing towards Bhagat Singh said.

"I wonder what that man is doing here at our political meeting. By God he is the same person whom I saw traveling in the same train with his wife and child and that too in a first class compartment when I was returning from Lahore, and today he is here sitting amongst us and I just cannot believe it."

"Maybe he is an intelligence agent for the British and has come here to snoop around," said Naren Sen.

"But are you sure that he is the same person," asked Dr Ghulam Hussein.

"Well I have no doubts and I will prove it to both of you when I confront that man once the meeting is over," said Debu Ghose very confidently.

Seeing the three of them periodically staring at him, Bhagat Singh thought that he was under surveillance by them and fearing that they could working for the British intelligence department he decided not to take any chances. So when the next speaker rose to address the gathering and the cheering began, he quietly slipped away and.quickly walked home. Therafter he changed his clothes and went to see the film 'Uncle Tom's Cabin,' which was showing at the Tiger Cinema on Chowringee.

While the Congress in Calcutta moved a resolution in favour of complete independence if dominion status was not granted to the country by the end of 1929, Bhagat Singh clandestinely met Jatin Das and sought his help and services for the manufacture of bombs. Inspired by his name sake Jatin Mukherjee who was also known as Bagha Jatin, the revolutionary who once killed a tiger with his bare hands, Jatin Das teamed up with Bhagat Singh to soon create history. It was however with more encouragement from his seniors that the grand idea occurred to Bhagat Singh and he was now determined to make the deaf British hear and he would do it in the heart of the new British capital of India, and that too right inside the massive Central Assembly in Delhi.

"I am sure a few harmless bombs thrown inside the Central Assembly will definitely make the British sit up and accede to some of our demands," said Bhagat Singh while discussing the methodology of the operation with the other core members of the HSRA. And while the members of the HSRA at Lahore, Saharanpur and Lahore got busy manufacturing bombs in their secret factories, at Chittagong in East Bengal, Surya Sen a nondescript local school teacher popularly known as Masterda having served his two years of imprisonment for his anti British activities was once again a free man. Having actively participated in Gandhi's non cooperation movement against the Rowlatt Act in 1919, and later convicted by a British court for his revolutionary ideas and activities, Masterda was seething with revenge. As a cover up for his future revolutionary activities, Surjya Sen now had promptly joined the Chittagong Congress District Committee and had become its secretary. A great admirer of both Rabindranath Tagore and Kazi Nazrul Islam, he immediately set about to organize a young band of dedicated and devoted revolutionaries who would give the British a run for their money. A brilliant and inspiring soul, the soft spoken and unpretentious school teacher soon got busy evolving a daring plan that would throw the British out from his own District of Chittagong if not from the whole of Bengal. Attleast so he thought.

Though the revolutionary spark in young men like Bhagat Singh, Jatin Das and Surya Sen galvanized the youth of the country to take up arms, in Bombay on 22nd February 1929, the spark to live died in a young well to do Indian woman. After 11 years of marriage and leaving a 10 year old girl Dina behind, the beautiful 29 year old Ruttie or rather Mariam the estranged wife of Mohammed Ali Jinnah was no more.With Jinnah's preoccupation initially with his profession and now with his political ambitions, they as a couple had been separated for quite some time. It was a marriage of complete incompatibility. Maybe the difference in age was too much for the beautiful Petit family daughter who while staying independently in a suite at the Taj Mahal Hotel in Bombay with her only daughter had practically become a mental wreck.

On hearing about her death, Jinnah immediately took the Frontier Mail from Delhi to be in time for his wife's funeral. In his first class compartment he was surprised to find Major Attiqur Rehman and Colonel Reginald Edwards. They were both on their way to Poona to attend a get together of decorated First World War veterans. On hearing the sad news both of them also got off at Bombay and they too went straight for the funeral ceremony.The tall handsome Jinnah who probably had never cried so much ever but on that day he wept like a little child as his wife's body was laid to rest in her grave. Reggie felt pity for the young old man and wished that like him Jinnah should have never married at all. That very evening Reggie and Attiqur called on Mr Jinnah at his palatial South Court Residence on Malabar Hill to offer their condolences.

Next morning while on the train to Poona Major Attiqur remarked.

"You know Sir I think it is not that Mr Jinnah did not love or care for his beautiful wife; it is simply that he had no time for her and his little daughter."

"Yes you may be right there but I also heard that during the initial few years of their married life, he was so much in love with her that before leaving for the courts for for the day's work, Mr Jinnah would invariably wake his wife up with a hundred rupee note under her pillow and that mind you is still a hellava lot of pocket money for a single day isn't it," said Reggie.

"Well I guess now that Ruttie is no more, Mr Jinnah will not only have more money in his pocket, but he will also be more active in politics too," said Attiqur Rehman.

Meanwhile having resolved to make the deaf hear and that to with a loud bang, Bhagat Singh with Batukeshwar Dutt arrived at Delhi and stayed at 15, Roshanara Mansion in Bazaar Sitaram. With the help of Jaidev Kapur from Hardoi who was also a student of DAV College Kanpur they had procured the visitors passes for entry into the Central Assembly. On 8th April, 1929, Bhagat Singh and Batukeshwar Dutt got dressed in their khaki shirts and shorts and before proceeding to the Central Assembly they even got themselves photographed in Ram Nath's studio near Kashmiri Gate. They had made up their minds to protest against the Public Safety Bill and the Trade Dispute Bill which was to be tabled that day in the Assembly and which if passed would reduce the civil liberties of the citizens of India. On arrival at the Central Assembly they produced their passes and had no problem in getting to their seats in the visitors gallery. The bombs, leaflets and the revolver that was carried by them had also gone undetected. With the Assembly in full session, they now waited for the right opportune moment to strike.

When the Bills were placed before the Assembly they were outrightly rejected by the Indian members of the Assembly. But as Sir George Schuster stood up to announce that the Viceroy had excercised his special powers in giving his consent to the bills and that he had been delegated to ratify them, Bhagat Singh and Batukeshwar Dutt boldly got up and threw the two hand made bombs in quick succession into the well of the house. The bombs exploded with a loud bang and soon the entire hall was filled with smoke. While there was complete pandemonium inside the assembly, Bhagat Singh and Batukeshwar Dutt like heroes stood up on their seats and on top of their voices shouted 'Inquilab Zindabad' 'Long live Freedom and Long Live the Revolution. And while those inside the assembly ducked for cover, both of them took out the bunch of red leaflets from their pockets and threw it into the well of the House. As the red leaflets carrying the messages 'Explosion necessary to make the deaf hear' and that 'It takes a loud voice to make the deaf hear' slowly floated down into the well of the house, there was look of triumph on Bhagat Singh's face. These were the same words that were uttered by Valiant a French anarchist and a martyr not very many years ago.

Following the loud explosion most of the members had dived for cover. A terrified George Schuster took cover behind a desk, while Motilal Nehru, Vithalbhai Patel, Mohammed Ali Jinnah and Mr Madan Mohan Mallviya kept their calm and remained in their seats. In order to draw their attention, Bhagat Singh then fired two shots in the air. Both the bombs were however harmless with only a few receiving some very minor injuries. A minute or two later after the pandemonium inside the Assembly had subsided, Bhagat Singh and Batukehwar Dutt both courted voluntary arrest. But seeing the revolvers in their hands the police at first were hesitant to even get near them. While addressing a shaken Sergeant Terry of the Police department who was on duty that day, Bhagat Singh very happily said.

"Do not worry Sergeant, we shall tell the whole world that we did it." Having made that confessional statement, both of them then surrendered their arms and on assurance from Bhagat Singh that they had no intention of using the weapon, the security staff arrested them. That is exactly what they had planned for and what they wanted to do. They wanted to be tried in court and use that as a forum for propaganda so that people all over India would become familiar with their movement and ideology.

While they were being taken to the Kotwali Police Station at Chandni Chowk in the police van, they passed a horse driven tonga. The tonga was carrying Bhagwati Charan, his wife Durgawati and their son Shachi to the railway station. Recognizing his favourite uncle inside the police van, an excited young Shachi cried out.

"Look look, there goes 'Lambu Chacha.' (Tall Uncle) But before the child could make a gesture and could utter something more, Durgawati quickly put her hand over the child's mouth.

After the arrest of Bhagat Singh and Bhatukeshwar Dutt, the man hunt for the other leaders of the revolutionary movement immediately started. Next day when Bhagat Singh's photograph featured in all the leading daily newspapers, Debu Ghose was stunned.

"My God.I just cannot believe it. This is the same man whom I saw dressed up like an Englishman travelling with his wife and child in a first class compartment when I returned from Lahore. Then again a week later the same man dressed as a Bengali Bhadralok was spotted by me sitting in one of the enclosures meant for the spectators during the Calcutta Congress and all the time I thought that he was probably a mole of the British intelligence service,'" said Debu Ghose to his wife.

"Well you thought wrong then," said Debu's wife Hena who was not the least bothered about the photograph in the paper.

"Yes and we would have looked like bloody fools had we confronted him that day during the opening of the Calcutta Congress of being a lackey of the British," added Naren Sen.

"Thank God for that and I must say both Bhagat Singh and his compatriot Bhatukeshwar Dutt are young men of true grit and courage," said Dr Ghulam Hussein.

"You bet they are and just imagine that the two of them while wearing only khaki shorts nearly took the pants off our British masters," said a delighted Naren Sen.

"And just look at their bloody guts. Of all the places they confidently sat in the member's gallery inside the Council Assembly, threw the bombs and the leaflets as planned and then heroically gave themselves up," said Debu Ghose

"But I only hope that the so called Gora Sahibs heard and understood what the two had to convey," said Naren's wife Shobha as she came in with three cups of hot Darjeeling tea for the men folk.

"Heard or not I cannot say. But one thing is certain and that is that the two young men will definitely go down in history," said Debu Ghose.

"There is no doubt about that, but having made the headlines today, I only hope and pray that the two of them will be able to sustain and stand up to the severe torture and punishment that they will be subjected to," said Naren Sen.

"But all said and done, the question still remains will this help in getting us our freedom," said Dr Ghulam Hussein in all seriousness as he called out to his Begum Sahiba to check if their son Nawaz Hussein had gone to sleep.

After the sensational bombing incident inside the National Assembly, the British police and their intelligence agents slowly and steadily started getting scent of the bomb making factories at Lahore, Saharanpur and Agra. Thereafter gradually and with the help from some of their own colleagues from the HSRA like Jai Gopal and a few others who had turned approvers because they could not stand the terrible torture inflicted on them, the game was up. Soon the police managed to nab the other key members of the HSRA who were directly and indirectly connected not only with the bomb throwing incident inside the Assembly, but also for the killing of Saunders. A few months later the trial of the persons allegedly involved in the 'Assembly Bomb Case' became a secondary issue and 'The Lahore Conspiracy Case' that resulted in the death of the British Police officer Saunders became the main one. Debu Ghosh as a lawyer therefore decided that he had to be in Lahore in case he could be of some help to the under trials there.

Everyday when the under trials arrived at the Court, they defiantly shouted slogans like 'Inquilab Zindabad,"Long Live the Revolution,"Long Live the Proletariat'and 'Down with Imperialism.' The slogans seemed to be fallout of the success of the Red Communist movement in the newly formed Soviet Union thought Debu Ghosh as he took his seat inside the courtroom as a junior judicial observer.

On the 6th of June,1929 when Mr Asaf Ali the defending lawyer stood up to read the full text of the statement made by Bhagat Singh and Bhatukeshwar Dutt, that day besides the usual slogan shouting, the under trials also sang patriotic songs. Debu Ghosh was visibly moved when he heard them sing 'Sarfarosh Ki Tamanna Hamare Dil Mein Hai' and 'Mera Rang De Basanti Chola.'The first song amply spelt out that the hearts of the young revolutionaries were filled with the desire for martyrdom, while the second song pleaded that their clothes should be dyed in the saffron colour, which to Indians since time immemorial has been the colour of courage and sacrifice. Despite the arguments by the prosecution and the spirited reply by the defence council to prove that the throwing of the harmless bombs inside the Assembly was not to kill or harm anybody and it was only to make the deaf hear, but to the learned Judge that did not cut any ice. He sentenced most of them to long terms of rigorous imprisonment. Once inside the prison the condemned revolutionaries were now subjected to various repressive measures and punishments.

In August 1929, on having heard about the plight of political prisoners in prison, Subhas Bose in Calcutta led a mammoth procession to protest against it. Dressed in uniform the protesters marched through the streets of Calcutta singing patriotic songs, shouting 'Vande Mataram' and some even kept reciting from the Hindu holy book of Gita. The police authorities were however quick to act and they immediately arrested Subhas Bose and sentenced him to imprisonment in the Alipur Jail. The Superintendent of the jail was Major Som Dutt. He was known to be a strict disciplinarian and often used the services of the hefty Pathans to straighten out the young Bengali revolutionaries crowding the jails.

"Though I am in jail, the fight against the British must continue," wrote Subhas Bose to his friends outside. Thanks to Debu Ghosh and his friend Edwin Pugsley, all such secret messages to and fro from the Alipur jail were now being routed through a few trusted young Anglo Indian boys who were employed by the jail authorities.

In July, all the under trials in the Assembly bomb case protesting against the inhuman conditions and treatment meted out to them inside the Lahore jail resorted to a mass indefinite hunger strike. They demanded they be treated not as ordinary criminals, but as political prisoners. Jatindranath Das had taken a vow that he would not eat unless the British asked for forgiveness for the death of their beloved leader Lala Lajpat Rai. Initially the British authorities mocked at his demand but when they realized that the young man meant business and was determined to fast unto death, they resorted to force feeding him. It was an exercise by itself as the prison doctor with the hefty jail wardens came twice a day armed with rubber tubes, funnels and jugs of milk to forcibly feed young Jatin. But Jatin knew how to outsmart them. Seven people were required to pin him down and he was forced to face upwards for the feeding operation. But once the rubber tube passed through his nostrils and reached his throat, Jatin would cough a bit and this would result in the tube being diverted to his mouth. Then as the doctor poured the milk through the funnel all Jatin had to do was to open his mouth and out it came. One fine day frustrated with his efforts the doctor came with three separate tubes. Two tubes were put through both his nostrils and one through Jatin's mouth. Now when the doctor poured the milk through the funnel and Jatin coughed his wind pipe got blocked and he couldn't even breathe. Jatin had violent convulsions and his face turned red. Realising his folly the doctor quickly removed all the three tubes but it was a bit too late. Jatin's blood now started showing symptoms of poisoning and on the 13th September 1929 at 4 PM in the evening the frail young Bengali with an iron will died.

The news of his death spread like wild fire as the jail authorities carried the bier to the outer gate of the jail. From there it was carried by his ardent admirers to the Lahore railway station. The compartment carrying his body was strewn with flowers and fruits, and as the train made its long journey to Calcutta, thousands came to pay homage to the courageous martyr at each and every railway station where the train stopped. At Calcutta a two mile long procession with some six lacs of people accompanied the proud son of India to the cremation ground. Amongst them were Debu Ghose, Naren Sen, Dr Ghulam Hussein and their aged fathers. A few days later, when all of them went to pay their condolences to the bereaved family, they were pleasantly surprised to read a telegram that was sent by the wife of Terence McSwiney, the Irish freedom fighter who also sacrificed his life under similar circumstances in Ireland. The telegram read "Family Terence McSwiney unites patriotic Indians in grief and pride of death of Jatindra Nath Das. Freedom will come."

"The sacrifice made by Jatin Das was not in vain. It would soon kindle the youth of India to take revenge," said Debu Ghose as they made their way back home.

While the young Indian revolutionaries in India kept the British busy, in England, the King decided to honour all the winners of the Victoria Cross from his British Empire. The date fixed was the 11th of November, 1929, which was a full ten years after the Armistice was signed and it would also coincide with 'Poppy Day' in England.

"With your kind permission, I would like to take young Ismail Sikandar Khan with me to London," "said Reggie to the Principal of the Prince of Wales Royal Indian Military College.

"You are most welcome Sir because the winter vacations are not very far away and young Ismail will also not be handicapped when he returns back to his studies," said the Principal.

A delighted Ismail Sikandar Khan with Reggie as his official guardian soon boarded a P&O ship from Bombay and three weeks later disembarked at London. On board were a large number of Indians, all winners or the near relatives of the winners of the Empire's highest gallantry award who had been invited for the occasion. After the remembrance service at the Cenotaph, young Ismail felt proud to see some 300 winners of the Victoria Cross, both young and old marching smartly as a body on parade. They were all proudly wearing the coveted medal and the Flanders poppy and Ismail wished that his father Curzon Sikandar Khan was there in their midst too. Also being missed by one and all and especially by Reggie was Field Marshall Douglas Haig, because he was the man who led them to victory and was instrumental in introducing the Flanders poppy. Unfortunately Haig the great soldier who loved India had died a year earlier.

Exactly on the dot of 10.59 AM, Prince Edward, the handsome Prince of Wales in his Welsh Guard uniform arrived in front of the Home Office. The King himself would have come to honour his gallant men, but he was indisposed that day. A minute later at 11 O'clock and standing next to the Prime Minister Mr Ramsay Macdonald when the Big Ben struck the first note of the Armistice hour, guns in the near distance boomed in salute. Then suddenly there was pin drop silence all around as each and everyone observed the two minutes silence and paid homage to those who had sacrificed their lives for the Empire. Seeing the solemnity of the occasion there were tears in the eyes of the 16 year old son of the hero of Gilgit, but later there was happiness in his eyes too when the Prince of Wales shook hands with him and said to Reggie.

"I am happy that the lad is doing well, but only make sure that he makes his career into the Indian Army as a regular commissioned officer and not as an ordinary sepoy now that the Government of India is considering having its own Sandhurst in India too. Moreover I notice that the lad still has my great grandmother around his neck like his late father used to and therefore it is all the more reason that he makes it to a regular commissioned officer," added the Prince in good humour.

"I definitely will see to that Your Highness,' said Reggie while saluting smartly.

On the 15th of December, 1929 while poet Nazrul Islam was being feted by Subhas Bose at the Albert Hall in Calcutta, elsewhere in India things were again hotting up for the British. While in Northern India at Delhi members of the HSRA were planning to target the Viceroy, in Calcutta, Chittagong and Dhaka members of various other revolutionary groups were identifying their new targets. The HSRA members had decided to blow up the Viceroy's special train when it was scheduled to arrive back with the Viceroy to Delhi sometime at the end of December. Unfortunately the bombs placed on the railway track were not powerful enough to cause any serious damage either to the train or to Viceroy Irwin. Gandhi was however happy that the Viceroy had escaped unhurt. In an article titled 'Cult of the Bomb.' the Mahatma thanked God for the Viceroy's narrow escape and he condemned those who had perpetrated the crime.

"Who the devil does he think he is," said an angry Bhagwati Charan as he sat down with Chandrashekar Azad in the room located above the Solomon Company at Aminabad Lucknow to write a rejoinder on Gandhi's article. The room was their secret den and they usually met there to discuss their future strategy, tactics and plans. Reacting strongly to Gandhi's article Bhagwati Charan wrote.

"We the revolutionaries stand for winning independence by all forces, physical as well as moral at our command and not only through Satyagraha or soul force that Gandhi believes in. We would like to advocate both soul force plus physical force to get rid of the British. Here in India, as in other countries in the past, terrorism will develop into a revolution and the revolution into independence, social, political and economic. There is no crime that the British has not committed in India. Their deliberate misrule has reduced us to paupers, and they have bled us white. As a race and a people we stand dishonoured and outraged. Do people still expect us to forget and forgive? We shall have our revenge—a people's righteous revenge on the tyrant. Let cowards fall back and cringe for compromise and peace. We ask not for mercy and we give no quarters. Ours is a war to the end to victory or death."

And while the young Indian revolutionaries kept raising their voices against the British, Debu Ghosh reached Lahore. It was in the last fortnight of December and like many others he was also a delegate at the Lahore Congress. At one of the meetings he found a young man distributing some pamphlets.

"Here please give me one too," said Debu Ghosh stretching out his hand.

"Sure Sir, but please do read it and do not throw it away as scrap, and I can assure you that the white Gandhi topiwallahs like you may learn a lot from it too," said the turbaned young Sikh as he handed over a copy of the HSRA manifesto that had been prepared by B C Vohra and signed by Kartar Singh, the President of the Hindustan Socialist Republican Association.

Though Debu Ghosh himself was not very upset with the contents of the manifesto, but others very much were. It was not only an open and blatant challenge by the young Indian revolutionaries to the British to get out of India, but it also was a warning to the Indian National Congress that they as members of the HSRA meant business. That evening, when Debu Ghosh returned to his room he lit another cigarette and then sat down to once again read the entire contents of that manifesto and analyze its implications. It began with the following sentence.

"The HSRA stands for revolution in India in order to liberate her from foreign domination by means of organized armed rebellion." In the next paragraph it attacked Gandhi and his policy of non violence. "Mr Gandhi is great and we mean no disrespect to him if we express our emphatic disapproval of the methods advocated by him for our country's emancipation. We would be ungrateful if we did not salute him for the immense awakening that has been brought about by his own non cooperation movement. But to us the Mahatma is an impossible visionary. Non violence may be a noble idea, but is the thing of the morrow. We believe in violence not as an end in itself, but as a means to a noble end. Terrorism of which we are being accused of is not the object of revolutions, nor do we believe that terrorism alone can bring us Independence. India today is bleeding under the yoke of Imperialism. Her teeming millions today are a helpless prey to poverty and ignorance. The future of India rests with the youth. They are the salt of this Earth and as the late Deshbandhu C R

Das had said that they are at once the hope and glory of our Motherland and the torch bearers on the road to freedom." The manifesto ended with the following call to the Indian youth. "Youths of India fall in, do not stand at ease, and do not let your knees tremble. Yours is a noble mission and respond to the clarion call of duty. Do not vegetate, but grow and let a new India arise." And it ended with the words. "Long Live The Revolution."

"It seems that the HSRA mean business," thought Debu Ghosh to himself as he wrote a letter to Naren Sen and enclosed the copy of the manifesto in it for his information. On 21st January 1930, Debu Ghose attended the court where Bhagat Singh with the others was being tried in the Lahore conspiracy case. It was also the death anniversary of Vladimir Ilych Lenin that day. Wearing a bright red scarf to show his solidarity with the Communist movement, Bhagat Singh while on his way to the court house, clarified that revolution does not necessarily involve just sanguine strife, and nor was there any place in it for individual vendettas. To him it was not the cult of the bomb and the pistol. All it meant to him was that that the present order of things which is based on manifest injustice must change and change fast.

As they entered the court room the group of under trials led by Bhagat Singh shouted. "Long live the Revolution." Long live Lenin" and' Long live the Communist International." For those few moments every Indian inside the court room including Debu Ghose felt proud of being an Indian.

And while the young revolutionaries of India while in jail kept shouting for the country's freedom, at midnight of 31[st of] December 1929 and 1st January 1930, in the historical city of Lahore and on the banks of the Ravi River the Indian tricolour was raised by Jawaharlal Nehru. As it unfurled there was a deafening roar as thousands of Congress delegates together with their sympathizers and supporters attending the historic Lahore Congress cheered wildly. It was their cry for Purna Swaraj or full freedom. In that exultant mood of that night Pandit Jawaharlal Nehru with a Pathani turban covering his receding hair joined the 200 odd wily Pathans from the North West Frontier Province in the merriment. As the drums thumped to a crescendo, they all locked their arms in a great circle and swayed with joy to one of the vibrant Pathan dances and the thumping of their feet only added to their new found elation. It seemed that for those few hours India was totally free, but she had still to prove it to their British masters. The declaration that night by the Congress party from India echoed the demand that was made by a small band of American colonials who on the 4th of July 1776, at Philadelphia voiced their own demand for total independence. The same demand was now being wholly supported by a tall well built Pathan from the small village of Utmanzai, a village not far away from Peshawar and the Afghanistan frontier. He also wanted that the Pathans of the North West Frontier should also join in the struggle for India's freedom, but in Gandhi's peaceful manner only.

It was nearly thirty two years ago on 22nd June 1897 at 11 O'clock in the morning under a clear blue sky, when Queen Victoria had touched her dainty fingers to the brass transmitting key in the telegraph room of her Buckingham Palace to commemorate the diamond jubilee of her reign. That day she sent her message of greetings telegraphically to her 372 million subjects spread over her vast Empire.

"From my heart I thank my people. May God bless them." On her sixtieth birthday, the Queen and Empress it seems had tapped the key somewhat a little nervously. Because on that very day while the great Queen dressed in black stepped into an open landau that was drawn by eight cream coloured horses and made her way to St. Paul's Cathedral for the thanksgiving ceremony, in the remote North West corner of India at Utmanzai, the 7 year old son of Behram Khan was using all his strength and effort to stop the wooden logs from floating down stream into the shallow Swat River. Hearing his father's call, the obedient boy ran back home. The youngest member of the family, Abdul Ghaffar Khan had two elder sisters and an elder brother Abdul Jabbar Khan and all of them were much older to him. That night on her 60th birthday, when Queen Victoria wrote in her journal that no one ever had received such an ovation as was given to her that day; in India young Abdul Ghaffar Khan an illiterate boy was fast asleep in his father's house at Utmanzai. But today on the declaration of Purna Swaraj the tall strapping Pathan was dancing with joy and keeping him company was the elderly Haji Abdul Rehman who had come all the way from Peshawar to Lahore to witness the historic declaration.

Abdul Ghaffar Khan belonged to the Pathan clan of the Mohammedzai tribe. They were known as the the sons of Prophet Mohammed. His ancestors originally hailed from Jalalabad in Afghanistan and Abdul Ghaffar Khan was no ordinary man. His grandfather Obaidullah Khan had gone to the gallows for a Pathan's honour. His father Behram Khan was a wealthy landowner and Chief of the Utmanzai tribe. His elder brother Abdul Jabbar Khan popularly known as Dr Khan Sahib had married a Scottish lady while studying medicine in England and had served as a doctor in the Indian Medical Service during the Great War. Though a Pathan from the North West Frontier Province, he was a true disciple and follower of Gandhi's non violent movement. A product of the Edwardes Memorial Mission High School, Peshawar, Abdul Gaffar like his elder brother Dr Khan Sahib was also a colleague and class mate of Attiqur Rehman, but he could not complete his school finals. While in the 10th class he was even offered a Viceroy's Commission in the famed Guides Cavalry of the Frontier Force Rifles which he refused. While studying in school he was devoted to the two large hearted Englishmen. One was the Reverened EFF Wigram, the headmaster, and the other the headmaster's younger brother who was a doctor by profession.On the recommendation of Reverend Father Wigram, Abdul Ghaffar as a young man would have sailed for England to pursue higher studies like his elder brother did, but fate decided otherwise. Even his passage was booked on a P&O ship. But because of his mother's pleading and request, the young lad decided not to carve his future on his mother's sorrow. In December 1915, an influenza epidemic swept through the province and he lost is wife. Grief stricken he left his two young sons Abdul Ghani and Wali with his mother and toured the villages with the aim of starting his own schools, and by 1918 he had visited practically all the villages in the Frontier. Though not even a matriculate, he took the cue from Father Wigram and started his own school at Utmanzai when he was not even 20 years old.

His name first came into public notice on 6th April 1919, when he led an agitation against the repressive Rowlatt Act. That day he presided over a protest meeting in his own village of Utmanzai and surprisingly a large number attended it. As a result of this he was arrested and put in prison, where his feet was kept in iron shackles which was too small for his long legs. When he came out of prison, his parents had found for him another wife. In 1920, he attended the Indian Congress Session at Nagpur and was inspired by Gandhi. On his return his father Behram Khan was warned by the Chief Commissioner of the North West Frontier Province, John Maffey to persuade his son not to open any more schools, but Ghaffar Khan refused. He was again arrested and sentenced to three years rigorous imprisonment and brutally tortured. His elder brother Dr Khan Sahib who had just returned from England went to see him and was in tears. That day in prison Dr Khan Sahib handed over a note from Maffey to his younger brother. The note from the Commissioner of the North West Frontier Province promised that the sentence could be immediately commuted if only Ghaffar Khan promised not to tour the villages and run his schools. Gaffar Khan tore the note up in disgust. A few days later he was transferred to the prison at Dera Ismail Khan. It was a prison for the habitual and hardened criminals. There with his hand and feet in shackles and with an iron ring locked around his neck he served the remaining part of the sentence. His crime according to the British was sedition. While in prison he learnt about his mother's death. In 1924, on being released from prison he returned to Utmanzai. Undeterred by the punishment suffered by him, he addressed a mammoth meeting of the Pathans and roared.

"Oh Pathans, do remember you are not sheep but lions. The pity is that you are still being brought up in slavery. Therefore stop bleating like sheep and roar like a lion." The message had its impact. The Pathans roared again and again and as the loud cheering and clapping echoed across the mountain ridges, they knew that they had found their true leader.

In 1926, his father Behram Khan died and Ghaffar with his sister and wife went on a Haj to the holy city of Mecca. He also visited Palestine, Lebanon, Syria and some other Middle East countries. There he found that Islam was in the midst of a renaissance. The Muslim countries who were also under the yoke of British colonial power now looked to India for inspiration and Ghaffar Khan clearly realized it. India was the corner stone of the British Empire and if only that stone was removed, the British Empire in the Middle East could collapse like a house of cards thought Ghaffar Khan. During that visit his second wife met with a tragic accident. While visiting Jerusalem she tripped and fell from a high flight of steps and died and Ghaffar Khan vowed not to marry again. He however encouraged the women of the Frontier to come out of the veil and become more progressive. Like his own dear sisters he encouraged them to remove the system of purdah and come out in the open to take part in his movement. This was undoubtedly a very daring and courageous thing to do and especially so in the North West Frontier which was highly conservative and more so where women were concerned. To them he gave the example of Sarojini Naidu who in December 1925 was made the President of the Congress party. On his return from Calcutta after having attended the meeting of the Indian National Congress in that city in December 1928, the burly bearded Ghaffar Khan roared again. He told his fellow Pathans.

"Oh Pathans if you want your country and your people to prosper, you must stop living for yourselves. You must start living for the community because that is the only way to prosperity and progress. What I need now are soldiers, but not the fighting type with guns and weapons but good, gentle, disciplined and non violent ones. We will have our own cadre and uniforms and we will be an army of unarmed but dedicated Pathans. Tell me what could possibly take more bravado than facing an enemy in a righteous cause without weapons, and neither retreating or retaliating. Isn't that the loftiest kind of honour?"

Ghaffar Khan knew that the word honour stirs the Pathan more deeply than anything else and without freedom how could there be honour. For a moment or two there was pin drop silence as the mammoth congregation of Maliks and tribesman waited with baited breath for their new found leader to continue, but Ghaffar Khan had nothing more to say for the moment. He had hit the nail on the head. Having surveyed the general mood of the huge congregation of his brother Pathans, Ghaffar Khan spoke again.

"Well then we will call ourselves the Khudai Khidmatgars, the true servants of Allah and our motto will be full freedom and our aim will be to do service to the people and to mankind. We will show to the world that ours will be the first professional non violent army. As God needs no service so shall we as Khudai Khidmatgars for by serving his people we will only be serving him and him alone? Therefore from today and from this very moment let us all therefore promise to shun violence and refrain from taking revenge on one another. Let us also stop taking part in our feuds and quarrels and thus stop creating enmity amongst ourselves. Let us promise to treat every Pathan as a brother and a friend. So let us us brave Pathans as true Khudai Khidmatgars take this solemn oath today."

Having said that, again for a while there was complete silence as Ghaffar Khan surveyed the faces around him. Soon the place started humming as they consulted one another. For a Pathan taking an oath was not a simple matter because once a Pathan gave his word it could not be broken, such was their code of conduct and even his sworn enemy could count on that. Soon slowly and steadily Ghaffar Khan drew his first recruits from the high school educated Pathans and others voluntarily followed.

After the Lahore Congress, Abdul Gaffer Khan was now on the verge of tormenting the British with his unique brand of non violence. In September 1929, he had formed the Khudai Khidmatgar—'The servants of God' as he called them It was a movement aimed at teaching the wily Pathans industry, discipline and self reliance by inculcating in them the love and fear of God. His nonviolent army consisting entirely of Muslims from the North West Frontier was based on the ancient Islamic principles of universal brotherhood, submission to God and the Service of God through the Service of his own creatures. To the British they were known as the Red Shirts because of the colour of the uniform that they wore. Meanwhile his elder brother Dr Khan Sahib from the Indian Medical Service who had been asked to join a military expediton against the Wazir tribe promptly resigned. With

Abdul Gaffar Khan's personality and commitment to the well being of his people, he was now affectionately and reverently called Badshah Khan or the Khan's Khan and the man was not even 30 years old.

One day sometime in early January 1930, Haji Abdul Rehman with his son Major Attiqur Rehman went to Utmanzai village to pay a courtesy call on the Khan Brothers.

"This indeed is a pleasant surprise and both of you are our honoured guests sent to us by Allah," said the bearded Khan while welcoming the two of them to sit with all the other participants and take part in the discourse about the role and duties of the Khudai Khidmatgars. While they all sat in a circle in the open under the warm winter sun and they kept bantering in Pushtu while sharing a common water pipe, Major Attiqur Rehman who was still in military service quietly slipped away. Though he was in civil clothes, Attiqur was afraid that meeting Badshah Khan and that to in his own domain may prove harmful to his career and he therefore went inside the house to play with Gani and Wali, the two young sons of the Badshah.

"But tell me Chachajaan (Uncle) why have you put both your sons, Gul and Aftab in the military college at Dehradun? Do you really want them to become soldiers and fight for the British who have shown no mercy on us and our people," said Gani. Attiqur Rehman for a second was stunned by the young boy's question and for a brief moment did not know what and how to reply. But after a long pause when he said that with Badshah Khan commitment and that of Mahatma Gandhi to free India, the British one day will have to give us freedom and then leave our country and India would then require its own well trained army officers to train others to defend ourselves, the young boys were generally satisfied.

That evening while returning home on hearing the call of a village muezzin for prayers, both father and son spread their small carpets in an open field and knelt down to pray. As the words 'Allahu Akbar' echoed through the distant hills and mountains, Haji Abdul Rehman truly believed that God was indeed great. Because that very morning he had been given the good news that his third grandson Arif Rehman who was 10 years old had topped his class with record marks in the Edwardes Memorial School and had been short listed by the Commissioner himself for entry into the next batch to the Prince of Wales Royal Military College at Dehra Dun.

"Well we will soon have all the three musketeers together at Dehradun. As it is I miss the company of the other two rascals, and now Arif will also go away, but I guess it is all for their own good," said the proud grandfather to his dear wife on reaching home.

"And when will I join them," said Shenaz his six year old granddaughter and the only girl in the family as she plonked herself comfortably on her grandfather's lap.

"That is a million dollar question which only the Prince of Wales can answer my love and that to provided he too gets married soon. Then we could expect the charming future Princess of Wales with her husband to once again visit India and open one such college for girls also. But it should not be in Dehradun."

"But why not in Dehradun grandfather," questioned the young and beautiful Shehnaz.

"For the simple reason that if such a girl's college does open in Dehradun, then the boys will not put their minds into their studies and it will be a a major distraction to them. Their teachers will also be unhappy and the chances of some of them falling in love and eloping from there cannot be ruled out either," said Haji Abdul Rehman while having a hearty laugh.

"Please oldman do not give our granddaughter such crazy ideas, afterall she is only a child," said the Begum Sahiba in her loud voice from inside the kitchen.

' But I was only joking and replying to her intelligent question," said Haji Abdul Rehman as he winked at Attiqur Rehman and called for his daughter-in-law Nafisa to get him some more of those mouth watering chapli kebabs.

While the Haji and his family were celebrating young Arif Rehman's progress in school and Bhagat Singh and the others were languishing inside the Lahore jail, at Allahabad, another young fiery member of the HSRA was planning his next move. Born on 23rd July 1906, in a mud plastered hut in an obscure village in the state of Alirajpur in Central India, the young man had risen to become the first Commander-inChief of the Republican Army. Born to Jagrani Devi and Pandit Sitaram Tewari, he as a young boy of 14 years had actively taken part in Gandhi's non cooperation movement in 1919-1920, and for which on one occasion he had also been brutally punished. When arrested and questioned by the magistrate about his name, his father's name and his place of residence, the young boy defiantly gave his name as Azad, his fathers name as 'Swatantra', and the 'Prison' as his residence. Provoked by the lad's cheekiness, the Magistrate sentenced the boy to 15 lashes of flogging in public. When he was stripped and tied to the flogging pole and the brutal whipping began, the courageous young 14 year old did not even flinch. With every stroke of that lash on his bare back he kept shouting 'Mahatma Gandhi ki Jai' and 'Vande Mataram.' Seeing the young lad's amazing endurance, courage and fortitude, the people added the title of Azad to his name. Chandrashekhar Azad, the revolutionary from the HSRA who had taken part in the Kakori dacoity, the bombing attempt on the Viceroy's train, in the shooting of Saunders and in many other such revolutionary activities was still at large and the British had placed a very high reward for his head.

After proclaiming the declaration of India's Independence on 26th January 1930, Gandhi came to an impasse in his fight with the British. He had made an offer to the Viceroy to accept his eleven point programme which included among others, reduction in land revenue, abolition of the salt tax, release of political prisoners, but it had evoked no response from the Government. In mid February, the Congress Working Committee met at the Sabarmati Ashram and invested Gandhi with full powers to launch the Civil Disobedience Movement at a time and place of his choosing. Debu Ghosh who had gone to Ahmedabad as a volunteer for the Congress Working Committee meeting on hearing about Gandhi's ingenious plan immediately wrote about it to his friend and brother-in-law Naren Sen.

"Dear Naren,

The matter I am about to write to you about must not be divulged to any one, not even to your wife till such time the new movement begins. The oldman Gandhiji has had another great brainwave and he will soon literally rub a lot of salt into the British Raj. Therefore salt my dear friend will soon become the focal point of the oldman's extraordinary nonviolent movement and will shake the British Raj like it had never been shaken before."

"As you are aware that the British have a total monopoly on the salt tax in India and the production and sale of this very vital ingredient for our daily consumption is not only prohibited, but it is also a criminal offence punishable by law. Gandhi realizes that each and every Indian requires salt and will shortly use the British monopoly as a catalyst for a major nonviolent civil disobedience campaign. He is going to appeal to all loyal Indians which will cut across all regional, class and ethnic boundaries and barriers to join him in this great movement, and I can bet you it will work wonders. That is because this item can be collected free of cost by most of us since it is available in abundance along our huge sea coast and even I was not aware that we were all paying for it and it is one of the biggest sources of revenue for our British masters. Undoubtedly with our climatic conditions we all must have some little salt everyday and that goes for even the poorest of the poor in this country. Now that Gandhi's 'Operation Salt'" will soon begin, I have decided to extend my stay here and take an active part in it. Only for heavens sake do keep this to yourself for the time being, but when the clarion call is given, do please also ensure that the whole of Calcutta takes part in it too.

On the 2nd of March, 1930 Gandhi wrote a letter to the Viceroy which was simply remarkable and unique in its style. In that he wrote.

"Dear Friend, I cannot intentionally hurt anything that lives, much less fellow human beings, even though they may do the greatest wrong to me. Whilst therefore I hold the British rule in India to be a curse, I do not intend any harm to a single Englishman or to any legitimate interest that he may have in India. With the vast inequities in the salaries paid to Indians and to British officials whereby while the average Indian earns two annas a day, the British Prime Minister earns Rupees 180 and the Viceroy Rs 700 per day, I therefore ask you on bended knees to seriously ponder over this phenomenon. The system of administration carried out in India is thus demonstratively the most expensive in the world and it only further impoverishes the nation. I would like to therefore mention that I intend to begin with breaking the salt laws for I regard this tax on salt to be the most iniquitous of all from the poor man's standpoint. As the Independence movement is essentially for the poorest in the land the beginning will be made with this evil. If my letter makes no appeal to your heart, then on the 11th day of this month I shall proceed with such co-workers of this Ashram as I can take, to disregard the provisions of the Salt laws."

On 12th March, 1930 from his Sabarmati Ashram at Ahmedabad, a frail and lean Gandhi with the walking stick in his hand led the historic Dandi March and Debu Ghosh as one of the 78 satyagrahis also set out with the Mahatma for the coastal village of Dandi. Gandhi told the people along the way that he on bended knees had asked only for bread from the Viceroy but what he got was only stone. The only woman leader in that great march to the sea was Sarojini Naidu whom not only Debu but everybody admired. All along the route of that 241 mile march, Gandhi addressed the large crowds and soon more joined in. Marching to the tune of Gandhi's favourite bhajan "'Raghupati Raghava Rajaram' they arrived on the 5th of April in the sleepy coastal village of Dandi on the coast of Gujrat.

Next morning after 23 days of marching and at 8.30 in the morning as the sun shone over the Arabian Sea, Gandhi picked up a handful of salt from the sea and having tasted it threw it up triumphantly into the morning air.

'Hail deliverer' shouted Sarojini Naidu with joy while complimenting the Mahatma for his indomitable courage and for setting an example to his own people. Gandhi's example soon set India alight as people from all walks of life broke the salt law nonviolently. It was a big slap in the face of the British authorities who now with impunity started arresting anyone and everyone who broke it or even attempted to break it. One of them to be taken to the Arthur Road jail in Bombay was 42 year old Mrs Perin Captain, a Parsi lady. She was arrested at Chowpatty for leading the women to defy the draconian salt law. As a young 18 year old girl, Perin had first met Mr Gandhi in 1906 at London. Gandhi was an invitee to the Parsi Pateti Day celebrations that was being hosted by Mr Jamshetji Tata on a boat on the Thames River that day. Dressed in a morning coat with stripped trousers and with a diamond pin stuck in his readymade tie, Gandhi looked a complete westerner in that outfit. He was in England to solicit support for his work in South Africa. When Perin was sentenced to three months of imprisionment in the Arthur Road jail, she simply smiled at the Magistrate and thought about Gandhi's complete change in lifestyle.

On the same day after Gandhiji broke the salt law at Dandi, at Allahabad, Motilal Nehru magnanimously donated his own huge mansion called Anand Bhavan to the Congress. Giving it the new name of Swaraj Bhavan, Motilal at a formal ceremony at Allahabad presented the keys of the house to his son Jawaharlal and who in turn as the President of the Congress humbly accepted the gift from his father.

"By God this is what I call true Indian patriotic spirit," said Shaukat Hussein as he with his old friend Sonjoy Sen sat on a bench in the great Calcutta Maidan after their routine early morning walk to read the morning papers.

"Yes and imagine the very man who not very many years ago admired the British, and who dressed himself in the best of English clothes from Saville Row, who liked his tot of scotch in the evenings and six days a week ate only western food sitting on a Victorian chair on his twenty four seater dining table at home, is today a devoted and a patriotic Indian." said Sonjoy Sen while enjoying the hot tea in the small earthen pot.

"Incidentally I must also tell you that when I visited Allahabad some years ago I was told by none other than Ashgar Ali, Mr Motilal Nehru's trusted butler that the huge house had two separate wings. One was the western wing and the other the Indian wing, and each wing was complete with two separate kitchens and two separate dinings rooms. The western wing was staffed by Muslims and Christians and the Indian wing by the

Hindus. Ofcourse on all Sundays and on all Hindu festival days it was always Indian food and they all sat on colourful little mats on the floor and enjoyed the delicious Indian meal that was served to all the house members and their guests in pure silver thalis with six or more silver bowls around it and a silver glass for drinking water. I must say that the man really lived in style. And I was also told that when he with his family went to Delhi for Jawaharlal's wedding to Kamla Kaul, the sixteen year old slim, beauitful and tall daughter of Arjun Lal Kaul, Mr Motilal Nehru had even chartered a complete railway train for the great event. It was called the Nehru wedding train and it was decorated from the engine to the guards van with ribbons, buntings and flowers," said Sonjoy Sen while enjoying the hot tea.

"And not only that, Mr Motilal Nehru had even established a complete tented camp outside the city and it was handsomely furnished too. Incidently my son Naren if you will recall also got married on that same Basant Panchnami day in 1916," added Sonjoy Sen, as they both slowly made their way home.

"But do you know Baba that once upon a time the Nehrus I believe were also Kauls," said Naren as he with his friend Dr Ghulam joined their fathers for the walk home.

"But how cand that be possible," asked Shaukat Hussein.

"Originally the Nehru family I am told was from the beautiful vale of Kashmir, but some 200 years ago and in 1719 to be exact, when the Moghul Emperor Faruksiyar visited the valley he was so impressed with the conduct of the learned Kashmiri Pandit Raj Kaul that he invited him to come with him to Delhi. On his arrival at Delhi, the Emperor presented Mr Raj Kaul with a house that stood on the banks of a canal and the word for canal in Hindi happens to be 'Nehar' and the Kaul family thus became popularly known as the family living near the 'Nehar' and the house itself was called 'Kaul-Nehar.' The name somehow later got corrupted and they thus became the Nehru's," said Naren.

"And that is not all and let me tell you something more interesting about the Nehru family. Jawaharlal's great grandfather incidently was I believe the first vakil or rather the first legal representative of the British East India Company at the Royal Moghul Court and his grandfather Mr Gangadhar Nehru was the Kotwal and the chief of police of the last Moghul Emperor and during the revolt in 1857 he with his wife and two teenage sons and two young daughters fled from Delhi. After initially staying for a while at Agra, Gangadhar Nehru died on 6th may 1861 and three months later Motilal was born. Indrani Nehru doted on her son Motilal and when Motilal became a senior and well known lawyer, both his son Jawaharlal and Mr Mohammed Ali Jinnah were his immediate juniors," said Ghulam Hussein.

"I must say both our boys are much better informed about the Nehru's than we are," said Sonjoy Sen as they stopped by near Burra Bazaar to do the monthly grocery shopping.

Meanwhile having completed the march to Dandi, Debu Ghose returned to Calcutta. He had a couple of important court cases to attend to. On reaching home he was surprised to get a registered letter from his father in Chittagong. It was marked confidential and was dated 1st April, but he received it only on the 15th which coincided with the Bengali\New Year's day. As Debu Ghose went through the contents he looked a bit worried. It seemed that his younger brother Hitu who was only 16 years old and was the youngest in the family had run away from home to do what was popularly known in Bengali parlance as 'Swadeshi.' In other words Hiten Ghosh had become a revolutionary and had joined Masterda Surjya Sen's secret outfit and about which Debu Ghosh had no clue at that time. However, to console his old father, Debu wrote back and said that there was nothing to worry about because that was the trend all over the country and that Hitu will probably be back to his studies soon.

That night while Debu Ghosh's thoughts went back to his younger brother Hitu, at Chittagong Masterda was busy finalizing his 'Death Programme.' Addressing a handful of his young dedicated lieutenants that included Nirmal Chander Sen, Lokenath Baul, Ambika Chatterjee, Ananta Singh, Ganesh Ghose and a few others, some of whom were still in their teens, Surjya Sen the middle aged school master dressed in a white spotless dhoti, kurta and a khadi Gandhi cap over his receding hairline said.

"I fully realize that it is not possible for us sitting here in this remote eastern corner of our dear motherland to liberate the entire country, but a beginning has to be made and it will be made here in our own Chattogram. Gandhiji has already declared and demanded that the British should free us from our bondage and slavery and we will therefore give the lead. But Gandhiji is also mistaken if he thinks that the British will so easily abandon their milch cow. We none the less need to give the Gora Sahibs a big jolt and we will do it in our style. You are all very young and I am not old either, but we have to stand up and fight the tyranny and the slavery of the British Raj which has made us spineless and impotent. The 'Death Programme' calls for your sacrifice for the motherland and I know you all have it in you to make that supreme sacrifice. The plan is simple but it has to be executed with boldness, guile, secrecy and pride, and which will set an example to the youth of our entire nation. We may not be able to emancipate and free the whole of India but we will definitely remove the District of Chittagong from British subjugation. The date for this emancipation comrade is Friday the 18th of April. It is the Easter week and it is one of the great festivals of the Christian church commemorating the resurrection of Christ. And while they paint their Easter eggs we will kick their bloody goose. We therefore need to catch them completely off guard and literally with their pants down because it is going to be a one night operation to begin with. For them it will not be a happy Easter Sunday this year I can assure you, atleast not in Chattogram if all of you young and bold leaders with your respective action groups carry out the tasks that I will now spell out to you in a little more detail."

Hiten Ghose, the younger brother of Debu Ghosh who was sitting beside his leader Ganesh Ghose with awe listened to every word as Masterda gave out the final plan.

"Comrades the Death Programme will start at 10 pm sharp on the night of Friday the 18th of April. The plan is to boldly strike and capture with lightening speed and with complete surprise the following key targets and that too simultaneously."

Like a well trained military commander, Masterda that morning using a hand made sketch of the areas that were required to be targeted gave out his final orders with full confidence. He was determined to make the sun set in atleast on one part of the British Empire and for the world to see.

Very early that morning of 18th April, 1930 Ananta Singh with the pistol in his pocket went to the garage to tune up his Baby Austin car. Thereafter he took it for a drive and did a quick reconnaissance of the given routes to the main objectives. On his return, he with Masterda, Lokenath Baul and Ganesh Ghose, meticulously went through the entire plan of mobilization and attack using the big hand made wall chart which they ultimately destroyed. It was a simple but daring plan that was to be carried out by some 65 odd armed dedicated young men and women in military uniform and with most of them still in their teens.

In the first phase the assault parties in small squads with lighting speed and with complete surprise were to attack the two main objectives, namely the main Police armoury and the Auxilary Force armoury in Chittagong and capture as many weapons and as much ammunition as possible. Simultaneously two other armed squads were tasked to attack the Central Telegraph and the Central Telephone Exchange and cut off all communication between Chittagong and the rest of the world. At the same time another well armed group was tasked to attack and storm the main

European Club and take hostage of as many English Officers as possible and in case they resisted they were at fully liberty to shoot them. Two other small groups with explosives were also dispatched to sabotage the railway line and to cut of the telegraph wires near the Dhum and Feni railway stations respectively. All these tasks were to be carried out simultaneously at 10 pm that night. Another party of 30 or so young revolutionaries was to be kept ready and in reserve inside the forested area that was located 200 yards from the Police armoury. Later that morning Ananta Singh left the Baby Austin car with Ganesh Ghose and went to the showroom of M/S J N Ray Chowdhury and Company to take delivery of the new and bigger Chevrolet car that was to be used for the operation.

At 9.45 PM that evening from Ganesh Ghose's house in Sadarghat the group of six dare devils that included Ananta Singh, Devaprasad Gupta, Himangshu Sen, Soroj Guha, Haripada Mahajan and Ganesh Ghose all dressed in full military uniform and armed with pistols and revolvers got into the big car. With Ananta Singh at the wheels, they made their way to the Police Armoury. When the car reached the water works which was adjacent to the police armoury, Ananta Singh slowed down. Near the bend of the road and as planned he spotted Masterda with the reserve group. Masterda was majestically attired in his full white dress of a white dhoti, a white khaddar long coat, white PT shoes and a spotlessly starched white Gandhi cap on is head. On his chest he proudly sported the metal insignia of the IRA, the Indian Republican Army Chittagong Branch. Standing next to him was his bodyguard, Binode Dutta. Having spotted the leader, Ananta Singh as planned blinked the head lights of the car for a moment and then switched it off. That was the recognition and identification signal for both the groups. When Masterda came on to the road, all six of them got out of the car, stood to attention and saluted him. On receiving the blessings from their Commander-in-Chief they happily left for their mission.

The Police armoury was located in the North Western end of the city on a hillock.And as soon as the car reached the base of the police armoury and halted, all six of them quickly alighted. With Ganesh Ghose and Ananta Singh in the lead, the group confidently climbed the stairs. Thinking that Ganesh Ghose and Ananta Singh were some senior officers who were on a surprise inspection visit, the lone sentry on duty even saluted them with his weapon. As the sentry's right hand hit the trigger guard of the weapon in salute, both Ganesh Ghose and Ananta Singh opened fire and the hapless sentry came tumbling down. The group then charged towards the guard room where the remaining five or six sentries on night duty were sleeping and resting. Two of them got injured in the attack and the rest were told to flee or else they too would also meet the same fate. In a matter of minutes the Police Armoury was in the hands of the young revolutionaries. Delirious with joy they shouted on top of their voices 'Inquilab Zindabad' and 'Long Live the Revolution, Thereafter the reserve party under Masterda with all the heavy iron tools and sledge hammers arrived to complete the mission. The reserve party soon went hammer and tongs with their sledgehammers to break open the armoury doors and it did not take them much time to get to their booty. But the number of weapons were more than they could handle or carry. With whatever arms that they could seize, Ganesh Ghose decided to give a quick demonstration to all the greenhorns on the drill for loading, firing and unloading of the weapon. Someone then set the Union Jack that was in the guard room on fire and a while later India's national flag was hoisted. To the joyous cheers and cries of 'Vande Mataram' and 'Inquilab Zindabad,' Masterda Surjya Sen with his young band of revolutionaries stood to attention and saluted the Indian tricolour.

While the solemn and historic flag hoisting ceremony was being conducted at the Police armoury, the second major other assault group under Loke Nath Baul had also successfully captured the Auxuliary Force armoury but albeit with a little more difficulty. Makhan Ghose the driver of the second car had at the appointed time stopped his vehicle at the landing of the armoury building. Then as rehearsed earlier, he smartly alighted and ceremoniously opened the door for Loke Nath Baul to get out. When Lokenath Baul with his party rushed towards the guard room, the sentry on duty once again thinking that he must be some senior officer on an inspection visit, therefore presented arms and was shot dead in cold blood, while the others fled in panic. The noise of the shooting attracted the attention of the English Sergeant Major Farrel who was residing with his family within the complex of the armoury and he immediately came out and shouted.

"Who are you and what do you want?"

Despite the warning given to him to get back, the Sargeant Major refused to listen. Then young Shanti Nag fired at him with his double barrel gun and knocked him out. When Mrs Farrel came out to rescue her husband, Farrel asked her to immediately alert the police headquarters. Lokenath Baul then ordered a member of his group to seize the bayonet of the sentry who had been killed earlier and bayonet the Englishman but not to touch the lady. The young revolutionary did exactly as told and while a dead Farrel lay in a pool of blood, the door of the armoury was forced open by tying the door frame to the car with a strong rope. And once as the car was set in motion the armoury door with its frame was broken open. A large number of 303 Enfield rifles and Lewis guns were captured but there was no trace of the ammunition. This was a gross and total failure of intelligence on the part of the revolutionaries. They were unaware that a new magazine for the ammunition had been recently built, but they had no idea of its location.

"Take whatever weapons possible and put them inside the car and then and set the place on fire," ordered Lokenath Baul. With the armoury in flames, Lokenath Baul and his party drove to the Police armoury to link up with the others.However, at the Police armoury another tragedy was unfolding itself. Masterda had given instructions that on conclusion of all the major tasks the entire force with the captured weapons and ammunition were to reassemble in the centre of the city, but Himanghshu Sen who was entrusted to set the police armoury on fire in his hurry to do the task did not take the necessary precautions and in the bargain got engulfed in the fire. Ananta Singh with Ganesh Ghose together with two other comrades and the badly burnt Himangshu Sen then got into the car and sped away towards the city. They wanted to get him to a safe shelter and have him treated for his burns.

In the meanwhile and as was planned earlier, Ganesh Ghose who had expected Masterda to lead the main group to the centre of the town so that he with Ananta Singh could meet up with him there never materialized. Due to the chaos and misunderstanding Masterda with the rest of the group kept waiting for Ganesh Ghosh and party to return to the police armoury and having waited for a long time when there was still no sign of Ganesh Ghosh and Ananta Singh, Masterda got worried. The group that was tasked to capture the British hostages at the European Club also drew a blank because the club was closed that day for Good Friday. Finally Amiya Chakrabarty a close lieutenant of Masterda advised that it would not be safe to keep waiting at the police armoury and neither would it be prudent for the entire group to go to the centre of the city since by now the authorities may have got wind of their actions. He therefore suggested that the entire force with their weapons and ammunition should move to a vantage point on the Jalalabad hills where they would be able to defend themselves more effectively if required.

It was only at 4 pm in the evening of 22nd April, that the Government troops and police from the regular British Indian Army spotted the revolutionaries on Jalalabad Hills on the outskirts of the city. A fierce firefight followed and there were quite a few casualties amongst the young brave hearted revolutionaries. When the Army with their heavy machine guns moved to a more dominating area and engaged the revolutionaries, Masterda realized that they were greatly out numbered and that it would be futile to take on the regular army in a set peice battle. He therefore ordered everyone to disengage and to slowly and carefully get away and go into hiding. A few weeks later under his leadership Masterda again regrouped his followers. This time he decided he would continue the struggle by engaging the enemy with guerrilla warfare.

As Masterda's young revolutionary army of mostly young teenagers lived to fight another day, in Calcutta on that very day of 22nd April 1930, the Superintendent of the Alipur jail in Calcutta, Major Som Dutt in order to sort out the young revolutionaries in his own jail had used the Pathans and some Anglo Indians to attack the politicals and teach them a lesson. This resulted in Subhash Bose being knocked out unconscious. In the next few days and as the news spread of the daring armoury raids at Chittagong by Masterda's young and spirited revolutionaries and of the injury to Subhash Bose, it gave the much needed impetus to the young educated Bengalis in the whole of Bengal to once again revive and step up their terrorist activities against their British masters.

While Masterda's small guerrilla groups faded away into the vast countryside and into the villages along the long sea coast of the Bay of Bengal in eastern India, a few days earlier far away in the North West Frontier of India on 18th and 19th of April, the tall bearded leader of the Khudai Khidmatgars whose ancestral home was originally in Jalalabad in Afghanistan had held his first official meeting with his followers in his own village of Utmanzai. A few days later Badshah Khan decided to proceed to Peshawar, the provincial capital in order to make a similar appeal to his people to heed to Gandhi's call and break the draconian salt laws, but only nonviolently. However, on the 23rd of April, before Badshah Khan could reach Peshawar, he with four of his close associates was arrested and on having been sentenced to 3 years of rigorous imprisonment was whisked away from the North West Frontier.

Meanwhile at Peshawar, the word of their beloved leader Badshah Khan's arrest spread rapidly. Soon thousands of Pathan demonstrators took to the streets and they soon surrounded the jail and declared themselves as Khudai Khidmatgars. The situation was now becoming very tense but there was still no violence. Fearing the the situation may turn for the worse, Dr Khan Sahib, the elder brother of Badshah appealed to the agitating Pathans to remain cool and nonviolent. By mid day a spontaneous general strike had paralyzed the entire city and the Frontier was now exploding, but nonviolently. The British were simply stunned. They just could not imagine that the Pathan of all the people will remain nonviolent. However, they decided not to take any chances. When a large crowd started gathering at the Kissa Kahani bazzar to protest against the unlawful arrest of their leader, the civil administration requested for aid from the Army authorities. Till then the protests was entirely peaceful and continued to remain so for a while. But all that suddenly changed, when on the scene arrived four British armoured cars. As the DC, the Deputy Commissioner sitting in the leading armoured car named 'Bray' entered through the Kabuli Gate of the city, he was greeted with brickbats and stones. Soon all the four armoured cars closed their hatches and headed for the nearby police station that was insde the city.

Haji Abdul Rehman who was there at the Kissa Kahani Bazaar that morning was trying to keep the tempers cool on both sides, and when he saw the four British armoured cars guided by the two motorcycle dispatch riders approaching, he waved out to the leading armoured car to slow down. But by now the crowd had become even more defiant and aggressive, and when some of them attacked one of the dispatch riders and lynched him to death, the situation became out of control. Seeing the soldier's body lying limp on the street when the second armoured car named 'Bullycourt,' which was following behind approached the body of their fallen colleague, Haji Abdul Rehman became a bit apprehensive. At this point it seemed that either the driver had lost control of the vehicle or he intentionally and without warning drove into the crowd to teach them a lesson. And when it finally came to a stop, Haji Abdul Rehman and a few others had already become the first victims of that dreadful carnage. Although bleeding profusely, a seriously injured and badly limping Haji Abdul Rehman stood up and loudly appealed to the crowd to remain peaceful.

"What has happened to me and to the few others who have been injured by the armoured car should not be of any consequence to the rest of you. Maybe it was only an accident. Therefore I beg of you my dear Pathan brothers, and to all our honourable Khudai Khidmatgars not to be carried away and in the name of Allah to stick to your resolve to remain nonviolent."

Surprisingly in spite of the grave provocation, the crowd heeded the elderly Haji's advice. They did not retaliate but came forward peacefully to collect the wounded. Meanwhile the news about the casualties amongst the peaceful congregation of the Pathans in the area of the Kissa Kahani bazaar had spread like wild fire. Soon more Pathans from all over Peshawar city and all of them claiming to be also true Khudai Khidmatgars started collecting in the area of the bazaar. Seeing the menacing mood of the ferocious looking bearded Pathans, baring their chests in open defiance and advancing towards the temporary District Headquarters that had been established in the area, the District Magistrate got panicky. He gave the troops the order to open fire and as a result of which several more innocent Pathans, both young and old were also killed. Despite the very serious injury to his spine, Haji Abdul Rehman bleeding from the hip again stood up and persuaded the crowd to disburse and for the civil administration to withdraw the armed troops and the armoured cars to their barracks. But neither side was willing to listen or give in. The unarmed Pathans were now in a more rebellious mood as they kept advancing towards the armoured cars. They were now prepared to receive the bullet and lay down their lives if required. Then the second round of firing started and when those in front fell down felled by the bullets, others automatically from behind came forward exposing their bare chests even more defiantly. It would have probably resulted in another Jalianwala Bagh tragedy, but for the refusal of the Indian Platoon commander from the crack Garhwal Rifle Battalion who simply refused to obey the order when asked to open fire on those unarmed Pathans.

"Sahib you may blow me and my sepoys from your gun if you like, but we will not fire on innocent, unarmed men, women and children and I as their Platoon Commander take full responsibility for my actions, but we will not at any cost shoot our unarmed brothers," said the courageous Garhwali VCO. A loud cheer for the defiant Garhwalis from the Pathans went up as the British Officer incharge ordered their immediate arrest. To the other British officers and Tommies it was a chilling reminder to them of the Great Indian Mutiny of 1857.Meanwhile seeing the hopeless condition of Khan Bahadur Haji Abdul Rehman who had collapsed on the street, the District Adminstration lost no time in rushing him to the Mission hospital in an army ambulance. But by the time he was brought in he was declared dead.

"My God what has happened to our loyal and disciplined officers and soldiers? Why did they have to resolve to such barbaric methods,"' said the indignant and upset British matron.

"It is indeed a great pity that the old revered Haji Abdul Rehman who had done so much for the troops and for the British civil administration throughout his life and who had never ever hurt even a damn fly had to be mowed down like this," said a visibly moved Mrs Lillian Starr, the same good lady who had risked her own life to rescue Molly Ellis.

The irony of his father being killed by a British armoured car did shock Major Attiqur Rehman when he received the telegram at Kohat, and he immediately rushed to Peshawar to provide the necessary succour to his aged mother. He however felt very proud, when at the public condolence meeting held in his late father's honour; not only the Pathan Maliks but also the senior British Officers from the civil and the military praised the work and deeds of the old man. His only regret was that for a man who was fighting fit at the age of 63, it was still too early for Allah to so cruelly take him away.

Chapter-5

The Half Naked but Bold Faqir

On the midnight of 4th/5th May 1930, Mahatma Gandhi was once again arrested and imprisoned without trial for his salt Satyagraha movement. At the dead of night, while Gandhiji was fast asleep in a cot under a mango tree at Dandi, the District Magistrate of Surat with a posse of armed police arrived. Shining his torch on Gandhi's face, the Englishman said.

"You are under arrest Mr Gandhi."

"Alright but where was the delay. I was expecting you much earlier," said the Mahatma as he smiled at the British police officer and got into his vehicle.

While Gandhi was on his way to prison, the handsome young Parsee gentleman and the first Indian to hold a flying license that bore the figure No I on it was on his first solo flight to London. He was competing for the 500 sterling pound reward that had been offered by the Aga Khan to the first Indian pilot who would complete the distance from England to India or vice versa in the shortest possible time, but not later than six weeks.Before taking off from Karachi on the 3rd of May 1930, young JRD Tata was surprised to be greeted by a retired British Colonel.

"Do you remember me young man," said Reggie as he extended his hand to the pilot and wished him the best of luck.

' Well not exactly Sir but anyway thank you Sir for the good wishes," replied JRD as they both shook hands.

"Well it was only in yesterday's papers that I heard about your taking part in the competition and since I happened to be in Karachi I decided to check and find out for myself if it was really you. I mean if you were the same boy who during the Great War while the German planes were on there way to bomb Paris and the air raid had been sounded, you kept on insisting with your mother that you would like to see those flying machines in the sky and I had to physically lift you up and take you to the air raid shelter below the hospital where your charming French mother voluntarily worked."

Oh of course now I do remember Sir though I was hardly 10 years old then. My name is very very long but the surname is short and you may call me Jeh," said an excited JRD as he got into the cockpit, while Reggie kept waving to the enthusiastic young pilot as he took off from Karachi's Drigh Road airstrip.

Competing for the same prize also were two other Indians who had decided to take off from England in the opposite direction. While JRD was refuelling at the Gaza airstrip in Palestine, another Gypsy Moth with the catchy name of 'Miss India' also landed there and a jovial Manmohan Singh who took delight in hunting for gazelles with his revolver whilst flying came out of the cockpit to greet his competitor.

"You know it is a pity that I lost my bearings twice, once over the English Channel and a second time because of heavy fog over Europe, and both the times I had to get back to Croydon airfield to start all over again," said a happy go lucky Manmohan as they shook hands.

"That I must say is real bad luck," said JRD as he sympathized with his rival.

"And it is not only that, but the damn Editor of 'Aeroplane' magazine even had the cheek to write that though Mr Manmohan Singh called his aeroplane 'Miss India,' he is most likely to miss Iindia too!'" On hearing that pun of Manmohan missing India, JRD burst out laughing and very sportingly Manmohan Singh joined in too.

"Good flying," said Manmohan Singh as JRD taxied to take off for the next leg of his long journey. When he landed at Alexandria in Egypt, JRD was even more surprised when he was greeted by another young Parsee who like him was also a flying enthusiast. The young lad was also competing for the same prize.

"My name is Aspy Engineer and I am stuck because I do not have an extra set of spare plugs," said the lad who to JRD seemed to be still in his late teens.

"Not to worry friend," said a sporting JRD as he took out four of the eight spare plugs that he was carrying with him and gave it to his rival.

"That is really very kind and sporting of you and to reciprocate your gesture may I offer you my Mae West life jacket because it will not be required by me anymore as I intend flying the rest of the distance mostly over the land route to India, but it might come handy and useful to you while you cross the Mediterrean and later the English Channel,"' said Aspy as he handed over the life jacket to JRD.

By the time JRD landed at Paris, Aspy Engineer had reached Karachi and had claimed the prize. When Reggie read in the papers that it would have been a much closer fight had not Mr Tata chosen to land at a military airport in Naples where there were strict instructions not to release any planes before 6 a.m, he felt pity for the man, but all the same he sent him a letter of congratulations for his adventurous spirit. And while young Aspi celebrated his aerial victory, Mahatma Gandhi galvanized his followers to keep up the spirit of defying the British and courting arrest. And by the time Gandhi himself landed up in jail, there were thousands of others and practically all Congress leaders who had heeded his call were already behind bars. Early next morning, while Gandhi was yet to settle himself in the Yerwada jail at Poona, at Lahore and inside Poonch House the 18 main accused in the Lahore conspiracy case for waging a war against the British were getting ready to attend the special tribunal court. 'Inquilab Zindabad,' and 'Long Live the Revolution' shouted all of them loudly as they entered the special court premises smiling away to all and sundry.

"I wonder what will happen now since all our leaders including the Mahatma are in jail, and the HSRA is also practically defunct with most of their young leaders caught and charged for sedition in the Lahore conspiracy case," said Dr Ghulam Hussein as he with Debu Ghosh and Naren Sen sat for their Saturday afternoon coffee session at the College Street coffee house.

"Don't worry and it is not all over yet because there are now clear indications that very soon a new and a more violent band of fiery young Bengalis will surface. And it will be like a rejuvenated Ansushilan and Jugantar organization," said Debu Ghosh very proudly.

"Then what happens to the Mahatma's teaching of non violence," asked Naren Sen.

That for the time being I guess will have to take a back seat," said Debu Ghosh very confidently.

As predicted correctly by Debu Ghosh, the next few months a spate of daring revolutionary and terrorist activities shook Bengal. On the morning of 25th August 1930, at the Dalhousie Square in Calcutta the two young revolutionaries Amiya Sen and Dinesh Mazumdar armed with home made bombs waited for the dreaded Police Commissioner, Charles Teggart's vehicle to pass by. Waiting astride the road which ran through the busy Dalhousie Square they kept facing each other.They were dertermined to get their man that day. But it was not to be so. The two young revolutionaries had not correctly judged the speed of the car as it drove past them. And when with 'Vande Mataram' on their lips, threw the bombs, they missed the target completely. Not only that, in the bargain poor Amiya Sen was killed and though Dinesh Mazumdar was injured, but he had managed to escape and Charles. Teggart was once again very lucky. He did not even have a scratch on him. Soon Dinesh Mazumdar and Surendra Nath Datta from Jorbagan who had made the bombs were both arrested. On that very day while Dinesh and Amiya were targeting Teggart in Calcutta, in Dhaka another young revolutionary, Benoy Krishna Bose successfully shot dead Mr Lowman, the British Police Commissioner of Dhaka. With the revolutionary movement gathering momentum, more young people of Bengal pledged support to Subhas Chander Bose. And on 5th September, when Subhas Bose was released from the Alipur jail, Debu Ghosh was thrilled as he with some other loyal supporters garlanded the young nationalist leader as he came out smiling.through the main gate.

"From today all of us will canvass for your election as the Mayor of Calcutta and you will definitely win," said an excited Debu Ghosh and how right he was. On 24th of September, 1930 Subhas Bose was sworn in as the new Mayor of Calcutta and he was yet to celebrate his thirty third birthday. But what Debu Ghosh was feeling bad and surprised about was the arrest on 2nd September of some of the young revolutionary leaders of Masterda's Chittagong outfit from the tiny French enclave at Chandanagore, which was not very far from Calcutta.It was way back in 1673, when the French dropped anchor in Bengal and a few years later after taking permission from Shayasta Khan, who was then ruling Bengal, Dupleix had secured the place at Boro Bishnupur for Rupees 401 only and it was now known as Chandanagore.

After the sucessful raid at the Chittagong police armoury and because of the serious burn injuries to one of their own colleagues whom they had taken to the doctor in the town to have him treated, Ganesh Ghose and his party had lost contact with Masterda. They were not aware that Masterda together with his band of followers had taken up a defensive position on the Jalalabad hills. But when Masterda realised that the defensive position was untenable and asked his followers to fade away in order to fight another day that Ganesh Ghosh with his party thought it prudent to go to Chandanagore. For them what could be a safer haven than a French possession in Bengal they thought? On reaching Chandanagore they took shelter in a house where Suhasini Ganguly and Shashadhar were staying. Both of them were genuine sympathizers and as members of the organization were only willing to help. Posing as husband and wife they had heartily welcomed them. But on 2nd September, after someone had squealed to the police it was all over. The British raided the place and a skirmish followed. This resulted in the death of Makhan Ghoshal, while the other three revolutionaries including Ganesh Ghosh, with their hosts Suhasini Ganguly and Shashadhar Mukherjee were mercilessly beaten and captured.

"But tell me how could the British so blatantly violate all diplomatic norms and walk into French territory to arrest Ganesh Ghosh and his party," said an higly agitated Debu Ghosh to Edwin Pugsley who had no clue whatsoever of what Debu was talking about. Though Edwin Pugsley was much senior in age to Debu, but they both liked each others company and they often met over a round of drinks in the small sleazy bars that had now sprung up unofficially around the notorious Karaya Road. Located just off posh Park Street, Karaya Road was the place where besides getting booze and girls for the night to enjoy in bed, one only had to pay a few extra rupees to the lady running the brothel to get the latest dope on what was happening and where in the city.And when Pugsley was told about the arrest of the Bengali revolutionaries from Chandanagore, he as usual in his wity manner remarked.

"Bloody men as far as the prostitutes are concerned for big money they will open their big mouths at both ends, and these kinds of den are ideal joints to ferret out valuable information. Moreover, most of these girls who are from abroad are not bothered at all about your Swaraj man," added Edwin as he signalled to the lone cashier at the counter to send two more large whiskies with sodas.

"I guess you are damn well right because if you and I can talk a whole lot of shit after a few drinks, then what stops them, who after fondling a big busty buxom woman enters her for pleasure in the missionary position and then spills the beans," said Debu Ghosh.'

"Yes and that is what is called mission accomplished because the lady being laid may well also be a police informer," said Edwin Pugsley as he paid for the drinks and wished Debu Ghosh a very good night.

Inspite of the set back at Chandanagore, the young revolutionaries in Bengal were now busy regrouping themselves. Meanwhile at Lahore, in the Lahore Conspiracy Case, the Tribunal on the 7th of October sentenced Bhagat Singh, Rajguru and Sukhdev to death by hanging. The warrant of execution to the Superintendent of the Central Jail at Lahore pertaining to Bhagat Singh read. "Whereas Bhagat Singh son of Kishen Singh, resident of Khawasrian, Lahore one of the prisoner's in the Lahore conspiracy case having been found guilty by us of offence under section 121 and section 302 of the Indian Penal Code and also under section 4(b) of the explosives substances act read with section 5 of that act and with section 102 (F) of the Indian Penal Code at a trial commencing from the 5th of May, 1930 and ending with the 7th October, 1930, is hereby sentenced to death. This is to authorize and require you, the said Superintendent, to carry the same sentence into execution by causing the said Bhagat Singh to be hanged by the neck until he be dead at Lahore."

The death sentence on the three courageous and brave Indians by the tribunal was received with great shock and sadness by the Indian people and especially so by Debu Ghosh and Naren Sen who had followed the court proceedings minutely through the eyes of a lawyer.

"Maybe all three of them should appeal and take the help of all the eminent lawyers who are now in the forefront of the national movement for Purna Swaraj," said Dr Ghulam Hussein.

"Yes you are right, but let me also tell you that on the 4th of October, just a few days before the judjement was declared, Bhagat Singh's father Kishen Singh without consulting his son had made a personal request to the tribunal stating that his son was innocent. When Bhagat Singh came to know about it, he was livid and he sent a strong rejoinder to his father. And this is what he wrote from his cell," said Debu Ghosh as he took out the news item that had been carried by a vernacular paper that was published from Lahore and started to read some important excerpts from it. The letter began thus.

"My Dear Father,

I was astounded to learn that you had submitted a petition to the members of the Special Tribunal in connection with my defence. It has upset the whole equilibrium of my mind. I have not been able to understand how you could think it proper to submit such a petition at this stage and in these circumstances. Inspite of all the sentiments and feelings of a father, I don't think you were at all entitled to make such a move on my behalf without even consulting me. My life is not as precious, at least to me as you may probably think it to be. It is not at all worth buying at the cost of my principles.There are other comrades whose cases are as serious as that of mine. We had adopted a common policy and we shall stand to the last no matter how dearly we have to pay for it individually."

"Father, I am quite perplexed. I fear I might overlook the ordinary principles of etiquette and my language may become a little harsh while criticizing or rather censoring this move on your part. Let me be candid. I feel as though I have been stabbed in the back. Had any other person done it, I would have considered it nothing short of treachery. But in your case let me say it has been a weakness and a weakness of the worst type. In the end I would like to inform you and my other friends and all the people interested in my case that I have not approved of your move. I am still not at all in favour of offering any defence. If I did my dear friends in the Borstal Jail will be taking it as a treachery and betrayal on my part. I want that the public should know all the details about this complication and therefore, I request you to publish this letter." And that letter ended with the sentence, your loving son, Bhagat Singh.

As Debu put down the paper cutting on the table at the India Coffee House in Calcutta, Naren Sen said.

"But damn it this is practically a confession and now it will be very very difficult for the defence to save him and his colleages from the gallows."

"No doubt, but look at the man's strong character and conviction, and the genuine feeling of love he has for his comrades,".said Dr Ghulam Hussein.

"Yes a man like Bhagat Singh will never cow down and he will even go smiling to the gallows," said Debu Ghosh.

While Bhagat Singh and his comrades were being tried by the Special tribunal at Lahore, on 30th September, the first trial on the Chittagong Armoury case also began. It was on 2nd September, that the Police Commissioner Charles Teggart having thrown all diplomatic niceties to the wind had raided a house in the small French colony of Chandanagore and the people inside were completely taken by surprise.as the policemen like a herd of cattle shoved them inside the police van that was popularly known as the Black Maria. Soon Ganesh Ghose, Lokenath Baul, and Ananda Gupta found themselves back home not in the safety of their own houses, but as criminals inside the Chittagong Jail.

Meanwhile the Commander-inChief India, Field Marshall Birdwood who was soon to relinquish his appointment at the end of the year was busy with his farewell parties. It was only in January of that very year that he with Mrs Birdwood had moved into the luxurious new appointment house of the C-in-C in New Delhi. Located not far from the Viceroys magnificent palace, the sprawling house with its huge garden and long driveway designed by Lutyen had only just been completed and he was the first one to occupy it. But to his bad luck he hardly got the time to stay in it. In November 1930, for his farewell and dining out as the Colonel of the 13th Frontier Force

Regiment, the famous Piffers, General Birdwood visited the 58th FF, more popularly known as the Aaatwanjas in Kohat. It was the Battalion that he had commanded during the 1908-1910 Mohmand Operations in the North West Frontier.

At the Officer's Mess party in the evening he was delighted to meet Major Attiqur Rehman who was a special invitee because of his having won the Military Cross while serving with the 59th FF in France during the 1st World War.

"How is everybody and your dear mother, and what is the total strength of your own family now," asked the C-in-C in his usual friendly tone.

"Still carrying on with one loving wife, three young healthy rascal boys and one pretty daughter, who is the youngest and who is now the darling of the family Sir," said Major Attiqur Rehman as they shook hands.

"Well four is not too bad as a score for an Indian, but come what may and for heaven's sake do not keep adding anymore. And now that you have brought them into this world, you must give all of them fair and equal opportunities in life to emulate the high moral standards set by you and by your late father," said the C-in-C while raising a toast to the Rehman family. That evening what impressed Major Attiqur Rehman the most was the send off that the C-in-C received from the Officer's Mess after the formalities of the guest night was over.

After the last and final toast was drunk and as was the custom, there were always the last ride of honour for the departing celebrity and the C-in-C was no exception to the rule. To the lilting music of the regimental pipers playing the Auld Lang Syne, and to the full throated shouting of 'He is a jolly good fellow' by his brother officers, the C-in-C was of all the things wheeled back to the flagstaff house in a mess soda water bottle cart and he seemed to have enjoyed every moment of it. But late that night, and after that delightful party in the officers' mess, there was sad news for Attiqur Rehman. A telegram had arrived saying that Begum Haji Abdul Rehman had died of a heart failure.That very moment a heart broken Attiqur Rehman left for Peshawar and he too realized now that he was no longer a son.

While Major Attiqur Rehman after his mother's funeral was debating in is mind what to do with his father's huge ancestral 'Haveli' and property at Peshawar, at Jammu there were celebrations of a different kind. News had just arrived that the fourth wife of the Maharajah of Kashmir, the beautiful Tara Devi, a commoner from the hills of Kangra had finally conceived.

"I only hope and I will pray for a son," said a delighted Hari Singh to his young wife as he confided with the doctor and asked him to take all the necessary precautions. Since this was going to be the first royal child in the family and with the Maharani being very young, it was therefore decided to have the delivery of the child in Europe where good doctors were also available.

"In that case I think the salubrious climate of southern France wiil suit all of us admirably and I too will get to play some good Polo in the Cote D'zur, and maybe also try my luck in the many casinos that dot the beautiful French Reviera," said a happy Hari Singh as he immediately told his Prime Minister to draft a letter to the Viceroy and send it through the British Resident in Srinagar requesting for the necessary permission to go to Europe.

With the happy young Maharaja of Kashmir looking forward to his holiday in France, the out going Commander-in-Chief of the Indian Army made his final farewell call to his own old regiment, the famous Probyn's Horse at Mian Mir Cantt in Lahore. Meanwhile the King and Emperor of India George the Fifth on the 12th of November opened the historic First Round Table Conference in the royal gallery of the House of Lords in London.

Under the Chairmanship of the British Prime Minister Ramsay Macdonald, the Indian delegation was there to discuss the Simon Commission Report. With one of the main recommendations made by the Simon Commission that India should have a Federal Constitution and be given Provincial Autonomy subject to over-riding powers to be vested in the Governor of the Provinces and with enlarged Provincial Legislative Councils, but with no responsible Government in the Centre, the Congress leaders rejected the Simon Report as it had not guaranteed a National Government and demanded India's right to secede from the Empire. The Congress therefore decided to completely boycott the proposed First Round table conference.

Knowing fully well that the conference on Indian affairs without the Congress participating would be nothing more than a meaningless exercise, nevertheless, a delegation led by the Aga Khan and with several eminent Indian leaders like Mohammed Ali Jinnah, Tej Bahadur Sapru and BR Ambedkar as members sailed for London. The First Round Table Conference however carried on aimlessly till the 19th of January 1931 with the British Government opposing the immediate grant of Dominion Status to India. The conference received its biggest set back when Dr BR Ambedkar, the man born in Ambavadi, a small village in the Ratnagiri District of Bombay Province demanded at the conference that the depressed classes of India of which he was also an unfortunate being be justly treated as a separate community for all electoral purposes. Likewise, the Muslim delegation too demanded their own pound of flesh and demanded adequate safeguards for the Muslims of India too.

Dr Bhimrao Ambedkar born on 14th April 1891 and whose original full name was Bhimrao Ambavadekar had returned with a PHD from the USA in mid 1917 and had now earnestly taken up the cause of uplifting the poor depressed and exploited minority Hindu communities of India. The Brtish were only too happy with this development. They now looked forward to their policy of divide and rule since the proceedings in London had proved abhortive.

Early on the morning of the 25th of November, 1930, Lieutenant Colonel Reginald Edwards called on the outgoing Commander-in-Chief, Field Marshall Birdwood to formally bid a final goodbye to him. Coincidently the last and final guard of honour for the outgoing "Jangi Lath' that was given to the Chief at his residence was by none other than the 69th Punjabees, Reggie's old Battalion and Reggie felt mighty proud as the smartly turned out guard paraded with the regimental colours. That evening there was a huge crowd at the Delhi railway Station to wave a fiinal goodbye to their very popular and capable C-in-C. Even Viceroy Irwin breaking all protocol was there with the Vicerene. As the guard blew his whistle and showed the green lantern to the engine driver, Reggie also got into his first class coupe on his last and final journey to England. He had now decided that he would return and finally settle down in India for good and was therefore on his way to dispose off what ever little property that he had inherited from his late parents.

On the 29th of November at Bombay, when the Field Marshall with Mrs Birdwood drove in an open car from the Governor's House to the Gateway of India, they were greeted by huge crowds on the road. When he with his wife embarked on the ship "Mantua", both of them were pleasantly surprised to see Reggie on board too.

"Well one thing is for sure and that is my wife and I both will surely have some good company all the way to England," said the Field Marshall as they firmly shook hands.

"I am sorry Sir but I will only be able to keep you and Mrs Birdwood company till as far as Naples, because from there I intend going to Rome and to the Vatican," said Reggie.

"But why to the Vatican and don't tell me that at this late stage of your life you intend to change from your bachelorhood to priesthood," said the Field Marshall jokingly.

"No chance at all for that in Vatican City Sir unless I convert myself from a Protestant to a Roman Catholic," replied Reggie in a lighter vein.

"Well if you know your Bible well, not even the Pope will know whether you are a Protestant or otherwise. Afterall you are a good Christian and that is what counts," said Mrs Birdwood.

"I guess you are absolutely right Maam and as a soldier it never ever bothered me because I always felt that one should always remain a good human being irrespective of what type of religion one follows," replied Reggie.

"Yes there I agree with you whole heartedly because our uniform is our religion and we in the army thank God we never discriminate," said the Field Marshall as the Skipper and Captain of the 'Mantua" came down from the bridge to pay his compliments.

While the 'Mantua'was on the high seas, Major Attiqur Rehman with his entire family arrived for a holiday during the festive winter season in Calcutta. Surprisingly on the very day that they detrained at Howrah railway station, the world famous and popular Hollywood actor and star and the heartthrob of many a lady also set foot in the Empire's second capital. Late that evening as the phaeton carrying the Rehman family got on to the pontoon bridge at Howrah there was a massive traffic jam.

"Look Look there he is Mr Douglas Fairbanks," said Ghulam Hussein to his two nephews Gul and Aftab who were both sitting perched up high next to the phaeton driver. Then as the phaeton slowly came to a complete halt on the crowded bridge, both the young lads now aged 16 and 12 repectively and wearing their impressive PWRIMC blazers sought their father's permission to move ahead in order to have a closer look at the Hollywood star, and if possible to also get an autograph from him.

"Alright you can try your luck but do not get lost," said the father.

Though the two young boys had managed to jostle their way through the big crowd, but there was no chance for them to get an autograph from the matinee idol since he was now being mobbed by his many fans. But they did manage somehow to get hold off one button from the great actor's blazer as a souvenier.

"How could you ever do such a thing like that," said an angry Nafisa as Gul Rehman very proudly showed the blazer button to his mother.

"But what could I do Ammijan, it was not I, but somebody else who had torn of the button and when it fell on the ground I just picked it up and if you so desire I will go and return it to him right now," said Gul Rehman looking somewhat peeved.

"There is no need for that," said his father sternly as he told them to get back on the perch and sit there quietly.

While they waited patiently for the crowd to disburse, Ghulam Hussein narrated to them a brief history of the charming lady who was to play host to the famous Hollywood actor.

"Mind you he has come all the way around the world as the honoured guest of none other than the charming Indira Devi, the Maharani of Cooch Bihar, and incidently the beautiful Maharni is also presently the regent of that small princely kingdom in North Bengal. Though Maharani Indira Devi is a Maharashtrian by birth and the only daughter of Sayaji Rao the Maharaja of Baroda but she had against the wishes of her parents married Jitender Narayan, the Prince of Cooch Bihar while both of them with their parents were holidaying in England in 1913. A week after the marriage her father-in-law Raja Rajinder Narayan the Raja of Cooch Bihar died. Then a few years later her brother-in-law who was the eldest in the family and who had succeeded his father to the Gaddhi also died. Thereafter her husband who was next in line became the ruler, but unfortunately the handsome Jitender Narayan too did not live long. On 20th December 1922 at the age of thirty Indira Devi who is still a ravishing beauty became a widow with five young children. Normally during the winter months the Maharani with her two boys and three girls comes to Calcutta to stay at the Woodlands, the big Cooch Bihar house in Alipur. After her husband's death in England, when she with her children returned to India, her eldest son who is popularly know as Bhaiya was proclaimed as the Maharaja, but since the boy then was only seven or eight years old his mother Indira Devi was proclaimed as the regent," said Ghulam Hussein.

"Well you seem to know her whole history and I hope there is nothing fishy about it,"' said Attiqur as he winked at his brother-in-law.

"No not really, but I must tell you about a fabulous party that took place in the Cooch Bihar palace in North Bengal and that was sometime in1925. Playing the good hostess that she always is, the Maharani had invited a large number of well to do and important Englishmen and their wives from the Calcutta officialdom to visit her State. They were all her honoured guests and I just happen to be at Jalpaiguri that evening when lo and behold what do I see. The Englishmen in dhoti kurtas and their wives in sarees all dressed as Bengalees were waltzing away to the band playing the Blue Danube and Over the Waves. Later I came to know that the Maharani had specifically mentioned this particular dress code on the invitation card and they all had willingly obliged," said Ghulam Hussein.

"But Uncle did some off the dhotis and sarees come off while dancing," asked an excited Gul Rehman.

I really would'nt know about that son since I wasn't there and I do agree that for ballroom dancing that dress is just not suitable," said Ghulam Hussein in all simplicity.

"Oh I am sure they must have come off and definitely after all the dancing and merry making was over," said Attiqur Rehman with a wicked smile on his face as Nafisa disapproved of that naughty comment from her husband.

"But I must give full credit to the lady. Imagine with rapid fire and in double time she had produced so many children, and if you look at her today you will never believe it because even now she still maintains a fabulous figure," said Ghulam Hussein somewhat proudly as he looked at his wife Suraiya who had put on quite a bit of weight.

"Well now I guess you will also tell us all about all her children," said Suriaya somewhat sarcastically.

"Yes and why not. For all I know, the eldest Ila is a girl and she was born in 1914, and then came Bhaiya a boy in 1915. He was followed I think by another son and then came two more daughters. The lovely Gyatri Devi or Ayesha alias May was born in England on 23rd May 1919 and Meneka the youngest was born a year later in 1920," said Ghulam Hussein with a big smile on his face.

"Now I guess you will also tell us even the time and the stars under which they were born," said a visibly annoyed Suraiya.

"I do not know about the rest of them, but I can tell you about Gyatri who is the prettiest of the lot.She was born at 8 am in the morning and because she was born in the month of May, her English nanny always addressed her as Princess May and needless to say that she being a princess was also born under a lucky star," said Ghulam Hussein as he had one more dig at his wife.

But my dear brother-in-law, the Princess is now only 11 years old and don't you go cradle snatching at this age," said Attiqur Rehman as Suraiya gave her dear and only brother a big smile.

"Just imagine five lovely children in only seven years and that I am sure must be some sort of a record for any royal family in India, dont you think so?" said Nafisa.

"Well come to think of it, we haven't done too badly either. We also produced four in ten years.

"And no more p;ease," said Suraiya while Nafisa blushed.

But to me it seems rather strange because inspite of being married four times, the young dashing Maharaja of Kashmir who comes regularly to Calcutta during the racing season and stays as a guest of Indira Devi at Woodlands because his horses are stabled there, he is still waiting to produce just one," said Ghulam Hussein.

"I think maybe he enjoys more playing polo, riding and racing his horses rather than galloping in bed," said Attiqur Rrehman as he squeezed his brother-in-law's hand and waited to see the reaction and response from the ladies.

Now I think this is too much and we should change the topic. After all the boys are not just kids anymore," said Nafisa with a tone of annoyance in her voice.

That evening there was a special dinner in honour of Attiqur Rehman and his family. It was hosted by the ageing Shaukat Hussein and his Begum Sahiba and they had invited all their old dear friends.

"I must say you have so many and such well behaved lovely children," said Sonjoy Sen as he walked in with his two grandsons Samir and Ronen who were now 13 and 11 years old respectively. Following closely him behind arrived Debu Ghosh with his wife Hena and their three sons Arup, Swarup and Anup aged 12, 10, and 8 and toddling behind all of them was their 5 year old sister Mona.

"Well well, I thought us Musalmaans from the North West Frontier only like to have large families, but these Bangalees are no less," remarked Attiqur Rehman jokingly.

"But why only you the Pathans and the Bengalees, because we also love to have big families," came the loud husky voice of Edwin Pugsley as he with his wife Laila trooped in with their two sons and three daughters. Besides being invited they had also come to bid farewell to the Hussein family.

Edwin had decided to leave Calcutta for good after the next Christmas season. Sean Pugsley the eldest son had just turned 19 and like his father he too had been selected as an engine driver and was leaving for his training at Mogulsarai soon. Edwin Pugsley was now in his late forties and had decided to finally settle down at Mhow near Indore where his late mother had bought a small property near the railway colony and which he had inherited from her.

"Now all of you go and play with the other children," said Laila to her two beautiful twin daughters Sandra and Debbie who had just got into their teens and to her second son Richard who had just completed his 10th birthday.

"And what about me Mamma, whom will I play with," asked the five year old Veronica.

"Since Mona and you are of the same age, I suggest both of you go inside and play with my little sister Hasina. She is only six years old and she has many nice dolls too," said Dr Ghulam Hussein's 13 year old son Nawaz Hussein as he cleverly lured the two little girls inside. And a little later, when Nawaz Hussein after taking due permission from his father announced that all those who were interested in playing dark room hiding should all move to the last room, all the other children were delighted.

"Certainly do go and play but no mischief, no fighting and no shouting and screaming too loudly," said Dr Ghulam Hussein's wife Suraiya as she gave the boys and girls a glass of sherbet and some sweets. The game began with Nawaz Hussein volunteering to give the den and as each one tried to find a suitable hiding place, Gul Rehman went behind the door where Debbie herself was hiding. Though she was only 13, she definitely looked much older than her age as Gul Rehman taking advantage of the small enclosed place squeezed in with her and having whispered softly into her ear not to mind, he tickled her ear with his lips. Giggling away, Debbie also took it all very sportingly.

With all the schools having winter December holidays, the children were soon having a ball in Calcutta. Chaperoned by their grandparents they went on picnics to the Botanical garden, to the Alipur Zoo, to the Strand, to the Victoria Memorial and to any other place that caught their fancy. For those few days while the Pugsley's were still in Calcutta, Gul Rehman could be seen constantly in the company of Debbie. An observant Shaukat Hussein in order to break the contact between the two, on 8th December decided to take only the senior boys for an educative tour of the Governor's House and of the nearby Writer's building.

"But why cannot the senior girls also come with us," said Gul Rehman not feeling very happy with the arrangement.

"That is because no women work there and therefore no girls are allowed," said the oldman looking a bit annoyed at Gul Rehman's question.

It was around 10 o'clock in the morning, when Shaukat Hussein and Sonjoy Sen with Gul Rehman, Arif Rehman, Samir Sen, Arup Ghosh and Nawaz Hussein in tow entered through the Eastern Gate of the Government House that was normally used by the working staff of the Governor. Seeing the Governor on his usual routine walk and busy talking to the Mr Reid the officiating Chief Secretary, Shaukat Hussein did his traditional salaam, while the boys in unison and in a loud voice and as briefed earlier by Sonjoy Sen wished His Excellency a very good morning.

"Oh so both you brothers are from the Prince of Wales College I see," said the Governor as he took another close look at their school blazers.

"Yes Sir," replied Gul and Aftab very smartly while the Governor instructed an aide of his to take all of them on a conducted tour and to not only show the young boys the lift which was a novelty in Calcutta, but to also give them a ride in it. But while they were on their way to the lift, a series of long loud police whistles were heard coming from the direction of the Writers building.

"I think there is trouble and so you all better go home," said Reid in fluent Bengali to Shaukat Hussein as he himself took leave of the Governor and rushed back to his office in the Writers building.

Three young Bengalee revolutionaries, Binoy Bose, Badal Gupta and Dinesh Gupta dressed in European clothes on the pretext of seeking an interview with Colonel N S Simpson, the Inspector General of Prisons had entered his office inside the Writers building and had shot him dead while the man was sitting at his desk. With the noise of the firing inside the IG prisons office, the security police inside the building had now been alerted and the three revolutionaries it seems had now been cornered well and proper. Their escape routes had been sealed and they soon became victims of a shoot out. Binoy Bose the young man who only a few months ago in August had killed Frank Lawson in Dhaka was shot in the head and died on the spot. When Badal-Gupta was cornered and he knew that he had no chance to escape, he took poison and committeed suicide. Dinesh was shot in the throat and though he did survive, but he was later tried and hanged. night the party for the Pugsley's at Debu Ghosh's house would have remained a tame affair had it not been for the ingenuity of young Gul Rehman who with Debbie and her twin sister Sandra livened the evening with their rendering of old popular English songs like 'Bicycle built for two' and 'Old Macdonald had a farm, E I E I O.'

On 26th January 1931, Viceroy Irwin revoked the illegality of the Congress Working Committee and released many of the Congress leaders who were languishing in jails. As an English aristrocat the elegant Irwin standing 6 feet 5 inches tall felt even taller that morning. In a gesture of amity and goodwill and with the hope that they the Congress would make the next Round Table Conference a success, he sat down under the bright winter sunshine in the well manicured lawns of his Viceroy's Palace in Delhi to draft a letter to the Secretary of State for India. He was now proposing to the Government in England that the time had come for him to have a heart to heart meeting with Mr Gandhi.

On the same very morning of that 26th of January 1931, come hell or high water Subhas Chander Bose had decided to celebrate the first anniversary of India's Independence Day. Gripping the pole of the National Flag in his hands, when he with his supporters approached the big Maidan to conduct the meeting, he was stopped by the policemen. Charles Teggart, the police commissioner had no doubt made massive arrangements to stop the celebrations, but Subhas Bose was not a person to be easily cowed down. Loudly chanting the words 'Vande Mataram'" (Glory to our Motherland) as he entered the great Calcutta Maidan, he was challenged by the massive police force. Ignoring their threats Subhas Bose resisted and a police lathi charge followed. Subhas was badly bruised and injured as Debu Ghosh following his leader went to his rescue. But it was too late. The Police whisked away the leader, produced him before the Presidency Magistrate and Subhas was back behind bars for a another six months of rigourous imprisionment.

And while Subhas was languishing in jail, the Viceroy invited Gandhiji for talks on the 18th of February, 1931. A day or so later, when all the major newspapers in India and some from even abroad carried a prized photograph of the small man in dhoti walking up the stairs of the Viceroy's House in Delhi. Naren was thrilled.

"Have a look and he has done it," said an excited Naren Sen as he showed the photograph to Debu Ghosh and Dr Ghulam Hussein. A day earlier the Mahatma had his famous meeting with Irwin and from that very day they had both hit it off well. But unfortunately a few days earlier India lost one of her most illustrious sons. The man who was born on the 6th of May 1861, which coincidently was also the birthday of Gurudev Rabindranath Tagore had been seriously sick for quite sometime. Only a year earlier on 1st January 1930, when a handsome Jawaharlal Nehru dressed in white tight trousers and a Sherwani made of white Khadi and with a Gandhi cap on his head rode majestically on a white horse to the venue of the Lahore Congress, the father felt extremely proud of his only son as he lovingly handed over the Gaddhi of the Congress party to him. This was the only time in the history of the Congress that the father gave the Party Gaddhi to his son and the date 26th of January was set for complete independence.But for Motilal Nehru that day was still very far away and he did not live to see it. A few days earlier suffering from a severe asthmatic attack and high blood pressure and when he knew that his end was near he had called Mahatma Gandhi to his bedside and said.

"I am not fortunate enough to see India free, but I have no doubt that you will have the good fortune and I only hope that I have rendered my bit of service to our motherland."

Motilal Nehru at the age of seventy on 6th February 1931 had breathed his last. That day as the son holding his dead father's head in his lap and with his lips trembling and eyes filled with unshed tears looked at his ailing mother, Gandhi having touched Motilal's feet put an arm around his griefing wife and said.

"Motilal is not dead. Men like him never die. He will always live long."

On the next day at dusk on the banks of the holy Sangam, the confluence of the mighty Indian rivers the Ganges and the Jamuna at Allahabad, while rendering the last melancholy service to his great father, Jawaharlal with a flaming torch lit the sandalwood pyre. For the 'Sharad Ceremony' of Motilal Nehru, Debu Ghosh had gone to Allahabad and once it was over he decided to stay back and spend sometime with a cousin of his who was also a lawyer in that city. On the evening of the 27th of February as usual Debu Ghosh with his cousin went for their daily evening walk to the Alfred Park and was surprised to see a large number of armed policemen there. The entire park area had been cordoned off by the police and on further enquiries from passerbys as to why the entry to the park had been closed, when he was told that the police were looking for an armed fugitive who had taken refuge inside it, Debu's cousin thought it was some kind of a joke. And before Debu could pose a question to one of the constables manning the gate, the sound of gun fire was heard. It seemed that the man had been cornered by the police force and was being fired upon by them, but he.was not the type who would give up very easily, as he too kept firing back at them intermittently. The exchange of fire carried on for a quite while and then suddenly there was a unerrie silence all round. Then a single shot from a pistol rang out and with that last bullet the much wanted man had killed himself. He was the same very man who had himself penned the Hindi couplet 'Dushman ki goliyan ka hum samna karenge, Azad he rahen hain, Azad he rahenge.' The brave young man who had written those words that he will gladly face the enemy's bullet but will always remain free had kept his word. Chandrashekar Azad, the Commander-in-Chief of the Hindustan Socialist Republican was finally eliminated. Nicknamed quicksilver by his own colleagues for his remarkable speedy reflexes, Chandrashekar Azad had come to the park to hold a secret meeting, but it seems someone had tipped off the police. When the deadbody was brought out from the Alfred Park, Debu Ghosh with folded hands bowed his head in honour and sorrow to the man who had become a big thorn to the British Raj in India.

On the 4th of March, at a meeting that lasted until midnight, Viceroy Irwin and Mahatma Gandhi finally came to an honourable agreement. And a few hours later at two o'clock in the early hours of the next morning Gandhi presented the 'Delhi Pact' to the Congress Working Committee.

"So the Congress has finally decided to attend the next Round Table Conference and once again discontinue the disobedience movement," said Debu Ghosh somewhat sarcastically.

"What else could the old man one do and in any case it has only been temporarily suspended," said Naren Sen.

"Moreover the pact is provisional and conditional too," said Dr Ghulam Hussein.

"But all the same I am sure not everbody in the Congress Party is happy with the outcome and certainly I am not because nothing has beeen promised or achieved and it is neither Independence nor Home Rule, though the Congress on the 5th itself had ratified it," said Debu Ghosh.

"I guess we had no other choice but atleast some sort of a beginning has been made," said Naren Sen.

While the three bosom friends, Dr Ghulam Hussein, Debu Ghosh and Naren Sen in early March of 1931 debated what would be the likely outcome of the Second Round Table Conference that was scheduled to be held in London sometime in August 1931, at the Hotel Martinez in the pleasure resort of Cannes on the Cote D'Azur in the French Reviera, Hari Singh the young dashing polo loving Maharaja of Kashmir checked in with his young 21 year old beautiful pregnant wife Tara Devi. The Maharaja and his entourage had occupied all the three suites on the third floor starting from suite numbers 318 to 320 and having assured his wife who was on her last stage of pregnancy that everything was under control and there was nothing to worry about, he got into his riding kit and was on his way for a few chukkers of fast polo. Invariably the round of polo was religiously followed by a lavish champagne party that was thrown by him and which normally ended with a sumptuous early breakfast of ham bacon and eggs. The child was due any day and with the Maharani's labour pains having been slightly delayed, the Maharaja was worried.

One evening, while the Maharaja was entertaining all his guests in the hotel with the choicest of wines and champagne, his own personal physician attending on the Maharani looked a much worried man too. When the Maharaja returned to his suite the doctor said.

"Your Highness, it will be indeed very encouraging if you could stay by the Maharani's side because the child should be due at any moment."

" Alright in that case I will park myself right next door to her," said the happy Maharaja.

When the Doctor got back to the labour room, he instructed the nurses attending on the Maharani to tell her that all she had to do was was to exert some more extra pressure and nothing more, and right enough on on the very next day the 9th of March 1931, she delivered the child. The Maharaja was finally blessed with a son. He was a lovely child, not very big built but with handsome features. Admiring his offspring sleeping peacefully next to his mother, Hari Singh said to his wife.

"Well keeping in mind his time of birth and the location of the various planets as told to me by the high priest, it has been ordained that the boy's name should start with the alphabet 'K' and therefore, I feel the name Karan Singh should be good choice. Don't you think so?'The tired Maharani simply smiled and nodded her head.

"Well your Highness, we could also give him the nickname of 'Tiger' too suggessted one of the Maharaja's senior aides who like the Maharaja was also very fond of Shikar.

"That is wonderful and it calls for celebrations," said the happy father as he instructed his senior most ADC to immediately flash the good news telegraphically to all his subjects and declare the next three days as public holidays in his kingdom. Without much ado, the delighted ADC ran to the nearest telegraph office.to declare 10th,11th and 12th of March as official public holidays in the Maharaja's state of Jammu and Kashmir.

That very week and on that very day when Karan Singh was born, Colonel Reginald Edwards happened to be in Cannes too. He had sold of his parent's property in England and was on his way back to India. Since he had now a little more cash to play around with, he on that very evening was trying his luck in one of the casinos and eventually came out a little richer. But by next morning, when the news about the rich and extravagant Maharaja from Kashmir rejoicing over the birth of his son and celebrating the event in royal style had become the talk of the town, Reggie immediately rushed to Hotel Martinez to congratulate his old friend.

"Oh what a pleasant surprise," said Hari Singh as he poured the chilled French champagne into a long fluted crystal glass and offered it to Reggie.

"Here's to the new born your highness and may he bring more prosperity and hapiness to you and to your people," said Reggie as they both clinked glasses. But when the Maharaja learnt that Colonel Edwards had finally decided to make India his home, he too was surprised.

'But why of all places India and not here in the beautiful French Reviera," said the Maharaja as he as a good host poured some more champagne into Reggie's glass.

"And why not your highness, afterall I was born in India and so were my parents and I therefore do have a legitimate and parental claim to be a part of that jewel in the crown, don't I?' said Reggie rather proudly.

"Undoubtedly so Colonel and with your magnimous gesture to have Ismail Sikandar Khan who is one of my subjects from Gilgit to serve as an officer in the British Indian Army in the near future, I am simply delighted," said the Maharaja while raising a toast to Reggie's good health and for his future happiness in India.

Four days later on the 13th of March, 1931, Viceroy Irwin expressing his frank views about Gandhi in a personal confidential letter to his King in England wrote-:

"Regarding Mr Gandhi who though he looks emaciated with no front teeth and with hardly or no personality, but one should not go by his looks alone. I have noticed that there is a force of character behind those sharp little eyes and an immensely active and acutely working mind. If the man gives his word, his words become absolutely secure for me and I can trust it implicitly. He wants to see India established in her own self respect and in the respect of the world. And he also wants to see India with Great Britain on terms of equality and vice versa. He will be satisfied if India gets Purna Swaraj or complete independence in association with Great Britain. If Great Britain will not help in the attainment of this Purna Swaraj then I am afraid he will have to persue it in isolation of Great Britain."

Meanwhile when Debu Ghosh heard that Subhas Bose was going to Delhi to hold a protest rally in Azad Maidan on 20th March against the death sentence that had been confirmed by the higher court on Bhagat Singh, Rajguru and Sukhdev, he immediately booked an inter class berth on the Kalka Mail.

"But where is the need for you to be there. In fact I would suggest that you go to Chittagong instead and help your old parents in tracing out your younger brother Hitu who I believe is still hiding in some remote village with Masterda and his young revolutionaries," advised Naren Sen.

"I will also do that when I get back from Delhi and Lahore. Afterall my brother hopefully is still living but those three young Indian patriots and freedom fighters who are languishing in the Lahore jail have only a couple of more days to live and I want to be there with them in heart and soul," said Debu Ghosh.

"Then just do as you please," said his wife Hena in disgust as she went back into her kitchen to get supper ready.

On the 20th of March, at the Azad Maidan in Delhi where some 25,000 people had collected to hear the Lion of Bengal, Subhas Bose eulogizing the true patriotic spirit of the three condemned prisoners once again appealed to the good offices of the British government to commute the death sentence to life imprisionment, but it fell on totally deaf years. Even Pandit Jawaharlal Nehru while appealing to the British Government wrote.

"Whether I agree with him or not, my heart is full of admiration for the courage and self sacrifices of a man like Bhagat Singh. Courage like that of Bhagat Singh is exceedingly rare. If the Viceroy expects us to refrain from admiring this wonderful courage and the high purpose behind it, he is mistaken. Let him ask what he would have felt if Bhagat Singh had been an Englishman and had acted for England."

When such strong appeals by influential Indian leaders to spare the lives of the three accused were reviewed by the Vicerroy and his council it was concluded by them that the hanging of the three should be secretly preponed or else there could be serious trouble now that the sentiments of the general Indian public were being aroused by their own leaders.

"Let us hang those blighters a day earlier than planned and that too in the late hours of the evening, which though is against all norms of the jail manual but it must be done very quietly and the bodies secretly disposed off immediately," suggested one of the senior members of the Governor's Council in Punjab. And the suggestion was immediately approved and accepted.

Originally the date for the hanging had been fixed for the early morning of the 24th of March, but neither Bhagat Singh nor Sukhdev nor Rajguru were surprised when the jail authorities on the evening of the 23rd told them to get ready and that the time had arrived for all of them to face the gallows. For the past two days Debu Ghosh had tried his best with the jail authorities as a lawyer to allow him only for a few minutes to meet the three condemned men, but his requests were turned down. Not even the members of their families were allowed to meet them on that day.

Just a few days before, Bhagat Singh had sent a letter to the authorities concerned demanding that he and his condemned comrades for waging a war against the King should be treated as prisoners of war and should therefore be executed by a firing squad rather than being hanged. But that appeal too was rejected.

A little before 7 pm on the evening of the 23rd of March 1931, after requesting for a cup of coffee that he loved to drink, Bhagat Singh with Sukhdev and Rajguru smilingly walked up to the gallows shouting 'Vande Mataram,'(Glory to the Motherland), and 'Inquilab Zindabad', (Long Live Freedom.). To get the honour of who should have the privilege of being hanged first, the three decided to toss a coin and the honour went to Sukhdev and who was to be followed by Bhagat Singh and Rajguru. And when all three of them very cheerfully climbed the platform, kissed the rope that they themselves put around their necks, even the executioner admired their courage. And when they told the jail authorities that they were ready and the hangman did his job, it was all over within minutes. Though the jail authorities had managed to keep the hanging a secret but it was not going to remain a secret for long. As per the jail manual the body must hang atleast for one hour and a certificate of execution of the death sentence with the seal of the Judicial Department and signed by the Superintendent of the Jail were also required to be submitted to the higher authorities. The norms accordingly were followed and a separate certificate for each one of them individually was submitted, but all this took a little time.In the case of Bhagat Singh the certificate read as follows.

"I hereby certify that the sentence of death on Bhagat Singh has been duly executed, and that the said Bhagat Singh was accordingly hanged by the neck till he was dead at Lahore Central Jail on Monday, the 23rd of March 1931, at 7 pm., that the body remained suspended for a full hour, and was not taken down until life was ascertained by a medical officer to be extinct; and that no accident, error or other misadventure occurred."

Then suddenly immediately after the mandatory hour was over there was high drama within the jail premises as the three dead bodies were slipped out from a gap that had been specially breached in the high wall to the rear of the jail for this very purpose. The bodies were then piled into a vehicle and taken secretly to the banks of the River Sutlej at Husseiniwala near Ferozepore for their final disposal.

With the contacts that Debu Ghosh had established with the menial staff working inside the jail, late that night word was soon passed to him regarding the disposal of the three bodies. Debu Ghosh therefore with a few other members from the Congress party left Lahore in a private car and they rushed to Husseiniwalla, but by the time they got there, it was already a bit too late. On reaching the banks of the Sutlej at Husseiniwalla, they found a large number of villagers and they had all a gathered around the wet and half burnt bodies of the three martyrs. The villagers had noticed that the bodies had been burnt collectively by the policemen and before they could be fully consumed by the flames, the police in their hurry and fear of being mobbed and lynched by the crowd had thrown the half burnt bodies into the River Sutlej and had vanished from the scene. The villagers had timely salvaged the bodies from the river and decided to once more do the unfinished cremation individually for all three of them.

"Believe you me this is going to be a bloody black Monday and maybe even a blacker Tuesday for the Englishman," said a young Sardar lad when he came to know the truth.

"Yes but let us not be impulsive. Let let us all collect the sacred ashes of our immortal heroes and let us all march to Lahore to protest against this inhuman treatment that even the devil himself would never have advocated against his worst enemy," said an elderly Sikh with a flowing white beard.

"Yes, and we must let the people of India and the world know about this inhuman and brutal attitude of the British even to our dead," said Debu Ghosh as he rushed off to the main telegraph office at Ferozepore to dispatch a ten line telegram to The Bombay Chronical.

Tuesday the 24th of March was a day of complete mourning in India as word got around about the death of the three brave young sons of the country. The people including the inmates of the jail in Lahore fasted in sorrow when they learnt that the families of the three young and brave sons of India had been turned away from the gates of the jail with the excuse that it was all over. They had only come early that morning to say a final goodbye and had to leave even without the ashes of their loved ones. That very night Debu Ghosh also dispatched an urgent telegram to his wife in Calcutta and followed it up with a detailed letter. He explained to her that much that he would have liked to return home, but he was now constrained with what had happened at Lahore and therefore was on his way to Karachi to confront the Mahatma who was expected there on the 29th. The Congress leaders were meeting at Karachi to officially endorse the Gandhi-Irwin Pact or the Delhi Pact as it was now officially known.

The Gandhi Irwin Pact had brought in a sense of understanding between the British Rulers in India and the Congress Party and it had also in principle given India the hope that someday she would be free. However, in England the Delhi Pact was not at all welcomed by the powers who ruled over the goose that laid their golden eggs. For Mr Winston Churchill it was a big let down as he openly called the great Mahatma nothing but a half naked Indian fakir. To Mr Churchill the nauseating and humiliating spectacle of this one time Inner Temple lawyer striding half naked up the stairs of the Viceroy's palace while correspondents from all over the world clicked away on their cameras, was nothing less than a bloody disgrace and a let down by the representative of the King Emperor in India.

A day before the Congress meet at Karachi, Debu arrived there on the 'Heat Stroke Express.' The train journey through the plains of Punjab and the Sind Desert to the port of Karachi was rather miserable as Debu sat all crammed up in a trhird class compartment. The train was like a moving inferno at that time of the year. With the execution of the three brave young sons of India, the political temperature at Karachi was even higher when Gandhiji arrived the next day. Annoyed by Gandhi for not doing enough to save the three young men from the gallows, a huge crowd had gathered to protest against his uncalled for silence on the issue.And as soon as Gandhi alighted from his third class compartment, the crowd at the railway station and on the streets of Karachi both Hindus and Muslims waving black flags loudly shouted.

"Go back Gandhi. Go back Gandhi. You and your Congress have let us down."

Leading a group of young Congress volunteers, Debu Ghosh pleaded with the Mahatma to make some statement praising the courage of the three dead souls. The very next day the Congress passed a resolution that was drafted by Gandhi himself and in that though he reiterated his disapproval of political violence in any shape or form, but he also admired the bravery and sacrifice of the three martyrs.

The Karachi Session also became memorable for its resolution on Fundamental Rights and the National Economic Programme. The resolution guaranteed the basic civil rights of free speech, free press, free assembly and freedom of aasociation as also equality before the law of all irrespective of caste, creed or sex and the neutrality of the State in regard to all religions. It also promised elections on the basis of universal adult franchise and to provide free and compulsory education to all. Under the terms of the Gandhi-Irwin Pact all political prisoners not convicted would be released, there would be remission of all fines not yet collected and the return of all confiscated land and property that were not yet sold to third parties, as also lenient treatment would be given to those government employees who had resigned.To further assuage the feelings of his countrymen on that very day when he arrived at Karachi on the 29th of March, Gandhiji in an article in Young India wrote.

"Bhagat Singh was not a devotee of non violence, bur he did not subscribe to the religion of violence. He took to violence due to helplessness and to defend his motherland. In his last letter Bhagat Singh wrote 'I have been arrested while waging a war. For me there can be no gallows, put me into a mouth of a cannon and blow me off. These three heroes had conquered the fear of death. Let us bow to them a thousand times for their heroism.'

On his return from Karachi, having received another telegram from his father that there was still no news about the whereabouts of his younger brother Hitu, Debu immediately left for Chittagong. Meanwhile on 7th April 1931 two young revolutionaries, Bimal Dasgupta and Jatgiban Ghosh from the Midnapur Group of Bengal volunteers shot dead in cold blood Mr James Peddie, the District Magistrate of Midnapur while he was presiding over the District Board Meeting and both of them had also made good their escape. Earlier on the 12th of March, Tarakeshwar Dastidar and Binode Dutta, both young lieutenants of Masterda were confronted by a police party near the village of Barama. Luckily both managed to escape after shooting Sashanka Bhattacharya the inspector from the Intelligence Bureau who was chasing them. On reaching Chittagong, Debu Ghosh started making discreet enquiries from reliable local sources both from Chittagong town itself and also from some of the locals who regularly frequented the town from the distant fishing villages along the Chittagong coastal area to dispose off their day's catch.

Then one day by chance he happened to meet a young girl by the name of Kalpana Datta. The seventeen year old daughter of a family acquaintance had completed her intermediate college examination in science from Bethune College, Calcutta and had only recently in May 1930 joined Masterda's revolutionary outfit. Being a good chemistry student, Masterda Surya Sen who was still in hiding had secretly assigned her with a very important task.

"I believe you have given up your studies for good. You were always a good student and must continue to become atleast a graduate," said Debu Ghosh.

"I will but at some other later date. And as far as your brother Hitu is concerned Debuda, do not worry he is well and safe and has also become a devoted 'Swadeshi'(Freedom Fighter) like me," said Kalpana Datta very proudly.

"That is fine but is 'swadeshi' with violence the answer to attain our freedom?asked Debu Ghosh.

"Maybe yes Debuda and if we just a handful of 65 young people under Masterda could take on the British for the worthy cause of freeing ourselves from British slavery, then imagine what could happen to them if the entire youth of this country rises in revolt against them. And whatever you may say but we have shaken the Britishers, haven't we?' added Kalpana Datta.

"I guess you have but at what cost when most of your young leaders are inside the jail," said Debu Ghosh.

"But they won't be there for long I can assure you and you just have to wait and see," said a confident Kalpana Datta as she took leave of Debu Ghosh.

On being assured by Kalpana Datta that his brother Hitu was in safe hands, Debu Ghosh convinced his aging parents that there was nothing to worry about and he returned back to Calcutta.It was in February 1931, that Masterda while still underground had prepared another daring plan. Having established contact with Ganesh Ghosh and Ananta Singh who were inside the Chittagong jail, Masterda had now planned to blow up the place in order to free his junior comrades. Masterda had heard that all of them were now being subjected to severe torture and he was desperate to get the plan going at the earliest.In February and on instructions from him, Kalpana Datta had gone to Calcutta. There with the help of Kamala Chatterjee, Renu Ray and Amita Sen of the Jugantar Revolutionary Party she had managed to procure the required large consignment of sulphuric acid and nitric acid for the preparation of gun cotton slabs and other explosives. Together with the help from Nalini Pal of Chittagong, some 90 pounds of that deadly material had been clandestinely smuggled into the town. With the formula that was sent by Ganesh Ghose and Anantha Singh from the Chittagong prison, Kalpana Datta while pretending to her parents that she was only revising her chemistry practicals, she now got busy preparing the required explosives for the daring escape plan.

By early May, and despite the dusk to dawn curfew that was still in force at Chittagong, small groups of Kalpana Datta's young task force with their innocent looks had managed to place the devastating explosive charges at some of the important designated targets. These were all located in the important and strategic centres of the town and included the District Court building, the bungalow of the Superintendent of Police, as also the Circuit

House where the three tribunal judges who were conducting the first Chittagong armoury raid case were housed. The 'Swadeshis,'the dedicated young revolutionaries had cleverly with the help of the local conservancy staff working inside the jail premises who were covertly sympathetic to their cause had even managed to smuggle in the large quantity of gun cotton slabs with the fuzes that were required to blow up a part of the high jail wall as planned. The task given to Kalpana Datta was the all important one to coordinate with her other team members and to ensure that they all physically and simultaneously ignited all the explosive charges that had been so far successfully placed at the important and vital locations inside the town. She was now only waiting for the final go ahead signal from Masterda, when the news arrived for them to abhort the plan completely.

On the morning of the 5th of May 1931, the police having received reliable information of the plot had started digging up the ground in front of the cells that were occupied by the under trial prisoners. Soon they found a cigarette tin that contained two 12 volt electric bulbs, a few daggers, knives and even some revolvers. The game was now up. It seemed that someone for the lure of a small monetary reward had squealed to the police. Kalpana Datta was therefore immediately directed by Masterda to go underground.

Disappointed with the failure of the plan to blow up the Chittagong jail and free his loyal lieutenants, Masterda now decided to spread out the activities of his Chittagong group to the neighbouring district also. On the 13th of June, he called for a special secret meeting at Dalaghat, a village not far from the town. Preetilata Waddedar, a young graduate and a school teacher by proffession from the new High School for girls was also one of the invitees to the secret conclave. Preetilata had become an ardent admirer of Masterda and to the cause. It seemed that the British authorities had got wind of this secret rendez-vous and when the meeting was in progress, the place was raided by Captain Cameron and his Gurkha troops. In the exchange of fire, young Nirmal and Apurbha Sen, two of Masterda's trusted lieutenants were killed. Masterda and Preetilata were however, lucky to escape.

During the end of April, while Kalpana Datta was busy giving the finishing touches to the daring Chittagong jail break, Maharaja Hari Singh with his young wife and the infant Karan Singh returned to India on the ship 'Kaiser-e-Hind.'.On arrval, he was greeted at the Ballard Pier in Bombay by a large retinue of his officials. On the 3rd of May 1931 as his special railway saloon steamed into the Satwari railway station near Jammu, a huge crowd shouted 'Jai De Maharaj,', 'Jai De Maharaj,'(Victory to the

Maharaja, Victory to the Maharaja.) From the railway station as he drove in his open carriage with his wife to his palace in the city, little Karan Singh following behind in a motor car was peacefully asleep with his head resting comfortably on the lap of Miss Doris, his English nurse. The two month old boy was oblivious of what was happening around him.

While in Eastern India Masterda with his small force of young and brave revolutionaries was still fighting against the British imperialistic rule, far away in Kashmir the young Maharaja Hari Singh was being confronted with a situation that would later cost him not only his very throne, but would remain a curse for India, the country that was desparately now clamouring for nothing else but Purna Swaraj or complete Independence from the British Raj. In Bengal seeing the increasing revolutionary activities of the Bengalees, the legislative council of Bengal had now passed new emergency ordinances, but in Kashmir the troubles were of a completely different kind.

Chapter-6

First Tremors in Paradise (1931-1932)

It was only two years earlier in March 1929, that Sir Albion Banerjee, a Bengali Christian and the Maharaja's Prime Minister had resigned on the grounds that the Maharaja's Hindu Government officials had no sympathy with the wants and grievances of the Muslims in the state and therefore he was not going to be a party to it. Albion Banerjee had immediately been replaced by Mr GEC Wakefield who hitherto had been incharge of the State Police and the Public Works Department.

On the 11th of May 1931, while Karan Singh's naming ceremony was formally being held in the Maharaja's summer capital at Srinager, not very far away from the venue, a tall handsome 26 year old Kashmiri Muslim who was born in the nearby village of Surah was conducting his own little meeting condemning the rule of his Hindu Maharaja. Sheikh Abdulla who had recently returned from Aligarh Muslim University with a Master's degree in Chemistry was not the type who could be easily brow beaten. The birth of young Karan Singh coincided with the emergence of this fiery young school master from the valley.

The Abdulla families, which had originally descended from a family of Kasmiri Brahmins and were converted to Islam in the 18th century, were not rich by any standards. The family traded in Pashmina shawls and Sheikh Abdulla was now only an ordinary school teacher on a salary of Rupees sixty per month. Though the young Sheikh Abdulla as a child had lost his father two weeks before his own birth, but he was one of the very few amongst the Muslims of Kashmir who was very well educated. That morning sitting in the small common reading room that he himself had opened at Srinagar he quoted the vital disparities between the Dogra Hindus, the Kashmiri Pundits and the Kashmiri Muslims. According to the Sheikh though the Muslims were the largest community in the State, but they were were being given the least opportunity in the Kashmir Government service, in the State Police and also in the Maharaja's State Forces. Addressing the small gathering in the heart of Srinagar, the young Sheikh Abdulla said.

"Why should we be discriminated in our own land? Why cannot we also be given equal opportunities like the other favoured classes? What crime have we committed? Maybe the Maharaja himself does not know what is happening in his own domain and I think it is time that we spoke out firmly justifying our legitimate demands."

Listening to him very attentively that day was 17 year old Ismail Sikandar Khan and his grandfather Sarfaraz Khan. Ismail Sikandar Khan had come on his summer holidays from the PWRIMC and was impressed by the speaker's personality and his command over the Kashmiri language. When the Sheikh while gesticulating with his long hands said on top of his voice that it was only for a measly sum of Rupees 75 lacs only that the Britishers had sold their sacred land to Maharaja Gulab Singh, everybody was surprised. This was something that only very few were aware of and when he further added that the Hindu dynasty was not even 100 years old and that the ordinary Kashmiri Muslim eversince that day was always treated as a slave, the crowd got a little restive. Finally when the meeting ended and Sheikh Abdulla vowed that he will not sit quiet till full justice for the Muslims of the state was dispensed with, Ismail Sikandar Khan knew that a future leader for the down trodden Kashmiris was in the making.

During that very month of May, Colonel Reginald Edwards was also holidaying in Srinagar and he was there to coach Ismail Sikandar Khan for a career as an officer in the Indian Army.

'Now do lease remember this is your final year at the PWRIMC and thereafter you must appear and also qualify at the entrance test for admission to the new military academy that will shortly be opened there and therefore we will spend all the vacation time preparing for it, said Reggie while advising Ismail to keep away from local politics.

Yes most certainly Sir," replied Ismail as he smartly saluted Reggie and showed him the homework that was given to him on the previous day.

Later that evening there was a grand party. It was being hosted by the Maharaja at the Shalimar Gardens in Srinagar and both Reggie and Ismail Sikandar Khan had also been invited. The famed garden built by the Mughul Emperor Jehangir looked like a fairyland with myriad lanterns and small oil lamps flickering from every crevice and all along the walls of the royal garden. As Reggie and Ismail dressed in proper dinner jackets walked upto Maharaja Hari Singh to pay their respects, Reggie noticed two other Englishmen standing nearby. They too were both elegantly dressed in their respective uniforms and one of them in the white mess dress of the Indian Political Department was Colonel George Drummond Ogilvie the British Resident in Kashmir and whom Reggie knew well. His beautiful daughter Vere Ogilvie was soon to marry Captain Christopher Birdwood, the son of the erstwhile Commander-in-Chief India, but the other handsome British Lieutenant in his mess kit of red, blue and gold dress seemed to be a newcomer.

Maharaja Hari Singh looked indeed very handsome in his tight white Jodhpuris and jacket which was emblazoned with stars and medals. His feet carried the gold encrusted Indian shoes locally known as 'jutties.' On his head was a saffron turban of the finest silk, while a large diamond adorned his big forehead. After Ismail Sikandar Khan had had done the traditional namaste and reached out towards the Maharaja's feet in obeisance as was the custom, Hari Singh shook his hand and said.

"I have been told that you are aspiring to become an Indian army officer and therefore you must do well in the entrance examination."

With that kind of encouragement coming from his own Maharaja, Ismail Sikandar Khan was now determined to do well as Reggie and he moved aside for the others to pay their obeisance to the Maharaja.

'Let me now present to you my new young assistant,'said Colonel Ogilvie very proudly as he introduced Lieutenant Francis Ingall to Reggie and Ismail.Born on 24th October 1908, Francis Ingall nicknamed Bingle was a product of the Sandhurst 1929 batch and was commissioned into the 6th Lancers. And with only two years plus service he had been loaned to the British Resident temporarily. The 6th Lancers were then stationed at Sialkot and the Maharaja's present Comptroller of the household was none other than their old Officer's Mess Dafadar Nischant Singh. Nischant Singh had started his life as a trooper in the 6th Lancers and it was his sister who was married to the Maharaja and bore him a son. The Maharaja and his brother-in-law Nischant Singh were now good friends and when Nischant Singh requested all of them to move to the lavish well stocked bar for a drink, Ismail Sikandar Khan realized how important luck played in a person's life. The ex Mess Dafadar from the 6th Lancers was also now a man to reckon with as far as Kashmir was concerned.

While everybody was enjoying the lovely party, suddenly there was a hue and cry as Maharaja Hari Singh blared loudly at his ADC and asked. "Where is Poonch?"

Poonch was one of the Maharaja's vassals and it seemed that he was late and the Maharaja was furious. A little while later, when the Raja of Poonch was seen running breathlessly towards the Maharaja, Ismail Sikandar Khan did not find it very funny. But when the Raja of Poonch prostrated himself before the Maharaja and clutched both his feet while asking for forgiveness, Ismail Sikandar knew that it must be something very serious. The fuming Maharaja with a scowl on his face called for his Prime Minister and they both went into a huddle inside a room. A little while later the entire cabinet including Colonel Oglivie the British resident was summoned for an urgent meeting that was being presided over by the Maharaja himself. The Maharaja's animosity towards the Raja of Poonch could be attributed to the fact that his uncle Maharaja Pratap Singh wanted to adopt him. When the Maharaja with his Prime Minister and Colonel Oglivie returned back to the party, Lt. Ingall said to Ismail Sikandar Khan.

"Now watch the bloody fun,"

So when the Maharaja livid with anger and in his loud voice which could be heard by one and all said.

"Gentlemen the action of Raja of Poonch today I regret to say is in utter disrespect to me. I have been insulted and that to deliberately in public. I want him to be deposed immediately," Ismail was simply flabbergasted.Then there was a hushed silence till Colonel Ogilvie pointed out that it would not be proper without taking the Viceroy's prior permission which is mandatory in all such cases.

"Alright punish him I will and that too right now and today," said an angry Hari Singh as he withdrew the two gun salute that the Raja of Poonch was entitled to. Ismail felt a bit sorry for the Raja who stood there sheepishly after being scolded like an errant schoolboy.

And while the Maharaja of Kashmir tried to ensure that he would not tolerate any indiscipline from any quarter, in India preparations were on to give the Indians a military academy of their own. Field Marshall Birdwood on relinquishing command had promised that India would soon have her own Sandhurst. And now the new Commander-in-Chief India, Field Marshall Chetwode, whose name would soon forever be etched in letters of gold, had given the Indian Sandhurst Committee the final go ahead and he was keen that the Indian Military Academy at Dehra Dun for the training of the potential Indian Army officers must commence by the end of the summer of 1932.

In mid June 1931, while the Indian Sandhurst Committee was busy selecting a suitable location for the academy, it was allegedly reported to the Maharaja of Kashmir that some Hindus in Jammu had disrupted a Muslim congregation for worship and that the Holy Koran had been insulted. On hearing that the Maharaja was absolutely livid and he ordered the culprits to be brought to book immediately. But by the time any action could be taken, the situation in the valley took a violent turn. The real trouble between the Hindus and the Muslims of the valley now started as the Maulvis from their pulpits of their mosques denounced the Hindus, while others condemned the despotic rule of the Hindu Maharaja and his coterie of advisors at public meetings and they even took out processions through the streets of Srinagar.

On the 9th of July, the Maharaja himself appealed to his own people to remain calm and peaceful. He in his proclamation that was titled "To My Beloved People" once again reiterated what he had said when he took over as the new Maharaja.

"At the beginning of my rule I announced to you my people, that my religion is justice. That announcement has guided all my public acts and policies and I shall always adhere to it. I have not made, and will not permit any discrimination against any class of my people on the grounds of religion. The humblest of my subjects have free and direct acess to me and any grievance my people may have can be submitted by them personally to me but subject to two fundamental conditions, which are firstly that all political activities should be confined to the laws of the land and secondly no outside intervention is sought in any shape or form."

In July 1931, the beautiful vale of Kashmir, the land of lotuses, quiet rivers and shining lakes exploded with unprecedented communal violence. A violence that would continue for decades together for the poor people of that Himalayan kingdom bringing in more misery to the innocent inhabitants who unfortunately had no say in the matter at all.

It all started on 25th June, 1931 when Abdul Quadir a Muslim who as some unconfirmed reports indicated hailed originally from the North West Frontier and who had come to the valley as a cook for a British officer. He had made a fiery inflammatory speech to the general public asking the Muslims to unite and revolt against the King and his Hindu Raj. He had aroused so much of communal passion that aid to civil authorities using the military state forces had to be called for. Soon the disturbances spread far and wide in the valley and Abdul Quadir was arrested on charges of sedition.

On the 6th of July, while Abdul Quadir was being tried by a Sessions Court, the local population of Muslims in Srinagar instigated by some others in large numbers soon started congregating outside the Court room and started demanding the release of the man. Seeing the tense situation, the court was immediately adjourned and the date 13th of July was fixed for the next hearing that was now to be held within the safe environments of the Srinagar Central Jail.

On the 13th of July, when the trial reopened a huge crowd had once again gathered outside the jail to protest against the trial of the accused and they also once again demanded his immediate release. That day afternoon unaware of what was happenning inside the tensed up city, Sarfaraz Khan having taken the day off from cooking in the royal kitchen had decided to visit the Hazratbal Mosque. Eversince the day Ismail Sikandar Khan went away to join the PWRIMC at Dehra Dun, Sarfaraz Khan whenever he got the opportunity he went and prayed at that big mosque and on that very day he had gone there to pray for his grandson's success in the forthcoming first entrance examination to the IMA. Ismail Khan was appearing as an open candidate and for which there were just 15 vacancies out of a total of 40 that had been earmarked for the first course at the Indian Military Academy.

The 13th proved to be an unlucky day for the aging Sarfaraz Khan. After the news had spread about the trial of Abdul Quadir, people had come out on the streets and were demanding his release. Though the DIG Police, Sheikh Aziz had taken adequate measures to control the crowd near the jail, but it soon got out of hand when the crowd decided to storm the jail itself. Soon the police baton charged them. Then the stone throwing began and the police had no other recourse but to open fire. When the bullets started raining on the agitators, they started running for cover, but this unfortunately resulted in a large number of demonstrators being either killed or wounded. The city of Srinagar and the peaceful beautiful Kashmir valley which according to poets and historians was like a big flower garden and a paradise on earth now became a virtual battle ground of hatred between the Hindus and the Muslims. The Muslims who were in the majority now started killing innocent Hindus and looting their shops and property. The situation had come to such a stage that Brigadier R O Sutherland who was the Chief of Staff of the Maharaja's State Forces himself with 50 sepoys from the Kasmir Infantry went to the Srinagar jail to establish order. In the meantime poor Sarfaraz Khan who was about to reach the mosque while trying to pacify the crowd that had gathered there to restrain themselves from unwanted killings and looting, soon fell victim to the angry crowd. A young Muslim lad thinking that Sarfaraz Khan was taking the side of the Hindus simply took out a long kitchen knife and stabbed him to death. That evening when his dead body was brought back to the palace, Ismail Sikandar Khan was shocked. He could never imagine that his own grandfather would become one of the first victims of communal frenzy in the valley.

Next day happened to be the 14th of July and Bastille Day. It was a day when the French people went against their own King Louis the XIV, when they had stormed the Bastille prison in Paris to free the many innocent people who had been jailed and demanded their own freedom. On that morning, while Reggie with tears in his eyes silently attended the burial of his old faithful cook at the Badami Bagh Cantonment, at the Jumma Masjid mosque inside the city the dead bodies of those killed in the firing were being handed over to their next of kin. At that very moment, when the bodies were being handed over, the young Sheikh Abdulla arrived. He was already a marked man and his mood showed the anger in his face. Brigadier Sutherland, who was present there, fearing that more trouble would be created if the Sheikh was allowed to open his mouth, therefore very quietly had him whisked away in a military truck to the Badami Bagh cantonment where he was kept under detention till such time the burial of those dead had been conducted.

That evening for the first time Reggie met the handsome young Sheikh Abdulla and as they discussed the tense situation that was prevailing in the valley, Ismail kept listening to them.

"It is indeed rather sad and very unfortunate that so many innocent people have lost their lives and that includes this young boy's grandfather also," said Reggie as he introduced Ismail Sikandar Khan to the young fiery leader.

"Yes it is indeed very unfortunate but this should also be taken as a wake up call for the Maharaja, or else the situation may become even worse in the days to come And I feel sorry for the boy," said Sheikh Abdullah as he conveyed his condolences to Ismail on the death of his grandfather. And a little later, when the Sheikh with tears in his eyes cursed himself for having been born in Kashmir, Reggie said.

Well let me tell you that only this morning I too was crying for a poor innocent soul, who too was a Kashmiri but who for no rhyme or reason became a victim of mob violence. And here you are as a young leader of the Muslims repenting on your kismet of being born in this beautiful valley, where according to your own confession you are nobody. But that I don't think is correct and what is destined to happen should be left in the hands of the Almighty. You never know maybe the 13th of July, 1931 may prove lucky for you and your people.in the long run. It could even be a blessing in disguise and maybe someday God willing you as a leader will be able to convince the Maharaja that the Kashimir Muslims are as patriotic as the Hindus in his state and therefore they should be looked upon as equals, because failing which I am afraid it would lead to a bloody catastrophe and from which none will be the wiser," added Reggie.

Hearing those words of wisdom coming from an Englishman there was now a smile on the young Muslim leader's face as he thanked Reggie for his kind words and encouragement.Soon the crises that erupted on that 13th of July came to be dominated by two Kashmiri Muslims. One was the Mirwaiz Mohammed Yusuf Shah, a religious leader and the acknowledged head of the entire Kashmiri Muslim community, while the other was the young school master, Sheikh Mohammed Abdulla. Strangely enough, it was also around this time that the Maharaja had Mr GEC Wakefield replaced by Pandit Hari Krishan Kaul as his new Prime Minister.

While an uneasy peace came back to the valley for a short while, in Calcutta on the 27th of July, Mr Garlick the District Judge who had tried Dinesh Gupta for the death of Mr Simpson, the IG Prisons was killed while seated in the court. It was an act of revenge by the young revolutionaries of Bengal. Then on 30th August, the young 16 year old Haripada Bhattacharya in broad daylight shot dead Khan Bahadur Assanullah, the Muslim Deputy Superintendent of Police, Chittagong in a crowded football field. Assanullah's crime was that he had been siding with the British and was instrumental in the capture of some of Masterda's young revolutionaries.

The British were only waiting for such an opportunity as they fanned the flames of communalism to pitch the Hindus against the Muslims in Bengal. Taking advantage of the situation the goonda gangs from both the communities now started looting each others shops and properties.

"You must go and look after your old father and mother and if possible convince them to come and stay with us in Calcutta till such time the situation in Chittagong improves," pleaded Hena Ghosh to her dear husband.

"Not a bad idea and maybe I could find my brother Hitu too and get him back to his books and studies in Calcutta," said Debu Ghosh as he got ready to pack his bags and leave.

While Debu Ghosh accompanied by his brother-in-law Naren Sen were both on their way to Chittagong, on the 1st of August, Sheikh Abdulla was released from his detention. But on the 26th he was again rearrested. This time under the supervision of Captain Pir Mohammed Khan, the Sheikh was kept as a prisoner in the lines of the 5th Kashmir Rifles at Badami Bagh. With trouble expected, Brigadier Sutherland, the Chief of Staff of the Maharaja's Army who was enjoying a short holiday with good golf at Gulmarg was also recalled.

Six days earlier on the 20th of August, 1931 Mahatma Gandhi boarded the SS Rajputana for his historic trip to attend the Second Round Table Conference in England. In the meantime in April 1931, soon after having signed the Delhi Pact, Viceroy Irwin had been replaced by Wellingdon who believed that the signing of the pact with the Congress was a major error and he was determined to crush the Congress.

The Second Round Table Conference opened in London on the 7th of September and Gandhi attended the Congress as the sole representative of the Congress party. But it ended in failure, when the conference got deadlocked on the minority's issue. The Muslims, the depressed Hindu classes, the Indian Christians, Anglo Indians and even the Europeans settled in India were now demanding separate electorates for themselves and Gandhi was totally against it. He knew that this would further divide India and he was not willing to be a party to it.

Meanwhile Debu Ghosh and Naren Sen had reached Chittagong and though they found the atmosphere in the town to be still tense, but the looting mercifully had stopped.

"I will make one more attempt to trace out Hitu but failing which I will take both of you Baba nd Ma back with me to Calcutta," said Debu Ghosh while touching their feet. For the next couple of days Debu Ghosh having made some reliable contacts with the local boatmen called 'Majhis' finally managed to trace out his dear brother Hitu. Some of these loyal Majhis both Hindus and Muslims had time and again ferried Masterda and his young revolutionaries from one hiding place to another in the riverine area around Chittagong.

'There is no need for any payment Hujoor and I will take you free,' said Majhi Aslam Mia as he grinned, and put one more big betel leaf into his fully reddened mouth that showed half his black teeth. And when they reached the hideout, Hitu was taken by completely surprise but there was nothing that would change his mind.

"I know Borda, (elder brother) that both Ma and Baba will be disappointed, but you do not have to mention to them that you have met me. Just return home and tell them that though you could not locate me, you were assured by the other young revolutionaries that I was safe and well and this is a fact isn't it?" said Hitu confidently.

"Alright if that is what you wish so be it and you are most welcome to come home anytime you want, but just be careful," said Debu Ghosh as he clasped his brother in his arms and wished him all the luck. The moistness in

Debu's eyes showed not only his fond love for Hitu, but also the respect and honour for the cause for which his youngest brother was fighting for.

"Well then good luck and all the very best to you, to Masterda and all his gallant young men," added Debu Ghosh as Aslam Mia safely guided the small boat through the dense swamps.

"I must admit that Hitu is not doing all this just for kicks. He is truly a dedicated Swadeshi and all that we can pray for is for his safety and well being," said Naren Sen to his in-laws when they reached home.

On the morning of the 22nd of September 1931, while the Mahatma was on his way back from London, at Srinagar where curfew had been imposed from dusk to dawn and which was announced by the firing of a gun from the top of Hari Parbat, the deserted streets of the city was soon filled with men, women and children. They were congregating at the Jumma Majid to demand the release of their beloved young Sheikh Abdulla.

Three days later on the 25th of September, Captain NS Rawat with two companies of his soldiers from the Kashmir Rifles on being informed that arms were being stored in a mosque inside the city and that local trouble creators had sought refuge inside it, they surrounded the place of worship. He then ordered Lieutenant Fateh Ali Khan with his Muslim troops to conduct the search, but nothing was found.

"I think we should be a little more discreet and careful while conducting such searches at such sensitive places," said Reggie to Brigadier Sutherland over a peg of good Scotch whisky.

"You are right there, but orders are orders and one has to carry them out without prejudice," replied the Brigadier.

"But this kind of sabre rattling or should I say a show of force I am afraid feel will only create more bad blood between the Maharaja and his Muslim subjects and it will only worsen matters," said Reggie.

The 5th of October was Maharaja Hari Singh's birthday and on that very day realizing the tense situation that had been created, the Maharaja magnanimously granted amnesty to all political prisoners and Sheikh Abdulla was once again a free man. That very evening Reggie called on the Maharaja and congratulated him for his statesmanship.

"So what shall it be Scotch or Champagne," said a happy Hari Singh as he instructed his ADC to doubly ensure that both the bottle of skotch and the French champagne were of the rare brand and of the vintage variety.

CHAPTER-7

The Honour of the Country Comes First Always and Everytime

While the tension in Kashmir subsided for a while, in Bengal the young Bengalee revolutionaries stepped up their activities against the senior British civil servants. On 28th October, the District magistrate of Dhaka was shot and wounded. With tension all around, the police laid siege to large areas of the city and started raiding various homes and educational institutions and whosoever was even remotely connected with nationalism and swadeshi were promptly arrested. When told about the activities of the police in Dhaka, Subhas Bose with Debu Ghosh who knew Dhaka well rushed to the first city of East Bengal. But when they landed by steamer at Narayanganj, the Superintendent of Police in Dhaka, Mr Ellison refused them entry. When they again tried to enter the city from a different route, they were both arrested and taken to the Dhaka jail.

"I wonder where will all this lead too if the British authorities like dumb goats do not realize that come what may they are not at all welcome to our 'Shonar Bangla' our Golden Bengal, a name that was given by no less a person than the Nobel Laureate, Rabindranath Tagore," said a demoralised Debu Ghosh on his release from the Dhaka jail to his wife Hena. On learning about her husband's arrest she with Naren Sen had promptly landed in Dhaka. '

"But I think that it is high time that you stopped all this party business and concentrated more on your legal profession. Afterall, the children are growing up and we are not getting any younger either and thanks to you even your own sister Shobha's eldest son, Samir Sen whom we all address as our dear Lallu, a nickname that was given to him simply because he was born during the Russian revolution, he too though he is not even 14 years old is today talking about becoming a Swadeshi. And with his influence I will not be surprised if our dearest eldest son Arup Ghosh who is always in

Lallu's company also joins him in the same endeavour," said a visibly angry Hena.

"Oh no, but why must you always look to the future in such a negative manner. I agree that the boys now should devote more time to their books and studies but they are not to be blamed if they worship such living heroes like Subhas Chander Bose and the late Comrade Lenin or patriots like Benoy, Badal and Dinesh who smilingly laid down their lives for their beloved country," said Debu Ghosh looking somewhat annoyed at his wife's attitude.

"Well then don't blame me if they too join Masterda's young group of revolutionaries like your brother Hitu has done," replied an angry Hena as they boarded the train. Thereafter for the rest of their journey back to Calcutta there was no further communication between husband and wife.

It was on the 17th of November 1931, that Mr Reid who in 1911 as a young ICS officer did the ushering duties at Prinsep Ghat when the King and the Queen visited Calcutta took over as the Commissioner of Chittagong. With his fluency over the Bengali language, he was soon able to get a grip over the menacing terrorist threat that loomed large over the coastal town and the areas around.

'Ammi jaani ke thomra shob chaho Azadi. Etta thomra nischoi pabe ek din kintu erom bhabe na.' (I know that you all want your freedom and independence. This you will definitely get some day but not in this manner,) said Commissioner Reid in fluent Bengali while presiding over a local college function.

And Mr Reid had hardly completed a month, when news arrived on the 14th of December that two young school girls, Suniti Chowdhury and Shanti Das who were still in their early teens had shot dead Mr Stevens the District Magistrate of Commilla District while he was sitting in his own very office.

"My God, now even the girls in Bengal are in this business,'" remarked Reid as he directed all the police officers and the District Magistrates to be more vigilant.

Though the revolutionary movement amongst the young in Bengal was gaining momentum, but it was still not very alarming and with the Christmas season approaching, Reggie with Ismail Sikandar Khan together with Major Attiqur Rehman and his entire family decided to spend it in Calcutta. They had met at Dehra Dun when they had gone to pick up their wards from the PWRIMC.

"And though it is vacation time but I am afraid while in Calcutta both of you, Gul Rehman and Ismail Sikandar Khan will have to devote most of your time preparing for your future career and therefore the two of you under my personal supervision will be coached for the first public service exam for entry into the IMA, the Indian Military Academy that will be held on the 14th of July and we do not have very much time left. But this is all subject to both of you successfully passing your Senior Cambridge examination first and for which you have just appeared. But that does not mean that you will not enjoy your holidays," said Reggie as he ordered for another round of tipsy pudding for the two boys. For Ismail Sikandar Khan this was his first meal in the the well laid out dining car of the train that was run by the caterers Brandon and Company.

After the Great War, ten vacancies were earmarked for the Indian aspirants to the Sandhurst Military College in England, but with the projected opening of India's Sandhurst at Dehra Dun, these vacancies had now been withdrawn once and for all. During the fag end of the Great War after a lot of pressure had been brought on the British for the excellent contribution by the Indian troops fighting the Germans, only a handful of Indians were given the King's Commission.

Popularly known as KCO's, these first few selected lot after through screening of their antecedents and education, were first trained at the Daly College, Indore and in 1919 were commissioned into the infantry and the cavalry regiments of the King's Indian Army. Among them was KM Carriappa a handsome lad from Coorg and an equally handsome Iskandar Mirza, a lad from a rich well to do feudal family from Bengal. Though it was way back in 1754 that the 39th Fuziliers, the first British regular troops that had been rented out to the East India Company had set foot on Indian soil, but as far as the Indians were concerned they could only aspire to reach the dizzy heights of a Subedar Major of a unit, and if luck favoured further they could even retire as Honorary Lieutenants and Honorary Captains, but nothing beyond that.

Winter was the season for the great polo matches and tournaments in Calcutta and both Gul Rehman and Ismail Khan who were not only good riders but also good polo players, they therefore were hell bent on seeing all the matches.

'We promise you Sir that we will study an extra two hours everyday and try our very best to join the IMA, but please do not deprive us off the thrills of polo," said both the boys to Reggie somewhat pleadingly.

'Agreed, and I hope that's a solemn promise,' said Reggie as they all got ready to go to the polo ground.

At 2.30 PM in the evening, Maharaja Jai Singh of Jaipur, the 21 year old dashing polo player for whom the game was always a passion rode in with his team to take on his opponents from the State of Kishengarh.

'Come on, Jaipureans, put in your best and you must win,' said the elegant and excited Maharani Indira Devi of Cooch Bihar as Maharaja Jai Singh doffed his pith hat to her in gracious acknowledgement.

Jai Singh was a lucky man who had got to the Gaddhi of the rich Jaipur State on being adopted by the late ruler. He was a product of Mayo College, Ajmer, a college that was meant only for the royal princes of India. The college was the brain child of the late Lord Mayo and was started by Colonel Walters the then Political Agent of the State of Bharatpur in Rajasthan. Jai Singh had just returned from England after completing his military training from the Royal Woolwich Military Academy in England. That academy was mainly a training institution for the artillery gunner officers and the engineer sapper officers. The polo match that evening though it ended in a exciting draw, but it gave the Jaipureans to advance further in the prestigious tournament.

A week later it was the finals. For the Jaipurians, the princely royal family that had entered the finals with their own young Maharaja leading the team it had to be a win win situation only.

'I know you will do it and get the coveted trophy,' said the beautiful 12 year old Ayesha to Jai Singh as he left Woodlands where he was an honoured guest of Indira Devi. Though a twice married man, Jai Singh had fallen madly in love with the young and charming princess Gyatri Devi.

"Thank you for all the good wishes and if we do win, then we will celebrate the occasion at Firpos and you will be my treasured and honoured guest," said Maharaja Jai Singh as he got into his car.

That evening the Jaipur team had won and Reggie with the two young lads smartly walked up to the young Maharaja to congratulate him.

"Do please join us for the party at Firpos tonight and get these two young enthusiasts of polo with you also," said Maharaja Jai Singh while dismounting from his polo pony to shake hands with all of them.

"Thank you your highness we will all be there dot at seven," said an excited Gul Rehman as he smartly doffed his grey felt hat in appreciation to the royal invitation.

'Firpos'the most sought after restaurant on Calcutta's busy Chowringee was not only famous for its Italian cuisine, but also for its cakes and pastries and the type of English food of fried Beckti fish and chips with tartare sauce that every Englishman and his wife loved.

"Maywe also have a taste of some chilled beer Sir," said Gul Rehman as Reggie scanned through the menu and the wine card.

"Don't you try and fool me young man, you and Ismail can have a glass of chilled beer, but don't tell me that you do not know the taste of it," said Reggie with a smile as he beckoned the steward to take the order.

"My God and isn't she really beautiful," whispered Gul Rehman to Ismail Khan when he saw the petite young Gyatri Devi dressed in a saree for the first time being escorted by the handsome Maharaja of Jaipur and his equally handsome young ADC to the reserved VIP table.

"Boy, you can definitely say that again, Yes she is really beautiful," said Ismail as he held the frothy mug of beer high above his chest and clinked glasses with his dear friend Gul Rehman.

"Well in that case let's raise a toast to the young princess and to the wonderful people of India," added Reggie very sportingly.

"That was indeed very thoughtful of you Colonel Edwards," said the young Maharaja while ordering half a dozen bottles of the best chilled French champagne that Firpos could offer. With the first bubbles in her flouted glass, the young, elegant, beautiful and charming Gyatri Devi though feeling somewhat embarrassed, raised her own glass to accept the honour.

For the two young lads Gul Rehman and Ismail Sikandar Khan that December of 1931 in Calcutta besides concentrating on their books to appear for the IMA entrance examination, they also had a rollicking time going on picnics and excursions with the Sen, Ghosh, and the Hussein families.

A week or two later it got even more exciting for the two young PWRIMC boys, when the final farewell partiess to the Pugsley's started. Whether it was lunch, dinner or just a tea party for the Pugsleys, all of them were there in full strength and the two boys Gul Rehman and Ismail Sikandar were always seen in the company of the two identical looking Pugsley sisters, Sandra and Debbie. Both the girls had just turned 14 and they were not only tall and beautiful, but they looked a few years older than their actual age too. One fine evening unable to bear the familiarity of the two young boys with the Pugsley girls, Begum Shaukat Hussein could take it no more and she confided to her husband and said somewhat seriously to him.

"I think it is high time that the these two young boys are put on hold or else matters could get complicated,"

"But why and what happened,' asked Shaukat Hussein looking a little surprised.

"Well the day before in the afternoon, while all of you fathers and sons were busy playing cards in the drawing room and we the ladies were busy gossiping inside our bedroom, and the rest of the younger children were taking their afternoon nap, these four, that is the two boys and the two Pugsley girls were playing a game of their own while hiding under the bed and this I noticed by chance and it was when I was on my way to the kitchen to make tea for all of you.Then again last evening at the get together at the Sen's house for dinner, I found the two of them with their respective partners quietly disappearing into the small kitchen garden and they were giggling and cuddling one another. And when they saw me, all of them with a sheepish grin on their faces quietly made their way inside. And this morning I have been told that were seen also sitting in pairs at the Eden Gardens."

"Oh I guess these things happen at this age and you can call it calf love, puppy love or infatuation, but nevertheless one must be careful no doubt. In any case it is a matter of another few days only and then the Pugsleys will be off for good to settle in their own little cottage in Mhow in Central India and there will be nothing more to worry about," said Shaukat Hussein.

However, not wishing to be a spoil sport for Gul Rehman and Ismail Sikandar Khan who were only a couple of years elder to his own grandson Nawaz Hussein, Shaukat Hussein put it very diplomatically to Major Attiqur Rehman.

"In case you really want the two boys to become officers then I think they need to devote more time to their books and stay indoors rather than waste time on picnics and excursions," said Shaukat Hussein. And the hint was immediately well taken by Attiqur Rehman and from that very day itself both Gul Rehman and Ismail Sikandar Khan once again got busy with their studies.

On Christmas Night, Reggie decided to host a final farewell party for the Pugsleys and to celebrate the occasion he also invited the Sen, Ghosh, Hussein and the Rehman families. But when only the husbands from all the three Calcutta based families turned up minus their wives, Reggie was a bit dissapointed. He was ofcourse very happy to see Major Attiqur with his wife Nafisa and the two young lads from the PWRIMC present for the yuletide party.Being fully aware that everyone was fond of good authentic Chinese food, Reggie had booked a table for 14 at a lesser known but a popular Chinese restaurant in Central Calcutta's China town. It was a sit down affair and Reggie wanted it to be done in real style with candlelights and with the choicest of wines. Very sportingly and conveniently he had also worked out the seating plan in such a manner that the two young Pugsley twins sat with the two boys in the farthest corner of the long table.A little while later and in order to bring some life into the party, when Edwin Pugsley suggested that a game of limericks could be played to liven the evening and that each individual should sportingly compose and recite his own limerick starting with the sentence "My name is—.' everyone unanilmously agreed.

"'Well then let us start seniority wise and therefore it is your turn Mr Sen," said Edwin Pugsley as he smiled at all the others on the table.

"But that is not being fair because my English is rather poor, but if you so wish I could recite in Bengali a verse from the popular 'Abol Tabol.' These are called nonsense verses composed by Sukumar Ray,"'said Sonjoy as he sportingly recited one and then pointed his finger at Edwin for him to continue with the game.

"Well then here it is said a happy Edwin as he did a bottoms up with his glass. But when he recited one of his self composed bawdy limericks that started with the sentence 'My name is Edwin", Reggie very diplomatically and on the plea that there were four teenagers on the table decided to call the game off and raised a toast to the charming Pugsley family. Nonetheless after the toast, when Sandra got up said.

"My name is Sandra but they call me Sandy, I love my parents and I also love my candy.When I am in school I try and play it cool, Because schools have too many rules.But those are only meant for stupid fools."

"That was rather good I must say," said Reggie as he handed over a bar of Kit Kat chocolate each to the four teenagers.That evening Sandra had become Sandy to Ismail and Ismail had become Smiley to Sandra as they tried to pull each other's leg with their own little limericks. Sitting opposite them Gul Rehman seemed to be in a world of his own world as he tried to explain to a bored Debbie the concept of the Indian Sandhurst at Dehradun.

The very next evening on the 26th of December, Boxing day the Pugsley family boarded the BNR mail, better known as the Bombay Howrah mail via Nagpur for their journey to Khandwa and then from there to Mhow. They were indeed very touched when they found all the family members from the Sen, Ghosh and the Hussein families with little gifts and food packets in their hands at the Howrah Station waiting to see them off. Conversing seriously with Edwin, Reggie asked.

"But how come of all the god damn places on earth did you have to select Mhow, that sleepy small military station in the middle of nowhere in Central India to finally settle down?"

"Well Sir it is both for parental and selfish interests, but do let me explain. The first and the most important reason is that my dear parents now dead have left me a small bunglow and some little property there and since I do not have any resources to buy any other property anywhere else, it suited me fine. Secondly, the small sleepy town of Mhow has a fairly large population of Chee Chees like us and they are mostly from the railway crowd too and therefore there will be no dearth of good company. Thirdly, Mhow also has a decent railway club where one can afford to have a cocktail of rum with milk that we chee chees call grog. Fourthly, I have been told that the place also has one or two good Christian Missionary schools where my children can get good education at a reasonable cost. Fifthly, being a military training station and maybe like my mother, my beautiful girls may also find handsome British Officers as their life partners and God willing they may take them back to Blighty. And finally I know for sure that both my wife and I will at least be given a decent burial with a church service after we are dead and gone," said Edwin Pugsley as he kissed Laila on the cheek. But a minute letter when the guard sounded his whistle, the man who was always smiling had tears in his eyes as the train slowly steamed off the number one platform of Howrah station.

"Do please come and stay with us at Mhow, or atleast do write to us and keep in touch," said Leila Pugsley as she wiped away her tears and while the rest of the family peeping through the windows of their reserved inter class compartment kept waving out. And as a grand finale, when the two Pugsley sisters in royal style sent flying kisses to all of them, Gul Rehman sent one back too.

That night when they went to bed both Gul Rehman and Ismail Sikandar Khan kept teasing each other.

"Dammit all and the way you kept waving out to her it seems that you have been badly smitten by Sandra," said Gul Rehman.

"And what about that flying return kiss of yours and which I am quite sure was meant for none other than Debbie. And you too will miss her wont you? said Ismail.

In that beautiful winter month of December in Calcutta, while champagne kept flowing at Maharani Indira Devi's sprawling Woodlands estate, far away in the North West Frontier Province of India as a sequel to the successful Gandhi-Irwin truce, Ghaffar Khan triumphantly returned home to his native place to revive his Khudai Khidmatgar movement. Much to his discomfort, the young spirited Badshah Khan was now being revered by his own fellow Pathans as a living Pir or Saint and who they believed could alone lead them to salvation. The distant hills of the North West Frontier were dotted with shrines and tombs of many such holy Pirs and Fakirs, and some of them could be found even on top of inaccessible mountains and cliffs. These sacred places more often than not were the real power centres of the tribesmen who live there. For the Pathan tribesmen in that part of the world, no tribe is without at least one such tomb or shrine. Praying at these tombs and Mazhars of these holy men, the Pathan takes his most solemn oath and vows. To his utter dislike the Pathans even named him the Frontier Gandhi. There was no doubt that the young Abdul Ghaffar Khan was very much unlike a Pathan for he had given up eating meat, spun his own clothes and as a supreme sacrifice had even given up his own land for the well being of his Pathan brothers. But he thoroughly loathed being referred to as the Frontier Gandhi, and one day he said so in as many words too. "Dear Pathans. Please do not compare me to Gandhi because he and only he and he alone is the true spritual leader of the masses and the giver of hope for all of us."

On his return back to the Frontier and much to the chagrin and annoyance of the British authorities, Badshah Khan once again started touring the land of his ancestors and visited as many villages as he could. He not only urged the wily Pathans to stand up to the imperialistic policy of the British Raj, but also asked the women to come out off the purdah and join their men folk in becoming true and loyal Khudai Khidmatgars and thus work for a prosperous, better and peaceful Frontier. After the end of the day having walked for miles and miles visiting the far-flung villages, he would seek shelter in some small village mosque that more often than not was just a tiny room of undressed rock and mortar. The tall Khan would soon be seen sweeping and cleaning the sacred place and before the sun went down he would kneel and say his final day's prayers to Allah. Seeing the activities of Badshah Khan, the Chief Commissioner of the North West Frontier Province, Mr Ralph Griffith the man who virtually ruled over these tribesmen soon became a worried man. Addressing his senior staff and the head of the police and the intelligence department he said.

"'Gentleman, the young Khan inspired by Gandhi and his teachings of non violence and satyagraha could become more and more dangerous if we do not keep a thorough check of his movements and activities and nip it in the bud. I would therefore like to have a full daily secret report from the head of the Intelligence Bureau on the man's activities and movements, including the places that he frequently visits and what he does there. So that when the time comes and without any excuses or trial we will have not only him but also his entire family if required behind bars."

During the third week of December, Major Attiqur Rehman took a few days casual leave and arrived at his late father's palatial mansion in Peshawar.

After his parents death it had become a deserted house and he therefore decided to give it on rent to a well to do and known Punjabi Hindu family who were in the business of dry fruits.One day while visiting the "Kissa Kahani Bazaar he was surprised to find Abdul Ghaffar Khan and his elder brother Dr Khan Sahib there. The younger Khan was holding an open jirga with other elderly Maliks and was requesting them to use their influence on their respective tribes to follow the path of non-violence while opposing the British Raj.

"Salaam Waileikum Badshah Khan," said Attiqur Rehman while cautioning him to be careful since there may be some plainclothesmen around watching and noting everything that was being discussed and planned for the future.

"But I am only holding a peaceful durbar and if the British want to listen in then they are most welcome to do so," said Badshah Khan with a big smile on his bearded face.

"That's seems alright, but all the same both of you still need to be careful because the British are only waiting for such like opportunities. And by the way I believe that the Chief Commissioner has also invited both you and Dr Khan Sahib for the grand party during Christmas week and I shall see you there," said Attiqur Rehman.

"'Yes the invitation is for the 22nd of December, but I have declined. I have of course thanked the host for the courtesy extended, but I also made it clear to the Chief Commissioner that I cannot socialize with him, while he keeps suppressing the Khudai Khidmatgars who are only peaceful servants of God looking for their own honour, respect and freedom in their very own motherland," said Abdul Ghaffar Khan.

"Well you do have a point there," said Attiqur Rehman as he wished both of them the very best of luck.

On the 24th of December, Christmas Eve, Mr Ralph Griffith the Chief Commissioner of the North West Frontier Province had Abdul Ghaffar Khan and his three young sons, Ghani, Wali and Ali together with his elder brother Dr Khan Sahib arrested. According to the Chief Commissioner, he was firmly implementing the orders of the new Viceroy Wellingdon who had given explicit instructions that by Christmas day the Red shirt movement must be crushed once and for all. By now some 80,000 Pathans had willingly and voluntarily joined Badshah Khan's Khudai Khidmatgar movement, and to the British administration a non violent Pathan had now become even more dangerous than a gun totting and trigger happy one.

And while the Frontier Gandhi kept motivating the Pathans to agitate peacefully against the British Raj, Mahatma Gandhi soon after his return from the indecisive Second Round Table conference in England, he together with the strong backing of the Congress Working Committee now called for the start of another disobedience movement. This was primarily in protest against the British decision to give separate electorates even to the Hindu minorities in the country.

However, the new year of 1932 therefore did not augur well for the Congress since the Viceroy Lord Wellingdon had decided to come down with a heavy hand. He was bent on crushing the Congress and for any revival of Gandhi's movement of non-cooperation and civil disobedience. Before the Congress could get organised to start the movement, the Government launched its pre-emptive action. The Viceroy promulgated new ordinances that were more draconian in character and gave the authorities unlimited powers to arrest without warrant anybody and everybody and throw into prison anyone they felt like. The Viceroy had therefore virtually brought in a total civil martial law in the country.

On the 4th of January 1932, they not only arrested Mr Gandhi but they also declared the Congress illegal and came down very heavily on its leaders. They took away all civil liberties and seized people and property at will. And during that month of January alone more than a lac of peaceful sathyagrahis were arrested and jailed.

While the police were busy rounding up the Congress leaders in India and the Khudai Khidmatgars in the Frontier, in the State of Kashmir, Maharaja Hari Singh was making elaborate arrangements to celebrate the "Annaprashan" of his one and only son Karan Singh. On the 8th of February, 1932 to the chants of Vedic hymns and mantras by the holy Brahmin priests in India's age-old language of Sanskrit that only a handful in the crowd understood, the infant Karan Singh was fed with a few spoonfuls of the fragrant basmati rice that was mixed with thick sweetened milk. Elsewhere, under the massive colourful awnings on the well-manicured lawns of the Maharaja's palace, the other invitees helped themselves to a variety of Dogri dishes that had been specially prepared for the occasion. Enjoying the hearty meal were Colonel ESD Colvin, the new Prime Minister of Kashmir together with his team of three new British ICS officer who had been specially selected and inducted by the Viceroy to look after the portfolios of Home, Revenue and Police in the State. Colonel Colvin from the Indian Political Service had replaced the Kashmiri Brahmin Hari Krishan Kaul as the new Prime Minister of the State and slowly, steadily and diplomatically the British therefore had started getting the young Maharaja under their own control.

Relishing the sumprtous meal that day with Colonel Reginald Edwards was the young 18 year old Ismail Sikander Khan with his ex Biscoe school mate Daler Singh Bajwa. Ismail Sikandar Khan had completed his senior Cambridge from the PWRIMC and was waiting to appear for the first entrance test to the yet to be commissioned Indian Military Academy at Dehra Dun. Daler Singh Bajwa from Muzzafarabad had also recently passed out successfully from the Kashmir Maharaja's own cadet school at Nagbani near Jammu and was expecting to be nominated as a State Force cadet to the IMA and for which a few vacancies had been given to the Kashmir State Forces.

""Well as far as the written examination is concerned, I have no doubts that both of you will definitely get through. But that is not all. Thereafter there will be an interview which both of you will have to face confidently and in that you have not only to do well, but qualify handsomely too, so that your names figure somewhere on top of the final merit list," said Reggie as he helped himself to some more of the delicious soya bean dal that was locally known as rajma and was a delicacy of the Dogras.

"Well Sir in that case may we request you to coach us on how to give the interview," said Daler Singh Bajwa as he too helped himself to some more of that special dal.

"Sure and with pleasure and it will also give me some time to keep myself purposefully occupied too," replied Reggie as he introduced the two young aspirants to Colonel Colvin.

And while the 'Annaprashan' celebrations of the royal Prince Karan Singh were being celebrated in Kashmir, there was bad news for the Emperor of India.On the evening of 18th February, 1932 the King and Emperor of India who loved children and who doted on his two beautiful and only grandchildren wrote in his diary." Lilibet and Marg came for lunch and my little cairn 'Bob' was fairly to them.' Then just as he was about to finish writing his diary for the day, a confidential paper on India from the Secretary of State arrived and the King's face fell as he read the contents.

"My God now even the young girls of Bengal have become dare devils," he said to himself while underlining in red ink the ages of the two girl revolutionaries. He was referring to the Suniti Chowdhary and Shanti Das, the two young girls who were still in their early teens and who as students of Class viii from a Girls' High School at Comilla had walked into the office of the District Magistrate, Mr Stevens and had shot him dead.

Then on the 6th of February, Bina Dass a young collegian from the Diocesan Girls College in Calcutta during the annual convocation ceremony while going up the aisle to get her degree whipped out a pistol from her bag and shot at the Governor of Bengal, Sir Stanley Jackson. The Governor however was lucky to escape. Providence had saved him. He was sitting on the dais and the bullet had ricocheted off the thick notebook that the Governor was carrying in his top breastcoat pocket and all he lost was a few more hairs from his balding head. Bina Dass a bright student was also immediately arrested, but the convocation ceremony carried on. The revolutionaries admiring Bina Das's courage christened her as Bengal's "Agni Kanya", the daughter of the Hindu Holy Goddess of Fire.

"My God what guts," said the King as he read the report and asked for another small scotch on the rocks.

With the re-emergence of young motivated and educated Bengali boys and girls with revolutionary ideals drifting into the world of terrorism and violence, the British Government in Bengal now felt that something had to be done on priority to divert the minds of the youth of Bengal from such volatile acts. There was no doubt that they had been encouraged and stimulated by the daring actions of Masterda's teenage dare devils in Chittagong and the time had come now for the British to try a different approach in order get these so called misguided youth of Bengal back into the schools and colleges. Using Gandhi's philosophy that violence would get them nowhere except to the jails, gallows and to the Andamans, teams of senior British Army Officers were deputed to visit important higher educational institutions in all the big provincial towns of Bengal to lecture the students on the futility of their taking up arms against the mighty arsenal of the British Empire and their Indian Army.

Debu Ghosh who happened to be in Dhaka at that time attended one such lecture as an observer. He only wanted to see what would be the reaction of the young listeners. Addressing the young boys of the Dhaka University, the tall and handsome Major John Hunt who loved the mountains and whose team one day would conquer the mighty Everest, exhorted the students to shun violence and to get back to their books.

"Gentlemen, violence and terrorism will not lead you anywhere; except that it will get you a free ticket on the boat to the Andamans concluded," the next speaker but none of the counsellors could cut much ice with their listeners that morning. A week or two later Debu Ghosh with Naren Sen attended another such counselling talk in Calcutta that was given by another British officer who very cleverly, delicately and diplomatically approached the subject. Addressing the boys he said.

"Gentleman, I have no doubts about your capabilities and I agree that all of you present here today have tremendous love for your motherland and you want to be free. But taking the path of violence like your own leader Mr Gandhi says is not the answer. There is no doubt that some day you will be totally free to run your own country and that is why His Majesty's Government has already conducted two round table conferences with your own leaders. But to run this vast and beautiful country with its teeming population of different castes, creeds and religion is not going to be a cake walk and it will not be an easy task either. For this very purpose you first need to be well educated and well trained in all disciplines that go to make good governance. The Indian Civil Service, the Indian Medical Service, the Indian Police Service and the Kings Commission in the Indian Army in the officer cadre and that to in the gazetted rank is already open to you all and soon you will have your own Indian Sandhurst to train your own army officers too. Besides that, you will also require eminent lawyers, judges, doctors, engineers and legislators, and for all this good education is a must. Today a large number of you are willing to sacrifice your very lives for the freedom of your country, but you do not realise that if the country loses you it will be so much the poorer. Because when the time eventually comes for you all to guide the nation, you will not be there, and it will be the uneducated and the half baked lot who will take advantage of your absence and it will be they who will grab the reins of power that some of you are now craving and aspiring for. The need of the moment gentlemen therefore is to spread knowledge, education and not violence and now if there are any questions or doubts or questions I will try and answer them," concluded the officer as he surveyed the reactions of the audience in the hall. When the British Officer concluded his talk with those words of wisdom, for a minute or so there was total silence and then a young student got up and asked.

"Sir all that you just stated is all very fine, but we can never ever have a level playing field when it comes to promotions and seniority. Because when it comes to giving us equal opportunities, it will always be you the white Englishmen who will take the cake and eat it too without sharing even a morsel with us."'

"That I must admit indeed is an intelligent and good question," said the British Army officer as he smiled at the lad and asked him to sit down.

"'All right now also let me tell you that we as the white Englishmen are not only ruling India, but we are practically ruling half the world that is known as the British Empire today. Needless to say that India is our jewel in the crown and we are indeed very proud and lucky to be a part of this great country. But the answer to all this conquest and governance is higher education and that to in every possible field and discipline and which we have given and will continue to give to those who desire it. Whether it be in medicine, engineering, law, art, science and even in the art of warfare and leadership, they are required. On the same analogy may I ask as to why in India is the Brahmin class considered a privileged lot. It is not simply because he has a sacred thread around his chest, but because he is considered to be a learned man who is well versed with the Vedas, the Gita, the Ramayana, the Mahabharata, the Puranas and the Upanishads. These books written by great sages are the very essence of India's great civilization and culture and which has produced great leaders and saints like Gautama Buddha, Guru Nanak, Rama, Krishna, Tulsidas and others. The learned Brahmin is therefore the one who guides the illiterates and the poor Hindus in all their actions and deeds in this country. But all the same I am sorry to say that some of these so-called Brahmins also exploit the ignorance of the masses by demanding additional favours and material benefits. They may not be directly demanding the same, but one hint from them could be considered enough for the illiterates to fall on to his feet. I will not hesitate to say that all Englishmen are also not saints. We too are humans and not every one is a good, clean and honest a man as one may perceive him to be.We also at times commit mistakes because to err is human and we at times are also carried away by temptations and greed. Therefore the need of the hour is not intimidation and violence, but reconciliation and understanding of one another's difficulties and have them solved in a peaceful manner and as advocated by the Mahatma himself. Therefore on this candid submission gentleman let me wish you all greater and better success in your academic career and for a bright and a prosperous future for you and for India."

Once again there was complete silence for a while and then the clapping started, there was no doubt that the British Officer had made his point very convincingly, but the question now was whether the young educated Bengalees would heed his advice.

In February 1932, when the trial of the 32 young revolutionaries from Surjya Sen's Indian Republican Army in the first Chittagong armoury raid case was about to be concluded, Debu Ghosh dashed off to offer his legal services free and to find the whereabouts of his younger brother Hitu. However, by the time he arrived at Chittagong it was already a bit too late and for his free services there were no takers.

On the 1st of March the judgement was delivered and12 of them still in their youth and who were considered as the the leaders were sentenced to transportation for life to the Andamans. Another three were given 3 years of rigorous imprisonment, while the remaining 17 were honourably acquitted. Though the British were now using the carrot and stick policy, the harsh sentences of 'Kala Pani' to the 12 young revolutionaries only fanned the desire of other diehards to spill more British blood.

On the evening of 30th April, while Mr Robert Douglas, the District Magistrate of Midnapur was presiding over a District board meeting, two young boys, Prabhangshu Shekar Pal and Pradyut Bhattacharjee barged into the meeting room and shot the DM dead.Meanwhile in Delhi, Field Marshall Chetwode on taking over as the new Commander-in-Chief of the Indian Army from Field Marshall Birdwood had now set the ball rolling once again for an Indian Sandhurst. Though the Skeen Committee under the chairmanship of Lt General Andrew Skeen the Chief of General Staff in 1925 with Motilal Nehru and Tej Bahadur Sapru and a few other eminent Indians as members had started working for an Indian Sandhurst, but it only remained on paper.

In July 1931, Field Marshall Philip Chetwode as Chairman of the newly revived Indian Sandhurst Committee submitted its final report to the Government. Not only would India have its own Sandhurst, but a few selected Indian Regiments with Indian troops would also be selected for complete Indianization. In 1932, from among the few selected regiments, the 2nd Punjab Regiment and the 59th Royal Scinde "Unnat" which had now become the 6th Royal Battalion Scinde Frontier Force Regiment were given this unique honour.

It was way back in 1754, that the first regular British Army Unit, the 39th Fuzilers arrived in India. They had been loaned on payment by the crown to the East India Company. It was however only after 1st November 1858, when Queen Victoria formally assumed direct government control over India that the British servicemen serving in India became part of the British Imperial Army. But for the Indians they could only join as sepoys and then work their way up the steep promotional ladder. Those who were good and lucky finally ended up as unit Subedar Majors and retired as honorary lieutenants or honorary captains. But there was no way by which they could get a regular commission in the officer cadre. But the valour and courage shown by the brave Indian soldiers in the fields of Flanders and in the Middle East during the First World War had now changed all that. To start with, the British first opened The Daly College at Indore for the training of selected young educated Indians for direct commission into the British Indian Army. The college was the brainchild of Lieutenant General Henry Daly who commanded both the Central India Horse and the Hodson's Horse and who later in 1870 was the Governor General's Agent in Central India. The instititution was initially started by him to provide British type of education to the sons of ruling chiefs of Central India and was called the Indore Residency College. Then his son Colonel Hugh Daly from the Indian Political Service who was also the British Agent in the court of the Holkar royal family at Indore in 1905 turned it into a full scale Chief's College. On 17th July 1920, a handful of young Indian cadets in the rank of Second Lieutenants passed out from this very college and were commissioned into the Infantry and Cavalry Regiments. And the first amongst them were 2/Lt KM Carriappa and 2/Lt Iskandar Mirza. Thereafter ten competitive vacancies per year were allotted to the Indians aspiring to join The Sandhurst Military Academy in England.

On 1st April 1932, Brigadier L P Collins, a much decorated tall and handsome British officer from the Gurkha Rifles with his team of dedicated skeleton staff arrived at Dehra Dun railway station to set up the Indian Sandhurst. Though it was April Fools day that day, nonetheless this was not a matter of joke as he meticulously went around the proposed selected site.

The small and beautiful town of Dehra Dun located under the shadows of the mighty Himalayas was a paradise for pensioners. The site selected was on the outskirts of the town and where till recently existed the old Railway Staff College. The old railway staff college with its inspiring central building and with one building block for its trainees and a number of decent staff quarters located not far from the Tons River was indeed a right and a good choice. Standing majestically in front of the impressive cream coloured central building, the imposing first Commandant of the Indian Military Academy said.

'Well Major Savory. What do you feel? Don't you think that this is the ideal location for the academy?'

'Most certainly Sir, and it also has the required infrastructure to begin with,'replied Major RA Savory, the Military Cross winner from the Sikh Regiment and the Alpha Company Commander designate.

'Well then let me get a second opinion and ask you Captain McLaren about the selection of the site and what do you have to say,' added the Brigadier with a smile.

'I think with all types of terrain in the neighbourhood it will be ideal Sir,' said Captain JFS McLaren the first Adjutant designate of the IMA.

And since we have ample area in front of the main building Sir, we could therefore lay the big drill square there,' said Regimental Sergeant Major F Fullbrook, the first RSM of the Academy as he looked towards Company Havildar Major Tara Singh for his views.

'Ek dum thik kaha Sahib. Abhi aap kuch fiqar matt karo. Hum sub gentlemen cadeton ko ekdam fit kar ke rakhdenge,' said the CHM designate of Alpha Company, while saluting the Commandant. (This is absolutely ideal and do not worry Sir I will make sure that the Gentlemen Cadets are drilled nice and proper)

'Shabash and that is the sprit CHM,' said the Commandant as they all walked to inspect the billeting quarters for the cadets.

On 14th July 1932, on Bastille Day, a day that symbolizes liberty, equality and fraternity, some 800 young men, and all of them Indians sat for the first federal public service examination for entrance to the Indian Sandhurst at Dehra Dun. The government had declared the total number off vacancies as 40 only and out of these just 15 vacancies were for the open entry candidates. Another 15 vacancies were reserved for candidates from the ranks of the Indian army and 10 were given to candidates selected from the various State Forces. The eligibility criteria laid down that all candidates must be British subjects of Indian origin and be within the laid down age limit of 18 to 20 years for the open entry candidates and not above 25 years for the serving soldier of the Indian Army. While there was no special education qualifications laid down for the open candidates appearing for the written test, except that they should be atleast matriculates, but they had to be first screened for their aptitude and suitability and also be recommended by their respective District Collectors and Political Officers. In the case of the service candidate, besides having passed their Army First Class Certificate of Education that was equivalent to matriculation, they had also to be recommended by their respective Commanding Officers and his superiors and all the way up the chain of command including the C-in-C himself. Those qualifying in the written test and those recommended from the Services would then have to appear before the four high-powered members of the Federal Service Commission interview board. The board consisted of two high-ranking British army officers with a Major General as the presiding officer and two non-official eminent Indians, one to be nominated by the Viceroy and the other by the C-in-C himself.

'Well best of luck to both of you,' said Colonel Reginald Edwards to Ismail Sikandar Khan and to Gul Rehman as they were about to enter the examination hall.

'Yes do well and answer all questions intelligently and carefully,' added Major Attiqur Rehman as he waved out to the two boys and did thumbs up to them for good luck.

A minute later, when a very fair young thin lad who was immaculately dressed in a well-creased shirt, trousers and a necktie and with his black leather shoes shining like a mirror jauntily and with big strides and with a perpetual smile on his handsome face walked into the examination hall and took his seat, Attiqur was highly impressed.

'But Sir I always thought and was also told that these vacancies for the Indian Sandhurst were only for the Indians, but what is the English lad who just took his seat doing here,' asked Major Attiqur.

'Maybe he is a fair Indian like you,' said Reggie.

'That is absolutely right Sir and he is a young Parsi lad who is a product of Sherwood College, Nainital and is presently a student of Hindu Sabha College, Amritsar and where his father is a well-known doctor,' said the examination supervisor as he ticked off the boy's name in the attendance roster.

'Not being fully convinced Attiqur said.'Oh is that so and what is his good name?'

His good name Sir is Sam Hormusji Framji Jamshedji Manekshaw,' said the supervisor as he loudly read out the long name from the attendance roster.

'Good lord is that a name or a damn history of the family said,' Major Atiqur Rehman in good humour.

'Well whatever his name maybe, I personally think that a lad with such a long and impressive name and who so very smartly walked into the examination hall full of confidence, will not only make it to the academy, but he will probably someday make it big in his career and maybe create history too,' said Reggie as he smiled at the examination supervisor and lit his Dunhill pipe.

About a month or so later, when the results of the written examination were declared, both Gul Rehman and Ismail Sikandar Khan were delighted. Their names had figured high on the list of the 360 who had successfully crossed the first hurdle.

'Well then with only 15 seats to compete for and with the odds having been reduced from a staggering 50 to 1 to 24 to1, I feel both of you have a good chance of making it and the two of you must therefore do exceptionally well at the interview stage also. Remember never to bluff and if you do not know the answer to a question say so frankly, but just be confident and answer all questions honestly and truthfully. Let me also warn you that the Army does not like bluffers,' said Reggie as he once again chalked out a programme to coach them on current affairs and on the finer points of appearing before an interview board.

That evening having scanned the newspapers that had arrived from London, Gul Rehman took out all the old copies of the Illustrated London News magazine and sat down on the floor with a pair of scissors to cut the glossy pictures of his favourite cricketers and for pasting them into his scrap book.

'Could you also please cut the photographs of our talented hockey players if there are any at all in the magazine,' requested Ismail as he read the editorial for the day in the Times of India that was published from Bombay.

Though both Gul Rehman and Ismail Khan were talented sportsmen and played practically each and every outdoor game, but Gul Rehman still loved his cricket, while Ismail Khan favoured the fast game of Indian hockey. It was around this time that Don Bradman, the twenty four year old Australian who was born into a modest carpenter's family was just about to emerge as a wonder batsman on the international cricketing scene.With England's cricket captain Douglas Jardine planning his bodyline bowling attack with Harold Larwood and Bill Voce on the Australians in order to win the prestigious Ashes, Gul Rehman's was looking forward to the forthcoming tour of the English cricketers to Australia. However, his favourite cricketer whom he admired the most was neither an Australian nor an Englisman. He was Kumar Duleepsingji an Indian from the royal family of Nawanagar in India and to his friends in England he was known as the popular Mr Smith. Duleepsingji was also the nephew of the legendary Ranji who had played test cricket for England. In 1932, Duleepsingji had become the Captain of the Sussex county team and Sussex was on the verge of winning the County Championship that year, but on the day for the crucial match, Duleepsingji fell very ill. When his uncle Ranji told him that he must play not only because he was the captain and the star player for his county, but also that he was from the royal blood of Nawanagar, the young obedient nephew promptly took the field. Though indisposed, he scored 90 solid runs and later collapsed. He was rushed to a hospital and then taken to a sanatorium in Switzerland for treatment. Soon the young dashing Duleepsinghji lost a lung and at twenty-seven was never fit to play cricket again. There were tears in Gul Rehman's eyes as he read the news and kissed the photograph of Duleepsinghji, the man who had mastered the late cut, a delicate stroke that could pierce any number of slip fielders that the rival captain could set for him. But for Ismail Khan it was always Dhyan Chand from the small town of Jhansi and a simple soldier of the Indian Army who was his evergreen hero.

'Just Imagine, we licked the Americans 24-1 at the Olympics that is being held at Los Angeles and that too in front of their home crowd and most of those goals came from the magic stick of the hockey wizard from India,' said an excited Ismail Sikandar Khan as he too kissed Dhyan Chand's photograph and pasted it in his scrap book.While the two friends Gul Rehman and Ismail Sikandar Khan discussed the finer points of cricket and hockey, in Calcutta on that Saturday August afternoon a visibly agitated Debu Ghosh walked into the College Street Coffee House with a copy of the Calcutta Statesman.

'Have you all read this shit,' said an angry Debu Ghosh as he flung the paper on the face of his two friends Naren Sen and Dr Ghulam Hussein.

'The bloody British having already given the other minorities in India like the Muslims, Sikhs and Christians their separate electorates they now want to divide and rule the Hindus too and therefore they have very wisely decided to give separate electorates to the Hindu minority classes also. As it is our so called minority Hindu communities of low castes and tribes are amongst the worst exploited by us and this will only further alienate them from the so called high class Hindus who are no doubt are in absolute majority in the whole of the subcontinent. And what is still worse is that the Angrez has the bloody cheek to call it the Communal Award, added Debu Ghosh as he lit a cigarette and ordered for his cup of coffee.

'But for heavens sake please also tell me in a lay man's language what does this so called communal award imply and how will it affect us,' said Dr Ghulam Hussein as he called out to the waiter to hurry up with the sandwiches.

'Well it simply means that each and every minority community in India, be they Hindus, Muslims, Sikhs, Christians and what else have you, they will all now be given the opportunity and the privilege to get elected to the various legislative assemblies on the basis of a separate electorate,' said Debu Ghosh somewhat angrily.

'But why are you getting so upset about it. 'You are not standing for any such elections are you,' said Naren Sen who had no particular interest at all in such matters, but always kept himself abreast of what was happening.

'And as for you Ghulambhai you are a doctor and will always remain one, and you will never be able to understand the nuances and the finer points of British governance and politics in India. By announcing such an award, the British have not only pitched one Indian against the other, but they have now with the communal card have also pitched one Hindu against the other also. Do not forget that because of the Hindus being in majority this land is also called Hindustan. In other words I feel that they are now trying to create a rift among the Hindus too by playing the high caste against the low caste,' said Debu Ghosh as he lit another cigarette to go with the special coffee that had been ordered for him.

'But tell me why you are being so worked up over this issue. I am sure Gandhiji with his other Congress leaders together with their vision for a secular India of tomorrow they to must be seized with the problem, and I am sure they will never accept this biased award,' said Naren Sen as they all pooled in four annas each to make the final payment for the coffee and snacks that they had ordered.

While the 360 odd successful candidates of the IMA written examination in the months of August and September 1932 were busy appearing for their interviews for admission to the Indian Sandhurst, far away in Eastern India at Chittagong, Masterda Surjya Sen's squad of youthful revolutionaries led by a young educated lady school teacher were meticulously planning an attack on the European Club at Pahartally.The Pahartally Club was an exclusive club for the British elite. It was a club only for the Whiteman that was located a few miles outside the Chittagong town and where practically every evening and specially on weekends after a hard day's work, the members with their families gathered to let their hair down over a few rounds of skotch and soda, a few mugs of chilled beer or a couple of large gins with tonic water. On such club evenings they could all be seen lounging on the long grandfather easy chairs, enjoying their drinks, playing cards and billiards and generally talking about their good old days in Blighty.Masterda, Surjya Sen was still in hiding but he was not the man to give up so very easily. He had decided to take revenge for those who had been sent to the Andamans. With his young supporters who worked in the Pahartally club as kitchen helpers, tennis ball boys and waiters, he had by now successfully infiltrated the premises. These boys were now his eyes and ears as they eavesdropped on the shop talk that took place within the four walls of the club. While listening in to their conversatuion they were sometimes able to send an early warning to Masterda and his men about the next likely target for a police and military raid and about their movements in the general area off Chittagong and in the nearby villages of that busy port town.

`On 16th September 1932, summoned by Masterda, Preetilata Waddedar and Kalpana Datta reported to him at Kaltali village. The village was not far from Chittagong and both the young ladies had to be very careful while getting to that place because they could not take the risk of being shadowed. From his hiding place near Kaltali, Masterda disclosed the final plan.

'Do remember this is a very bold plan and it won't be an easy task. Therefore before deciding on the final date and time of the attack on the Pahartally Club, you must carryout a thorough reconnaissance of the entire area. I do not want it to be another fiasco like the one we had, when we attacked the European Club at Chittagong on the night of the 13th of April, which happened to be Good Friday, and there was not a soul in the Club. Your task with your motivated young group of revolutionaries will therefore be to kill as many of those white bastards, and then once and for all destroy the bloody place so that they will never be able to use it again. Have I made myself clear?'

'It will be done as per your wishes Masterda,' said Preetilata as she took the blessings from her revered Commander-in-Chief.

"Best of luck then and Vande Mataram,' replied Masterda as he too made his way back to his hideout.

The very next day while Kalpana Datta was on her way back to Chittagong, she was arrested by the police on suspicion. And it was simply because she was dressed in a male's attire. However, a few days later she was released for want of any concrete evidence regarding her links with Masterda's Indian Revolutionary Army.

While Preetilata was busy finalizing her plans to attack the Pahartally Club in Chittagong, the three bosom friends kept meeting regularly at the coffee house in Calcutta. Regarding Gandhi's attitude towards the Communal Award announced by the British, Naren Sen was dead right. Opposing it tooth and nail, Gandhiji on 20th September went for a fast unto death. He maintained that the representatives of the so called Hindu depressed classes were first and foremost Hindus and they should be elected by the general electorate under the laws of universal common franchise. He knew that the separate electorates for these depressed Hindu classes whom he now called Harijans or the sons of God would only separate them further from the other Hindus and consequently the Hindus themselves will be divided. By accepting the Communal Award the Congress would only be playing into the hands of the British. Having studied the rigid Hindu caste system and by offering the depressed Hindu classes an electorate of their own, the British had hit the nail on the head, Supporting the move for a separate electorate was non other than the highly US educated Dr BR Ambedkar who was now the leader of the depressed Hindu classes. Gandhi or no Gandhi he was determined to have it his way. With Gandhiji's resolve to fast unto death on this very issue, the Congress leaders were now in a dilemma, and in order to reach at some compromise and save Gandhiji's life, the Congress despatched a high level delegation to meet Dr Ambedkar in Poona.

On the evening of 24th September, 1932 while Gandhiji was on the 4th day of his fast unto death, Preetilata Waddedar with his young band of revolutionaries decided to strike. As the sun went down over the Bay of Bengal, the young school teacher dressed in a soldier's uniform with her squad of seven highly motivated and armed young men slowly and carefully made their way to the Pahartally European Club. When the party was a few hundred yards short of the Club, they took cover behind the thick undergrowth to check their weapons and ammunition. Once that important drill was over, Preetilata in a hushed tone said.

'Remember we have to shoot and kill the Europeans and then destroy the place and it has to be done as quickly as possible. And once the mission is accomplished all of us must quickly fade away in small groups by taking different routes into the countryside, and nobody will wait for me because I will still have yet another important mission to fulfill tonight. Therefore now let us kiss the ground that has given us birth and say a prayer for the early freedom of our motherland,' added Preetilata as she closed her eyes to invoke the blessings of Ma Durga for the last and final time.Repeating silently the words 'Vande Mataram,' Preetilata and her small group consisting of Pannalal Sen, Shanti Chakravarty, Prafulla Das, Bireshwar Roy, Mahindra Chowdhury, Sushil and Kalikinkar Dey now very cautiously and carefully made their way to the Pahartally Club. A few minutes later the sound of their weapons firing in short bursts echoed across the hills of Chittagong. The members all of them Europeans who were enjoying the evening were simply stunned as the young revolutionaries with their guns blazing entered the lounge and opened indiscriminate fire that left them with 13 dead and a larger number seriously wounded. The young revolutionaries had successfully completed their mission.And while all the other members of the group made good their escape into the countryside, Preetilata Waddedar stood her ground. She walked on to the pathway leading to the gate of the club, took out the vial of poison that she was carrying on her person and gulped it down. She had already decided to end her life and had even taken Masterji's blessings for it. It was not out of fear of being caught that she took her own, life but she wanted to prove a point to the people of India. That point was revealed, when the police found the suicide note written by her on the breast pocket of her uniform. In that she wrote.

'I formally declare that I am a member of the Chittagong Branch of the Indian Republican Army which is inspired by the lofty ideal of uprooting imperialistic British rule in India. It also aims at introducing democratic movement in my Motherland, India after its liberation. I feel myself fortunate for being enrolled as a member of an organization that is crowned with glory. I have taken part in the armed struggle for the freedom of my country and the assault today on the European Club at Pahartally is a part of that struggle for freedom. When the highly revered and respected leader of our party, Masterda Surjya Sen called me to lead the assault party today, I really felt proud to have been given that honour. I thought that after a long waiting period the long cherished ambition of my life was fjnally achieved. I accepted the assigned duty with a full sense of responsibility and I think I am bound to account for my action to my countrymen. Unfortunately there may yet be many among my dear countrymen who would question this. Nursed in the high ideal of Indian womanhood they may ask, how can a woman engage in such a ferocious task of murdering and killing people? I am pained at the distinction being made between a man and woman in the struggle for the freedom of the country. Today if our brothers can enlist in the war of independence, we too the women should be allowed to do the same and why not? With this hope in my heart I am proceeding today for self immolation. Vande Mataram. '

Two days later on the 26th of September, while in prison at the Yerwada jail in Poona, Gandhiji gave up his fast unto death. It was not because of the self-sacrifice made by Preetilata Waddedar far away in Chittagong, but on the compromise that had been reached by Gandhi's emissaries with Dr BR Ambedkar at Poona on that same very evening of the 24th when Preetilata Waddedar took her own life. At first Dr Ambedkar, the revered leader of the backward classes in India just would not budge from the stand taken by him to have separate electorates for his depressed Hindu classes and therefore for Gandhi's negotiators he was a difficult nut to crack. A bitter and angry Ambedkar had argued and said.

"But tell me why should Gandhiji who never objected earlier when the Muslims, Sikhs and the Christians were given their separate electorates object to our demands now when we the depressed Hindu classes who have been for ages been exploited by the very Hindus of the upper class who consider themselves to be superior just because they came out of the womb of a so called high class woman.? And now just to save Gandhiji you expect me to give up looking after the interest of those backward and downtrodden classes who by right are also Hindus! If that were the case I am sorry you all are mistakened.'

When Ambedkar said those words, for a brief moment or so there was complete silence and it was only broken by Palwankar Baloo, a low caste by birth from Dharwar. He was a member of Ambedkar's Dalit delegation and one of India's best spin bowlers of cricket of his time. In fact he with his three brothers, Shivram, Ganpat and Vithal Baloo had all played for the Bombay Hindu Gymkhana in the early 1920's.

'All right we have got the Mahatma's point amd since you are not willing to give us the untouchables our separate electorates then tell us in what manner will we be compensated, or else give us another practical solution to the problem,'said Palwankar.

'Well we could come to some mutual understanding and compromise whereby we could jointly demand from the British a larger number of reserved seats out of the general electorate quota for the Dalits, both in the Provincial Legislatures as well as in the Central Legislature as compared to what they have offered so far,' said Madan Mohan Malaviya.

'All right in that case we could agree,' said Dr Ambedkar though somewhat reluctantly. And two days later on the 26th, when the Congress and Gandhiji decided that it will be fair to reserve atleast 10% of the seats for the Harijans as Gandhiji called them, the Poona Pact was implemented and Gandhi broke his fast and Dr Ambedkar gave up his demand for a separate electorate for his minority Hindu depressed classes.

Meanwhile the daring attack on the Pahartally European Club and the death of young Preetilata Waddedar made headlines in almost all the leading vernacular newspapers of India. Overnight the young lady to some of the young men who were on their way to Dehra Dun to join the Indian Military Academy, Preetilata Waddedar had suddenly become their own Joan of Arc.

'Just imagine of all people a young lady and that too a school teacher in a soldier's uniform wielding a gun and leading an attack on the Europeans. I just cannot believe it. She must have been a very highly motivated revolutionary,' said Ismail Sikandar Khan to his friend Gul Rehman as the train on which they were travelling steamed into the main platform of the Dehra Dun railway station.

By 30th September 1932, all those who were lucky to have been selected for the first course at the IMA reported for their training at the Indian Sandhurst at Dehradun. They were a total of only 40 of them and they were therefore rightly called the 'Pioneers.' On their arrival at the Academy, they were greeted by the tall and towering Regimental Sergeant Major.

'Now all of you Gentlemen Cadets bloody well and in double time fall in quickly,' roared RSM Fullbrook as he blew the whistle. When all 40 of them scampered and stood to attention in front of him, Fullbrook in his stentorian voice proudly addressed them for the first time.

'Gentlemen consider yourselves to be very lucky because from today you will be writing history. A history of an institution called the Indian Military Academy. Your job is to learn and ours is to teach. Therefore without much ado be prepared to lead a life that will make you both an officer and a gentleman. Let me also drum it into you all once again that this is not a bloody place for sissy's and cry babies. It is a place for only the fucking brave and courageous men. This is the place for the men of future India and where discipline is the key word and while you are here you will be drilled into it day in and day out both physically as well as mentally. And do remember that the word of command by your teachers and superiors here at the IMA both on the drill square and off it is sacred and must be obeyed implicitly at all times. Now I hope that is clear to all of you once and for all.'

But when to that last sentence by the RSM there was hardly any response from the cadtes, Fullbrook roared again. After repeating that last sentence once again when all the 40 freshers in unison shouted 'Yes Sir' it brought a slight grin on the face of the RSM who had never ever been seen before to smile while on duty.Then opening the file that was in his hand, RSM Fullbrook loudly read out the names of the individuals and allotted them their Company's.

'Mr George Issacs, GC number!, A for Able company ; Mr Umrao Singh; GC number 14, senior GC A coy. Nipender Singh Bhagat, PWRIMC, Naik Mohammed Musa, Hazara Pioneers, Jemadar Smith Dunn 2/20 Burma Rifles, GC number 30, Senior GC B for Bravo Company. Lance Naik Mohan Singh 2/14 Punjab Regiment GC Number etc etc.'

Both Ismail Sikandar Khan and Gul Rehman luckily were allotted to the A Company, but GC Daler Singh Bajwa from the Kashmir State Forces was allotted to the B Company. When the final allotment of the rooms to the cadets were over, and the Company Havildar Majors took charge of their respective gentlemen cadets, the RSM brought the parade to attention and with a smart salute gave the report to Captain JFS McLaren the Academy Adjutant. Captain McLaren always a man of few words simply said.

"Gentleman welcome to the IMA and be ready from tomorrow and for the next two and a half years, that is for the next five terms to slog it out for the single star that you all are aspiring to proudly wear on your not so broad as yet shoulders. Of course and it is needless to say that at the end of each term, you will also be given a nice long break to go home and let your hair down. And tomorrow morning at first parade and after the address by the Commandant, the count down will begin." With those few words when the meticulously turned out Academy Adjutant rode off on his magnificent horse, the 40 Gentlemen Cadets of the first IMA course realised that it was not going to be easy going at all.

The accommodation block earmarked for the Gentlemen Cadets consisted of 40 independent and well-furnished rooms and for every four cadets there was one civilian orderly. Not very far away was the mess for the cadets with eight well laid out tables for dining. A little distance away was the barber's shop where on that very first afternoon there was a long line off the gentleman cadets and some of whom were waiting rather sheepishly to take their close cropped first military crew cut. Supervising all such needs and requirements of the Gentleman Cadets was Rai Bahadur Prem Nath, an efficient and hard working contractor who was responsible to provid all the cooks, waiters, masalchis, orderlies, barbers, dhobis etc etc and they were all his employees.

That evening in the cadet's mess, when all 40 of them assembled to have their first meal together and came to know each other a little better, they found to their surprise that the first three in order of merit were all from Government College Lahore and topping the list was GC Aga Abdul Hamid Khan. At the 6th spot was the Parsee with the long name who soon became Sam to everybody. A few days later on the 5th of October, after a simple ceremony by the Commandant Brigadier LP Collins, the main building of the Academy was christened as the Chetwode Block and the main hall inside the building as the Chetwode Hall. It was indeed a fitting tribute to Field Marshall Chetwode, the resourceful and dynamic Commander-in-Chief of India. For the parents of those lucky 15 open candidates it did cut a big hole into their pockets as they had to shell out a fairly large sum of Rupees three thousand eight hundred and fifty for the entire two and half years of training that their sons would now have to undergo, and this also included the Rs 20 pocket money per month for their wards. However, for the GC's from the ranks and the Services it was a boon. For not only was the entire training free for them, but they also collected a monthly stipend of Rs 60 per month.

For Ismail Sikandar Khan the cost of his training was borne by his late father's 2nd Punjab Regiment, while the monthly pocket money was to be taken care of by Colonel Reginald Edwards. But there was still only one glaring disparity for those passing out with a King's Commission from the Sandhurst Military College in England and those who would now pass out from the IMA in India with an Indian Commission. Whereas the KCIO, the King's Commissioned Indian Officer on being commissioned got a whopping pay packet of Rs 500 per month, his Indian counterpart as an ICO, the Indian commissioned officer would only be getting just Rs 300. However, the only consolation was that henceforth no more Indians would go to Sandhurst for their training.

'What the bloody hell! It is Monday today and it is nearing 7 o'clock in the morning and there is still no sign of that that bloody orderly of mine. That bugger Bachulal doesn't realise that it is the Adjutant's drill parade today and that bloody fool has yet to show his bloody face,' said an angry Gul Rehman to Ismail as he rushed out totally naked from the bathroom and ran along the long corridor to look for the orderly.Soon thereafter appeared Bacchulal muttering his apologies and giving lame excuses as usual for his late appearance." Maff karma Sahib, mera bacche ko doctor ke pass lejana bahut hi zaroori tha Sahib. Woh bahut bimar hai, isliye thodi si deri ho gayi,' said Bacchulal with a straight face. (I do beg pardon Sir, but my child had to be taken to a doctor as he is very sick and hence the delay). 'Oye Beimann, thoo toh kabhi nahin sudrega.' (You liar you will never reform), said Gul Rehman, while rubbing his shaved chin to check that there were no more stubs left on it. And having ordered Bachulal to get his drill uniform ready he casually remarked.

'Well to me it seems that members of your family conveniently fall sick only on Monday mornings. Last Monday it was your wife, and the Monday before that it was your father, and the Monday before that it was your mother and today it is your child and next Monday I guess it will be your turn to fall sick too. Now for heavens sake stop fibbing and get on with your bloody.job. And by God if I get checked today for a filthy turn out then God only help you. Not only will I do those bloody extra drills but I will make sure that you to do them too in front of Rai Bahadur Prem Nath. Now is that clear,' said an angry Gul Rehman as he waited for Bachulal to hand over the drill boots to him.

Bacchulal who hailed from the nearby village of Doiwalla gave as usual his sly smile and using the spit and polish attacked the drill boots with vengeance. There was no doubt that Bacchulal was a honest and hardworking orderly, but his only weakness on weekends was his love for "tharra" the local and potent country made liquor.

As far as Ismail Sikandar Khan was concerned, his orderly Saligram was the dope of the highest order, but he was an extremely hard working person and always reported for duty on time. He was a tall well built man with a big and curly handle bar moustache. He was from the Jat community and was once a good wrestler, but he had more brains in his legs than on his damn head. Orderly Saligram however steadily became very attached to Ismail Khan after he learnt that Ismail Khan was an orphan and came from a poor family.

The formal opening of the Academy by Field Marshall Phillip Chetwode, C-in-C Indian Army was scheduled for the 10th of December 1932, and a few days before that Saligram said very humbly.

'Sahib aap, aapne jigri dost Gul Rehman ke bare mein ekdum fikar matt karo. Hum salla Bacchulal ko apne kabse mein aisa rakhoonga ke woh salla apna Nani tho kiya aapna Dadi ka naam ko bhi bhul jayega. (Sahib please do not worry about your dear friend Gul Rehman. I will ensure that I will have Bacchulal under my total control and that man I assure you will forget both his own and his grandmother's name too)

'Magar woh kaisse' (But how will you ensure that) asked Ismail looking a bit worried at Saligram's sudden belligerent attitude.

'You just leave that to me Sahib,' said a confident Saligram as he smiled, twirled his big handle bar moustaches and showed his mighty biceps. However, among Rai Bahadur Prem Nath's many civilian helping hands, Ismail Khan's favourite was the short jovial and ever smiling Goan mess waiter Joseph Pinto. Joseph knew that GC Ismail Khan was an orphan, but he also knew that he was the son of a Victoria Cross winner. So invariably on Sundays and on holidays Joseph Pinto would serve him a double and even a triple breakfast at times.

'Just eat to your hearts content Sir, because for breakfast today there will be always as usual four or five absentees and by that I mean those lazy lumps that on Sabbath day would prefer to sleep it out rather than have their breakfast. So you just enjoy yourself at Mr Prem Nath's expense,' said Joseph as he laid another plate of scrambled eggs on toast with a boiled tomato and fried liver and which Ismail simply loved.

At the IMA since Ismail Sikandar Khan, Gul Rehman and Daler Singh Bajwa were always seen in each other's company, therefore to all their course mates they soon became known as the three musketeers.

The 10th of December 1932 was a red letter day for the IMA. That morning the Commander-in-Chief India, Field Marshal Philip Walhouse Chetwode, popularly and reverently referred to as 'the Bart' not just because of his aristocratic lineage as a Baronet, but also for his suave manners and style had consented to do the formal opening of the institution that day. A cavalry man with an impeccable record of service, he had taken part in the Boer war in South Africa, and also led the cavalry charges at Flanders and Gaza during the Great War. He had arrived not only with his wife and daughter Penelope, but he also brought along with him Sir BL Mitter, Captain Sher Mohammed Khan and some others who had helped him to prepare the comprehensive report on the need for an Indian Sandhurst. Sitting among the invitees were also Colonel Reginald Edwards and Major Attiqur Rehman.

On that beautiful winter morning of 10th December and under a clear blue sky and with the Union Jack fluttering proudly in the breeze from atop the Chetwode building at exactly on the dot of 9.45 a.m. the parade was marched in. With Gentleman Cadet Lance Corporal Smith Dunn in command and to the music of the pipe band of the 2nd Battalion of the 8th Gurkha Rifles, the 40 Pioneers smartly marched on parade. At 9.58 after the Commandant Brigadier LP Collins had taken his salute, the fanfare heralded the arrival of the Commander-in-Chief. Marching smartly like a young cadet himself, the C-in-C now stood on the centre of the rectangular dais to take the general salute. Commanding his first ever-ceremonial parade, Lance Corporal Smith Dunn did it in real style. After the impressive parade a very happy C-in-C addressed the gathering and this is what he had to say.

'Ladies and gentlemen I wish I could have welcomed these Gentlemen Cadets of the new IMA on the day they made their first appearance here. For it was indeed a memorable day in the history of the Indian Army. I could not do so because it was pointed out to me that they had not yet received their uniforms and nor were they sufficiently drilled to make an inspection or a parade possible. At the request of the Commandant I therefore postponed my visit until today when he said he would be ready to receive me. I have also taken this opportunity of my first formal inspection of the IMA to invite a large number of distinguished Indian gentlemen and specially those who assisted me as members of the Indian Sandhurst Committee. They are also present here today as my honoured guests.'

As he concluded that last sentence there was thunderous clapping by all those present. After the parade, the C-in-C escorted by the Commandant together with the other main invitees entered the Chetwode Hall to do the formal opening of the momentous military institution. On conclusion of the opening address by the Commandant, the dapper Commander-in-Chief gave his memorable and historic speech. Speaking to them with his usual nasal drawl he said.

"Let me remind you the Gentlemen Cadets the gravity of your tasks and the challenges before you. We have got the men who will soon serve under you in the rank. No better material exists in the world and they have proven it in many stricken fields. But hitherto we have led them and now they are to be led by you. That great task is before you and for those who will follow you here. You have therefore to prove that you are fit to teach these gallant men in peace and gain their confidence and lead them in war. Let me therefore conclude gentlemen by saying that "First of all the safety, honour and the welfare of your country comes first always. Second, the honour and the welfare of the men you command come next. Third, you own ease, comfort and safety comes last, always and every time." And the C-in-C having said those last few inspiring sentences, the Pioneers of the first IMA course vowed that come what may they will all live upto it. And rightly so, because those famous words written in golden letters would soon adorn the walls of the Chetwode Hall.

When they all moved in for a cup of tea with the C-in-C, Reggie having got hold of the three boys said.

'Now let me tell you three musketeers that those final thought provoking sentences that was uttered by the Commander-in-Chief of India will one day immortalize the institution and will bring all glory and joy to your motherland. Therefore, all that Major Attiqur Rehman and I desire is that the three of you should live up to it both in spirit and in deeds. Is that understood?'

'Yes Sir,' said the three of them as they smartly came to attention and saluted.

Later that afternoon, the C-in-C had lunch with the gentlemen cadets in the cadet's mess. Thanks to Mrs Collins the mess looked a lot more homely with the eight flower vases with flowers adorning all the eight tabled which she had presented. The C-in-C later in the afternoon also witnessed a well-fought hockey match between the Academy and the PWRIMC.

'My God you are really a very good hockey player,' said the C-in-C while presenting a small souvenir to Ismail Sikandar Khan. When the C-in-C was told that the cadet was the son of the late Curzon Sikandar Khan a Victoria Cross holder, he promptly saluted the boy to honour his late father.

Chapter-8

Inching Forward Towards a New Dawn

While the training of the gentlemen cadets were in full swing at Dehra Dun, far away in Chittagong and elsewhere in Bengal, the Army, the Police and the Intelligence agencies intensified their search for Masterda and his revolutionaries. Slowly and steadily the net was closing in on them. Since the uniform found on the dead Preetilata Waddedar was identical to what Kalpana Datta was wearing when she first got arrested a week earlier, the police again took her in custody. She was once again arrested, interrogated and detained. However, after a month in custody when she was released on bail, Masterda now sent word to her to abscond and Kalpana Datta immediately went underground. The very next day after she was found missing, her photograph appeared on the most wanted list. Debu Ghosh who had come once again to Chittagong to trace out his brother Hitu was surprised to see the photograph of the fair tall girl with long hair at one of the police stations not far from his father's house. While he was reading the short description of Kalpana Datta that was pasted below her photograph, a middle aged man in a torn dhoti and who had just been brought in for some minor offence of theft also looked at the photograph and said in Bengali.

'Don't you worry she is "Amader Mey" meaning thereby that Kalpana Datta was everyone's daughter and that she is safe and will be looked after. And while the hunt for Masterda was still on, there were Christmas week celebrations at the IMA.On the 25th of December 1932, on Christmas Day the Commandant's bungalow over looking the picturesque Tons River and the snow capped Himalayan peaks in the far distance had a festive look. The colonial structure with its elegant wooden panelling, beautiful manicured lawns and the artistically laid out vast landscaped garden which was the sole creation of Mrs Collins, together with the beautifully decorated and colourful pine Christmas tree was all set and ready for the grand Christmas party that was scheduled for the afternoon. Mrs Collins the energetic and loving hostess who was like a mother to the Gentlemen Cadets went around urging the young men to help themselves to as much of the food as possible.

'Come on you three musketeers, just don't stand there like statues with empty plates and do not please feel shy because it is your party too,' said the gracious lady.

'Yes and do go an attack the damn barbecue and help yourselves to some chilled beer if you so desire,'said the delightful host.

Taking the cue from Gul Rehman, the three musketeers made a beeline for the cadet's beer bar. While the Gentlemen Cadets with their officer staff and their families were enjoying the Christmas party at Dehra Dun, far away in the North West Frontier on the direct orders of Viceroy Wellingdon to crush the Red Shirt movement, a large and strong army column occupied the provincial capital of Peshawar. Though Badshah Khan was undergoing imprisonment in the Hazaribagh jail in Bihar, his Khudai Khidmatgar movement had become so very active that he was now being hailed as a miracle man for having raised an entire Army of non violent Pathans from among the most violent peoples in the world. Elsewhere in the eastern corner of India in the Chittagong District of Bengal, the police and the army further intensified their search to capture Masterda Surjya Sen dead or alive. On the 12th of February 1933, Masterda with Kalpana Datta, Shanti Chakravarty and a few others from his small revolutionary group reached the village of Goirala. Everyday as per Masterda's instructions they would all have an early evening meal and then disappear into their hiding places in the open fields outside the village to sleep, and get back before dawn the next day. On the 16th of February, having had their early supper and as they were in the process of getting out of the village to go to their respective hide outs, they were challenged by an army patrol.

'Stop who goes there,' shouted an armed sepoy loudly. Without batting an eyelid the group of 6 revolutionaries led by Masterda made a dash for safety and cover. Seeing them running away, the army personnel opened fire. But since it was dark there were no immediate casualties. Kalpana Datta held on to Masterda's hand as Brojen Sen the local guide led them through a different route. While running for their lives, Kalpana Datta slipped. She fell into a ditch and got separated from Masterda. Together with a few others who were following behind they all crawled into a pond. Being winter it was miserably cold, but it proved to be a good and safe hiding place. They braved the cold weather and once they were sure that the cordon around the village by the army had been lifted, they crawled out. Shivering in the cold and in their wet clothes they made their way to the hut of their beloved

Khirod Mashima.(Khirod aunty) The elderly lady was their universal aunt and sympathiser. Often all of them used to take shelter there. When Kalpana Datta peeped through the slit in the door, she found the lady packing all their belongings and putting them in a bag probably with the intention of hiding them some place else. Not wishing to disturb the elderly lady, as also for their own safety and that of Khirod Mashima, they quietly slipped away and in the darkness made their way to the village of Baghdandi. It was dawn by the time they arrived at Baghdandi and they were indeed very lucky to have got out of the army and police dragnet safely. On arrival at the village she was surprised to find Hitu Ghosh there.

'What the devil are you doing here,' asked Kalpana Datta with a look of disbelief in her face as Haren Chakravarty another devoted follower of Masterda led them to a secluded and a safer hiding place.

'I was on my way to meet Masterda at Goirala village to convey an important message regarding the deployment of additional troops and police force at Chittagong and in the general area around the city and warn him to be doubly careful, but I lost my way. Anyway but where is Masterda? " asked Hitu Ghosh with a worried look on his innocent face.

'I too do not know. We got separated from him after we were challenged by the army at Goirala and I only hope that he is safe and out of harms way,' said Kalpana Datta, as she enquired from the village folk if anyone had seen their leader.And while the tired group of young revolutionaries were drying their wet clothes, their arms and ammunition, cleaning their weapons and generally relaxing with a hot cup of tea under the pleasant winter sun, the elderly Mr Dey, the owner of the barn where they were camping walked in and without mincing any words in a most humble and apologetic manner said.

'I know that you all are "Swadeshis" and young Freedom Fighters and I too am proud of you. But considering my old age, my family, I would not like to get into trouble with the authorities. However, I can supplement and compensate you all with some dry rations and some food,' added the man with folded hands.

Respecting Mr Dey's humble request Tarakeshwar Dastidar the 23-year-old leader of the group immediately said.

'We fully understand your predicament Sir and we will move out as soon as we finish having our tea and once again thank you for looking after us.'Andfive minutes later, the young band of revolutionaries quickly picked up their meagre belongings and made their way to another village.

For the next couple of months with the police and the Army on their hot trail, they kept hopping from village to village. Finally on the 16th of May, 1933 they reached the seaside village of Gahira and where they found shelter in the hut of Purno Talukdar. Three days later on the 19th of May a well armed body of soldiers having established strong picquets at all the entry and exist points to and from the village, cordoned the hut where they were staying. Soon a fierce firefight followed. Though the Army warned all of them to surrender, the revolutionaries however refused to do so. In the heavy exchange of fire PurnoTalukdar and his family were trapped, and then suddenly a voice rang out.

'Please stop firing, my elder brother and the master of the house, Purno Dada has been killed,' pleaded someone loudly from inside the house while the women and children wailing and crying with fear crouched together for safety. It seems the owner Purno Talukdar had been shot when he obeyed the order to come out. One.trigger happy soldier mistaking him to be also a member of the revolutionary group had shot him dead a soon as he stepped outside his door. His lifeless body was now lying motionless in a pool of blood. However, the exchange of fire continued.When Nishi Talukdar the younger brother of Purno together with an unarmed Hitu Ghosh came out to retrieve the body and carry it to safety, they too were caught in the cross fire and were killed. Then Manoranjan Das another young rebel also became a victim to an army bullet. Realising that the family members of Purno Talukdar were now in terrible danger of being caught in the cross fire, a worried Kalpana Datta said to her leader.

'I think it is no use resisting any further Fotuda because only the innocent are being killed and moreover we are running out of ammunition too.'The young Tarakeshwar Dastidar popularly known as Fotuda initially was not in favour of surrendering, but when he too realised that they would soon be out of ammunition, he agreed though some what reluctantly.A few minutes later as they all came out with their hands and weapons above their heads; it was indeed a pathetic scene. When they all passed by the fallen bodies of Purno Talukdar and their erstwhile young own comrades in arms, they felt somewhat guilty. The blood was oozing out from their bullet ridden bodies and there was nobody willing to help. Seeing the women folk wailing and slapping their heads and faces with the blood of their beloved ones, Kalpana Datta said a small prayer and asked for forgiveness from the family. Strangely when all of them were handcuffed and taken away, there were tears in the eyes of the villagers, both Hindus and Muslims.

It was on the next day, when they reached the Chittagong Police Station that Takakeshwar Dastidar the 4th year college student and Kalpana Datta came to know the details about Masterda's arrest. On the 16th of February, when they got separated, Masterda to his bad luck while trying to escape in the darkness of the night inadvertently collided with a Gurkha soldier. There was a minor scuffle, but the soldier managed to pin Masterda down. And when the powerful spot light was switched on, the Army knew that they had got their prized catch. As a reprisal poor Khirod Mashima's hut was burnt down and she too was arrested. Masterda was put in shackles and the police secretly brought him to Chittagong where he was now undergoing brutal torture.

On learning about Hitu's tragic death, his old father too collapsed and died. Debu Ghosh together with his brother-in-law Naren Sen and their families rushed to Chittagong. With the Second Armoury Raid supplementary trial scheduled for hearing in mid June, the eminent barrister Sarat Chandra Bose, the elder brother of Subhas Chandra magnanimously offered his services free of cost to all the under trial prisoners. With him as the Chief Defence Counsel to all the three main acused, Surjya Sen, Tarakeshwar Dastidar, and Kalpana Datta respectively, both Debu Ghosh and Naren Sen decided to stay back and assist the eminent lawyer if required. However, despite the thunderous and heroic defence by Sarat Chander Bose, the final verdict seemed to be a foregone conclusion.

On 14th of August, 1933 the judgement on the three main accused were passed. Surjya Sen the revered Masterda of the 65 gallant young revolutionaries and the majority of whom were still in their teens together with his trusted lieutenant Tarakeshwar Dastidar were sentenced to death by hanging. Kalpana Datta the brave and spirited young lady was sentenced to transportation for life.However, the arrest, trial and the death sentence of their beloved Masterda did not deter the spirit of some others who undoubtedly worshipped him. On the evening of 2nd September, while Masterda was languishing in jail waiting to be hanged, at Midnapore, the District Magistrate BEJ Burge himself a keen football enthusiast and a fairly good player was on his way to the local football ground to participate in the match between the local Town Club and the famed Mohammedan Sporting Club of Calcutta. As soon as he arrived at the football field and got out of his car, two young boys Anantha Panja and Mrigendra Dutta whipped out their pistols and shot him dead at point blank range. In the bargain they too were also killed, when the District Magistrates armed body guards fired back on them.

During that winter and while young Bengalis in Bengal were gearing up to revive Masterda's revolutionary zeal, at the IMA the three musketeers were looking forward to their winter term break. On the conclusion of the third term in the Academy and during the winter vacations of 1933 at the behest of his bosom friend Gul Rehman, Ismail Sikandar Khan went to spend his holidays with him and his family at Quetta where his father Major Attiqur Rehman had only recently been posted. Derived from the word "Kuwetta" which means a fort in the local language and situated at an altitude of 5000 feet above sea level it was the prime city of Baluchistan and the Aldershot of India. With its strategic location commanding some of the important passes like the Bolan, Kojak and the Lak, it was another gateway to India from Central Asia and Afghanistan. The place came under British rule when Robert Sandeman subdued the Khan of Kalat and made Quetta the capital of his Political Agency. With its pleasant climate practically through out the year it was one of the biggest and beautiful military cantonments of India. Moreover, it was also the place where the prestigious Indian Military Staff College was located. Throughout the year it was full of life for the Officers and their families who were posted there and it was especially so in winter. With weekly Sunday hunts, golf tournaments, picnics, weekend balls, bingo and cricket matches at the ever popular Quetta Club, it was one of the most sought after military stations of India. But it was also known for its notoriety too as scandals pertaining to some officers stealng the affection of another brother officer's wife was not very uncommon. Some of the young bachelor Indian Officers from Sandhurst who were posted on staff or were attending the Staff College, they too were lucky at times in sharing the bed with a Memsahib, while her husband was away. But those were very rare occasions and normally ended with a onenight stand.

Gul Rehman and Ismail Sikandar Khan were both now 19 years old. Though still under training to become officers of the Indian Army, they were young, tall and handsome. At times they felt embarrassed, when some of those sexy grass widows, all English Memsahibs with large breasts gave them the come hither look. Some of the middle aged Memsahibs at times were a sexually frustrated lot. Practically all of them were separated temporarily from their dear husbands because of exigencies of their husband's military service in the Frontier, and with most of their children away studying in Blighty, they did at times feel lonely for company and for some fun too. To get rid of their boredom they regulary patronised the Quetta Club and especially so on Saturdays, when the weekly dances were held. A few of them discreetly also had an affair or two with other single officers, or at times even with a married one in the station. These sporting ladies at times also enjoyed dancing with the two young Gentlemen Cadets from the IMA and which more often than not ended up with cheek to cheek dancing as the music got slower and softer, and the lights dimmer and dimmer. Then as they danced to a slow foxtrot some of the Memsahibs would conveniently whisper a casual invitation like.

'Son, why don't you drop in for high tea tomorrow and maybe I could teach you to dance the Charleston and the tango? Or how about keeping me good company while we look for berries and mushrooms in the forest?.Or maybe you would like to learn how to play Bridge, Mahjong or Canasta etc etc.'.

It did not therefore take long for Ismail Sikandar Khan and Gul Rehman to realize what those invitations were meant for. Soon they too at the weekly dances started taking advantage of their lady partner's willingness to dance a little closer than what was normal. And as they glided to a slow foxtrot and moved into the far corner of the dimly lit dance floor with some cheek to cheek dancing, they felt emboldened too. And with no serious objections comimg from their partners who seemed rather delighted in getting themselves rubbed by their young manhood, all of them would enjoy the fun and the petty smooching that went with it. But as soon as the dance was over both the gentleman Cadets would be seen charging towards the Men's rest room to relieve themselves off. But the two of them never went beyond that, atleast not within the precints of the Club.Then one evening it all happened, and it was during the gala Christmas week. It was one of the many festivity dances and social evenings during the festive season at the Quetta Club, when Mrs Cynthia Lindsay the vivacious and sexy middle aged wife of a senior army British Colonel decided to take the plunge with the young and handsome Ismail Sikandar Khan. Her husband was the commanding officer of an Indian Regiment and was posted at Bannu. While Colonel Lindsay was busy fighting the tribesmen of the North West Frontier Province, a sex starved Mrs Cynthia Lindsay could not take her lonliness and frustrations any longer. Her biological clock was ticking and she was not the least bothered.Having danced a few close dances with the two young Indian Gentlemen Cadets that evening, she now desperately craved for some one like young Ismail Sikandar Khan to share the bed with her. That evening while they danced cheek to cheek under the soft lights to a slow foxtrot, Mrs Lindsay while lovingly holding on tightly to her partner's hand suddenly lowered it to a position from where she could now feel Ismail's throbbing manhood. Giving it a loving squeeze she softly whispered into his ears.

'You want it too, don't you?'And when the five peicer string band suddenly switched on to play a fast quick step, Cynthia said somewhat coyly into Ismail's ears. 'Come let's go out into the garden and enjoy the moon light for a while'. And before Ismail Sikandar Khan could even reply, he found himself being led away across the sprawling lawns towards the small wicket gate to the rear of the Club.

'Come on quick let us get out of here,' said the lovely and excited Cynthia as they both got on to the lonely dark pathway that led to the Officers married quarters below the club. Squeezing Ismail's hand she dragged him behind a huge bush and having placed the big woollen shawl that was around her shoulders, she spread it on the ground and then quickly laid down on her back. And soon thereafter, when she lifted her shapely long legs and took off her panties and with a bewitching smile on her face beckoned Ismail Sikandar Khan to come on top of her, Ismail Sikandar Khan could take it no more. He quickly lowered his trousers, got on top of her and pushed his hand up her skirt to feel Cynthias's beautiful shapely legs and thighs. When their lips met and they started kissing each other like hungry animals, Mrs Lindsay gently and softly caressed Ismail's throbbing manhood. After a minute or so they got into doing a 69 as Cynthia opened her legs wide while Ismail lovingly fondled and kissed all over the place.

'Please kiss me there while I kiss yours;' said the lady as she expertly guided Ismail's lips into her wide-open pleasure hole. Leave alone fucking any woman, Ismail Sikandar Khan had never ever before seen or explored a woman's treasure trove even with his hands. With the auburn coloured pubic hairs tickling his face, he now dived into Cynthis's gaping hole and with his fleeting tongue like that of a wiper snake, he now licked it through and through. As he kept licking and kissing her and fondled her big breasts, Cynthia swooned with ecstasy till she could take it no more.

.'Please darling that will be enough and now just put it put it inside me and do it to me nice and hard,' pleaded the lady as she expertly and slowly glided Ismail's throbbing manhood into her well-lubricated hole. And as the thrusts increased in tempo, she closed her eyes and moaned for more. Raising her legs high with both his hands, Ismail kept doing it to her faster and faster and within minutes of that deep rapid thrusting action it was all over. The smile on Mrs Lindsay's face as she planted a motherly kiss on Ismail's forehead said it all. There was no doubt that Ismail Sikandar Khan on his first ever-maiden sexual experience had performed brilliantly and later that night while thinking about Cynthia, and before going off to sleep, he jerked humself off one more time. When he surfaced late next morning, young Ismail Sikandar Khan felt like a new man. He however did not disclose his manly conquest to anybody, not even to his best friend Gul Rehman.

That day being a Sunday, Ismail Sikandar Khan generally wanted to relax and when he was about to enter the bathroom he found to his surprise Gul Rehman all dressed up in his new English white flannels and cricket boots

'Now where the hell are you off too early morning,' asked Ismail Sikandar Khan as Gul Rehman picked up his Gunn and Moore cricket bat and practised the cover drive?

'Well chum when you disappeared from the club for quite a while last evening, doing what I would not know, I was selected by the District Commissioner to open the innings for his team in today's annual cricket match against the Military Staff College,' said Gul Rehman with a sly smile on his face.

'Good for you then and wish you the best of luck and in the meantime let me also get ready so that I can come and cheer you up. And mind you I would like to see you score at least a half-century if not more,' said Ismail Sikandar Khan with a broad guilty grin on his face.

'Yes and do come soon and do not forget to bring the entire family along with you,' replied Gul Rehman as he doffed his blue county cap and ran out of the door happily waving his favourite bat to his dear friend.

That morning the Rehman family in full strength with their young house guest Ismail Sikandar Khan descended upon the Quetta Club cricket ground to witness the prestigious annual match between the army and the civil administration. For the whole lot of them and especially for Mrs Nafisa Rehman it was a nice day out for a family picnic though she had little or no knowledge of the game.

'Go on son show them how to bat like a champion,' said a proud Major Attiqur Rehman as Gul Rehman with the score reading 10 runs for 2 wickets on the black board walked out to take his guard at the batting crease. A stylish left-hander with a wide array of all round strokes, young Gul Rehman soon had the fielders running all over the cricket field. With delightful cover drives, late cuts and leg glances he batted like a true master and soon runs were flowing from his bat on both sides of the wicket.

' We want a six.' 'We want a six,' shouted the whole family and their supporters as Gul crossed the half-century mark with a scorching square cut to the fence.

'Change the bloody bowler, change the bloody bowler' shouted the Commandant of the Staff College and some other supporters of the military team, as Gul Rehman with hooks, pulls and cuts raced to his nineties. However a pall of gloom fell over the Rehman family, when at his personal score at 99, Gul Rehman while attempting a big hook to clear the fence was smartly caught deep at long leg. While all the spectators including the fielders gave him a standing ovation as he walked back to the pavilion, his little sister Shenaz was in tears.

'They are all cheaters,' shouted the petite girl as she too rushed out to hug him. Being the favourite of her dearest eldest brother who always pampered her and even allowed her to play cricket with the rest of them, she just could not bear to see her brother being given out one short of his well deserved hundred.

'Never mind my sweetheart this is all in the game,' said Attiqur Rehman as he bought her some pop corns and a candyfloss.

That evening after the match and as they all sat down for the evening meal, Major Attiqur Rehman who was also fond of the game asked all those present starting with the junior most to name their favourite cricketer. Promptly Shenaz with a big smile said. "My favourite is Bhaijan ofcourse.'

"And what about you Arif and who is your favourite? '

'My favourite is Jack Hobbs,' replied the 12 year old.

'That's a good choice too and now how about you Aftab

.'But I only like Don Bradman,' said the second son who frankly speaking was not very fond of the game though.

'Alright now let us ask Ismail and hear his choice,' said Attiqur as he put another big ladel full of biryani into the boy's plate.

'My current favourite Sir is a young man from Lahore and his name is Lala Amarnath. And only the other day while making his debut for India against a formidable English team led by none other than Douglas Jardine at the Bombay Gymkhana ground, this 22 year old stylish right hand batsman scored a memorable 118 runs and that too against the bowling attack of Hedley Verity and John Langridge,' said Ismail Sikandar Khan very proudly.

'That is absolutely right and let me also tell you that with that hundred of his, Lala Amarnath has entered the record book as the first Indian to score a test century,' said Attiqur Rehman.

'In that case I must get a big photograph of the Indian hero and paste it on the cover of my scrap book,' said Gul Rehman as Shenaz having finished her food cuddled upto him and said.

'And who is your favourite Bhaijan?'

'Well with my old favourite Duleepsingji not playing the game any longer, I guess my choice too is Lala Amarnath, because not only is the Lala a capable batsman but he is also a good bowler and he I believe is very energetic in the field too. In other words he is a perfect all rounder,' replied Gul Rehman.

'And now that we have all given our choices, but tell us who is your favourite Abbajan,' asked Gul Rehman.

'Well I am not trying to be partial or parochial, but my favourite is a man in a military uniform from the Holkar State Forces and he is none other than Colonel CK Nayudu. And if you ever get a chance you must watch him bat because he does not believe in scoring by ones and twos, but only by hitting fours and sixes,' said Attiqur very proudly, when the Begum Sahiba walked in with a huge chocolate cake.

'Well in that case why not also ask Ammijaan about her favourite cricketer,' said Attiqur as he winked at all the children.

'I must say with that question you and your children have got me stumped no doubt, but with my son Gul Rehman having been declared as the man of the match today there can be nobody else but him,' said the mother very proudly.

For Ismail Sikandar Khan that winter holiday with the Rehman family was indeed a very memorable one.With all the love and affection that was showered on him he now practically considered himself to be a part of that very family as he helped out the Begum Sahiba in the kitchen and little Shenaz with her school home work everyday. To the nine-year-old Shenaz he was now Ismail Bhaijan and she became so much attached to him that she invariably took his side if and when any controversy between the brothers took place. And on the day when Gul Rehman and Ismail Skandar Khan left Quettta for their journey back to the Indian Military Academy, the poor girl was in tears as the train steamed out of the railway station.

On the 7th of January 1934, just five days before Masterda was to face the gallows, at Chittagong four Bengalee youths, Krishna Chowdhary, Ranjan Sen, Himangshu Chakravarty and Haren Bhattacharya attacked the British spectators at the Paltan Maidan. That morning the 'Gora Sahibs'; while enjoying the winter sun under a clear blue sky were witnessing a friendly cricket match between the two English teams. When suddenly from the middle of nowhere and armed with bombs and revolvers and despite the tight security arrangements that day, the young revolutionaries managed to sneak inside. Suddenly the four of them assaulted the terrified English families and inflicted on them quite a few casualties. The armed police immediately retaliated and Himangshu Chakravarty and Ranjan Sen were killed. Krishna Chowdhury and Haren Bhattacharya however had managed to excape but they too were caught subsequently and were sentenced to be hanged. Three days before Masterda was to face the gallows, the severed head of the greedy landlord from Goirala who had betrayed Masterda was found not far from the village itself. The head had been completely severed from the trunk. The young revolutionaries had taken their revenge.

On that fateful day of 12th January 1934, in the early hours of the morning and before being sent to the gallows Masterda Surjya Sen and Tarakeshwar Dastidar were brutally tortured for singing Vande Mataram. Masterda's teeth and joints were broken with a hammer and his unconscious body was dragged to the gallows for hanging. Like Bhagat Singh, Rajguru and Sukhdev. Masterda's and Dastidar's bodies too were not handed over to their parents and relatives. Instead they were secretly taken on board the British naval cruiser "Renown" which sailed out from the port into the open seas and their bodies were thrown into the Bay of Bengal. They were not even given a proper cremation as per the Hindu rites. Ironically and strangely the British warship bore the name "Renown. With their daring deeds, the names of Surjya Sen and his brave band of loyal young followers who sacrificed their lives at the gallows would also now be immortalized forever. Their names too would now become renowned and legendary not only in Bengal but in India too.

'Tell me with the death of Masterda, do you think the revolutionary activity in Bengal will meet its own silent death,' asked Dr Ghulam Hussein while the three friends met for their usual Saturday afternoon coffee at the Coffee House.

'Well if you ask me it has been a very bad setback to the movement no doubt and can only resurface if they find another courageous and humble leader like Masterda to lead them,' said Naren Sen.

'I agree but not whole heartedly though,' said Debu Ghosh.

'But why'? asked Dr Ghulam Hussein

'Because I feel that this will now definitely bring in an attitude of revenge from those diehards who literally worshipped Masterda and one should not forget that Masterda was highly inspired by the Irish revolutionaries and especially by Dan Breene whose book "My Fight for Irish Freedom" was like a bible to him. And like Breene, Masterda's followers too will now look for a reprisal to avenge his death and it could lead to an attempt to kill somebody who is important in Bengal and in the British Government,'said Debu Ghosh and how right he was.

Though Gandhiji in April 1934 had once again suspended the civil disobedience movement, but on the 8th of May, the 22 year old Sushil Kumar Chakravarty with Madhusadan Banerjee and Anshu Kumar Ghosh, all three college students of Dhaka University were waiting to assassinate John Anderson the Governor of Bengal. Of all the places they had decided to finish him off once and for all at the Lebong Race Course in the beautiful hill station of Darjeeling. That afternoon after the Governor with his pair of binoculars had seated himself in his special box to enjoy the races, shots rang out but luckily for him he escaped the attempt. And all the three college students were arrested and on 12th September they too were awarded the harsh sentence of transportation for life to the Andamans.

Having suspended the civil disobedience movement, Gandhiji threw himself into the upliftment of the Indian villages in order to motivate and ready the masses of the nation for a final push and drive towards eventual Swarajya and full Independence. To achieve that aim he decided to locate himself at a place in Central India which would be not only equidistant from the remotest four corners of the country, but also from the four major metropolises of Calcutta, Bombay, Delhi and Madras, Gandhiji thus chose to set up camp in an obscure village not far from Nagpur.The place chosen was a snake infested area close to the little town of Wardha. The only importance of Wardha was that it was a major railway junction on the Indian rail map.

'We will call our new village Sevagram, a village that will solely be dedicated for service to our motherland and it will also be an Ashram and shelter for the service to the poor, and it will also be our new capital,' said the Mahatma as he went about earnestly to set up the place with his small army of dedicated workers and followers. Knowing the importance of the man, the British soon established not only a telephone service to Sewagram to keep in touch with the man, but also established a police post to keep a close eye on him and also a post office. Sitting on the mud floor of his hut, Gandhi soon started dictating terms to his Majesty's government in England and to their Viceroy in India.

On 27th August 1934, the two Khan brothers, Abdul Ghaffar and Dr Khan Sahib after serving nearly two years were released from prison. At the Hazaribagh prison in Bihar they were treated as ordinary criminals and were kept in solitary confinement and were denied newspapers, letters and contact with the outside world. The release of the two brothers was however conditional. They were not to enter at any cost the land of their birth, the already truncated land of the proud Pathans, the North West Frontier. On hearing that, Gandhiji had invited them to his Sevagram Ashram and the two brothers happily arrived.there.

Ever since the success of the Salt Satyagraha movement, Mahatma Gandhi at the age of 65 had now become an international figure. Correspondents from all over the world with their typewriters and cameras now congregated to the once unknown and obscure village to have a glimpse of the man and to talk to him. The frail half naked man in a hand-spun dhoti had shown the people of India and the world how to fight and win and that too non-violently. Soon Abdul Ghaffar Khan also taught himself to spin, while Dr Khan Sahib opened a small free clinic to treat all and sundry including the poor villagers from the nearby areas. For everyone in the ashram the evening prayers were something that they all looked forward to after a hard days work. Sitting under the big neem tree each and everyone, irrespective of his caste, creed or religion learnt the valuable lesson that all religions of the world were the same. The Ram of the Hindus, the Rahim of the Muslims and the Christ of the Christians were the manifestation of the same God whose message to the world was to preach love and shun hatred. It was always an evening of true worship where hymns from the Holy Bible were sung, and prayers from all the holy scriptures were read. Sitting next to his mentor and his Guru, Badshah Khan religiously read the Koran sometimes even borrowing the reamless spectacles of the Mahatma because he had forgotten to bring his own from the small little hut that he occupied. One day after the evening prayers were over, finding Ghaffar Khan alone by himself Gandhiji took him aside for a little private talk. He wanted to ask him something confidential but he did not know how to put it diplomatically across to him.Knowing fully well that Dr Khan Sahib had an English wife Gandhiji finally asked.

'But tell me is your elder brother's wife a convert now?' On being asked that question, Ghaffar Khan simply smiled and said.

'Gandhiji, though I am myself a devout Muslim and I pray five times a day, but I am also very broad minded. And since God, Bhagwan and Allah according to you and me are one and the same, then why should marriage alter ones faith. And as far as my elder brother is concerned, my good sister-in-law is at complete liberty to follow her own religion if she so desires,' added Badshah Khan.

'That is indeed a splendid answer and therefore to spread the same thoughts amongst your lovely children and in order for you to be closer to them, why don't you get them and let them also work and study in this very Ashram,' said the Mahatma.

Gaffar Khan was delighted with that offer and by November 1934 he was once again reunited with his entire family. Ever since that fateful Christmas Day of 1931, when he was arrested and then sent to the jail at Hazaribagh, Badshah Khan had not seen his children and when Gani, Wali, Ali and his 14 year old daughter Mehar Taj arrived at Sevagram, it was an occasion to celebrate.

In October 1934, Badshah Khan with Gandhiji went to Bombay to attend the annual session of the Congress Party, but to his discomfort when he found that he was being acclaimed as a hero, the humble man did not like it one bit. The organizers had named the main pavilion after him and he was not in favour of it, and when he was offered the Presidency of the Congress even that he humbly declined. Debu Ghosh who had come to Bombay as a delegate found the man to be no less than a saint and was thrilled to hear the man, when on the 27th of October with surged up emotion he spoke boldly to the members of the Indian Christian Association about his land and his people.

Unveiling his deepest feelings for his fellow Pathans he said "What is our fault. But let me tell you very plainly that our greatest fault is that our Province, the North West Frontier was and still is the gateway to India. For us who live there the British call us their gate keepers. So how can they give any reforms to their own gate keepers because if they start giving them anything at all then India which is their golden goose will be out of their hands? Therefore, if we gate keepers seriously join hands with you Indians, the British will not be able to rule India. It is for this very reason that our peaceful Khudai Khidmatghar movement was crushed brutally at the outset. The saddest part is that we were born in the Frontier Province and that is why we are doomed."

Debu Ghosh had become so attached to the mighty Pathan that he did not miss a single of his many speeches that he made in Bombay. On his last day in that city while speaking to the Women Unity Club he praised them to high heavens for the sacrifices made by the thousands of them who had voluntarily and boldly joined the freedom struggle. When he concluded his address with the words that if the women of India were awakened once again, it would not be possible for any power on Earth to keep India under slavery, the tall Pathan Badshah Khan was once again greeted with a thunderous applause.

On his return to Wardha, Ghaffar Khan had planned a trip to Bengal. He had decided to work out a programme of reforms for the millions of poor Bengali Muslims who resided there. He was scheduled to leave for Calcutta on the 8th of December, but the British Intelligence after his provocative speeches in Bombay had kept a close tag on him. They could not afford to have Ghaffar Khan in a Province where even a slight spark could once again reignite the revolutionary instincts of the Bengalees. Therefore on the 7th of December, the day before he was to leave for Calcutta, the police arrived at the Sevagram ashram and arrested the man on the charges of having made seditious speeches in Bombay. To Debu Ghosh who had talked so much about the man to his dear friends Ghulam Hussein, Naren Sen and others and who was eagerly looking forward to the stately Pathan's visit to his house, it all ended up with one very big and sad disappointment as the Frontier Gandhi was once again sentenced to another long term in prison.

During the month of October, while Gandhi with Ghaffar Khan were busy attending the Annual Congress session at Bombay, the Gentlemen Cadets of the first course at the Indian Military Academy, Dehradun were busy with their own sports competitons and rehearsals for the institution's first passing out parade that was scheduled to be held a few weeks later. At the first ever hockey match that was played against the formidable Government College team from Lahore and which was held at Dehra Doon on 28th October, 1934 the IMA team was unlucky to lose by a narrow margin. But having excelled with their brilliant stick work and play in that match, both Ismail Sikandar Khan and Gul Rehman were both awarded the Academy Blues in hockey. Three weeks later on 18th November1934, the Indian Military Academy received its first King's Colours and the King's banner, and it was indeed a very proud day for the academy. With the final academic examinations over, the Gentlemen Cadets now eagerly waited for the 22nd of December, when they would pass out of the Academy in the first batch as full fledged and gazetted Indian army officers with their Indian commissioned personal numbers prefixing their ranks of second lieutenants The same IC's, the Indian Commissioned magic numbers would also reckon their inter se seniority and their military competence and promotion in the years to come.

While Gandhiji on 17th December announced his earnest desire to retire from politics, the young gentlemen cadets under the command of their fiery Regimental Sergeant Major Fullbrook and Company Havildar Major Tara Singh were getting their act together on the drill square, the most sacred and revered piece of ground in the academy. Bellowing in his rich stentorian voice, Fullbrook said.

'Gentlemen today there are only a handful of you and if you 100 plus bloody fools cannot even march in step and in one bloody straight line then

I am afraid you do not deserve to become bloody officers and definitely not officers of the gallant and brave Indian Army. Then turning towards CHM Tara Singh he loudly added.

'CHM inko thoda aur ragda lagao.' (CHM drill them properly some more) CHM Tara Singh was delighted to have been given the honour to bullshit the very people who tomorrow probably would be ordering him around.

'Thik hai Sahib,' shouted Tara Singh as he with sheer delight ordered all the Gentlemen Cadets on parade less the senior key appointments to lift their rifles over the heads and do two quick rounds of the drill square.

'Come on yaar for heaven sake take it easy,' said Gul Rehman as the keener ones in the group took off at a fast pace.

'Kissne bola take it eegee. Humko bhi angrezi aata hai,' (Who said take it easy. I too know English.) said CHM Tara Singh as he instinctively ordered the parade to mark time in order to find out who the culprit was.

'Aur unchha uttao ghutne ko aur aap log tab thak uttathe rahenge jab tak mere ko mera sawal ka jawab nahin milta. (And now you will all keep lifting your knees higher and higher till such time I get my answer)" said CHM Tara Singh swinging his drill baton with a feeling of mutual pride and sympathy.

'Kasoor vaar mein hu' (I am to be blamed) CHM,' said Ismail Sikandar Khan as he took one step forward and kept marking time with the rifle over his head and with his legs raised even higher than demanded. Ismail Sikandar Khan had sportingly taken the blame in order to shield his bosom pal Gul Rehman Khan who even at the fag end of his training was still under going 14 days restrictions. It was only a week earlier that GC Gul Rehman had been punished for violating good order and military discipline, when he was caught loitering in an out of bound area in Dehra Dun and had been apprehended by the military police. Ismail Sikandar Khan was apprehensive that a second disciplinary charge while on parade today may prove rather costly for his dear friend and he therefore had decided to take the blame on him.

CHM Tara Singh was however confident that Ismail Sikandar Khan could not have been the culprit, because he was not the type. He however liked the young man's espirit de corps and with a straight face commented. This is indeed a very good example of aapas mein dosti aur aisa hi hona chaiye zindagi mein aur khas kareke ladahi aur yudh ke dauran'. (This is indeed a sign of good comradeship between friends and that is how it should ever remain in life and especially so during battle and in war) said a beaming

Tara Singh as he brought the parade to a complete halt and gave them a few minutes of well deserved rest.

A fortnight before the final passing out parade, Major Savory, the Alpha Company Commander during the Academy dinner night informally asked some of the Gentlemen Cadets from the passing out course about their choice of arms and service.

'Well Sir, if given a choice I would opt for the infantry,'said Gul Rehman confidently.

And so would I Sir,' said Ismail Sikandar Khan.

'That indeed is very heartening, but what about your friend, the third musketeer from the Bravo Company. What is his choice?.'

'Unfortunately Sir Gentleman Cadet Daler Singh Bajwa has no choice but to join the Kashmir State Forces and thereafter I guess his superiors will decide on his arm or service,' said Ismail Sikandar Khan.

'Well that settles the arm of service and now what about the choice of regiments,' added Major Savory who was himself a veteran World War hero and the winner of the Military Cross.

'I would like to join the Punjabees Sir,' because it is the oldest regiment in the Indian Army and moreover my father had also served as an RMO with them at Flanders' said Gul Rehman.

'And so would I Sir, and moreover I have a parental claim to it also don't I, Sir?'said Ismail Sikandar Khan.

'Yes that you definitely have a parental claim and it could be a plus point for you, and now that I have got your first preferences let me see how best I can help both of you out, but I am afraid both of you cannot be commissioned into the same Punjab regiment and definitely not into the same Battalion. I will therefore recommend you Gul Rehman for commission into the First Punjabees, and as for you Ismail Sikandar Khan you will ofcourse join the Second Punjabees, your late father's regiment which will always and forever be proud of Naik Curzon Sikandar Khan, the winner of the Victoria Cross at Loos.'

In his heart of heart Major Savory was keen that both Gul Rehman and Ismail Sikandar with their proficiency in games and especially in hockey should join his own Sikh Regiment, but seeing the young men's enthusiasm for the Punjabees, he decided to close the matter there and then and once and for all.

Under a clear blue winter sky on the morning of 22nd December 1934, and to the music of the 2nd Batallion the 8th Gurkha Rifles pipe band, the contingent of the Gentlemen Cadets of the Indian Military Academy smartly marched on parade. For the Gentlemen Cadets of the First Course, the Pioneers as they were now called that day was indeed a day to cherish and remember. They would soon create history and become the first regular course to pass out from the IMA as commissioned officers of the Indian Army. It was indeed a historic day for the institution as Gentleman Cadet Under Officer Smith Dunn commanding the parade waited eagerly for the fanfare to be sounded and for the chief guest taking the salute to arrive. Looking smart in their blue mess jackets and with the red tabs shining from the shoulders of those holding appointments, the parents of those passing out sitting in the spectator's stand felt indeed proud of their sons. Amongst them were Major Attiqur Rehman, Sardar Gurcharan Singh, father of GC Daler Singh Bajwa and Colonel Reginald Edwards. Though none of their wards held any appointments or got any of the top awards, but they were none the less part of the First Pioneers and that by itself was an honour to be a member of that great team.

After the award of the Gold Medal for standing first in order of merit was presented to Gentleman Cadet Nripendra Singh Bhagat and the coveted sword of honour for the best all round Gentlemen Cadet to Under Officer Smith Dunn, the parade was now ready for the final march past.

'Eyeeeeees right,' shouted Smith Dunn as he smartly saluted with his sword, while the passing out course in perfect well coordinated rhythm marched past the saluting base to the clapping of hands by the spectators. They were now no longer Gentlemen Cadets but proud subalterns of the Indian Army. The unassuming strong Pathan and ex Lance Naik Mohammed Musa who was third in order of merit went ultimately to the Piffers, while the young and handsome Sam Manekshaw 17th in order of merit was also commissioned into the famous Piffers, the 4th Battalion of the 12th Frontier Force Regiment, which was also commonly known as the "Chawanjas" or the 54th Sikhs. And as far as the three musketeers wwere concerned, Gul Rehman got his 1/1 Punjabees, while Ismail Sikandar Khan went to the 1/2 Punjabees and Daler Singh Bajwa was commissioned into the Maharaja of Kashmir's 4th Kashmir Rifles, which was also known as the "Fateh Shibji" battalion.Though the 1st Pioneers passed out from the Indian Military Academy Dehra Dun on 22nd December 1934, however their dates of first commission as well as their seniority in the government of India's gazette was concerned, it was notified as 1st February 1935.

As per the policy laid down, all the young officers had to first do an attachment for a year with a British Infantry Battalion before being reverted to their own parent Indian unit. For 2/Lt Sam Manekshaw the attachment was with the 2nd Battalion the Royal Scots, while for 2/Lt Ismail Sikandar Khan and 2/Lt Gul Rehman it was the First Somerset Light Infantry and the 2nd Black Watch Regiment respectively.Both the British Battalions had very long affiliations with India and they were highly decorated units too.

'Well, I must say both of you are indeed very lucky to get the pick of the British Battalions and therefore you must train hard with them and learn the best from them too,' said Colonel Reginald Edwards as he congratulated the two young subalterns.

'Yes and do also remember that the British officers are sticklers for protocol and especially when it comes to mess rules and etiquettes, therefore just do as you are told. For even in the thick of Indian summer you will be expected to put on a damn tie at social evenings at the clubs and the officers' mess,' said Major Attiqur Rehman while presenting the three Musketeers each with a set of the Punjab Regimental Ties and with handerkerchiefs to match.

CHAPTER-9

Wake Up Call for the World, the British Empire and for India too

On 5th February 1935, in England the draft bill for the proposed Government of India Act 1935 was presented in the House of Commons and thereafter it was debated both in the House of Commons and in the House of Lords. But after the failure of the Third Round Table conference, both the Congress and the Muslim League had decided to oppose the Act. Under the Act a Federation of India was promised comprising both the Provinces and States. The Indian Council was to be abolished and a Central Legislature formed which had the right to pass any bill, but the bill required the approval of the Governor General before it could become law. Thus the British Governor General remained the head of the central administration and enjoyed wide powers concerning administration, legislation and finance. Under this act both Burma and Aden were to be separated from India and two new provinces of Sind and Orissa were to be created. One-third Muslim representation in the Central Legislature was guaranteed. Autonomous provincial governments in 11 provinces, under ministries responsible to the legislatures were to be set up. The Reserve Bank of India was to be established and a Federal Court was required to function from the Centre. Initially both the Congress and the Muslim League opposed the Act, but with the provincial elections due in the winter of 1936-37 they decided to participate in it.

While the debate on the Government of India Act 1935 was still being discussed in England, in India on 26th of March 1935, the Maharaja of Kashmir, Hari Singh signed a sixty year lease deed with Mr L E Lang, the British Resident in Kashmir, thus giving away temporarily the territory and the Agency of Gilgit to the British. It was mutually agreed that though the British would assume the civil and military administration of the area, the area however would continue to be included within the Dominion of His

Highness the Maharaja of Jammu and Kashmir and the flag of His Highness would continue to fly at the official Headquarters of the Agency. The 60 year lease was to begin from 1st August 1935 and to doubly ensure that there would be no back tracking by the Maharaja, on the 3rd of April, the Viceroy; Lord Wellingdon promptly ratified the treaty. With Maharaja Hari Singh saddled with his own problems of containing the demands of Sheikh Abdulla for more Muslim representation in the Government, the British took full advantage of the situation.

On the very day that the treaty to give Gilgit away was ratified, Major Attiqur Rehman MC was promoted to the rank of Lieutenant Colonel. It also happened to be his 48th birthday that day and he decided to celebrate it with his close friends in Quetta. Amongst them was a twenty eight year old Indian officer in the rank of a Major He was popularly known as Timmy and Timmy with his very charming young wife Nina was then posted at Quetta.

Born in Mercara the handsome Coorgi officer had completed his schooling from the Bishop Cotton School Bangalore. When he was a little over 15 years old he was selected to be in the first batch of cadets to join the PWRIMC at Dehra Dun. That was in 1921 and it was well before the Prince of Wales formally inaugurated the College officially. From there he qualified for admission into the Sandhurst Military Academy in England and on being commissioned in 1926 he was posted on attachment to the 2nd Battalion of the Highland Light Infantry which was then stationed luckily at Bangalore, a city that he loved. With his good looks and suave manners, Timmy soon became a big draw for the young girls who frequented the Bowring Institute. It was a popular club that was patronised by the large Anglo Indian community of the City.

On that evening at Colonel Attiqur Rehman's promotion party, the young handsome Coorgi officer was in great form. Major KS Thimmaya from the 4th Battalion of the 19th Hyderabad Regiment had everybody in splits as he narrated his exploits at the PWRIMC and during his short nine years of service.

'Alright tell us a little more about your first few months at the PWRIMC, or rather the first day at Dehra Dun. Didn't you feel homesick?' Asked Nafisa as she with her11year old daughter Shenaz brought in a few more plates of hot sheek kebabs to go with the drinks.

'Well it was like this. I was just 15 plus and a few months under age, but that did not really matter. Though I knew I was probably the youngest, there were however some who were not boys but young men to say the least. They were all well over 20 and one Muslim fellow was even 25 plus, but more about him later.On the very first day when I arrived at the Doon railway station accompanied by my father, we were pleasantly surprised to be welcomed by none other than the Principal himself Mr JGC Scott. But what surprised me even more was the presence of Mrs Scott, his beautiful wife on the platform. She too was very much a part of the reception committee and she instantly made us feel at home Initially on landing at Doon frankly my morale was not very high, but after seeing and being introduced to the charming pretty lady my morale went sky high,' said Timmy.

"Undoubtedly you always were and probably still are a lady's man,' commented someone in jest as Timmy helped himself to another scotch.

'But how many of you were in that first batch,' asked Colonel Attiqur.

'We were only 32 of us Sir, and we were grouped into three sections, Rawlinson, Roberts and Kitchener, The sections were named after the old British Commander-in-Chiefs of India, and I was put in Rawlinson where our section master was one Mr Kittermaster, a superb athelete and who had just arrived in India. Thanks to him I concentrated less on studies and more on games of which cricket was my favourite,' said Timmy.

' And who was the Commandant and what was he like,' asked Dr Henry Holland, a well known medic of Quetta who ran a hospital for the poor.

'Well Sir the Commandant, Colonel J L Houghton, DSO was a wonderful person. He was a real fatherly figure and a man of principles. He was from the 11 Sikhs and with his 6 feet three inches height he was not only a towering personality, but his very presence both off and on parade injected a lot of pride in all of us.' added Timmy.

'And what about the Sergeant Major. What was he like? Was he generally a typical bull shitter like most Sergeant Majors are,' asked Colonel Attiqur Rehman.

'You could'nt be more right Sir. Sergeant Major Gorman from the Durham Light Infantry was a bloody big bull shitter, but only on parade. And off parade he was a thorough gentleman. With his beefy figure, crimson face and a well-waxed moustache he was a bloody terror on parade. As the chief drill and the physical training instructor he was the most feared man in the College, and when he bellowed out his orders in his thundering voice, it was like an earthquake' said Timmy while clearing his throat in order to give live a demonstration

'No not here please and definitely not inside the house and you may give the demonstration later in the lawn outside if you so wish,' said his wife Nina.

'Alright you win as always,' said Timmy as he poured himself another whisky.

'But if I remember correctly you did mention something about a Muslim cadet who was well over 25 years old but what was he doing there?' asked Nafisa.

'Oh yes there were quite a few of such stalwarts. Besides Mohammed Zafar Alam who was the senior most age wise, we also had for company the two elderly Pathan brothers, Khalid Jan and Ahmed Jan. They were from a distinguished family of the North West Frontier Province but to me it seems that they were there only for fun. Well now coming back to my senior friend the 25 year old Mohammed Zafar Iqbal, he I must say was quite a character. His father was the Chief Detective Officer to the Viceroy and Zafar's only interest it seems was Urdu poetry or what is popularly called in the local lingo as, "Shair and Shairy". Physically Zafar was a very weak cadet and Sargeant Major Gorman who had a terrific sense of humour would invariably let him have it on the parade ground,' added Timmy as he requested little Shenaz darling to go inside the kitchen and get some more of those delicious hot sheek kebabs. And as soon as little Shenaz was out of sight, Timmy with a mischievous smile continued with his story.

'You see as I said earlier Zafar Iqbal was very weak in PT and he hated the wooden horse. One day during PT, Gorman got so fed up with Zafar's halfhearted efforts to vault over it that he bellowed loudly to him.'

'You bloody man why are you trying to bugher that wooden horse. Don't try to get into it, just go over it. But when poor Zafar Iqbal gave it one more try, and the result was still the same, Gorman also gave up. Zafar's problem was that he was mortally scared of horses, and it was irrespective of whether it was a wooden one or a real one. Once during equitation class and either by design or otherwise he was given a rather frisky horse. When Gorman gave the order for all of us to mount, poor Zafar Iqbal just could'nt make it to the saddle and Gorman was once again livid.

'You bloody nitwit, if at this age you cannot mount even a bloody horse, how the bloody well will you ever mount a bloody woman.'

Timmy's anecdotes no doubt drew a loud laugh from the male audience, but as far as the ladies were concerned they only kept blushing. Therefore in order to change the subject Attiqur therefore very diplomatically said.

'Hey Timmy why don't you tell all of us about that chance meeting of yours and of some of your colleagues with the late Mr Motilal Nehru."

'Well that was in 1929 when I was with my battalion at Allahabad. One day dressed in my military uniform I together with three other Indian officers went to see a stage play. In between the acts there was a short break and we all went for a drink to the bar. Standing there with a drink in hand was an elderly Indian gentleman and on seeing us three young Indians in military uniforms he in his impeccable English asked me very candidly.

'Now tell me young man what does an Indian officer feel wearing the uniform of a British ruler?' And without batting an eyelid when I simply said flippantly, 'Hot Sir' and the gentleman gave a big smile, I knew that he was one of our kind. But till then I had no idea whatsever of who he was till he gave me his calling card and extended an invitation to all of us to call on him at his palatial Anand Bhavan residence,' said Timmy as Nafisa announced that dinner was served.

While the ladies made a beeline for the dining table, in the adjoining room, Timmywwith a few others including Colonel Attiqur Rehman made a beeline for the open air bar in the garden.

'Alright now that the ladies are busy hogging away, I must tell all of you so called bachelors this one, and mind you this is real juicy stuff and I am not bluffing,' said Timmy as the small group of bachelor officers huddled around him.

'Come on and let the juice flow man before your better half sends you the summons for dinner' said one of Timmy's close bachelor friends as all of them topped their glasses with the usual but never ending one for the road excuse.

'Well then listen and listen very carefully because the grape wine has it that one Indian officer from a Sikh Regiment and without taking names is presently believed to be having an affair with that striking American blonde who everyone knows is the wife of a British officer and that I must say is indeed a great achievement. Because by all given standards she is undoubtedly the glamour girl of the station and therefore all of you I am sure know who the lady is,' said Timmy as he poured himself one more for the road.'

'Boy that is really great news because in good old days when their wives were away from India, the Angrez used to have their own 'Bibi Khanas,' and therefore it is heartening to know that atleast one Indian officer has his own little secret 'Mem Khana' and that to here inside the Staff College itself,' said Colonel Attiqur Rehman as he too helped himself to another whisky. And when another bachelor officer came up with another more spicy and juicy story everybody was aghast.

'No it simply cannot be true,' said one of them who refused to believe it.

'But by God its gospel truth and this is an exclusive orgy club and its membership is restricted only to those married British couples who want to join it voluntarily. Presently it is being run by a small select group of four English couples who are doing the staff college course and they undoubtedly are having a rollicking time it seems,' said the bachelor officer.

'I must say that's news to all of us no doubt, but what are the rules for admission to it? asked a friend of his and who sounded rather serious.

'It is no use your trying because firstly you are a thoroughbred 'Kalu"(Black) Indian and secondly you are unmarried and you don't have a wife,' added Colonel Attiqur Rehman while requesting all of them to move in for the dinner.

'But there is still no harm in asking as to how this so called exclusive orgy club carries out all its nefarious activities and that to so very discreetly,' said the bachelor officer sounding even more enthusiastic this time.

'It is all very simple and it works on a mutually agreed lottery system. The venue is a pot luck get together and it is taken by turns. The performing stage is the quarters of the officer hosting the pot luck and it is generally held on weekends. Once everybody is in, first the drinks and snacks are served and it is follwed by bawdy jokes, stories, music and dancing. Then the host puts the name of all the members in a hat and depending upon your luck and pick of the draw, you are then paired off with your respective partners and the first session begins. Thereafter it is all rotational and it entirely depends on each other's sexual desires, fantasies and capabilities and that's about all. It is all very straight and simple and with each one getting an equal opportunity to lay the other its great fun too I guess. Moreover it is a free for all and with no questions asked,' said the officer as he too poured a drink for himself.

'But for how long does this kind of an orgy party carry on,' asked another officer.

Well in order to add a little more colour and spice to it, sometimes they even combine it with a kitty party during a weekend lunch, and which is then followed by a pound and pint party in the evening and ends with strip poker the next day,' said the officer as one of the ladies who had overheard the concluding part of that dialogue asked.

'Well what party are we talking about now and though I do not know how to play poker, nontheless I won't mind learning,' added the lady.

'Oh they were only talking about some give and take party where you take some and give some and everything is mutually shared without any heart burning. And as far as the game of poker is concerned I would rather advise you Madam to stay away from it. That American gambling game has ruined many a good soul and it is not worth it,' said Colonel Attiqur Rehman with a straight face as he remined the tipplers at the bar that dinner was getting cold.

After dinner that night, when they were about to bid farewell to their gracious host and hostess, Timmy said.

'Sir next time when your son 2/Lt Gul Rehman and his dear friend 2/Lt Ismail Sikandar Khan visit Quetta, do please ask them to call on us. Maybe we could exchange notes on the type of training they received at the IMA at Doon vis a vis what we had to go through at Sandhurst. Moreover with their interest in hockey and cricket we could also play a few friendly matches between The "Kallus" (Blacks)verses the Goras (Whites) or maybe as Indians verses the Rest and beat them all handsomely too,' added Timmy very proudly.

After passing out from the Indian Military Academy Ismail Sikandar Khan was very keen to make one last visit to Gilgit before the area came under complete British control. But because of the severe heavy winter snowfall and continuous bad inclement weather, his friend Second Lieutenant Daler Singh Bajwa who too was now now a commissioned officer in the Mahraja's State Forces dissuaded him from doing so.

'You can always visit Gilgit when it is beautiful during spring and summer and may we will go there together later. And as for now why don't you come with me and be my guest at Bagh,' said 2/Lt Daler Singh as the one horse tonga carrying them crossed the custom post at Domel made its way to the New Sher-e-Punjab hotel at Muzzafarabad. Next day, when they reached Daler's ancestral village of Bagh, Daler's parents, Harbir Kaur and Sardar Gurcharan were simply delighted.

'Wahe Guru ki kasam he looks a perfect carbon copy of his late father Curzon Sikandar Khan,' said a delighted Harbir Kaur as the family congregated at the local gurdwara to seek the Wahe Guru's blessings.They were all feeling very proud and were therefore celebrating the homecoming of Daler Singh Bajwa who was now a full fledged officer in the Maharaja's 4th Kashmir Rifles.

'And mark my words, but this very Ismail Sikandar Khan like his brave father will also someday bring glory to his family,' said Gurcharan Singh Bajwa as he put another big ladel full of the "Kadha Prashad", the traditional sweet dish also known as halwa and which is served on all such occasions at the Gurudwara into the young man's already over full plate.

'And as far as our own munda (son) Daler Singh is concerned, I can tell you he will be no less than our very own and legendary General Zorawar Singh, the conqueror of Leh and Ladakh,' said one of the village elders, a retired Subedar from the State Forces. When the congregation finally disbursed with a loud and shrilll rendering of "Bole Sonehal' by Ismail Sikandar Khan, the village reverberated with an even louder: Sat Sri Akal".

After the death of Sardar Harbhajan Singh, Daler Singh, loving grandfather who died at Jalianwala, the small community of the Bajwas at Bagh was now a big joint family. Though Bagh was traditionally and predominantly a Sikh village, but it also had a sprinkling of Muslims and Hindus too, and all the three communities always lived in complete harmony. But of late and due to the demands of Sheikh Abdulla for better representation of the Muslims of Kashmir in the Maharaja's overwhelming Kashmiri Pundits and Dogra dominated government, the tension between the Muslims and the non Muslims were also now being felt in these border areas of Philandri, Poonch and Muzzafarabad too, and Bagh was no exception. On seeing a Muslim officer being felicitated by the Sikh community, the local Muslims felt very happy that afternoon, but two or three days later, when it dawned on them that Ismail Sikandar Khan though a Kashmiri from Kashmir was not part of the Maharaja's State Forces they took it as another insult because to them it was another example of discrimination by the Hindu ruler of Kashmir. Sensing that he was indirectly becoming the cause of unnecessary bad blood that was being spilt between the two communities, Ismail Sikandar Khan therefore after a few days very diplomatically giving the excuse that he had to go urgently to Rawalpindi to give trials for his new uniforms and mess kit at the tailors and then from there go to the Second Punjab Regimental Centre to buy the rest of the accoutrements that went with the uniform, he very gracefully took leave of his friend and host.

A week later Ismail was in Quetta with the Rehman family. One evening over a cup of tea he met the charming Thimmaiyas and was completely bowled over by them. After his leave was over, young 2/Lt Ismail Sikandar Khan with his bag and baggage that included his new set of uniforms and the new mess dress which he picked up from Rawalpindi and for which he had to pay quite a packet simply because the tailoring firm boasted that it had been appointed by no less a person than the Commander-in-Chief of the Indian Army was on his way to his new British unit. After spending a day at Rawalpindi, Ismail Sikandar Khan took the Frontier Mail to Peshawar and from there in a military convoy made his way North to Mardan where the 1st Somersets were located and with whom he was required to do his initial attachment before finally joining his parent unit the 2nd Punjabees. Likewise from Quetta, 2/Lt Gul Rehman Khan took the train to Pathankot where the broad gauge railway network terminated. Pathankot was not only the gateway to Kashmir, but also to the small beautiful exclusive British military hill stations and cantonments that dotted the approach to the British summer capital at Simla. It was around mid afternoon, when the train arrived at Pathankot and 2/Lt Gul Rehman smartly dressed in his new military uniform and feeling very hungry entered the Pathankot railway restaurant.

While sitting inside the railway restaurant that proudly displayed on its glass fronted cupboard at the entrance, bottles of Worcester sauce, Pan Yan Pickles and the popular Becks beer, Gul Rehman Khan noticed a tall handsome Englishman sitting a few tables away reading a book. He was probably his own age or may be a few years older, but he looked every inch an army officer. The man was in civilian clothes and was enjoying his bottle of Becks beer with the railway restaurant's standard bill of fare of mulligatawny soup, chicken curry rice and caramel custard. He seemed engrossed with his book and intermittently while enjoying his meal he also kept smiling at Gul Rehman. A few minutes later the smartly dressed liveried waiter having done his customary long salaam handed over a small hand written note to Gul Rehman. On reading that note, Gul Rehman immediately got up and joined the Englishman at his table.

'Welcome to the Indian army and my name is Mr John Masters and I am from the 4th Gurkha Rifles,' said the Englishman as they shook hands.

'Delighted to meet you Sir and my name is Mr Gul Rehman Khan and I am from the 1st Punjabees. But right now I am on my way to Dalhousie to do my attachment with the 2nd Blackwatch Regiment Sir,' replied Gul Rehman very confidently.

'Just cut off the bloody Sir and have a chilled beer,' said John Masters as he shouted "Koi Hai" to place the order.

'Thank you Sir for the offer, but my bottle of beer must be on its way since I have already ordered for it,' said Gul Rehman.

'All the same and in that case we can always share that extra bottle, because I was the one who invited you to my table and as per Indian hospitality you will have to split it with me. Moreover, I consider myself to be a half Indian because I was born in Calcutta and eversince 1805, three generations of my family have been here in this very fascinating country and about which God willing I will write someday,' said John Masters.

John Masters had passed out only a few months earlier from Sandhurst. He had won the coveted Norman Medal for topping the list of cadets opting for the Indian Army and was very proud of it. He had passed out second in order of merit and that too with a much-needed scholarship. While enjoying his chilled beer, John Masters took out a parchment paper from his leather valise and placed it on the table. It was signed by no less a person then the King of England and it read as follows.

'From George the Vth by the grace of God and of Great Britain, Ireland, and British Dominions beyond the seas, King, defender of the faith, Emperor of India. To our trusty and well beloved John Masters, greetings. We reposing special trust and confidence in your loyalty, courage and good conduct, do by these presents constitute and appoint you to be an officer in our land forces from the 30th day of August 1934. You are therefore carefully and diligently to discharge your duty as such in the rank of Second Lieutenant or in such other rank as we may from time to time hereafter be pleased to promote or appoint you to, and of which a notification will be made in the London gazette. Given at our Court, at St James, the twenty first of August in the twenty-fifth year of our reign.

It was Johm Masters letter of commission in original and when they parted company, John Masters simply said.

'You know it is a real pity that only we the Britishers are today allowed to join and command the Gurkhas, and I can tell you that they are not only the most loyal troops in our army, but as Nepali Hindus they are probably more orthodox in their customs than the Hindus in India!'

'Yes Sir there you absolutely right, and it is because of this may be that Nepal to you is an important country because it also serves as a good buffer between British India and China,' replied Gul Rehman.

'There is no doubt about that and there is no disputing the fact that they the Gurkhas are great fighters and are totally loyal provided they have your full confidence and trust. But once that confidence and trust is lost they can be deadly enemies too,' added John Masters as he ordered for another bottle of chilled beer.

It was around 2 PM in the afternoon, when Gul Rehman boarded the last bus for Dalhousie. The driver a young Sardar seemed to be in one helleva hurry as he constantly honked away while negotiating the many hairpin bends along the dusty, narrow hilly road. When the bus reached its final destination all the passengers including Second Lieutenant Gul Rehman Khan breathed a sigh of relief. Besides being a military station, the hill station of Dalhousie was also a popular tourist resort for the Europeans during the summer season. With the local coolies carrying his big steel trunk, the holdall and the standard kit bag, Gul Rehman finally arrived at the Officer's Mess of the 2nd Black Watch Regiment.

The Black Watch a Highland regiment was raised on the banks of the River Tay at Aberfeldy, in Perthshire in 1739. Their uniform was the dark tartan and hence they were known as the " Black Watch." To fight the Red Indians they even went to America and seeing them dressed in kilts, the Red Indians thought they were probably their own distant cousins. During the American war of Independence they even fought against George Washington and his forces. Now the King himself was the regiment's first Colonel-in-Chief and with a red hackle on their berets, they were all very proud of their achievements.

The Officers Mess and the bachelor's quarters had no electric lights, and a hurricane lamp had been provided by the unit to the young subaltern. Others who were well off had a petromax or an Alladdin lamp in their rooms. Gul Rehman's room had a narrow wooden bed, a heavy wooden chest of drawers, a wooden cupboard, two hard top and one cane easy chair, a writing table and a bookshelf. Attached to the room was another small room that served as the bathroom and it had a wooden platform to stand on and have a bath, a table holding an enamelled basin, a soap dish and a jug. In one corner was the thunder box which was nothing but a wooden chair with four legs and a round hole in the middle of the seat to which was fitted a detachable enamel pot popularly known as the top hat. After one had finished the drill of shitting into the pot, the sweeper would dispose the stinking shit, clean the enamel pot and put it back into place.

The Officers Mess was the most sacred and revered place next to the Unit Quarter Guard.and the 2nd Black Watch like any other British Regiment was proud of their mess silver. However, once inside the mess it was taboo for an officer to talk shop. The dress regulations laid down for the mess had to be religiously followed and a regimental dinner night was a drill that was compulsory for all to attend.

For the regimental dinner night, the first bugle call was like a warning call for the officer to get ready and to head for the Officers Mess. Then followed the second call as everybody congregated inside the mess lounge. And this was followed buy a couple of rounds of drinks before everyone moved in and took their appointed seats in the beautifully laid out dining table. Normally it was a four course dinner and the unit pipe band in their ceremonials played outside, while the food was served. The change of music by the regimental band indicated the end of a particular course and for the start of a new one. The well trained mess waiters most of whom were the officer's personal civilian orderlies provided the necessary table service. After the final toast to His Majesty, The King and Emperor was raised and drunk for his good health, the Pipe Major from the Band was invited to play inside and have his share of rum. And as soon as he gulped down his tot of neat rum, the silver cigar and cigarette cases were passed around. Thereafter the officers moved back into the ante room for a cognac or two before calling it a day, and then as per protocol they all left the premises in their order of seniority and with the junior most officer being the last to depart.

The 2nd Battalion of the Black Watch was part of the Bareilly Brigade and the Indian Meerut Division and the unit during the Great War of 1914-1918 had fought magnificently at Givenchy and Loos in France and thereafter in the Middle East. Being the only Indian in a completely British unit, it took quite a while for the British Officers and staff to accept the newly commissioned Indian army officer into their fold, though it was only for an attachment for about a year.

For the first few weeks, Gul Rehman felt like a fish out of water. But in early May, when the Brigade inter battalion officers small arms competition took place and young 2/Lt Gul Rehman was declared the best firer and the trophy was won by the Blackwatch, Gul Rehman suddenly became very popular both with the Tommies and the officers. Then a week later, when the 2nd Blackwatch also took the hockey trophy thanks to a hatrick by Gul Rehman in the inter battalion brigade hockey competition finals, he now became the oldman's favourite.

'Well son for all the effort and laurels that has been brought by you to the battalion, you are hereby granted 7 days casual leave with effect from tomorrow and therefore let your hair down and enjoy yourself, and we will see you back here with us for the inter company patrolling competition which is scheduled to begin from the 3rd of June,' said the Commanding Officer as he with gusto patted the young Indian officer on his back.

Early next morning putting all the medals and trophies that were won by him and a few change of clothes into the small suitcase, Gul Rehman caught the first early morning bus for Pathankot. In the afternoon and before boarding the train for Quetta, he sent off an urgent telegram to his dear friend Ismail Sikandar Khan who was doing his attachment with the 1st Somersets in the North West Frontier.

When 2/Lt Ismail Sikandar Khan reported for his attachment with the Somersets from the very first day itself he was warmly received by all the officers and the men of the unit. This could be attributed to the fact that he was after all the son of a Victoria Cross winner who had so gallantly fought and had died for the glory of the British Empire. The Somerset Light Infantry was raised in 1685 and in 1822 had sailed for India. In 1842, the First Somersets after having been besieged at Jalalabad during the First Afghan War had sallied out and routed the forces of Akbar Khan and were given the title of "Prince Albert's Regiment of Light Infantry." It also took part during the 1857 uprising and in the First World War in France.

On receiving the telegram from Gul Rehman, Ismail also requested for a few days casual leave and on being granted five days leave, he immediately left for Quetta. It was a memorable short holiday not only for the two friends, but also for the Rehman family as they went on picnics to the nearby Urak Valley and the beautiful emerald Hanna Lake. Known as the fruit basket of the Frontier with its numerous orchards growing the best of fruits from plums to cherries, they all enjoyed the outing as they stuffed themselves with the large variety of delicious fresh fruits which they plucked straight from the trees. Fed up with the typical English type of mess food that was served in the officers mess, the two young officers were seen every evening savouring the delicious Sajji, the roasted leg of a tender lamb, or biting into the juicy bits of tender kebabs at the many roadside eating joints of the city. Quetta was a food lover's paradise and with its innumerable numbers of small road side cafes one could get a variety of spicy and mouth watering non vegetarian dishes and at very reasonable rates too.

On the 30th of May 1935, a day before they were scheduled to depart for their respective units, the two young officers together with Lieutenant Colonel and Mrs Attiqur Rehman and a few others who were Timmy's close friends were invited by the Thimmaiyas to a dinner party at their residence. Perfect hosts that they were, both Timmy and Nina kept their guests thoroughly entertained as they all enjoyed the evening drinking and chatting on the lawns of their well kept bungalow. Adept in playing the mouth organ, Timmy regaled his guests with popular English numbers and even sang a few Punjabi songs of which not a word he understood though. It was Mohinder Singh from the Bedi clan and the second senior most cadet and colleague of his at the PWRIMC who had taught him a few of those fast Punjabi numbers. However, after the second Punjabi song, when Timmy went to get a refill from the bar, Colonel Attiqur took him aside and whispered into his ears.

'I must say that you do sing very well in Punjabi also, but thank God that none of the gentlemen and ladies around here tonight are Punjabees or else you could have had a few chappals and shoes thrown at you.

'.But why,' asked Timmy looking quite surprised.

'Because bloody man some of those lines that you sang were hair raisingly obscene and that is why,' added Attiqur as he also helped himself to one more small whisky.

'Oh Shit I never knew that and I had no clue whatsoever that some of those lines were obscene and bawdy and I always sang them with pleasure,' said Timmy as he laughed heartily and poured a large one into his own glass.A little later, when Timmy walked up to the two subalterns who were standing in one far corner and asked them how they were doing with their beers, Ismail said.'

'Sir, please tell us some more stories of you exploits at the PWRIMC and of your days at Sandhurst.'

'Or may be you would like to tell us about the most nervous moment in your life,' butted in Gul Rehman.

'Oh that nervous moment is there practically every day in my life and especially on evening's like this when I have a few more than my normal quota, and my wife looks at me like a tigress. But nevertheless I still manage to put one away for the road. But domestic secrets aside, my most nervous moment in life was when I walked in for my final Sandhurst interview with the Viceroy of India. On that day as I stood behind the huge door waiting to be marched in, I was thoroughly confused as to how I should address His Excellency, and before I could ask anybody the great door swung open.and I entered the majestic room with my knees shaking. I tried to confidently march across the acres of thick soft carpets and on reaching the appointed place I also managed to click my heels sharply. And there in the centre of that big palatial room and in a great big chair sat the Viceroy and immediately behind him and on both sides stood a phlanx of other senior British officers. While I kept standing at attention, Viceroy Reading first looked at the paper that was placed in front of him and then looking me straight in the face said, "You're Thimayya?" For the next few seconds I was totally confused and I did not know on how to respond and wondered how I should address the Viceroy. Initially I thought I should say Yes My Lord, or rather Milord as the Englishman normally address a judge in a court room. But then some others had blundered earlier by addressing him as "Our Lord" or "Good Lord" and one even went one better with " Oh Lord." Finally I decided to delete the word lord altogether and said simply "Yes Sir.' And when I noticed the smile on Lord Reading's face I knew I had crossed my first hurdle successfully and thereafter it was plain smooth sailing. The interview with the Viceroy did last for about 10 minutes and his parting comment was.

'I hope you enjoy Sandhurst.' But that did not register in my dull brain at that moment till I walked out of that door and was greeted by my British guardian officer who offered me a glass of port wine to celebrate my success and that was the second time in my young life that I tasted an alcoholic drink. The first one was thanks to Colonel Houghton who had offered me a Tom Collins cocktail at his residence since four others and I had successfully passed the open written examination for Sandhurst which was held at Simla,' added Timmy.

When dinner was announced and unaware that Colonel Attiqur Rehman was a Pathan, one of the Indian invitees a junior Bengali officer from the civil service department who had only recently been posted to Quetta as an engineer joined Timmy and Attiqur for one last drink at the bar.

'But tell me is it true that the Pathans of the North West Frontier are extremely fond of boys because so I have been told,' said the Bengali gentleman as he clinked glasses with the senior medico Colonel Attiqur. Without disclosing that he himself was a Pathan, Colonel Attiqur in all seriousness said.

'Yes that is bloody well true and you better be careful youngman for the saying goes that for a Pathan, the woman is for business, a boy for pleasure and a goat for choice.'

When Timmy heard that he just could not help laughing and then very sportingly added. 'Yes there is even a very popular Pathan song. It is called "Zakhme Dil" or "Wounded Heart" and the song begins with the words "There is a boy across the river with a bottom like a peach, but alas I cannot swim."

'How very right you are and mind you during one of the attacks by the 40th Pathans at Flanders during the First World War I heard their pipe band playing this very song and it did raise their morale sky high as they routed the Germans that day,' said Colonel Attiqur Rehman. Then as a passing shot to the hapless young Bengali, Attiqur squeezed his hand and said. 'Incidently I am a hardcore Pathan too, but don't worry you are safe.' On hearing that the poor Bengali did not know where to look as he apologised profusely to Attiqur and to his host.'

'Well in that case lets all do the bottoms up and I do not mean it literally,' said Attiqur as he gulped down his whisky and went for his dinner. Surprisingly though Quetta was in the midst of the long Indian hot summer, strangely that night it was unusually cold as the Rehmans made their way back to their house.

'I do not know why this sudden change in weather, and in order that none of us catch a cold and fall sick, I suggest we all sleep indoors tonight. Moreover both of you Don Juan's will have to leave for your units very early tomorrow morning and both of you should therefore go to sleep straight away. And in any case it is already well passed midnight,'added Attiqur while wishing everyone a very good night.

That night because of the sudden change in weather, most of the inhabitants of Quetta slept indoors and had no idea what was in store for them. Quetta was the Aldershot of India and the biggest garrison station of the British Empire. Besides a regular Brigade stationed there, the Defence Services Staff College too was located in that very cantonment and there was no dearth of good social life during that part of the year. There were polo weeks, tennis tournaments, hunts, cricket matches, club nights, whist drives, bumper bingo evenings followed by dances.

Both Gul Rehman and Ismail Sikandar having enjoyed each others company for nearly a week were now feeling sad since they would have to go back to the daily grind of regimental duties and for which they would have to catch the train early next morning. Therefore that night after the party at the Thimmaiyas was over, both of them while lying in bed and having switched off the lights kept talking to each other. They also nostalgically recalled those happy carefree days as young boys at Dehradun and the lovely holiday that they had spent together in Calcutta a few years ago. Ultimately when the topic centered around the Pugsley family and the two young and pretty Pugsley sisters Sandra and Debbie, Gul Rehman having loosened his pyjamas in advance said.

'Arre Saala tu kuch bhi bol yaar, dono bahenon iitni choti umar mein bhi bahut hi khoobsorat cheez thi, aur aab shayed dono hoor bangayen honge. (Bloody hell whatever you may say, but both the sisters even at such a young age were real stunning beauties and by now I am sure both of then must be like beautiful teenage fairy queens.)

'And even their mother the voluptous, Aunty Laila in spite of having produced five children she too was very sexy and a good looker too. Wasn't she!?

'Yes undoubtedly so, and both the mother and the two daughters must be now painting the small town of Mhow red,' said Ismail, when he suddenly felt that the bed was shaking a bit under him. At first he thought that Gul Rehman probably was on one of his solo flight of fancy missions and was jerking himself off. But when Gul Rehman suddenly jumped out of the bed and raised an alarm, Ismail realised that it was an earthquake. And he knew it for sure, because as a child he had often felt such tremors in Gilgit. As he too jumped out of the bed, he could still feel the strong tremors. Therefore without wasting any more time, they both ran to the adjoining room where Arif, Aftab and Shenaz were sleeping and having woken them up they all ran quickly outside.

It was just after past 3 am on that morning of the 31st of May, 1935, when the earthquake struck and luckily both Gul Rehman and Ismail Sikandar Khan were wide awake. Colonel Attiqur Rehman standing on the lawns of his big bunglow with all the members of his family thanked Allah, and when he checked the time on his wrist watch by shining the torch on it, the time was about five minutes past three in the morning. Luckily they were all still alive and the bungalow surprisingly was still standing. Exactly at 3.03 AM at that unearthly hour of the morning, when the people of Quetta were deep in their sleep, the massive earthquake had struck the city, and within a minute or two practically the entire city was flattened. But by some fate of luck and inspite of the fact that the epicentre of the terrible earthquake was not very far from Quetta, the seismic waves had mercifully spared the cantonment area of the city where the military and the civil lines were located and it had escaped the wrath with only minor damages. The earthquake was so great in magnitude that the tremors were felt even as far away as the city of Agra which was some 400 miles away from Quetta as the crow flies. After about five minutes, when the tremors had finally subsided, Colonel Attiqur Rehman with the two young subalterns went inside the bungalow to fetch some warm clothing for the family. He then got into his uniform and with Gul Rehman and Ismail Sikandar in tow all of them rushed to the Military hospital. Luckily there was not much of physical damage to the hospital, but physcologically the patients inside and especially those who were completely bedridden, for them it was a traumatic experience as the two young subalterns with the other staff members either carried or wheeled them out into the open.

Within half an hour from that terrible moment, when the earthquake struck, Major General Henry Karlslake the Quetta Military Station Commander and the Commandant of the Defence Sevices Staff College was on the scene to formulate and execute the massive rescue operations that he was about to face with. He was once an ADC to His Majesty King George the Vth, the reigning monarch and was witness to the cool manner in which the King reacted to such cataclysmic situations that were many in the vast

British Empire. The General was a gunner by profession and a Frontier specialist too. To assist him ably was Bunch Parsons the British Resident in Waziristan. An ex Sandhurst graduate Bunch too had served in the Scouts and in the Frontier as a political officer for nearly two decades and spoke near perfect Pashtu in several dialects. A highly informal person both in dress and manner Bunch Parsons had a complete distaste for pomp and show. On occasions when a red carpet was laid out for him, Bunch Parsons would purposely walk in the dust alongside it. If some junior officer addressed him as Sir, he would give him a look of disapproval and then add "Please cut out the honorifics."

By the time the Sun came up on that terrible morning, the mobile patrols sent earlier by General Karlslake to assess the damage had reported back to him. The damage was mild boggling as far as the civilians and the city was concerned and General Karlslake immediately declared an emergency and the entire Quetta garrison including the student officers and the directing staff of the Quetta Staff College were mobilized for the rescue operations. It was already daylight, and while the mobilization was still in progress, hordes of well armed Afghan tribesmen from the nearby villages and hills descended on the city to loot and plunder. They did not even spare the dead, not even the women and children as they mercilessly hacked off their limbs for a few pieces of gold and silver ornaments. Seeing the situation, General Karlslake immediately declared martial law and ordered the troops to shoot at sight at such miscreants. Ordering Bunch Parsons to take over all relief operations, General Karlslake set up his own headquarters at the Quetta Race Course where a gigantic tented refugee camp was about to come up.

In order to evacuate the wounded and bury the dead, complete labour companies and battalions were organised from the officers and troops in the station. Irrespective of the fact whether they were Hindus, Muslims, Sikhs or Christians, all these officers and soldiers worked shoulder to shoulder rescuing people from the rubble and disposing of the dead. For the next few days they not only worked side by side but even ate out of the same plates and dishes. Both the young subalterns, Gul Rehman and Ismail Sikandar voluntarily did their bit too as they physically laboured with the troops to rescue people who were trapped under the debris. Setting an example to the others they even physically lifted the decaying dead corpses and put them into the wheel barrows for final disposal. It was immaterial to both of them to what creed; colour or religion the dead man belonged to.

Timmy with his wife Nina had converted their own bungalow into a medical rehabilitation centre cum mini hospital and so did the Atttiqur Rehmans. Both Nina Thimmaiya and Nafisa Rehman worked relentlessly and without rest for the next 96 hours thereby saving as many lives as possible. For their gallant humanitarian services both were later awarded the Kaiser-e-Hind medal of honour.For the nexl seven days, the city of Quetta was practically cut off from the rest of the world. It was one of the worst natural disasters of the 20th century that took away more than 20,000 lives. The casualties would have been much higher if an epidemic had broken out, but.thanks to General Henry Karlslake and his team of dedicated staff officers which also included Colonel Bernard Law Montgomery, the son of priest who had just finished command of the 1st Warwickshires at Poona and who was now an instructor in Staff College, that disaster had been avoided. The disaster management team not only had successfully planned the relief operations, but they also executed them very efficiently, and for General Karlslake and his dedicated team of officers and staff it was probably their finest hour.

During those difficult days of relief work at Quetta another young British Officer, also a son of a priest and who was born in Mussoorie in the foothills of the Himalayas had also set an example to the others. Lieutenant John Guise Cowley from the Corps of Royal Engineers with his party of Sappers was the first to start the relief work at the Civil Hospital where the walls of all the wards had collapsed and the roof had fallen on top of the unfortunate patients. As his men with a Herculean effort raised a part of the roof for short periods of time, Lt Cowley crawled under it and dragged out many survivors who were trapped below the debris. Regardless of the warning that they were all patients in the hospital and that some of them were suffering from serious contagious diseases, and that some were even lepers, the gallant young officer truly demonstrated to his men and his superiors that he was indeed a true Catholic and a man of God.

It was only three weeks earlier on the 6th of May that the King Emperor celebrated 25 years on the throne. It was the silver jubilee year of his reign and despite his weak health the King and the Queen attended all the ceremonies. A few months earlier there had been a sharp renewal of the King's bronchial problem. A problem that it seemed he had inherited from his late father. On the morning of the 31st of May, the King was playing with his two favourite and lovely grand children Lilibet and Margaret when the news about the severe earthquake at Quetta was conveyed to him. He immediately asked the Secretary of State for India to convey his deep felt grief and condolences to the bereaved people of Quetta, while at the same time directed the Viceroy to spare no effort in organising the relief work.

It was only in the first week of June that Ismail Sikandar Khan and Gul Rehman reported back to their respective units. One day Ismail was surprised, when he was told by his Commanding Officer that the Commander Peshawar Brigade would interview him the next morning. Having ensured that his turn out was meticulous, Ismail Sikandar waited outside the Brigade Commander's office waiting for his turn to be marched in.

The name plate on the board read Brigadier CJE Auchinleck. OBE When the Brigade Major, Major CH Boucher from the 2/3rd Gurkha Rifles marched him in, Ismail clicked his heels and saluted smartly.

'Do sit down and lett me first congratulate you young man on your valuable contribution to the relief effort at Quetta which has been brought to my notice by Major General Karlslake. And it only proves that you are a worthy son of your late father and you will someday I am sure will live up to his excellent reputation and bring greater glory to the 2nd Punjabees. I am myself from the Punjabees and commanded the First First not very many years ago, and I am also very proud of them. Incidently it was I who as the recruiting officer at Jhelum had recruited that gallant soldier, your late father Curzon Sikandar Khan and though he is physically not with us today but his spirit always remains in our blood,' said the tall well built Brigade Commander with a big smile on his face.

Ismail Sikandar Khan was not aware of this fact and felt very proud that the man who recruited his father was none other than "The Auk" himself, his own Brigade Commander. That evening he was even invited for a drink with the oldman. A few days later the Peshawar Brigade under Auk was successfully conducting the "Mohmand Operations" against the Pathans of the Khyber and 2/L Ismail Sikandar Khan lived up to the expectations of his Brigade Commander, when he successfully led a platoon attack against the fanatic Pathans of that area.During the operation Ismail Sikander Khan came across a very fine English gentleman by the name of AJ Dring who was once a Piffer himself, but was now in the Frontier Political Service. During the Khudai Khidmatgar movement he was posted at Charsadda and he had some very interesting stories to tell regarding his transformation from an ex Sandhurst military officer into the not so heaven born Indian Political Service.

'And let me tell you it was no cake walk son,' said Dring as the liveried mess waiter brought in the first round of drinks. To begin with I had to bloody well pass a series of damn examinations, which also included some stupid subjects like the Indian Penal Code referred to in short as the IPC, the revenue law, the civil procedure code, treasury regulations, and even the excise law. Once I was through with all that I had to undergo secretariat training and pass another departmental test in the history and background of the State or the region that I was to be posted to. And that is not all. I even had to learn the art of rapidly enciphering and deciphering coded messages and documents. All this took a lot of time and it was only after three years of service and slogging as a probationer that I finally became a full fledged member of the service that I am now in. And to further top it all I even had to spend from my own damn pocket for this evening tail coat with the dark blue cuffs which is our our mess dress,' added Dring as he walked up to the bar for a refill.

While Dring was busy at the bar, a handsome Indian gentleman who was also dressed in the mess kit of a political officer said.

'Sir may I have the pleasure of raising a toast to the gallant officers and men of the Peshawar Brigade for the success of the Mohmand Operations.'

'Yes you may, but before you do that Mr Iskandar Mirza let me introduce you to those who may not know you at all,' said Dring as he called for another round of drinks for everybody.

'Gentlemen Iskandar Mirza like me was also and not very long ago in the Indian army. He is from a well to do feudal family of Bengal and one of the previleged few who was selected and got his Kings commission after attending the special course at the Daly College at Indore. Incidently his friend and colleague Major K C Carriappa is today the Brigade Major of the Kojak Brigade in Waziristan where I also started my second life as an Assistant Political Officer. But Iskandar hasn't done too badly either. I have also been told that Iskandar had once very cleverly managed to disburse an angry tribal mob by simply inviting all the tribal Chiefs and Maliks to some exquisite refreshments in his office. The Maliks were not aware that those special sweets had been cleverly laced with a medicine that invariably made all those who relished it to run to the damn loo and that was the end of the Jirga that day and believe you me gentlemen it was one helleva achievement under those murderous circumstances for a young Indian Muslim and that too a non Pathan.

'Three cheers for Mr Mirza.' said an excited Ismail Sikandar Khan as he walked up to the elegant and charming Assistant Political Officer and introduced himself.

'But tell me Sir is the job of a Political Officer serving in the Frontier really dangerous?.'

' Yes in a way it is, but it is not as dangerous or risky for those like you in military uniform. And if you can speak their language, respect their customs and don't interfere in their personal lives, then there is really nothing to fear. Sometimes they do come up with ridiculous demands, but if you are well versed with Pashtu then you can with a little persuasion talk them out of it. Nontheless, one has to tow a very fine diplomatic line while handling a Jirga and one has also to be very tactful while dealing with them. In other words if an agreement on the demands of the Maliks and the tribal chiefs cannot be reached with honour, then some bargaining is required to be done and a compromise has to be reached, and that to without making them feel small. The Pathan is a very sensitive and a very proud human being and to reach that stage of mutual respect and understanding one is required to have a lot a patience,' said Iskandar Mirza.

'Yes and besides that we have also to keep our eyes and ears open all the time and cultivate reliable sources in order to expand our intelligence network in this very highly sensitive and strategic area of the British Empire. In brief gentlemen it is all about personal contacts, a friendly approach and a thorough knowledge of the tribes, their many customs and the terrain in this God forsaken land. And as far as possible one should avoid the use of military force because the Pathans are on both sides of the Durand Line and they are not dumb either. They are clever fighters too,' said Mr Dring while raising a toast to the high fighting qualities of the tribesmen in the North West Frontier.

On the 1st of August 1935, when the Gilgit Agency was formally handed over to the British on a long 60 years lease by the Maharaja of Kashmir and the news was reported in all the leading English newspapers the next day, Debu Ghosh in Calcutta was surprised.

'This is typical of the British policy to give with one hand and take away with the other. On the one hand they give us hope of self rule by proclaiming the Government of India Act 1935, and now at the same time in order to secure their own territorial interest in India, they have very conveniently and cleverly forced the Maharaja of Kashmir to sign the long lease deed over Gilgit,' said Debu Ghosh to his friends Naren and Ghulam Hussein, when they met for their routine weekend coffee session at the College Street coffee house.

'It could also be a fall out of the recent troubles in the valley between the Muslims and their Hindu Raja, and maybr the British are conveniently taking advantage of it,'said Naren Sen.

'Or maybe the Maharaja for the safety of his own self and his kingdom needs the Britishers too,' said Ghulam Hussein.

'Well whatever it is, the fact still remains that the Government of India Act passed by the British recently is only applicable to the 11 Provinces that are ruled and governed by them and not to the Princely States. And if India has to attain full and complete freedom then the 500 odd princely states and kingdoms which form very much a part of our land mass they too must fall in line and there is no denying the fact that Kashmir is one of the biggest or maybe the biggest area wise, and it is also the one which is most strategically located,' said Debu Ghosh.

'I think we should leave all this to the Indian National Congress and our politicians, and therefore now let us talk about something more stimulating and interesting,' said Dr Ghulam Hussein as he called for another round of coffee.

'Well I do know that coffee does stimulate and as a keen student of modern world history let me also tell you gentlemen that during the past one year or so far more exciting things have been happening in this world and specially in Europe, and this could lead to a very serious and grave situation in the not too distant future,' said Debu Ghosh.

'In that case and with your wide knowledge about international affairs, why don't you elaborate a little more and educate and enlighten us too,' said Naren Sen as he took a puff from Debu's cigarette. Having gathered his thoughts, Debu Ghosh began chronologically.

'Well to start off with, on the 30th of June 1934 it was the 'Night of the Long Knives' in Nazi Germany and on that night that madman of Germany who is known as Hitler had 77 of his own people both friends and foes executed because he simply did not trust them. Then four months later on 10th September, King Alexander of Yugoslavia while on a state visit to France was assassinated by a Croation. Early in January last year, Sergei Kirov a close associate of Marshall Stalin was assassinated and this led to a massive purge in the Communist Party of Russia and to the elimination of leaders like Zinoviev and Kamenev. Consequently a very large number of them who were anti Stalin were sent to the many concentration camps in Siberia. And immediately to our north and not far away from the Indo-Chinese border, Comrade Mao Tse Dung, the leader of the Chinese Communist Party in October had to perforce set off with his followers for his long march in order to regroup, so that he and his men could fight the Koumingtang Army of Chiang Kai Shek another day. Early this year on the 13th of January 1935, and as per the Treaty of Versailles a plebiscite was held in the Saar Region of

Europe and where the people were given the option to either join France or Germany and 90% of them voted in favour of unification with Germany. This resulted in the German Reich under Hitler expanding for the first time territorially. In fact on the 16th of March, Hitler had the audacity to announce to his people and the world that he was abrogating those clauses of the Versailles Treaty that limited the size and weapons of the German Forces. Moreover, Hitler and his Nazi Party have off late also been actively advocating for the territorial expansion of the Third Reich. Therefore gentlemen all these are indicative of what the future may hold both for the world and for us in India and to me personally it looks rather very ominous. And since India is the Empire's biggest and fattest milch cow, and in case there is another world war then the British I am sure will not be foolish enough to give us our freedom so very easily,' said Debu Ghosh as he took one last drag of his cigarette before stubbing it off.

'By Jove you should have become a damn professor of modern history than a stupid lawyer and that too with out a brief,' said Dr Ghulam Hussein jokingly.

On the very day that the Maharaja of Kashmir formally handed over the Gilgit Agency to the British, and which would now become the sole authority to administer and defend this strategic area, the British Resident in Srinagar threw a grand party. That night at Peshawar Mr John Dring in order to reciprocate the hospitality of Brigadier Auk the Commander of the Peshawar Brigade invited him and his staff for dinner to his house. Since Colonel Reginald Edwards was also in station, he and the young 2/Lt Ismail Sikandar Khan had also been cordially invited. And it was only at that party that Ismail Sikandar Khan became aware of the new status of Gilgit, his own home town, when the senior British officers with a drink in their hand started discussing the pros and cons of the Government's decision.

'Well Sir let me tell you that the people of that area are not a homogeneous lot and like the Frontier people here, they too love their independence,' said Ismal Sikandar Khan.

'Yes and the young man is dead right because he and his forefathers are from that very area and I have also served in that desolate region,' added Reggie.

The host, Mr Dring sensing that the topic was not conducive for a happy jovial evening therefore quickly changed it to a personal monologue of his experiences as a young Political Officer.

'You all may not believe it, but in our service too there is also a lot of 'Yes Sir' and 'No Sir' and as a new inductee I was more like a glorified ADC to the Resident. My sole job was to carry out all his orders and that also included organizing a sit down dinner for his guests. But it was only he and he alone as the Resident who decided who should be invited and and who should not be, and what should be the menu. My only damn job was to ensure that the invitations were sent in time, the RSVP's received and to arrange the seating plan. And making the seating plan was quite an exercise by itself and at times it could also be very complicated and mind boggling if you did not know who was senior to whom or who was not getting along with X, Y or Z, and who was having an affair with whom in the station and so on and so forth. And woe to the Political Assistant if he got it wrong,' said Dring as he poured himself another small skotch.

'But Sir what did you mean by getting it wrong,' asked Ismail Sikandar Khan innocently.

'Well if one knew that so and so lady was not pulling along well with another lady and protocol wise their dear husbands were in the same bracket, then it would be damn well stupid and foolish to have the husband of one seated next to the wife of the other. Similarly if you knew that Mr X a bachelor was sleeping with Mrs Y and it was also the talk of the town, then it would be criminal to have then seated next to one another also. And God forbid if you inadvertently made such fatal mistakes then it would surely ruin the whole damn party, and you would be the one to face the wrath of the old man next morning,' said Dring.

'Good Lord and in such a case it would be even criminal to make them sit across the table facing each other because that would give them an opportunity to play footsie under the table', said Major Boucher the Brigade Major in good humour.

'And Sir what was the menu like on such sit down formal dinners,' asked Ismail Sikandar Khan.

'Initially I really didn't know because it was all transalated into French and that too from a special little book that was provided only for this very purpose. Thereafter it was sent to the appointed printing press where they were printed with bold gold lettering and placed into the silver menu cards on the dining table. Nevertheless, the food on that day was definitely a lot more appetising than what we were generally served with day in and day out by the khansama, the local Indian cook and who like all good cooks was very very moody and temperamental,' said Dring when the butler came in and announced that dinner was ready. The Politicals and the Heaven born were not to be left behind as far as bullshit was concerned and it was quite evident on the dining table too. The exquisite rosewood dining table was laid with official fine china crockery and shining silver cutlery and every piece was smugly embossed with the motto of the erstwhile East India Company "Heaven's Light our Guide." 2/Lt Ismail Sikandar Khan being the junior most invitee on scrutinizing the seating plan that was prominently displayed on a board outside the entrance to the dining room quietly made his way to the far end of the table. He had also been nominated as the Vice for the formal dinner that evening. Mr Dring always a good host was in great mood as he narrated some of the hilarious faux pas and anecdotes by some of the young Politicals in service.

'Well there was one over enthusiastic Political Assistant who had only recently started his life and career in the Political Department, when it was abruptly cut short because of a simple spelling error that was unintentionally made by him. He was from the ex Poona Horse, a fine cavalry regiment of the Indian Army and had only recently been posted as the Political Assistant to our Resident in Rajputana. One day, when he was asked to send an invitation to one Miss Hoare, he inadvertently spelt it with a;'W" and that too incorrectly and the lady was livid and she complained to the Resident. The Political Assistant was summoned and when he replied that he knew no other way of spelling it., he was immediately shown the door,' said Dring as the soup was served.

'How about telling us about the rules of accepting gifts,' said Reggie.

'Well though the rule is amply clear and forbids the acceptance of any gift from the rulers of the princely states or from influential civilians like the contractors etc, but there were certain occasions when you could accept and these were on certain specified festival days only. Even on such occassions also you could only accept a basket of fruits, vegetables and sweets, but that too in limited quantities only. And in case any other gift was sent with that basket, then one was required to politely return it back to the sender and without offending the person concerned. And if that also could not be done or be avoided diplomatically, then the same as per rules had to be deposited into the general pool and a return gift of the same value was picked up from the many in the same pool and had to be sent back to the generous giver. However, there was an interesting case in the not to distant past, when a ruler of a fairly well to do princely state presented to the newly posted Resident with the usual basket of fruits for Christmas. The Resident who had a weakness for plums and the delicious apricots while delving deep into the beautifully decorated wicker work basket for more was simply horrified to find 100 gold mohurs at the bottom of it. Furious at being offered a bribe, he wrote an angry letter to the ruler admonishing him for the indiscretion. When the concerned ruler received the letter he simply replied.

'Sir, I have checked my own records and have found that it was customary to give a 100 gold mohurs to the honoured resident on every Christmas. However if that is not considered good enough, then the Resident may please indicate what and how much is considered as suitable.'

'The Resident was appalled with the reply and he immediately ordered an in house investigation. To his surprise he found that what the Maharaja said was in fact correct but it was the Residents retinue of servants who would quietly and conveniently pocket the year ending windfall,' added Dring.as the main course was served to the guests.'

'But let me also tell you that everything was not so honky dory as far as Vicerene Lady Wellingdon was concerned. She was a very shrewd woman and knew how to get around the rulers. She therefore did not strictly adhere to the laid down rules, while giving the excuse that she was the one who was instrumental in influencing the rulers to handsomely contribute to the welfare of his own people by building schools, hospitals, training and welfare centres for women etc etc. On one occasion, when she was asked by a well to do ruler as to what gift would she and the Viceroy prefer for Christmas, the first lady without batting an eyelid said.'Oh His Excellency I am sure would like a golf set, and as far as I am concerned I would love an emerald necklace.'.

'Well you seem to know quite a few secrets about the Wellingdons,' said Reggie.

'Yes and why not. After all I was once summoned for an interview to the Viceregal Palace for the post of Assistant Private Secetary to His Excellency and since it was on very short notice and I had just arrived from the Frontier, I did not even have time to get myself a new decent suit stiched for myself. So I conveniently borrowed one from one of his ADC's, but lo and behold Lady Wellingdon who always a very sharp eye had caught me red handed. And as soon as I was introduced to her, she gave me one look and simply said. "Young man I see you have Cecil's suit on,' and believe you me I did not know where to look. But though she was tough, she was also considerate, thoughtful and a kind lady. But her biggest handicap was that she was a big bully and could be very demanding too,' said Dring as the main course of chicken a la Kiev with boiled vegetables was served by the smartly liveried turbaned waiters.

' But tell me how did the Viceroy tolerate all this,' asked Reggie.

'I guess he had no choice and when at times he found that Her Excellency was becoming a bit too over demanding, then all he did was to comfort himself with half a bottle of champagne by mid morning,' said Dring as Ismail Sikandar Khan hearing that burst out laughing and said.

'Then in that case the poor ADC'c must have had a very tough time coping with her.'

'Yes you are dead right young man. Most of the time they were all exasperated with her many demands, and so was the Viceroy who in such situations would sometimes barge into the ADCs room for a chat with them. And one day, when the Viceroy unintentionally overheard one of the ADC's telling the other.

'Bloody hell I cannot take her any longer and I am therefore requesting for a posting back to my regiment,' the Viceroy on hearing that simply retorted by saying.

.'Well son you atleast have a choice, but I don't have a regiment to go back to.'

'And as a result of that witty comment by the Viceroy, the young ADC who only a few seconds ago was venting his anger against the first lady of India was himself in splits of laughter and the Viceroy very sportingly called for some champagne for them too.'

When it was turn for the dessert to be served, Ismail read the gold lettering on the menu card. The menu card neatly written and elegantly displayed in a small silver frame on the table was written in French and Ismail could make no head or tail out of it. But when it was served it was none other than his favourite tipsy pudding. While waiting for the service to be over and for the toasts to begin Ismail Sikandar Khan said.

'Sir I believe that big game hunting is quite a sport with the Viceroys of India and it is I believe quite an event whenever it is organised. But isn't it dangerous. Afterall the Viceroy is the King's representative in India and he should not take any chances and risk his life hunting tigers and other such wild big game.'

'No on the contrary, It is not dangerous at all and big game hunting is considered to be a status symbol for the high and mighty, and this also gives the Maharajas and Rajas who organize it an opportunity to become a little more familiar with the Viceroy. And more often than not the hunt is also very cleverly stage managed, and that too with the full connivance of the British Resident of that princely state. Afterall he has to also justify his existence and he therefore has to also ensure that the Viceroy does not go back without bagging the largest animal,' said Dring.

'But how is it stage managed,' asked Ismail.

'Now let's take for example the tiger hunt and for which the Viceroy has been invited. A day or two before the arrival of the Viceroy, the well briefed beating parties are sent out deep into the jungle. And once the tiger is tracked and cornered by the beaters, the host conveniently ensures that the Viceroy is given the pride of place in the best machan.Thereafter it is was for the beaters to bloody well ensure that the tiger moves only in the direction of the Viceroy's machan, and when the tiger is in the killing field the Viceroy is told to fire first and this is immediately followed by a volley from a dozen or so double barrelled 12 bore guns of the other good shikaris taking part in the hunt. The poor tiger therefore has no chance at all and kicks the bucket immediately. With a dozen or more hits on the unfortunate animal it becomes therefore axiomatic that the first bullet had been that of the Viceroy and therefore it automatically goes into his bag," added Dring as he lightly tapped the small silver gong on the table with the well polished small wooden hammer and raised a toast to His Majesty the King.When they all moved in for some cognac inside the drawing room, Reggie said.

'But all the same John, though you too were once in an army uniform the fact is the Political Officer is still a shade below the heaven born ICS officer who having done his apprenticeship in a remote district normally gets posted to a privileged appointment in one of the many neatly laid out military cantonments in this country, while the Political Officer has to rough it out in some remote part of the subcontinent'.

'Yes and not only that, the bloody ICS man then comfortably settles down in a sprawling bungalow in the prestigious civil lines area of the cantonment and he with his platoon of servants and helpers then starts calling all the bloody shots. And every evening after a game of tennis, squash, or badmington or whatever the exclusive whiteman's club has to offer for exercise, the heaven born leisurely take his bath, gets dressed in his evening clothes and thereafter setlles down comfortably in one of those long easy chairs either in the veranda or on the well manicured lawns and gives the "Koi Hai." On hearing that 'Koi Hai' and the Bada Sahibs familiar voice, the liveried head waiter with a big turban on his head then quickly serves him his first sundowner for the evening. Then with a drink in his hand he either plays a game of billiards, or a rubber or two of bridge or browses through books and periodicals in the library and if he is the extra social type then he joins the others in the bar and they all talk about good old Blighty,' said Dring as he helped himself to another small Napoleon cognac.

'Well whatever one may say, but they also work hard for their living and it gets even harder when they they have to visit the many remote villages under their jurisdiction. Sometimes on these extended tours and in the heat of the Indian summer they too literally sweat it out. And it is certainly not a joyride for them when they have to travel cuddled up in their small dhoolies and they have to keep listening to the dhoolie bearers chanting their never ending well syncronised "Hun Hunnas". Yes when they get back from these tours then these heaven born really let their hair down and especially on Sundays and holidays when they enjoy a round of good golf at the local Golf Course and follow it up with some chilled beer and a sumptous lunch. Incidently the game of golf which originated in England and was established in 1754 at the Royal and Ancient Golf club at St Andrews has now indeed become very popular after the world's second golf course was set up in the Empire's second city of Calcutta in the last century and that was way back in 1829. And in India if you have not played at the RCGC, the Royal Calcutta Golf Club located in the lovely wooded Tollygunge area of the city then you have not played golf at all. There on that course I have seen Golfers carrying with pride their own golf bags for the simple reason that their golf bags were especially made from the long penis of the elephant that they had themselves shot and that was considered the ultimate for the golfer,' said Reggie.

"My God and how I wish I could be in their shoes,' said one of the young British officers from the Brigade staff. On hearing that remark coming from one of his own staff, Auk who loved his soldiering commented somewhat little sarcastically.'Gentlemen first learn to deserve and then desire.'

As the year 1935 came to a close, the King's health with his chronic bronchial problem progressively kept deteriorating, and with the New Year approaching it only got worse. The advent of 1936 wasn't a happy new year for the royal family as the King lay sick in bed and on the 17th of January the King with his hands trembling made the last entry into his diary. The hand writing was practically illegible as he struggled to complete the last sentence and in which he wrote.

'"A little snow and wind, Dawson arrived this evening. I saw him and feel rotten." After that last entry that was made in his own handwriting, he requested his wife the loving Queen to write the diary on his behalf everyday and till he was alive, and she did it religiously. But she only had to write it for the next three days. By the afternoon of the 20th of January the King's condition became very serious and every one and even the King knew that death wasn't very far away. That night at 9.25 PM, Lord Dawson drafted the last bulletin on his Majesty's condition that would inform the world and the people of the British Empire that no hope remained.'The Monarchs life he wrote is moving peacefully to its close.'

That evening on hearing the King's condition over the radio, in India his subjects both Indians and Europeans prayed for his recovery, but it was already a bit too late. As the King's life slowly ebbed away from his body, his near and dear ones standing by his bed with folded hands prayed to God to work a miracle, but that miracle never occurred and at 11:.55 that night the King passed away. On that day too the final entry in the Kings diary was made by the grieving but brave Queen Mary. In her own hand writing she wrote. 'My dearest husband, King George Vth, was much distressed at his own bad hand writing to the entries till the 17th of January and begged me to write his diary for him till he was alive. He passed away on 20th January at five minutes to midnight.'

No sooner had the King died the calm but broken hearted Queen took her eldest son's hand and kissed it. Edward had now become the King, but he too broke down and cried like a child. The forty year old monarch still a bachelor became hysterical, cried loudly and kept on embracing his mother. It was however early in the morning of the next day, when India awoke to the sad news.

In the morning after the death of his father, the new King with his younger brother the Duke of York flew to London. It was an historic flight because it was the first time that a British Monarch had flown in an aircraft. The next day the Garter King of Arms at St James Palace as per the tradition proclaimed him King Edward the VIIIth, while his lady love Mrs Wallis Simpson viewed the ceremony from a nearby window. The King was first introduced to her in early January 1931 by none other than Lady Thelma Furness when they met at her country house near Melton Mowbray. As the then Prince of Wales and the Empire's most eligible bachelor he was alleged to be having an affair with Thelma. Earlier to her it was Mrs Freda Dudley Ward and now it was Mrs Wallis Simpson, an American lady who was twice married and once divorced.

Born Wallis Warfield on 19th June 1898, she was only two years younger to the King. Her first marriage to Win Spencer a handsome American naval officer did not last very long and soon ended in a divorce. A decade later in July 1928, she married Ernest Simpson a man with an English father and an American mother who had served for a brief period with the Coldstream Guards, but was now in the family shipping business and they had settled down in London. Though still married, her relationship with the future

King was therefore always viewed with disdain by the late King who virtually ignored her existence. It was all the more evident in November 1934, when the King struck her name off from the list of invitees for the evening party at Buckingham Palace which was being held in honour of the Duke of Kent's wedding. But thanks to the Prince of Wales and his younger brother, Wallis was very much present that evening much to the annoyance of the King. On the very next day the King gave orders to The Lord Chamber to ensure that Mrs Simpson was not invited to the Silver Jubilee function or to the Royal Enclosure at Ascot. On 31st December1935, during the New Year's Eve fancy dress ball at Melton where the theme was '1066' when the threesome of Mr and Mrs Simpson and the Prince of Wales all dressed up as pirates entered the hall, a whispering campaign followed. That evening, when Mr Simpson was seen nursing his drink in some far corner while his wife in the company of the Prince of Wales kept dancing away, it was quite evident that they were madly in love with each other.

And while the royal affair in England became the talk of the town, in February 1936, after his attachment with the 1st Somersets, 2/Lt Ismail Sikandar Khan reported to his parent unit the 2nd Punjabees, which was stationed at Barrackpore, near Calcutta. With his late father Naik Curzon Sikandar Khan revered as a hero of the Regiment, Ismail Sikandar Khan had little or no problems adjusting to the life in his own unit. Though it had a mixed composition of Punjabi Mussalmans, Dogras and Sikhs, Ismail Sikandar Khan felt completely at ease with the Dogra troops of his company to which he was now attached for training, and a few months later he could be heard conversing to them in their own Dogri language. With the British officers in command, the routine unit and mess life was no different from what he had experienced with the Somersets and that included the typical English mess food. Therefore for a change in his taste bud he would routinely visit the company cookhouse during the lunch hour and on the pretext of inspecting the hygiene standard of the cooks and the cook house, he would also taste the food in plentiful. A few months later the unit celebrated its raising day and Ismail Sikandar Khan got into the thick of it by organizing the various events. It was a two day celebration starting with a Pagal Gymkhana, the inter company hockey finals, a Bara Khana for the troops and a party in the officers mess.

For the Pagal Gymkhana the football field was converted into a 'Mela' ground and stalls had been put up by all the companies for games of skill and for eateries, and prizes were also earmarked for the best decorated stall in each of these categories. For the troops and their families there were games of skill and luck for all age groups. Starting from the lollipop race for the kids, there was the needle and thread race for the married soldiers and their wives, a three legged race for the bachelors or forced bachelors, breaking the chatty blind folded for the VCO's, the lemon and spoon race for their wives and a musical chair for the officers and their wives. After the games were over, and all the prizes had been distributed, the merry makers then descended on to the other stalls of skill like the lucky dip, shying the coconut, ringing the duck, shooting the balloon etc etc. To a limited extent even a bit of gambling with cards was also permitted on that day.To attract the crowd the Havildar or the Naik with his team of helpers manning the stall in the best of traditions would shout and shriek till their voices ran out. Some others who were not interested in gambling could be seen in groups of four under a tent playing cards with muted noises and they seemed to be driving great pleasure as they with full force hurled each card on to the mat. And at the end of the day when all the profits were counted, they were all handed over to the Battalion Subedar Major and it became a part of the unit's welfare fund.For the traditional Bara Khana in the evening, everyone including the officers with their families was required to share a common meal with the troops and their families. It was an evening of camaraderie as the officers mingled with the men and drank the potent triple x rum that was offered to them. During the Bara Khana, the unit drama party entertained everybody with their hilarious skits, songs and dances. Finally at the close of the entertainment programme, the officers joined the participants in doing the time honoured and vigorous Punjabi bhangra and the Pathan's Khattak dance.

It was only after two months of his reporting to the unit at Barrackpore that Ismail Sikandar Khan finally took a weekend off and made a trip to Calcutta. The outing basically was to renew his contacts with the Sen, Ghosh and the Hussein families. That day happened to be the 15th of April and the Bengali New Year's day, when Ismail Sikandar Khan with a box of Bengali sweets from the famous Darricks shop at Bhawanipore knocked on the door of Debu Ghosh's house on Lansdowne Road.

'Dhako Baba ke eshechey" (look Papa who has come) said a delighted 11 year old Mona Ghosh as she opened the door and ran inside to fetch her father.Born in 1925, Mona after her three elder brothers Arup, Swarup and Anup was the youngest member of the Ghosh family and needless to say being the only girl she was her father's favourite and thoroughly spoilt too.

'My God what a pleasant surprise,' said Debu Ghosh as he warmly hugged the young handsome army officer and asked.

'But where is your luggage young man, and I must say that you are bang on time for the celebrations. Because today on the auspicious Bengali New Year's Day my friend and dear brother-in-law Naren Sen is having his house warming party which will be preceded by a religious ceremony and we cannot afford to be late. He has built a new bungalow on Southern Avenue which is not very far from this place and you are coming with us right now. But first have a cup of tea and some refreshments and later after the lunch is over you will get back to your hotel and come back with your bag and baggage and that is an order,' said Debu Ghosh with a smile as little Mona came in with two cups of tea and a plateful of rosshogullas

' I must say our little Mona has really become a big girl now,' said Ismail Sikandar Khan as he lovingly squeezed her cheeks and presented her with the the box of Darrick's sweets. An excited Mona immediately ran back inside the kitchen and give it to her mother. While having his tea sitting in the well furnished but small drawing room of Debu Ghosh's apartment at 217, Lansdowne Road, when Ismail Sikandar Khan noticed the four framed photographs on the wall that had fresh garlands around them, he knew who they were, but kept quiet till Debu Ghosh himself opened the topic.

Well I guess old age has to ultimately catch up with all of us some day, but my father was not very old and he died of shock when he heard about my younger brother Hitu's death a few years ago, Six months later my poor mother died heart broken, and a year later both my in-laws at Dhaka passed away. Soon thereafter my brother-in-law Naren Sen too lost both his parents when the boat that was ferrying them from Belur Math to Dhakineswar capsized mid stream while it was crossing the Ganga during the Monsoon season. And within a few months of their passing away, my good friend Dr Ghulam Hussein also lost both his parents.And as the saying goes it never rains, but pours and therefore these past couple of years have been full of tragedies fo all of us. But nonetheless life must carry on I guess, because what is destined to happen will happen.Therefore as of now the first generation of our families have now gone into our family history books and now we from the second generation are left holding the flag,' said Debu Ghosh as his wife Hena walked in with a plate of that typical Bengali delicacy called 'Shondesh.'

'You will have to have atleast eat two because I have made them,' said Hena Ghosh as Ismail in true Bengali tradition and custom got up to touch her feet." "Thak thak Baba' (That is alright) said the lady of the house as she blessed Ismail with long life. That afternoon after the long religious ceremony by the high Brahmin priest that was primarily meant to keep away all evil spirits from Naren Sen's new house was finally over, and as per the local custom the select group of fat pot bellied so called high caste Brahmins, sat down as chief guests for an exclusive meal, for Ismail Sikandar Khan it was a kind of a new revelation. He could never imagine that one single person can consume so much of food at one sitting. The twelve high caste Brahmins seemed like professional eaters as they kept hogging and hogging till they could hog no more and all this was much to the delight of the host and the hostess who simply kept egging them to have more. Then as they got up one by one and kept belching away to glory, there was a sigh of relief on the face of the catering contractor. Apprehensive of the fact that he may run short of food, the caterer had very wisely kept the fire in the makeshift kitchen burning. And it was only when all the other guests had finished their meals and had been seen off by the host and the hostess, that the three old friends Debu Ghosh. Dr Ghulam Hussein and Naren Sen with their families sat down to enjoy their meal. While the fathers and sons were served on tables and benchess that were laid under an awning on the terrace, all the wives with their daughters enjoyed their food sitting on the matted floor in an enclosed room. As per tradition all the preparations which were far too many to count was served on big rectangular banana leaves and for Ismail Sikandar Khan this was a new kind of experience and he enjoyed it thoroughly. But what struck him the most was the manner and kindness with which the host and the hostess later served the poor people who had gathered outside their gate.

During the meal while sitting down with the rest of the boys Ismail Sikandar Khan had done a quick mental exercise to recollect all their names. The Ghosh family was the largest and their three sons Arup, Swarup and Anup were now 17, 15 and 13 years old respectively, while the only daughterl Mona was 11. The Sen Family too was not lagging far behind either. Their eldest son Samir was 18, Ronen was nearing 16 and their one and only daughter Purnima was 10. The Hussein family with just two children seemed quite satisfied with their size. Their only son Nawaz Hussein was now 17, while Hasina their only daughter had just celebrated her 10th birthday. Their total would have also been three, but in 1921 the Begum Sahiba lost her second son soon after he was born. The boy whom they had named Irfan only lived for a day.

That evening Ismail Sikandar Khan wrote a long letter to his friend Gul Rehman who was also now posted to his parent unit the First Punjabees at Jhelum. In that letter he described the big new house that Naren Uncle had built and also drew the family tree of all the three families that he now once again had the pleasure to meet. The names of those elders who were no more were lightly shaded in black. After he had put the letter into an envelope, he took out another piece of plain paper and drew a family tree of his own family and that of his dear friend Gul Rehman. As far as his own family was concerned there was none else but him and Colonel Reggie and as far as Gul Rehman was concerned he was now 22, his brothers Aftab and Arif were 18 and 16 respectively while their one and only sister Shenaz was 12 years old. Then he suddenly realized why should the Pugsley's be left out and when he calculated he found that the eldest Shaun was 24, the twin sisters Sandra and Debbie were 18, the second brother Richard was 15 and the youngest Veronica was 10 or 11 years old.

'My God Sandy is now an adult too' he thought to himself as he nostalgically remembered those lovely holidays in Calcutta not very many years ago.In end April 1936, Reggie visited Barrackpur.and stayed as a guest of Ismail Sikandar Khan and the 2nd Punjabees, the unit that he had commanded during the Great War. In his honour the Commanding Officer had organised a special durbar that was followed by the traditional 'Bara Khana" with the men.In his talk to the troops, Reggie highlighted the sacrifices made by the Indian soldiers of the battalion in the various battles during the Great War and he also made a special mention of the late Curzon Sikandar Khan, the proud winner of the Victoria Cross, the highest gallantry award of the British Empire.

With the 1936 Berlin Olympic Games scheduled to be held in Berlin during August, Colonel Reginald Edwards therefore decided to go on a long holiday to Europe. He was very keen to witness the games and more so the hockey competition, because that was the only event India was taking part in and the Captain of the Indian team was none other than the mercurial Dhyan Chand who was also from the Punjabees. Since Reggie was going to be away from India for the next six months, he had therefore come to Barrackpur to say goodbye to Ismail Sikandar Khan.

'Do write to me about the games on picture postcards,' said Ismail Sikandar Khan as they reached the Howrah railway station in the nick of time. The Bombay Mail via Nagpur was about to steam off as Reggie got inside his first class coupe. Early next morning, when the train halted at Bilaspur station, Reggie with a dressing gown over his night suit walked up to the A H Wheeler bookstall and there to his utter surprise he was greeted by Naren Sen. He was also travelling with his eldest son Samir on the same train and they were also going to Bombay.

'It is indeed a pleasant surprise to meet you again Sir, but I wish while you were in Barrackpur you should have come and spent some time with us in Calcutta as my guest now that I have my own house.'

'Never mind, that can wait for some other occasion and I only had a week at my disposal, but tell me where are you off too with your eldest son Samir.'

'I am going to London with him because I want him to complete his law from there and then join me as my junior,' said Naren Sen. Well then in that case for all you know we will all be on the same boat too,' said Reggie.

It was end of May 1936, when Naren Sen with his eldest son Samir reached London. Samir had little or no interest in becoming a lawyer and while in College in Calcutta he had come under the influence of the All India Student's Federation which had only recently been founded in India. And as a result of which he had also become an ardent admirer of the late Vladimr Ilych Lenin, the architect of the Great October Revolution in Russia. Besides his interest in the world communist movement and of the teachings of Karl Marx and Frederich Engels, his only other interest was in the game of cricket and in art. Without having any formal training he was quite good in making pencil portraits and those of Lenin, Marx and Engels made by him he proudly displayed in his room. In order to ensure that his son concentrated on his books Naren Sen had appointed an old friend of his in London as his son's legal guardian. The gentleman was a Bengali and he was working in India House.

The India House in London was built by Sir Herbert Baker, the same gentleman who was also the architect of the Parliament House in Delhi. Samir Sen was highly impressed as he entered the Indian High Commission building in Aldwych, London. The building was inaugurated by the late King George the Vth on 8th July 1930, when he opened the gate with a golden key. It was like a mini museum with works of art by four selected Bengali artists who had been commissioned after a very stiff competition in India, and then trained at the Royal College of Arts, London. The big murals at the entrance depicted the six seasons of India and these were done by Ranada Charan Ukil and Sudhanshu Sekhar Choudhury. The magnificent central dome with its richly coloured murals depicted the four epochs in the history of India from the time of Alexander the Great and the defeat of Porus to the reign of Akbar the Great who is shown discussing with his architect the plans for his new capital at Fatehpur Sikri. And the work of each epoch was done by each of the four Bengali artists that included, Lalit Mohan Sen from Lucknow, Ranada Ukil from Delhi, DK Deb Barma from

Shantiniketan and Sudhangshu Shekar Choudhary from Calcutta. There were a lot many more works of art in the various other rooms, but Samir Sen that day did not find time to see all of them. The credit for the selection of the themes typically Indian was that of Sir Atul Chatterjee who was from the 1896 ICS batch and who was Indian the High Commissioner in London from 1925 to 1931.

'But Mesho (Uncle) why don't you convince Baba that I would rather prefer being an artiste than a lawyer,' said Samir Sen as he touched Mr Sanyal's feet.

'That is entirely between your father and you my son, but let me also caution you young man that in this profession of painting and art money comes in rather slowly and till such time you establish yourself it could be just a hand to mouth existence Incidentally all the four artists whose brilliant works that you saw in India House were paid only one pound per day for their effort besides their boarding and lodging of course. Therefore you make up your mind what you want to become,' said Mr Sanyal.

Mr Sudhangshu Sanyal the only son from a very well do Bengali Zamindar family was a contemporary of Naren Sen and Debu Ghosh, when they all came as students to England to do their higher studies in law. Sudangshu however soon fell in love with a young English nurse, forgot about his studies and he married her quietly. His old man was so very angry with him that he expelled his son for good both from his home and property. Since there was no other option, Sudangshu first worked in a British shipping company as a booking clerk at Tilbury and then after India House was ready, thanks to Sir Atul Chatterjee and Sudangshu's good command over the English language, he was taken on the staff of the High Commission as a junior laison and protocol officer.

A fortnight later after his father took the boat back to India; Samir Sen was seen more on the cricket and football fields of London and England than in the law college. An Indian cricket team under the Maharaja of Vizanagram as Captain was touring England that very year and he was not going to miss all the action. The captain of the Indian cricket team was Vijaya Anand. He was from a princely family of Benaras and was popularly known as "Vizzy". But Vizzy was no wizard as far as the game of cricket was concerned and was appointed captain primarily because of his princely status.

Samir Sen's manifestation against anything connected with the rich and the mighty was clearly brought out when he raised a banner of revolt against the Maharaja on the eve of the first test at Lords.

'But why the hell did you send back our best young all rounder you stupid man,' shouted Samir as Vizzy the Captain walked into the ground for the toss. Samir was referring to the promising young cricketer Lala Amarnath from Lahore who was also the first Indian to score a Test century against DR Jardine's formidable eleven. Lala was an atheletic all rounder and had a very promising future ahead of him. In the match against the Minor Counties eleven after being told to pad up by the Captain and be ready to go and bat at two down, the young dashing Lala kept waiting and waiting and was only sent after seven wickets were down and that to when there was only 10 minutes of play left. In the earlier two matches and even against Essex Lala Amarnath had scored two back to back centuries and he simply could not fathom as to why he had been relegated in the batting order. On that day, when he returned back to the pavilion with his score reading one not out, Lala was livid. Once inside the dressing room he lashed out at his captain with the choicest of expletives in his mother tongue Punjabi.

'Saala machod Captain usko khudko tho kelne saala aata nahin aur saala angrezon se sirf aapna gaand marata hai." (Bloody mother fucker he doesn't know how to play the game himself and all he does is to get himself bughered by the Englishmen or words to that effect).Hearing that an angry Vizzy immediately reported the matter to the team manager a British army officer by the name of Major Jones. The British Major a stickler for discipline straight away ordered Lala's return to India. Despite pleadings by CK Nayudu, Wazir Ali, Vijay Merchant, Mushtaq Ali, Mohammed Nissar and other members of the team to give the young Lala another chance, Major Jones was adamant and all their pleadings only fell on the deaf ears of the team Manager. The very next morning Lala Amarnath Nanik Bhardwaj was on the boat train from Waterloo Station for his journey back to India.

With Lala who was also Samir Sen's favourite on his way back to India and skipper Vizzy scoring no runs whatsoever even during the first class matches and hardly any in the tests, Samir Sen before the start of the first days play on the third test at the Oval with a VIP guest pass in his hand confidently walked into the Indian dressing room. That pass he had managed through the kind offices of Mr Sanyal at India House. On noticing the chubby Indian Cricket Captain, Samir said rather disparagingly in his half Bengali and half Hindi. 'Shala bokachoda Angrez ka chamcha. Tui jhodi nijhe khelte na parish, kom she kom onno bhalo player der tho chance de.'(You bloody fool, nitwit and a stooge of the whiteman, if you do not know how to play yourself, atleast give the other good players a chance). Hearing that tThere was a subdued chuckle from some of the Indian players as Samir Sen walked out confidently from the dressing room shouting. "Long live India. Long live the Peoples Revolution and Long Live the Hammer and the Sickle". And from that very day at the Oval, young Samir Sen became a marked man with the British Intelligence.

Before going for the Summer Olympics to Berlin, Colonel Reginal Edwards decided to spend a month or so in London to look up his old colleagues and friends. The main topic doing the rounds in London was whether the New King will give up his love for Mrs Wallis Simpson and remain as the King Emperor, or will he sacrifice his throne for his lady love. Some who were in the closer circle of the English royalty even started referring to Mrs Simpson as the shadow Queen.since she now more and more overtly and without her husband's consent started spending almost every weekend with the King at Fort Belvedere. When the King sent her for the Ascot races in a royal carriage a leading politician could not but help remark angrily. 'Dammit all the people of this country do not mind people fornicating but they loathe adultery.'

While the King of England pined away for the twice divorced and elderly Mrs Simpson, in London in that very year the twice married but not divoced handsome young Maharaja Jai Singh of Jaipur proposed to the 17 year old stunning beauty from India as he drove her around Hyde Park in his Bentley car. Young Gyatri Devi the ravishing Princess May of Cooch Bihar having done a year at Shantiniketan and having completed her matriculation and her course from a finishing school in Switzerland was then staying at the Dorchester Hotel. The dashing polo playing Maharaja Jai Singh was also in England at that time and they were noticed by Reggie quite often whenever they met clandestinely at the Berkeley Hotel and from where they went on their long drives in his shining Bentley. And as a good sport Reggie deliberately avoided confronting them.

It was on the 30th of July, that Reggie arrived in Berlin for the Olympic Games. Berlin once earlier in 1916 had beeen awarded the Games, but due to the Great War no Olympics took place that year. In May 1931, the International Olympic Committee had awarded the games to Berlin and at that time Germany as the Weimar Republic had returned back into the folds of the world community after her defeat in the First World War. But two years later in 1933, the Nazi party leader on becoming the Chancellor had turned the nation's fragile democracy into a one party dictatorship. The Nazification of all aspects of German life now extended even to sport as Germany as the host nation fielded the largest contingent. Reggie had heard a lot about the racism in the land of Hitler; and about the prosecution by the Nazis of the German Jews, and about also Herr Hitler's resolve to make Germany a country only fit for the blonde haired and blue eyed Aryans. But when he arrived at Berlin for those two or three weeks the Fuhrer's dictatorship had successfully camouglaged its otherwise racist and militaristic character of the new Germany. The anti Semitic posters that had littered Germany before the Games had suddenly disappeared and the German capital with flags and swastikas could be seen fluttering from every important monument and also from the houses of the proud German people.

On 1st August, 1936 to the musical fanfare that was especially composed as an Olympic Anthem by Richard Strauss on the orders of the Fuhrer himself, Hitler opened the XIth Olympiad. The Olympics was now the perfect arena for the Nazi propaganda machine, as the Nazi Party with warm hospitality staged elaborate public spectacles and pageantries for the foreign spectators and participants, and Reggie too was impressed. As greetings for the excellent conduct of the Games poured in from all over the World, personally for Joseph Goebbels the German Minister for propaganda it was a personal triumph.

Throughout the conduct of the Games the medals tally showed the home contingent well ahead of the nearest rivals the Americans. In most of the events they proved their supremacy, but in Athletics it was the American contingent with the sensational black wonder called Jesse Owens who called all the shots. With a 10.2 seconds world record in the 100 meters dash, and a haul of four gold medals, even the Fuhrer acknowledged the supremacy of the blacks in the track events though some what reluctantly. Reggie however felt very proud as he walked up to the son of a Negro sharecropper and the grandson of a slave to personally congratulate him on his unique achievement of setting up four world records in each of the events that he had taken part in.

Reggie had basically come to Berlin to witness the hockey tournament and he did not miss a single match whenever the Indian team played. After the team's arrival in Germany they had played a friendly match against the Germans and when they had lost 4-1, the Manager of the Indian team was in a quandry. The Manager Mr Jaganath and his assistant Mr Pankaj Gupta immediately asked for the services of a young Indian army officer by the name of Ali Iqtidar Shah Dara. And once AIS Dara joined the team, there was no looking back. With Dhyan Chand as centre forward and Dara as the inside right the opponents were no match for the Indians. The combination of their stick work literally drew circles around their opponents, while Babu

Nimal and Joseph Pillay from Kirkee near Poona together with goal keeper Richard Allen kept the enemy strikers at bay. After the 10-0 massacre of France in the semi finals, India was now all set to take on Germany in the finals and India had not till then conceded a single goal.

The finals was originally scheduled to be played on the evening of the 14th of August, but it rained so very heavily that day that the entire ground was completely water logged. The match was therefore rescheduled to be played at 11 O'clock in the morning of the the next day 15th of August. Before taking the field, Reggie visited the Indian team to wish them luck and found the team saluting the Indian Congress tricolour that had been produced by Pankaj Gupta the Assistant Manager of the team.

'Do remember you are playing for India, your own country and you have to win,' said Reggie as the Indian team took the field. The ground was jam packed with some 40,000 spectators mostly Germans, but there were also the Maharaja of Baroda, the Princess of Bhopal and a large number of Indians too who had congregated from all over Europe for the grand occasion. Even Samir Sen was there.

Soon after the bully off, the Indian team stormed the German defences repeatedly and by half time the score read 4-0 in favour of the Indians. Then a ball rebounded of goal keeper Allen's pad and the Germans finally scored. It was now 4-I.

'Bloody well just give it back to them nice and proper,' shouted Samir Sen as the Indian team took the field after lemon time.

'Oh tussi fikar mat karo yaar" (Just don't worry friend) said a spirited young Sikh as he looked up towards the sky and asked for his Wahe Guru's blessings. Immediately thereafter an elderly Muslim gentleman turned his face towards the East, knelt down and offered his prayer to Allah. Reggie also kissed his rosary and invoked the blessings of Jesus Christ. When the final whistle was sounded, India had trounced Germany by 8 goals to 1 and out of those 8, three were scored by the Indian Captain Dhyan Chand and two by AIS Dara. India had now won the Olympic hockey gold for a record third time in a row and everybody was jubilant. Even the Fuhrer was impressed and he even offered to elevate Dhyan Chand to the rank of a Colonel if the star centre forward decided to migrate to Germany. But that offer according to Reggie was only an excuse for the German leader to hoodwink the world that there was no racial discrimination in his country.After the medal ceremony was over, and when Reggie personally went to congratulate the Indian team, he was surprised to find young Samir Sen also there.

'What the hell are you doing over here young man? Don't you think you should be concentrating on your law books in London, rather than ogling at the big built German blonde girls here in Berlin,' said Reggie with a smile.'

'I fully agree with you Sir, but the Olympics do not come everyday and in anycase to me law has no meaning. I am a very poor liar and will be more of a liability to my father in his law business. I have therefore given it up and will be going back to India to study fine arts at Shantiniketan,' said Samir Sen.

'Well good luck to you then,' said Reggie as he patted Dhyan Chand the star player who was from his own Punjab Regiment and requested him to give his autograph on the cover page of the Olympic brochure that he had bought as a souvenir for Ismail Sikandar Khan.

'Do sign your name boldly and write with best wishes to 2/Lt Ismail Sikandar Khan. He too is a great fan of yours and he is from my Second Punjabees,' said Reggie very proudly. But being poor in English, the hockey wizard simply wrote his name in Hindi.The very next day after an impressive closing ceremony, a proud Reich Chancellor, Herr Hitler declared the XIth Olympiad closed. 49 countries had taken part and Germany the host country headed the medal tally with 33 golds, 26 silvers and 30 bronze medals.

'I wish the Soviet Union had also taken part Sir and I am sure had they done so, they would have licked the Germans hollow,' said Samir Sen very assertively.

'I am not too sure about that because as a nation they may be very big in size both physically and in numbers, but as a homogenous country and with so many ethnic groups they have yet to find their feet. Yes maybe in the years to come they might be a force to reckon with,' said Reggie.

'But do mark my words Sir and that day is not very far away, when the Communist Party of the Soviet Union will rule the world,' said Samir Sen very proudly as he presented Reggie with a library edition of Tolstoys "War and Peace."

'I thought you were going to give some thoughts and speeches of Comrade Lenin,' said Reggie with a mischievous smile on his face.

'Maybe I will Sir someday, but only after I visit that great country,' said Samir Sen rather pompously.

A few days later the Indian hockey team boarded a train at Pottsdammer railway station to commence their post Olympic tour of the Continent. For their superb performance they were also given a week's holiday in London and the Indian High Commissioner, Sir Feroze Khan Noon made their stay in the British capital a really memorable one.

On 17th September Samir Sen boarded the P&O steamer "Strathmore" for his journey back to India and was pleasantly surprised to find not only the Indian hockey team on board, but also a host of other Indian VIPs that included the Indian Cricket Captain "Vizzy", the Nawab of Pataudi and Colonel Reginald Edwards. There was even a large crowd of Indians at the docks in London to see the team off.On the morning of the 29th of September the "Strathmore" docked at the Ballard Pier in Bombay and to his utter surprise Samir Sen found that there was practically no one to welcome and cheer the victorious Indian team.

'What b[oody nonsense and is this the way we treat our world famous hockey heroes,' said a visibly angry Samir Sen as he lashed out at Mr Behram Doctor and Mr Mukherjee the two junior officials from the Hockey Association who had come to receive the team.

'Dammit it all even in England and Germany our great team was cordially welcomed by the huge crowds where ever they went, and in our own damn country except for the welcome monsoon rains there is just nobody to give them even a 'shabash'. (A pat on their backs) Shame on us,' added the young Samir Sen as he waved out the tricolour which the Indian team was carrying.

'That was very well said young man,' remarked Reggie as he patted Samir Sen for his timely outburst.

'And even I too will write a complaint and a stinker to the Indian Hockey Association, because this is certainly not the way to honour our hockey heroes who have done the nation so very proud,' said Reggie as he with young Samir Sen came down the gangway to be welcomed by Naren Sen and Debu Ghosh who with their wives Shobha and Hena it seems were waiting for them.

By God there are more people to welcome Samir than the victorious Indian team, but where was the need for all of you to come all the way to Bombay and Samir could have easily taken the train to Howrah and you all could have received them there,' said Reggie as he shook hands with Naren and Debu and did the traditional namaste to the two ladies

'You are right Sir, but the purpose of our coming to Bombay is slightly different and our receiving you and Samir was just a coincidence. We have been invited by a young budding cinema actor who had just made a break in Hindi cinema and he desired that we all come for a special screening of the film "Achyut Kanya". I first met him by chance on the train when I with my son Samir travelled with him in the same compartment. And that was when you were also on the same train. You were on your way to London and that was only a couple of months ago. The well mannered young Bengali who was in his mid twenties had got into the same inter class compartment at Khandwa railway station, and by the time the train reached Victoria terminus we both had hit it off very well. The young man's father Kunjalal Ganguly is a practising lawyer in Khandwa and he too wanted this eldest son like I did to become a lawyer. As a matter of fact he had sent him to Calcutta to pay the Rupees 35 for his examination fees, but like Samir, the young man too was not interested in studying law. Therefore instead of paying his fees, he utilised the money for his train ticket to Bombay. But the man who was primarily responsible for his change of career was none other than his own brother-in-law, Mr Shashadar Mukherjee who was married to the youngman's sister and he was working as a sound recordist at the Bombay Talkies studios at Malad.

'The Bombay Talkies studio was the brain child of Mr Himanshu Rai and his beautiful wife Devika Rani. She was a grand neice of Rabindranath Tagore and the daughter of Colonel MN Chaudhuri of the Indian Medical Service. In 1928, Himanshu Rai had produced a movie titled "Shiraz". In 1930, Devika Rani then 26 years old joined Himanshu Rai as a set designer, while he was producing another film titled "Throw of Dice'. Thereafter they became husband and wife. Both of them had gained good experience in film making in Germany and had now employed a team of qualified German technicians for the production of Hindi feature films for the Indian public in their Bombay Talkies studio at Malad. With a capital of Rupees 25 lakhs, Himanshu Rai had converted Mr F E Dinshaw's summer mansion in far away Malad into a modern cinema studio. They also wanted other staff as junior technicians and Shashadar Mukherjee therefore had got the young man, his brother-in-law the job of an assistant cameraman on a start of Rs 150 per month. Thereafter the youngman shifted to editing and also worked as a lab assistant on a pay scale of Rs 250 per month. Malad was an out of the way place which was thickly forested and the young Ashok Kumar Ganguly stayed in one small room which had just one cot and two chairs. When he got those first two hundred and fifty rupees he was simply thrilled, but fearing that it might be stolen, he hid it inside the wool of his pillow. Then one day lady luck smiled on him. The director Himanshu Rai was on the look out for a new hero for his new film "Jeevan Naiya" "The Boat of Life". One day by chance, when his eyes fell on the young man who had taken a short break to have a cigarette, he liked the manner in which the youngman held the cigarette in his mouth and then lit it very stylishly.

'Come here and what is your name,' asked the Director Mr Himanshu Rai.

'My name is Ashok Kumar Ganguli Sir' said the youngman looking rather nervous in front of his boss.

'No that is too long a name for a future film hero and therefore from today you will be only known as Ashok Kumar and nothing more and nothing less. Now get ready for the screen test.'

'But I cannot act at all Sir,' pleaded the youngman, but the Director would have none of it.

'That we shall see,' said Himanshu Rai as he firmly told the German cameraman to roll the camera. For the screen test young Ashok Kumar had to only walk up and garland Devika Rani the heroine of the film. But she was 6 years elder to him and she was also the wife of the Director himself and Ashok Kumar naturally was very nervous.

'Cut said the cameraman as a nervous Ashok Kumar fumbled with the garland, but after a few more takes and much to his own dislike he had no other option but to become a hero,' said Naren Sen as he invited Reggie to come with them for the special screening of the Ashok Kumar, Devika Rani starrer "Achyut Kanya".

'Yes sir you must see the film. It has a good social message about the evils of untouchability in our Hindu society, and Mr Nehru with his young daughter Indira and even the nightingale of India, Mrs Sarojini Naidu will also be there as special guests,' added Debu Ghosh.

'Well in that case I will join you all definitely, and needless to say that it will also be my first Hindi film too,' said Reggie as he got into the phaeton with his luggage and made his way to the Taj Mahal Hotel on Appollo Bunder.

It was two days later, when the Bombay Talkies staff did a special screening of "Achyut Kanya" for the few exclusive invitees.

'My God I must say that Panditji is really a very handsome man,' said Hena Ghosh as Jawaharlal Nehru took his seat.

'Yes he definitely is except that his hairline is fast receding,' said her husband Debu.

' Please don't say it so loudly, its bad manners,' said Naren Sen's wife Shobha as Reggie walked inside the hall and took his seat next to Debu. Pandit Nehru with his young and goodlooking daughter Indira and Mrs Sarojini Naidu were seated only two rows behind them and keeping them good company was the Director of the film Mr Himanshu Rai andhis beautiful wife Devika Rani. When the song "Khet ki Mulli, Bagh ka aam" which was part of the film came on the screen, Sarojini Naidu could not but help ask.

'But tell me who is that young man and he sings well too.'

'He is our new hero and his name is Ashok Kumar,' said the director very proudly.

When there was an interval for tea and snacks, Ashok Kumar was seen standing in the company of Naren Sen and his other guests in a corner with a cigarette dangling from his lips. And when he saw Mrs Naidu heading his way, he immediately handed over the burning cigarette to Debu Ghosh and felt indeed very proud, when Mrs Naidu said.to him

'I must say that you do have a lot of talent in you young man, but for heaven's sake don't let it go waste. The medium of the cinema has come to stay in this country and it can be very educative for our illliterate masses if such like films are produced more often. It reminds me of Gurudev Tagore's dance drama 'Chandalika', and the moral of the story is not very different from that of 'Achyut Kanya".

'Yes and undoubtedly so,' said Pandit Nehru who having noticed an elderly foreigner in their midst and fluently conversing with the others in Urdu walked up to Reggie and said.

. 'Do pardon the interruption, but where did you learn such good Urdu Sir'. And I am sure that many amongst us present here today are not as fluent in that language as you are.'

When Reggie told him who he was and that having been born in India he had now decided to even die in this country, Mrs Sarojini Naidu who was standing nearby having heard the whole conversation wittingly remarked

'Well Sir I only hope that you are an exception to the rule because otherwise if all Englishmen decide to settle permanently in India and also die over here then we will never ever get our Independence.' That remark by the nightingale of India was greeted with a big applause by everybody as Reggie congratulated Mrs Naidu for her subtle sense of humour.

That evening after the film was over, Debu Ghosh accompanied Reggie back to his hotel room.

'Now tell me Sir what is your hunch. Do you think the new King will give up the throne for his ladylove?"

'Well if you ask me I think this is entirely his own personal affair, but if he does give up the throne, then England will lose a good King and a wonderful human being too,' said Reggie.

'Yes I think so too and that will be a sad day for the Empire and for India in particular,' said Debu Ghosh.

'But what makes you say that and why particularly India,' asked Reggie as he poured another chota peg into Debu's glass.

'For the simple reason Sir because as a human being the King is a wonderful person. He is full of compassion and one who is always keen to help the poor and this was quite evident in the dignified manner in which he conducted himself when he visited India as the Prince of Wales in 1921. And looking at his attitude towards the Indian people I wont be surprised if he as the King and Emperor accedes to Gandhi's views and those of the Indian National Congress and decides to free India from Britain's slavery earlier than expected,' said Debu Ghosh.

'That I am afraid is wishful thinking because it is not entirely in his hands and moreover India is the most important jewel in his crown and with a mad Hitler in Europe wanting to promote and expand his Nazi cult beyond Germany's existing borders that I am afraid will be suicidal for England,' said Reggie.

'You are right and if there is another war in Europe then India will have to contribute both militarily and economically as she has always been doing or else the sun may gradually set over the mighty British Empire,' said Debu as he took leave of his gracious host.

On 16th November 1936, at a dinner in Marlborough House the King for the first time told his mother about his plans to marry Mrs Simpson. On that evening Queen Alexandar had nothing much to say to her son, but there was no doubt that she was very upset. The divorce of the Simpsons was also now very much on the cards. On 27th October having heard the divorce proceedings the learned Judge had already granted a decree nisi for the divorce, but it was only a provisional one. For the decree absolute there would now be an agonizing wait for the mandatory six months and it could be annulled in case it could be proved that it was collusion between the couple seeking the divorce. There was no doubt that there was collusion and it was indeed very sporting of the British press to observe such an honourable restraint, thought Reggie.

On the 3rd of December, and, before matters could get worse, the King bid Mrs Simpson a tearful farewell as she quietly got into the car at Fort Belvedere for her journey to Cannes in France. And a week later on the 10th of December from Windsor Castle in England and over the radio, the King addressed his subjects for the last and final time. That very morning at Fort Belvedere in the presence of all his brothers, the King had signed the Instrument of Abdication. A stunned British public listened with rapt attention as the ex King spoke with all humility and said.

'You must believe me when I tell you that I have found it impossible to carry the heavy burden of responsibikity and to discharge my duty as King as I would wish to do, without the help and support of the woman I love. I now quit all together public affairs and I lay down my burden. And now we all have a new King. I wish him, and you, his people, happiness and prosperity with all my heart. God bless you all. God save the King.'

After the broadcast, the ex King went back to take leave of his family. There was sadness no doubt all around as he gave his final bows to his younger brother the new King George the VIth and got into the waiting car. A few hours later at 2 AM early morning while Britain slept the ex King on board the battle ship "Fury" sailed across the English Channel to be reunited with his true love in France.

'My God he has actually done it,' said an excited Debu Ghosh to his wife Hena as he walked inside the kitchen with the copy of the Calcutta Statesmen early that morning.

'Now what more has your Mr Gandhi done,' said Hena with a look of disgust in her face as she handed over another cup of tea to her politically minded husband.

"No not even Gandhiji could have done what he has done,' said Debu Ghosh as he read the headlines. "The King Abdicates. George VIth is the new King Emperor."

' This is more like a fairy tale of once there was a King,'said Naren Sen as he walked in with his copy of the Bengali newspaper "Ananda Bazaar Patrika."

'But whatever you all may say, the handsome King must be terribly in love with the two time divorcee and I hope they get married soon,' said Hena as she had one more closer look at the ex King's photograph in the newspaper.

'Well dear brother-in-law now that you have lost the bet with your wife, you better start making plans to take her to London for the coronation of the new King,' said Naren Sen

'Oh about that bet I also completely forgot, but now I remember that I had taken that bet with my husband when all of us had gone to spend a few days of summer holidays with our children at Darjeeling when one day my dear husband proudly showed us a photograph of the King with his lady love on board some yacht called :Nahlin" and I said that come what may the

King will definitely marry her one day and Isnt that right Naren Babu and you were a witness to it also, weren't you?, said a beaming Hena Ghosh.

'Yes that is absolutely right and in order to refresh Debu Ghosh's failing memory let me remind him as to how and why the bet was taken,' said Naren Sen as Debu lit a cigarette and scratched his head.

'Well the King at that time was on a cruise of the Mediterreanean with some of his bosom friends which also included Mrs Simpson and everyone of us that day debated the hot topic of,' will he or will he not' and Hena was the only one who said that if required the King will even give up his throne to marry that woman and to which Debu boastfully committed that it was next to impossible, and if that ever happened then he would take Hena for the new King's coronation to London.'

'But dammit all he hasn't married her yet,' said Debu Ghosh.

'But he will I am sure otherwise why should he abdicate,' replied Hena with a frown on her face.

'Why he need not get married, and moreover the decree absolute regarding her second divorce is still to be announced. But ofcourse he can always keep her as his privileged girl friend,' said Debu Ghosh.

'Alright let us not fight over the issue, but if the King proclaims to marry her then you will have to take Hena for the coronation whether you like it or not, and if you require extra finances for the trip you can always borrow it from me,' said Naren Sen as Dr Ghulam Hussein joined them with his copy of the Calcutta Statesman.

. 'Well in that case I too with my better half in tow will keep Debu and Hena Ghosh company' said the jovial doctor while requesting the hostess for a real hot cup of tea.

'Oh that will be simply superb and I hope the old King marries soon so that both Suraiya Bhabi and I can do a lot of shopping in London and in Europe too', said Hena as she ran inside the kitchen to prepare the tea for Ghulam Bhai.

A few weeks later, when it was officially announced that the coronation of King George the VIth would be held at the Westminster Abbey in London on the 12th of May, 1937, both Hena and Suraiya were thrilled.This would be their first trip abroad with their husbands and they had already started making preparations for it well in advance. In early April, they boarded a P&O ship from Bombay and on the 20th after a comfortable long voyage they arrived in London as guests of the Sanyals. Mrs Anne Sanyal though an English lady was a perfect hostess and the three ladies got on wonderfully well with one another as they helped each other out with all the household chores. The hot topic in England was whether the old King would marry before or after the coronation. Hena and Suraiya were firmly of the view that the ex King since he was already out of the country with his lady love, he would marry before the coronation, but their husbands however felt that the coronation being a more important event would be held first.

'Alright then let us have another bet on that,' said Hena crossing her fingers. If the Ex King marries first then both of you will take us for a second honeymoon to the French Riviera, and if the coronation comes first then we will not step outside the British Isles and that's a promise,' said Hena

. 'Agreed' said Debu Ghosh very confidently as he whispered something into Dr Ghulam Hussein's ears.

'Well in that case I think we are on a strong wicket,' said Ghulam Hussein to Debu. The fact of the matter was that the absolute decree for the second divorce was yet to be announced and the mandatory waiting period of six months was yet to be over and Debu Ghosh being a lawyer was fully aware of it.

'This time you will certainly loose the bet my dear wife,'said a confident Debu Ghosh as he opened a bottle of scotch for his host Mr Sudhangshu Sanyal.

To Debu's bad luck the decree absolute granting Mrs Simpson the divorce from her second husband came through on the 3rd of May and on the very next day the ex King hopped on to the Orient Express which was especiaily stopped for him at an out of the way place some 45 miles from Paris. He was now quietly on his way to join his sweetheart at the Chateau de Cande in Touraine. On the 8th of May, when Mrs Simpson changed her name by deed poll to Wallis Warfield, Debu Ghosh and Ghulam Hussein got jittery. There were now only 6 days left for the coronation and not being very sure of what was on the mind of the ex King, Debu Ghosh very diplomatically asked for the cancellation of the bet

' No that is being totally unfair.' said Mrs Anne Sanyal and whether the Ex King marries or doesn't marry, or has a honeymoon or doesn't have one, it is none of our business. And now that you all have come all the way, I would suggest that you must visit beautiful Paris and the French Reviera and catch the boat to India from Marseilles. Maybe one of you will run into luck in some casino at Cannes and go home a lot richer.'

'That I think is a splendid idea, and after the coronation whether you all like it or not, we will all go to Paris and also to the beautiful French Reviera,' said Hena.

On the 12th of May, Debu Ghosh, Ghulam Hussein and Sudhnagshu Sanyal with their wives waved out to their Royal Highnesses as they drove in the royal carriage for the coronation ceremony at the Westminster Abbey.

'What a handsome couple they make and the two little princesses Elizabeth and Margaret are like two little angels aren't they,' said Anne Sanyal as the royal cavalcade passed by.

'Yes darling, you are absolutely right, but the one big problem with the new King is that he stammers,' said Mr Sanyal.

But how the hell does that matter after all he is the King Emperor now and whether he stammers or stutters that is none of our business,' said Hena Ghosh in support of her hostess.

I am not disputing that at all, but none the less it is still a handicap for the monarch who as the King Emperor will now have to give speeches both in private and in public and that to more often,' said Debu Ghosh as he lit one more cigarette and ruled the topic to be closed.

'All right so he has finally got her,' said an excited Debu Ghosh as he came home with a copy of the London Times that carried a wedding photograph of the Duke and Duchess of Windsor as they were now called. They were married the previous day on the 3rd of June at Chateau de Cande in France.

'Well the saying that men get naughty at four zero forty and woman get flirty at three zero thirty is absolutely right, and therefore why not celebrate the last weekend with our guests from India with some Bingo at the India House and then follow it up with some delicious Indian food at the "Yatra" restaurant on Dover Street. It is probably the first or one of the first Indian resturants in London and the food is simply out of this world,' said Sudhangshu smacking his lips.

'We can go only to one place in the French Reviera and that too only for two or three days maximum so therefore decide where do you wives want to go,' said Ghulam Hussein as they boarded the boat for Pas de Calais at Dover.

'That we will decide only after we see Paris,' said Hena Ghosh.

'That's fine but we only have forty hours to spend in Paris and no more, and that also includes the shopping and sightseeing too', added Debu Ghosh.

'That is rather unfair, but where is the frightful hurry. After all it is not everyday that one comes to Paris, and in two days what can you see anyway. You cannot even finish seeing the Louvre,'.said Suraiya somewhat angrily.

'Alright then by popular demand we will make it three days and extendable by another one day provided we get reasonably good accommodation at a reasonably good price in some pension, or at some decent hotel in the centre of the city and the ladies restrict themselves to 200 Francs each for their personal shopping,' said Debu Ghosh.

'Yes and let me also remind you ladies that the French people can be quite curt and nasty if you do not tip them well, and they get even nastier if you speak to them in English. Therefore for the next 24 hours starting from this very moment and till we get to Paris I with my limited knowledge of French, which I learnt in School at St Xavier's, Calcutta, I will try and teach all of you some common words and phrases that hopefully may prove useful while we are in the land of Napoleon Bonaparte,' said Dr Ghulam Hussein as he opened the small English to French easy guide for beginners.

'Alright lesson number one, always speak through your nose and remember that the French language has no neuter gender. Lesson number two the little "Le" is for masculine and" La" is always for for the feminine gender. But sometimes when you hear someone say " Ooh.La La", that should be taken as a compliment and the French love complinents. Therefore let's take for example that young good looking lady standing there in the far corner of the boat,' said Dr Ghulam Hussein as he discreetly pointed her out to the others.'And now if I smile and say 'Ooh La La; isn't she really beautiful,' then that is taken as an expression of appreciation and nothing more,' added the wise doctor.'

'Arre bloody Doctor Babu thum bhi lagta forty cross karne ke baad hero bangaye ho. Raat ko gharwali se jhoote padhenge (You bloody doctor now that you too have crossed the forty mark you also have become a damn hero it seems. Therefore do not be surprised if tonight you get greeted with a shower of shoes from your wife.) said Debu Ghosh in good humour.

'But you do not have to take it literally, I am just giving an example you see. Similarly let us say we order some French food and we find it really delicious then all that one has to say is "Ooh La La C'est Magnifique" meaning it is simply magnificent and that's about all. And now finally for the golden rule and that is when in doubt just say "Pardon" stressing the letter "N" with a long nasal sound. And never forget to say "Merci Beaucoup" pronounced as in the English word mercy and beaucoup as in the word beau for bowtie and coup as in coup d"etat.'

'But what does it mean,' said an irritated Suraiya who was fed up with her husband's corny sense of humour.

'It only means thank you in English, "Shukriya" in Urdu, 'Dhonnobad' in Bengali and 'Danke' in German replied Dr Ghulam Hussein very proudly.

'But why bring in the German language into all this now? As it is the French is going over our heads,' said Hena.

'No there may be a requirement for learning German in the not to distant future too looking at the speed and the manner in which the Fuhrer is arming Germany and shouting himself hoarse from the roof top of the Reichstag for more space in this world, And I wont be surprised if one day you find the Germans doing their goose steps in the very heart of Paris while keeping their right hand perpetually raised and screaming 'Hail Hitlet.' As it is they are already sitting next door in the Saar region, which is now a part of Germany, and the rumours are that he is seriously contemplating to include Austria too because that is the country where he was born, and he therefore feels that it is his birthright to include it as part of his Greater Germany,' said Debu Ghosh as he demonstrated the German salute with a 'Hail Hena'.

'Oh come on why cant we talk of something more interesting and entertaining,' said Suraiya as she distributed the cheese and chicken sandwiches that Anne Sanyal had made for all of them.

'Alright meri jaan(my love) you win again and therefore let us talk about the sites of Paris that you ladies would like to see,'said her husband as he put the small English to French phrase book back into one pocket and took out the tourist guide book from the other.

On arrival in Paris a historic city created some 2000 years before, they checked in at the Hotel Montholon since it was very centrally located, relatively cheap and close to the railway station Gare Du Nord. That very day with the help of a tourist map and having studied the layout of the Paris Metro, Debu Ghosh chalked out the three and a half day itinerary for the group and started his running commentary on the famous tourist spots of the city.

'Alright without wastimg any more time and after our breakfast we will start visiting the following tourist spots. First we will see The Louvre. It was once a medieval fortress and the palace of the Kings of France and bears witness to more than 800 years of history. The museum which is one of the oldest in Europe was however established in 1793.'Next we will cover the famous Eiffiel Tower. This is a piece of architectural wonder created by Mr Gustav Eiffel for the International Exhibition that was held in Paris in 1889 as also to commemorate the centenary of the French Revolution. Then we will move on to the Notre Dame, a beautiful creation of Gothic architecture constructed seven hundred years ago. Following that we will walk along the Champs Elysees to the Place de la Concorde which was built by architect Jacques-Ange Gabriel in 1763 to cleberate the glory of King Louis XV. But tragically it also saw the beheading of his successor Louis XVI on 21st January 1793 during the French revolution. From there we shall land up at the very impressive Arch de T'riomphe. The triumphant arch was commissioned in 1806 by Napeoleon Bonaparte to commemorate his victory at Austerlitz, but was completed only in 1836. Incidently beneath the Arch is the tomb of the Unknown Soldier and there we must pay homage to our old friend Curzon Sikandar Khan who so gallantly had laid down his life in the battle of Loos during the First World War.'Finally on our last evening in Paris while you two ladies finish doing your shopping and get back to the hotel by sunset to have your early supper and then to bed, we the two menfolk will take off for Montmartre to see the Can Can dance at the Moulin Rouge,' concluded Debu Ghosh

'But why can't we also go and see the Can Can,'said a defiant Hena.

'It is simply because the dance performance by the artistes will only embarrass both of you and nothing else,' said Debu Ghosh.

'And though the place mind you has been immortalised by no less a person than the painter Henri de Toulouse-Lautrec since 1889, it is still not meant for ladies of virtue,' added Dr Ghulam Hussein.

'And ever since Toulouse Lautrec patronised the place, the cabaret artistes have been kicking their legs higher and higher for the entertainment of the viewers, and that I am sure will not interest you ladies,' added Debu Ghosh.

'Alright let them go and have some fun on their own, but on condition that we get atleast 5 full days on the French Reviera, and it should include not only Cannes but Monte Carlo also and with an additional allowance of 100 Francs each at both these places in order to try our luck at the many casinos there,' said an excited Suraiya. And before the ladies could change their minds and demand something more, Debu Ghosh immediately took out a 100 Francs from his wallet and gave it to Hena and Dr Ghulam Hussein too promptly followed his friend's example.

The French Reviera was generally a place for the rich and the famous, but it mattered to the two Indian couples, when they checked in at one of the cheaper hotels in Cannes. They were more interested in enjoying the beautiful weather of the Cote D'Azur, swim in the warm waters of the Mediterranean and try their luck in the casinos. The ladies had purchased their swimming costumes in Paris and though they were a little reluctant at first to wear them but they reconciled to the idea fast when they found that on the lovely sprawling beaches nobody was even bothered about who was wearing what. But nevertheless it did turn a few eyes as the two good looking Indian middle aged ladies with their naturally tanned skin and long black hair in big buns under their hair nets threw away the towels and entered into the cool waters of the calm sea. After a while, when they came out to relax on the beach to their utter surprise they found another young Indian couple relaxing under a sun umbrella and not very far from where they were sitting. The girl who was around 18 was a stunning beauty and the two it seemed were having some sort of a lover's tiff. Then a little while later, when the girl picked up the man's shoes and angrily threw it into the water, it was evident that the young lovers were probably having a little spat.

'My God the beautiful girl sure has some temper,' remarked Debu Ghosh as they in order to leave the two of them alone made it back to the hotel.

Two days later, when Debu Ghosh was on his way to the Cannes railway station to do their booking for their journey to Marseilles, he found the same couple alighting from a chauffer driven luxury car. As soon as the couple entered the station platform Debu Ghosh asked the chauffer who they were and was pleasantly surprised to learn that the gentlemen was none other than Maharaja Jai Singh of Jaipur and the pretty lady was Princess Gyatri Devi from Cooch Bihar. It seems that the lovers tiff between the two was now over as Debu Ghosh saw the young and pretty Gyatri Devi running the whole length of the platform holding the hand of the handsome Maharaja as the train carrying him steamed off from the station.But when he returned to the hotel and narrated the incident, none of the ladies would believe his story.

'Please stop bluffing my dear husband and you must have been dreaming,' said Hena as she got up to get ready and dress up to go and try her luck at the cassino.

'And do pardon my saying so Debuda but you sure can make up such juicy stories, but we are not biting it,' added Suraiya.

'Well if you both do not believe me then let's have a bet and If you ladies win then you will get an extra fifty francs to gamble at the casino, but if you lose the bet then I am afraid the trip to Monte Carlo will have to be called off,' said Debu Ghosh rather confidently.

Unfortunately that evening all four of them had miserable luck not only at the roulette table, but also with the Black Jack and at the Poker table. And as a result of which their trip to Monte Carlo was automatically off.

' Well I guess the popular saying lucky in love and unlucky in cards even now holds good for all of us too, and may be we shall make it to Monte

Carlo some other time,' said Debu as they took the next available train to Marseilles.

It was end June 1937, when the two couples finally returned to India and soon as Debu reached Calcutta he called on Subhas Chander Bose at his house on Elgin Road. Subhas Bose after his forced exile in Europe and detention in India had only recently been released, and the stormy petrel of Bengal was once again in action.He had returned to India and to his home after a lapse of four long years. It was on 22nd February 1933 that a seriously sick Subhas Bose was released from prison on condition that he went to Europe for his medical treatment. He boarded a ship at Bombay and entered Dr. Furth's sanatorium at Vienna on 11th March where he met Mr Vithalbhai Patel, the elder brother of Vallabhai, but the veteran Congressman and patriot was practically now an invalid. Both Vithalbhai and Subhas were very upset when they heard on 8th May in Vienna that Gandhi had suspended the civil disobedience movement in India. And promptly on the very next day they jointly wrote to the Congress Party a strong letter which categorically stated that firstly the events of the last thirteen years have demonstrated that a political warfare based upon the principles of maximum suffering for us and minimum suffering for our opponents cannot possibly lead to success. Secondly it was futile to expect that with Gandhiji's policy of non violence the Congress party and the people of India can ever bring about a change of heart in our rulers merely through our own suffering or by trying to love them. And that the latest action of Mahatma Gandhi in suspending the civil disobedience movement was a confession of failure so far as the method of the Congress is concerned. And in conclusion both Subhas and Vithalbhai were both clearly of the opinion that as a political leader Mahatma Gandhi had failed

In end 1934, when Subhash lost his father, he was permitted to return, but only for the funeral. He arrived on 10th January 1935 but sailed again for Europe a few days later. In March 1936, he boldly proclaimed that he was returning to India and inspite of receiving a formal warning that he would be arrested on landing he was not in the least deterred. He reached Bombay on 8th April and while coming down the gangway, when the firebrand Bengalee shouted loudly to the crowd that had assembled there to greet him to keep the flag of India's freedom flying high, the police promptly arrested him and whisked him away in the Black Maria. Debu Ghosh was also present that day at Ballad Pier in Bombay, but the police cordon around the Indian leader was so very tight that he had no chance to personally meet or greet him.

'Now that you are back and your health has also started improving do please get back into the mainstream of politics. Soon we are also going to have our own Provincial Governments in the Provinces and for which the elections have already been held and declared and we will be in power in 9 out of those 11 provinces. We the Congress have got a clear majority in Madras, the United Provinces, the Central Provinces, Bihar and Orrisa, and we are also coalition partners in Bombay Province, the NWFP, Sind and Assam. The only two provinces that we lost were Bengal and Punjab. In Bengal it was Fazlul Haq's Krishak Praja Party that emerged as the leader and here too we could have easily formed a coalition with them and I do not know why we backed out from it thereby giving Mr Jinnah's Muslim League the much awaited opportunity. And as far as Punjab was concerned the Unionist Party under Sir Fazal-i-Hussein was the clear winner. However, what is of significance is that not only Mr Jinnah's Muslim League failed to form a government in any of the Provinces, but even in the Muslim majority province of Punjab it won only two measly seats. Therefore, what India requires now Subhash Babu is your dynamic leadership and thus I and others like me as your well wishers would earnestly request you to stand for the Presidency of the Congress party at its next session which is scheduled to be held in early February next year,' pleaded Debu Ghosh as he lit one more cigarette to go with the hot cup of tea.

'Well my becoming the President of the Congress is not left to me by choice, because this is a decision that has to be taken by the Congress Working Committee and by the Mahatma. Nevertheless, it would be quite an honour if I am raised to that pedestal,' said Subhas Bose who on that very day of 17th March had been brought home from the Calcutta Medical College Hospital where he was interned for treatment. He had come to see his mother, and when a few minutes later the Deputy Commissioner of Police walked in and handed over the order for his unconditional release from detention, it was celebration time again.Subhas Bose was once again a free man.

'Bring in the box of sweets,' said a delighted Debu Ghosh as he sat with Subhas Bose and a few other close friends of his to chalk out the strategy for making Subhas the next Congress President. Without wasting anymore time, Debu Ghosh decided to get back into Congress politics and a week later told his wife Hena.

'I know this will upset you, but I have decided to accompany Mr Nehru and his party to Kashmir and from there to the North West Frontier.

'But what ever for?. Don't you have responsibilities towards us and the children? Our eldest son Arup is not getting any younger and he will soon be twenty years old and I do not see any future for him. He seems to be living up to his nick name of 'Laloo' and like his cousin Samir has lost all interest in his studies and now only boasts about the new world order of communism and nothing else,' said a visbly angry Hena.

'But thank God he has atleast passed his BA, and even though it is only in the third division, I will try and get him some clerical job with one of the box walla companies or as a clerk in some government department. Thereafter we will get him married to a nice homely girl and he will soon forget about the Red Flag and the Hammer and the Sickle,' said Debu Ghosh.

'That is only wishful thinking Borda (eldest brother) said Debu's sister; Shobha Sen as she walked in with a plateful of freshly made delicious Bengali 'Shondesh' for her loving eldest brother.

Despite the opposition from his family members, Debu Ghosh went to Kashmir and there for the first time like Pandit Nehru he came across the fiery young Kashmiri who had raised the banner of revolt against the Maharaja's repressive policies not very many years ago.'The man from the small hamlet of Sura situated north of Hari Parbat in Srinagar was now a much married man. Sheikh Abdulla in October 1933 had married the charming Akbar Jehan. She was the daughter of Mr Michael Harry Nedou whose father had come from Europe and had started a series of good posh hotels for European tourists at Lahore and Srinagar. Her father though an Austrian had fallen in love with a Kashmiri Gujjar peasant girl. The peasant girl's father used to deliver milk to the Nedous Hotel at Gulmarg. When Michael Harry Nedou's proposal to marry her was turned down, he converted himself into a Muslim and took the new name of Sheikh Ahmed Hussein. Soon therafter he married her and Akbar Jehan was their daughter and she was no ordinary girl. She had completed her Senior Cambridge from the English Missionary Convent School at Murree and had been married once earlier at a very young age to one Karamat Shah a Muslim high priest in Bombay. But that marriage did not last long. And inspite of having lived in cosmopolitan Bombay she fitted in easily with her second husband Sheikh Abdullah. Despite her mixed origin and cosmopolitan upbringing, Debu Ghosh found that the young charming lady was a devout Muslim who always stood by her husband in his hour of need.This was the first time that Debu Ghosh visited the beautiful vale of Kashmir and was enchanted by its natural beauty.

'This is really heaven on earth and yet the people are so very poor,' remarked Debu Ghosh as he with Sheikh Abdulla visited a few villages not far from the capital Srinagar.

Undoubtedly so and this is what I call exploitation of the people by the Maharaja and his cohorts and this is what I have been fighting for during these past six years,' said the tall handsome Sheikh with a look of disgust in his face.

Well I hope with your efforts and those of your people and the National Conference of which you are the undisputed leader, things will improve. And as you are now aware that after the recent Provincial elections in the country, the Congress is now in power in 9 out of the 11 Provinces and this also includes the NWPF where the population is predominantly Muslim and the Chief Minister there is none other than Dr Khan Sahib, the elder brother of the Frontier Gandhi. So therefore, as we now inch forward or rather crawl towards our Independence, the Princely States will also have to sometime or the other fall in line with us and that is the time when men and leaders like you will play a decisive part in the making of a new and resurgent India,' added Pandit Nehru.

Chapter-10

The Return of the Royal Bengal Tiger

As soon as Debu Ghosh returned back to Calcutta from Kashmir, he once again called on Subhas Chander Bose at his house on Elgin Road to enquire about his health. It was already end September and the Congress was yet to announce the name of the President elect for the 51st session of the Indian National Congress that was to be held at Haripura on the 19th and 20th of February 1938.

'There are I believe two serious contenders and you are one of them,' said Debu Ghosh.

'But who is the other,' asked Subhash. 'The other person likely to foot the bill and this I have confidentially come to know is Dr Pattabi Sitaramayya. But your chances seem to be greater as the Mahatma I believe is also in your favour,' said Debu Ghosh.

'Well may the better man win,' said Subhash Bose while inviting Debu to share the dinner with the family.

In early of November 1937, Gandhiji was in Calcutta and in that very year at the Lahore Congress, Pandit Nehru was elected as Congress President, but Panditji did not accompany the Mahatma to Calcutta. Moreover, Gandhiji was not keeping good health and Dr Bidhan Chandra Roy and his team of doctors were now worried. Sarojini Naidu who had accompanied the Mahatma to Calcutta on 13th November and on the eve of Pandit Nehru's birthday wrote a very interesting letter to Jawaharlal. On that very day Debu had also gone to pay his respects to the Mahatma and when he by chance was shown that letter, he got so fascinated by the writer's mastery over the English language and her subtle sense of humour that he actually memorised most of it. When he returned home and narrated it to his wife the letter verbatim, she was really touched. The letter read as follows-:

'My Very Dear Jawahar,

I am writing from the modern version of the Tower of Babel. The little man is sitting unconcernedly eating spinach and boiled macaroni while the world ebbs and flows about him breaking into waves of Bengali, Gujrathi, English and Hindi. Bidhan and his colleagues are in despair over his stubborn indocility as regards his health.He is really ill, not only in his brittle bones and thinning blood, but in the core of his soul, this most lonely and tragic figure of his time-India's man of destiny on the edge of his own doom.

To you, the other man of destiny, I am sending birthday greetings. It will not reach you in time because of intervening eyes that must scan your correspondence. I have been watching you these two years with a most poignant sense of your suffering and loniliness, knowing that it cannot be otherwise.'

'What shall I wish for you for the coming year? Happiness? Peace? Triumph? All these things men hold supremely dear are but secondary things, almost incidental. I wish you my dear unflinching faith and unfaltering courage in your via cruces that all must tread who seek freedom and hold it more precious than life. Not personal freedom but the deliverance of a nation from bondage steadfastly and along that perilous path. If sorrow and pain and lonliness be your portion, remember liberty is the ultimate crown of your sacrifice—but you will not walk alone.' The letter was signed your loving Sarojini.

'I must say that the lady is a real genius and her English is flawless and the manner in which she conveyed all that she had to say in just a few sentences only speaks of her greatness,' said Hena.

'Undoubtedly so and the rumours are that Subash Bose is most likely to succeed Jawaharlal Nehru as the next President of the Congress Party and if that happens it will be another step towards Purna Swaraj, full freedom,' said Debu.

Not knowing what was in store for him, Subhas Bose on 18th November 1937 left India by air for Europe once again. Having visited Badgastein in Austria he arrived in Rome on 21st December. To greet him there was none other than Emilie Schenkl who had been his secretary during his stay in Vienna earlier from 1934 to 1936. Now she was to become his wife, his secret confidante and his constant companion for the next few weeks.

In January 1938, Subhas Bose after a gap of 17 years arrived in London, On the 18th of January, while he was in London, the Congress General Secretary, Mr JB Kirpalani in India formally announced that Mr Subhas

Chandra Bose had been elected as the Congress President for the Haripura Congress. Without further ado Subhash Bose left for India for his political coronation.

On arrival at Haripura his Presidential car was drawn by 51 bullocks for the 51st session of the Congress. As it passed through the 51 gates of honour he was lustily cheered by the mammoth crowd that had gathered to welcome him. Adding colour to the proceedings were the innumerable posters depicting the rural aspects of India that were displayed prominently on the gates and in the huge pandal. These series of paintings were all done by Nandlal Bose who at the request of the Mahatma had come to Haripura from Shantiniketan and did it all for free. Debu Ghosh who had also arrived there a few days earlier as a volunteer was often seen assisting the renowned painter; as Nandlal Bose with a towel round his head climbed on to the bamboo ladders to asthetically adjust the various painted panels.

After the session was over, Debu Ghosh was mighty pleased with the performance of the Congress President. Subhas Bose had done full justice to his speech that ranged from the Congress policy both from the national point of view and from the international point of view also, and he exhorted the Congress Party that they should look forward to retaining power when finally complete freedom and Purna Swaraj is won. On his return back to Calcutta Debu talked about Subash Bose so much to all his family members that his second son Swarup who was now just 17 years old decided to join the freedom movement.

In 1939 at the Tripura Congress, when Subhash was re-elected as Congress President by defeating the Mahatma's nominee, the stage was set for a split. Gandhi had announced that he regarded the election of Subhas Bose as a personal defeat and even hinted that he might even retire from politics.

In the meantime the world was now moving to the brink of another World War. On the 12th of March 1938, Hitler had occupied Vienna without even firing a single shot. And with England in difficulty Subhash felt that this was the ideal opportunity under the threat of massive civil disobedience to demand self determination within the next six months. This was a bold resolution that was proposed by him, but it was eventually defeated. His short presidential address was read out by his elder brother Sarat Chander as Subhash himself was running high fever and he was bought on a stretcher to the Congress podium. A month later at the end of April with the deadlock still unresolved, he had to face the All India Congress

Committee and with a hostile Congress Working Committee unwilling to tow his line, Subhash Bose had no other option but to resign.

On the 3rd of May 1939, Subhas Bose announced the formation of the Forward Bloc, and in August he was suspended from the Congress for three years. It was a sad day for Debu Ghosh to see the downfall of his dear friend, and it was made even sadder when his eldest son Arup having come under the sway of the Commintern movement left home and made his way to the Soviet Union. The change in Arup's attitude was largely due to the influence of the now elderly Mr MN Roy.

Mr Roy whose real name was Narendra Nath Bhattacharya was born in 1887 in a village in the 24 Parganas of Bengal. With his knowledge of engineering and chemistrty that he had studied and gained from the Bengal Technical Institute, he in his youth had also learnt the art of bomb making to help the Indian revolutiuonaries. Thereafter, under the pseudonym of Charles Martin he went to Germany to procure arms and ammunition for the revolutionary movement in India.In the summer of 1916, he sailed for San Francisco and while in America in order to evade arrest he changed his name to Manabendra Nath Roy. In 1917, when America declared war on Germany and USA started rounding up all German sympathisers, Roy fled to Mexico. There he met Mr Michael Brodin an emissary of Lenin and got fascinated with Lenin's idea of power to the proletariat. In July-August 1920 with the Soviets in power and on being invited by Lenin to take part in the Second World Congress of the Communist International, MN Roy arrived in Moscow. From there he went to Tashkent to establish the Asian Bureau of the Communist International and on 17th October 1920, while at Tashkent he formed the Communist party of India. In 1930 he clandestinely returned to India under the name of Dr Mahmud, but a year later was arrested by the British and was tried for sedition. He was sentenced to 12 years with hard labour. After serving six years in prison, in November 1936 he was released and joined the Indian National Congress and became a great supporter of Subhas Bose and his policies. While in America he had married Evelyn Trent and when she left him he again remarried in 1937. With the many stories that Arup had heard from Mr MN Roy about equality of opportunities in the Soviet Union and of the rapid progress of the the Communist movement and that the real power was now resting with the working classes and the tillers, he decIded to become a dedicated communist. Arup was convinced that it was better to stay as an Indian and as a freeman in the Soviet Union rather than languish as a slave and a second class citizen in his own country.

A month later with Subhash Bose out of power, when Debu's second son Swarup with an offer for better prospects in South East Asia decided to leave Calcutta, Hena was very upset. The job offer was from one of his friends, a Sikh lad from his college in Calcutta and whose father had a thriving business of gems in Burma, Malaya, Siam and Singapore. So on the day when Swarup sailed for Singapore, Hena gave it back to her husband.

'This is precisely what happens when the head of the family gets too involved in stupid politics and gives no time to his children when they need it most,' said a heart broken Hena as she with her husband and the rest of the family saw off the second son at the Khidderpur docks.

With the two elder boys Arup and Swarup on their way to far off lands to seek their own fortunes, there was despair and sorrow in the Ghosh family. Their only consolation was that their third son Anup who had just turned 16 and their only daughter Mona who was getting on 14 were still living with them. Anup after completing his matriculation with a third division had now also lost interest in his studies.

As far as the Sen Family was concerned, things were not too bad. The eldest son Samir had completed his fine arts course course from Shantiniketan, but like his father was more interested in politics, but that of the Gandhian kind for the emancipation and upliftment of India's helpless poor castes of Harijans. Their second son Ronen now 18 years old having excelled in his studies at St Xaviers with a first class first in his matriculation examination was about to complete his graduation with English honours from the Presidency College in Calcutta. Ronen had decided to compete for the heaven born and was simultaneously preparing for it. Their only daughter Purnima so called because she was born on a full moon night had just got into her teens and was studying in school.

Things were however brighter for the Rehman family. Gul Rehman now 24 years old was a Captain in the Indian Army. Their second son Aftab was in the Indian Military Academy and was due to pass out as an officer in another six months time. The third son Arif having done very well in his Senior Cambridge examinations from PWRIMC had joined Government College, Lahore He was only in his second year, but had made up his mind to compete for the Indian Civil Service, or at best for the Indian Police Service. He would have probably also opted for the Army, but thanks to his mother Nafisa, she had convincingly talked him out of it. With all the three brothers away from home, there was only their 15 year old sister Shenaz who kept constant company with her parents.

The Hussein family too was doing fairly well. Dr Ghulam Hussein and Suraiya Begum's 20 year old and only son Nawaz Hussein had decided to follow his father's footsteps. He was now in medical college and aspired to become a surgeon and that to with a post graduation degree from London. Their one and only daughter Hasina at 13 years had just completed her eighth standard from the Gokhale Memorial School that was located on Harish Mukherjee Street. A creation of Mrs Sarala Ray, the wife of the first Indian Principal of Presidency College, the school was opened in 1920 primarily to provide educational opportunities to the Indian girls with a blend of both Eastern and Western fussion of culture. Her best friends were Mona Ghosh and Purnima Sen and they were all in the same school and in the same class too.

In the Maharaja's kingdom of Kashmir, the Bajwa family from Bagh were not doing too badly either. Gurcharhan Bajwa the father of Captain Daler Singh Bajwa had now become a very prosperous and successful businessman and a military contractor at Muzzafarabad. With his own two younger brothers now looking after the New Sher-e-Punjab Hotel and other interests of the big joint family, Gurcharan with his wife Harbir were back in their village of Bagh and were now busy in renovating the old Gurdwara. Their 29 year old son Captain Daler Singh serving with the 4th Jammu and Kashmir Regiment was engaged to the daughter of another well do Sardar family from Jammu and the marriage was to be solemnised in the coming summer. Gurcharan's only daughter Satwant Kaur was happily married in a well to do Sikh family who were settled in Poonch, which was not very far from her own parents ancestral village of Bagh.

As far as the Pugsley family was concerned, Mr Edwin Pugsley though still not very old was leading a relatively quiet retired life tending to the roses in his garden, and doing an honorary secretary's job on weekends at the small Railway Institute at Mhow. His wife Laila now in her early forties was still a stunning beauty and besides looking after the house, she also taught partime in a local missionary school. Out of the two goodlooking twin sisters Debbie last year on her 19th birthday met her match in a friend of her elder brother who was also in the railways and they promptly got married. Sandra now 20 was still single. She had completed her teachers training from St Mary's Training College, Poona and was presently employed as a teacher in the kindergarten section of the local convent missionary school at Mhow. Richard now 17 being poor in studies had joined the Indian Army as a Signaler, while the youngest Veronica having just got into her teens and being the favourite of his father was away at Sanawar in the boarding school there.

In December 1938, Captain Ismail Sikandar Khan while on courier duty witnessed a very interesting incident. He was on his way to the Quetta Military District Headquarters to deliver some classified documents. At around 11 in the morning, the motorcycle carrying him was stopped by a large crowd of Baluchis at an unmanned railway level crossing not very far from the city. The gateless level crossing was on the highway that connected Quetta with Chaman and Fort Sandeman. Then a long hooting of a railway engine was heard and a few minutes later with a clank and a clong and accompanied by the hiss of the steam engine, the railway engine with it tender first together with just two passenger coaches packed with British, Eurasians and local railway staff and with a brake van separating them came to a grinding halt right in the middle of the highway. They were all mourners and in the brake van was the coffined body of an elderly Englishman. No sooner had the train stopped, the coffin was ceremoniously lowered from the brake van and it was handed over to and six pall bearers from the British community. Led by eleven clergymen the procession slowly moved along the road to the Christian cemetery located about 500 yards away. After saluting the coffin, Ismail too joined the procession to find out who had died. Then suddenly from a gap in a thorny hedgerow appeared six strong unarmed tribesman led by a Mulla. They were all dressed in spotless white garments, baggy pantaloons and waist coats and their dark feet were adorned with rawhide hobnailed chapplis with curling tips. They now suddenly blocked the road and stopped the funeral procession and for a brief moment everybody was stunned. Then the Mulla standing in front of his men salammed the coffin and with great dignity and humilty said.

'Dear Friends and please believe me and there is no cause for alarm. The Padre Sahib whose body is now being carried to his grave has for the past 45 years been the father and mother not only of all the Frontier tribes in our land, but also of those across the border. The name of Padre Cumming is as well known today to our generation as that of good Sandeman Sahib in the past. Padre Cumming Sahib's life and work was solely devoted to the poor, sick and the helpless. May Allah rest his soul in peace. All that we as Muslim tribesmen humbly request is to give us the privilege to pay our respects to our benefactor by permitting us to carry his body on our shoulders from this spot to the grave.'

Immediately after the request was granted, the six Muslim pall bearers led by the Mulla carried the coffin on their shoulders and gently placed it near the grave site. Then with tears in their eyes they solemnly bowed, did their salaam and backed away.Ismail however observed that one man who was crying the most was the engine driver whose name was Nadir Shah. On enquiring Ismail was told that Nadir Shah was a Baluchi who hailed from a nearby village and thanks to the English Padre he from the age of nine had been employed by the North Western Railway first as a general fag on a salary of four annas a day and thereafter as an engine driver. To Nadir Shah the Padre was everything to him. Reverend James Whilliam Nicol Cumming from 1890 to 1922 had served in the Political Office of the British Agent to the Viceroy of India in Baluchistan. Thereafter he became an ordained Minister and served in Quetta till he breathed his last.

After the funeral service was over and in order to console the driver and to save him from the wrath of his foreman, Ismail accompanied Nadir Shah in his old 'L' Class locomotive to the railway yard. Nadir Shah it seemed had a heated argument with his foreman that morning and despite his orders had taken the funeral special out driving it tender first. And when the foreman at Ismail's request pardoned Nadir Shah, the Baluchi engine driver was so touched by that gesture that he immediately invited Captain Ismail Sikandar Khan for a meal to his house that evening.

A month later In January 1939, Captain Ismail Sikandar Khan was on his way to attend a short course on the medium machine gun at the small arms school at Saugar in Central India. On the termination of the course he bought a second hand Norton motorcycle from one of the British officers stationed at Saugar and having been granted 14 days of casual leave he decided to drive down to Poona where his unit had just moved to. While studying the road map, when he came across the name of the small military cantonment at Mhow which was enroute, he decided to give the Pugsley family a pleasant surprise. The name of the small military town as Mhow it is believed was derived from its designation Military Headquarters of War when the British set it up there during the 1857 uprising in Central India.

It was evening, when Captain Ismail Sikandar Khan after making a few enquires at the Mhow railway station knocked on the door of the small bunglow located on the Station Road. The door was opened by Sandra and she got the surprise of her life when the handsome army officer introduced himself.

'My name is Smiley and you must be either Sandy or Debbie.'

'Debbie is already married and gone and I am Sandy and do please come inside,' said the young beautiful girl as she happily called out to her mother and father. There was no doubt in Ismail's mind that Sandy was no longer the young pig tailed teenaged school girl that he knew in Calcutta. She was now a tall, graceful young lady and with an hour glass figure and a flawless complexion. She was indeed a real beauty.

On seeing the dashing, tall and handsome Indian Army officer both Edwin Pugsley and his wife Laila were simply delighted. They were even more thrilled as Ismail took out the few small gifts that he had so thoughtfully bought on his way from Indore and presented it to them.

'Thank you for the bottle of Scotch eh and you are not going anywhere from here man and by order you will park yourself right here with us,' said the host as he tightly hugged Ismail. Initially Ismail had decided only to spend one night at Mhow, but with the instant cordial hospitality shown by the Pugsleys, and more so by Sandra, he now decided to atleast spend a few more days with them.

With Sandra as his constant companion on the pillion of his Norton bike they went on picnics to the nearby Bercha Lake, the lonely forests near Choral and also to the famous tourist spots of nearby Mandu and Ujjain. Normally in the evenings they would drive down to some lonely spot that was not far from the town and where they could find a cosy secluded spot to be in each others company. Soon they were madly in love with one another as Ismail kept on extending his stay.

On the last Saturday, the day before he was finally to leave for Poona, Ismail was invited by the Pugsleys to an evening of Bingo and dancing at the local Railway Club. Though the host was very keen that Ismail and Sandra should join them, but the young couple wanted to be left to themselves.

'I tell you Ismail that you will love the grog that we serve there.It is a cocktail of rum mixed with sugar and milk and besides that there will be plenty of good looking females around for dancing too man,' said Mr Pugsley as he tried to convince his young guest that he must not lose the opportunity. But with both Ismail and Sandra wanting to be alone together, Ismail already had an excuse ready.

'But Sir, please do excuse us as both Sandra and I have already accepted another invitation. We have been invited by one of my old army friends in this town for a party in his Officers Mess and it will not be proper for us at this late stage to back out,' said Ismail

'Yes ofcourse and if that be the case then both of you must honour the invitation. After all it is not very often that a member of the Pugsley family is invited to a British officer's mess,'said Laila a little sarcastically.

After the elder Pugsleys had departed for their own evening at the Railway Club, Sandra quickly got busy in the kitchen making some cheese and egg sandwiches.

'Don't forget to carry a blanket or two because it will be cold outside in the open,'said Sandra as Ismail got busy in organizing the mini bar with a bottle of gin, and a few bottles of tonic water to go with it.

'Alright let us not delay any further and we will go to the Bercha Lake,' said Ismail as he tenderly pecked Sandra on her cheek and gave the Norton a kick start and soon they were on their way for their own exclusive moonlight picnic.

Spreading the blanket on the ground, Ismail remembered the night that he had spent in the open with the voluptuous Mrs Lindsay at Quetta. That night he had been seduced by the middle aged lady, but tonight with Sandra it would be one of sorrowful parting thought he as they both lay motionless on the blanket squeezing each other's hands.Then suddenly Ismail turned around and holding Sandra tenderly in his arms he smothered her with kisses all over her beautiful face. He started with her forehead then switched on tenderly to her eyebrows, her eyes, her ears, her cheeks, her slender neck and it finally ended with a tight kiss on her inviting lips.

'Oh I am going to really miss you my darling and why don't you for my sake extend your leave by a few more days,' swooned Sandra as she whispered those words into Ismail's ears. Holding her tightly in his arms, Ismail lifted her skirt up and felt her beautiful shapely legs while he kept kissing her passionately on her lips. Suprisingly Sandra that evening on purpose or otherwise had no other under garments under her warm woollen skirt or under her woollen sweater as Ismail's fingers tenderly explored her mount while his lips lovingly sucked her pink and aroused nipples.

'Please be careful love,' begged Sandra as she spread her legs a little wider and Ismail got on top of her.

'Do be gentle my darling and don't put it inside please', pleaded Sandra but Ismail it seems had come fully prepared.

'Just don't worry and it will be very safe, I promise' said an excited Ismail as he unrolled the rubber band over his throbbing manhood. Very wisely he had bought them from the only chemist's shop that was inside the local Bombay bazaar. Holdingly it lovingly, Sandra then very gently slided it into her gaping hole. For both of them it was now an ecstasy of a different kind as they let themselves go and climaxed simultaneously. Within a couple of minutes when it was all over, Sandra having adjusted her crumpled skirt got up and got ready to serve the sandwiches that she had made for her one and only Smiley.

"And when do we meet again and try and come back soon,' said Sandra as she held the sandwich to Ismail's lips.for him to take the first bite.

'But I am afraid these sandwiches alone darling will never ever satisfy my hunger and love for you ever. What I need is you and you alone all the time,' said Ismail as they once more stretched themselves on the blanket. A minute or so later and giving the excuse that the ground below was hurting, Sandra climbed on top of Ismail and having lifted her skirt a wee bit higher said rather coyly.

'Don't you think this way it will be more thrilling and comfortable.'

Having got the hint, Ismail promptly lifted her blouse up and with his soft hands kept fondling her pear shaped breasts. As he kept rolling his palms gently over her taut nipples, Sandra closed her eyes and using her right hand she once again slowly guided Ismail's stiff manhood into her love box.

It was around midnight, when they both reached home and luckily for them the elderly Pugsley's were still at the club.

'Tomorrow morning my darling and before I leave, I am going to ask your parents formally for your hand, but the engagement ceremony and the marriage I am afraid will have to wait for a while longer because getting leave after doing an army course is well nigh impossible,' said Ismail as he knelt and kissed Sandra's hand to formalize the proposal. Sandra was delighted and as they kissed once more she said.

'All these days I have been waiting to hear those words and I really will miss you most terribly.'

'Don't worry I will be back soon, and I only hope that your parents will not have any objections to the marriage since I am not a Christian,' said Ismail as he brushed of all the mud, dust and the tell tale signs on the blanket and on his clothes.

Next morning, when Ismail announced his decision, the Pugsleys were simply delighted.

'Though we are Protestant Christians and you are a Muslim so what and that does not matter because we are all human beings. After all Abraham or Ibrahimn, Joseph or Yusuf, Mary or Marriam are one and the same. They all came from the same stock, but the pity is that some of our so called living preachers and politicians whether they be Hindus, Muslims, Sikhs, Jews or Christians, all of them are bloody hypocrites of the first order. Instead of binding mankind together, they are hell bent to separate them only for their selfish gains and now only the God Almighty with whatever name you may call him can save this wretched selfish world,' said the retired engine driver as he hugged Ismail and reminded him to drive slowly and very carefully.

In early March1939, after completion of the medium machine gun course at Saugar, Ismail rejoined the Second Punjabees in Poona. But a week later they moved out for collective training at the unit level and that was followed by formation level exercisies under the newly raised 4th Indian Division.

With the possibility of another world war looming large in the horizon, the top brass of the Indian Army were taking no chances whatsoever. A kind off unofficial mobilization and urgent recruitment to fill in the defficiencies of man power was already in progress. But despite the strenuous training schedule with his Dogra Company, Ismail without fail and religiously everyday while sitting unde his 180 pounder tent somewhere in the wilderness would write to his sweet heart Sandra. Ismail had so far only confided in his decision to marry Sandra to his bosom friend Captain Gul Rehman whose unit the 1/1 st Punjabees were now part of the 5th Indian Division and they too were conducting training exercises in and around Secunderabad.

It was on the first of April that Ismail received a very long letter from his dear friend Gul Rehman informing him about his forthcoming marriage to some girl called Zubeida. Initially he thought it to be a prank for the April Fool's day which Gul Rehman with his sense of humour was quite capable of executing, but when he read the entire contents he was convinced that it was not a joke. In his long letter Gul Rehman wrote.

'I do not know when you are going to tie the knot, but my marriage is fixed for the 3rd of August at Peshawar after my parents return from their second honeymoon and this time the venue for their wedding anniversary is a luxury ship which will soon be sailing to the Far East . . . My marriage is an arranged one and though I don't remember ever meeting Zubeida, but according to my mother I had first met her when she was three year old toddler and I was around eleven. That was sometime in 1925, when both our parents were posted in Rawalpindi and as per my mother, I had even carried her quite a few times in my arms whenever we all went out together for picnics. This does sound rather funny doesn't it? It virtually amounts to cradle snatching, but that is how it is and now she is soon going to be my wife. Needless to say she was my mother's choice and I immediately consented to it. Therefore I do not want to hear any lame excuses such as exigencies of service, or out on test exercise and suck kind of crap and bullshit. Therefore keep all your seniors in good humour and particularly the oldman and ensure that you reach Peshawar atleast a week in advance. Also keep your fingers crossed till my D-Day is over and you have to make it because without you by my wedding will forever remain incomplete.'

Surprising a day later a wedding card with a letter arrived giving the happy news that Captain Daler Singh Bajwa would be getting married at Jammu on 20th Jun and Ismail wondered when his turn would come to tie the knot with Sandra.

In the hot summer month of May 1939, though the war clouds over Europe were once again thickening, Colonel Rehman with his wife and daughter Shenaz together with Colonel Reginald Edwards for good company were not going to miss the opportunity of visiting Singapore and Hongkong. The SS Canton was on her maiden voyage from England to the Far East and they were already booked on it.

'To hell with Hitler and his bloody Nazis and war or no war, I am not going to let go of this opportunity,' said Colonel Attiqur Rehman as he hugged and bid goodbye to his son Gul Rehman who had come to see them of.

'Yes Sir you are absolutely right and the last time I was here which was not very many months ago to board a ship for England, the Military Police on duty at the very last minute got me off the gangway with the excuse that the war could start anyday and my damn leave was cancelled and I had to rush back by the return Frontier Mail to my dear Kanchas from the 4th Gurkha Rifles. It seems that Mr Hitler simply cannot decide when to let go the bloody balloon. Well for whatever he is worth or not worth, now that leave has once again been reopened, I will be the last person to get off this boat,'said Captain John Masters as he smiled at Gul Rehman, shook hands with him and ran up the gangway.

'But how do you my son,' asked Colonel Attiqur as the SS Canton slowly sailed out of the Bombay harbour.

'Oh we met by chance and we got to know each other over some beer and lunch at the Pathankot railway restaurant a few years ago and it is a pity that he is not accompanying us. I wish he did then I too would have had some real good company too,' said Captain John Masters.

'Never mind, for we will have you as our company,' said Colonel Reginald Edwards.

The very next day during supper, the young and handsome John Masters was seen in the company of two young American ladies and both of them seemed very much impressed with his status as a King's Commissioned Officer of the Indian army.

'Oh so you are the King's man in India,' said one of the ladies as John Masters tried to explain to them that he was only one of the King's humble servants in the country.

'Not only that my dear ladies, but he is also the winner of the Norman medal from the prestigious Sandhurst Military Academy in,' said Colonel Reginald Edwards while ordering for a bottle of chilled rare French white wine to go with the continental menu of chicken and fish delicacies that was on the bill of fare for that evening.

'With my compliments,' said Reggie as the smartly dressed ship's steward in a black bow tie and a liveried waiter with élan slowly poured the contents into the two crystal wine glasses that Reggie had specially asked for.

'I must say Colonel that chivalry in the Indian Army is simply par excellence and may be we will see more of each other in the days to come,' said one of the young ladies who was overwhelmed by the hospitality.

'You will definitely see more of us the two old foggies, but we as husband and wife are now more or less a spent force as far as the Indian Army is concerned,'.said Colonel Attiqur Rehman while introducing his wife and daughter to the two American ladies.

A day or two later, when the games and dances started on board the ship for those in the higher classes, little Shenaz was thrilled. She soon learnt how to play the game of Bingo and Canasta and everytime she saw the young Captain John Masters dancing on the floor, she went back into her cabin to practice the steps.

One evening, when she saw him teaching the two American ladies the Lambeth Walk on the ship's deck, she in desperation went upto him and said.

'Sir didn't you say that that you are a good friend of my dear eldest brother but you don't seem to care for us because we are Indians I guess. I too would like to learn to dance the way you do but you seem to be interested only in the Americans,' said an angry Shenaz with tears in her eyes as she ran back into her cabin.

A few minutes later Colonel Attiqur came out and apologised to the two American ladies and to Captain John Masters for his daughters uncalled for outburst.

'It's alright Sir, but I guess she too was right in her own way. It maybe because she has no one on board of her own age to keep her company, but we will soon make up for it,' said Captain John Masters.

That very evening when there was a lot of more such interesting games on the upper deck, Captain John Masters joined Colonel Attiqur's table and with young Shenaz as his partner took part in most of them and Shenaz was thrilled. A little later, when the compere announced the last and final game for the day and declared it open to all the passengers irrespective of their gender and age, Shenaz was delighted. It was a simple game that required all the participants to run from one end of the deck to the other and from the long table that was placed at the far end to pick up two cream cracker biscuits and chew them as fast as possible and thereafter the participants were required to entertain the crowd by whistling at least four lines from any popular English tune. To ensure that everyone took part enthusiastically, the Captain of the ship also declared three fabulous prizes to the winner, the runner up and the second runner up. To be fair to all the ladies and to the tiny tots the total running distance was also reduced for them accordingly. And In order to ensure that the verdict would be a fair one and that it should go to the deserving candidate, Colonel Reggie being the senior most was appointed as the chief judge.

'No cheating ladies, gentlemen and children and remember each one of you will have to chew not just one or one and a half, but two full cream cracker biscuits and the whistling has to be fairly audible and as per the original tune or else I am afraid you will be disqualied.'.

'When the compere over the ship's megaphone announced the start of the novel race and game, everybody was excited. Once everybody was ready and the final whistle was sounded there was a regular stampede to chew those biscuits, and it was young Shenaz who took the lead. Thereafter it was quite a comic scene as each competitor kept munching away those cream cracker biscuits, but when it finally came to whistling a proper recognisable tune most of them got eliminated. Little Shenaz was not the type to give up so very easily as she tried desparetly to whistle the popular 'Bicycle Built For Two' song which was her grandfather's favourite and the only one that she knew, but with the crumbs of biscuit still in her mouth, the task was next to impossible.

'Never mind and well done and atleast you tried your best young lady,' said the ship's Captain while giving a special prize of a box of Swiss chocolates to the spirited girl. And as far as Colonel Attiqur was concerned he did slightly better and could manage to faintly whistle the first line only of that same very song. But it was finally the young handsome Captain John Masters from the Fourth Gurkha Rifles who merrily walked away with the first prize. With his remarkable rendering of 'The Alexander's Rag Time Tune' he was now considered as a hero And when he came back with the grand prize to the table where the two American ladies were sitting, and he found that they too were trying their best to get the hang of how to whistle, Colonel Attiqur very sportingly gave a loud wolf whisle and invited all of them and Colonel Reggie to cocktails that evening.

On the 19th of June 1939, both Captain Gul Rehman and Captain Ismail Sikandar Khan arrived at the Satwari railway Station near Jammu to attend their friend Captain Daler Singh's wedding. The wedding in the local gurdwara next morning was a simple but yet a very dignified affair as the young couple walked around the holy Guru Granth Sahib and took their vows.Once the wedding was over, the dimunitive, shy and pretty seventeen year old Simran Tej Kaur dressed in a heavily brocaded bright red traditional Punjabi wedding costume and with gold, diamonds and other precious stones glittering from her head to toe sought the blessings of all the elders.

'No Bhabiji you do not have to touch our feet. We are the bum chums of your dear husband and from today you are our loving sister-in-law,' said Ismail while blessing her with a gold necklace set, while Gul Rehman presented her with a pure silver photoframe. With all the formalities in the Gurudwara over, it was now the time for merry making, eating and drinking at the Jammu Brigade Officer's Mess and it was followed by the traditional Punjabi Bhangra and Giddha dancing which carried on late into the night. And when Ismail and Gul Rehman were about to call it a day, the elderly and happy Harbir Kaur, the mother of the groom said.

'Now that musketeer number one has tied the knot, how about the two of you, and don't forget to invite us for the wedding. And even if you all don't I will still be there and with my husband too,' said the jovial lady while presenting them with a big box of sweets each.

'Ofcourse they will invite us' said Gurcharan Singh as he hugged the two young Captains and thanked them for having taken all the trouble to come for the wedding.

It was on the 1st of August 1939, when Captain Ismail Sikandar Khan with Second Lieutenant Aftab Rehman Khan the younger brother of the groom who had recently been commissioned into Ismail's 2nd Punjabees arrived at Peshawar. They had been granted only a week's leave and though a good four days alone would be taken up with travelling only, but they could not miss the grand occassion. Gul Rehman was there at the railway station to receive them, and when Ismail confidentially told him that he was madly in love with Sandra and requested that the matter be kept a secret between the two of them till the wedding date was finalised, Gul Rehman readily agreed. However, he cautioned Ismail not to delay it for very long because there were strong rumours about a war shortly breaking out in Europe and the possibility of the newly raised Indian Divisions going overseas was very much a possibility too.'

'Frankly speaking I would'nt mind marrying her tomorrow, but I don't think the boss will give me permission since I am not yet twenty five, and moreover I have got to generate a reasonable bank balance to run a family,' said Ismail.

'Don't worry about the money yaar that we will look after and you can pay us back later,' said Gul Rehman as they got into the car for the drive home.

That day and from the very moment that Ismail set foot at the huge Rehman family mansion at Peshawar, the preparations for the wedding was put in top gear.as he with the 15 year old Shenaz, the sister of the groom got busy with all the decorations and the food arrangements for the big occassion. This was going to be the first wedding in Colonel Attiqur's family and it had to be something more than special. It was also an occasion for a grand reunion of old friends and relatives from far off places and especially the three musketeers. From far away Calcutta and in the company of Dr Ghulam Hussein and family in an especially reserved second class railway coach arrived the Sen's and the Ghosh's with their wives but minus their grown up sons. But all the daughters had accompanied them. The Bajwa clan from Muzzafarabad was all present in full measure and even Colonel Reginald Edwards had arrived three days ahead of schedule. Only the Pugsley family from Mhow was missing. They had expressed their inability to attend the wedding but they did send a gift by parcel post.

'My isn't the bride really beautiful,' said Hena Ghosh when she and the others among the senior ladies present were introduced to Zubeida after the Nikaah ceremony was finally over.

Zubeida was the eldest daughter of Major Aslam Khan and she too came from a renowned Pathan family of Peshawar. Attiqur and Aslam had become good friends from the day Major Aslam Khan, a greenhorn Lieutenant from the Indian Medical Service first reported for duty as the Regimental Medical Officer of the 2nd Punjabees and that was just after the Great War. Major Aslam was a couple of years junior to Colonel Attiqur Rehman both in age and service andt they had served together in quite a few military stations in the North West Frontier. A year ago and after completing 20 years in the army, Major Aslam Khan had taken premature retirement and was now a general practioner with a roaring practice in the important port town of Karachi.

'Arre Colonel Sahib aapne to waqai ek chand ko zameen mein lay aaya. Maasha alla aapki Bahu bahut hi khoobsorat hai. Hum wahe guru se prathana karenge ke ye jodi ko har waqt khush aur sai salamat rakhe" (I must say Colonel Sahib that you have literally brought the Moon down to Mother Earth. By God she is really very beautiful and I will pray to our Wahe Guru that the young couple always remain happy and healthy.) said a happy Gurcharan Singh while blessing the bride.

'Please aap aur nazar mat lagaye hamare nahin dhulaniyan ko,' said Harbir Kaur to her husband as Shenaz with her cousin Hasina and her new found friends Mona Ghosh and Purnima Sen all dressed in traditional and colourful Muslim long dresses of Ghagra Choli entered with the' Paans' on silver trays.

'Abhi tho inkee bari aani walee hai, tho aur der kis baat ki. Maine tho mera beta Nawaz ke liye uski jodi pasand kar hi llya hai (Now it will soon be the turn of these young girls and we must not delay and in anycase I have already selected the girl for my son Nawaz) said Dr Ghulam Hussein as he loving pinched Shenaz's cheek.Hearing that remark all the girls started blushing and to add a little more spice to that comment, the grooms two younger brothers, Second Lieutenant Aftab Rehman Khan and Arif Rehman Khan who were standing nearby jokingly added.

'Arre Allah bachaye in hasinon se, yeh sub tho bhar denge apne hone walle shaur ko pasine se" (God help the men who get such partners because if they do, then it will be only one big sweat for them).'

'Wah Wah, Kiya Farmaya., Muqarrer Muqarrar' (That was indeed well said and needs to be repeated, shouted the other young men as the three girls' giigling and blushing ran into the adjoining special shamiana that was meant only for the ladies.

While Gul Rehman with his beautiful wife Zubeida were enjoying their honeymoon in the Kashmir Valley, in Europe the winds of war were blowing towards a dark future for the world. It was on 19th August 1934, that Hitler had become the Fuhrer of Germany and within a few months on 16th March 1935 he blatantly violated the terms of the treaty of Versailles by introducing compulsory military conscription in the German Armed Forces.

On 10th of February 1936, Hitler placed his German Gestapo above the law and 21 months later on 5th November 1937 at 4.15 PM he held his top secret conference with his trusted lieutenants in the Reich Chancellery and after swearing them into secrecy had spelt out Germany's future expansion plans

'We the German people need more living space and we shall have it at all costs. The aim of this German Policy is to make sure and to preserve the racial community and to enlarge it. It is therefore a question of space,' added the Fuhrer as Colonel Frederich Hossbach meticulously took down the minutes. Six months later in mid March 1938, Hitler announced his so called union with Austria as his German troops marched unopposed into that country and on 12th August the full mobilization of the German Army was ordered.On the 30th of September, 1938 the British Prime Minister appeased Hitler at the Munich conference and the threat of another world war receded albeit only temporarily though. Emboldened by his foreign policy, the German troops on 15th October occupied the Sudentenland and the Czech government resigned. On 27th October some 15,000 Jews of Polish origin were expelled from Germany and without any warning were forcibly packed like sardines into railway boxcars and were dumped at the Polish border. Amonst them was the family of Herschel Grynszpan a young 17 year old who was then working and living in Paris. In retaliation for the inhuman treatment meted out to his father and his family, Herschel on 7th November, 1938 shot Erns Vom Rath the third secretary in the German Embassy in Paris. On the very next day 9th November when the death of the German embassy staff was announced, the German mobs, aided by Nazi storm troopers, the dreaded SS and the Hitler Youth inhumanly beat up the Jews, murdered quite a few of them, looted their property and burned their synagogues. That became known as the Night of the Broken Glass.

In mid March 1939, the Nazis had taken over Czechoslovakia and with the Spanish civil war having ended on 28th March, Hitler's Germany on 22nd May signed the "Pact of Steel" with Mussolini's Italy. The German southern flank was now fully secure. On 23rd August, 1939 the Germans also conveniently signed a non aggression pact with the Soviet Union thereby securing their eastern flank too. And with Poland serving as a convenient buffer.to be carved up subsequently between the Russians and the Germans, Britain and Poland quickly signed a The Mutual Assistance Treaty two days later. The stage was now set for Hitler to launch "Operation Case White", the invasion of Poland.

Chapter-11

The Armageddon Begins

Early in the morning at 4.45 AM on 1st September 1939, the three massive German Army Groups spearheaded by German armoured formations and consisting of 1.8 million German troops practically walked into Poland. And on the very next day of 2nd September, both England and France sent Germany a 24 hour ultimatum and threatened Hitler with dire consequences if the German forces were not withdrawn immediately from Poland. Meanwhile on 1st September itself Britain had declared general mobilization and ordered that all men between the ages of 20 and 22 years were liable for conscription, but Hitler couldn't care less. And as far as the Jews in Germany were concerned, from 1st September they were all ordered to remain indoors and were not to be seen outside their houses after 8 PM in the evening. On the 3rd of September, 1939 after the ultimatum expired Britain declared war on Germany.

'What bloody cheek and who the hell is Viceroy Linlithgow to decide about India declaring war on Germany,' said Debu Bose as the three friends met at the Coffee House for their usual Saturday get together.

'Yes and you are damn well right because this war is between the Europeans and why the hell are we being unnecessarily dragged into it,'said Dr Ghulam Hussein.

'I will tell you why. We are being dragged into it because we are the bigest milch cow of the Empire and they have a big well trained Indian Army that is being commanded by them and which when required could be used as cannon fodder,' said Naren Sen.

'But atleast the Viceroy could have consulted the Indian leaders of the Central Legislature before making such a unilateral proclamation at his own initiative,' said Ghulam Hussein.

'Yes we dumb Indians have not yet understood the psyche of the clever Britishers and I guess we never ever will,' said Debu Ghosh while asking for the bill.

'In anycase I suggest Daktar Babu now that the war has been officially declared, I do not think it will be wise for you to send your son Nawaz to England for his higher studies in medicine,' added Naren Sen.

'Yes I guess you are right and it is all because of the damn stupid Hitler who is the cause for all this', said Dr Ghulam Hussein as the three old friends made a beeline for the Tiger Cinema Hall where the latest Hollywood film 'The Adventures of Robin Hood" was being screened. It was a 1938 Hollywood release starring the handsome and swashbuckling Errol Flynn and was an Oscar award winning movie.

When the Viceroy at the behest of the British Government asked the Congress Party for its support for the war effort, the Congress agreed provided the British were ready to give India full Independence. Seeing the attitude of the Congress, the Muslim League also chipped in with their full support for the war provided they too were given justice and fair play for their demands. However, the Muslim Premiers of Bengal, Punjab and Sind which were neither Congress nor Muslim League ministries pledged unconditional support of their respective Provinces towards the cause of the allies. Not to be left behind, the Princely States too either individually or through the Chamber of Princes also pledged their support to the King and Emperor. By now total mobilization of the Indian armed forces had also been ordered by the Government. And on the 28th of September, when the 2nd Punjabees by a special train arrived in Bombay, Ismail sent an urgent telegram to Sandra to come and meet him there at the earliest.

'I regret our engagement and marriage will now have to take a backseat since we will be sailing on the 'SS Erinpura' for some unknown destination from Bombay in the first week of October. Therefore do try and make it before we sail off. We are camping at Colaba Military station and it is near the Afghan Church which is quite a famous landmark of the city. I miss you so much love and hoping to see you soon.Your's forever Smiley.'

Due to the orders for mobilization there was mounting pressure on the Indian post and telegraph department who had to first give first priority to the call up telegrams and to all government messages and as a result of which Ismail's telegram to Sandra got inordinately delayed and by the time Sandra received it and she arrived in Bombay, the SS Erinpura had already sailed for the Middle East.

'Sorry Maam you are only 12 hours too late, but there is a small parcel and a letter waiting for you,' said the duty officer at the Embarkation Headquarters to a heartbroken Sandra Pugsley as he handed over the envelope and the small gift wrapped parcel that Captain Ismail Sikandar Khan had left for her.

There were tears in Sandra's eyes as she read the long love letter from her Smiley, which repeatedly stated that hopefully the war will be over soon and then they would be together finally again as husband and wife. 'I pray to God that your words come true,' said Sandra to herself as she did the sign of the cross, kissed the diamond ring that he had left for her and caught the next train back to Mhow.

A month or so later the Viceroy categorically stated that the British Government's war aims had not yet been defined and that the British policy in India still retained the goal of Dominion Status. And to this he also promised that at the end of the war the modifications of the 1935 Government Act would be once again considered in the light of Indian views. But when he ruled that during the war a consultative group would be established consisting of all the major political parties and the Princes, all the Congress ministries in the Provinces promptly resigned.

With no Muslim League Governments elected during the formation of the Provincial Ministries in 1937, Mr Mohammed Ali Jinnah realized the need to unify all the Muslims in India in order to build for himself a mass base and for the Muslims of India a mass party. He therefore had now started touring the Muslim populated provinces of India. In Bengal he had sided with the Fazlul Haq ministry and in December 1938 had presided over the Muslim League meeting at Patna and now with all the Congress ministries resigning on 31st October 1939, he was a very happy and a relieved man. For him it was a blessing in disguise as he vigorously set about to once more mobilize all Muslim support for the Muslim League. He now appealed to the Muslims and the other minorities in India to observe 22nd December, 1939 as the 'Day of Deliverance and Thanksgiving' and followed it up by calling for another session of the Muslim League to be held this time at the historic city of Lahore in March 1940.

It was on 28th January 1933 that a forty year old Muslim graduate, Chaudhury Rehmat Ali residing then in England at 3, Humberstone Road, Cambridge had dreamt of the land of the pure and had aptly given it the name of Pakistan. He had dreamt of a separate independent nation of Muslims in the subcontinent. That very afternoon he meticulously wrote out the draft of what he considered should be included as part and parcel of his separate Islamic Nation.

To the Muslims there was but one Allah the Almighty, Bismillah Rehman-e-Rahim. These were the three names of the same Allah that was recited at the start of each Muslim prayer. The Holy Koran forbade the representation of Allah in any shape or form whatsoever because Allah was always omnipresent, debated Mr Jinnah in his mind as he put his heart and soul in drafting a speech that would soon shake the Indian subcontinent and its people.

In the third week of March, 1940, a colourfully decorated train with green flags mounted on the steam engine and with the emblem of the Muslim League, the Crescent and the Star prominently displayed steamed out of the Delhi railway Station with Mr Mohammed Ali Jinnah and other Muslim League leaders and their supporters. The destination was Lahore. It was on 9th October 1938, at Karachi that the Muslim League's green flag with the silver crescent moon and star was hoisted for the first time by Sir Sikandar Hyatt, but now it flew in all splendour on top of a gigantic tent at Lahore's famous Minto Park.

In the afternoon of 22nd March 1940 the gigantic tent was packed with some 60,000 Muslim supporters of the man who was now acknowledged as their supreme leader. At 2.25 PM the tall and handsome Mr Jinnah impeccably dressed as usual in a Saville Row suit entered the venue to the thunderous cheers of his supporters. All of them stood in respect as the man briskly walked to the rostrum to give his historic address. He started first speaking in Urdu, but soon switched over to English. Though some in the audience objected, but a cool and confidrnt Mr Jinnah having lit in what was probably his 25th cigarette of the day.surveyed the huge crowd with his piercing eyes. Then placing back the tin of his Craven A cigarettes back on the table, he contemplated for a while and then again started in English. He know spoke for the next two hours and those who understood the language listened to him with rapt attention.Expounding the rationale behind the Lahore resolution, he asserted that the Muslims of India were a nation by any definition and this he said very categorically and emphatically.

'Gentlemen it is always been taken for granted mistakenly that the Mussulmans are a minority. But I say that the Mussulmans are not a minority. They are a nation by any definition. Even according to the British map of India, we Mussulmans occupy parts of this country where we are in big majority and these include Bengal, Punjab, Sind, the North West Frontier and Baluchistan. If the British Government earnestly and sincerely believes in the happiness of this subcontinent then the only course open to them is to give us our separate homeland by dividing the country into autonomous national states.

'In India, Islam and Hinduism are not religions in the strict sense of the word, but are, in fact different and distinct social orders, and it is a dream that the Hindus and the Muslims can ever evolve a common nationality. The Hindus and the Mussulmans gentlemen belong to two different religious philosophies, social customs, and literatures. They neither inter-marry nor inter dine together. And indeed they belong to two different civilizations which are based mainly on conflicting ideas and conceptions. We also derive our inspiration from different sources of history. They have different epics, different heroes and different episodes. Often the hero of one is the foe of the other. Hence to yoke together two such nations into one, one as a numerical minority, the other a majority, will only lead to discontent and destruction of one another. Therefore, the Muslims of India cannot accept any constitution that will result in a Hindu majority Government. This will only amount to Hindu Raj and we cannot or will not accept it and if it is forced upon us it will only lead to Civil War. Therefore, we must be prepared to face all difficulties and consequences and to make all the sacrifices that may be required of us to achieve the goal we have set in front of us. We must have our own homeland, our own Pakistan and that is our ultimate aim.' those words, when Mr Jinnah concluded his address there was thunderous clapping all around except from one far corner where sat Colonel Attiqur Rehman and a few others Indian Army doctors. They were not there as delegates but as individual listeners and observers. Colonel Attiqur and his group were on their way to Bombay and from there to the Middle East. He had been given command of a newly raised field ambulance unit and he wondered where will all this lead to as he boarded the Frontier Mail from Lahore. Personally Colonel Attiqur Rehman now in his early fifties was not at all in favour of Mr Jinnah's call for a separate Muslim nation.

While Mr Jinnah was talking about a possible civil war between the Muslims and the Hindus in India, in the Middle East the 4th Indian Division was now getting ready to go hell for leather against the enemy. Raised at Ahmednagar near Poona in 1935, the Indian Division had arrived in Egypt and had set up their Divisional Headquarters at Mena House, in Cairo. The Infantry Division was now camping and training under the shadows of the world famous Pyramids and were getting ready to take on the Germans and the Italians. On 12th December 1939, the War Office in London had authorised the Division its new formation sign. It was the Red Eagle on a black background and their motto was "Jo Hukam" (At Your Command).

Promoted to a war time rank of acting major, Ismail Sikandar Khan commanding a Dogra company of the 2nd Punjabees was detailed to do an Italian language course in Cairo. The Italian Army under the orders of their Duce, Benito Mussolini since October 1935 had overrun Ertirea, Somaliland and Ethopia, but had yet to declare war on England and France. Ismail Sikandar Khan being proficient in languages, excelled on the course.at Cairo.

On the morning of 19th May 1940, the man who managed to enter The Royal Military College at Sandhurst, England after three tries and coaching in a crammer with a big cigar in his mouth prepared his speech for the people of his country. The man who was part of the awkward squad at Sandhurst and needed smartening up and who as a young cavalry officer from the 4th Hussars had served in India and also in South Africa during the Boer War and from where after being taken prisoner he carried out a daring escape was a man of letters too. A week earlier on the 10th of May, Mr Winston Churchill, the First Lord of the Admiralty had taken over as the new Prime Minister from Mr Neville Chamberlain. Mr Chamberlain having met Hitler at Munich in 1938 had promised the so called "Peace in our time". But it was war now and peace was far from Mr Churchill's mind that afternoon as he spoke to the British people as their Prime Minister for the first time over the radio. He was now going to tell them what he had told the members of his coalition cabinet on the 10th of May and later on the same day to the honourable members of the House of Commons. That day he had said I have nothing to offer but blood, toil, tears and sweat. And today he was telling his countrymen to do the same and defeat the monstrous enemy. He concluded his speech by saying "Arm yourselves and be ye men of valour, and be in readiness for the conflict; for it is better for us to perish in battle than to look upon the outrage of our nation at this hour."

In India it was only after the fall of France, the near disaster at Dunkirk, and Italy's declaration of war against England and France on the 10th of June 1940 that the Congress Working Committee decided to throw their full weight behind the defence of Britain, but on two major conditions. The first being that the declaration of full Independence to India must be guaranteed and it should take effect immediately after the war ended. And the second being of more pressing need was for the formation of a Provisional National Government at the Centre which should be such so as to command the confidence of all elected elements in the Central Legislature. However, the above proposals were not fully acceptable to the Government and to streamline matters, the British cabinet decided to send a new mission to India under Sir Stafford Cripps.

While the British Expeditionary Force in Western Europe was reeling under the German Blitzkrieg, in early March of that very year a well dressed Indian in western clothes who was born in the small Indian village of Sunam in the Punjab in 1899, and who as a teenage water carrier had been an eye witness to the senseless massacre of helpless innocent Indian men, women and children at the Jalianwala Bagh walked into the India House in London.

'This is it,' he said to himself as he read the notice that had been placed on the notice board. It was an invitation by the Association of retired and serving British colonial officers to all like minded people who had served in India for a meeting and a get together at the Caxton Hall in London on 13th March 1940. But what really thrilled the middle aged Indian reading that notice was the name of the Chief Guest for the occasion and who was also going to be one of the speakers that evening.

'Now I will get him and a few others too and teach these British bastards a lesson of their lives,' vowed the man as he underlined the name with his newly acquired Swan fountain pen. The man had been stalking his British prey for very many years in England and was only waiting for an opportune moment where in full view of the British public and other past and present colonial dignitaries he would shoot him dead in cold blood and take his revenge.

It was thirty one years ago on the 1st of July 1909, when a young educated Indian from a well to do family from Punjab who had gone to England to study mechanical engineering had shot dead the first Englishman in his own country and that victim was not just an ordinary Englishman. The victim was Sir Curzon Wyllie, the political aide to Lord Morley, the Secretary of State for India. That Indian's grudge too was that Britain cannot treat Indians as their slaves and that she had no moral right to rule over India. To the Indian reading that notice at India House, Madan Lal Dhingra was a true patriot and he too like Bhagat Singh, Rajguru and Sukhdev had happily faced the gallows when he was hanged at the Pentonville prison in London. On Madan Lal's death, the Irish press had hailed him as a hero, and Anne Besant had said that more Madan Lal Dhingras was the the need of the time. Even Mr VS Blunt, a British Member of Parliament had noted in his diary that no Christian martyr ever faced the judge more fiercly and with such dignity then Mr Madan Lal Dhingra.

'Well now more Udham Singhs, alias Ram Mohammed Singh Azad's were needed to teach the English a lesson,' thought the man as he got dressed for the occasion.In a well tailored suit and tie, Udham Singh on 13th March, 1940 entered the Caxton hall and took his seat not very far from where the honourable speakers were seated on the dais. When Sir Michael O' Dwyer the erstwhile retired Lieutenant Governor of Punjab and the chief guest for the occasion got up to address the gathering, Udham Singh too joined in the clapping. The man who had so arrogantly said that if the gathering is being held at Jalianwala Bagh on Baisakhi Day then we will do all people to death did not know about his own fate that evening as he walked up to the rostrum. The audience listened to his speech with rapt attention while occassionaly punctuating it with some clapping. Then no sooner had he concluded his talk and graciously acknowledged the standing ovation, Udham Singh walked up, called out his new name and greeted the man with a smile. And as the 76 year old Michael O'Dwyer gracefully acknowledged the greeting, returned the smile and he turned around to go back to his seat, Udham Singh pulled out the revolver and shot him dead. He also shot and wounded Lord Lamington and Sir Louis Dane. Then a scuffle ensued and some people including a few women in the audience with their combined effort managed to pin Udham Singh down. On the 31st of July 1940, Udham Singh was hanged in the same Pentonville prison and like Madan Lal Dingra, his death too found no place in the British and the Indian press. The prison authorities like in the case of Madan Lal Dhingra simply dug a grave within the premises of the prison and threw his dead body into it. Justice Atkinson on the orders of the Government had ruled that no statement of the accused or his conviction be made public, and the British press dutifully honoured the ruling. Udham Singh alias Ram Mohammed Singh Azad, the name he had coined for himself and which during his trial he insisted he was in flesh and blood had sacrificied his life as a martyr. Even while the noose was being tightened around his neck, he reiterated his passion for Hindu, Sikh and Muslim unity for an emerging India.

While the trial of Udham Singh was in progress in London, in Calcutta Subhas Bose on 2nd July 1940, under a cloudy monsoon sky organized a demonstration to protest against the existence of the memorial to that tragic event in history, when innocent people became the victims of what had become famous in Indian History as the "Blackhole of Calcutta". He was now out of the Congress Party, but not out of reckoning as he in a fiery speech exhorted his Forward Block supporters to rise against the slavery of the "Gora" Sahibs, the Whitemen and fight for India's freedom. He was promptly arrested, charged with sedition and put in prison.

The British and the French were on the losing side now as the German juggernaut swept through France, and the Benelux countries. Hitler was now planning "Operation Sea Lion" to bring England and her Empire to its knees but this was conditional and it was only if Britain sued for peace with Germany. Surprisingly Hitler had left Great Britain off the hook, when he stalled the pursuit and the rout of the British Expedtionary Forces while they were stranded at Dunkirk. Whether it was intentional or otherwise, it was very difficult to tell. But for England it came as a blessing in disguise as' Operation Dynamo' for the evacuation of British Forces at Dunkirk went into full swing

Earlier in January, rationing of sugar, butter and bacon in England had already been enforced, and in April in order to raise more funds for the war effort, the tax on beer and whisky had been raised marginally. And in May 1940, Britain also raised the conscription age to 36. On the 4th of June, an inspired and courageous Mr Churchill declared in the House of Commons. "Gentlemen we shall fight on the beaches, we shall fight on the fields, we shall fight on the streets and we shall fight on the hills, but we will never ever surrender."

'That was indeed a very good speech by the new British Prime Minister, but without the support of the Empire's milch cow India and the other Dominions of the Empire she will land up nowhere. After all by themselves they hardly have any worthwhile raw material resources inside the British Isles to fight the mighty Germans. Infact they hardly have anything at all to sustain a long drawn out war," said Debu Ghosh as he thumped the table and put the copy of the Calcutta Staesman on it, while Naren Sen ordered. "Teen garam coffee. (Three hot coffees). As the liveried waiter took the order, three old friends sat down for their weekly Saturday pow-wow at the Calcutta Coffee House.

'Yes and I too am totally surprised as to why Mr Hitler having had them cornered at Dunkirk did not deliver the knock out punch,' said Dr Ghulam Hussein.

'May be he has something bigger up his sleeves, but I must say that the planning and execution of the military operations by the German General Staff in Western Europe has been simply superb,' added Naren Sen.

'That is all very well, but what will happen to our own country now that Mr Jinnah has opened his bid for a separate land for the Mussulmans, and with Gandhiji and the Congress supporting the war conditionally, and your good friend Subhash Chander Bose languishing in Alipur jail? 'said Dr Ghulam Hussein as Debu Ghosh lit one more cigarette.

'I really cannot say, but knowing Subhas he is not the type to sit idle in jail and I bet he must be planning something out of the ordinary even while he is inside,' said Debu Ghosh confidently as he took another long sip of the aromatic coffee and followed it up with a long drag of the Cavenders navy cut cigarette and paid the bill.

CHAPTER-12

The Great Escape

By the end of 1940, while Subhash Bose was still inside the Alipur jail in Calcutta and was waiting for his trial on sedition charges to begin, the war had taken an ugly turn as it spread across North Africa, Southern Europe, and Eastern Europe and into Asia. The Battle of Britain was in full swing as the German Luftwaffe and the British Royal Air Force together with the British Navy fought tooth and nail for the command over the British skies and the English Channel. Germany and Russia both having occupied their share of Poland had partioned the country to their own advantage. Concentration camps for the Jews of Poland and of Europe had been opened at Treblinka, Lublin and at Auschwitz near Krakow. Under the orders of Reinhard Heydrich, the Warsaw Ghetto with a population of 4 lac Jews and the Lodz Ghetto with half that number had been sealed off and all the Jews locked inside. All Jews had to now wear the arm band with the yellow star and the final solution for them was soon to begin.

In Asia, Japanese forces were well inside China and Hong Kong too had been blockaded. In Southern Europe, Italian and German forces had attacked Albania and Greece. Only in North Africa after a swift drive by the Italians into Libya there was a set back for the Axis Forces. The Italian formations in Libya under Marshall Grazianni had been ordered by the Duce on the 19th of August to invade Egypt, but they failed to do so and were routed by Field Marshall Wavell's Western Desert Force which included the 7th British Armoured Division and the gallant 4th Indian Division.

On 13th September, Marshall Grazianni with five Italian Divisions and 200 tanks had crossed the Libya-Egyptian border and had advanced and captured Sidi Barrani which was 60 miles inside Egyptian territory. But Wavell with a swift and surprise counter attack in mid December had routed Grazianni's numerically larger forces and had captured more than 38,000

Italian prisoners. By the 20th of December 1940, there were no more Italian soldiers on Egyptian soil.

During the battle of Sidi Barrani, Major Ismail Sikandar Khan of the Punjabees for his daring attack on a well fortified Italian position was recommended for the Military Cross and in early January he was decorated with it by Field Marshall Wavell at a special investiture parade on the battlefield. He was only 26 years old and had just six years of service. That evening after the party was over in the Alfha Mess of the Red Eagle Division, Ismail with the help of a lantern in his small tent wrote a long love letter to his darling Sandra.

Meanwhile inside the Calcutta Alipur jail Subhas Bose was feeling very frustrated.'I am not going to sit and keep twiddling my thumbs languishing inside this damn prison,' thought Subhas Bose to himself as the news of Hitler's Germany subjugating the whole of Europe started doing the rounds of the prison. It had become a popular subject of discussion among the political inmates. Subhas Bose also felt that if he was not seen in public life, he too would soon fade away and his dream of freeing the country from British slavery would remain unfulfilled. He had to therefore get out of the prison but the question was how! And on the 29th of November 1940, he got his answer.

'I will fast unto death and die rather than be at the mercy of the bloody 'Gora Sahibs', said Subhash Bose to the jail authorities as he began his fast unto death that day.'

'Do not let that bloody man die came the orders from the very top as the jail authorities tried to forcibly feed him. But Subhash was no ordinary prisoner. He vehemently resisted the force feeding. As it is he was never in good health and the British fearing that his death in custody could spark another mass uprising not only by the hot headed Bengalees, but by the countrymen at large too and with the Indian soldiers shedding their blood for the Empire, they could not to take any chances. On the sixth day of his fast, Subhas Bose was released, but on condition that he would go home and not step out of the house till the 26th of January, when he would be produced in the court for his trial.That evening on arrival at his home in Elgin Road, he was warmly received by members of his family, friends and supporters.

'So now what next?' said Debu Ghosh as he garlanded his old friend.

'Well do not be surprised if I tell you that I am going to quit this mad game of politics, renounce this wicked world and become a hermit,' replied Subhash Bose very seriously.

'But how can you do that now, when the country needs you so very badly to lead us to our goal of total independence,' said another of Subhas Bose's close friend and admirer.

'Well as far as I am concerned, I think we should leave that to Mr Gandhi's Congress and Mr Jinnah's Muslim League, because I am tired of all this now and I sincerely want to have my own peace of mind,' added Subhash Bose.

From that very day Subhash Bose stopped shaving and started growing a beard. He was now working on his next secret plan of action.

'Do keep me regularly posted about the surveillance measures outside the house,' said Subhash to his nephew Sisir as he wrote a secret letter to one of his Muslim friends in the Punjab. A fortnight later arrived from Naushera, Mr Akbar Shah to enquire about Subhash's health. He had actually come to finalize the daring escape plan.

'Yes I can tell you it will work provided we go about it in a very serious and meticulous manner,'said Subhas Bose to a few of his very close and trusted confidants.

'But first of all for those few of us who are involved in the plot must maintain utter secrecy, and number two it must be doubly ensured that on the night of the escape there is no police presence or surveillance during the late hours of the night and during the very early hours of the following morning,' added Subhash Bose as he casually walked to the window of his room which was on the upper floor and which overlooked the big iron gates of his father's house. It was primarily to check and to show his face to the plainclothesmen from the police department who he knew would be watching. After another few days when it was more or less certain that the surveillance over the house late at night was nothing to be alarmed about, the date for the escape was finally fixed.

'My trial is to begin on the 26th of January but I will require enough lead time to get out of the country and before the police get wind of it. And therefore for the plan to succeed, I need atleast a week if not more before the cover story is let out of the bag,' said Subhash Bose.

'Alright then let us plan for the night of the 16/17th of January to be on the safe side,' said Akbar Shah.

'Yes and that will give me nine to ten days of good lead time and if that is agreed to then as planned I will start my meditation in complete seclusion inside my room after dinner on the 16th of January,' said Subhash Bose as he explained in detail to his small group of well wishers and plotters the modus operandi of the great escape.

Early on the morning of 16th January, Subhash Bose told his mother.

'Ma today's evening meal will be my last with the family before I go into total meditation and therefore please prepare all my favourite dishes. Because thereafter I will not stir out of my room and nor will I see anybody's face or speak to anyone, because while doing my meditation I would not like to be disturbed at all. Consequently, all my meals starting from tomorrow morning Ma should be sent only through Ila my neice and she will slide it into my room.'

Without asking any further questions, Subhas's mother immediately gave all the necessary instructions and the menu to the kitchen staff for the special supper for the family get together that evening.

Later that afternoon Sisir Bose on instructions from his uncle Subhash Bose accompanied Mr Akbar Shah for some shopping. And as they were leaving the house, when Subhash hugged Akbar Shah and instructed his nephew Shisir to see his friend off at the Howrah railway station after the shopping was done, the first.phase of the escape plan was set in motion.

'Inshallah the plan will work,' said Akbar Shah as Subhas Bose wished him 'Khuda Hafiz,' and for a safe journey home.

On the way to the railway station, Akbar Shah did all the necessary shopping. He first bought a new attaché case, then a couple of pairs of baggy pyjamas and shirts and of the type that the Muslims and Pathans normally wear. To that he added a pair of Kabuli sandals, a coarse blanket, a fez cap and a new Koran. Once all the items were inside the attaché case, Akbar Shah put the initials "MZ" in bold letters on top of it.

'Alright, now that my shopping is over, you may drive me to the railway station,' said a beaming Akbar Shah as they got into the car. And on reaching the railway station at Howrah, Akbar Shah handed over a set of visiting cards to Sisir Bose and said.

'Be very careful with the attache case and do not forget to hand over these visiting cards also to your Chacha-Jaan' said Akbar Shah as he got into his second class compartment.

'Salaam walem kom Kaka,' said a happy Shisir very softly as he handed over the set of visiting cards to his uncle Subhash and quietly put the new attaché case in one far corner of Subhash's room. From that night Subhash Bose had become Mr Mohammed Ziauddin, the travelling salesman of the Empire of India Insurance Company, Civil Lines, Jabalpur Cantonment.

At around 8 o'clock that evening, the 43 year old handsome Subhash Bose impeccably dressed in a silk dhoti and kurta and with a warm woollen shawl draped around his shoulders sat down for his last meal with the family.

He was in a very jovial mood as he pulled the legs of his nephews and nieces and joked about his young days in England when he made the white skin Gora orderlies to polish his shoes. Once the meal was over, Subhash Bose having thanked everyone present including the servants, solemly touched his mother's feet and retired into his room.

'I still have a couple of hours to go before I start my meditation,' said Subhash Bose to his nephews Shisir, Dwighen and to his neice Ila.

'And do please remember my meditation can only be a success if all of you keep your cool and do what you have been told, and mind you have been sworn to utmost secrecy. The most difficult act will be for you Ila, but you do not have to eat all the food. Just eat what you like on my behalf and the rest you may put it down the drain if you so desire. But do remember to keep the fish bones back on the plate before you slide it back outside from under the door' added Subhash Bose.

'My God Kaka you really do think of every little detail,'said Ila as she with Shishir got ready to ensure that their favourite uncle got dressed flawlessly as Mohammed Ziauddin, the Insurance inspector.

At 1.30 AM on that cold unearthly hour of the morning of 17th January 1941, Shishir having ensured that the entire household was fast sleep got into the driver's seat of the German Wanderer car. A minute or two later, Dwigen standing on the porch of the house cleared his throat to give them the all clear signal. Subhas Bose then bid a silent farewell to his favourite neice Ila, as Aurobiundo with the luggage and the attaché case escorted him to the car. Soon the car sped away through the deserted streets of Calcutta to Shisir's elder brother's house and as soon it got there, Ashok also jumped into it. The car then left for its final destination.

Speeding away on the Grand Trunk Road, a road that was build by Sher Shah Suri during the Moghul period they reached Gomoh, a small railway station in Bihar some 210 miles West of Calcutta. It was nearing midnight of the next day when the two nephews touched their Uncle's feet and watched as Subhash Bose with a sleepy porter carrying his luggage walked across the railway over bridge to the platform on the other side of the railway track. Luckily the Howrah-Kalka Mail was not very late and as soon as the train steamed off, both the nephews gave a big sigh of relief. Though they felt sad that their Uncle was leaving on a long and perilous journey, but they also felt very proud of his courage and determination to fight for India's Independence while in self exile.

Next day evening, Subhash Bose boarded the Peshawar Mail at Delhi and on arriving at Peshawar was received by his friend Akbar Shah who had booked him for that night at the Taj Mahal Hotel. Though the hotel had a very impressive name, but it was a low budget hotel in the heart of the city. Next day Akbar Shah moved him into a rented house.

'Just do not worry, these two gentlemen will take you safely across the Durand Line and to Kabul,' said Akbar Shah while introducing Bhagat Ram Talwar and Abid Shah to Subhash Chander Bose.

'From tomorrow you will become a deaf and dumb Pathan and I will become Rehmat Khan and having been in the Frontier for very many years I can speak fairly good Pushtu too,' said an excited Bhagat Ram as he embraced Subhash and then sat down to explain the plan.

Early on the morning of 22nd January, 1941 Abid Shah sitting behind the wheel of a 1932 model Chevrolet together with Bhagat Ram picked up the deaf and dumb Shubash from the Kabuli Gate of Peshawar city. He was now dressed in an old Pathani outfit from head to toe. As the car headed towards Jamrud, Bhagat Ram said.

'Abid remember you and only you will do all the talking with the sentry on duty at the Jamrud barrier and you will have to convince the sentry that we are not going all the way to Landhikotal, but to the sacred shrine of the Pir Baba which is only a few miles ahead of the barrier and off the main road to pray for this deaf and dumb man. But that is only in case we are questioned. Otherwise we just drive on.'

'Fine,' said Abid Shah as he stepped on the accelerator.Luckily there were no questions asked at the Jamrud barrier as the old Chevrolet after going for a few more miles branched off on to a motorable track and soon they were in Afridi tribal territory. When they reached the foot track that led to the village of Pishkam Maina, Abid Shah having bid goodluck and goodbye to both of them, reversed the car and made his way back to Peshawar.

After walking for a good few hours, a dead tired "Rehmat Khan "with his deaf and dumb companion reached the village of Pishkam Maina. There they stayed the night in biting cold winter weather in a "Serai," a local rest house for travellers with 25 other inmates. The next day was 23rd January. It was Subhash's 44th birthday as he sat on a mule early that morning to make his way to Kabul. It was midnight by the time they reached the first Afghan village across the Durand Line and by early next morning they had hit the main road to Jalalabad. Waving out for a lift they managed to stop a passing truck. The middle aged Afghan driver was a kind and jovial fellow.

'Agar tum bhi kabool tho hum bhi kabool. Toh der kis baat ki. Chalo hum subh chale Kabul'. (If you are ready then I am ready too.So why delay. Let us all go to Kabul) said the driver in good humour as he openly and shamelessly showed his manhood to Bhagat Ram and went for a leak. Though there was hardly any vehicular traffic on the road, but by the time they reached Kabul's Lahori Gate it was well passed lunch time. Though it was the capital of Afghanistan, Kabul was more like a big glorified village with only a few brick houses and cemented buildings, which included the King's Palace and a few apartments and offices of the foreign embassies and consulates. Once again in Kabul they secured a room in one of the dirty local serais and waited for the next day to make their subsequent move.

Subhash had already decided that on the very next day which happened to be the 25th of January, he would boldly walk into the German Embassy and offer himself for political asylum in that country. But when that morning they were on their way to the German Embassy, they saw the Russian Ambassador's car with the red flag standing on the road. It had broken down and the driver was trying to repair it.

Let me try him first,' suggested Bhagat Ram as he asked Subhas to wait on one side of the road and then walked up to the Russian Ambassador. Bowing his head in reverence Bhagat Ram said.

'Please excuse me Sir, I have Mr Subhash Bose, the Indian revolutionary from India with me and he wishes to seek asylum in the Soviet Union, so could you please help him." The Russian Ambassador having had one good look at Subhash who was in his Afghan clothes, shaked his big head as if he did not understand, or maybe he was not sure of the man's correct identity and got back into his car. The duo then made their way to the German Embassy where a young embassy officer who had some idea of who Subash Bose was, but he told them that he would first have to inform Mr Pilger, the German Ambassador because only he and he alone after consulting Berlin could take the decision. He then asked them to come back after a few days.

Meanwhile in Calcutta next morning on the 26th of January, 1941 a great drama was being enacted at Subhas Bose's Elgin Road house. As planned on the night of the 25th, Ila did not eat the food and instead raised the alarm. The household members and staff searched every nook and corner of the house, but Subhash was nowhere to be found. They immediately informed the police who also conducted a fruitless search. Sarat Bose the elder brother who was aware of the entire plan had very cleverly parked himself at his country house in Richra. This was primarily done so as not to create any suspicion about the involvement of any of the family members in the disappearance of his younger brother. When on the morning of the 26th of January a few members of the family came to Richra to give him the news, he feigned complete ignorance and came back immediately to Calcutta. Late that morning while Subhash was still in the Serai at Kabul, Sarat Bose at Elgin Road in the presence of plainclothesmen from the police department presided over a family durbar. The news of Subhash's disappearance had spread rapidly and friends and relatives too joined in the congregation.

'But I simply cannot believe that he has just walked away from the house without telling us anything at all. I am sure some of you can give some clue as to what was in the man's mind,' said a visbly disturbed Sarat Bose.

'Well Bordda (Elder brother) after he came home from the prison he did mention very seriously that he was contemplating to leave this dirty world of politics and become a hermit or a sadhu,' said Debu Ghose who too was taken aback by Subhas Bose's sudden disappearance.

'Yes that is right, and he also talked about it to his mother and he would not lie to her I am sure, would he? said another elderly gentleman who was also a close friend of the family Finally when the meeting broke off, the consensus was that Subhash Bose after his long meditation in complete solitude had most probably decided to become more spiritual and he therefore had left the house to go on a long pilgrimage. But to where that nobody knew.

'But the bloody man just cannot vanish into thin air,' shouted the Calcutta Police Commissioner as he bullshitted and fired his staff for their ineptness and negligence. Then a manhunt for the most wanted man in India was started. Every province and every Princely State was alerted as the police went on a wild goose chase searching for their prey in every big pilgrim centre in India, starting from the Himalayas in the north to Rameshwaram and Cape Camorin in the south. But it was all in vain.

On the 9th of February 1941, at 9.40 PM the Director of Political Department, Government of Germany in Berlin sent out a secret telegram to their German Ambassador in Moscow which was received the next day at the German Embassy. The telegram read. 'Subhas Chander Bose, fighter in the Indian Freedom Movement now in Kabul, intends to travel to Germany through the Soviet Union. He was also twice President of the Indian National Congress. Please enquire cautiously whether the Soviet Union is willing to permit his passage through Soviet territory and to instruct the Soviet Ambassador in Kabul accordingly. The request must indicate that Germany considers it more as a personal asylum without according it any particular political significance.'

To this the German Embassy in Moscow on the 3rd of March replied that the Soviet Government had no objections of Mr Subhas Chander Bose transiting through the Soviet Union on his way to Germany.

'Amader Kakababu tho Gorasahib der ullu baniye shothi shothi hariye gache. Aaj puro derd mansh hote chol lo aar aakhuno onar kono khobor nahin (Uncle has really made a fool of the white skin sahibs and now he seems to have got lost completely. Because already a month and a half has passed and still there is no news of his whereabouts at all) said Shisir in Bengali to his father confidentially.

Well as the English say no news is good news my son, so let us all pray that all is well with him and he is happy wherever he is,' replied the proud father.

Meanwhile in Kabul, Mr Pilger the long standing German Ambassador to Afghanistan on learning about Subhas Bose's escape, or rather vanishing trick from India had now contacted the Italian and the Russian Ambassadors. Having taken them into complete confidence he had sent a secret telegram to Berlin but was still awaiting a reply.Subhash still masquerading as a deaf and dumb Afghan Pathan was now finding it difficult to hide from the prying eyes of the local policemen as he kept moving from one Serai to another incognito. Then on 22nd February and after a very long and agonizing wait he decided to try his luck with the Italian Embassy. There he met Mr Pietro Quarani, a senior Italian diplomat who seemed helpful and friendly.

'OK we will try our best to get you to Germany but you have to give us time,' said Mr Quarani as Subhash thanked him and went back to a new place that Bhagat Ram had hired. It was now really becoming very difficult for Subhash Bose to keep up the false front. Then one day luck smiled on the two fugitives as Mr Uttamchand Mehrotra, a very old resident of Kabul and a dear friend of Bhagat Ram offered to give them shelter in his own house. Finally on the 15th of March, while the police in India and elsewhere in the British Empire including the Scotland Yard, the MI5 and the MI6 were still searching for their man, at the Italian Embassy in Kabul the good news had arrived. Subhash Bose with an Italian passport and under the care of the Italian Embassy in Kabul could now leave for Berlin via the Soviet Union.

Three days later on 18th March, 1941 after an affectionate farewell from the Uttamchand family, Subhash Bose was now finally on his way to Germany. With an Italian diplomatic passport under his new name Orlando Mazzota, he together with Dr Wagner a German Engineer, an Italian courier and a driver were on their way to Samarkand. As the car drove away, Subhash Bose looked back, smiled and waved out his hand to the members of the Uttamchand family. It was quite a torturous and tiring journey as the car wound its way through high mountain passes of the Hindu Khush range to the Soviet border via the north Afghan city of Mazar-e-Sharif which was only a 100 miles from the Uzbegistan-Soviet border. Though it was a small impoverished town rather than a city, it was of great strategic importance to Afghanistan. During the entire journey and with the hope that he would one day return triumphant along the same route to liberate India, Subhash kept making his own notes. When they reached the Russian border, Subhash Bose alias Mr Mazzotta was even greeted with a smart salute by the Soviet sentry on duty and after a hot cup of tea they drove to Samarkhand. It was here at Samarkhand that Alexander the Great during his conquests is believed to have fallen in love with Rushnak the beautiful princess and the legendary beauty of the city. He named her Roxanne and married her. It was also the city of the dreaded Timur the Lame and it was also from here that Babur the great Moghul king came to rule India. Subhash now dreamt that he to would one day with Hitler's help free India from the British Raj. At Samarkhand, Subhash boarded the train for the long journey to Moscow that took him across Central Asia and through the Ural Mountains to the capital of the Soviet Union.On arrival at Moscow he was put into an aircraft and on 28th March 1941he flew to Berlin.The war was now in its third year and still going Hitler's way. On 3rd April, the Political Department of Germany after having interviewed Subhas Bose sent a confidential note to the Fuhrer that read.'Subhas Bose arrived in Berlin yesterday 2nd April and has expressed his desire to set up an Indian Government in exile in Germany. Bose stated that the British Indian Army of today has a total strength of over 300,000 men, of which only 70,000 were Englishmen. He also reiterated that out of the remaining all of whom were Indians, he was confident that the majority of them would defect if they were told to do so by him and even if he gets one lac such soldiers with modern equipment and weapons, it would be adequate to free India from English rule.'

The note also reiterated that the presence of Mr Bose in Aghanistan will continue to remain a secret and so will be his travel through the Soviet Union and arrival in Germany. The Fuhrer was now very busy planning "Operation Barbarossa." the mighty offensive against the Soviet Union and he did not have much time to give a thought to the request of Mr Subhas Chander Bose. Subhas Bose then decided to go to Italy and and seek the help of the Duce also.

While Subhash Bose got busy planning for his visit to Mussolini in Italy, the 4th India Division, the Red Eagles as they were now called under their new General Officer Commanding Major General Frank Walter Messervy, the son of a bank manager and a product of Eton and Sandhurst and a veteran of the Great War having routed the Italians in Eithopia had now under the orders of General Wavell moved back to the Western Desert. General Messervy while in command of 9 Indian Infantry Brigade and the Gazelle Force of the 5th Indian Division in Eritrea had led a daring attack and had successfully stormed the vital fort of Dologorodoc in the Karen sector. He had now established himself as a brave and courageous commander and was now looking forward as GOC 4 Indian Division to give the Germans a bloody nose in North Africa.Though from the Armoured Corps and from the famed Indian Cavalry Regiment of The Hodson's Horse, Messervy on the raising of the 5th Indian Division was its General Staff Officer Grade one and it was he who had suggested the "Red Ball Of Fire" as its formation sign. He was highly impressed by young acting Major Ismail Sikandar Khan's knowledge of the Italian language and had now recommended him for a special course in Interrogation of the Italian Prisoners of War. The four week course was to be conducted at the Italian prisoner of war cages on the outskirts of Cairo and after which the Italian prisoners would set sail for India.

For Ismail Sikandar Khan the Interrogators course was like an on the job training and he relished every moment of it as he talked informally to the more important Italian prisoners who were of senior rank in their own language and tried to ferret out important tactical, political and other related intelligence of value from them. By the time he got back to his unit and formation he was so fluent with the Italian language that he was now often called by the higher formations to act as an interpreter during the interrogation of other captured senior Italian officers.

Then in mid June 1941, Ismail Sikandar Khan received a very long and interesting letter from his very dear friend and coursemate, acting Major Gul Rehman Khan. The letter was dated 19th May and was post marked "Field". Both of them were from the Punjab Regiment and they intermittently shared some of the lighter moments of the war by exchanging letters through the military despatch service couriers. Major Gul Rehman Khan was serving as the Brigade liaison officer of his Infantry Brigade that was under command of thef 5 Indian Division. In this particular letter Gul Rehman wrote-:

My Dear Ismail,

I am writing this letter sitting on a big boulder at a place called Amba Alagi somewhere in Abbysinya which geographically is also known as Eithopia. This morning at 11.15 a.m. the defeated remnants of the Italian Army marched out eight abreast from their Amba Alagi defences to formally surrender in a memorable fashion to the Red Ball 5th Indian Division. This was a unique surrender ceremony, but more about that later. First let me relate to you in brief and in chronological order as to how it all happened.

It all started early on the morning of 16th May, 1941 when our GOC, General Mayne was about to set out for his last reconnaissance of the Italian defences on Alma Alagi and thereafter to give out his final orders for the attack. Just then news arrived that two senior Italian Officers claiming to be envoys from the Duke of Aosta, the C-in-C of the Italian Forces with white flags flying had presented themselves at the Headquarters of the Skinner's Horse. The two Italian officers were blind folded and quickly brought under escort to our Divisional Headquarters and Colonel Tramontano the senior of the two then told the GOC that in the name of humanity they were asking for an armistice. General Mayne and all of us initially were taken quite by surprise to this sudden change of heart by the Italians who were sitting pretty fully armed on the formidable heights of the Amba Alagi defences. We only came to know later that by a quirk fate of luck our artillery shells had struck their POL dump that was sited on the reverse slopes of Amba Alagi and as a result of which all their petrol and oil reserves had flowed down hill and it had badly polluted completely the Duke's last remaining source of fresh drinking water. Fortunately this lucky strike by our gunners also saved many lives of the Red Ball Division now that the attack was finally called off and the preparations for the surrender began.

The GOC then promptly deputed his GSO1 (General Staff Officer Grade 1) Colonel Dudley Russel to negotiate the surrender with the Italians. At three o'clock that afternoon Pasha arrived at the given rendez-vous to meet the Italian General Volpini. Colonel Russel was nicknamed "Pasha" because of his bushy black moustache and his suave manners. That afternoon he was wearing a Sam Browne belt over his khaki shirt and shorts and a broad brimmed hat upon his head that was secured with a chin strap beneath his firm jaw. On his feet and over the black stockings was a pair of open leather chapplis. Under his arms was his favourite walking stick.Pasha while serving with the Royal West Kent Regiment during the First World War was wounded in France. Thereafter he was transferred to the Indian

Army and had won the Military Cross at Palestine. He had also served for four years in the North West Frontier as a Recruiting Officer for Pathans. At the outbreak of war he commanded the 6th Royal Battalion Frontier Force Rifles. A Piffer to the core and a thorough gentleman at heart, Colonel Dudley Russel returned disappointed, when news arrived that General Volpini had been murdered by a group of free lance Abyssinians while he was on his way for the meeting. The negotiations were therefore postponed for the next day.

At around midday 17th May, after a long tiring climb, Pasha with his team and escorts finally reached the venue for the meeting. It was on top of Amba Algi. He was first greeted with half a glass of neat brandy which he gulped diplomatically to ease the tension around, and when he arrived at the tent that had been put up for the conduct of the negotiations, General Trezzani insisted that Pasha should have a glass of neat whisky before the talks began. This too Pasha drowned with a smile. At this stage I felt a bit apprehensive since I was part of the escort. Were they trying to get Pasha high I thought to myself. But when I saw the glint in Pasha's eyes, I knew that even a few more glasses would not have made any difference to our beloved Pasha.

At about half past five in the evening, the terms of the surrender, one in English and the other in Italian was signed by both sides and Pasha pocketed the English copy. It was going to be "Surrender with Honour" as desired by the Duke of Aosta himself. The Italians would hand over the battlefield clear of all mines, booby traps and there would be no destruction of arms, ammunition, weapons, equipment and stores whatsoever. And we in turn would accept the surrender at noon on the 19th of May with a parade and a guard of honour.

On the 18th of May, our forces without a single bullet being fired occupied the positions on top of the impregnable Amba Algi defences. At 11.15 am on the 19th, as the Italians eight abreast came down merrily from Amba Algi, the special guard of honour comprising of one officer and twenty five other ranks from each Battalion of the 5th Indian Division presented arms. As the Italians marched towards the saluting base on the road to the music of the 1st Transvaal Scottish pipe band, General Mayne impeccably dressed in his service uniform took the salute. Once the march past by the Italians was over, the Italian Chief of Staff, General Borgini was presented to our GOC. His companion General Trezzani who had signed the surrender document was in tears. Surprisingly the Duke of Aosta, the senior most

Italian officer was not present at the formal march past and capitulation when the Italian forces laid down their personal arms.

Amadeo Umberto Isabella Luigi Fillipo Mario Giuseppe Giovanni, Prince of Savoia-Aosta, Duke of Puglie and Aosta, the nephew of King Victor Enamuel of Italy with his long name and innumerable decorations turned out to be a damn squib. A day earlier before the surrender ceremony the Duke had invited the GOC and a couple of his senior Brigade commanders for lunch at his own Headquarters which was nothing more than a dark and dank room hewn out of rock. It was like a cavern and the menu was bully beef, hearts of antichokes and tinned peaches with Italian Chianti or whisky soda as desired. During that lunch the tall and slender Duke in his early forties and who spoke perfect English having lost his status as the Italian Viceroy had requested the GOC to spare him the ignominy of a personal surrender and this our GOC had graciously agreed to. On 20th May, the Duke accompanied by Brigadier Marriot came down from Amba Algi to the main road where three officers and fifty men from the 1st Worcestershire's presented him with a guard of honour which he inspected with General Mayne by his side. Thereafter with our GOC for company, the Duke was driven away to Quiha and thus ended this unique "Surrender with Honour" ceremony of our dear Italian adversaries here. Hope you found it interesting and do keep writing more often.

'At present with the collapse of the Italians, the war on this front is getting a bit boring indeed. Incidently and before I forget, let me tell you that my only son Aslam Rehman who I named after my father-in-law and who is also your nephew will soon be celebrating his second birthday on the 31st of May and my wife Zubeida desires that both of us should be present on the occasion. But much that we would like to, but under the present circumstances its like asking for the moon.

'What news from Sandy and when do you propose to tie the knot with her. Bloody Hitler and his friend Mussolini have upset everything and let us hope and pray that this damn war ends soon. With fond love and regards, you're loving friend Gul Rehman.'

On reading Gul Rehman's fascinating letter, Ismail Sikandar Khan too wrote back to him immediately about some interesting and hilarious incidents that he had encountered while brushing up his Italian and while interrogating some of the senior Italian prisoners of war at Port Said. During one such interrogation, a senior Colonel from the Italian army when he was asked as to why so many thousands of Italian soldiers and officers kept surrendering without putting up a fight, he very candidly answered that it was better to become a prisoner in the hands of the enemy than that of the Duce. According to him both the Duce and his friend Hitler were mad Facists of the highest order and if he had his way he would have them shot dead by a firing squad.'

Another Italian soldier when he was told that he was being sent to India as a prisoner of war, and who had no idea where India was simply said. 'Thank God. Just send me anywhere and even to hell if required, but for God's sake do not send me back to Italy or Germany. I am tired of this bloody war.'

On 28th May 1941, at 11.40 PM a most urgent telegram was sent by the Director Political department to the German Embassy in Italy that read. 'The well known Indian Nationalist Subhas Chandra Bose, who has escaped from India and has been staying here in Germany secretly for almost three months with an Italian passport under the cover name of Mazzota, will be arriving in Rome by plane on 29th May at the invitation of the Italian Government. He is accompanied by his secretary, the Reich German Emilie Schenkl. The Italian Government has been informed through their Embassy in Berlin regarding the talks that have been held with the Indian leader. The intention is to work together very closely with him in all Indian matters. Upon his arrival in Rome, Bose will establish contact with the German Embassy there. Please receive him in a friendly manner and afford him any help he desires. In Rome he is the guest of the Italian Government.'

In Berlin, Subhas Bose had asked Ribbentrop for an Axis declaration on Indian Independence which was turned down and in Rome too, when he now got a negative answer from Count Ciano the Italian Foreign Minister and the son-in-law of the Duce on the same very proposal, he was dissapointed. Both of them gave the same excuse that it was too early to even consider it. Without an Axis declaration to guarantee India's Independence it was pointless broadcasting any anti British propaganda thought Subhas Bose as he with his secretary cum wife Emilie Schenkl decided to return to Berlin.

Subhas had first met Emilie in June 1934 in Vienna. She was an Austrian and during his forced exile and recuperation in Europe they had fallen in love. In December 1937, before returning to India he had secretly married her and it was a very well kept secret just between the two of them though they were many exchanges of letters even while he was in prison in India. On 22nd June 1941, while Mr and Mrs Bose were still in Rome, they heard about the German invasion of Russia. Early that morning at 3.30 AM, the three massive German Army Groups with their Panzers divisions in the vanguard, and comprising of 183 full strength Divisions of three and a half million combat troops on an 1800 mile front from Finland in the North to the Black sea in the South launched the biggest military operations in history.

Hitler's overall objective by the end of autumn that year was to destroy all Soviet forces in Western Russia and to occupy the line Archangel-Urals-Volga-and Astrakhan. Though the "Lucy" spy ring had warned the Soviet Union of the impending German attack, but Stalin and his Generals were not convinced. They could never believe that Hitler would stab them on the back. By the end of April, the Italians and the Germans had already conquered Yugoslavia and Greece and this also gave the Germans a good jumping off point to direct Operation Barbarossa towards Crimea and further to the East.

However in North Africa and in East Africa, the Italians were getting a drubbing by the allied forces that were under the command of General Wavell. Therefore, in order to help out the Italians, Hitler approved of "Operation Sunflower" to give military support to the beleaguered Italian forces who had been surrendering in the thousands. The 4th and the 5th Indian Divisions had already taken the Karen fort and there were no more Itlalian forces now left in Eritrea. The Australians too had captured Tobruk and Bengazi by mid February. On the 12th of February 1941, there arrived on the scene Lieutenant General Erwin Rommel with his Afrika Corps. By March, Rommelhad successfully captured El Aghelia and having trapped the Australians at Tobruk, he was now racing along the coast towards the Egyptian frontier.

Meanwhile on 1st March, Himmler had paid his first visit to the Auschwitz Concentration Camp for the Jews in occupied Poland and had ordered Commandant Hoss to begin a massive expansion of the place as more Jews in thousands were expected to arrive there soon. A week later all German Jews were ordered into forced labour and the dreaded German SS Einsatsgruppen were formed into murder squads. Now all Jews from occupied Europe were also being mustered for the "Final solution".

In the Far East the Japaneese war machine also rolled on relentlessly towards Indo China as they took the strategic islands in the Pacific as future bases. On the 21st of May, the German battleship "Bismarck" had met its watery grave in the Atlantic after she had sunk the British battle cruiser "Hood" Surprisingly on the 5th of May, Rudolf Hess, Hitler's deputy and a former First World War fighter pilot on a solo flight landed in Scotland. His primary aim was to convince the anti Churchill lobby in England to stop the war with Germany and adopt a neutral attitude so as to allow Germany to completely eliminate the Bolshevik menace in Russia. Hess was promptly arrested, interrogated and put behind bars.

Thus by the middle of 1941, while Subhash Bose was in Germany, a fairly large body of Indian prisoners of war who had been captured by Rommel's forces in North Africa had also now started arriving both in Italy and in Germany from the large prisoner of war cages in Cyrenaica. A camp at Annaburg near Dresden in Germany was created for the Indians. Soon these captured soldiers from these prisoner of war camps were all for Subhash Bose and his idea of forming an Indian Legion in Germany, a legion that would spearhead the German advance into the subcontinent once the Russians were defeated and the whole of Central Asia too would be in the Fuhrer's hand.

Chapter-13

The Ugly Face of Hitler's War.

While Hitler's ugly war was waging in the Middle East, Maharaja Hari Singh of Kashmir having inspected the State Force Troops fighting in that theatre of operations arrived in Bombay and he bought a block of flats at 94, Napean Sea Road. He lived on the 6th floor, while his only son Karan Singh with his guardian Colonel Kailash Narain Haksar a Kashmiri Pandit and a large man with bushy eyebrows stayed on the first floor. Having completed his primary schooling from the Presentation Convent at Rajbagh in Srinagar that was run by the Irish nuns and where Sister Anunciate took good care of him, the young and quiet Karan Singh was now admitted to the prestigious Cathedral School in Bombay. Also known as the John Cannon School, it was one of the oldest English schools of Bombay and a couple of year's senior to him and in the same school was the young Zulfiqar Ali Bhutto, a flamboyant, loud mouthed intelligent boy from a rich Sindhi family of Larkana in Sind.

During the winter months and during the Monsoon season, the Maharaja was generally busy with his stable of horses. He had developed a passion for horse racing and was a regular at the Bombay's Mahalaxmi and the Poona race courses. On practically every race day he could be seen sitting in his special box with his big binoculars watching his horses and fillies in their scarlet and gold colours run for the honours and the money.

On the 7th of December 1941, which happened to be a Sunday, while the Japaneese rocked Pearl Harbour in the East and Rommel's Panzer forces in the western desert were being pursued by General Claude Auchinleck's Army in "Operation Crusader", at the Bombay's Mahalaxmi Race Course, Colonel Reginald Edwards immaculately dressed in a three peice pin striped suit and a matching felt hat took his seat in the specially reserved enclosure for the members to watch the main event for the day. Suddenly he heard a loud voice beckoning him. 'Hello there Colonel do please come up here and keep me company,' shouted Maharaja Hari Singh to his old friend Colonel Reginald Edwards. A minute later one of the Maharajas ADC's in his ceremonial military uniform escorted Col Edwards to the royal box.

'My God what a pleasant surprise to see you here of all the places,' said the Maharaja as they warmly shook hands.

And on which horse are you going to put your money on, the one running for the Axis powers or the one running for the Allies,' added the Maharaja in good humour as the runners for the main race made their way from the paddock to the starting rails.

'Fortunately Mr Adolf Hitler has only horse sense and nothing more and he will be the ultimate loser you will see,' said Reggie very confidently.

'Yes and I hope you are damn well right,'said the Maharaja as he asked about the whereabouts of Ismail Sikandar Khan. When he was told that Ismail Sikandar had won the Military Cross in North Africa, the Maharaja was simply delighted and added.

'After all he is a son of my soil, isn't he.' And having said that he very proudly introduced Mr Rosenthal to Reggie and invited both of them to spend the coming summer as his guest in the valley.Mr Rosenthal was a prominent rich jeweller from France and he with his family had migrated from Russia during the revolution. He was now a very good friend of the Maharaja.and shared all his varied tastes that ranged from art and culture, good food and drinks and also to breeding of race horses.

And while the war in Europe, North Africa and in the Far East gathered momentum, the British Indian army in India kept recruiting more and more Indians both as soldiers and officers to fight for them.

'I wonder what that moustached mad man who was born in Austria and who wanted to become a painter but became only a corporal during the First World War is up to now. And one wonders as to how a man of his intelligence could become the leader of the Nazis and the so called Fuhrer. And it is beyond my comprehension,' said Naren Sen as the three friends took their seats for their usual Saturday meeting at the CalcuttaCoffee House

'But Hitler is not mad at all. He is only very egoistic, and when something gets into his nut it simply refuses to get out. And this great gamble by him to finish a country like the size of Russia will not be easy at all I can tell you,' said Debu Ghosh as he lit his newly acquired Dunhill pipe.

Since when have you switched on to this new novelty,' asked Dr Ghulam Hussein looking rather surprised at Debu's new style of smoking a pipe.

'Not that I wanted to, but with the war on, the damn cigarettes have become expensive and with a pipe in your mouth you not only smoke a lot less, but it looks more dignified too. And moreover, my days of becoming a photograph with a garland around my neck in my own house hopefully also gets a bit delayed too,' said Debu Ghosh as usual jokingly.

'God bless you. But tell us, is there any news at all about your old friend Subhash Bose. It seems that he has really renounced the world and vanished into thin air,' said Dr Ghulam Hussein.

'Let me tell you, Subhash is not an escapist and knowing him as I do, he must be somewhere in this wide world scheming and planning his next move to free India from the British Raj, and I only hope and pray that he is safe and sound where ever he is,' said Debu Ghosh.

'I must say you are quite an optimist Debu,' added Naren Sen as the three of them went for a walk to the Maidan.It was on the morning of 8th December 1941, when Debu Ghosh while tuning in to the shortwave radio station of the BBC, the British Broadcasting Corporation in London on his German make Pilot radio to hear the latest news accidentally tuned in to some new radio station that called itself the "Azad Hind Radio". And though the reception was very bad, but the radio station was spitting venom on the British while asking them to get out of India. On hearing that a jubilant Debu Ghosh immediately rushed across to Naren Sen's house to announce that it was very much possible that Subhash was alive and he could be the architect of the secret radio station.

'Maybe you are right but have you heard the latest. Yesterday the Japanese celebrated their Sunday holiday with the bombing of the Pearl Harbour, the big American naval base in Hawaii and they did it with great precision and effect too. And as a result of this the Americans have also now formally declared war on the Japs, and as of today England too has followed suit,' said Naren Sen as he called out to his wife Shobha and requested her for two cups of hot tea.

'Sorry no more sugar for the tea but if you all want it with desi gur, jaggery as a sweetner then both of you can have it. Sometimes I wonder what this war is all about. It is only bringing in more and more misery into this world and I simply do not understand as to why food in India has to be rationed. Today there is no sugar. Tomorrow there won't be any rice, and probably the day after there will be no fish or meat either,' said an angry Shobha Ghosh as she placed the two cups of the black looking tea on the centre table.

'You are absolutely right my dear and with the Japanese expanding their empire by leaps and bounds, I wont be surprised if we are forced to drink Japanese tea in the near future and that too with you ladies all dressed up in a Japanese kimono rather than a sari,' said Debu Ghosh to his sister Shobha in his usual jocular manner.

By the end of 1941, though the Japanese were expanding their empire in the Far East and South East Asia, Hitler's military adventure and prophecy to wipe out Bolshevism and Communism from the Soviet Union was not at all going according to his plan. It was all so very near and yet so far as the Russian resistance kept gaining in strength from day to day.Hitler's forces in December 1941had knocked on the doors of Moscow, but the stubborn and determined Red Army just would not let them in. On the Leningrad front too the Germans continued with the siege of the city. In fact in October, when the German Army Group Centre launched "Operation Typhoon" to capture Moscow from their jumping off points at Kursk and Kharkov, Hitler had boasted that the Russians were finished and would never rise again. On the 5th of December, the Germans were only 19 miles from the capital city, when "General Winter" once again came to Russia's rescue. And as the temperatures dropped to minus 37 degrees centigrade, the Germans had to call off the offensive.

Meanwhile in the deserts of North Africa with General Claude Aukincleck having taken over from General Wavell as C-in-C Middle East in July, the plans for "Operation Crusader" to relieve the trapped Australians at Tobruk and to reconquer Cyrenaica from Rommel's Africa Corps was being planned out. At 6 AM on the 18th of November, Operation Crusader was launched by the British XIIIth and XXXth Corps which were now part of the British 8th Army. On 8th December, the besieged Tobruk garrison was relieved and on that Christmas day of 1941, Benghazi was also retaken. Rommel's forces were now in full retreat.

In Southern Europe on 2nd December, Hitler issued Directive Number 38 tasking Field Marshall Kesselring the C-in-C South to gain full air and naval superiority over the Mediterranean and to deny British supplies to Malta and to Libya. On 11th December 1941 Italy also declared war on the USA.

In the war in Asia, the Japanese war machine was constantly on the move and General Wavell in July had now taken over as C-in-C India. By mid December, the Japanese had overrun Thailand, Malaya, Shanghai, Hong Kong and Singapore. On the 23rd the Japs had bombed Rangoon and on the 25th of December, Christmas day Hong Kong too finally surrendered. Three days later on the 28th of December, General Wavell took over command of the British Forces defending Burma and India.

'Are these Hitler's Nazis human beings or savages,' said an angry Debu Ghosh while showing his two bosom friends the gruesome photographs of German soldiers brutally executing Russian men, women and children. And thereafter when he added that on the 30th of December, the Congress Party had declared its support for the British war effort, but this in turn had alienated Gandhiji who according to latest reports has resigned from its leadership it took everybody by surprise.'

'Well you started with Hitler being a savage and ended abruptly with Mr Gandhi quitting the Congress. Now tell us what savagery has Hitler's goose stepping Nazi's been up to,' said Dr Ghulam Hussein.

'Those German bastards have commenced the extermination of the Jews in all of occupied Europe and also inside their own damn country. According to a secret report released by an underground Jewish organization in Europe, Marshall Goring in July had instructed Reynard Heydrich the German butcher to prepare for the "Final Solution." So without wasting any time on the 3rd of September the Jews who were forced to wear the Yellow Star were stripped of their clothes and like cattle were herded into the gas chambers at Auschwitz where for the first time the Germans experimented with the deadly Zyklon B, the hydrogen cyanide gas that was let loose on those poor naked helpless Jewish, men, women and children for giving them a bath unto death. And that is not all. On 29th September, the SS it is believed massacred around 90,000 Ukrainians and out of which more than one third were Jews. Here they did not use gas because they did not have any. They simply took them to a deep ravine near a place called Babi Yar some 30 miles from Kiev and shot them in cold blood,' said Debu Ghosh as he called out to his wife Hena to serve the food.

'My God I thought the men like Aurangzeb, Mohammed Ghazni, Timur Lane and Nadir Shah were cruel people, but this Mr Hitler really takes the cake,' said Hena while calling out to the men folk to wash their hands and sit down for the special silver jubilee wedding anniversary dinner.

'And that is not all on 8th December, 1941at a place called Lodz in occupied Poland the bloody Germans introduced the mobile gas van, whereby as they drove the Jews to their burial place, enroute itself they would release the carbon monoxide from the engine's exhaust into the sealed passenger compartment and by the time the victims arrived at the burial site they were all dead,' said Debu Ghosh.

'Now please can we all talk of something more pleasant today. After all it is not everyday that some lucky couples celebrate their twenty five years of existence in the midst of rationing and rising prices,' said Dr Ghulam Hussein as he invited everyone to the late night show of Ashok Kumar's latest hit film "Jhoola' and sang the first four lines of the popular song " Chali re Chali re meri nau chali re. " from that very film.

'Wah Wah' that was indeed very good daktar babu but do also please note that though Ashok Kumar's boat may be sailing merrily, but the Japanese boats are not too far away from India's shores either. And I only hope and pray that their boats capsize in the Indian Ocean because secret reports from the Far East indicate that the Japs are equally inhuman when it comes to dealing with their enemies and they make no difference between blacks, whites and yellows. Therefore, like the handsome Prithviraj Kapoor playing the role of Sikandar it is time for General Wavell with his Indian Army, Navy and Air Force too keep them away from our soil,' said Naren Sen as he presented Debu Ghosh with a bottle of Haig's Dimple Skotch whisky and Hena with a set of KL Saigal's latest hits on 78 RPM's records.

'Now remember Bhabhi whenever you play the song "Karoon kiya aas Nirass Bhayi" think of your beloved Debu. He is undoubtedly your Master's voice but he is not your 'Dushman' or enemy either. In fact he loves you so much that he just cannot do without you,'said Dr Ghulam Hussein somewhat seriously.

'Oh come on tell me another one. He is even trying to compete with Mr KL Saigal not only as far as hitting the bottle is concerned, but even in his love for hot chilly pickles,' said Hena.

Alright we have all got the point and now to liven up the evening a little more let me request Daktar Babu and Suraiya Bhabi to sing for us a duet of a some popular Bengali song,' said Naren Sen. And promptly the sporting couple sang for them Rabindranath Tagore's "Jodhi tor dak shune keyu na aashe tohbe akela chalo re" (Even at your beck and call if others do not come and join you, then go it alone).

'This I believe is now also Gandhijis favourite song and he too has now decided to go it alone,' said Dr Ghulam Hussein as others applauded and clapped.

Though the war as yet had not come close to the Indian soil, but a large number of well educated young men were now undergoing the officer's training at the two Officer's Training Schools that had recently been established at Mhow and at Belgaum. On completion of their training they were to be commissioned as Short Service Commissioned officers. But as far as England was concerned the Battle of Britain was still in full swing.

While the Battle for the Atlantic and the Battle of Britain raged on and in order to keep the spirits and the morale high of the British people and the British Forces fighting on all fronts, the BBC introduced a special musical request programme for them. They named it "Sincerely Yours" and it soon became very popular. It was also rumoured that through this programme secret messages were also being sent to the "V Army", who were members of the underground resistance movement fighting against the Germans inside occupied Europe.

Eversince Hitler invaded Poland, and Britain declared war on Germany, the listeners to the programmes on the BBC and especially for the world news had grown manifold in India. Under the influence of Colonel Reginald Edwards, and the British way of life in the the Indian Army even Captain Ismail Sikandar Khan and Captain Gul Rehman had become avid listeners of the programmes over the British Broadcasting Corporation and they were also now fond of popular English music too. Their current favourites were Vera Lynn and her beautiful rendering of "We'll Meet Again" and "White Cliffs of Dover." And as far as good jazz was concerned it was "In the Mood" by Glenn Miller and his Orchestra, Eddie Duchin on the piano, Benny Godman on the clarinet and the golden voices of Perry Como and Bing Crosby was always a morale booster for them.

Since its humble beginning in 1922 as a private firm that had set up a 6 kilowatt transmitter at Chelmsford to make long distance transmission of both speech and music, the BBC by now had become a repertoire of information and culture. The first Director General John Reith was indeed a very far sighted man. He had divided the programmes into value education and entertainment and soon from a Company it became a Corporation. The radio had revolutionised the whole world and BBC took full advantage of it.

On the evening of the 15th of February 1942, Ismail Sikandar Khan while listening to the number "We'll Meet Again" sung in the melodious voice of Vera Lynn and thinking about his beloved Sandra Pugsley, heard an announcement over the BBC that Singapore had fallen to the Japanese and that General Percival had shown the white flag of surrender. The very next day when the civil post arrived from India there was still more tragic news for Ismail. It seems that Sandra in the middle of January while visiting her twin sister Debbie who was expecting her second child had fallen victim to the dreaded cholera and died in the small railway hospital at Jhansi. It came as such a shock to him that he could not even cry as he kept reading again and again the beautiful pathetic and yet courageous letter that was written by Sandra's father. The last line read.'Do not grief for our darling Sandra who was also your only true love in life. Maybe she will again come back to you in her next birth and that is what we wiil always hope and pray for. Let her now from heaven protect you all the time my son and please do not take it amiss because I am returning back to you your last precious and final gift to our beloved Sandra, the beautiful diamond ring.'

Ismail just could not believe that his beloved Sandy was no more. And as he read the last letter that she had written to him and which was received by him only a fortnight ago and in which she wrote how very proud and lucky she was in finding a man like Smiley, he broke down. As he read that letter again and again, he kept looking at her photograph that was in his purse. Unable to control himself he started crying softly and as the tear drops fell on the letter and smudged it partially, he closed his eyes.

Meanwhile in Germany, Subhash Bose had opened the Free India Centre at Number 10, Lichtensteinallee in the Tiergarten Area of Central Berlin and he too had moved into his new apartment at 6-7, Sophienstrasse, in the fashionable Charlottenburg complex of the city. This was the same house where not very long ago stayed the Military Attache of the United States of America. Though Subhas was still working under the name of Orlando Mazzotta, but with the fall of Singapore on the 15th of February to Japan Subhash had now become ecstatic and he In his broadcast from the clandestine and secret Azad Hind Radio station declared. 'I have waited silently and patiently on the course of events and now that the hour has struck, I can now come forward and speak to my fellow Indians. Here was certain proof of the collapse of the British Empire and India must rejoice. Finally when he closed the broadcast with a loud 'Jai Hind', Debu Ghosh was overjoyed.

Just two days earlier on 13th February 1942, at a big recreation park in Calcutta an excited Mohammed Ali Jinnah had hoisted the Muslim League flag and called upon all Muslims to unite and demand for their own independent Pakistan. Meanwhile the Congress kept striving for a secular Independent India which would include the Muslims too.

Debu Ghosh now as a habit everyday tuned in to the so called radio station of "Azad Hind Radio", and on that evening of 15th February after hearimg that broadcast by Subhas, he immediately went to Subhas' Elgin Road house to convey that Subhas was very much alive. There he came to know that Subhas Bose was now in Germany and the Indians there had christened him as "Netaji". He also became aware of the fact that Subhash

Bose had raised a small Indian Legion there and that the official greeting amongst all the Indians was 'Jaihind 'and the national anthem chosen was Rabindranath Tagore's Jana Gana Mana. From the captured Indian prisoners of war, Subhash had also set up a camp at Annaburg near the city of Dresden.

It was around April 1942, and much after the fall of Singapore that Debu Ghosh and his wife Hena after a break of nearly a whole year received a long letter from their second son Swarup. In his letter, Swarup mentioned that while at Bankok he had joined the India League that was led by Mr Rash Behari Bose and that having married a Sikh girl, the daughter of a local granthi, the priest in the Gurudwara he himself had become a follower of Guru Nanak Ji but minus the turban. Swarup Ghosh also mentioned in his letter that he had now joined the Indian independence movement and he described in brief how it had all started. He wrote that it all began on a wet Monsoon day in mid December 1941, when he with his wife and a few other passengers were on their way in a rickety old bus from Bankok to Singapore. But as soon as they crossed into the Malayan border and were nearing the small border town of Alor Star, they were stopped by a strong Japanese patrol. The Japanese searched the bus and then took them to a small wayside tea shop for questioning. The patrol it seemed was looking for the remnants of an Indian army unit that was being led by a British Colonel. It was raining cats and dogs that morning, when suddenly from the opening in the nearby jungle appeared a British Colonel with two Indian Officers and a large group of Indian soldiers. They were fugitives and survivors of the 1/14th Punjab Regiment and had surrendered to the Japaneese forces. All of them were being escorted at gun point by a group of Japanese soldiers to the Japanese military headquarters at Alor Star. The officers and the men were in a pitiable condition and they all looked famished and half dead as they marched sluggishly in torrential rain and in their tattered uniforms that were totally covered with mud and slush. Swarup, his wife and the other passengers had to perforce stay at Alor Star for the next couple of days because the Japanese authorities would not permit them to go any further. Thus Swarup's and his wife's trip to Singapore fo visit his in-laws ended abruptly at the small Malayan border town of Alor Star and it was during those two or three crucial days at Alor Star that he had finally made up his mind to work for India's freedom and he described it as to how it all happened.

According to Swarup on the 15th of December 1941, there arrived on the scene at Alor Star a Sikh gentleman by the name of Pritam Singh. The very fact that he came in a car with the Indian National flag flying meant that he was definitely a man of some importance. Like his own father-in-law, Pritam Singh too was a Gyani and a well respected holy man who too was diligently working for India's Independence. He had come there with one Major Fujihara from the Royal Japanese Imperial Army to convince the Indian officers and soldiers of the 1/14th Punjab Regiment that it was time for them to switch over allegiance and with the help of the Japanese military to raise an Indian Army of Independence. While Major Fujihara stood erect in his full ceremonial military uniform and with a sword by his side, Pritam Singh with a strong nationalist fervour spoke to the gathering. After Pritam Singh had concluded his talk, Major Fujihara without mincing any more words in a firm yet friendly tone said.

'I am Major Fujihara of the Royal Japanese Imperial Army and from now onwards I will be in charge of you all. You are all Indians and will be treated with respect and dignity and not as prisoners of war, but as honoured friends provided you agree to join the Gyani's movement and as far as the English Colonel and British officers are concerned they I am afraid will remain as prisoners of war. '

That very evening thanks to Sardar Pritam Singh who knew Swarup's father-in-law very well, both Swarup and his wife were taken to the Gyani's house and where they stayed as his guests. Giani Pritam Singh was himself a revolutionary who had escaped the dragnet of the British Intelligence in India and from 1933 had found refuge in Siam. In June 1941, when he came to know that Japan was willing to help the Burmese nationalist group led by Aung San to throw out the British from their land, the Giani too contacted the Japanese authorities in Siam and started working with them for India's Independence. The Giani was now the spokesman for all Indians and for the Indian Independent League. That very evening of the 15th of December 1941, Major Iwaichi Fujihara taking help from the Gyani, brainwashed the two Indian officers from the 1/14 Punjab Regiment to switch sides. The senior most among the two was Captain Mohan Singh, the only son of Tara Singh and Hukam Kaur from the Ugoke village in the Sialkot District of Punjab. Born into a poor peasant family, Mohan Singh never saw his father because his father died two months before he was even born. He was brought up by his mother and on passing high school had joined the Punjab Regiment as an ordinary soldier. He was intelligent and hard working and seeing his potential to become an officer, he was sent for six months special training to the Kitchner College at Nowgong. In 1932, he joined the first IMA course at Dehradun and got his commission as a 2/Lt two and a half years later. After his one year compulsory attachment with the British 2nd Border Regiment, Mohan Singh joined his parent unit the 1/14th Punjabees. In December 1940, while the battalion was undergoing intensive training at Secunderabad for overseas service in Malaya and Singapore, he got married to Jaswant Kaur, the sister of a brother officer. On the day they surrendered they were trying to escape from the Japanese who were now driving southwards from Siam and along the narrow Malayan Peninsula towards Singapore. In that confusion the battalion had disintegrated and the Commanding Officer with some remnants of his unit decided to head south. But without any fire support and food they were now stragglers who had lost their way in the thick tropical jungles of Northern Malaya.

Politely and diplomatically addressing the two Indian officers inside his own hut, Major Fujihara said. 'Well gentlemen if you really want freedom for your country then you must aspire to do something worthwhile and that worthwhile thing would be to raise an Indian National Army and become our allies to fight the British.'Two days later on 17th of December 1941, Major Fujihara took Captain Mohan Singh to see the Japanese C-in-C and by the end of the month Captain Mohan Singh agreed to raise and organise the Indian National Army. Gyani Prtiam Singh was thrilled when Swarup too decided to pitch in by joining the Indian Independence League. When the Japanese started sweeping through South East Asia and the countries in the Pacific region, Major Fujihara the Japanese Intelligence Officer together with Gyani Pritam Singh and nine other Indians that included the young and enthusiastic Swarup Ghosh went all out to recruit and get the support of over eight lac Indians who were then based in Siam and in the other neighbouring countries of South East Asia.Swarup's next letter to his parents was dated 17th February 1941, and it was datelined Singapore. In that letter he vividly described the British surrender.

'Dear Baba at noon on the 15th of February, General Percival the C-in-C British forces with his staff and senior commanders approached the Japanese with a white flag and at 4.30 that evening a ceasefire was ordered. Yesterday the British forces surrendered all their arms and then the Japanese separated the Britishers from the Indians. The British officers and the Tommies were lined up on one side of the road, while the Indian officers and soldiers were lined up on the other side. Then the Regimental Medical Officer from the famed Cokes Frontier Force Rifles, Captain Chowdhury was ordered to march all the Indian officers and troops to the Farrer Park. While they were being marched off, a number of Indian soldiers broke rank and ran forward to salute, shake hands, and say a final goodbye to their British Officers. At times the scenes were quite touching as some of them hugged one another, while some others had tears in their eyes. After the Indian contingent left, the British were marched off to the notorious Changi Camp to work on the "Death Railway.

After the fall of Singapore In February 1942, Captain Mohan Singh having promoted himself to the rank of a General was handed over 45,000 Indian Prisoners of War by the Japanese Military authorities to raise the first Indian National Army. The British also feared that with their capitulation at Singapore, the Japanese would now sail unopposed into the vast Indian Ocean. With the fall of Singapore, and Japanese assurance at the Tokyo Conference in March 1942 to free India from British rule, Rash Behari Bose, the Indian revolutionary who had master minded the abhortive 1915 uprising in India and had later fled to Japan now decided to shift his base to Bankok. He soon arrived in South East Asia to become the President and leader of the Indian Independence League. With the motto, Unity, Faith and Sacrifice, Rash Behari Bose together with General Mohan Singh, Mr N Raghavan, Mr PK Menon and Colonel GQ Gilani became founder members of the Council of Action for the Indian Independence League and they soon got busy to get their act together. They hoped that with the might of the newly formed Indian National Army and with the backing of the Japanese government and the military they would soon march victoriously into India and give to the Indian people their much desired freedom, but it was not as simple as it looked.

In the subcontinent of India and in South East Asia the British Empire seemed to be crumbling. Mr Churchill's coalition government not only needed India's support with trained military manpower, but it also needed the huge material resources that the country possessed to keep the war going. To appease the Indian politicians with promises that Independence will be given to them when the time demands, the British Governemnt had sent out a special high level mission under Sir Stafford Cripps to India. After the first few rounds of talks with the Indian leaders, the mission soon realised that they were heading nowhere.

On 13th March 1942, while the Cripps Mission was still trying to find a way out to break the impasse, Subhas Bose made a second proclamation to the Indian people over the Azad Hind Radio in Berlin. He told them that the Cripps mission ito India was only eyewash and that it was a meaningless exercise and a waste of time to even talk to them. He instead suggested to the Indian leaders that they should rather talk to the Japanese Prime Minister

Mr Tojo, now that the Japanese Imperial Army was in full control of South East Asia.

Finally on 30th March 1942, Sir Stafford Cripps decided to broadcast his message to the people of India over the radio from Delhi. He began his address or rather appeal by saying.'Let me tell you what the main object of this mission were when we came to India. Our object primarily was that the British government and the British people desire that the Indian people should have full self government and with a Constitution as free in every respect as our own in Great Britain, or as any of the great Dominions of the British Commonwealth of Nations. India therefore will be equal to them in every respect and in no way subordinate in any aspect of its domestic or external affairs. But there are those who claim that India should be divided into two separate countries. We can only provide the lead, but it is now in your hands and in the hands of your leaders to decide your future destiny and attain your own freedom. If you fail to accept this opportunity, the responsibility for the failure will rest on you alone.'

'Now what do you thing Gandhi or Jinnah will do or say to Mr Cripps diplomatic and clever manoeuvre,' said Naren Sen as he read out the contents of the speech in the Statesman to Debu Ghosh and Dr Ghulam Hussein and then ordered the coffee for their weekly coffee session at the India Coffee House.

'I think it is a master stroke to keep us divided and still rule as before' said Dr Ghulam Hussein.

'Undoubtedly so and the Goras are no fools. They know how and where to create a rift between the Muslim League and the Congress, and it will once again become a demand for total full Independence by Gandhi's Congress versus Jinnahs demand for a separate Muslim nation, and the war will carry on as usual,'said Debu Ghosh with a look of apathy in his face.

'But I believe now that the American forces having landed in India, even President Roosvelt the President of the United States is in favour of India getting full Independence, but it seems that Mr Churchill is still harping on granting India only Dominion Status,' said Naren Sen.

'That is rather unfortunate too, but I think now with all the American military might being thrown in to counter the Axis Powers, the day is not very far when we will get our Independence,' said Dr Ghulam Hussein.

' Yes we will but at what cost,' said Debu Ghosh as he very magnanimously paid the bill.

On the 8th of March 1942, a very high level delegation from America arrived in London to hold strategic level talks with their British allies.

It was led by Mr Harry Hopkins and General George C Marshall, The Chairman of the American Joint Chiefs of Staff Committee. Harry Lloyd Hopkins was born in Sioux City, Iowa in 1890. A close friend of the American President FD Roosevelt and his wife Eleanor, he during the Great American Depression was instrumental in pushing federal programmes to provide government sponsored jobs for the unemployed and was now the American President's unofficial chief emissary to Winston Churchill and Joseph Stalin. On the other hand General George C Marshall was a seasoned soldier. Born on 31st December 1880, the son of the owner of a prosperous coal businessman from Pennsylvania, he opted for the armed forces and graduated in 1901 from the Virginia Military Institute. Having served in the First World War in France, he worked his way up the ladder to be appointed by President Roosvelt in 1939 as Chief of Staff with the rank of a full General. Now as Joint Chief of Staff, he with the firm backing of the President of America had proposed the major landings of the allied forces on the French coast in the summer of 1943, but the British were still not fully prepared for such a daring venture at this stage. It was accepted in principle though and soon the Allies started making preparations for such a landing.

By the middle of February with the Japanese onslaught through Burma towards India, the 17th Indian Division started their withdrawal across the Sittang River and on the 8th of March 1942 with Rangoon falling and the 17th Indian Division trapped at Pegu, the situation on India's eastern borders was indeed very grave. While the Japanese were advancing rapidly through Burma, at Anand Bhavan, the Nehru Family's 'Abode of Happiness" in Allahabad frantic arrangements were being made for the marriage ceremony of Jawahar Lal Nehru's only daughter Indira.

Born on 19th November 1917, Indira Priyadarshini had her early schooling at the Pupils Own School n Poona. Founded in 1928 by Mr Jehangir Vakil, a graduate from Oxford and his wife Coover Bai the patriotic Parsee couple were true nationalists. The school provided a home and a place of learning to the children of imprisioned freedom fighters. Housed in an old Portugeese colonial building in Poona and with classes being held in the open air, the day started with military drill, salutation to the Congress flag and the singing of Vande Mataram. Even as a kid, little Indira had formed her own children's army and took pride in commanding those who joined it. In July 1934, she joined Rabindra Nath Tagore's Shantiniketan, but after just nine months had to leave as her father was in prison and her mother Kamla Nehru was very sick and she had to accompany her to Germany for her specialised treatment in a sanatorium there.

A frequent visitor to the sanatorium in Bavaria was a young handsome Parsee lad by the name of Feroze Gandhi. He was also born in Allahbad and it was probably in the sanatorium that the two of them fell in love with each other. On 28th February 1936, 19 year old Indira lost her young 36 year old mother. In February 1938, she joined Sommerville College in Oxford to study Modern History. Feroze was also there studying at the London School of Economics and soon he started courting Indira by sending her flowers and taking her to the theatre. With the war on, Indira Priyadarshini accompanied by Feroze Gandhi returned to India. At first there were objections by some of the family members since it was going to be an inter caste marriage and the family had tried to keep it a well guarded secret. But on 21st February 1942, while Nehru was in Calcutta for talks with Mr Chiang Kai Shek of China, the newspaper "Leader" published from Allahabad had leaked out the story.

On 26th March, 1942 and on the auspicious day of "Ram Naumi" Indira and Feroze were happily married. One of the very important guests at their wedding at Anand Bhavan was Sir Stafford Cripps. During the reception and dinner, a pretty and smiling Indira Gandhi looking beautiful and charming in her wedding saree humourously said to Sir Stafford. "Do also have some potato Cripps please" After all the ceremonies were over, the young married couple went for their honeymoon to the enchanting Kashmir valley.

With the Cripps Mission heading for a total disaster, on 2nd April, the Working Committee of the Indian National Congress passed a momentous resolution. It stated that the people of India as a whole clearly demanded full Independence and has repeatedly declared that no other status will be welcomed or agreed to. This was followed by another resolution by the All India Congress Committee three weeks later, when it reiterated that they would oppose tooth and nail any proposal that would lead to the disintegration of India.

By now the British Forces in Burma were in total retreat, and on 9th April, 1942 with the arrest of the Mahatma, the talk with the Cripps Mission finally broke down once and for all. It was during this time in the summer of 1942 that Colonel Reginald Edwards decided to visit the vale of Kashmir once again. This time he would be going there as a guest of the Maharaja to take part in the duck shooting competition on the Hoksar Lake near Srinagar. From Bombay Reggie did the first leg of his journey by boat to Karachi. After disembarking at the port, he was surprised to see the large number of shoe shine boys on the streets of the city and they all seem to be targetting only the newly arrived gum chewing American soldiers, sailors and airmen.

'Famous boot polish of Karachi Sir and it will shine like a mirror,' shouted one as another in an even more louder tone said.

'Karachi's mirror shoes shine only for two annas.'

It seemed that all of them were doing fairly brisk business as the American GI's got there boots and shoes polished and then merrily threw their money with a big smile on their faces. Seeing the enthusiasm on the faces of the shoe shine boys, Reggie also decided to try it out with one of the polishwallas. He found that with their spit and polish, the young boys had become quite adept in their new proffession and some had even picked up pidgen English to solicite customers for a fling in the evening at the whore joints which had suddenly mushroomed all along the harbour in that port city.

'For you too Sir I can get good young grandma to spend evening with,' said the young shoeshine as he smudged some Kiwi black polish on Reggie's black calf leather shoes. Then having literally spat on it, the young boy with a flourish ran the cloth over it.

'Thanks for the offer young man, but there is no time for such mundane pleasures for men of my age and incidentally I am not an American, I am British. But maybe an elderly American will gladly take up the offer,' said Reggie as he smiled and paid the boy four annas. That was double the amount what the Americans were paying and thrilled with the money in his pocket, the boy jumped up to salute Reggie though he was not in uniform any longer.

Late that evening, Reggie caught the Heat Stroke Express for his next stop over at Rawalpindi where he would renew his friendship with Lieutenant Colonel D R Thapar and be his guest there. Lt Col Thapar from the Indian Medical Service because of the heavy demand for qualified nursing assistants, stretcher bearers and other junior qualified medical hands for the Indian formation and units engaged in fighting the enemy was now busy organising an Army Medical Corps training centre in Rawalpindi.

The very next day after his arrival, Reggie was witness to an unusual and extraordinary special durbar that was being conducted by the Commanding Officer, Lt Col DR Thapar himself. Being a mixed training centre under canvas and located fairly far away from the Rawalpindi Cantonment, the troops had expressed their desire to have their own places of worship within the training centre and for which they were also willing to contribute handsomely.And what took Reggie and Colonel Thapar with utter surprise was when the Subedar Major of the Centre gave out the methodology of how this fund raising was to be achieved. Having taken permission from his commanding officer to speak, the Subedar Major saluted and said.

'Sahib we have all decided irrespective of our rank, caste, creed or religion that we will all contribute a minimum of one rupee each to build a Mandir for the Hindus, a Masjid for the Mussulmans and a Gurdwara for the Sikhs. And all this will be done in our own spare time and after parade hours by using only our own man power resources and that to voluntarily. Now for the information of everyone present here today Sahib I feel proud to announce that the Hindus have volunteered to build the Masjid for their Muslim brothers in arms. The Muslims in turn have volunterred to build the Mandir for the Hindu troops and all of us tlogether as a unified force will build the Gurdwara for our Sikh brothers. Therefore all that we now require Sahib is your blessings and approval to start the project,' concluded the Subedar Major once more clicking his heels and saluting in traditional military style.For a couple of seconds there was stunned silence. Then a smiling Colonel Thapar stood up and vigourously pumped the hand of his Subedar Major as the entire durbar broke into a huge applause

On the very next day Reggie was witness to another glorious chapter of communal brotherhood, camaraderie, love and respect amongst the various communities and religions which was the corner stone of the Indian Army, when Colonel Thapar the proud commanding officer laid the foundation stone of the three religious institutions. On them was recorded for posterity the fact of who build what and for whom and that too voluntarily.

'This is simply marvellous and I wish all the leaders of the Hindus, Muslims, Sikhs and those of the Backward Classes of this great country take a lesson from this,' said Colonel Reginald Edwards, while congratulating the officers and soldiers of the training centre.

Later that evening, Reggie also visited all the reputed military tailors of the Rawalpindi Military Cantonment which included Kirpa Ram and Bros, Mohammed Ismail and the expensive Rankin and Company. It was from these very tailors that he had most of his uniforms made during his long service with the Indian Army and it started right from the day when he first landed in India as a young subaltern.A week later Reggie from Rawalpindi made his way to Srinagar. It was in a chauffeur driven big convertible navy blue Studebaker car which belonged to Lt Col Attiqur Rehman. The car had been sent to him for his visit to the valley from Peshawar by his old friend. On the way he stopped for a cup of tea in a wayside inn at the picturesque hill station of Murree. The legend says that the hill station derived its name from Virgin Mary whose tomb it is believed is located on a hilltop. The local

Muslims revere her as Hazrat Marium, the mother of Isa (Jesus) and when the British first arrived at Murree in 1850 to establish a new hill station, the people of the area referred to it as "Mai Mary da Asthan" or the resting place of Mother Mary. That day being a Thursday Reggie also visited the ancient shrine and together with the Hindu and Muslim devotees of the area lit an earthen lamp and prayed for Ismail Sikandar Khan's safety. His next stop was at Nathaigali and to the old British Club with its panoramic view of the Pirpanjal mountain ranges. Sitting in the verandah on a sprawling wickerwork Rattan chair he ordered a chilled beer with his favourite fish and chips for lunch.

Later that very evening he stopped by at the Bajwa family's old hotel at Muzzafarabad, 'The New Sher-e-Punjab' for a hot cup of tea. Located on the only main highway to the Kashmir Valley, it was no longer a small inn. It was now a regular hotel with 20 odd clean well furnished rooms with attached baths. It also had a fairly good restaurant with a well stocked liquor bar attached to it. For its efficient service and delightful North Indian and Frontier cuisine, the hotel was very popular with the rich middle class Indian tourists who had now started visiting the vale of Kashmir in larger numbers. Surprisingly, the hotel was still being run by Sardar Gurcharan Singh Bajwa who was simply delighted to meet Reggie after so many years. They had last met nearly a decade ago at the passing out parade of the Pioneers from the IMA, when Daler Singh Bajwa with Ismail and Gul Rehman popularly known as the three musketeers got their first pips. It was a very nostalgic evening for both of them as they talked about those good old days.

'Imagine how time has flown,' said Reggie as Gurbachan Bajwa showed him a few photographs of his new born grandson Montek Singh Bajwa and his proud parents.

"He was born on 25th December 1941 on Christmas day in the Christian Mission hospital in Baramulla and the good Irish nuns there nicknamed him "Jingles" from the popular Christian yuletide hymn "Jingle Bells" said the proud grandfather.

"Well where I can meet little Jingles and his parents, 'asked Reggie as Gurcharan Singh poured him another cup of the hot Kashmiri Kava tea from the silver samovar.

'I guess you will meet little Jingles definitely by tomorrow evening, when you get to Srinagar. My son Daler Singh is now an acting Major and he is on the staff of Brigadier HL Scott, the Chief of Staff of the Maharaja of Kashmir's State Forces and he has a nice comfortable house in Badami Bagh cantonment,' added Gurcharan Singh while giving out the menu to his head cook for the special evening meal for his honouredl guest.

Early next morning Reggie was on his way to Srinagar. According to the programme made by the Maharaja's efficient staff, he stopped for lunch at the Maharajas Hunting Lodge on the banks of the roaring Jhelum River at Rampur. There he was greeted by none other than Major Daler Singh Bajwa who had been specially deputed by the Maharaja as Reggie's personal liaison officer.

'Welcome once more to the valley of the Gods Sir,' said Daler Singh Bajwa as the liveried smart waiter on a silver tray brought in the two silver mugs and a bottle of chilled Munchen German beer.

'This is like aiding the bloody enemy, Hitler and his damn Nazis,' said Reggie jokingly as Daler Singh poured the German beer into the two silver mugs.

'Just cannot be helped Sir, because His Highness the Maharaja will not lower his standards, war or no war,' said Daler Singh as Reggie raised a toast to the health of the three musketeers.

The very next morning the grand hospitality of Mahraja Hari Singh of Kashmir was even more evident, when Daler Singh before setting out with Colonel Reginald Edwards for the duck shoot at the Hoksar Lake handed over to him his gun and a big box full of cartridges. To this was added the special haversack lunch and a bottle of rare French red wine to go with it. The small invitation card on the tiffin box with the Maharaja's coat of arms on it read.'Good shooting Colonel and best of luck,' and it was signed with compliments from Maharaja Hari Singh.

'Well, well I must say your Maharaja really has style. I am sure even our royalty in England would think twice before arming his guest with a box of high calibre gun cartridges and a bottle of booze to go with it,' said Reggie humourously as he tested one of the cartridges by firing the gun in the air.

And while Reggie was enjoying his holiday in Kashmir, Rash Behari Bose was busy in the Far East drafting the Bangkok Resolutions for the Indian Independence League, and in the West in Germany Subhas Bose was still trying his level best for an Axis tripartite declaration. Japan had come around to the proposal and Mussolini too was not averse to the idea, but Hitler was still reluctant. Subhas Bose had initially thought the Germans would have a cake walk through the Soviet Caucauses and that they with there mighty military machine would soon be knocking at India's western door in the North West Frontier. From there Subash reckoned that he with his Indian Legion that was being raised trained and armed in Germany by the German officers he would triumphantly march into India and the independent minded Pathans would also join them whole heartedly in throwing out their British masters. He had hoped and planned that with his three Indian battalions of the Indian Legion comprising of the captured Indian prisioners of war and with a company of irregulars that would form part of the German Fifth Column, he would be in the vanguard and that they would be the first to set foot on Indian soil. Subhas Bose was also over confident and thought that as soon as he and his Indian Legion entered their own revered motherland, the Indian soldiers and Officers of the Indian Army would automatically turn against their British superiors. But this was all wishful thinking and soon became a mirage as the Russian defence of their own motherland became stronger and stronger day by day. The last proverbial straw that really broke Subhas Bose's stout heart was on the 29th of May 1942, when Subhas Bose met Hitler for the final time. He once again tried to get Hitler's final nod for the tripartite declaration, but Hitler seemed adamant. Subhas Bose therefore returned to Berlin a disappointed man. Without an official tripartite declaration Subhas Bose was not even in a position to broadcast anti British propaganda over the German radio because that would be of no real use.That day he had met Hitler in his Field Headquarters and told him candidly that he with his popularity and contacts in India could rouse the country through Germany's time tested propaganda machine from outside, and this in turn would help the Axis powers in the overall war effort.'I have only to give it a small push and the people of India would revolt,' he told the Fuhrer. But Hitler was not at all impressed. Instead he simply took Subhas Bose to the Operations Room and standing in front of the big military situation map with his usual flourish explained the reason why.The Fuhrer pointed out to him on the map the latest German and Italian positions on the Russian front, in North Africa and in the Middle East. He then related their dispositions to the long distances geographically by the land route to the Indian frontier and said very candidly.'But Mr Bose our combined forces are still very far away from the frontiers of India and it will be foolish on my part and on part of the Duce at this stage to make any such declaration and promise. We cannot therefore at this juncture promise India her Independence from British rule.' On that very evening a dejected Subhash Bose decided to turn his eye towards the East and to Japan for help.

While Subhas Bose was still debating about what his next move should be, Samir Sen the eldest son of Naren Sen decided to try his luck as an art director with the Bombay Talkies Studios at Malad. He was 24 years old and was still without a regular job. His parents were now insisting that he should get married, but Samir was in no frame of mind of joining the matrimonial club. With a letter of recommendation from his father Naren Sen for Mr Ashok Kumar Ganguly, the up and coming hero of many a Bombay Talkies production and whom he and his father had first met on the train to Bombay some few years ago when he with his father was on his way to England, Samir Sen now arrived in Bombay, and with his knowledge of art, Samir Sen started working on the different types of sets that were required to be prepaid and painted for the various types of scenes to be shot indoors. He actually wanted to become a cameraman under the expert guidance of the Germans, but with the war on, all the Geman staff and technicians of the studio had been interned and the studio therefore required new hands and new faces to keep going.

On his very first day at work in the studio in May 1942, Samir Sen was witness to a very amusing incident. The new 19 year old plus handsome well built Pathan from Peshawar and the new hero had never faced the camera before. This was going to be his first film and he had been selected as a Bombay Talkies artist by none other than Devika Rani herself who was now in control of the studio after the untimely death of her husband Himanshu Rai a year ago. The young widow was quite a fire brand. She it seemed had discovered the new man and the young Yusuf Khan having given up his job as a military canteen manager at Poona was now looking for stardom with his new found screen name of Dilip Kumar.

Born at Peshawar on 11th December 1923, in the North West Frontier Province of India the young well educated Dilip Kumar was basically an introvert by nature. That day for the scene to be shot for the film "Jawar Bhata" he was rrequired to run and rescue the heroine from drowning. The heroine Mridula was also a new leading lady and as soon as director Amiya Chakravarty shouted action and roll camera, the young and energetic Dilip Kumar who was himself a good sportsman ran like hell. It was as if he was running a 100 meters race. 'Cut, cut, cut' shouted the Director as he summoned the young man over the megaphone.

'Orre Baba run slowly, the camera cannot follow you at that speed,' explained the director as he guided the new comer with the speed that was required for the retake. Then for the actual rescue shot, Dilip Kumar was required to physically touch the young lady and he became very very nervous and self conscious. Inspite of having taken a few retakes of that scene, the Director who was now behind the camera was not at al satisfied and while he was explaining his requirement to the new hero, suddenly somebody from the unit cried out loudly in Bengali. "Ore bacha bhabar kichu nahin, karoor kichu hobena, aar keyu doobe na. Ahkun puro mon diye scene ta koro, nohile ammra ekhneyi yehi clapper boyer shate atke thakbo shara deen.' (Young man there is nothing to think or fear about and nobody will drown. Therefore apply your whole mind and soul into the act or else we will be stuck with this clapper boy for the rest of the day.)

' Well I guess this is quite natural with any young new comer into the world of films and even Ashok Kumar in his first film with me was a nervous wreck too, when all that he was required to do was to put a simple garland around my neck. So please get on with the act and do the scenes a lot more realistically,' said the charming Devika Rani as she looked somewhat sternly at the other young new comer who too had been given a small roll in the same film. The extremely fair Punjabi lad with chubby cheeks and with the screen name of Raj Kapoor was standing in a far corner of the studio giggling away. Seeing the look on Devika Rani's face he quickly went out to have a cigarette. Surprisingly Ranbir Raj Kapoor too was born in Peshawar on 14th December 1924 and his father Prithviraj Kapoor was already a big name not only in Indian Films, but on the Indian stage also.

Being a restless person, Samir Sen after a couple of months found the work in the studios rather boring. He wanted to learn more about camera work and was told that Germany was the best place to go to. So one fine day after having worked for three months he collected his dues from Bombay Talkies and without saying goodbye to anybody he quietly in September 1942 boarded a cargo ship from the Ballard Pier in Bombay and set sail for Europe.

In the meantime with his futile meeting with Hitler having being made public, Subhash Bose now felt helpless sitting in Germany. Therefore, on being offered the leadership of the Indian Independence League in the Far East, he willingly and gladly accepted it. With over three million Indians in South East Asia and with the positive response and assurance by the Japanese government to help India in attaining her Independence, this was for Subhas Bose his best option. He immediately wrote to the leading members of the Bangkok conference that the Indian Independent Movement whether inside India or outside was one and the same and that India must not solely rely on the efforts of others, but should achieve their Independence through their own hard work work and industrious endeavour.

On the 15th of June 1942, at Bangkok an enthusiastic large crowd of Indians heard with animated joy the message sent by Subhash Bose to the members of the Bangkok Conference. He was now unanimously invited by them to assume the leadership of the League and the INA as soon as possible. However, nearly a full year was to pass before he could physically present himself and take complete charge of the fast changing situation.

In the meantime the command of the Indian Red Eagles had changed hands once again. In early January 1942, Major General Francis Tuker took over the command of the 4th Indian Division from Major General Frank Messervy. Five days earlier on Christmas day Messervy's troops had entered Bengazi, while General Rommel was forced to lift his siege of Tobruk.

General Francis Ivan Simms Tuker from the 2nd Gurkha Rifles of the Indian Army had just arrived on the scene of action after his stint as Director of Military Training, Army Headquarters India. He was soon to prove to the British people and the Empire the stuff his Red Eagles were made off.

With the British supply lines over extended, Rommel having received fresh reinforcements from Tripoli had now launched a counter attack and had recaptured Bengazi on 29th January 1942. General Claude Auchinleck's forces were now once again on the retreat. By the middle of the year 1942, the war situation on all the fronts was in a state of flux and there were no clear winners in sight.On 26th June 1942, the Fuhrer had promoted Rommel to the rank of a Field Marshall. By the end of the month after very heavy fighting Rommel had taken Mersa Matruh while his Panzer spearheads had reached the outskirts of El Alamein. On the 29th of June a jubilant Mussolini arrived at Derna in Libya. He was now hoping to make his triumphant entry into Cairo along the only coastal road that hugged the blue Mediterranean Sea. On the very next day the brave but demoralzied and disorganised Headquarters of the British Eighth Army in Cairo thinking that all was now lost had started destroying all their classified secret and top secret documents. They were preparing to evacuate to Palestine, when the C-in-C Middle East, General Claude Auchinleck forbid any further withdrawals. He had on that very day received a very authentic intelligence report that Rommel was preparing to attack El Alamein the next day and he ordered everyone to stay put and fight.

On the Russian Eastern Front on the 1st of June 1942, Hitler arrived at Poltava, the Headquarters of his Army Group South to review the military situation. Three days later on 4th June the Fuhrer received the sad news that Reinhard Heydrich his blue eyed boy who rose to the rank of a Brigadier General in the dreaded SS before he was even thirty years old had died of his wounds. Nicknamed the "Blonde Beast" by the Nazis and "Hangman Heydrich" by others, the buthcher of Jews had become a victim of an assassination himself. The act had been carried out by the Czech underground in their capital city of Prague. The so called assasins had been trained in England and were parachuted back into their own country to carry out the killing.

Born on 7th March 1904, in the German city of Halle, Reinhard Eugen Tristan Heydrich came from a musical minded family. His father was an opera singer and his mother an accomplished pianist. As a young boy he had trained as a violinst which when not killing people remained as his life long passion. At the age of eighteen he had joined the German Navy as a cadet, and by 1926 had risen to the rank of a Second Lieutenant. It was rumoured that he had some Jewish blood in him and this always haunted him when his batchmates for his love for classical music taunted him with the name "Moses Handel. In 1931, he was forced to resign his naval commission for conduct unbecoming of an officer and a gentleman. He had being accused of having sex with the unmarried daughter of a shipyard director, but refused to marry her when asked to do so. With his naval career in ruins, Heydrich in 1931 at age twenty seven joined the Nazi Party and soon became a member of the Schutzstaffel, the dreaded SS. The SS was an elite organization of black coated young men who were fanatically attached to their Nazi leaders and their belligerent policies.Heinrich Himmler the SS Reichsfuhrer seeing the enthusiasm and dedication of the young man soon appointed Reinhard Heydrich to create the intelligence gathering organization for the SS. It was called the Sicherheitsdienst or the SS Security Service and was referred to as the SD. A master conspirator Heydrich was also responsible for the downfall of Werner Von Blomberg the German War Minister and Werner Von Fritsch, the Commander-in-Chief of the German Army, when in 1937 they both opposed Hitler's long range war plans. Planting false stories about their personal character both of them were disgraced and dismissed thus paving the way for Hitler to become the Commander-in-Chief. Heydrich was also the one who engineered a fake Polish attack on a German radio station at Gleiwitz thus giving Hitler the excuse to pounce upon Poland. After the invasion of Poland, Heydrich was given command of the newly formed Reich Main Security Office, also known as the RSHA. This was the all powerful office which combined the activities of the SD, the Gestapo, the Criiminal Police and the Foreign Intelligence Service that terrorised the entire continent of Europe with mass murders and annihilation of the Jews. It was again Heydrich who on 20th January 1942, had convened the Wansee Conference in Berlin to coordinate the programme for the success of the Final solution.

'The whole of Europe from East to West will be combed of all Jews,' declared Heydrich very proudly as Adolf Eichmann took down the minutes of that conference. On 27th May that very year at Prague as his car slowed down to take a sharp turn on a road bend, the Czech revenge seekers opened fire. The person whom Hitler called 'The man with an iron heart" was no more. His iron heart had stopped beating for good.

Hitler's forces on the Eastern Front were still fighting a ding dong battle against the die hard Russians who were now not prepared to give even an inch of their sacred land to the Hitlerites without a fight. The Germans were still in the process of capturing the fortress of Sevasthopol on the Crimean coast as the Russian offensive kept pushing the Germans back further and further from Moscow. Though Leningrad was still under siege, but fighting had broken out there too. On the 26th of May, 1942 Britain and the Soviet Union signed a treaty in London pledging their will to fight on until final victory was achieved and under no circumstamces would either of them ever make a separate peace with the enemy.

On the 28th of June 1942, a furious Hitler ordered 'Operation Blau' for the capture of Sevastopol and for the drive to the Caucasus and to the rich oil fields of that region. His summer offensive did make some initial progress, but it soon got stalled with the Russians hanging on to their defences tooth and nail. To ease the pressure on the Russian defence line, the courageous and brave Soviet Partisan Groups sabotaged, attacked and harrassed the long German lines of communication. The German high command now launched "Operation Hanover" to catch, kill and destroy the Partisans, but it was not such a simple and easy task. When a desparate German high command contemplated the use of poison gas against the Soviets, Prime Minister Winston Churchill sent out a warning that if the Germans used the poison gas on the Eastern Front, then the Allied forces would also use it against the Germans. The warning did have a salutary effect on Hitler and the German General staff. In the meantime in the Far East and in the Pacific, the Japanese were busy carving out there own larger Empire and they had also to be stopped.To push them back from the strategic islands in the Pacific Ocean and from the Phillipines came back on to the scene, General Douglas MacArthur and Admiral Nimitz of the American armed forces.

CHAPTER-14

The Turn of the Tide

Born in 1880, Douglas MacArthur was the son of an army officer. His father Arthur MacArthur as a teenager had won the Congressional Medal of Honour when as a member of the Union Army he led a courageous assault up Missionary Ridge in Tennesse. Douglas graduated first in the class of 1903 from West Point. As a Brigadier General he led the Rainbow Division during the First World War in France. It was a formation created out of the National Guards. Later he also became the Superintendent of West Point. In 1928, after the divorce from his first wife Louis, Douglas found solace in the Phillipines where his father had served as a Military Governor during the Spanish Civil War. Douglas was returning now to take command of the Army's Phillipine Department. He too like his father would have become the Governor of Phillipines had not President Hoover appointed him for the top job of Chief of Staff in 1930. In 1935, with the blessings of his old friend Manuel Quezon now the President of the Phillipines Commonwealth, Douglas once again returned at his invitation to head the US military mission and with the task of preparing the Islands of the Commonwealth for full Independence in 1946. It was the best years of his life as he fell in love with the 37 year old Jean Marie Faircloth from Tennesse and at the age of 58 years became the proud father of a son. After the Japanese surprise attack on Pearl harbour on 7th December 1941, and with the Japanese superiority both in the air and on the seas soon MacArthur's air force was also destroyed. Now he had no other option but to retreat with his forces to the Bataan Peninsula where they struggled to survive. From his command post on the island of Corregidor at the mouth of the Manila Bay, Douglas MacArthur now watched his world fall apart. But he was not a man to give up so easily. He had vowed that he would return and this was exactly what he was now doing.

Born on 24th February 1885, Fleet Admiral Chester Whilliam Nimitz also wanted to go to West Point but finally joined the navy. A product of the US Naval Academy, Annapolis, Chester had passed out with distinction in his class of 1905. Though he was court-martialled for grounding the USS Decatur, but he did not lose heart. In fact he became more resolute and committed to his profession when he became a submariner. He then commanded in succession a series of submarines and redeemed his service career in the US Navy. In December 1941, he was designated as Commander-in-Chief Pacific Fleet and Pacific Ocean Areas, and he too was now waiting to take revenge on the Japanese Navy.

While the Allies were getting ready to teach the Axis Powers the lesson of their lives on the sea, in the air and on the ground, at Bombay, Mahatma Gandhi was gearing up to show the British Masters of the country the door from where to get out from India. On the 7th of August, 1942 at Birla House in Bombay where Gandhi was staying and where the Congress Party leaders had gathered for an important meeting, Pandit Nehru moved the Quit India resolution.

'Yes, enough is enough and they must Quit India," repeated the old frail man on the 8th of August 1942, while addressing the meeting of the All India Congress Committee at the Tejpal Hall at Gowalia Tank.'We must strike and strike now and it is a matter of now or never,' said a very worked up Mahatma.as Debu Ghosh and others heard him with rapt attention. Debu who had come all the way to Bombay as an observer for this historic session felt inspired with those words. After the resolution was passed unanimously, the Mahatma once again addressed the session and it was nearing midnight when he said.

'I therefore want complete freedom immediately, this very night and before dawn, if it can be had. Freedom now cannot wait for the realization of communal unity. If that unity is not achieved, sacrifices necessary for it will have to be much greater than would have otherwise sufficed. But the Congress must win freedom or be wiped out in the effort. And forget not that the freedom which the Congress is struggling for will not be for the Congressmen alone, but for all the forty crores of the Indian people and I am not going to be satisfied with anything short of complete freedom. So here is the "Mantra", a short one that I give you. And you may imprint it in your heart and that mantra is "Do or Die" "Karo ya Maro."

With the Intelligence snoops listening in to every word that the Mahatma spoke that night, it was immediately reported to the highest British Headquarters and early next morning they were ready to swoop down on all the Congress leaders and put them in prison. The first one to be arrested was the Mahatma himself from Birla House. The next in line was Pandit Nehru. He was staying with his youngest sister Krishna Hutheesingh affectionately called Betty at her Sakina Mansion flat on Carmichael Road and the Police had kept it under close surveillance ever since the time Nehru arrived there. It was around 5 o'clock early that morning, when the police knocked on the door and a sleepy Mr Hutheesingh opened it. Both Betty and her husband were taken by total surprise, but Pandit Nehru was cool as a cucumber.

'Tell them to wait while I get ready and please make for me my favourite breakfast,' said Jawaharlal to his sister. After a heavy English breakfast of eggs and bacon, Pandit Nehru sat inside the police Black Maria and was taken to the Victoria Terminus Station. From early dawn, Bombay's Victoria Terminus station was teeming with scores of policeman as the arrested Congress leaders arrived one by one to be escorted to their seats on the train to Poona. As Kalyan flashed by, they were all taken to the dining car for breakfast. Thereafter all hell broke loose all over India as the news of their arrests spread like wild fire. In Bombay, the young Tturks from the Congress Party led by a pretty young married lady in a spotless white saree congregated at the Gowalia Tank ground to voice their protest

Born Aruna Ganguly the 33 year old Bengali lady was the wife of Mr Asaf Ali a senior Congress leader from Allahabad and a lawyer by profession. He too had been whisked away by the police that morning. Aruna Asaf Ali after completing her schooling from the Sacred Heart Convent at Lahore and Protestant School Nainital did her graduation and for a while also taught at the Gokhale Memorial School in Calcutta. At the age of 19, she had met Mr Asaf Ali, a man 23 years her senior and despite parental objections married him. Her first major political involvement was in 1930 during the salt Satyagraha and for which she served a year in prison also. Today she was in a fiery mood and police or no police she was determined to hoist the Indian National Flag at the venue from where only a few hours earlier the Mahatma had given the mantra of do or die

By the afternoon a massive crowd had gathered at the Gowalia tank maidan shouting slogans for the British to get out of India. The police too now had started arriving in strength with batons, rifles and tear gas shells. But the courageous young lady with other young second rung leaders of the Congress party was not the least bothered as she exhorted the crowd to defy the policemen and got ready to unfurl the Indian flag. As soon as it started fluttering in the monsoon breeze on that cloudy day, the police fired the tear gas shells into the crowd. Debu Ghosh with a few other volunteers rushed towards the police cordon and seeing them the crowd too joined in. Now the firing started and soon a large number of them became innocent victims. Debu Ghosh too got a bullet in his leg and had fallen down, but luckily he did not get trampled in the stampede, or else he too would have met with sure death. Fotunately a young Congress volunteer had seen him fall and had carried him piggy back to a nearby house. There Debu was given immediate first aid and later that night violating the curfew orders a local doctor was summoned and he removed the bullet. The injury providentially was not very serious as Debu Ghosh with Aruna Asaf Ali, Usha Mehta and others from the second rung of the Congress ladder went underground to fan the movement.

Not to be cowed down by the retaliation from their colonial masters, the Indians all over the country now went on a rampage. For the next six weeks they attacked all visible signs of British authority. With vengeance they went after the courts, the post offices, the railway stations and offices. Workers in factories struck work. Students in schools and colleges boycotted their classes and even villagers in some villages across the country courted voluntary arrest. Over 60,000 people were now under police custody while a large number of others were flogged for violating orders. Around 900 people had been killed in the firing in various parts of India. The British had under estimated the reaction and the fall out from the mantra that was given by the Mahatma. It was a mass upsurge the likes of which the British had not seen for a very long time. The non violent Mahatma had turned violent it seems. This time however the Mahatma was not put in an ordinary jail. He had been interned inside the Aga Khan Palace in Poona, which was not very far away from the Yerwada prison.where he had been imprisoned earlier.

The construction of the Aga Khan Palace was started in 1897, when the city of Poona and the area around were faced with a severe famine. In order to provide employment to the famine stricken people, His Highness the Aga Khan Imam Sultan Mohammed Shah, the spiritual leader of the Khoja Muslims had initiated the project and the construction was supervised by none other than his wife Mata Saalmaat Lady Ali Shah.

While Gandhi was interned inside the huge palace, most of the other Congress leaders including Pandit Nehru were taken to the Ahmednagar Jail, a hundred miles to the east of Poona.By now the British had armed themselves with draconian powers. They completely suspended all civil liberties and even the press was gagged. But this only added in driving the movement further underground. From the second rung of the young

Congress leaders, men and women like Achyut Patwardhan, Aruna Asaf Ali, Ram Manohar Lohia, Sucheta Kripalani, Chotubhai Puranik, Biju Patnaik, Jai Prakash Narayan, Usha Mehta and the newly married couple of Feroze and Indira Gandhi and other such like nationalists and patriots kept the fire of freedom burning. With their dedication and courage they guided the underground movement and soon others too secretly joined the faction, while staying over ground. They provided to those in hiding with money, shelter, information and logistical support. Soon a clandestine Congress radio network also started broadcasting songs, news, views and anti British propaganda from a secret location inside Bombay. The time for the British to quit India had now begun, but the question remained as to when would the world war be over and which side would finally emerge victorious.

While Indira Gandhi returned to Allahabad, Feroze Gandhi who was wanted by the police for his anti British activities went underground. Having grown a moustache, the fair complexioned and handsome Feroze Gandhi got himself an army haircut and dressed in an old Khaki uniform and pretending to be an Anglo Indian soldier, he boarded the Bombay-Calcutta Mail via Allahabad from the majestic Victoria Terminus railway station. As he sat quietly in a second class compartment he was joined at Kalyan junction by another tall, well built and handsome Anglo Indian.

'Hey Buddy where to?,' asked the 21 year old Richard Pugsley from the Corps of Signals as he placed his army kit bag against the door and offered Feroze Gandhi a cigarette.

'No thanks. I don't smoke,' said Feroze as he tried to avoid further conversation with the jovial Anglo Indian.

'Alright no minor vices I guess, but please do wake me up at Khandwa station which comes early in the morning because I want to be with my dad and mom for every moment of my short 10 days leave at Mhow before our unit sails for the Middle East,' said Richard Pugsley as he switched off the lights in the compartment and went off to sleep. Seeing the serviceman snoozing away, Feroze Gandhi breathed a sigh of great relief.

The next day evening and before the train reached Allahabad, Feroze Gandhi got off at a small wayside station and went into hiding in a congested part of the city. Here Indira met him secretly in the homes of their non political friends. The British Intelligence now started tracking her, and soon she too went underground and into hiding with her husband. At Allahabad, Feroze started operating a clandestine Congress radio station, but it was not before long when both of them were arrested and on the 10th of September, 1942 they were both sent to the jail at Naini.

On the 15th of August 1942, seeing the volatile mood of the Indians, the Government of the United States of America issued a bulletin for the guidance of all American military forces that were based in India. The bulletin stated that the sole purpose of the American Forces in India was to prosecute war of the United Nations against the Axis powers and they were not to indulge even in the slightest degree in activities of any other nature. They were also categorically told not to participate in India's political movement and problems and in the event of any internal disturbances they were required only to resort to taking defensive measures for their own personal safety and protect the American military bases in India.

The do or die call for the British to quit India given by the Mahatma on 8th August at Bombay had also boosted the morale of Subhas Bose in Germany. Thinking that revolution in India was imminent, he opened two more radio stations there. Calling them as "Congress Radio" and 'Azad Muslim Radio" he decided to contribute to the tension in India through vigorous propaganda oriented talks. Subhash Bose also felt that with Mahatma Gandhi now opting for a now or never attitude, there was no difference in their respective attitudes as far as the British masters were concerned. Therefore with the Indian prisoners of war from the North African front now in Germany, he also now went full throttle to organize and train them as a fighting force. Calling it the Indian Legion they were now under the strict supervision of German officers. By October 1942, the first of the three battalions of the Indian Legion was inspected by Subhas Bose at the German military centre at Koenigsbrueck in Saxony. After Lieutenant Colonel Krappe the German Commanding Officer had addressed them, the oath was taken. With due solemnity, the oath was administered by the German officers to six Indians at a time as they touched the officer's sword. Subhas Chandra Bose accompanied by Colonel Yamamoto, the Japaneese Military Attache in Germany stood to attention and in silence as the Indian legionnaires loudly repeated the words.'I swear by God this holy oath, that I will obey the leader of the German State and People, Adolf Hitler as Commander of the German Armed Forces in the fight for the freedom of India and in which fight the leader is Subhas Chandra Bose and that as a brave soldier, I am willing to lay down my life for this oath.'Once the oath taking ceremony was over, Subhash Bose presented to the Legion the new standard. It was the Indian tricolour of green, white and saffron of the Indian National Congress that was superimposed with the figure of a springing tiger. It was a moment of great pride and emotion as the Indians in German uniforms with the springing tiger as their formation sign on their arms listened to Subhas Bose their leader.

'Freedom is not given, it is taken and I shall lead the Army when we march to India together,' said Subhas Bose while concluding his address with a loud Jai Hind." But in his heart of hearts he knew that with just three Indian battalions and inspite of they being a part of the German war machine it was still a distant dream at this stage to even think of getting anywhere near India from the west. With the Fuhrer and the Duce still unwilling to make a tripartite declaration, Subhas Bose was only waiting to get to South East Asia where the Mahatma's call to "Do or Die" had invigorated the large expatriate Indian population and the Indian prisoners of war there. Now even young girls and ladies were coming forward voluntarily to bolster the movement for full freedom. At this juncture Subhas Bose was also saddled with a personal dilemma. In July 1942, Fraulein Emilie Schenkl his personal private secretary who was also secretly his wife left for Vienna to deliver his child. In September he would become a proud father of a pretty baby girl.

On The 1st of August, the Japanese had established a puppet government in Burma and the defeated army of General Bill Slim's 1st Burma Corps having retreated into India by end May were now getting ready once again to launch their counter offensive in western Burma and in the Arakans. The defeat of the British and their withdrawal from South East Asia in the face of the Japanese onslaught also had created a very negative image in the minds of the Indian people in those countries. Whereas the British evacuated their own white people, they left their own Indian subjects to their fate. Now for the Indians in India and especially those in the North East, Assam and Bengal there was genuine apprehension that the British may repeat the same and desert them when the Japanese start knocking on India's eastern door. Demoralized by the news of British betrayal in South East Asia, the struggle against the existing colonial power at this juncture needed a decisive momentum and a big push. The British now had started using every resource of even the poor Indian people as they kept mustering and requisitioning their boats, their food and their accommodation in Bengal, Assam and the North East. All this was now leading to shortages as prices of essential commodities like rice, food grains and lentils spiralled up at an alarming rate and which would soon spell disaster. The faith in the British was steadily reaching an all time low and the time had now come to take full advantage of this by the Indian Independence League in South East Asia. But in India with the top Congress leaders in jail and without the Muslim

League giving any support to the Quit India movement, the enthusiasm of the Indian masses inside the country was now also steadily waning away.

By the end of August 1942, more than 40,000 Indian prisoners of war had signed the pledge to join the INA under their self proclaimed leader General Mohan Singh. On the 10th of September, the first combat division was ready for action, but for Mohan Singh that was not good enough. He now demanded from the Japanese a second division to be armed and trained from the 24,000 surplus volunteers that he was still holding with him. He told Colonel Iwaguro the head of the Japanese liaison organization in South East Asia that with the overwhelming support of the Indians in Malaya and Burma he was capable of raising an army of two and a half lacs and the Japanese authorities must help him out with all the wherewithal to equip and arm them. But that was not to be as the Japanese kept delaying even giving due recognition to the INA. Then as reports started coming in that the Japanese had started usurping the properties of the Indian community also, and which rightfully belonged to the India Independence League, Mohan Singh could take it no more. He told the Japanese authorities point blank that India did not need Japanese bogus support and if need be he was prepared to even order the disbandment and dissolution of the Indian National Army. The Japanese authorities now dismissed him from his command and sent him into quiet internment to a remote part of the Singapore Island.

It had been earlier resolved by the members of the Council of Action in the Bangkok Resolution and of which Mohan Singh was very much a member that the INA should be in the hands of Indians themselves and this had been signed by Rash Bihari Bose, the President of the Indian independence League himself on 30th June 1942. It had also been agreed to by the Japanese government that the INA would also be accorded the powers and status of a Free National Army of an Independent India on a footing of equality with the armies of Japan and other friendly powers. But now it seemed that for the Japanese the Council of Action had no status at all and only the Japanese local cadres irrespective of their seniority could lay down all the ground rules.

With Mohan Singh out of rekoning, the Indian Independence League was in a dilemna. The formation of the INA had gone into a limbo and Rash Bihari Bose had to now get busy to salvage the INA. When Mohan Singh had suggested that the INA be dissolved, the Japanese promptly declared that the Indians could now go back to the prisoner of war camps. The question now arose whether the INA should continue or not and if at all they did under what terms should it continue. Luckily news had now arrived that Subhash Bose would soon be on his way from Germany to Japan and they therefore decided to leave the final decision to him.

Meanwhile in the North African Desert, Field Marshal Rommel's Afrika Korps was still struggling to breakthrough the British defences of the 8th Army at El Alamein, when Churchill himself arrived on the scene to review the situation. He now decided to replace General Claude Auchinleck with General Alexandar as C-in-C Middle East. A major change was also made in the command of the British 8th Army, but the aircraft carrying the Army Commander designate General Gott was shot down while it was enroute to Cairo. The command of the 8th Army was therefore now given to General Bernard Montgomery who took over on 11th August 1942.

General Aukchinleck was now being sent to India as the new Commander-in-Chief designate. Born on 21st June 1884 at Aldershot, General Claude John Eyre Auchinleck was now 58 years old. A Sandhurst product and a proud First Punjabee he simply loved India. He was returning at a time when Gandhi and the Indians were shouting at the Britishers to quit their country and the Japaneese war machine was advancing through the jungles of Burma towards India. His unusual surname was derived from the Gaelic words "Ach an Leach" meaning the field of the flat stone and Auk as he was now popularly known would leave no stone unturned to ensure that the sacrifices made by the Indian soldiers did not go unsung. A late entry into the matrimonial club, he got married at the age of 36. He had met his future wife the 21 year old Jessie Stewart, the daughter of a Scotsman while both the families were holidaying in the South of France. There they fell in love and soon the marriage followed. In 1930 having commanded the 1/1 Punjabees, the very battalion that had brought him up, Auk felt miserably sad when he took leave of them and boarded the train at Jhelum to take up his new assignment at the Staff college at Quetta. As the train steamed off to the thunderous cheers of "Auk Sahib ki Jai,' there were tears in his eyes. But that was very many years ago, when India was relatively a peaceful place, but now after the Mahatma's call to quit India and with the Japanese at India's doorstep it was a very dicey situation indeed.

While Auk was on his journey back to India, at El Alamein the new 8th Army Commander was inspecting the defences and issuing out his orders and instructions. The son of a Bishop, General Bernard Montgomery was born on 17th November 1887, and he had spent his childhood years at Hobart in Tasmania. On passing out from Sandhurst Military Academy he was commissioned into the Royal Warwickshire Regiment. He wanted to be in the top 30 so that he could opt for the Indian Army, but he had passed out 36th in order of merit. As a cadet at Sandhurst, Monty as he was popularly known while holding the appointment of a Lance Corporal was demoted to a Gentleman Cadet for setting fire to a junior cadet's tail coat. And the same man was now eagerly waiting to set fire to the tail coats of Rommel's Afrika Corps as he reorganised his defences on the El Alamein line and waited for the additional men and material that was badly required to get the 8th Army back into the offensive mode.

Strangely on the very first day of his taking over command of the 8th Army in the Middle East, one of the first messages that he sent to all the formation and units under his command took both the officers and the troops by complete surprise. He ordered that no official brothels will be set up for the troops near the Army camps in the rear or elsewhere near the troops. This may have been entirely for security resons, but the regulars including the officers however turned a blind eye to the order. Hotels like the Mimosa in Beirut and some others in Cairo and Alexandria were simply high class brothels which the officer class normally frequented. For the ordinary soldier there were brothels that had been especially and officially established in areas closer to their camps and these were done under the strict supervision of the RMO, the unit regimental medical officer.

In the second week of August 1942, a newly raised Field Ambulance unit of the Indian Army Medical Corps with Colonel Attiqur Rehman in command arrived in Egypt. They set up their tented camp for desert training in a far away suburb of Cairo. This camp was previously occupied by some other medical unit which had now been moved forward. One fine day after a fortnight of their arrival, when he was told by his Adjutant who was himself a qualified doctor that there was a middle aged lady waiting outside his office to see him urgently, Colonel Attiqur Rehman who was a thorough gentleman immediately asked the Adjutant to escort the lady inside. Colonel Attiqur now in his mid fifties had volunteered for service in the Middle East and though he had only a year more to serve before being superannuated, he simply wanted to be closer to his two sons, Gul and Aftab Rehman.

As soon as the big built lady stepped into his tented office, Col Attiqur immediately stood up and offered the lady a seat. Till that time he had no idea who she was. The fat buxom lady, half Egyptian and half European in a silk skirt and a low cut sleeveless blouse from which her huge breasts were about to fall out smiled, thanked the commanding officer for the courtesy, and then stated in fairly good English that she had come primarily to lodge a complaint against the Indian troops under the Colonel's command.

When the Adjutant in Urdu told the Commanding Officer who the lady really was, Colonel Attiqur immediately summoned his Subedar Major to be in attendance. Initially Colonel Attiqur Rehman thought that the fat buxom lady may have come for medical advice and medicines, but now on seeing the heavy make up and those dumble size arms and legs he knew who she really was.

'Yes now please shoot what is your complaint and what can I do to help you out,' said Attiqur Rehman rather firmly.

'You can do a lot Sir if you want to because I am losing a helleva lot of business and all this thanks to your clever and calculating Indian soldiers,' said the lady with a look of pathos and grief on her heavily made up face.

'Come to the point madam because I have a lot of other important things to attend to,' replied Colonel Attiqur Rehman somewhat a bit curtly this time.

'Alright in that case let me be candid about it Sir because if it carries on like this I will be ruined. This is my bread and butter and so is it for all my girls. But your young men from India are too very demanding. They want the best for the least price and I cannot afford that,' said the Madam.

'Please just get to the point madam and I will see how best we can help you out,' said Colonel Attiqur this time with a wry smile on his face. The lady then took out a Elizabeth Arden compact from her bag and having applied it to her face, added.

'Sir, the problem is two fold. Firstly your men visit the brothel always in pairs calling each other as buddies and while one performs the other insists on watching and if I object they say that those are the orders that have come right from the and that as buddies and with the war on they simply cannot be separated for security reasons. With the result that while one Indian soldier has a good time with the girl and pays for it, the other has a good time relieving himself off free of cost and once that is over he is in no mood to perform right then. This is rather unfair isn't it Colonel'?

'Technically you may be right Madam, but those are the orders from the high command. They simply just cannot perform together at the same time because as buddies they cannot leave each other out of their sight, and if somebody does not perform, why the hell should he have to pay,' said Colonel Rehman as he asked his office orderly to fetch a glass of cold water for the lady who was now sweating profusely.

' Alright Madam the first problem I am afraid we just cannot do anything about it, and the most you can do is to levy a small cover charge on the second person for watching the fun from a ringside seat. But to be fair to him too, if the second one also performs thereafter then the cover charge should be returned to him,' said Colonel Attiqur Rehman as he took approval of the suggestion from his Subedar Major.

"Bilkul tikh kaha aapne Sahib. Agar hamara sepahi karega to who paisa zaroor bharega. Lekin agar woh nahin karega tho paisa nahin bharega. Iss mein koi shak ki baat hi nahin hai. (You are absolutely right Sir. If the soldier performs he pays, but if he doesn't perform then he doesn't pay and there is no ambuigity in this at all.) said the Subedar Major as he came to attention, loudly clicked his heels and saluted.

'Alright that settles your first problem Madan and now tell me what is the second one,' said Attiqur Rehman while appreciating the Subedar Major's concern for the troops.The Madam having applied some more rouge on her face took a deep breath, looked at the Subedar Major somewhat pleadingly and said.

'For reasons unknown Sir, but most of your men I regret to say try to adopt all kinds of weird positions for performing on my girls and their favourite is doing it from behind. But my girls are not amazons. They are very frail and they complain of severe backache thereafter. With the result that they now demand to be kept off business for the next two to three days and consequently my business suffers. That is not only a great loss for me, but for my girls too. And when I ask them why they adopt such weird positions they confidently quote some book called the '"Kama Sutra' and that's that.'

'Well in that case all I can suggest to you Madam is that you put up a notice in bold capital letters in Urdu and Hindi and for those who cannot even read an illustration outside your joint saying "Only missionary position permissible;'. 'So either they do it in that position or they leave it.' added Colonel Attiqur this time with a poker face.

There was now a mischievous smile on the face of the Adjutant as he expressed his sympathy with the lady and said.somewhat matter of factly.'I am terribly sorry Madam but with the latest orders from Monty, your business I am afraid will see even worse times. For not only will you be out of business, but our boys too will have to do the jerking drill more often.'

'But who the hell is this Mounty? How can he put a spoke in my business? And if he cannot perform himself and mount he has no right to stop others,' said the Madam rather angrily.

'Madam his name is not Mounty, it is Monty and if we violate his orders he will mount on us and that I can assure will not be liked by anybody, not even by you,' added the Adjutant.

'What bloody nonsense is all this. Well whoever this Monty maybe, but can I have his telephone number and address. He may be some big bloody General for you all, but he cannot ruin my whoring business. As it is all of you, including your Monty have descended on my motherland without any proper invitation and we have welcomed you as our honoured guests. Now your job is to fuck the bloody Germans and the damn Italians, and my job is to see that your soldiers are in a happy and fit condition to do so. This is a biological requirement and it is good for their morale too Colonel. And if it is not periodically released with a woman in bed, than I am afraid quite a few of you will soon become active members of the gay club, and that may not be a healthy alternative,' said the brothel owner as she walked out in a huff.

After the Subedar Major was dismissed from this unsual orderly room, Colonel Attiqur Rehman with a big smile on his face narrated a nice joke to his Adjutant and to his Second in Command. And this he narrated for the simple reason because it had a good moral behind it.

'Well Chaps there was once this rich Arab Sheik from the Middle East who had a huge harem which was quite some distance away from his sprawling palace. And there were so many beautiful girls inside the harem and from so many different parts of the world that the Sheikh could never remember their names or nationalities. So for quick recognition he had all of them numbered from one to hundred and more. For the security and safety of the girls inside the harem, the Sheikh had employed a platoon of eunuchs to guard them. One day the Sheikh felt a bit more randy than usual and he ordered his young and strong ADC eunuck to run and fetch Number 10. The eunuch ADC quickly ran over the wall, jumped over the fence, sprinted to the harem and returned with number 10 on his back and presented her to the Sheikh. The Sheikh had a good time, but he still was'nt satisfied. Therefore he now ordered for Number 61 to be brought to him. Once again the eunuch ADC ran over the wall, jumped over the fence, sprinted away as fast as he could and came back panting with number 61 on his back. Once again the Sheikh had a good time, but he was still not satisfied. This time he asked for his favourite number 91. Again the poor young eunuch ran over the wall, jumped over the palace fence and with number 91 on his back came back with his tongue hanging out. Then having presented the girl to the Sheikh he gave a smart salute and fell dead at the Sheikh's feet. Now gentlemen the moral of this very tragic story is that it is not the fucking around that kills you, but it is the running around" said Attiqur Rehman as all of them burst out laughing.

Not to be left behind, his witty Second In Command also came up with another naughty one. Quoting a verse from one of Lord Byron's famous poems he said that the great English poet was once an eyewitness to a rape case. After he was put on the dock on oath to give evidence as a principal witness for the prosecution, and the prosecutor asked. 'Now Mr Byron could you please describe to this Court and to the honourable members of the jury what you actually saw with your very own eyes.' Having surveyed the courtroom, the great poet simply said. "Milord he was plain and simple forcibly fucking her and nothing more and nothing less.' Hearing that, there was sudden laughter inside the courtroom as the honourable Judge banged the table and, shouted order order, and then asked the learned poet to describe it in a more refined and dignified manner. The bard closed his eyes for a minute or two, thought for a while and then in his imitable poetical style said.'Milord his pants were down and her legs were bare; his balls were dangling in the air. His you know what was in her you know where and if that wasn't fucking I was'nt there.'

'That I must say was indeed a very good one and therefore gentlemen today the drinks in the Mess prior to lunch will be on me,' said Colonel Attiqur Rehman as they closed shop and went to the Officer's mess for a couple of mugs of chilled beer and that was to be followed by some delicious spread of Frontier food.

That day also happened to be Colonel Attiqur Reman's fifty fifth birthday, but he had not disclosed this to anybody else as yet. And when the first round of drinks were about to be served suddenly to the pleasant surprise of the oldman walked unannounced and inside the big EPIP Officer's Mess tent his eldest son Major Gul Rehman Khan from the 1st Punjabees and Major Ismail Sikandar Khan from the 2nd Punjabees. And each one with two big identical chocolate cakes that had a big 55 written on them greeted the old man.

Both the Punjab battalions were now part of the 161 Motorized Brigade of the Red Ball Division and the Brigade was now holding a very important defensive sector on the Ruweisat Ridge near El Alamein. Another half an hour later there was another surprise for the oldman as his second son Captain Aftab Rehman who was also from Ismail's Second Punjabees popped in with another huge cake. That afternoon it was also a double celebration as both the friends Major Gul Rehman and Major Ismail Sikandar Khan announced that they had been nominated for the next Staff College course at Quetta. Because of the war, the staff college course had now been reduced to six months and they had been selected to attend the one that was scheduled to begin in mid 1943.

'I thnk that will suit all of us admirably,' said a delighted Attiqur Rehman while announcing with pride that the wedding of his daughter Shenaz with her cousin Dr Nawaz Hussein, son Dr Ghulam Hussein had been fixed tentatively during the winter of that very year.

And while Colonel Attiqur Rehman's birthday was being celebrated in Cairo, at the Aga Khan Palace in Poona the Mahatma was mourning the death of his dear friend and Secretary Mahadev Desai. Tragically Mahadev Desai who was like a shadow to the Mahatma had breathed his last on 15th of August 1942 and it was not even a week after the Mahatma's arrest. It was also a great loss for Gandhi's wife Kasturbaji who with her husband had so much faith in that man. Both Mahatma and his wife who were now interned in the sprawling Aga Khan palace would now miss him forever.

In mid November, with his bullet wound having healed and the Quit India movement dying its own natural slow death, Debu Ghose came out of his hiding in Bombay and decided to return to Calcutta. His family was not very much perturbed because they kept getting regular information about him from friends and Congress social workers, but Debu Ghosh did not want to take a chance. With a help of a friend in the East India Railway Company who was based in Bombay, he travelled as a part time waiter in the dining car of the Bombay Calcutta Mail via Allahabad. On reaching Allahabad station the next day, he bought himself a copy of the late edition of the Calcutta Statesman and was delighted to read about the Hazaribagh jail break. The paper also carried the photograph of the mastermind and for whose capture the British had announced a very rich reward.

Born on 11th October 1902, under a thatched shed in the small village of Sitabdiara located 50 miles from Patna which was once the ancient capital of the great King Ashoka, the 40 year old middle aged Congressman imprisioned in the Hazaribagh Jail for his anti British activities during the Quit India movement was determined to get out of this high security prison.In 1922, leaving his young sixteen year old wife Prabhavati in Gandhiji's ashram, he had gone to the USA for his higher studies. And there to earn a decent living and to pay for his studies in America he did odd jobs including that of picking grapes in California at 40 cents an hour. In 1929, a week before the great Wall Street crash he sailed back for India with a Masters degree from Columbia University. After taking part in Gandhi's Salt Satyagraha, he together with other young Indian Turks like Morarji Desai, Ram Monohar Lohia, Ashoke Mehta, Minoo Masani and the elderly Bhulabhai Desai were imprisioned for over two years in the Nasik Road Central Prison. When Gandhi gave his call for Quit India he was in Hazirabagh prison and now he had resolved that he must escape to sustain the Mahatma's movement.

'Gentlemen I have planned the escape for the 8th of November on Diwali night, when most of the prison guards will be busy celebrating the evening by watching the entertainment programme and the fireworks that has been planned for us inmates by the jail authorities,' said Jai Prakash Narayan to the group of political prisioners who had shown their willingness in executing the plan.

At 10 PM on that auspicious Diwali night of 1942, having sought the blessings of Goddess Kali, Jai Prakash Narayan with Joginder Shukla and eight others on their bare feet stealthily tip toed their way through the prison courtyard towards the high wall of the jail. Colonel Nath the Jail's Superintendent of Police too was celebrating Diwali at home. Once the big high wooden table was placed against the jail wall, four out of the ten who had decide to sacrifice their freedom by staying back in the prison removed the table and they went back to the Diwali celebrations to regale the prison guards with songs, jokes and cigarettes. While these four inmates kept entertaining the jail guards with hit songs of actor and singer Kundan Lal Saigal like 'Main Kiya Janun Kiya Jadoo Hai" (What do I know of Magic) from the film Zindagi meaning 'Life' and "Duniya rang rangili Baba' (The world is indeed colourful") from the film "Dhartimata" meaning 'Motherland,' the rest of them one by one and with the help of the knotted dhotis that were used as a long rope and with Jai Prakash Narayan in the lead climbed the jail wall and jumped out into freedom.

And early next morning, when the jail break was discovered, it was already a bit too late. By then helped by the hours of darkness, JP having hitch hiked his way kept moving towards the holy city of Budh Gaya. Meanwhile a reward of Rupees five thousand for the capture of JP and his party had been announced and his face in particular found a prominent place in all the leading newspapers of India. But JP was determined not to get caught and be put back behind bars. Travelling incognito in a bullock cart and with a heap of jute bags covering him totally, JP with a two weeks growth of beard on his face reached the outskirts of Gaya. Carerfully making his way to the railway station he got into a third class compartment and made it to Benaras and to the Benaras Hindu University where he had some reliable contacts. From there moving in various kinds of disguises he finally crossed into Nepal. In Nepal he joined the "Azad Dasta", a guerrila army of liberation that was being trained by three Indian officers who had deserted from the British Army while they were fighting the Japanese in Burma. But luck was not his side, for soon he and Ram Monohar Lohia were both caught by the Nepalese local police. A few days later, when both of them under an armed police escort started the long march back to the Indian frontier; it seemed that JP was destined to go back to prison once again. But luckily JP had managed to send word to the other members of the guerrilla group of their capture and the guerrilla group now started tracking and shadowing the police escort.

On the 5th night of their long march and while they rested in a wayside dak bunglow that was being guarded by the policemen, the guerrilla group purposely set fire to a nearby hairstack. The sentry immediately raised an alarm, and when the rest of the police party went to fight the fire, JP with Ram Manohar Lohia once again escaped. Though they were chased by the police force, but they manged to across the Indian border safely and made their way to Bhagalpur. Since the hunt for him was still on, JP for months together kept moving from one hideout to another. From Bhagalpur he made his way to Calcutta and then to Delhi. At Delhi he waited for an opportunity to go to Peshawar and to the North West Frontier in order to direct the revolutionary movement from there.

On the 20th of December 1942, while Debu Ghosh with Naren Sen and Dr Ghulam Hussein were enjoying their coffee at the Coffee house and predicting the future course of the war, the city of Calcutta was greeted with loud air raid sirens. A few minutes later Japanese aircrafts bombed Calcutta for the first time.

'My God they are now at our very own doorstep,' said Dr Ghulam Hussein as the sound of blasts and anti aircraft fire was heard from the direction of the great Calcutta Maidan. Leaving their cups half empty, they ran out to see the action. It seemed to be a short and sweet affair for the all clear was sounded a little while later.Late that night they again met at Naren Sen's house to once again review the war situation on India's Eastern Front.

'No no, no I do not agree with you at all. The Japanese will treat us even worse if they get here. Of whatever little that I have heard about the atrocities that are being committed by them in South East Asia on innocent civilians, they will treat us like muck and confiscate even the little that we have as our own private property,' said Naren Sen to Debu Ghosh.

'But also please do not forget that the Japanese Government and their military leaders are the only people today who have recognised the Indian League under Rash Behari Bose and chances are that Subhas Bose will soon be joining them as their undisputed leader and Commander-in-Chief of the Azad Hind Fauj,' said Debu Ghosh with a lot of authority.

'That is all very well said, but we should get to that once Subhashda physically shows his presence in Bangkok or Singapore or Rangoon. Now the dinner is getting cold and if we wait any longer the Japs might come and eat it,' said Debu's wife Hena in good humour.

In that case Boudi I suggest that all you ladies should start learning how to prepare Sukiyaki, the delicious Japanese dish and how to also wear the kimono too', said a smiling Dr Ghulam Hussein as he called out to his Begum Sahiba to check whether she had brought the Biryani and the kebabs for the pot luck that evening.

While the British and American servicemen were celebrating Christmas week in Calcutta and strengthing the air defence of the city, far away in Vienna, Austria a worried Subhas Bose was spending a little time with his wife Emelie and his infant daughter Anita. And It was around this time that Samir Sen the eldest son of Naren Sen having hitch-hiked his way through Italy and Switzerland arrived in Munich.And just for curiosity sake he visited the now famous beer hall where on 8th November 1923, the ex corporal of the German Army Adolf Hitler with Goring, Himmler and other Nazi Party followers had staged their abhortive Beer Hall Putsch. They had hatched a plot to kidnap the leaders of the Bavarian Government and force them at gunpoint to accept Hitler as their leader. At 8.30 pm on that fateful evening, while Goring had surrounded the place, Hitler and his storm troopers burst into the beer hall with weapons causing instant panic. The putsch however lasted only for a few hours, when next morning they were challenged by Munich's armed police. In the firefight that took place in the centre of Munich, Goring was hit in the groin and Hitler suffered a dislocated shoulder and then it was all over, as Hitler was taken to the Landsberg prison for his public trial.

That evening Samir Sen parked himself leisurely on a bench outside the Munich railway station, and wrote a long letter to his parents in Calcutta describing in great detail his adventure after he had sailed from Bombay in a small cargo carrier. On that wintry cold morning of Christmas day, though the German capital had a festive look with the German Swastikas, Nazi banners, Christmas trees, Santa Clauses, and big cut outs of Hitler hanging from government buildings, but the fact was that the Axis troops both on the Russian front and in the North African desert were being beaten and routed by the Allied forces. Hitler's Sixth Army under Field Marshall Paulus was badly trapped in Stalingrad. Paulus's troops were literary starving and for Christmas that year all that they would receive as their last rations was horse meat. In North Africa, Field Marshall Rommel's Africa Corps after the mauling by General Montgomery's 8th Army was in disarray and in full retreat. It was under these unknowing circumstances that Samir Sen had landed up at the movie studio in Berlin to pursue his life's ambition of becoming a fully trained cinema photographer. But to his bad luck the studio had closed down. Wandering what to do next and while he was aimlessly loitering through the streets of the German capital he was arrested by the German Gestapo who took him to be a gypsy.And he would have surely been deported to a concentration camp in Poland where all young able bodied Jews, Gypsies and others who were not of pure Teutonic blood were being sent initially to do forced labour and then for the final extermination. But luck was on Samir's side.During his interrogation by the notorious SS, he produced the letter of introduction that had been given to him by one of the German cameraman from Bombay Talkies Studio. He was then promptly released and despatched to the Free India Centre. At the Free India Centre under the guidance of Mr A.C.N. Nambiar an Indian left wing journalist who had vast experience of working in Europe and who was now Subhas Bose's deputy, Samir Sen took up the job of a news editor, news reader and a propagandist of the "Azad Hind Radio". In January, he together with a few trusted others led by NG Swami were trained by the Germans in methods of espionage that included use of secret inks, codes and the use of portable transmitters. The team after their training was earmarked to work as spies and they were waiting to be secretly sent back to India.

In mid 1942, Egypt the hub of a geo-strategic network and the gateway to India and the Far East through the Suez Canal was about to fall to the Axis Powers. At that time there was all possibility of an Axis offensive thorough the land of the Pharoahs to link up with the German drive through the Caucasus. During the battle of Gazzala, Rommel had taken back the initiative and the fall of Torbuk was considered by Churchill as a disaster. The British had been driven back along the coast where the railway and the road ran through the small little village of El Alamein. On 1st July 1942 there had been panic in Cairo as the British Middle Eastern Command Headquarters and the British Embassy in Cairo burnt piles of classified papers showering the city with ash and charred documents. From that infamous "Ash Wednesday' Monty's well equipped and trained 8th Army had now turned the tables on his adversary.

In early November, at El Alamein with the launching of "Operation Surcharge" by Monty's 8th Army, his armoured divisions had broken through the German's last crust of defences. For the first time in England church bells rang after many years. This was a major defeat for Hitler and Mussolini and it had restored the much needed self confidence and prestige to the Allied Forces. By now "Operation Torch" under General Eisenhower had also been launched and as the Anglo American Forces landed in North Africa, the Axis forces were now squeezed from both sides.

On 26th January 1943, at Berlin on India's Independence Day, Subhash Bose celebrated the occassion in style as six hundred honoured guests drank to his health. Two days later on 28th January, despite the German debacle at Stalingrad and at El Alamein, Subhas Bose declared the day as Legion day. He was now referred to as Netaji and was just waiting for the day, when the German high command would help him to get to Tokyo and to the Far East. The day was not far and to conceal his secret departure, Subhas Bose recorded two speeches that were scheduled to be broadcast "live" from Berlin on 28th February and 4th March, 1943 respectively.

On 8th February, Subhas Bose with Abid Hussein his principal staff officer and Adjutant in utmost secrecy boarded a motor launch in Kiel harbour. In the early hours of that morning as the motor launch made its way to the waiting German submarine U 180, Emilie Schekl waved out to her husband for the last and final time. Two days later on 10th February, the German radio made a special broadcast of Bose's special message which was tape recorded earlier in order to indicate that Bose was still in Germany. As the U boat with Subhas Bose made a wide sweep of the Atlantic Ocean towards the Cape of Good Hope, Eisenhower's forces in French North Africa faced fairly stiff resistance from the Germans at the Kasserine Pass. The German High command in Berlin in order to keep Bose's journey a closely guarded secret had even communicated to the staff of the Free India Centre in Berlin that their revered leader had gone on a long mission to the Russian front.

While the German submarine with Subhas Bose slowly and stealthily made its long journey, at the Howrah railway station in Calcutta Richard Pugsley from the Corps of Signals joined fourteen others from the Calcutta Light Horse for a secret mission. All of them dressed in civies boarded the train at Howrah for their journey to Cochin. At Cochin they went aboard an old antique barge and hugging the coastline they were now on their way to the Portugees enclave of Goa. Though Portugal was still neutral, reliable intelligence reports had confirmed that the Germans had set up a clandestine radio station there. After Richard Pugsley had successfully tracked the location of the clandestine radio station, the Calcutta Light Horse boys who were part of the Territorial Army carried out a raid and destroyed it. Soon thereafter Signaller Richard Pugsley with a few others of a newly raised Signal Monitering Unit was on their way to North Africa to join the Divisional Signal Regiment of the Indian Red Eagle Division.

On 31st March 1943, Colonel Attiqur Rehman at the age of fifty six and after 31 years of meritorious service having said a final goodbye to the Indian Medical Service and to the Indian Army in North Africa arrived back in India. He had taken leave pending retirement in order to make all the preparations for his only daughter's wedding which was planned for December that year. At the Ballard Pier he was received by his wife Nafisa, his third son Arif Rehman who was now 23 years old and the beautiful tall charming 19 year old Shenaz.Arif Rehman had aspired to join the heaven born, but because of the war, the entry into the ICS had been suspended. He therefore had now qualified and was selected for the Bengal Provincial Civil Service Cadre.

'Well I guess we will start shopping for your wedding trousseau from right here, from Bombay and from today itself,' said a delighted Attiqur Rehman as he affectionately hugged his daughter. On their way to Peshawar, they stopped by at Delhi to do some more shopping and for the first time they stayed at the magnificent Imperial Hotel near Connaught Place.

Having read in a newspaper that the Muslim League was holding its annual session in Delhi, Colonel Attiqur Rehman just for curiosity sake decided to attend one of its public meetings. Looking elegant in his new flannels and blue blazer he took his seat somewhere in the rear. A map of future Pakistan as visualized by the Muslim League adorned the dais and the banner on top of it read. "Freedom of India lies in Pakistan."

'What bloody bullshit,'said Attiqur Rehman to himself as Mr Jinnah in a white spotless Sherwani with a gold button engraved and pinned to his starched collar addressed the gathering and kept harping on the two nation theory. A disappointed Attiqur Rehman on returning back to the hotel told his wife Nafisa that if ever Mr Jinnah does get his Pakistan then God help this country. First of all there will be hell to pay from both sides because both the Hindus and the Muslims will each ask for their own pound of flesh and for the forty crores of poor people of this subcontinent who are shouting for Independence it will only add to more miseries.

'Yes and all these years we have been saying that only the British know how to divide and rule and it will be a real pity if this country gets divided on communal lines,' added Nafisa as she poured her husband a stiff scotch on the rocks.

Meanwhile after an adventurous journey of well over two months and cooped up in that small German U boat and living on plain bread, soup and insipid food, Subhas Bose on 28th April was transferred to a Japaneese submarine that was lying in wait in the Mozambique Channel of Africa which was in neutral Portugeese territory. The I-29 under its Japaneese skipper Captain Mesao Teraoka then made its way stealthily across the Indian Ocean and through the mighty Pacific Ocean till it safely reached Tokyo on13th June. On the very next day he was ceremoniously received by the Japanese Prime Minister Hideki Tojo.

`Nicknamed "The Razor", Tojo was born in Tokyo on 30th of December 1884 and had served during the First World War as his country's military attaché in Germany. An ex military general, Tojo on being appointEd Prime Minister in 18th October 1941, had advocated the surprise attack on Pearl Harbour. On 16th June 1943, a delighted Subhas Bose heard Tojo's historical declaration in the Japanese Diet. Speaking with measured tones, the bespectled 57 year old Japanese leader said.

'Japan is firmly resolved to extend all means in order to help, to expel and eliminate from India the Anglo Saxon influences which are the enemy of the Indian people, and enable India to achieve full Independence in the true sense of the term.'

With the full blooded assurance from no less a person than Hideki Tojo, a confident Subhas Bose on 2nd July, 1943 arrived in Singapore to a tumultuous welcome by the Indian community there. Two days later on 4th July which coincided with America's day of Independence, Subhas Chander Bose in the presence of the League representatives accepted the Presidency of the League and the allegiance of the Indian National Army.

On the very next day the 5th of July, he reviewed an impressive parade by the INA, the Indian National Army that was held in front of the Singapore Municipal Building and announced its existence to the world by giving it the new name of Azad Hind Fauj and with the battle cry of "Chalo Delhi." (Onward to Delhi). On the 9th of July, at Singapore in pouring rain he addressed the 60,000 Indians who had gathered there to hear him. To them he made a fervent appeal for man power and monetary contributions.'All I need is three lakh good trained soldiers from amongst you all, and thirty million Singapore dollars to realise our great dream of marching victoriously into India,' said Subhas Chander Bose as the crowd roared to give him all possible support. On the 12th of July, Subash Bose asked for recruits for his Rani of Jhansi Regiment and for the Red Cross units. The response was overwhelming as large numbers of young girls and ladies readily volunteered. Amongst them was Yeshwant Kaur, the wife of Swarup Ghosh.

And while Subhash Bose was making his secret trip to the Far East, Field Marshall Rommel after the defeat of his forces at El-Alamein was still licking his wounds.In early March 1943, Rommel returned to Germany for good on Hitler's orders and the command of the Afrika Korps fell on the shoulders of General Von Arnim. On 13th May, 1943 the 4th Indian Division under Major General Tuker having routed the Germans South of St Marie du Zet in Tunisia started their mopping up operations. When a Gurkha patrol party from the 1st Battallion of the Second Gurkha Rifles reported that they had stumbled upon the Headquarters of the German Army Command in North Africa, General Tuker immediately asked the nearest formation to cordon off the area with men and weapons lest the Germans escape. The Dogra Company of the Punjabees under their resourceful and courageous Company Commander, Acting Major Ismail Sikandar Khan rushed immediately. But they were the second sub-unit to reach the spot. A sub unit from the First Battalion of the Second Gurkha rifles had beaten them to it. The next day in the arid hot desert climate of North Africa another ceremonial surrender ceremony took place, when over a thousand German officers and men including quite a few Generals stood on parade. To Ismail Sikandar Khan it looked more like a ceremonial parade than a surrender ceremony as the clean shaven Germans in their neatly pressed military uniforms with their button shining on their tunics and shoes polished stood at attention and laid down their arms. For the 4th Indian Division there was a new war trophy as the military caravan of General Arnim's was ceremonially driven away. Thus by end of May, 1943 as far as the war was concerned, it was all over in North Africa as 250000 German and Italian troops surrendered unconditionally.

On the 19th of June, 1943 King George VIth and Emperor of India visited the Red Eagle Division in North Africa. He was delighted to be with his Indian troops who had done the Empire proud with their courage and heroism in every battle that they had fought. On being introduced to Major Ismail Sikandar Khan and Major Gul Rehman who were both now proud winners of the DSO, the Distinguished Service Order, the King invited a contingent from the Red Eagles to visit England on a short two week holiday in August. However, neither Ismail Sikandar Khan nor Gul Rehman could avail of this opportunity as they were detailed to attend the prestigious Defence Services Staff College at Quetta. A day after the King's visit, Major Ismail Sikander Khan from the Second Punjabees together with his bosom friend Major Gul Rehman Khan from the First Punjabees with a full shipload of Italian prisoners of war sailed for India. The final destination of the Italians would be the prisoner of war camp at Dehra Dun which ironically was also the birthplace of the IMA and from where the cream of the Indian Army were now being produced in much larger numbers. On arrival in India and before reporting to the Staff College at Quetta, Major Ismail Sikandar Khan with Colonel Reginald Edwards decided to visit Kashmir and Gilgit at the invitation of the Political Agent, George Kirkbride and his wife Nancy.

At Gilgit Ismail Sikandar Khan for the first time stayed at the Agents bunglow where his grandfather-in-law Sarfaraz Khan was once a a cook and his own grandfather Sikandar Khan was once the Chiefmate. It was a nostalgic home coming for Ismail as he played with the eight year old Mary and the six and four year old Mike and Tim, the three young children of the Kirkbrides. George Kirkbride had also brought along with him his own attractive sister as Governess to his three unruly children, but she soon fell in love with a British officer from the Gilgit Scouts and they got married on the lawns of the bungalow on the very day that Ismail arrived at Gilgit. What impressed Ismail most was the children's attitude towards their orderly Alif Khan. He was their friend, guide, playmate and guard. The only time the boys were beaten by him was when they leap frogged over him while Alif Khan was deep in his prayers. For the two days that he was in Gilgit, Reggie recalled his days, when he was the Political Agent and that incidently was a good forty years ago.

In the summer of 1943, while Netaji was busy organising the Azad Hind Fauj at Singapore, a disastrous famine struck Bengal. The occupation of Burma by the Japanese forces had disrupted the flow of rice imports to India and coupled with the British policy of destruction of all essentials to deny them to the advancing enemy who were on the gates of Eastern India, the prices of rice had more than doubled from its pre war level. The people most affected were from the rural areas of Bengal and by July 1943, Calcutta was flooded with over a lac and a half of poor destitutes who had migrated to the city in search of food. Rising to the occasion, Netaji made an offer of 100,000 tons of rice to be shipped to Calcutta as a humanitarian gift from the Indian League, but the British ignored the request. Early that year, the 23 year old Ronen Sen, the second son of Naren and Shobha Sen had qualified for the Bengal Provincial Civil Service and he together with Arif Rehman were now both undergoing their preliminary training in various departments at the Writer's Building in Calcutta.

While some blamed the famine catastrophe on the Muslim League Government in Bengal, others blamed the hoarders and those who indulged in the lucrative black market trade. During weekends the two friends Ronen Sen and Arif Rehman voluntarily worked with the non official relief agencies that were organised under the astute leadership of Dr Shyama Prasad Mukherjee and Badridas Goenka. Son of the great scholar Sir Ashutosh Mukherjee, Shyama Prasad was born on 6th July 1901 and had himself become like his father the youngest Vice Chancellor of Calcutta University. With his dynamic leadership he rose above narrow party alignments and worked night and day to organise the relief kitchens to feed the destitute. Sir Badridas Goenka though a rich business man had become in 1933 the first Indian Chairman of The Imperial Bank of India and he too spared no effort to help feed the poor village people who came in thousands every day for some food to Calcutta. But it was still not enough as thousands of peasants died like flies on the road everyday from hunger.

One Saturday afternoon as Ronen Sen in the company of his friend Arif Rehman were returning home from one of the relief kitchen camps on Dharamtolla Street, they found a middle aged lady in salwar kameez behind the Grand Hotel serving soup to some of the hungry poor people on the road. On enquiring Ronen found that the lady was none other than the wife of the owner of that place and whose husband had only recently on the second of June 1943 had been conferred the title of Rai Bahadur by The Viceroy of India for services rendered by him to the British Army. Promptly the two of them went inside the hotel to thank the owner for the food being given to the poor.

I wish my wife and I could give more,' said the stocky 43 year old Rai Bahadur Mohan Singh Oberoi as he offered the two young civil service officers a glass of beer which they politely declined and settled for coffee instead. The Grand Hotel in the midst of the great famine thanks to the war had become a big money spinner for the dynamic and enterprising hotelier. That evening, when Ronen Sen very proudly told his parents the story of that remarkable hotelier and his devoted wife Ishran Devi, they too were pleasantly surprised and highly impressed with their magnanimity.

Rai Bahadur Mohan Singh Oberoi was born in the small village of Chakwal in Punjab on 15th August 1900 to Sardar Attar Singh and his young wife Bhagwanti. The only issue of his parents, his father at the age of 22 had died of influenza while on a railway track laying job at Peshawar when the infant Mohan singh was only six months old. His mother with her infant child came back for good to her own village of Bhaun, that was eight miles from Chakwal. After his primary education in the village school, when Mohan Singh was fourteen his mother sent him to the Dayanand Anglo Vedic (DAV) School at Rawalpindi. After passing his matriculation in 1916, Mohan Singh did his Intermediate and thereafter quit studies to work as a young manager at his paternal uncle Sunder Singh's shoe factory at Lahore.In 1919, after the Jalianwala massacre the shoe factory closed down and on returning home to Bhaun his mother promptly got him married to the neigbours fifteen year old daughter Ishran Devi. When the shoe factory again reopened, Mohan Singh returned to Lahore. But one fine day in 1922, the young Sikh finding the hair on his head was more of a burden and a big hindrance he came back home with a nice hair cut. The uncle a pious Sikh was livid and threw him out immediately. A desparate young Mohan Singh Oberoi now much married and with a small daughter whom he had named Rajrani was out of work and was afraid to face his mother and family at Bhaun.

On the advice of some friends he went to Simla the summer capital of India to sit for the PWD examination but failed in the interview. Discouraged and demoralised he was about to return home, when one day he confidently walked into the Cecil Hotel, the best hotel in Simla that was owned by the Italian John Faletti. Dressed in his only well pressed worsted trouser, shirt and tie he had entered the hotel to look for a job, but was thrown out by the hall porter. A few days later once again smartly dressed in a shirt and tie, Mohan Singh Oberoi confidently walked up to the Hotel Manager Mr D W Grove as he came out of the hotel on his way home for lunch and offered himself for any job that the hotel could give him. Mr Grove was impressed and took the young man as a clerk at Rs 50 a month. Mohan Singh Oberoi was delighted and he soon moved his family into his dingy, dark cold one room tenement at the bottom of the hill. He then put his heart and soul into his work and soon gained the full confidence of the management.In 1924, his first son was born and he named him Tilak Raj, the anointed one. On 14th August 1934, a day before his 34th birthday after pawning his wife's jewellery most reluctantly at his wife's insistence and having borrowed some money from good friends and well wishers, the young man became the sole and exclusive owner of the Clarke's Hotel not only at Simla but also at Delhi. He wanted his eldest son Tilak Raj to join the Indian Army and for his education had sent him to the PWRIMC at Dehradun. But the boy was rusticated on disciplinary grounds for driving away the Headmaster's car without his permission. In 1938, at Delhi, when Mohan Singh was told by a friend that there was a nice big hotel on

Chowringee for grabs in Calcutta, he immediately boarded the very next train to that place.

Once a mansion of one Colonel Grand, it had initially started as a boarding house by an Irish lady and was called Mrs Anne Monk's Boarding house and later was purchased by the shrewd and enterprising peddler from Armenia, Stephen Arratoon who converted it into a 500 room hotel. In 1937, and after six occupants died in the hotel for bad sanitation and water which also included the late Stephen's widow, Gregory Aratoon the son-in-law had the massive gates shut for good. The Second World War was round the corner, when the 38 year old Mohan Singh took over the rat and rodent infested closed down hotel. Working like a mad man Mohan Singh with his wife Ishran Devi and two young handsome sons Tiki, and Biki as he lovingly called them on 21st December 1938 once again opened the massive gates of The Grand. But the once luxury hotel whose only rival was the Great Eastern and The Spencers on Dalhousie Square was soon destined to become a cheap transit camp for solders and officers alike as the war dragged on.

But Mohan Singh Oberoi was a born optimist to the core and knew how and where to cash in. When the British Army authorities in Calcutta put up a notice on his hotel that the premises were being requisitioned by them for billeting of troops that included officers and soldiers, Mohan Singh thought he was finished. The very next day all he did was to thank the Army Quarter Master General concerned at Fort Whilliam for the notice and immediately offered him both boarding and lodging at Rs 10 per head which was a full two Ruppees less than what was budgeted for by the Army authorities

'All yours at Rs 10 Mr Oberoi 'said the British Quarter Master General as they shook hands over the deal. With the big spending American GI's thronging Chowringee, Park Street and the nearby Karaya Road, where one could get a woman of one's choice from any part of the world, Mohan Singh's Oberoi Grand Hotel had now become a money spinner. The Casanova Bar for the Corporals and the Sargeants with two or more flirty butterflies from Karaya Road interlocked in their tattooed arms was choker block full as liquor flowed like water througout the day and also throughout the night. For the more sedate who loved dancing to the music of Sonny Lobo and his Band, while Teddy Weatherford and Kitty Walker belted out their favourite numbers, the "Prince's" restaurant was the place to be seen. Not worried whether they would be dead or alive the next day, the men in Khaki made the best of it as they ate drank and made merry while the going was still good for them. While the cash registers at The Grand Hotel jingled all the 24 hours, the counting of the big bucks at the end of each tiring day became problematic for the resourceful and vibrant Rai Bahadur. The money therefore was simply stuffed away in huge jute bags and kept for counting and depositing into the bank the next day.

Ronen Sen had been so fascinated by the Rai Bahadur's good simple nature and magnanimity that he one day invited him and his wife home for a simple Bengali meal of rice, dal, and fish curry.

'I must say that the "Shorshebata mach" was simply out of this world,' said the hotelier who loved his food as he thanked Naren Sen, Debu Ghosh and Dr Gulam Hussein and all their family members for the hearty meal and reciprocated the gesture by invitng all of them to be his guests for drinks and dinner at the "Princes" on the coming Saturday.

'I think it was wise of us to regret the inability of our wives and daughters to attend the Rai Bahadur's party at The Princes,' said Naren Sen to the others as all of them dressed smartly in dinner jackets and lounge suits with neckties as was the order, walked through the foyer of the hotel. The hotel was a sea of British Tommies and American GI's with some lounging on camp cots in the corridors of the hotel, while others escorted their new found Anglo Indian babes of mixed descent to the popular Casanova Bar. Inside the over congested bar, Mr Ellis Joshua the Manager kept a watchful eye on those who were looking for a scrap.

Once inside The Princes, they were ushered in and seated on a table reserved for seven, when a smiling Rai Bahadur walked in to welcome his guests.

'It is a pity that the ladies and the girls didn't join us and rightly so I should say because the culture here is definitely not conducive to our own high Indian morals and standards. But courtesy demanded that I invite them all the same,' said the Rai Bahadur as he apologised for the absence of his wife Ishran Devi and other members of his own family who he said were all busy at their duty stations in the sprawling hotel.Having ordered the drinks and the starters, the polished, suave and elegant unassuming host with his witty sense of humour kept them company for sometime while enjoying his daily tot of scotch with his favourite chicken tikkas.

'I will see you all again after an hour or so once I complete my evening round of the hotel and in the meantime do keep enjoying yourselves,' said the debonair hotelier as he excused himself and instructed the manager in charge to look after his guests.

With an excuse to see and explore more of what was happening inside the other parts of the hotel and to keep away for some time from their father's and uncles who were all now in their early or mid fifties, the two young bureaucrats, Ronen Sen and Arif Rehman with Dr Nawaz Hussein on being permitted by the elders walked into the jam packed Casanova Bar for a glass of chilled draft beer that was being served straight from the fountain

'I think a smoke with the draft beer and wih some French fries and cocktail sausages will go well with the beer,'said Ronen as he ordered for a tin of Three Castle Cigarettes. Resting their arms on the elbow bender and oblivious of the fact of which soldier was smooching whom in their happy blissfull semi-inebriated state, the three friends sat in one lonely corner of the bar to enjoy the beer and snacks and to talk about the future of India and their own future if the Japanese with the help from Subhas Bose's INA did manage to throw the British out from the country.

'I sincerely hope the Japs don't come soon because my sister's wedding is very much on the cards and we will all have to be there to celebrate the occasion. Incidently both my eldest brother Gul Rehman and his friend Ismail Sikandar Khan who are now attending the Staff College at Quetta will also be there at Peshawar to bless the bride and the groom, but unfortunately my other brother Captain Aftab Rehman who will be 26 soon and who is fighting the Germans and the Italians in North Africa will miss all the fun,' said Arif Rehman as he fondly and gently ribbed Dr Nawaz his future brother-in-law in the stomach.

'And unfortunately though the three Ghosh brothers, Arup, Swarup and Anup may not be there for the solemn occasion, but I will make sure for Ronen's sake atleast that Debu Uncle and Hena Aunty bring along their pretty 18 year old daughter Mona. And to make it hundred percent sure, I have also bribed my younger sister Hasina who is her best of friend in college to set the ball rolling from right now,' added Nawaz Hussein somewhat seriously, but with a mischievous smile on his face and which had Ronen blushing.

' And in order to doubly ensure that Mona Ghosh will be definitely there for the wedding, I would sincerely recommend that you put your sister Purnima Sen too on the job, since she also is part of the same group,' said Arif Rehman as he put a friendly arm around Ronen to give him more courage and to face the fact that Ronen was in love with his own cousin.

'For you Muslims marrying one's own first cousin is not only accepted, but it is also encouraged. However, for us orthodox Bengalees who believe in caste, gothra, stars, planets and horoscopes etc etc even mentioning it is taboo,' said Ronen Sen as he lit one more of his Three Castle Cigarrettes and ordered for one more round of beer.

"However, if you are really serious about her, then I would suggest that you diplomatically broach the subject with her parents soon and before it is too late, or else some other unknown lucky guy from nowhere will arrive, do the seven ritual rounds around the holy fire and walk away with her, while you will keep sucking your damn thumb,'said Nawaz Hussein.

'Yes and he is damn well right, but what news from the Pugsley's, and aren't you going to invite them for the wedding? Asked Arif Rehman.

'Unfortunately they have all gone inncommunicado after Sandra's tragic death and the last we heard was that the oldman Edwin with his wife Laila were leading a quiet and lonely existence in Mhow, while their eldest son Shaun and his sister Debbie's husband had both risen to become foremen in the railways. Their youngest 22 year old son Richard was now a signaller in the Indian Army and he did drop in for a while sometime ago, when he was on his way to Cochin on some secret mission. And as far as their youngest daughter Veronica is concerned, she is a boarder at Sanawar and will be appearing for her Senior Cambridge examinations later in December this year,' said Nawaz Hussein.

'But you must atleast send an invitation to the oldman and his wife from your side at least,'said Ronen Sen.

'Yes that I am sure my father will do,' said Nawaz Hussein.

As Nawaz completed the sentence, there was a sudden commontion inside the jam packed bar. The Casanova Bar had become famous for the usual daily brawl between the EnglishTommies and the American GI's and tonight it was no different. As usual it was over a woman from Karaya Street who was sitting initially on a table with the Tommies, but had been lured away by a group of quick spending American GI's. When the challenge by the British Tommies was thrown in for a fight to a finish, the ever smiling manager in a crisis, Ellis Joshua together with the head bouncer walked up to the two warring factions and politely requested them to settle scores outside.

'I thought they were all allies waiting to have a go at the Japs, but instead they love fighting amongst themselves and that too over some lousy whore,'remarked Ronen softly as he settled the bill and they all joined their fathers for the sumptuous continental dinner with red and white French wine that was being served in style to them by the white gloved liveried waiters at the more dignified and posh Princes Restaurant in Calcutta.

A few days later, when Debu Ghosh and Naren Sen were on their way to the Calcutta High Court, they were horrified to see a unit from the New Theatre Studios shooting the pathetic scenes of the hungry and famished poor people of Bengal dying of starvation and fighting for small crumbs of bread on the streets of the empire's second city, while another group of destitutes kept scraping and scavenging clean the city's stinking dust bins for the left over food particles.

Born in July 1909, the cameraman was non other than Bimal Roy who was the son of Hem Chander Roy from East Bengal, and when he was confronted by Debu Ghosh, he said that he was doing it as a duty and not for any pleasure as the crew had been commissioned by the British authorities to do a documentary on the Great Calcutta Famine.

'But what are they trying to prove or show to the world and instead of wasting money on such hideous and nonsensical absurd ventures, the authorities could do well by giving them some food instead,' said an angry Naren Sen.

And while the poor people of Bengal were dying of hunger, far away in Southern Europe the allied forces were getting ready to devour the Germans. On the night of 9th July 1943, with the US 82nd and British 1st Airborne Division parachuting into Sicily, "Operation Husky" had begun, and by the very next day 12 Divisions from the British Eighth and the US Seventh Armies from North Africa landed on the South East Coast of the island. The Germans and the Italians offered some stiff resistance initially and they also took a few prisioners which included the fair and handsome Lance Corporal Richard Pugsley, but they also knew that probably the end was near.

Unaware to the Germans, the British now had a new secret weapon. It was called the "Radar" and it was a device for radio detection and ranging. Richard Pugsley by virtue of his good knowledge about German radio communications and having qualified both as a parachutist and a radio locater had been seconded temporarily to the British 1st Airborne Division. But due to some serious navigational errors by the pilots some of them had been dropped well off the designated targets. On the night of the landing, Richard's party of 30 such parachutists were immediately taken prisoners and shipped to mainland Italy. By the end of August and after making their journey in filthy cattle trucks they arrived at Stalag 24 in Altengrabow, a few miles West of Berlin. It was a prisoner of war camp for the Australians. Despite his repeated pleadings to the Stalag Kommandant that he was neither English nor Australian but an Indian with a fair complexion from the 4th Indian Divisional Signal Regiment and who was temporarily attached to the British First Airborne Division, it had no effect on the poker faced German officer.

'Give me more positive proof dammit,' demanded the officer. Then one fine day by sheer chance Richard Pugsley found his old Indian Army pay book. It was in one of the pockets of his old Indian dungaree.

.'Look Sir I am a hardcore Indian from the Corps of Signals of the Indian Army and not an Australian, American or an Englishman,' declared Richard Pugsley with full confidence as he stood at attention and produced the pay book for verification at the Kommandant's very next orderly room.

'That is all very fine, but you will have to stay here till I find for you an alternative accommodation at some Stalag that is exclusively meant for the Indian prisoners of war,' said the Kommandant.

A week later in strict secrecy, Richard Pugsley was offered his freedom. But it was provided on condition that he was willing to join the Indian Legion of Subhas Bose that was now deployed in northern Holland and he was ready to fight for the Germans under oath to the Fuhrer.

While the Allied Forces slowly and steadily squeezed out the Germans and the Italians from the land of the so called Mafias in Sicily, on the 25th of July, 1943 a high drama was being enacted on the steps of the Italian King's Palace in Rome. On that Sunday summoned by the King for an audience with him, the Duce at sharp five o'clock in the evening drove into the porch of Villa Savoia. At ten past five just before the Duce came out from his meeting with the King, an Italian police officer on duty in the palace went up to Ercolo Boretto, the Duce's loyal chauffeur who was reading the newspaper while sitting in the car park and told thim that there was an urgent phone call for him. When Ercolo casually walked to the porter's lodge where the phone was kept, he was told that there was no more Duce and he was promptly arrested and taken to Trieste. Then as the Duce walked down the steps of the Villa Savoia looking for his car, a Captain of the Caribeneri came and saluted. The Duce had so far only been told that he had only been dismissed, but as soon as he returned the salute, he was arrested and was forced to get inside the waiting Red Cross ambulance. Initially the Duce did put up violent resistance, but the armed escort simply pushed him in. And as the ambulance with its siren blaring and with the Duce and his armed escort inside sped through the streets of Rome on that Sunday evening, the people on the streets were blissfully unaware of the bloodless coup that had taken place inside the King's palace a few minutes ago.

After being confined for a week at different places, the Duce was put on a light train that ran upto Campo Imperatore, a favourite spot for Italian winter sports. And no sooner the train arrived at the top of the 6500 feet high Gran Sasso he was taken to the Hotel Imperatore and kept as a prisoner there. Situated in the Appenine Mountains, Monte Corno at 9000 feet above sea level was the highest peak that overlooked Gran Sasso. But Mussolini was not destined to be there for long as his friend Hitler would soon come to his rescue.

And on the 8th of September 1943, when the Italian radio transmitted the news about Italy's capitulation, the guard over Mussoline was doubled. Shortly thereafter Hitler summoned Captain Otto Skorzeny, a dare devil officer of Silesian and Slavic origin to rescue the Duce and bring him back to Germany safe and sound.

Born in Vienna on 12th June 1908, the 6 feet 4 inch tall officer had joined the Austrian Nazi Party in 1930 and was also appointed as one of Hitler's bodyguards. In 1940, he joined the German Army as an artillery officer.

The 12th of September 1943 was again a Sunday. In the very early hours of that autumn morning while the heights of Gran Sasso were still enveloped with heavy mist, the roar of aeroplanes through the clouds were heard. A few minutes later after the roar of the aeroplane engines had died down; the German commandoes led by Captain Otto Skorzney like vultures looking for its prey swept down from their gliders and whisked away the Duce to safety. It was indeed a very daring operation, but Otto Skorzeny had kept his word with the Fuhrer. And while the Duce was enjoying the hospitality of the Fuhrer, Richard Pugsley was on his way to join the Indian Legion in Holland.But by the time Richard Pugsley in his new German uniform and with the sign of the springing tiger on his arm reached the military training camp of the Third Battalion of the Indian Legionaires near Zwolle that was just behind the fertile coastal strip of the Dutch Zuider Zee, he found that the unit was now being sent for duties to the French coast on the Bay of Biscay.The First and the Second Indian Battalions had already left and the Third was now in the process of moving and joining the other two. To his pleasant surprise and good luck he found Samir Sen as part of the Battalions Signal outfit.

'Of all the damn places what the fucks are you doing here,' said Richard as they embraced one another.

'I was about to ask you the same fucking question,' said Samir Sen as the two kept exchanging notes. After his training in German Ciphers and codes, when Samir Sen in March 1943 with the small party under NG Swami was scheduled to leave for Japan to join their chief Subhas Bose, he unfortunately came down heavily with a bout of influenza and had to be left behind. And after his recuperation, Samir Sen too had joined the 3rd Battalion of the

Indian Legionaires on the Dutch coast as a qualified cipher operator and signaller.

Before dawn on 3rd September 1943, the allied forces were in occupation of the toe of Italy and as they raced northwards at a brisk pace and tempo with "Operation Baytown" in full swing, the morale and the fighting spirit of the Italians crumbled like a pack of cards. Unknown to the others and to the German High Command it was on the 3rd of September itself and after the allied forces had occupied the toe, an unofficial armistice with the Italians had been secretly concluded. It was a very well guarded secret till five days later on the Eighth of September, when General Eisenhower publicly announced that Italy had unconditionally surrendered. The very next day all the Italian forces within the German controlled areas of Italy, Southern France, Yugoslavia, Albania and Greece were disarmed without a fight and they were all made prisoners of war by their very own friend and ally the Germans. The pact of steel with the Germans had now melted to a pact of need for the Italians with their new found allies and saviours.as the Italian King appointed Marshal Bagdalio a hero of the First World War as Italy's new Prime Minister.

In October 1943, while the Indian Brigade in German uniforms were getting fully deployed under the overall command of Field Marshall Von Rundstedt's German Army Group West on the Bay of Biscay coastline which was not far from the important port of Bordeaux, in faraway Singapore, Subhas Chander Bose was getting ready to make his historic proclamation to the world. Earlier Subhash Bose had made it very clear to the Japanese military commanders that any liberation of India secured through Japanese sacrifices would be worse than even slavery and he therefore insisted that the Indians must shed their own very blood to gain their own Independence. General Terauchi therefore agreed to employ one Indian regiment from the Azad Hind Fauj on a trial basis, and if he found the formation upto his required standards then he would employ more Indian troops for the proposed Imphal offensive.During September 1943, the hand picked men of the 1st INA Division was formed under Captain Shah Nawaz Khan from the erstwhile 1/14th Punjab Regiment for extensive training and it was named The Subhas Regiment.

On 20th October 1943, over endless cups of hot coffee and cigarettes, Subhas Bose in his own hand writing compiled and drafted the proclamation of the Provisional Government of India which he would announce the next day. On the morning of the 21st and before going to the venue, he took out the small Hindu holy book of Gita and with the rosary in his hand said a final prayer. On the afternoon of 21st October 1943, the Cathay Cinema in Singapore had a completely new look. With banners, slogans and the Indian and Japanese national flags hanging from the walls, when Subhas Bose immaculately dressed in his well pressed starched military uniform and high boots walked up to the dais majestically to make the historic proclamation, Swarup Ghose took a few photographs. Thereafter with General Yamamoto by his side, when he took the sacred oath and the press with their retinue of cameras clicked away, the tiger of Bengal under the blinding barrage of the flash bulbs spoke into the array of microphones that were lined up in front of him.

'In the name of God, I Subhas Chander Bose take this sacred oath to liberate India and the 38 crores of my countrymen, and I will continue this sacred war of freedom till the last breath of my life.'

No sooner had Subash finished taking his oath, the other members of his newly formed cabinet followed suit as they too in turn repeated the pledge one by one.Then followed the rendering of Free India's National Anthem in Hindi by a choir that was set to the music of a young Indian soldier who had composed it under the direction of Subhas Bose himself. And when the cinema hall reveberated with Rabindra Nath Tagore's Jaya hey, Jaya hey, Jaya hey, every one stood to attention not only inside the hall but even outside on the streets also. On that day a visibly moved Subash Bose.with tears of joy in is eyes felt that the day of India being free had finally dawned.

Two days later at midnight on 23rd October, 1943 Subhas Bose's Provisional Indian Government declared war on Britain and on America. For the Indians in Malaya and Singapore an oath of allegiance to the Provisional Government was required to be signed. It was printed on a small blue card and issued by the Indian League and all Indians were required to sign it in the presence of the chairman of the local League Branch in each district. On the very next day Swarup Ghose and his wife Yeswant Kaur also signed on the dotted line and it read as follows.

'We Swarup and Yeshwant Ghosh, members of The Azad Hind Sangh do hereby solemnly promise in the name of God and take the holy oath that we will be absolutely loyal and faithful to the Provisional Government of Azad Hind, and shall always be prepared for any sacrifice for the cause of the freedom of our Motherland, under the leadership of Subhas Chander Bose.'

In a gesture of goodwill, and with Japan having recognised the Provisional Government of Subhas Chander Bose, it was therefore decided to hand over the Andamans and Nicobar Islands to the Indian leader. And in order to bring in the spirit of Azaadi, Subhas Bose promptly named the iislands as "Shaheed" (Martyr) and "Swaraj" (Independence) respectively.

While Subhas Bose and the members of his council were busy designing the currency notes, coins, stamps and medals for the Azad Hind Government, on 16th September 1943, at the Delhi railway station, dressed in a proper English suit, Jaiprakash Narayan having checked the reservation slip which was under the pseudo name of Mr Mehta got into the four berth first class compartment of the Frontier Mail for his journey to Peshawar. The other three berths were in the name of one Mr Khan and his family and. since the Khans did not show up, JP changed into his night suit and got into his reserved upper berth. Meanwhile the manhunt for him was still on and in the eyes of his countrymen JP was now a hero and more so because the prize money for his capture had been raised to Rs10, 000. With no one to disturb him in his spacious first class compartment, he soon went off to sleep. After a peaceful night's rest, when the train arrived at Lahore railway station next morning, JP opened the door and having requested the pantry car waiter to fetch him a pot of tea, he gain relocked it. But after a few minutes there was a loud knock again and JP thinking the the waiter had brought the tea, he opened the door only to find a well dressed Englishman in civilian clothes. Thinking him to be a passenger, JP said very politely.

'Please do please come in. I am alone and all the other three berths are unoccupied.' But to that, when the Englishman very sternly said,', but may I see your ticket please', Jai Prakash Narayan very confidently said.

'Well if you are a railway official in civvies to catch ticketless travellers then you have come to the wrong man,' replied JP as he produced his valid first class ticket.

'No I think I have come to the right man and you must be Jai Prakash Narayan,'said the Englishman as he kept looking at JP and the photograph of his that was in his hand.

'But what kind of a joke is this. I am none other than Maharaj Mehta. That is my name and it is also on the reservation slip and I have a proper valid ticket to travel,' said JP very confidently.

Colonel Attiqur Rehman with his wife Nafisa and daughter Shenaz having finished their final shopping for the wedding were also at Lahore that day and they were waiting on the platform with a retinue of porters to board the same train to Peshawar. But when the Englishman demanded to conduct a search of JP's luggage and a heated argument followed, Colonel Attiqur in good faith tried to mediate. But when the Englishman disclosed his true identity, Colonel Attiqur got a shock of his life. The man was none other than the Senior Superintendent of Police, Lahore and the two Sikh policemen standing nearby in plain clothes were part of his CID team. And when they quickly put the handcuffs on a struggling JP, Colonel Attiqur felt very sad.indeed. Minutes later and outside the railway station, when they physically shoved JP into the waiting Black Maria and took him to the Lahore Fort for interrogation, Colonel Attiqur Rehman wondered as to why the Indian officers and soldiers were shedding their blood for the British Empire.

'It is indeed a rather strange world. On the one hand our brave Indian soldiers are sacrificing their lives for the British Empire, while on the other hand the British Government in India are arresting our poltical leaders and throwing them into prisions.' remarked Colonel Attiqur Rehman as the train guard finally blew his whistle and waved the green flag, for the engine driver to resume the journey.

Chapter-15

Towards Victory and More Sacrifices.

On the 29th of December 1943, while Subhas Bose set foot at Port Blair on Indian soil as the head of the Provisional Government of Free India, in Peshawar the grand marriage of Nawaz Hussein with Shenaz Rehman was being celebrated in royal style. Dr Ghulam Hussein the father of the groom had reserved an entire inter class bogie for the journey with his dear friends Debu Ghosh, Naren Sen and their families. Even Colonel Reginald Edwards now in his early sixties who had settled down in the hill station of Kasauli with his snow white handle bar moustache was there to greet the newly married couple. It was a grand reunion for all of them as Colonel Attiqur. Rehman with all his family members played host. Soon thereafter, Major Gul Rehman and Major Ismail Sikandar Khan having successfully completed their Staff College left for their new staff appointments. Major Gul Rehman was posted as GSO 2 Operations with The Red Ball 5th Indian Division. The Division was now back in India and were training in jungle warfare in Central India for induction into Burma. Major Ismail Sikandar Khan with his knowledge of Italian was posted as GSO 2 Intelligence with the Red Eagle 4th Indian Division. The Division was now on their way to Italy from North Africa.

On the 25th of January 1944, the 4th Indian division under Major General Tuker joined the British Fifth Army on the outskirts of the small town of Cassino. The town named after Mount Cassino was in the hands of the Germans and so were the features dominating the town. Mount Cassino was the central bastion of the German defences on the well fortified Gustav Line. Situated only 25 miles from the sea, the great buttress of stone jutted into the junction of the fertile Liri and Rapido valleys. Behind the Rapido valley and amidst the group of high mountains stood tall the snow capped summit of Mount Cairo. It was like a monster brooding over the fertile valley. From Monte Cairo the spurs ran down to merge into the

Cassino Promontory. At Monte Cassino was the principal monastry of the Benedictine Order that was was founded by Saint Benedict somewhere around 530 AD. The town and the monastry was first destroyed by the Lombards in 585, and then by the Saracens in 884, followed by the Normans in 1046 and by a massive earthquake in 1349. Now it was waiting to be ravaged by the war. The Germans had now converted the place into a formidable fortress and at the foot of it stood the small Italian town of Cassino. The town and the mountains overlooking it were on the route to Rome and to get to the Italian capital one had no other option but to cut across the Rapido valley which passed through Cassino. Route 6 was the only major road to Rome and it ran through the town and thereafter along the base of the mountain and into the neigbouring Liri valley. The monastry hill dominating the vital road axis was the nerve centre and the master key to the enemy's defences. For any further advance it had to be captured in order to open Highway 6 to the old Roman capital city.

On 4th February, 4th Indian Division, the elite Red Eagles as part of the newly formed New Zealand Corps had been tasked to capture the vital ground of Monastery Hill and Point 593, and thereafter cut highway 6 and capture Monte Cassino from the west. But on that very day, when Major Ismail Sikandar Khan as the GSO 2 Intelligence was out on a recce with his General Officer Commanding Major General Tuker, the General fell seriously ill and he had to be immediately evacuated to a field hospital. This was going to be the second battle for the capture of Monte Cassino since the first battle that began on 12th January had resulted in sheer disaster for the allied forces. The 36th US Division had fought gallantly and had come to 1000 yards of the monastery, but was stopped by the network of German machine gun posts. It was also the same story while fighting to capture the town of Cassino where every building had been turned into a strong point by the German 90th Panzer Grenadier Division.

Late that evening under the cover of darkness and in freezing weather conditions, Major Ismail Sikandar Khan with a small recconnaissance patrol from the forward troops of the Punjabees returned to the outskirts of Cassino town to seek help from the locals. He knew that they were the only ones who could tell him in greater detail the tracks and approaches that led to the top of the monastery. But no one was willing to come forward as they were all terribly scared of the repercussions that may follow since the Germans were sitting pretty on the dominating heights.

'I can very well understand your problem but you will have to trust me. Because not only ours but your lives too are at a great risk and danger, and we must get to Rome at the earliest,'said Ismail Sikandar Khan in fluent Italian to an elderly Italian gentleman.

That broke the ice as an elderly man asked him to join him for a cup of tea in a secluded hut that was well away from the town.

'I am an Italian but an Italian Jew and this is my grand daughter Gina Rosselini,' said the elderly man as he introduced the young and beautiful 20 year old to Major Ismail Sikandar Khan.'

'She is all that is left of my family after the Germans massacred my son, his wife and their two young sons as an act of revenge.'

'ut why and how did that happen,' asked Ismail while offering his condolences to the oldman.

'It was just bad luck I guess. They had all left for Rome to attend a marriage leaving behind this grand daughter of mine to look after me. And Rome as you know son is only 75 miles from here and my son had gone with the rest of his family to attend the marriage of Antonio, the only son of a wealthy Jewish family friend of ours. That was on 30th September last year and a day after General Eisenhower and Marshal Badoglio met aboard HMS Nelson to sign the full armistice. The German high command were now controlling only Northern Italy and they had already started the process of sending all Jews to the transit concentration camps that they had set up at Bolzano, Fossoli and other places in Northern Italy. The Fascist Black Brigade acting as informers to the Germans had reported the congregation of Jews for the marriage in the synagogue. While the solemn ceremony was being conducted, a truck load of the German SS fully armed with automatic weapons arrived and took all of them into custody. They were immediately put into cattle trucks and under escort were despatched to Bolzano. While they were on their way, the convoy halted to refuel near a lonely village. It was getting dark and my son with his family and a few others decided to take a chance. On the pretext of easing themselves they had moved to the edge of the road, but the German sentries were alert. They only needed an excuse and in order to teach all the others a lesson, they simply opened fire killing all of them mercilessly,' said the 70 year old Alberto Rosselini with anger and hatred showing on his shrivelled face.

'I now therefore only pray to God that someday if not I, than my grand daughter should take revenge against these German savages,' added the oldman as he with a pencil indicated on Ismail's map and on the enlarged sketch some of the foot tracks and the goat tracks leading to the monastery.

'I will be indeed very grateful if both of you could help me in getting some more information about the Germans defences in this area,' said Ismail as he looked appreciatively towards Gina and said a big thank you to her in Italian, while she served him and all the other members of his patrol with the refreshing hot coffee.As she stood there, the beautiful tall dark haired Italian girl with dimples on her rosy cheeks reminded Ismail a lot about his belovedSandra.

'My grandfather is quite old, but if required both of us could contribute in whatever little way we can in getting rid of these barbarians from our soil,' said Gina.

As Ismail smiled in appreciation and thanked Gina for the instant and positive response, he also gave them an option.

'Well considering the dangers that lurk because both of you are Jews, and keeping in mind that the town is in the line of fire of the artillery guns and mortars from both sides, may I therefore suggest that both of you move back to a safer place in the rear where our field hospital is located and there Gina could work as a nurse and you Sir as a medical assistant. Then from there if need be we could work as a team in getting more authentic information about the German defences not only on Monte Cassino but beyond it too,' said Major Ismail Sikander Khan very confidently.

'Not a bad idea at all provided we can get some shelter and some food with it,' said the oldman as he looked approvingly at Gina who simply smiled. And before it was dawn, Ismail with Gina and the oldman together with their meagre belongings of clothing and other necessities were huddled into an old requisitioned civil truck and were taken to the rear headquarters of the Division.

Meanwhile in Calcutta on the 4th of February 1944, there was rejoicing in Debu Ghosh's house. At long last and after more than two years of silence there was finally a letter from their eldest son Arup and the letter was datelined Lvov-USSR. Under the Influence of M N Roy his mentor, Arup Ghosh had become a staunch supporter of the Soviet communist movement and had married one Galina Alexandrovna, the pretty daughter of an influential member of the Communist Party of the USSR. Samir with his proficiency in the Russian language had become now not only a war correspondent of "The Morning Star", the Communist Party organ of Great Britain, but also an official interpreter. His wife Galya as she was popularly called by her friends and parents too had learnt a little bit of Bengali from her husband and she now looked forward to visiting India and her in-laws in Calcutta.

In his long letter, Arup Ghosh described in great detail not only the tremendous resilience and toughness of the men, women and children of the Soviet Union, but also of the atrocities that were being commited by the retreating German Army on the innocent Russian people in general and on the Russian Jews in particular. In that detailed letter to his parents from Lvov, a town near the non existent Polish-Russian border he wrote-:

My dear Baba and Maa,

I know I am guilty for this long unwanted and uncalled for silence on my part, but it was not entirely of my doing. All the same if this letter reaches you God willing, please do pardon me for being the cause of worry and anxiety to all of you.

What I write today will probably never become history, but it has to be written and told for the sake of posterity. The Germans are now on the run as the massive Russian offensive after routing the Germans in the greatest tank battle at Prokhorovka near Kursk in September 1943 are poised to enter Hitler's own so called fatherland. A few days ago, I interviewed some of the German prisoners of war and though most of them are still pro-Fuhrer, but there are others who condemned this war and the atrocities committed by them on the helpless Jews. One of them a Waffen SS soldier was in Warsaw during the Ghetto uprising and he described to me as to how the ZOB, the Jewish Fighting Organization consisiting of 22 groups with each group having only 20 to 30 men, women, girls and boys had fought heroically against the German using a maze of cellars, sewers and other hidden passages in that city. On 19th April, 1943 during the Jewish feast of Passover, when the elderly Jews were telling their children the story of their exodus from Egypt and were in the process of eating the Matzo, the unleavened bread to celebrate the occasion, 2000 Waffen SS soldiers under the command of SS General Jurgen Stroop attacked the ghetto with tanks, artillery and flame throwers. A fierce battle erupted and the Jews repulsed the attack. This carried on for four full days till an infuriated Himmler, the exterminator of Jews ordered Jurgen to burn down the entire ghetto block by block. Yet the Jews kept fighting while moving from one building to another. They preferred being burnt alive rather than being caught and tortured to death by the Germans. For a full 28 days the small bands of these heroic and gallant Jews fought on till the 16th of May, when Stroop sent his battle report that the former Jewish quarter of Warsaw was no longer in existence. Not only that, the blood thirsty Germans at around 8 o'clock that evening even blew up the Warsaw Synagogue.

A few weeks earlier and while I was passing through Kiev, the capital of Ukraine as a war correspondent with the advancing Russian forces I had by chance met a middle aged Russian Jew who told me another story of horror and degregadation about the wholesale massacre of practically all Jews, men women and children who were once residents of this big city in Ukraine. He could tell me the true story because he was amongst the very few who were lucky to have survived that brutal mass killing.This barbaric act happened more than two years ago, when the German blitzkrieg captured the city on 19th September of 1941. The Einsatsgruppen from the 'C' division of the dreaded SS who were nothing but mobile killing units that followed the advancing German armies soon rounded up all the Jews inside the city. They had been tasked to liquidate all Jews.On the 24th of September a series of large explosions had rocked the city. These had been organised by the NKVD, the Soviet Secret police. The very next day the high ranking SS and Wermacht officers decided to exterminate all the Jews in the city as a punishment.

On 28th September, the Germans issued an order for all the Jews including the young and old, the sick and the poor to assemble in the centre of the city. They told them to come with their documents, valuables, winter coats etc as they would be resettled at a place outside the city limits and where they would work as labourers in the proposed labour camp which thay were setting up there. Since the area indicated for the proposed labour camp was situated near the railroad, the Jews believed the story.For the next two days from the given rendez-vous of the proposed labour camp area, the Jews, including men, women and children were marched in large groups like herded cattle to the area of Babi Yar. It was an area full of naturally fomed ravines on the outskirts of the Ukrainian capital city of Kiev and had been barbwired by the Germans. There they were all stripped of their possessions and ordered to undress. Then they were told to walk up to the edge of the ravine and as soon as they reached there, a burst of machine gun fire from behind greeted them. As the corpes fell like nine pins with one on top of the other, the dastardly massacre continued till everyone the Germans thought had been eliminated. The riddled bodies were then covered with thin layers of earth. When the next group arrived the same drill was followed. This senseless massacre carried on for the next forty eight hours and in which more than 34,000, helpless, innocent Jews were mercilessly put to death. Comrade Vassily Danchenko who told me this story was lucky to survive. Though he too had been hit by a bullet, but he lay doggo for over three days under the heap of dead copses that covered his body. At the dead of night on the third day, when the German murder squads had left the area, he wriggled his way out to freedom.

I am sorry if I have bored you with such dreadful stories about this war and I wonder where this will all end. I am enclosing a photograph of self with wife that was taken a day prior to my moving out from Moscow for this current assignment as a war correspondent. Though I am wearing the uniform of a Captain in the Red Army but do not worry I have not joined it. The uniform is my legal passport to cover this miserable war.

What news about my two dear brothers Swarup and Anup and my dear little sister Purnima. When is she getting married? I read about the terrible famine in Bengal. I think it was a man made disaster.Do convey our warm regards to Hussein and Naren Uncle and also to the members of their family. There are some wild rumours here about Subhas Bose seeking help from the Russians. But at this juncture it is simply out of the question since the three big wigs of this war, namely Churchill, Roosevelt and Stalin in their meeting at Tehran in late November 1943 have already chalked out their future game plan and stategy against the Axis Powers. Chances are that a Second Front as requested by Stalin will be soon in the offing.

Whatever one might say but I miss my India and you all. If time and circumstances permit, I will write to you more often.

With fond regards and pranams to you and Ma,
Your wayward son,
Arup.

As Debu finished reading the long letter, his wife Hena with the edge of her saree wiped away the tears that had swelled in her big black eyes.

'Thank God atleast he is doing something good and useful, and so what if he has married a Russian girl,'said Debu Ghosh as he tried to console his wife.

Meanwhile in France a dangerous game was being played by Richard Pugsley and Samir Sen. After having contacted the French underground, both of them had deserted from their unit during the Christmas week of 1943. With the help from members of the French Resistance Movement and after having proved their credentials to them they were now recruited by the SOE, the Special Operations department which was Mr Churchill's brainchild to wage a guerrilla war against Hitler's forces in occupied Europe. As desired by Mr Winston Churchill, the members of the SOE would soon set the continent of Europe ablaze. Organized by Mr Hugh Dalton after the fall of France in 1940, the SOE had set up its first Headquarter in two nondescript family flats on London's Baker Street. The senior staff members were all from reputed British Public schools and from Oxford and Cambridge, but the agents that they recruited were from all walks of life and included even the daughter of a Brixton motor car dealer. The head of training and operations of the SOE was Brigadier Colin Gubbins from the British Royal artillery who had won the Military Cross while serving on the Western Front during the First World War and immediately after that in 1919 he also served under General Anton Denikin in the White Army that fought against the Bolsheviks inside Russia. The top secret training establishments were set up in mansions that were far from the madding crowd. There under Gubbin's expert guidance those selected were given rigorous training in arms and ammunition, sabotage and subversion till they were parachuted behind the enemy lines or were landed by boats on the French coast.

At a secluded house near Welwyn Garden City in Hertfordshire, the SOE even employed budding scientists to invent unique weapons of war that included among others the single shot cigarette pistol and the submersible canoe. In North London, 'The Thatched Barn' a former roadhouse was converted as the Headquarters of the ingenious camouflage section which was run by the film director Elder Wills. Here an army of ex prop makers from the world of cinema created countless illusions out of papier mache and plaster and with many of them lethally deadly. The backroom operations included the false documentation section which provided the agents with their false identities. A fashion company even outfitted the agents with the type of clothing that were usually worn by the people of the area they were to operate in. With these agents in action one did not need a whole squadron of Bombers to disrupt the German war machine. With most of the members of the secret underground organization of the "Prosper Network" set up by the SOE inside occupied France that was led by Francis Suttill and which was betrayed by a German spy who had infiltrated into the organization, Maurice Buckmuster who controlled his agents from England was now in a quandary.

Born in 1910, Buckmaster had served with the British Expeditionary Force in France in 1940. In September 1941, the young 31 year old Buckmaster was placed in charge of the SOE and was tasked to build an organization that would carry out acts of sabotage, gather information about the enemy and give all necessary help in terms of money and equipment to the French Resistance. With preparations for "Operation Overlord" to land a strong invasion force on the beaches of Normandy currently in full swing, Maurice Buckmaster now required more trained agents and saboteurs who would provide vital information not only about the deployment of German forces on the beaches of Normandy, but also of the location of the German Panzer Reserves in the rear. He also needed very badly courageous men and women to sabotage and disrupt all rail and road communication leading to the selected beaches on D-Day.

In late October 1943, while working late till the early hours of the morning in his office in Baker Street as was his habit, Buckmaster received a secret coded telegram mentioning that the last and only wireless operator, Noor Inayat Khan from his 'Prosper Group' had also now been arrested by the Gestapo in Paris. It was a very big set back not only for him but also for those who were banking on the SOE's inputs for the planning the invasion of Europe.

Noor Inayat Khan, the great great great grand daughter of Tipu Sultan was born on New Years Day 1914 inside the Kremlin in Moscow. Her father Inayat Khan had married an American and had served for a while in the Tsar's Imperial Court. Just before the outbreak of the First World War, the family first moved to England and later settled in France. Noor lost her father when she was only 13 years old. After taking a degree in child psychology from Sorbonne University she began her career as a free lance writer and she also wrote short stories for children. In 1939 Figaro published "Twenty Jataka Tales", a collection of traditional Indian stories that was written by Noor. In 1940, with the Germans approaching Paris the family made their way to Bordeaux and from there because her brother Vilayat as the name indicates was born in England, they managed to get on the last boat that was evacuating all British subjects from that port town. Back in England, Vilayat Khan joined the Royal Air Force and Noor in November 1940 joined the WAAF, the Women's Auxillary Air Force. With her good command over the French language and after her interview with Captain Jepson from the SOE which took place in a dingy little room of the Victoria Hotel on Northumberland Avenue, Noor Inayat Khan was selected and trained as a wireless operator for the SOE. Given the cover name of Jeanne Marie Regnier, a children's nurse maid and the code name of 'Madeleine', Noor on the night of 17th June 1943, climbed out of the Lysander aircraft of the 161 Special Operations Squadron in a moonlit meadow a few miles north-east of Angers not far away from where the Rivers Loire and the Sarthe met. From there she made her way to Paris to join the "Prosper Group.".

For the next three and a half months the ever smiling Noor Inayat through her wireless set had sent vital important information to Buckmaster. By September, with German locating vans closing in on her, and with most of the members of her group arrested, she was told to return back to England. But giving the argument that she was the only wireless operator left in the group, she kept sending back vital information and even made attempts to rebuild the "Prosper Network". In early October it was all over, when a woman who called herself Renee betrayed her to the Gestapo. Strangely the address where she was staying and operating the wireless set from was only a few minutes walking distance from the Gestapo headquarters on the Avenue Foch. The soft voice and the fine indomitable sprit that glowed in her dark quiet eyes would soon be silenced for ever at the Dachau concentration camp inside Nazi Germany.

With Samir Sen's expertise in German codes and wireless set operations together with Richard Pugsley's invaluable knowledge about the functioning of British wireless sets and radio locating skills, the Indian duo made quite a formidable team for the French Maquis who worked hand in glove with the SOE agents. The problem arose that though Richard Pugsley with his looks and fair complexion could possibly pass of as a Frenchman, but it was not so with Samir Sen. Keeping in view the dangers of the group being exposed with Samir Sen moving around with them for clandestine operations, it was decided a month later to smuggle him across the Pyrenees Mountains into Spain and from there to London where his services could be better utilised for signal intelligence gathering, now that the German "Enigma Code" without the Germans being aware of it had been successfully compromised by the code breakers working in wooden huts at Britain's Bletchley Park.

In February 1944, Richard Pugsley became a member of one of the French Maquis Groups which was now being organised by Nancy Wake. She had only recently parachuted into the mountains of Central France and with the bands of Maquis she was now setting up ammunition and arms drops for the French resistance. Nancy Wade a 29 year old Australian who was fluent in French was not only an expert in the use of plastic explosives, but was also familiar with the use of all small arms and grenades. A born leader, Nancy some weeks later even led a raid on the German Gestapo Headquarters at Montucon and Richard Pugsley simply adored her guts.

And while the Maquis in France was being better organized, Subhas Bose or Netaji as he was now called on 30th December 1943 had unfurled the Indian tricolour at Port Blair. A week later on 7th January 1944, Subhas Bose with key members of his cabinet and military brass arrived in Rangoon to discuss with the Japanese Commander-in-Chief General Kawabe about the coming invasion of India. The Japanese General suggested that the Subhas Regiment earmarked for the operation with the Japanese forces should be split into small groups for attachment with the Japanese formations, but to this Subhas Bose did not agree and said.

'I am sorry General. The first drop of blood to fall on Indian soil will be that of an INA soldier and nobody else can be given that honour.'

On 3rd February with tears of joy in his eyes Netaji bade farewell to the Subhas Regiment which was leaving for the front.'Blood is calling blood. It is now time to arise and take up arms. We have no more time. The road to Delhi is the road to freedom' said the C-in-C.as he shouted at the top of his voice ' Chalo Delhi and Jaihind' while, the special trains of the Azad Hind Fauj steamed off from the railway station to take on the allies.

By now the Second INA Division was also ready to go into action. It was under the command of the young ex Captain of the Indian Army and the officer was non other than Colonel Nripendra Singh Bhagat, an ex engineer officer from 17 Field Company of the Bonbay Sappers and a gold medallist from the "Pioneers", the first batch of officers from the Indian Military Academy, Dehradun. With over 10 years of service, he was also getting ready to take on the allies. The week before he with his Field Company surrendered to the Japanese at Singapore on 15th February 1942, Nripendra Bhagat had received the good news that his younger brother who was also an engineer officer from the Royal Bombay Sappers had been awarded the Victoria Cross by Lord Linlithgow, the Viceroy of India.

Commissioned on 15th July 1939, Second Lieutenant Preminder Singh Bhagat on the night of 31st January and 1st February 1941 at Gallbat, Gondar in Eithopia during the pursuit of the Italians had with complete coolness and in the face of the enemy and for four full days and over a distance of over 44 miles had cleared 15 minefields and Nripendra the eldest of the four Bhagat brothers, all of whom were ex products of the Prince of Wales Royal Indian Military College PWRIMC was indeed proud of him.

Though the Second IMA Division had been raised, but desertions by the Indian ex Prisoners of War who were part and parcel of it were now on the rise as news of allied victories in North Africa and Italy kept reaching them. It was a cause of great worry to Subhas Bose who now gave strict orders to shoot such traitors and cowards.

In 1942, and before Subhas Bose arrived on the scene, the Indian League had infiltrated in small groups through Burma a espionage network into India with the task of reporting vital military and political intelligence, but it was a total failure. Even from the group of parachute agents that were dropped into Eastern India in March 1943 nothing was received or heard off. On taking over as C-in-C, Subhash Bose had also lost faith in the Hikari Kikan, the Japanese Indian Laision Group which was headed by a Japanese officer. Their task was to operate the spy network, to spell out the propaganda policy, to be a link between the Japanese government and the Provisional Government of India, as also provide supplies and material to the INA forces. When Subhas was told that the Japanese officer heading the Hikari Kikan was diverting the material meant for the INA to the Japanese Forces, he was lived and made sure that it only worked henceforth as a simple military liaison cell and nothing more.Therefore after taking over charge as Prime Minister of the Provisional Government of India, Subash Bose had now revamped the entire espionage and spy network. These specially trained men were now to operate in small groups. The "Bahadur Groups" as they were called were required to operate behind enemy lines and to carry out sabotage, espionage and subversion, while the "Intelligence Groups" were tasked to collect battlefield intelligence, and the "Reinforcement Groups" were detailed to collect Indian Prisoners of War and indoctrinate them to join the INA.

On 8th December 1943, on the instructions of Subhas Bose another network of trained agents with powerful wireless sets and codes under the command of Mr SN Chopra, an Indian school master from Batu Pahat in Penang in a Japanese submarine clandestinely landed on the Kathiawar coast of India. After landing, it soon split up into smaller groups and was now sending political, military and economic intelligence in ciphers to Subhas Bose's INA Headquarters.

In January 1944, Subhash Bose met Captain Mohan Singh for the first time and interviewed him. Captain Mohan Singh agreed to serve under Netaji, but Subhas Bose was apprehensive that as the founder of the INA, Mohan Singh could create more trouble with the Japanese. Considering Captain Mohan Singh' poor health he diplomatically and conveniently sent him to Sumatra to a healthier and safer surrounding. was around this time in early January 1944, that Major Gul Rehman after his staff college course reported to the 5th Red Ball Indian Division in the Arakan region of Burma. He had been posted as GSO 2 Operations (General Staff Officer Grade 2) of the Division. Having fought the Italians and the Germans, the Division had arrived in Bombay during the first week of June 1943 and was immediately sent to the area of Chas, Lohardaga and Ranchi in Bihar for jungle warfare training. The Division was now ready to take on the Japanese and it soon came under the man who was better known as the soldier's general. Lt Gen WJ Slim was now the 14th Army Commander. He was commissioned into the 6th Gurkha Rifles, and he had now vowed that he would be back to convert defeat into victory and this is exactly what he was now preparing to do against what was still now a fanatical and ruthless enemy.

A month earlier in mid December1943, the Red Ball Division at Arakan had been visited by none other than the Supreme Allied Commander, South East Asia. It was Lord Louis Mountbatten first visit to an Indian Division. Resplendent in his spotless white naval uniform he proudly shook hands with even the lowest rank Indian sepoy. With the three Urdu words of praise, thank you and keep fighting.'Shabash, Shukriya and Ladthe Raho' that he had learnt by heart, Mountbatten soon won over their hearts. To the Indian soldiers he was now "Mounting Baton."

During January 1944, Major Gul Rehman's 1/1 Punjabees as part of Brigadier DFW Warren's 161 Brigade had suffered very high casualties while taking part in "Operation Jericho". The Brigade had been tasked to oust the Japanese from the Razabil Fortress, but had failed to do so. In March, 161 Brigade was again ordered to attack and capture the same fortress but this time under "Operation Markhor". Seeing the high casualty figures of both officers, JCO's and men of his parent unit, Major Gul Rehman requested for a posting back to his unit and it was immediately granted.

On 4th February, Major LS Misra's INA forces in the Mayu valley had succeeded in cutting off a part of Major General's Messervy's 7th Indian Division and Subhas Bose was thrilled. On that very day the advance party from the INA's 'Subhash Brigade" left from Rangoon for Prome and in the next subsequent two days, the main body also followed. Swarup Ghosh having joined the Azad Hind Dal, the Political Arm of the INA also moved with them.

At Arakan, Brigadier Warren also popularly known as "Daddy Warren" reminded the officers of his 161 Brigade in a conference that the Japanese were not super human beings and what was required of them was to set an example of sheer guts and courage while leading their troops in battle.'Simply be determined and fanatical if need be. For we will now get them nice and proper from behind,' said the bespectacled pipe smoking Brigade Commander while congratulating Major Gul Rehman and other officers who after spending several days of reconnaissance deep behind the enemy lines had now returned safely back to base with favourable patrol reports about the enemy's dispositions and obstacles on the given objective that was to be captured.

A few days later in the early hours of the morning as the heavy bombardment of own artillery guns echoed against the Mayu Range, the 1/1 Punjabees in their sub-units leading the Brigade Vanguard had in single file moved to their forming up place. At dawn they attacked their objective Point 1267. The Japanese were taken completely by surprise and soon the formidable Razabil Fortress was in the hands of 161 Brigade. However, during the mopping up phase, the 1/1 Punjabees lost their beloved Commanding Officer. Lieutenant Colonel D I Morrision popularly know as "Digger." Digger was cheerfully smoking his cigarette, when a bullet from a Japanese sniper ripped his lungs.

Meanwhile in North Burma, the Japanese military high command with the elements of the INA's Subhas Brigade posed a serious threat to India. On 19th March 1944, the Japanese troops with the irregulars from the Azad Hind Dal and with the forward elements of Subhash Brigade of the Azad Hind Fauj had crossed the border into India. On 21st March, Prime Minister Tojo stated in the Japanese Diet that on entering India, the Provisional Government of Subhas Bose would be responsible to administer all occupied Indian Territory and that indeed was a big shot in the arm for Netaji as he strongly appealed to the Indian people to actively cooperate with the combined forces of the advancing Japanese and INA trrops. He now appointed Major General AC Chatterjee the ex IMS Captain as his trusted lieutenant and right hand man. Chatterjee who was an excellent organizer and he had also been nominated to take over as Governor of the newly liberated areas.

Gen Renya Mutagachi the GOC-in-C Japanese 15th Army with three Japanese Divisions and elements from the INA had launched "Operation U GO". The aim was to destroy the British Indian Forces at Imphal and Kohima and then to invest the plains of Assam. While the Japanese main force was to attack and take Imphal, the 31st Japanese Division was tasked to advance rapidly in three strong Brigade Columns to cut the Kohima-Imphal road and to simultaneously envelope Kohima from three sides.

On 22nd March, on the very next day the Japanese with the elements of the INA had broken through the screens and forward elements of the allied forces on the Imphal front. Advancing from the North and West they encircled the allied defences at Imphal, and by 29th March had successfully cut of the only road axis to Kohima. With the elements of Major General Kiani's 1st Indian Division from the INA and that of Shah Nawaz Khan's Subhash Brigade, the Japanese Forces now laid siege to Imphal. Hearing the good news, Netaji was ecstatic as he announced the first list of the Azad Hind Fauj's gallantry awards and decorations for his officers and soldiers.

In the first week of April 1944, as the 31st Japanese Division under Major General Sato together with elements of the Subhash Brigade under Colonel Thakore Singh were knocking at the doors of the strategically located village of Kohima in the Naga Hills, Netaji from Rangoon moved his Tactical Headquarters forward to the small hilly town of Maymyo near Mandalay in Central Burma. He was expecting the fall of Imphal and Kohima very soon and he wanted to be in the forefront. Then just before leaving Rangoon, Netaji in a surprise move dismissed Colonel Nripendra Singh Bhagat from the command of the 2nd Indian Division on charges of insubordination and disloyalty. The letter of dismissal personally signed by Netaji and which was personally handed over to the officer read. 'You have been disloyal and defiant and your conduct cannot be overlooked.'Colonel Bhagat did not get a fair chance to answer those charges as he was taken into protective custody immediately.

When news of the rapid advance of the Japanese was reported to General Slim, the Fourteenth Army Commander, he immediately airlifted Brigadier Warren's 161 Brigade from Dohaziri in the Arakans to Dimapur in Assam. On landing at Dimapur, the units of 161 Bde which included the 4th Royal West Kent Regiment and the two Indian Battalions of 1/1 Punjab and 4/7 Rajputs were rushed to Kohima by road transport. While the 4th Royal West Kent was deployed on the Garrison Hill Ridge, the other two battalions because of paucity of space took up defences at Jotsoma, 2 miles West of Kohima. The small beautiful Angami village of Kohima situated at a height of 5000 feet above sea level and surrounded by thick forests was the Headquarters of Mr Charles Pawsey, the British Administrator and District Commissioner of the hard working Naga tribes of that area. It had only a small garrison of Assam Rifles, the 1st Assam Regiment and other small administrative army units holding the defences there.

On the night of 5th/6th April1944, the Japanese opened the attack on Kohima against the Royal West Kents and the small Kohima Garrison and they were surprised by the tenacious fighting spirit of both the British Tommies and the Indian soldiers. The Kohima Ridge overlooking the village of Kohima and consisting of the tactical features of Garrison Hill, Jail Hill, Field Supply Depot Hill, Detail Issue Hill, the Hospital Hill and the DC's Bungalow Hill were held by the West Kent's and others and they practically fought to the last man and last round as Brigadier Warren from time to time kept reinforcing them from the troops deployed in the Jatsoma area.

On the 7th of April, while passing through the defences of the 4th Royal West Kent on the feature named ' Detailed Issue Hill' and DIS Hill for short, Major Gul Rehman was witness to a deed of extreme valour, heroism and raw courage by a simple young English Lance Corporal.Lance Corporal John Harman, a trained sniper from the Delta Company of the famed Queens Own Royal West Kent Regiment having observed that a Japanese team had occupied one of their own captured trenches; he without asking anybody's permission simply crawled forward from his own slit trench to take them on single handedly. Before the Japs could react, Harman sprinted the last 35 yards and having flung himself down a few yards from the enemy, he pulled out the pin from his grenade and counting three of the four second fuse, threw it at the enemy. Having killed both the Japs he triumphantly walked back with the Japanese light machine gun on his shoulders. Not satisfied with his dare devilry Lance Corporal John Harman on the very next day when the Japanese resumed their attack on DIS Hill, he with his fixed bayonet charged at the five Japanese soldiers who were in the process of deploying another light machine gun to fire at them. Firing from the hip, Harman shot his way and wiped out the position single handedly. As a tired Harman made his way back and while his comrades told him to run, the brave English soldier was hit by a burst of enemy machine gun fire. As he reached and fell on his own defensive position, his last words were.' I've got to go. It was worth it. I got the lot.'

When Major Gul Rehman narrated the English soldier's deeds of courage, valour, daring and guts in the face of the enemy to the men of his battalion, the morale and the fighting spirit of the unit went sky high. A few weeks later the news arrived that the gallant Lance Corporal John Harman had been decorated with the Victoria Cross. It was the highest gallantry award of the British Empire, but unfortunately it was again a posthumous one.

On the 8th and 9th of Aprill, 1944 having laid siege to Kohima, the Japanese launched a series of ferocious attacks on the British and Indian positions, pushing them back slowly from the ridge. Soon the main battle centred on the DC's bungalow and the tennis court adjacent to it. With the deeds of Lance Corporal Harman fresh in their minds, the gallant troops of Major Gul Rehman's Dogra Company from the First Punjabees were now determined not to give even an inch to the Japanese, It was now a fierce hand to hand combat match on the tennis court and in the garden of the DC's bungalow, as both sides went hammer and tong against each other with hand grenades and bayonets.

Every night the men under the cover of darkness crawled to the only running water tap in the DC's garden that was just 35 yards from the enemy positions to fill their water bottles. Water had now been rationed to only half a mug a day for each man. This carried on relentlessly till the 13th of April as the Dogra and Sikh troops celebrated Baisakhi by giving it back to the Japanese with vengeance, while Colonel John Young and his medical team of surgeons and doctors carved, chopped, hacked and stitched the open bleeding wounds in the makeshift Operation Theatre, which was nothing but a dugout under a tarpaulin.

Mr Charles Pawsey the DC who had spent a score of years among his beloved Nagas dressed in his grey flannels and old trilby hat walked through the fighting trenches encouraging the troops to fight on. Then surprisingly the very next day on the 14th of April which happened to be the Bengali New Year's day eve that year, the Japanese for the first time did not put in any attack. That night over a drink with Major Brodie, the officiating Commanding Officer of the 1/1 Punjabees inside the small operations bunker of the battalion, Major Gul Rehman jokingly remarked that the cause for the lull in the battle could be because, the Japanese Commanders wanted Subhash Bose not to be unduly disturbed on such an auspicious day for the Bengalees.

'Well Cheers to that.' said Major Brodie while announcing that the new commanding officer Lt Colonel EHW Grimshaw who was earlier the Brigade Major of the Brigade was expected to take over the next day.

161 Infantry Brigade had now come under the command of Major General Grover's 2nd British Division that had been flown in from over a distance of 1500 miles and was now being inducted into the area. On 15th April, after a series of attacks on the Japanese positions by the 161 Bde and 5 Bde of the Red Ball Division and their subsequent link up on Milestone 41, the Dimapur-Kohima-Imphal road was once again open to the British Indian Forces.

On the 16th of April 1944, the 1/1 Punjabees under the command of their new commanding officer were once again in occupation of the Kohima ridge. That day the dare devil pilots of the Royal Air Force, the Royal Indian Air force, and the United States Air force saturated the small dropping zone with water, rum, rations, chocolates, grenades, and ammunition. It was much to the respite and delight of the heroes and defenders of Kohima as they celebrated the much needed air drop that day with some good food and rum.That evening inside the dug out of an improvised Officers Mess of 161 Bde, the Commanding Officers of 4/7 Rajputs and 1/1 Punjabees drank a toast to the heroic officers and troops of the 4th West Kent Regiment who had withstood the Japanese onslaught day after day and night after night for nearly a fortnight. The gallant action of the officers and men of the 161 Infantry Brigade in the battle for Kohima was the turning point of the Burma campaign. Strangely it would also be a turning point in the battle for Kashmir a few years later by the same 161 Infantry Brigade but under completely different circumstances as comrades and friends in arms would soon become enemies and adversaries in a never ending war with one another.

In June 1944, 161 Brigade came under the command of Major General Messervy's 7th Indian Division and relentlessly pursued the retreating Japanese 31st Division to Imphal and beyond. By the end of June, Imphal had been also saved. On 23rd September 1944, Brigadier Daddy Warren took over command of the Red Ball Division while handing over 161 Bde to Brigadier RGC Poole.

While the formations of the 5th Indian Red Ball Division valiantly pursued the retreating Japanese and INA Forces in Burma, in Italy, the Red Eagles, the 4th Indian Division having made desperate efforts to knock the Germans off from Monte Cassino had also suffered heavy casualties. Though with the help of Gina Rosselini and her father who were now working as informers and who were even risking their lives at times while working behind the German lines, Major Ismail Sikandar Khan had now produced a good intelligence appreciation regarding the enemy's strength and dispositions on Monte Cassino, but Lieutenant General Bernard Freyburg, the Corps Commander of the newly formed New Zealand Corps and of which the Red Eagle was very much now a part was not fully convinced.

Gina had brought in very reliable information that the Germans were not physically occupying the monastery since those were the strict orders from none other than Field Marshall Kesserling, the German C-in-C in Italy and who had even prohibited the German soldiers from entering the sacred place and had also posted a guard at its entrance. But the allied higher commanders' right from the Divisional Commanders in the chain of command to the Corps Commanders refused to believe it. To them it seemed inconceivable that the Monastery was not defended, and with the large number of casualties suffered during the First battle Of Cassino, the higher allied military brass now demanded for heavy artillery and air bombardment of the Benedictine Abbey that crowned the Monastery Hill.

'I want it reduced to rubble before we go in for the Second Battle of Cassino,' said Corps Commander Freyburg as the 4th Indian and the 1st New Zealand Divisions went into the details of planning their attacks.

Besides the monastery of Monte Cassino being the strongest point on the powerful German defences on the Gustav Line, the seemingly unending succession of mountain ranges, rivers and ravines of the terrain demanded the soldierly qualities of fighting, valour and endurance of each and every individual of the unit, irrespective of his trade and qualifications. Be it the infantryman from the leading section or the stretcher bearers of the medical units, or the muleteers with their mules bringing up supplies and ammunition, each and everyone had an important and big task in their hands.

On 15th February 1944, under a clear blue sky while Gina Rossellini who was doubling up during daytime as a cover to work as a nurse in the military field hospital watched wave after wave of medium and heavy bombers drop their 500 and 1000 pound bombs on the historically famous Abbey, her heart went out to the civilians inside it. Soon it became a roofless shell as the heavy, medium and field artillery guns together with the mortar batteries also pounded the place relentlessly and without remorse. It was a bombardment of a single target that now pulverised the area.

On the night of the 16th the Red Eagles on orders of their Officiating GOC, Brigadier HK Dimoline opened the attack and it carried on relentlessly for the next two subsequent days and nights with the full fire support of all available artillery and mortar batteries and air strikes. But unfortunately the overall attack plan was no different from the first one that was launched by the Americans earlier. The Red Eagles had been tasked to capture the redoubtable Monastery Hill and Point 593 and thereafter to cut highway 6 and capture Monte Cassino from the West. And the New Zealanders moving in across the plains were required to capture the railway station and the town of Cassino. But there was too much of delay after the total destruction of the monastery for the move forward of troops earmarked for the initial assault. And as luck would have it they used the same approaches to the objectives as the Americans had done during the first battle of Cassino. When the leading battalions moved in closer to make their final charge, they were taken by complete surprise as the troops from the German 1st Parachute and the!5th Panzer Grenadier Division who having now taken full advantage of the ruins mowed down the leading troops with accurate automatic machine gun, artillery and mortar fire. The Germans had now cleverly converted the ruins of the monastery into a formidable fortress.

The attackers simply had no chance as the leading troops were pinned down by the heavy accurate fire and by the anti personnel mines that had been laid in abundance by the German defenders. The Germans were well trained diehard troops who had received a special directive from no less a person than the Fuhrer himself which read.'Even if no military purposes were served, it was necessary on political grounds to hold this key bastion to the death.' And with that diktat from the Fuhrer, the German garrison on Monte Cassino were determined to honour it as they held on to Monte Cassino now even more doggedly and tenaciously.

While the Indian and British troops and those from New Zealand renewed their attacks on Monte Cassino, but it was a task now beyond them. The slopes of the feature were scraggy with great boulders, sharp ledges and with patches of scrub. These natural hideouts and the man made ruins sheltered the determined German Spandau teams and bomb squads, and though the enemy defences at places were not even a hundred yards away, the slightest movement drew deadly retaliatory fire from them. There was not even elbow room for deployment, or for effective cover for the leading troops as Major Ismail Sikandar Khan moved forward to the tactical headquarters of 7th Indian Brigade to make an on the spot assessment of the situation. The attacking troops were effectively pinned down by the enemy and by the morning of the 19th of February, 1944 the attack had to be called off completely. Now the forward elements dug in and clung on to the vital little piece of ground that had been captured by them, while their own senior commanders prepared for their next plan of attack.

The new plan of attack was planned for take off on the 24th of February, but the weather was not at all on the side of the Allies. The winter rains and snow together with low clouds, fog, mist and the freezing cold weather had made it impossible for the artillery gunners and the air force to guarantee the infantry soldier the much needed all important close fire support. The miserable weather continued for the next three weeks, as operations planned were postponed day after day. In the meantime the Germans let off a propaganda offensive as they shouted loudly the names of the captured prisoners over the loud speakers and megaphones. And while they made promises to them of giving them a dignified comfortable living as prisoners of war, they also thus tempted the others who were willing to desert or surrender to them.

With the weather playing foul, the planned third battle for Cassino got progressively delayed thus enabling the Germans to reinforce and consolidate their defences on Monastery Hill. With a little more time to spare, Gina and Ismail were now seeing more of each other. It was not necessarily for gathering of enemy intelligence as they met sometimes clandestinely in somebody's abandoned bombed out house or hut or in a deserted barn far away from the front line. They were now madly in love with one another.

On 13th March, 1944 and two days before the third battle of Cassino was to begin, Major Ismail Sikandar Khan took his beloved Gina to an abandoned lonely hut well away from the front line and proposed to her. And the same diamond ring that he had once left for Sandra Pugsley at the Embarkation Headquarters in Bombay when he first sailed for the Middle East and which was returned to him by the magnanimous Mr Edwin Pugsley was now on the dainty middle finger of his would be future wife.

'Please be very careful my darling while approaching the enemy's forward defences. They have quite a few ace sharp shooters and snipers who have been tasked to target senior officers,' pleaded Gina as she thanked and kissed Ismail passionately on his lips.

'But I am only a piddly damn Major and that to an acting one and I do not think that the German sniper will waste his bullet on me,' said Ismail with a smile as he pulled Gina under the pair of coarse army blankets that he had taken on loan from the field hospital. With the stacks of hay piled up in the middle of a small room serving as a bed, Ismail softly laid Gina on it and slowly undressed the beautiful shapely Italian girl. As he lifted her tight sweater and blouse over her golden brown hair and kissed her pear shaped breasts and taught nipples, Gina closed her eyes and lovingly held on to his head asking for more. Then Ismail's hands went under her skirt and as he fondly caressed her beautiful hips and thighs, Gina sportingly removed her skirt and all her under garments. Ismail could now wait no longer as he hurriedly took off all his clothes. With both his hands and fingers now slowly rubbing and fondling her breasts, Ismail while lying on top of her kissed her all over her face and lips. Then lowering himself slowly he kissed her neck, then her stomach and navel. As she swooned for more, Ismails lips explored her beautiful inner thighs and legs.

'Please, let us do it now pleaded Gina as Ismail and Gina got into the 69 position. And while the foreplay continued and when Gina could take no more, they reversed position. Now as they naked bodies in unison rocked together, they both went into an ecstasy and simultaneously came to a climax. For a while they lay in each others arms in total silence. Then Ismail guided her hand once again to his manhood.

'Let us do it once more before we get those bastard Germans,'said Ismail with a smile as he pulled Gina on top of him and played with her well formed breasts. Then as they made love, Ismail kept holding her in a tight embrace. Once it was over, Gina once again whispered into his ears.

'Do please be very careful my love and don't give those bastard German snipers a chance.'

That night before saying good night to her, Ismail requested Gina to keep the engagement a secret for the time being while promising to marry her as soon as the war was over.

'But why cannot we marry now, tomorrow or the day after or the day day after because God only knows when this dirty war will end,' said a depressed Gina.

'Alright in that case I promise I will marry you soon after Monte Cassino is in our hands, but as is the custom in the army I will have to first seek the blessings of my superiors,' said Ismail as he held her tightly in his arms. Gina was thrilled as she thanked and kissed Ismail passionately on the lips and bid him goodbye.

The Third Battle of Cassino began on 15th March 1944 with yet more bombing from the air and heavy artillery and mortar shelling from the ground. This time the town of Cassino was flattened. The British and Indian troops of the elite 4th Indian division once again courageously attacked the high ground, while the New Zealanders bludgeoned their way into the town of Cassino itself, but the German parachutists holding the town and the high ground grimly and firmly held on to them. Now a house to house fighting erupted in the ruins of Cassino with often the same building being occupied by the opposing forces at times. Major General Howard Kippenberger the New Zealand Divisional Commander lost both his legs as his jeep ran over a landmine while he was on his way to the forward positions of his brave New Zealanders. The fighting inside the town was so intense and heavy that at times it became simply nerve racking when small sub units lost contact with their company and platoon commanders. This carried on till the 25th of March, when a great blizzard swept through the town, but the heights beyond. Monte Casino was still very much in the hands of the enemy.

In the six weeks of bloody fighting for Cassino, the Red Eagles had lost 4000 men killed or wounded. Though it was a bitter experience for the Division as a whole, but for the brave infantrymen it was the supreme ordeal. Their lot would have been much worse off had it not been for the courage and devotion to duty of Colonel RL Raymond, the ADMS, the Assistant Director of Medical Services of the 4th Infantry Division and his team of dedicated doctors, nursing assistants, nursing orderlies, stretcher bearers, and ambulance and jeep drivers who did an admirable job under such trying and difficult conditions and saved so many precious lives. One of them was Sepoy Chet Ram a jeep driver from the 4/16th Punjabees who made more than a hundred trips evacuating the wounded from the battlefield to the Field Ambulances and to the Mobile Casualty Clearing Station in the rear. But luck was not in his side for he was also wounded and later died. So was the case with a dhobi washerman Bashir Mohammed who too voluntarily made many dare devil trips to the front lines and brought back a large number of wounded who lived to tell his tale. He was immediately decorated with the IDSM, the Indian Distinguished Service Medal.

As the blizzard subsided, Major General AWW Holsworthy from the 3rd Gurkha Rifles who had just taken over command of the Red Eagles very reluctantly ordered his gallant troops to pull back as he handed over charge of his Divisional Sector to GOC 78 Division. The gallant 4th Indian Division now pulled back to recoup and to fight another day.

After informing and having taken permission from Mr Alberto Rossilleni of his intention to marry his charming grand daughter Gina, Major Ismail Sikandar Khan as was the custom in the army applied formally and in writing to his immediate boss, the GSO-I Operations and through him to the new General Officer Commanding the 4th Indian Division.

'Dear Sir, I have the honour to state that it is my earnest desire to take the young Miss Gina Rosellini to be my legally wedded wife. And I will very grateful if the necessary permission is given to me for the same so that it can be solemnized at Cassino in the next few days.'

On reading the short and sweet application, the General was delighted and invited both Ismail and Gina for a drink in his caravan. His only request to them was that the marriage should be solemnised only after Monte Cassino was captured by the Allies so that both the events could be celebrated in royal style.

'Well Sir I can get hold of a Mulla and a Padre too but from where the hell do I get hold of a Rabbi to read Gina her vows,' said Major Ismail Sikandar Khan in a lighter vein.

'Alright in that case I could request Colonel Moses Cohen of the RIASC and my Director Supplies and Transport who is a Jew from India to officiate if need be. I am sure he will be able to at least read out the "Ketubah,' the wedding contract which is mandatory before the actual wedding, so that it is ensured that you Major Ismail Sikandar Khan, MC will promise to feed, clothe and care for your future, beautiful and talented wife who I believe has been not only a great source of information to you, but to the Division also as far as those bloody Germans are concerned,' added the General in good humour.

'That I think is a splendid idea Sir and one thing is for sure and that is with Colonel Cohen being from the Supply Corps presiding over the marriage we will at least get the best of rations and booze to celebrate the occasion,' said the GSO 1 Ops.

'Yes and I will also ensure Sir that all the officers of the General Staff Branch are present in full strength to hold the tradtitional "Chuppah" the canopy over the heads of the lucky couple,' said the GSO 2 ops as all of them drank a toast to the charming couple.

While Major Ismail Sikandar Khan waited anxiously for the fall of Monte Cassino, in India, Colonel Reginald Edwards with his friend Colonel Attiqur Rehman and his wife Nafisa were on their way to Poona at the invitation of their old friend Colonel DR Thapar from the Indian Medical Service. The city and the military cantonment at Poona always had a special place in Reggie's heart. It was here as a young boy that his father had bought him on his eighth birthday his first cricket set from Oberoi Sports, and the large retinue of cooks, chaprasis, abdars and the gardners had taught him the field game of hockey.

'Oh I must show both of you the old palatial bungalow on 5 Parade Ground Road where we lived, provided of course if it is still standing,' said Reggie as the Frontier Mail steamed into the Bombay Central railway terminus on the morning of 14th April 1944.

I tell you what, first let us all go to the Victoria Terminus railway station to keep all our stuff in the cloak room since we have to catch the Deccan Queen only in the evening from there to Poona. Then having done that we could go on a shopping cum sight seeing trip of the city and thereafter get to the "Sea Lounge Restaurant" of the beautiful Taj Mahal Hotel facing the waterfront for a few drinks and a sumptuous lunch followed by tea if required too' said Reggie.

'I think that is a splendid idea Sir,' said Colonel Attiqur Rehman as they all got into the rear seat of the big American Dodge taxi.And it was around 2.30 in the afternoon, and after a little bit of sight seeing along the Marine Drive, Hornby Road and the Bombay Harbour they finally arrived at the luxurious Taj Mahal Hotel on Apollo Bunder and made themselves comfortable on a table for four at the Sea Lounge.

'Let's have a tall gimlet for the Doctor, an ice cream soda for his charming wife and a chilled beer, the best you have for me. And please make it in double time because all of us our indeed very thirsty,' said Reggie to the well dressed steward.

While the three of them over their drinks and snacks discussed the war and the terrible hardships being faced by the millions of poor people around the world, it was soon time for them to place the order for the food.

'Please Sir, do allow me to host the lunch atleast,' said Colonel Attiqur Rehman as he summoned the steward to take the order.

'Over my dead body and if you insist then I will summararily court martial you right here in the very presence of dear your wife,' said Reggie in good humour as he took away the beautifully velvet bound menu card from Attiqur's hands and gave it to Nafisa to make her choice first.

'Alright Colonel I think I will have your much loved fish and chips with tartare sauce and I am sure my husband will have his favourite giant lobster thermidore with garlic bread,' said Nafisa as Reggie called for one more round of drinks and ordered for himself a chicken a la Kiev.

It was nearing 3.45 pm, when they ordered the dessert to be followed by hot coffee and were busy talking about their plans to visit Kashmir during the coming summer season, when suddenly a series of very loud explosions rocked the hotel.

'Don't tell me that the bloody Japs have reached here too,' said Attiqur Rehman as he with Reggie rushed to the long verandah of the hotel and looked up towards the sky.

' Very strange there are no aircrafts in sight and yet the bloody place is being bombarded relentlessly,' said Attiqur Rehman when some of the big glass panes from the rooms and windows above came crashing down.'

'I thing it will be safer if we move into the garden near the swimming pool,' suggested Nafisa looking a little frightened.

'Alright let us go outside and see what is happening,' said Reggie as he chivalrously helped Nafisa to get up from her seat and offered her his arm. now not only had the explosions become louder, but there were debris falling from the skies into the streets and buildings nearby.

'My God this is simply terrible,' said Nafisa as somebody's limb oozing with blood landed in the garden. And seeing that terrible sight when all of them ran back into the safe confines of the hotel, Reggie said.

'I wonder what the hell is happening, because to me the explosions do not sound like gun fire at all.' Just then somebody who had just arrived at the hotel from the dockyard said that a ship loaded with ammunition had caught fire and it was only later in the night that the true story was revealed.

On the 11th of April, 1944 the SS Fort Stikine, a big cargo ship had berthed at the Victoria docks that was adjacent to the Ballad Pier and the Ballad Estate. The handsome two year old 7000 ton grey painted cargo ship had arrived with cargo that was both hazardous and glamorous. Dangerous and hazardous because it had in its cargo holds nearly 1400 tons of lethal war explosives and that included artillery shells, torpedoes, mines, small arms ammunition, signal rockets, magnesium flares and also some incendiary bombs. And in addition to all this it was also carrying in its holds 31 crates that were full of bars of gold and each crate that weighed a solid 28 lbs contained 4 big and solid gold bars. This was the property of the Bank of England which was valued at over a million pounds sterling and was being sold to India in order to alleviate the ill effects of the war time economy of their jewel in the crown.

Strangely the 14th of April also coincided with the Bengali New Year's eve and the 32nd anniversary of the sinking of the Titanic. Besides the gold that was meant to stabilize the rapidly falling Indian economy, the ship was also carrying a large quantity of hessian, sulphur, fish manure and resin. These were also all highly inflammable material. To literally add more fuel to the fire there were 10 more ships berthed in the same dock. And some of them were also loaded with inflammable cargo.

The fire it seems had started at around one o'clock in the afternoon in the number two hold of the ship, but being lunch hour nobody had noticed it. And it was only at about 2 PM that Captain Brinley Thomas Oberst, the British army officer at the Embarkation Headquarters in charge of explosives and ammunition in the Bombay docks area was informed about the fire that the alarm was sounded. Foregoing his half finished lunch, Oberst got on to his powerful motorbike and rushed to the docks. Meanwhile unaware of the lurking danger, the citizens of Bombay were merrily going about their business as usual. Then the clanging of the big brass bells of the red fire brigade engines disturbed many of those who were enjoying their afternoon siesta as the fire fighters raced towards Victoria docks from all parts of the city. The ship unfortunately could not be scuttled as the valves designed were only to let out water and not to let in. By 3.30 that afternoon thirty two fire hoses from the fire brigade engines snaked across the decks of the Fort Stikine to put tons and tons of water into the ships number two hold. The brave firemen from Mr Coombe's Bombay fire brigade standing in four inches of scalding hot water fought on bravely to put off the fire. At exactly six minutes past four the big hands of the dockyard clock stood still as the massive explosion flung out men and material like flying saucers into the streets and buildings in and around Colaba, Crawford Market, and the Fort areas. So strong was the blast that it created a massive tidal wave on the otherwise calm and serene sea and which in turn reduced the neighbouring 12 ships in the dock to scrap iron and 300 acres of the Bombay docks to rubble and dust. But that was not the end of the terrible tragedy that afternoon because half an hour later at 4.40 PM Bombay was rocked by even a bigger blast which literally threw up the Fort Stikine high up into the Bombay sky. To the citizens of Bombay it proved to be a terrible disaster as the dead and wounded bodies of their near and dear ones unknown to others were blown to bits. But to some it also proved lucky as parts of the gold bars landed in their homes or were found by passer-by's on the streets and bye lanes of Bombay's busy business district.

'Let us forget about going to Poona now,' said Reggie as he with Colonel Attiqur Rehman and Nafisa offered their services to the government of Bombay. By early next morning medical teams from the army hospital in Poona had also arrived. For the next seven days all three of them visited the hospitals and the city morgues rendering whatever aid they could and consoling the relatives of the unfortunate victims of the accident. On the third day, Colonel Attiqur Rehman while on his way to the government hospital in the Fort area noticed a shining object at the base of the Emperor of India's equestrian statue near the Prince of Wales museum and not very far from the popular Regal Cinema Hall in Colaba. The area which the locals called the Kala Ghoda meaning the black horse was a big landmark of the city. Through sheer curiosity when the Colonel picked it up and on close examination found that it was a piece of solid gold that was probably worth a fortune, he was quite puzzled. But like a good honest and disciplined soldier, he immediately went and surrendered it at the nearby Colaba police station. He felt that it would be criminal on his part to get richer at the cost of so many gallant men from the Bombay fire brigade who had sacrificed their lives doing their duty. A month later, when a reward of rupees one thousand was announced for him, Colonel Attiqur Rehman gladly accepted it. But on the very next day he gave the money to Reggie as his contribution to the Poppy Day Fund for the Indian soldiers who were disabled and maimed during the First World War.

And while Bombay was still recovering from the deadly blasts, the battle for the capture of Mount Cassino was further intensified by the allied forces. To give it a more deadly punch, the fourth battle for Cassino was now incorporated into "Operation Diadem," which was the code name for the coordinated and well planned spring offensive by all the Allied forces into the heartland of Italy. The full fledged massive attack commenced on the 11th of May at 11 a.m. along the entire front with a gigantic air and artillery bombardment. The German response was equally savage. This time it was the turn of General Anders 11 Polish Corps to deal with Major General Richard Heidricks paratroopers who once again were grimly defending Monte Cassino.

On the 16th of May, the Polish Carpathian and Kresowa Divisions attacked again with vengeance. Then savage fighting took place against the stubborn German defence. In the meanwhile the two fisted heavy punch by the formations of the US 5th Army and the 8th British Army operating along the coastline and in the LIri Valley respectively had breached the German defence at many places on the Gustav Line. Realising that to escape and fight once again would be a better option rather than to be cut off and be surrounded which would eventually lead to more deaths and a shameful surrender, General Heidrich with whatever was left of his brave paratroopers now decided to slip away and this he did with well planned tactical withdrawal operation on the night of 17/18 May.

Suddenly on the morning of the 18th of May 1944, as dawn broke over the mighty mountains there was no more firing from the ruins of the monastery. And as the sun came up, the heroic Polish soldiers triumphantly occupied of whatever little was left of the historic Benedictine Monastery. Monte Cassino had finally fallen to the Allies. Two days later on the 20th of May in a simple ceremony with Major Aftab Rehman his junior colleage from the 2nd Punjabees and the younger brother of his best friend Gul Rehman as witness, Major Ismail Sikandar Khan and Miss Gina Rossellini were declared man and wife as they signed on the dotted line of the marriage register and in front of the local registrar of marriages. This was followed by a grand party in the tented Alpha Mess of the Red Eagle Division that evening as the Pipe Band of the 2nd Punjabees went merrily round and round the tent playing their traditional popular Dogri, Pathani and Scottish tunes. A little later the officers with Gina and Ismail in the centre danced the "Bhangra' and the "Khattak' much to the delight of Mr Alberto Rossillini who was the chief guest that evening.

'No more bloody fighting for you for the time being and you will by order take your pretty bride for a week's honeymoon to any place of her choice in her own Italy,' said the GOC as he proposed a toast to the couple's good health and happiness and presented them with a silver photo frame. Not wishing to lag behind, Ismail then ordered the Mess Havildar to quickly bring in the tray of French Champagne and the fluted champagne glasses that he had specially ordered for the occasion.

'Gentlemen I would now like all of you to drink a toast to the Red Eagle Division and to my dear newly wedded wife Gina. And I must also confess that, without her and her grandfather's active involvement and cooperation with the Red Eagles, the Germans would probably be still be sitting on Monastery Hill and I as the GSO 2 Intelligence would have probably remained a bachelor all my life,' said Ismail to the thunderous cheers of his colleagues, comrades and friends.

That evening both Gina and Ismail with an atlas of Italy in front of them surveyed the places of tourist interest that were to the south of the country and had already been liberated by the allied forces. They wanted to go to some quiet place for their honeymoon that had not been ravaged by the war. And as they kept studying the atlas, suddenly Gina's eyes fell on the small coastal town of Sorrento. It was located South of Napoli and which she as a young girl with her parents had visited that place while they were on their way for a holiday to the beautiful small island of Capri. Sorrento was also the birthplace of her favourite legendary Italian poet Torquato Tasso and it was blessed with a salubrious and healthy climate too.

'You've said it darling and therefore Sorrento it shall be' said Ismail as they made love practically the whole night before departing next morning in a specially decorated military jeep for the railway station at Casserta.

On return from their honeymoon, Ismail packed up his kit bag and was soon on his way to rejoin his Division. The Red Eagles were now in hot pursuit of the retreating Germans. On the 4th of June, the news arrived that Rome had fallen. The very next day on the 5th of June 1944 in his fireside chat over the radio, the American President, Franklin Delano Roosevelt very proudly proclaimed that it was one up and two to go indicating that the time was not very far for Berlin and Tokyo to fall also.

Oblivious of what was happening in the battlefields of Italy and in Burma, Richard Pugsley on the evening of 1st June as usual routinely tuned in to the special broadcast of the BBC's programme in the French language. When the others from his Maquis outfit heard the code which meant that someone special from the SOE would be soon on his way, and that arrangements for his reception at the appointed dropping zone must be kept a closely guarded secret, the commander of the Maquis team immediately briefed all his men. At around midnight they all waited eagerly in the forest area that was closeby to the designated dropping zone for the parachutist to land. An hour later the drone of a transport aircraft was heard and a few minutes thereafter "Emile" was safely down on French soil.

Emile was the code name of the young British special agent George Millar. Starting his life as a journalist on the outbreak of the war, George later enlisted in the British army and had served in the Western Desert till he was taken a prisoner by the Germans. While being taken to the prisoner of war camp in Germany from Italy he with a fellow prisoner of war Wally Binns made a daring escape by jumping off from the running train. With the help of the local resistance they managed to get to Spain and from there back to England. His main task now was to train and organise the French Resistance to sabotage, kill and harass the Germans in support of the expected landings of the Allied armies on the beaches of Normandy.

Next day at around midnight they once again under the leadership of "Emile" assembled near the dropping zone. At around 2 a.m. they heard the drone of the expected transport aircraft that were to drop the goodies. These were special containers packed with machine guns, carbines, pistols, explosives, grenades, wireless sets, and ammunition. With the all clear given by the perimeter patrols, the Maquis Groups under George Millar and his French deputy George Molle from the village of Vielly together with the horse carts got ready to receive the precious cargo. As the "parachutages" gently floated down in the still of that dark morning, Simone Deleury, the 17 year old daughter of the team leader of the recovery group handed over the sets of torches to the members who were responsible to spot and recover with great speed the valuable containers and load them on to the horse carts. There were very strict orders that no trace whatsoever of the parachute drops in and around the dropping zone should be seen or detected by the Germans, and the Maquis had to now doubly ensure that.

It was only a week ago, that Richard Pugsley had met the 17 year old freckled faced young Simone, when he was invited for tea by her father at their small house in the village. Tall and slim, Simone with her light blue eyes and golden brown hair had a very innocent look about her, but it was her smile which captivated Richard every time she said "Merci Beaucoup" which meant thank you very much in French for the small piece of chocolate that Richard often shared with her. Chocolates were part of the survival rations that were dropped for the SOE agents in occupied France. Sometimes Simone would quietly follow Richard into the forest to have a puff of his "Pall Mall" cigarette that were also part of the composite rations and which was kind courtesy Mr Buckmaster.

Acting as a courier, Simone because of her age and innocent looks was also used by the Maquis to give them early warning of German patrols and about check points being established by the enemy for conducting physical searches of the village folk and their horse carts. She would be often seen in a blouse and skirt cycling ahead of the horse carts that were carrying the special cargo hidden under the village produce or under the haystacks, and which were being transported for distribution to the Maquis groups. At times she would Invariably stop at the German check point for the mandatory physical search to be carried out on her and on her cycle and greet the men on duty with her charming smile. Often in order to distract their attention, Simone would on purpose adjust her stockings in such a manner so that the sex hungry German sentries got a good view of her shapely long legs and inner thighs.

On the evening of the 4th of June, 1944, Simone on her bicycle acting as usual as the early warning element was on her way to a nearby fishing village on the coast of Normandy. She was on a mission to deliver a special message for the French Resistance. Following half a mile behind her was a horse cart full of arms and ammunition that were hidden under the overloaded bundles of haystacks.And under the haystack and escorting the consignment for delivery to the Maquis was Richard Pugsley with a loaded pistol in his hand. Suddenly from behind, the noise of a motor cycle was heard. It was a German despatch rider with a companion on the pillion seat. They were on their way to deliver the mail to the German troops deployed on the well fortified French coast which formed a part of the formidable "Atlantic Wall". The driver of the horse cart an elderly French farmer kept his cool and smiled at the two Germans as it overtook his cart. Then seeing the lonely Simone cycling ahead, the German motor cycle driver increased his speed and overtook her. Soon thereafter at a lonely spot on the bend of the road and at the edge of a forest, the German suddenly braked and stopped his motorcycle.The man on the pillion also got off the bike and then both the Germans started molesting Simone. Simone immediately shouted loudly for help and tried to put up a fight, but both the burly Germans were too much for her.

'I think the poor girl is in serious trouble,' whispered the horse cart driver as he with his stick nudged Richard Pugsley under the haystack. Without batting an eyelid, Richard scrambled out of the hay stack and with the loaded revolver in his pocket ran to Simone's rescue. Meanwhile the the two Germans having parked the motorcycle on a nearby village track had forcibly and physically carried the struggling Simone into the nearby forest.

Having spotted the two of them and hearing Simone's pleas to spare her, Richard silently stalked and closed up on them.Then as the two German soldiers with their pants down were getting ready for the act, Richard simply shot them in cold blood. He did not even give them a warning or time to react. And to make sure that they would not live to tell their story; he pumped in a few more bullets into their bodies.Then he told a terrified Simone to carry on with her mission and not to mention anything about this to anybody, not even to her parents till such time he had sorted out the issue completely. He also conveyed this to the elderly horse cart owner.

'But what excuse will I give if somebody questions me about my torn blouse and my dirty clothes,' said a visibly shaken Simone as she clung on to Richard for moral support'

'Just do not worry about that my child. I will get you a set of fresh clothes from the next village,' said the cart owner confidently.

While Simone on her cycle and with the horse cart following her made a dash towards the nearest village, Richard Pugsley discarded his French farmer's dress temporarily and put on one of the uniforms of the dead Germans. Sitting on the motorcycle he went at full lick to a nearby village and came back with a pair of picks and shovels.

'There must not be any trace left of the Germans, their weapons and the motorcycle,' thought Richard to himself as he pushed the motorcycle deep into the forest and camouflaged it. Then turn by turn he carried the dead bodies of the two Germans deeper into the forest. There he stripped them completely naked and having sprinkled the dead bodies with the petrol from the motorcycle, he set them on fire. While the bodies kept burning, he frantically started digging. There was hardly and hour left for the sun to set and the curfew time to begin and he had to complete his job by that time. Finally he did manage to throw the two burnt out bodies with their clothes, weapons and, equipment into the deep pit that he had dug. Then he covered it with twigs, leaves and branches and having done that he filled it with the freshly dug mud. Finally he put some more leaves and branches over their combined grave. Since there was no more time for him to dig a large pit for the motorcycle, he deflated both the tyres and waited till dawn to get on with the job. It was around sunrise on the next day, after he had dumped the motorcycle into a pit and had covered it with mud that he got back into his French farmers clothes and made his way for the secret rendez-vous with Simone and the French Resistance Group.

For the brave and courageous girl like Simone the incident was traumatic no doubt, but as promised by her she kept it entirely to herself. She knew that within the Maquis too there could be moles and she had to be very careful. From that day onwards she was ever grateful to Richard. He had not only saved her from being gang raped, but also from possible death by the two sex hungry barbarian Germans.

On the very next evening of 5th June, while Richard Pugsley was on listening watch and he kept waiting for the important coded message over the BBC's routine broadcast in the French language, George Millar once again briefed the Resistance Groups on the importance of their tasks. As it is because of the bad weather over the English Channel the allied landings had been postponed by 24 hours, and any further delay could pose a big danger not only to them, but also to the gallant paratroopers and soldiers who would be in the vanguard of the expected invasion force on the selected five beaches of Normandy and to the areas immediately behind them on D-Day.

'Gentlemen the key to the success of "Operation Overlord" depends on a great deal also upon us. The first 24 to 96 hours will be crucial for the successful establishment of the bridgeheads on all the five beaches at Omaha, Utah, Juno, Sword and Gold. Therefore, come what may we must ensure that the German tactical and strategic reserves located in depth and behind the forward German defences at Normandy are harassed and sabotaged in such a manner that even if they do get there, they should be rendered ineffective,' said George Millar.

While the sub groups from the French Resistance once again coordinated their movements and tasks, at 9.15 PM that evening the BBC made the broadcast of those memorable lines from Verlaine's famous poem "The violins of autumn". Suddenly there was pin drop silence as the rich baritone voice over the BBC announced "Blessent mon coeur d'une longueur monotone" and repeated it for a second time. Translated into English it meant "Wound my heart with monotonous languor."

'Yes that's it gentlemen, It is on,' said George Millar with a smile on his face as he in his hushed but excited tone gave out his final orders.

'Alright now all groups must rush to their battle stations and let us give Hitler the bastard and his fucking soldiers on your sacred French soil a bloody licking of their lives. And Incidentally and geographically today is also the longest day of the year and a day for which we have all been looking forward to,' added George Millar's deputy George Molle as he did the good old thumbs up sign to the various groups, while they stealthily faded away into the countryside to carry out their assigned tasks.

Meanwhile another group under the SOE operating from behind the areas near Pas de Calais were dutifully carrying out their equally important task of wireless deception. They were a part of "Operation Fortitude'. "Operation Fortitude" was a well coordinated deception plan that was made at the highest level to convince the German High Command that the main landings for the invasion force would be in the Pas de Calais area and that the landings at Normandy were just a diversionary feint. This operation was orchestrated by the XX or the 'Twenty Committee," which was the name given to it because of the numerals used. But to some others it was also known as the Double Cross Committee because this secret committee had successfully employed double agents for the task. The most important of them was "Garbo", the code name given to the Spaniard who was highly regarded by the German Abwehr. The Abwehr was the focal point of all German Intelligence gathering operations, but Garbo was now very much a part of the "Fortitude" team since the Germans were now on the losing side and Italy had already joined the Allies.

While the allied strategic deception plan kept cleverly and realistically inundating the enemy with false captured documents, maps and identities of officers and men already dead and gone as and when they were skilfully landed from the air or were washed ashore from the sea towards the enemy defences. Samir Sen operating his wireless network from the coast of Kent was also in a small way responsible with the other networks to create the fictional First United States Army Group that the Germans now believed was the main allied operational group located in South East England and it was this major force who they surmised would land in the Pas de Calais area.

That night as the huge armada set sail for the beaches of Normandy, General Dwight Eisenhower, the overall military commander of the Allied Forces popularly known as Ike together with his staff raised a toast to the success of Operation Overlord. Meanwhile George S Patton, the Commander of the fictitious First US Army Group based in South West England helped himself to another cognac as his dummy fleet with their signal network ensured the total success of "Operation Fortitude".

During the weeks preceding the invasion, Allied Air Force had dropped more bombs on the Pas de Calais area than anywhere else in France. The Germans had become so convinced that nineteen of their divisions including their main Panzer reserves that were waiting to give the Allies a bloody nose were deployed in the Pas de Calais area, and stood idle on the day of the invasion waiting for the Allied assault that never came.Though the German intelligence had also managed to learn that those two lines of Paul Verlaine's poem over the BBC would be the final warning to the French Resistance to get ready for the invasion, but they were not aware as to where the invasion would finally come. On hearing those two lines, the German 15th Army in the Pas de Calais area went on high alert, but strangely enough Rommel's Army Group B headquarters in Normandy did nothing at all. The weather was so damn foul that no one believed that any invasion was possible. Ironically and to the good luck of the Allied Forces many of their senior field commanders from the German 7th Army were in Brittany attending a military exercise designed to simulate an allied landing in Normandy. Field Marshall Rommel too was in Germany. He had gone home with a pair of new shoes for his dear wife to celebrate her birthday.

While the Allied Forces in England were getting ready to land on the beaches of Normandy, in India Mahatma Gandhi having been released from his detention from the Aga Khan Palace in Poona on 6th May, found himself to be a very lonely man. To protest against the British policy he had undertaken a fast unto death since February and his condition became so very bad and critical that the British fearing that the man might die and as a consequence of which there could be a severe backlash, they had even made secret preparations in all major towns and cities to forestall it. At the Aga Khan Palace the British had even very discreetly smuggled in two Brahmin Pundits with piles of sandal wood to conduct the Mahatma's final rites. Though the Mahatma survived, but the sandalwood fed the flames of his dear loving wife and companion.Kasturbaji. She died on 24th February. Thus in a spate of just six months, the frail Indian leader had lost both his loyal secretary and his devoted wife.With all the other Congress leaders including Nehru and Patel languishing in prisons, the Mahatma immediately on his release in his usual humble way wrote a polite letter to Mr Jinnah who with his sister Fatima were holidaying in Kashmir at that time. In that letter he only reiterated his plea to him to fight for a united and independent India. He also made a similar appeal to Nehru who was still serving his sentence in Ahmednagar jail, but it had no affect on either of them it seems.

An adamant Mr Jinnah whose sights were set on carving out a country for the Muslims of India, and who never ever went to jail simply refused to recognize the Mahatma's claim that he and only he represented not only both the Hindus and Muslims, but also the Sikhs and other minorities of India. A dejected Gandhi now felt that both Jinnah and Nehru by their rigid attitudes were more inclined to carve their names in history rather than follow their own conscience of keeping India united. The Mahatma now felt that he had been cheated not only by the Englishman, but even by the so called leaders of his own people, be they Hindus, Muslims or the leaders of the minorities from the scheduled castes and tribes. The man who on the night of 8th August 1942 at Bombay had given the call of "Now or Never" nevertheless decided to once again strive for a free and fair united India.

And while the Mahatma was contemplating his next move to keep India united, the codeword to launch 'Operation Overlord' had been given. And att first light on D-Day 6th of June 1944, as the great armada of 25,000 ships and boats of every description on a ten lane axis, and on a twenty five mile wide front appeared on the horizon of Normandy stretching between Vierville on the Sea to Caen, there was a big smile on Richard Pugsley's handsome face. He and Simone with their Maquis Group had not only sabotaged a railway engine turn table on an important railway junction, but they had also succesfully derailed a German military goods train that was carrying artillery ammunition to the Normandy front. By the end of D-Day the SOE had become a much feared organization as they with the Maquis groups were able to strike at will at the Germans anywhere and at anytime. However, the most vulnerable were the SOE wireless operators and Richard was also one of them.

A few days later on the night of 9th and 10th of June, as the bridgeheads on all the five beaches were being successfully held and expanded by the Allies albeit with very heavy casualties that had been suffered by them, Field Marshall Gerd Von Rundstedt, the Commander-in-Chief of all German troops in Western Europe requested for the release of the strategic Panzer Reserves from the German High Command, But when he was told that the Fuhrer was fast asleep and that he could not be disturbed, he first thought that it was some kind of a joke. But when he learnt that it was actually true, a frustrated 69 year old Rundsedt cursed the German High command for being so meek and subservient to Hitler. And with that the Germans lost the one and only chance that they had to throw back the allied forces back into the English Channel.

That very night Richard and Simone also got the sad news that Simone's father who was instrumental in blowing up an important railway track had been caught and executed on the spot. Richard and Simone therefore immediately left for Oradour. Oradour was Simone's grandparent's village and her mother with here two young boys aged 14 and 10 had temporarily moved there on the evening prior to D-Day.It was around midday of that Saturday, when they both quietly sneaked into the village and when Richard found everyone inside the house was in a state of complete mourning, he after offering his heartfelt condolences to the bereaved family said to Simone's mother.

"Don't worry Mademoiselle I will teach these German bastards a lesson to avenge the death of your dear husband". It seems that the family had seen so much of suffering under the German occupation army that they were not even crying. It was a strange kind of a silence as they all sat for their afternoon meal that day. And as Simone's grandfather raised a final toast for his brave and devoted son-in-law, his words got drowned by the roar of vehicle engines. A convoy of German half tracks and trucks with a company of the dreaded SS troops armed with automatic weapons had surrounded the village. They were on a mission of vendetta to settle scores. It seemed that the day before, while the 2nd Panzer Division that was known as "The Das Reich" was moving to the Normandy area through the village of St Junien, it was sniped at and as a result of which two German soldiers had been killed.

'I order all of you, men, women and children, young and old to come out of your houses and assemble in the village market square at once. We are here to carry out an identity check,' thundered the young Lieutenant Colonel Adolf Diekmann, the commanding officer of the 1st Battalion of the SS Regiment.

'Please we have no time to waste. We have to hide you or else not only yours, but all our lives will be in danger too,' said Simone's grandfather to Richard Pugsley as he with Richard's help removed the carpet, pulled the bed to one side in the bedroom and opened the trap door on the wooden floor.

'May I also keep him company,' said Simone as he hugged the old man.

'Sure my dear girl and just remain there till we get back,'said Simone's doting grandfather. Once they were safely inside the secret hiding place, the old man with his daughter quickly swept the area, put the bed and the carpet back into its proper place and very confidently with the rest of the family boldly walked out of the house to join the rest of the village folk in the market square.

Adolf Diekmaan now ordered the men, women and the young children to be separated from the men folk. And once that drill was completed, the 450 odd women and children were ordered to move inside the village church. And as soon as they were inside, the Germans locked the church. Thereafter Adolf's execution teams took the men folk in small groups to the nearby barns and shot them in cold blood. And once that was completed, the sadist Adolf Diekmann now trained his sights on the poor helpless women and children who were trapped inside the village church.

'I want no bloody survivors,' yelled Diekmaan to his executioners as the Germans lobbed smoke grenades inside the church through the naves. The church was not very far away from where Richard and Simone were hiding and they could therefore faintly hear the shouts and cries of help, but there was nothing that they could do.

Not being content with the suffocation technique which was taking too much of time, Adolf Diekmaan now ordered his troops to get inside the church and open fire with their automatics. The village now reverberated with the rat a tat of their machine guns as helpless innocent women and children were mowed down without remorse or pity.

'My God I do not know what is happening there. Please for heaven's sake let us get out and check. Afterall my entire mother, my brothers, and my grand parents they are all there,' said Simone sobbing away.

'I understand my love, but do not be stupid. We have to live for them, and remain alive to tell the world, and if we go out now we will be dead ducks too and there will be nobody to tell this tragic inhuman story of the massacre,' said Reggie while consoling her.

The Germans had now set the church on fire, but there was one middle aged woman who though she was suffocating inside the church had decided to take the chance. Under the cover of thick smoke, Marguerite Rouffanche, the 47 year old neighbour and a close friend of the Simone family took the risk and jumped out of the church window and ran into the nearby forest. The Germans were preoccupied elsewhere and did not notice her escape. Marguerite Rouffanche also had lunch that afternoon with Simone's mother and with that fall though she had broken a leg, she hid in the forest and waited for the Germans to leave. As soon as she heard the noises of the vehicles and half tracks fading away into the distance, she came limping back to Simone's grandfather's house, opened the trap door and fainted. When Richard and Simone came out and saw the terrible carnage they just could not believe that the German soldiers could be such barbarians. There was not a single survivor except for the two of them and Mrs Rouffanche. Simone was now hysterical as she saw the charred bodies inside the church and she could not even recognise her own mother and brothers.

Early next morning as the two of them carried a delirious Mrs Rouffanche in a wheel barrow to the neighbouring village, the young couple had made up their minds to become man and wife. That day and in the presence of all the villagers, Richard proposed to Simone and both of them also they vowed to take revenge on the Germans.

'Please do not think I am doing all this through pity. I really love you Simone and I sincerely do and therefore will you please marry me,' said Richard Pugsley as he chivalrously knelt on the track, kissed her hand and gave Simone a piece of chocolate.

'I love you too,' said the tall freckleD faced girl as she with tears flowing down her cheeks kissed Richard on his lips.

Meanwhile the allied landings at Normandy had not taken Hitler completely by surprise, because he too had expressed that the area around Normandy was suitable for a bridgehead and accordingly Field Marshall Rommel had heavily fortified the beaches with a series of obstacles and heavy artillery weapons. But when the German defences at Normandy slowly started to crumble, Hitler was furious. And as a measure of reprisal against the British people, he now decided to employ his secret weapon the V-1 rocket bomb. Derived from the Greek word "Vergeltungswaffen" literally meaning reprisal, Hitler ordered a hundred of them to be launched from Peenemunde on the Baltic coast. The massive rocket attack was primarily aimed at London to teach the British a lesson. It commenced on the morning of 13th of June 1944, while people in London were on their way to work, and the children were on their way to school. That morning a mad Hitler struck with sheer vengeance. The deadly rockets that were developed by German scientists and built mainly through Polish slave labour at the huge underground factory near Nordhausen was Hitler's last secret weapon. The V-1's were launched from short length catapults that the Germans had constructed at Peenemunde and they were shaped like small aeroplanes. While in flight it made a distinct buzzing sound and the deadly rockets would now spread terror and suspense on the people of London, Kent and Sussex.

On that morning of 13th June and at around 10 o'clock in the morning, Samir Sen was on his way to work at Belchley Park. As usual on that day he had stopped by at Mrs Morrison's wayside café near Trafalgar square for his customary butterless toast and sugar free black coffee. When he heard the strange buzzing noise, Samir Sen first thought it to be some aircraft that was in trouble and he therefore went on to the curb to look for it in the sky. Suddenly there was a momentary silence and seconds later the bomb exploded with a deafening noise as it hit the ground where Samir Sen was standing. The rocket bomb with its 1870 pounds of warhead had devastated the entire place. There was nothing left of Mrs Morrison, her café and Samir Sen. He had become one of the first victims of the German dreaded V-1 rocket. Luckily some shop keepers in the neighbourhood who were friendly with Mrs Morrison and who knew the young Indian, they immediately informed India House about his death.

On that very day the SOE had also successfully targeted the tanks of the 2nd Panzer Division that were moving to the Normandy front on rail transport. On reaching their final destination and as they disembarked to move on their tracks, all the tank engines had seized. Richard and Simone as part of the Maquis group had successfully siphoned off the axle oil and had replaced it with abrasive grease. And while they were celebrating their success, the tragic news arrived about the capture of Violet Szabo by the SS.

Born Violet Bushell in Paris on 26th June 1921, she was the daughter of a French mother and English father. Her parents had first met, when her father fell in love with her mother while he was serving in France during the First World War. Her father was a second hand car dealer in England and like her mother; Violet too at the age of nineteen fell in love with Captain Etienne Szabo a dashing French Foreign Legion Officer and married him. But the marriage was not even year old, when Captain Etienne died fighting in North Africa. At that time Violet was pregnant and she soon gave birth to a pretty girl whom she named Tanya. With her good knowledge of French she soon joined the SOE and did some very valuable work for them.On a moonlit night in April 1944 as the dare devil pilot of the Lysander aircraft from the 161 Special Operations Squadron with its rudimentary navigation equipment took off from the Tangmere airfield with young Violet whose code name was "Corrine", her bosses knew that she would deliver the goods. She had been tasked to get authentic information about the German Atlantic Wall on the Normandy coast and this she did with great risk to herself and had returned with the needed inputs. On Day plus1 Day, Corrine was parachuted into the Limoges area in Central France to coordinate the resistance activity there, but she was captured and taken prisoner by the SS. Richard Pugsley and Simone had only met her once and had a very high regard for her and after her capture, both Richard and Simone had now offered their services to the "Jockey Network" that had been set up by the SOE at Lyons and were active on the Mediterranean coast and on the Italian and Swiss frontiers.

A few days later, and while the allied forces on the beaches of Normandy were getting ready to break out from there, the Sen's, the Ghosh's and the Hussein family with all their daughters had gone to a music function that had been organised by The New Theatre group to honour their versatile and talented music director Mr RC Boral.

Rai Chand Boral the son of a musician himself was born in 1903 in Calcutta and he was the first one to introduce playback singing into Indian films. He was now also the most sought after music director of both Hindi and Bengali films. That evening the audience was regaled with all his hit numbers. And they were sung live on stage by none other than the versatile

Kundan Lal Saigal, Pankaj Mullick and Kanan Bala Devi. But after the function, when they all reached home, a pall of gloom and grief greeted them. A telegram by Mr Sanyal from India House had arrived giving them the sad news of Samir Sen's death in a German rocket attack over London.

In the meantime on 22nd June 1944, after the Japanese siege on Imphal was lifted, the hopes of Subhas Bose and his Indian National Army marching to Delhi with the slogan "Chalo Delhi" also became a distant dream. But Subhas Bose or Netaji as he was now reverently called was always an optimist. The Japanese had now decided to abandon the Imphal campaign, but Subhas Bose was not aware of it. On the 6th of July, 1944 Subhas Bose confidently in a broadcast over the radio from Burma assured the Indian people that the day was not very far when his forces would liberate India.

On hearing Subhas Bose's speech, a happy Naren Sen who was not aware of the actual war situation on the ground in India's North Eastern Frontier decided to treat all his friends including their wives to a movie.

'Now please listen to me everybody. My old friend Ashok Kumar the famous actor was in Calcutta a few days ago for the release of his hit film: 'Kismet' and he, had very kindly given me six passes. They are for the evening show at Chitra talkies tomorrow and that too in the box seats. I therefore do not want to hear any excuses, and all of us with our wives, and I repeat with our wives will go to see the film,'said Naren Sen with a big smile on his face as he showed the six passes to both his bosom friends. On hearing that, Dr Ghulam Hussein who was very fond of Hindi film music immediately started singing the hit song from the same film. "Door hato hai Duniya walon Hindustan hamara hai."

'Really and how very apt are those words, but the British Gora Sahibs do not seem to be keen at all to leave our sacred land,' said Debu Ghosh in good humour as he took out the half smoked fat cigar from his pocket and lit it again.

'Now since when have you become Winston Churchill,' said Ghulam Hussein light-heartedly as he sang the first four lines once again.

'But tell me did you really meet Ashok Kumar in person while he was here, and if you did why did you not tell us. We and our wives would have met him too,' said Debu Ghosh.

'Well it just so happened that the actor was here only for a day or two, and since he was very busy he had asked me to meet him at the New Theatre's film studio where the rushes of another good Bengali film was being screened. Incidentally the name of the Bengali film is "Udayer Pothey"

(Lighting The Path) and it will soon be released at the "Aleya" cinema at Gariahat.'

'But what is the star cast like,' asked Debu Ghosh.

'Well the hero of the film is the handsome Radhamohan Bhattacharjee, and the heroine is Maya Basu and the Director is none other than Bimal Roy. The same Bimal Roy if you remember with whom we all had a heated argument while he was shooting famine scenes on the streets of this city last year. The music is by RC Boral and the song "Modhugandhe Bhora 'sung by Binota Roy and Hemanta Mukherjee is already a big hit,' said Naren Sen very proudly.

'My God since when have you become such a serious cinema buff?' remarked Debu Ghosh as he put his arm around his dear brother-in-law and thanked him for the generous offer. And to reciprocate the gesture Debu poured himself another drink and loudly announced.

'All right in that case next week it will be my turn to treat every one of you including our daughters to the hilarious Charlie Chaplin film titled "The Great Dictator " which is now running to packed houses at the Metro. And the film too has a lesson for the mad Hitler who I don't think will last very long, now that the Allies are screwing the Germans from Italy in the South, from France in the West and from Russia in the East, said Debu Ghosh.

'Well in that case why should I be left behind? Therefore the week after next it will be my turn to take all of you to the Oscar winning film "Gone with the Wind" starring the handsome Clarke Gable as Rhett Butler and the vivacious Vivien Leigh as "Scarlet O'Hara," said Dr Ghulam Hussein.

'But I have been told that the film has some very torrid kissing scenes and therefore it may not be suitable for our young daughters,' said Naren Sen.

'What bloody bullshit and all our daughters starting from your Purnima Sen, to Daktar Babu's Hasina and my own Mona Ghosh are not little children any longer. They are all grown up college girls and for all of them we are all now looking for suitable life partners and I don't think there is any harm in their seeing the film too. Afterall the film is based on history and on the American civil war and there is always the first time to everything,' said Debu Ghosh while quoting a passage from Margaret Mitchell's best selling book.

'But let me also tell you all a few very interesting things about the making of this great movie and about the author of the book. This thousand plus page romantic novel set during the period of the American Civil War was written by an unknown author by the name of Margaret Mitchell. This was her first novel, and when Producer David O. Selznick bought the rights to the film by paying the record breaking price of fifty thousand dollars in 1936, everyone in Hollywood had labelled the film as "Selznick's Folly." But today it has broken all records and created history,' added Debu Ghosh in his imitable style as he had one more long drag of whatever little was left of his Corona cigar.

'Come now let us cut out all this filmi business and let us get back to serious politics. Tell me now that the Mahatma has been freed from his detention, do you think he will once again give the cry of "I want freedom now and at any cost,' as he did on 8th August 1942,'? asked Naren Sen.

' Well some of my Muslim friends who are members of the Muslim League have told me that the Mahatma is now in correspondence with Jinnah, and let us hope that some good comes out of this,'said Ghulam Hussein.

'Yes let us hope so too, and as far as giving another cry for quit India is concerned, I do not think that it will now be necessary as the one eyed Viceroy Wavell has now given clear indications that once the war is over India will get her independence, come what may,' added Debu Ghosh

'But when will that be,' said Naren Sen.

'I do not think that the day is very far because with Italy having capitulated and both Germany and Japan on the retreat, it could be another few months when this world will see peace again, but I am afraid it will not be a United India,' said Debu Ghosh.

'That I am afraid will be even worse because that would lead not only to the partitioning of the country, but it could also lead to communal violence, loot and rioting,' said Mrs Shobha Sen as she with her daughter Purnima brought in the tea tray and the plate full of hot onion pakoras.

'Yes I think Shobha is right because what is bugging the Mahatma is not when this country will get Independence but will it get divided because Mr Jinnah and his Muslim Leaguers are hell bent on getting their own Pakistan even if it is a moth eaten one," said Hena Ghosh as she brought in the plate of the Puja Prasad.".

'Now since when has Mrs Ghosh become so very interested in Indian politics," said Naren Sen some what teasingly as he helped himself to a bit of the shondesh that was part of the offering made by Hena Ghosh to the Goddess Kali after her usual weekly visit to the Kalibari at Kalighat.

'My interest in politics started from the day I got married to my politically crazy husband,' said Hena as she blushed and covered her pretty round face and her head with a little more of the plain red bordered white saree that she was wearing, and one that matched with the big red roundel of sindoor on her forehead.

'I do agree that we belong to different religions, but that by itself does not justify the demand for different nations. The Sikhs too have their own religion and so do the Parsees and the Chiristians, the Buddhists and the Jains and even the Jews who are also very much a part of this country. I also agree that they are in the minority but so are we the Muslims as compared to the Hindus. So what prevents the others from asking for their piece of the cake too,' said Dr Ghulam Hussein.

'Yes you do have a point there my dear husband, but will Mr Jinnah or Mr Gandhi or their followers agree to this logic,' said Suraiya Begum as she with her silver paandan started making a few more paans with a touch of jarda for Debu, Shobha, Hena and for herself.

'Yes and I think she is right and we also have over 500 princely states, some big, some small and some insignificant ones too, and most of them also have a mixed population. Now imagine what will happen if they too start demanding their own independent existence,' said Naren Sen.

'But why go that far. Let us take the case of our own very Bengal, where the population mix of Hindus and the Muslims is practically equal today. Yes, today we have a Muslim led government in the chair but we all speak the same mother tongue which is Bengali. Does it mean Bengal will be part of Jinnah's Pakistan, or Nehru's Bharat or shall we ask for a separate independent "Banglastan," or will be again be divided, 'said an agitated Debu Ghosh as he took out his small notebook and rattled out the population stastics of Hindus and Muslims in the Bengal Presidency that besides Bengal also included, Assam, Bihar, and also Orissa.

'There is no doubt that the Moghuls and other Muslim conquerors came to this land and ruled over us and some of them are still doing so like the Nizam of Hyderabad and the royal family of Bhopal and that of Rampur in the United Provinces, and as time went by a large number of Hindus converted to Islam. But then so did the British, the French, the Portugeese and even the Greeks under Alexander who had conquered parts of India and a lot many of us became Christians too. Therefore going by that logic does it mean that those Indians and Hindus who have taken to Christianity should also rightly demand an exclusive independent enclave of their own in some corner of India? The fact still remains that Hinduisim in India flourished much before the other great religions like Christianity, Islam, Buddhism, Jainism, Sikhism and Judaism came into this world. But that does not mean that we and only we as Hindus have a right to rule over the others in this country. The need of the moment is to show unity, trust and solidarity and hold each other's hand instead of going for each other's throat,' added a visibly angry and agitated Debu Ghosh.

'I think we have had enough of this lousy topic for the day and it is time to talk of something else that is more stimulating and exciting,' said Hena Ghosh as all their three pretty young daughters, Purnima Sen, Mona Ghosh and Hasina Hussein walked in with a big cake and twenty five small candles.

It was Debu's and Hena's 25th wedding anniversary that day and only the girls seemed to have remembered the date. The 20 year old Anup Ghosh, the youngest son of Debu and Hena also had remembered the date as he too walked in to convey the good news that he had been selected for the post of a junior clerk in the British firm of Balmer Lawrie. Touching his parents feet for their blessings, Anup presented them with a red rose each and wished them a very happy wedding anniversary.

'Thank God atleast this son of mine is still with us and hopefully will remain so and not runaway to some other far away country like the other two did,' said a happy Hena Ghosh as she put a big piece of the Kalimata 'prasadam' in her youngest son's mouth.

While the war raged in France and elsewhere, the Mahatma on 17th July 1944 striving for a united India once again wrote to Mr Jinnah and in his letter the Mahatma said.

'Today my heart once again says that I should write to you and we should meet whenever you choose. Do not disappoint me.' To that Mr Jinnah replied promptly and they decided to meet on 9th September at Mr Jinnah's Malabar Hill residence in Bombay.

Three days later on the 20th of July, 1944 there was an attempt to assassinate Hitler, but it was kept a well kept secret for a few days as the dreaded Gestapo and the SS started rounding up the plotters and started either executing them or forcing them to commit suicide. The Germans were now at the receiving end of the war and the plotters had thought that it was only by killing Hitler that could they stop this bloody ordeal and the misery that had befallen on the German people.The full details of the plot and its fall out was dramatically revealed to Arup Ghose when a middle aged and middle rung German officer who while fighting on the Russian Front had deserted on the very next day after the abortive attempt was made on the Fuhrer and he had now given himself up to become a prisoner of war. With a mixed Jewish blood, the German officer was fairly well versed in the Russian language and had served as an interpreter during the interrogation of Russian Prisoners of War on the Stalingrad Front. Though he was not a major cog in the plot to kill Hitler, but he was very knowledgeable about it. His only request to Arup was that his real name should never be revealed to anyone and whosoever he may be.

As the German officer kept talking about the plot, Arup took down the salient points in his small pocket diary. According to him it all started in the winter of 1941, when the Germans as per Hitler's directive could not capture either Moscow or Leningrad or Stalingrad, the three major Soviet cities. At that time the first German resistance cell that was composed of senior German officers had surfaced secretly on the Eastern Front. The main architect of this cell was Colonel Von Treschow, the Chief of Staff Army Group Centre. However, the prisoner of war also revealed that ever since Hitler decided to conquer Europe and get fully rid of the Jews and the non Teutonic races from the Continent, there was already a group of very senior German officers who were silently plotting to get rid of the mad Fuhrer. And these included not only the Chief of Abhewr, the head of the German intelligence Admiral Canaris and his deputy Lt Col Hans Oster, but also Colonel General Ludwig Beck the Chief of German General Staff who had resigned in protest against Hitler's expansionist policy and General Franz Halder who had taken over from Beck. Serving in the Army Group Centre during the first eighteen months of the Russian campaign was another German officer who too was totally disillusioned with Hitler's expansionist dreams and barbaric policies of extermination of those who were not of pure German blood. It was during this time that the officer concerned who was to carry out the deed became very friendly with Colonel Treschow.

The officer concerned was Claus Philip Maria Schenk Graf Count Von Stauffenberg. He was from an influential Catholic noble family from Southern Germany and was born on 15th November 1907 at Griefsteen Castle, Jetingen, some 60 miles west of Munich. In 1930, he graduated from the Miltary Academy while standing first in his batch and joined the 17th Cavalry regiment of Bamberg. In 1936, he as a Captain joined the prestigious German General Staff and had seen action in Poland, France, and Russia. He had also fought in the Deserts of North Africa with Rommel's Afrika Korps where he had been decorated for valour and bravery with the coveted Iron Cross.

In August 1942, with the ex corporal Hitler as the Supreme Military Commander directing the German war machine virtually as a dictator, Stauffenberg while on the Russian front had commented to Colonel Treschow that Hitler was mad and that only his death could retrieve the terrible mess that were now all in. On New Year's Day of January 1943, when Hitler refused to allow the German troops of Field Marshall Paulus's Sixth army that was trapped in Stalingrad to escape, Count Stauffenberg requested for a transfer to North Africa and was posted in Tunisia as Operational officer with the 10th Panzer Division.On 7th April 1943 during an enemy air raid on his headquarters somewhere near the Kasserine pass, the Count was seriously wounded. He lost his left eye, his right hand and the fourth and fifth finger of his left hand too. He was therefore sent to a hospital in Munich to recuperate, and it was in that hospital that he had finally decided come what may Hitler must be killed and the Nazi regime overthrown.

On 13th March 1943, Colonel Treschow had himself made an attempt on Hitler's life when Hitler visited the Headquarters of Army Group Centre on the Eastern front. That day he had concealed and placed a time bomb on Hitler's aircraft, but the bomb failed to detonate when Hitler flew back to Germany.

In October 1943, Stauffenberg having recovered from his war injuries was now posted as Chief of Staff to the General Army Office in Berlin. At Berlin with Colonel General Beck's blessings he now started his own planning to kill Hitler. The plan envisaged that immediately after Hitler's assassination, the coup led by the military conspirators that included 22 senior serving and retired Generals and Field Marshalls like Rommel and others would first totally neutralize the Gestapo and the SS Black Shirts and install a military government. Thereafter having taken full control, they would end the bloody war unilaterally. From that very day Stauffenberg had organised and had made plans to kill Hitler. Several attempts had also been made earlier to get rid of him, but as luck would have it with the heavy security cordon around the Fuhrer all the attempts had to be aborted at the last minute. Finally on 1st July 1944, after he was promoted to the rank of Colonel and was appointed as Chief of Staff to the General Officer Commanding the Army Reserve, Stauffenberg knew he had got his chance. He was now in a position to carry out the assassination himself and that too with comparative ease and therefore took on the responsibility with full confidence.

As the principal staff officer of Army Reserve he now had the opportunity to attend the top level War Council meetings with his immediate superior oficer. These were held at the "The Wolfsschanze" the Wolf's Liar, which was Hitler's dug out command post near Rastenburg in East Prussia. With his medical disability, he knew he would be the least suspected and therefore could get close to Hitler without even being searched.

On 11th and 15th July, 1944, he did get an opportunity but maybe it was his nerves that failed him and he aborted the plan at the last minute. But for the next War Council meeting that was scheduled for the 20th of July, Count Stauffenberg was determined to get rid of the mad Fuhrer. With the bomb hidden inside his leather briefcase he got into the aircraft that would take him to Rastenburg. On landing there he motored down to the Wolf's Liar and confidently with the bomb in the leather briefcase entered Hitler's command post. Inside the big underground bunker Hitler as usual was presiding over his top military commanders and ridiculing some of them for their incompetence. Count Stauffenberg seizing the opportunity carefully primed the time bomb that was inside his briefcase and carefully slid it back under the table. Then making an excuse that he had to make an important phone call, he came out of the bunker and walked towards the waiting staff car. A minute or so later at 12.40 in the afternoon there was a violent deafening explosion and thinking that he had finally got rid of the mad man, he asked the staff car driver to take him post haste back to the airfield where a waiting aircraft was waiting to fly him back to Germany. Thinking that Hitler was finished once and for all, he therefore contacted Berlin on the wireless set and gave the code word "Valkyrie" confirming that his mission had been successful. "Valkyrie" which meant the chooser of the slain was the code word for the coup to begin. But the Count was sadly mistaken. Hitler had survived the attempt with only minor injuries. Ironically the bomb was one of the many British make ones that had been confiscated by the Abhewr. By late evening most of the key coup leaders had been arrested and on that very night itself Oberst Claus von Stauffenberg was executed by a firing squad in the courtyard of the German war ministry. It was simply bad luck for the plotters and even Field Marshall's Rommel's life was not spared.

'On 17th July, three days before the unsuccessful attempt on Hitler, Rommel's staff car was strafed by a pair of allied fighter aircrafts and he was severely wounded. He was therefore immediately taken to a hospital and thereafter had returned to Germany to convalesce. Once the plot was discovered, Hitler's once favourite General was given the option either to face the execution squad or commit suicide. Rommel chose the second option', said the captured German officer with tears in his eyes.

'Oh How I wish Hitler had been eliminated. That would have not only shortened the bloody war, but it would have also saved many more lives,' said Arup Ghosh as he sat down to send an exclusive despatch of the plot to his paper the "Morning Star"

By end July 1944, the war in Europe was heading towards victory for the Allied Forces and to bolster the morale of his Indian troops in Italy, the King Emperor George the Sixth visited them in their battle positions. He had earlier visited the 4th Indian Division in Tripoli and that was in June 1943, when the front was relatively quiet. But this time he was visiting them again right in the battle zone and at a time when the 3/12 Frontier Force Regiment was getting ready to launch their attack on Campriano, a strong German defensive position on the crest of a ridge some three kilometres east of the road to Florence. While watching the heavy concentration of artillery fire from a forward observation post that was being directed against the enemy defences, the King having recognised Major Sikandar Ismail Khan who had accompanied his GOC said to him

'Well Major Ismail I hope you still have the lucky gold coin with my great grandmother's face on it, and congratulations for adding the DSO to your MC. I have also been told that you have now mastered the Italian language too.'

'Not only that your majesty but he has also married a nice and homely Italian girl,' added Major General Halsworthy, the General Officer Commanding the Indian Red Eagle Division.

'Well then congratulations once again,' said the jovial and sporting King as he expressed his desire to personally decorate Sepoy Kamal Ram from the 3/8 Punjabees for his having won the coveted Victoria Cross in an action on the Liri River on 12th May 1944 and during which the sepoy was badly wounded. It just so happened that Sepoy Kamal Ram was convalescing somewhere in the rear but nobody knew exactly where he was. So a desperate search for Sepoy Kamal Ram now began and frantic messages were sent over the wireless to locate him. In his excitement the duty operator from the divisional signal regiment despatched the message in all directions enquiring for a Colonel Ram instead of Kamal Ram. Luckily Kamal Ram was found well in time for the investiture that was scheduled to be held with a ceremonial parade for the King in another 48 hours.

In late July 1944, while the German SS were busy rounding up the plotters, Richard Pugsley with Simone reported for duty at the "Jockey Network" in the Rhone valley. The Jockey network was being run by Francis Cammaerets and Cristine Granville. Son of Belgian father and an English mother, Francis Cammaerts was born in England. After completing his Masters from Cambridge he first became a school teacher. But after the death of his brother who was in the Royal Air Force, Francis who was once a pacifist in July 1942 was recruited into the SOE. In March 1943, he was flown to Compeigne where he joined the "Donkeyman Network". But after the network had been penetrated by the German intelligence, Francis under the code name of "Roger" shifted to the Rhone valley.

Richard and Simone were also delighted to meet "Roger's young and pretty deputy, Mrs Christine Granville. The 26 year old lady born in Poland was married to Jersy Gizycki and when Poland was invaded by the Germans they happen to be in Addis Ababa. And from there like many other Poles they went and settled in exile in England. Expressing her desire to fight for Polish freedom she was eventually recruited by the SOE. Richard could hardly imagine that the young lady in a simple skirt and blouse, with delicate features, without any make up and with her short dark hair that she always carelessly combed could ever be a spy. But she had also been employed earlier in quite a few hazardous missions inside occupied Europe and had been arressted not once but twice by the Gestapo earlier. The first time it was on the Slovakian Polish border and then later in Hungary, but the courageous and spirited lady both the times had managed to escape from custody. On D-Day 6th of June, Christine was dropped into occupied France to join the "Donkey Network."

Nicknamed L'ami Anglais, or the friendly Englishman, the tall and dashing "Roger" was loved by one and all. He was a man who took risks and adhered strictly to the basic and simple principles of security. He never used a telephone, neither did he visit cafes or bars and never ever ate the huge meals that were available only on the black market. If arrested he would tell others to confidently give out their cover names and occupation and thereafter in order to put the Germans off, he would tell them to bite their lips hard, swallow the blood and then keep frequently spitting it out. The Germans who were shit scared of the tuberculosis disease would then give up interrogating them and this was one novel way of getting them off their backs.

On the 10th of August, Simone had a very narrow escape. A coded message had arrived indicating that the allied landings would also soon begin in the South of France and that the Jockey network should be fully geared up to assist the operations through sabotage, disinformation and assassination of important and senior SS officers. The number one target for them would be the butcher of Lyon, Klaus Barbie. Klaus Barbie, the son of a school teacher was born in the village of Bad Godesburg in 1913 and in 1937 at the age of 24 became a member of the Nazi Party. He was now the head of the dreaded

Fourth Section of the Gestapo at Lyon. A dedicated sadist by nature, Klaus Barbie had only a month ago captured and deported to Auchwitz 44 Jewish children in the age group of four to thirteen. Though they were hidden in the village of Izieu, but Barbie had found them. Klaus was also responsible for the arrest and torture unto death of Jean Moulin on 8th July 1943.

Jean Moulin born on 28th June 1899 was a great patriot. In September 1941, having contacted General Charles De Gaulle and other French leaders in exile in London, he was parachuted back into France on New Year's Day 1942 with the daunting task of organizing the French resistance. He moulded eight other major resistance groups to form the CNR, the National Council of The French Resistance. Though he was brutally tortured to death, the brave and audacious Jean Moulin who never even carried a gun did not reveal his true identity and role to the Gestapo that "Max" was his cover name. He had been betrayed and had died like the valiant and legendary Joan of Arc.

Simone was a very great admirer of the French Hero and martyr. On the morning of 11th August,1944 she was on a solo mission to deliver the coded message to a Maquis Group regarding the expected allied landings between Cannes and Toulon in the area of the Cote D'Azur. Code named 'Operation Dragoon' by the allies, the landings were originally scheduled to coincide with D-Day, but because of shortages of landing crafts it was now scheduled for the night of 14/15 August. When Simone got into her railway compartment at Lyon, a squad of the SS storm troopers with two ladies in German uniform entered the carriage to carry out a physical search of all the travellers and their respective baggages. The SS it seemed had been tipped off by an informer that weapons and ammunition were being smuggled out for distribution to members of the French Resistance. Without flinching Simone bit her lower lip as hard as she could and then started coughing. By the time her turn came to be searched she had spitted out enough blood for the search party to be convinced that she was suffering from acute TB. The coded message giving details of the tasks to be conducted by the various Maquis groups was written on a length of a toilet paper roll which Simone had concealed inside her lower undergarments. Luckily the search on her was only a cursory one since the Germans were scared of even touching her. Had she been caught the whole game would have been up and Simone too would have faced the firing squad with the two other men who were caught with a dozen small arms and ammunition. Three days later, on the afternoon of 15th August, Simone together with the fisher folk people of Provence in Southern

France warmly greeted the American GI's of General Patch's US Seventh Army. "Operation Dragoon' had commenced successfully.

Sometime in the afternoon of 11th August, while Simone was on the train to the French Reviera, Richard Pugsley and Christine Granville at Lyon got the terrible news that Francis Cammaerts with another agent who were on their way for an important meeting in Southern France had both been arrested and taken to the Gestapo headquarters in Digne.Instructing Richard to pass on the message immediately to Buckmaster, Cristine Granville took a bold decision to personally go to the rescue of her leader. Late in the evening of 14th August as the paratroopers for the allied landings in Southern France were getting ready for the final count down, a calm and courageous Christine at the risk of her own life boldly walked into the office of Albert Schenck, the liaison officer between the French Prefecture and the Gestapo. In very plain language she told Schenck that the Maquis were aware of what has happened to their leader and if he valued his own life then he should help in getting the two men released immediately or else he too should be prepared to face death. She also conveyed to Schenck that not only was she a British agent but she was also Cammaerts wife and a neice of General Montgomery. Ofcourse it was all a big bluff because neither was she married to "Roger" nor did she ever come across Monty in her life. But she confidently pulled it off very well. Schenck who was now fully aware that the days of the Germans in occupied France were numbered and with the two million francs promised for the release, he immediately contacted the Gestapo Chief Max Waem. On receiving the payment both men were released unconditionally. The next day it was all celebrations and Richard Pugsley's admiration for Christine had now gone up sky high.

By the 15th of August 1944, General George S Patton's Third US Army had broken through the German defences at Avaranches in the Cotentin Penisula and his armoured columns together with the French 2nd Armoured Division under the command of Major General Leclerc now wheeled westwards and were heading hell for leather towards the French capital. A frustrated and maniacal Hitler now ordered his Generals to stem the rot but in doing so they themselves were caught in a trap inside the Falais Pocket. The Fuhrer now contemplated to burn Paris and ordered the German garrison commander of Paris, General Dietrich Choltitz to get ready for the task.On that very day in Paris there was a strike by the police and the metro, and a call had been given by Colonel Rol and other French patriotic leaders to the people of France to start an insurrection. Two days later on 17th August, in order to augment the signal network for the likely insurrection by the Parisians to liberate their own city. Richard Pugsley with Simone arrived in Paris.

For the next seven days and till the evening 24th of August, street combats inside the barricaded city continued intermittently. General Eisenhower had initially ordered his advancing forces to bypass the city, but later on being convinced personally by General DeGaulle that the Germans inside Paris were willing to capitulate and surrender unconditionally, Ike ordered the advance elements of the 2nd French Armoured Division to head for Paris. At around 9 PM on 24th August, 1944 Captain Drone with a few tanks arrived at the Hotel de Ville. That night a crest fallen General Choltitz and his staff who regularly enjoyed the nightlife and the food and wine of Paris knew that it was all over. Cholitz loved Paris and had decided to disobey Hitler's orders to burn the beautiful city. On the very next afternoon at 1530 hrs on the 25th of August, General Choltitz signed the instrument of surrender.

'Well I guess now that Paris is once again free I think its time now for us to get married, too' said Richard to Simone as they together with the vast crowd of Parisians and French people gathered near the Arc de Triomphe on that lovely Saturday afternoon of the 26th of August to acclaim and greet General De Gaulle and his valiant Free French Forces.

Born in Lille on 22nd November 1890, Charles De Gaulle the son of a school teacher after graduating from the French Military Academy was wounded thrice during the First World War and was taken prisoner by the Germans at Verdun. After the German invasion in 1940, he refused to honour the French Government's truce with Hitler and while in England formed the Free French Governent in exile.

As Richard and Simone walked with the huge long procession behind the tall French hero to Notre Dame, Simone kissed Richard and expressed her wish to get married inside the historic and famous cathedral.

'So it shall it be,' said an elated Richard as he happily lifted Simone high up in his hefty arms and returned the kiss. On Thursday 31st August and on the day the seat of the French Provisional Government was transferred to Paris, there inside the holy church of Notre Dame, Richard Pugsley and Simone Deleury were pronounced man and wife.

Through out the month of August, while the Allied Forces kept up the pressure on the Germans both on the Western and Eastern Fronts, Gandhi and Jinnah too kept corresponding with one another on the issue of a united India or a divided India. Meanwhile inside the Ahmednagar prison, when Pandit Nehru also received the happy news that on 20th of August he had become a proud grandfather of a buxom boy, he promptly wrote a congratulatory note to his daughter Indira who was then in Bombay and in that he also mentioned that the new born was probably the 4,000,00001st Indian born that day. A few days later Indira Gandhi wrote back to her father and she attached with it a list of 12 probable names that had been selected by her aunt and Pandit Nehru's sister Mrs Hutheesingh for the new child. The names ranged from Satyavarta, Suvarta, Abhimanyu, Indrajeet, Rajeeva, Rajat and few others including the name Rahul. Giving her own choice from the attached list Indira had preferred the name Rahul though she also mentioned in the letter that Rajat and Rajeeva were nice names too. However, she gave her father the privilege to choose a name of his own liking for his first grandson.

On the 4th of September, Pandit Nehru received another letter. This was from his sister and wherein when she mentioned that the family had already started calling the infant Rahul, Pandit Nehru somehow was not pleased at all with the name and he also gave his reasons for it too. He conceded that the name Rahul wasn't a bad choice, but wrote back to say that Lord Buddha's only son was also Rahul. However, when Buddha came to know about the birth of his son he exclaimed that coming into this world of Rahula at a time when he himself was planning to renounce his kingdom was going to act as a new "Bandhan" or a fetter for him. Pandit Nehru therefore wrote back to his daughter to send him a few more names for his selection. Then having had her son's horoscope made, Indira Gandhi also attached an English copy to the original Gujrati version and send it to her father.And in that she wrote that Rajeev had five planets in one house and according to the Jyotish that was indeed a very good sign. And from that day Rahul became Rajeev.

And while Pandit Nehru in jail was celebrating his first grandson's birth, the Allied Forces in Western Europe were going hammer and tong against the Germans. With both the important capital cities of Rome and Paris now in the hands of the allies and the Vichy Government In France having fallen, and with Mussolini's writ no longer running in Italy, Hitler decided to wreck havoc on England's capital London.

In September, with vengeance he unleashed his new V2 rockets. The V2 was a deadly liquid filled rocket that travelled at supersonic speed and carried 2000 lbs of high explosive warhead. The allies had no weapon initially to counter the destruction that the V2 bombs were now causing both in terms of devastation and the loss of innocent lives.

'We will give it back to them,' said Winston Churchill while directing his Air Chief Marshall to muster the maximum number of heavy bombers for daily raids on Berlin and the rich industrial areas of the Ruhr.

On 3rd September 1944, while Pandit Nehru and other Indian political leaders of the Congress were still languishing in jail, the 2nd World War entered its sixth year of devastation and misery, and on that day England also solemnly observed it as a national day of prayer. In India too Gandhi prayed for the early end of the war and for a rapprochement between the Congress and the Muslim League. Six days later on 9th September, Gandhi called on Mr Jinnah at his sprawling bungalow in Bombay to resolve the differences between their respective stands. But the talks failed as Gandhiji was opposed to the two nation theory, while Jinnah insisted that Muslims of India where ever they were in majority in any particular state they deserved the right for their own self determination. Disputing Gandhiji's claim that he and he alone stood for the whole of India and irrespective of class creed or religion, Jinnah simply refuted the argument by saying that it may be true for all the Hindus but definitely not for the Muslims.

And while in India the one eyed Viceroy Wavell got busy trying to find a way out of the Gandhi-Jinnah impasse, in Italy, the Italian Army joined the advancing Allies with bands and flags flying to defeat the Germans. In early September, the three Indian divisions, the 4th, the 8th and the 10th now also were ready to evict the Germans from the Gothic Line. It was one of the greatest defensive barriers on the high Appenine Mountains which began on the Adriatic plains and among the rolling ridges that was anchored to the buttress of the tiny city republic of San Marino.

Till a month ago life in the big German occupied Italian cities in Northern Italy was very gay and lively for the German senior commanders as they attended parties galore night after night and returned home in the wee hours of the morning to sleep until noon. But it was no longer the case now as active Italian partisan groups sought their prey in dark alleys, in the woods and on lonely roads. They also acted as eyes and ears for the advancing allied forces while providing them with real time and authentic intelligence about the whereabouts of senior German officers and commanders.

One day in mid September, when Major Ismail was informed through a reliable source that the same General Heydrich who was last heard of at Cassino was planning to hold a lavish farewell dinner party at his palatial villa in Florence before moving to his tactical headquarters on the Gothic line, he decided to make the party for General Heydrich and his guests even more livelier with some real fireworks. So while the party was in full swing with champagne flowing like water, the allied bombers zeroed in on to the lucrative target and pounded the place, while Heydrich and his guests ran helter skelter looking for cover under the tables and behind the well stocked bar.

In early October, news arrived that the Red Eagles should be relieved immediately by the 10th Indian Division since they were urgently required for operations in Greece. Major Ismail Sikandar Khan because of his fluency in the Italian language was therefore now posted as the new GSO2 Intelligence of the 10th Indian Division under Major General Reid. While the relief was in progress, Ismail Sikandar Khan was surprised to receive a letter from his wife Gina informing him that she was pregnant. In her letter she also mentioned about the reprisals that were being carried out by the Germans and especially by the dreaded SS and the Gestapo against Italian collaborators and Italian Jews. According to Gina it all began from the day the Italians threw in the towel and it progressively became more and more repressive after the fall of Rome.The brutal example for such ruthless killings of innocent Italians and Jews however started after 23rd March, 1944, when on that day in the Via Rasella area of Rome's historic centre, a group of Italian resistance fighters targeted a marching company of German SS military police troops with bombs and grenades. The Via Rasella attack was planned and executed by a few young men and women and included a laboratory worker, a government clerk and a bunch of highly motivated Italian university students. They had observed that the German military police company routinely used the same route and sang the same damn song while passing through the narrow passage way of the Via Rasella on their way back from the shooting range to the barracks. As a result of this attack, 33 German soldiers had died and a large number were seriously wounded. Hitler's orders for the reprisal were very specific. He wanted 10 Italians killed for every German soldier and demanded that the executions must be carried out within the next twenty four hours.

The man who finally received that order to execute that macabre task was the senior most SS officer in Rome, Lieutenant Colonel Herbert Kappler wrote Gina. Herbert Kappler in turn delegated this task to two of his junior SS Officers, Karl Hass and Erich Priebke. On 24th March, Herbert Kappler in order to meet the Fuhrer's twenty four hour deadline compiled a list of 335 civilians that included petty offenders who were already serving minor sentences in the jail, a few for their anti fascist activities and 75 innocent Jews who according to Karl Hass were going to die sooner or later in any case either at Auschwitz or at some other Nazi extermination camp. To be on the safe side, Kappler also added an extra five to the 330 required by him. This was the same Gestapo organization that had eliminated her own family and had also despatched a few thousand of innocent Italian Jews from Rome to the Auschwitz gas chambers only a few months earlier added Gina in her letter.

According to her information the 335 Italians old and young, and some of them still in school were huddled into military trucks which took them to the Adreatine caves. With their hands tied behind their backs in groups of five they were then taken inside the cave and executed with a bullet each on the back of their heads. In the last paragraph Gina wrote that she was sending the letter in a sealed envelope through a young Italian Captain who had come home to Cassino on a spot of leave. The young Captain was a friend of the family and according to him he was presently attached to some unit of the Fourth Indian Division and she therefore hoped that Ismail would receive the letter.She finally closed the letter by saying that she too probably would be getting closer to him in time and distance as she was planning to visit some old friends of the family at Milano. But that would be only when the Germans also surrendered which according to her should not take very long, now that the Italian people and the Italian army were part of the allied forces. She also mentioned that though Hitler and his Nazi Party were still backing the Fascist Mussolini and his cohorts in Northern Italy, but their numbers were slowly dwindling since the Italian Partisan Groups were now actively shadowing and eliminating them.

Ismail felt delighted in receiving Gina's letter and was even more thrilled when he knew that soon he too would become a father. Now that the Italian postal services were returning back to normal in central and southern Italy, Ismail Sikandar Khan replied back immediately expressing his undying love for Gina and the child. He ended the letter with a word of prayer to his Allah and to Gina's Moses.

'My dearest darling let us pray to the Almighty to end this war soon and to bless us with a son whom we shall name after Monte Cassino that beautiful ruined town of yours where I first met you. We shall name him Cassinolini Ismail Khan. '

By early October 1944, in Italy the 10th Indian Division of the British 8th Army had reached the Gothic Line, but the German's fought on heroically. The American 5th Army too had had crossed the River Arno and were advancing towards Bologna. In France the American 3rd Army under General George S Patton had broken the back of the German defences and was now racing towards the German frontier. On the Eastern Front the Russian armies under Marshall Zhukov were also making rapid progress towards the Polish-German border. And in the Far East and in Burma, the Japanese forces on land and on the sea too were being relentlessly pursued by the Allied Forces.

On 26th July, the Japanese Prime Minister Tojo had resigned and by then in Subhas Chandra Bose's INA there were desertions by the hundreds. The fighting qualities of the INA and their positive effect on the morale of the Indian troops of the British Indian Army on which Subhas Bose had so heavily counted upon was simply not there. In order to see what was happenning, Subhas Bose left for North Burma and all he witnessed was the miserable state of his once proud Azad Hind Fouj. Starved and suffering from all kinds of tropical diseases they were in a pitiable state. A born optimist though, Subhas Bose returned to Rangoon to take the salute at a ceremonial parade to honour those who had fallen and those who had returned as heroes to fight another day.

On that autumn day of October, 1944 as Subhas Bose dressed immaculately in the military uniform of a General with shining boots and a side cap over his head walked up to the dais to take the general salute, he was cheered by the huge crowd which also included a few Japanese generals, Burmese ministers, prominent Indian residents and Burmese citizens. While addressing the parade that listened to him attentively and in complete silence he reiterated that all was still not over. Subash Bose also reminded them about the solemn oath that each one of them including him had taken to fight or die for the country. Finally he concluded with the words. 'Ladies and Gentlemen let us fight for victory till death. For there can be no greater sacrifice than that in a true soldier which you all are.'

With the address over, the march past soon began. Leading the parade was the women's contingent from the Rani of Jhansi Regiment. But as they neared the saluting base an air raid siren was sounded. Soon thereafter was heard the drone of aircrafts which grew louder by the seconds. Within the next minute or so the group of British Royal Air Force fighters came sweeping along to raid the Burmese capital. As the spectators ran for cover, the parade contingents kept marching on and Netaji stood calmly on the dais to take the salute. On noticing the lucrative target, the fighters now swooped down over the parade ground and straffed the area. The parade had been caught off guard as half a dozen of them were killed and a fairly large number were wounded. Amongst them was Swarup's young wife Yeshwant Kaur from the Rani of Jhansi Regiment. Swarup Ghosh who was witnessing the parade seated in the official's gallery with the help of an Indian resident immediately rushed her to the nearest hospital in the gentleman's own small Austin car, but by the time she was brought to the operating table she was no more. A sad and heart broken Swarup Ghosh in order to avenge the death of his dear wife that very evening with the permission of the high command donned the INA soldier's uniform. He was no longer willing to remain in the back ground and decided to serve as one of Netaji's many bodyguards.

On that day of 14th of October, when Yeshwant Kaur died in Rangoon, a strange tragedy was unfolding itself in Field Marshall Rommel's house at Herrlingen inside Germany. Rommel after the air attack on his car was still convalescing, but he had been under suspicion for the plot to kill Hitler. His wife and only son Manfred who was now 15 years old were aware of it. Early that very morning Manfred had returned home on a spot of leave from the anti aircraft detachment that was deployed nearby and in which he was serving as a member of the crew. That morning the father and son after a long time had breakfast together and till noon everything seemed to be alright. Then a dark green car with a Berlin number plate stopped in front of the gate and two German General Officers got out and came inside the garden. When they clicked their heels, said Hail Hitler and saluted, the Field Marshall. Rommel was not in the least surprised. He was in fact expecting them any day. General Burgdorf and General Maisel then took Rommel aside and said something to him very softly. Requesting them to sit in the drawing room, Hitler's once blue eyed Field Marshall then went up to his wife's room and told her that in the next quarter of an hour or so he will be a dead man since the option available to him is either to die quietly by taking the poison that the two Generals had brought with them, or face a firing squad and be condemned in public. The poison would kill him in three seconds and that according to Rommell was the best option. Firstly it would save his own family and secondly there will be no further harassment of his staff as promised by the High Command. Moreover a cover story would also be made saying that the Field Marshall had died of a sudden stroke and he would be given a proper State funeral with full military hoinours in his own town of Ulm.

After convincing his wife, son and his ADC Captain Aldinger that they too were all now sworn to secrecy, Rommel went to his room to change into his Field Marshall's uniform. He donned the brown civilian jacket over his Afrika Korps Field Marshall's uniform. That was always his favourite because it had an open collar; He then looked himself into the mirror for the last and final time to adjust his peak cap and then returned back to the hall for his final journey to eternity. As soon as he entered the hall his little daschund jumped up to greet him. Having patted the dog, the Field Marshall like a true soldier with the Field Marshal's baton in his hand walked proudly out of the house. The two Generals waiting at the gate raised their right hands in salute and while the SS driver stood to attention and swung the car door open, Rommell with his Field Marshall's baton under his left arm once again shook hands with his son Manfred and his loyal ADC and got into the car. As the car drove off quickly, Manfred and his mother said a prayer. Soon it went up the hill and then disappeared round the bend on the road.

The car travelled for about half a mile or so and stopped on the curb of the road adjacent to a wooded area. A squad of SS armed men had already secured the place by blocking the road to all civilian traffic. They were also instructed to open fire on the Field Marshall in case he resisted or tried to escape. A minute or so later General Maisel and the SS driver got out of the car. General Maisel then ordered the driver to disappear for ten minutes. Once the driver was out of sight, General Burgdorf sitting next to the Field Marshall took out the poison capsule and gave it to Rommel. Without showing any signs of forgiveness, Rommel simply put it to his mouth. A couple of seconds later with his mouth frothing Rommell slumped on his seat and the Field Marshall's baton that he was so very proud off carrying slipped out of his hand. Twenty minutes later as planned the telephone rang in Rommel's house to announce that while Rommel was being taken for his treatment to hospital, he had succumbed to his war injuries. At his funeral in his own hometown of Ulm the representative from the German High Command, a senior General by rank eulogised the hero of Germany before finally placing the wreath that bizarrely was sent by Hitler, his executioner.

And while the Germans mourned the loss of their dynamic Field Marshall, in late October, Major Gul Rehman from the First First Punjabees was granted a week's casual leave to visit his wife and family who were now in Calcutta. Zubeida was expecting her second child and in order to be a little more nearer to her husband she had decided to have the delivery of the child at her aunt Suraiya's new sprawling bungalow at the junction of Harrison Road and Mirzapur Street.

On 23rd October, 1944 while Major Gul Rehman was waiting at the Dimapur airfield to board a returning American Air Force Dakota flight to Dum Dum, he was pleasantly surprised to be greeted by Major Daler Singh Bajwa his old pal from the Indian Military Academy days. Major Bajwa with his company of Sikh troops from the Maharaja of Kashmir's 4th Jammu and Kashmir Infantry, which was also known as the "Fateh Shibji" Battalion was also waiting to be air lifted to the Burmese front. The 4th KI as it was popularly known was not only the oldest, but it was also a crack State Force Battalion and had been specially selected by Maharaja Hari Singh himself for operations in Burma. It was now under the command of their new Commanding Officer Lieutenant Colonel Narain Singh Sambyal and had been earmarked to be part of 9 Infantry Brigade of the Indian Red Ball Division. It was a grand reunion for both the officers as they hugged and exchanged notes about each other's family and about Major Ismail Sikandar Khan who had found for himself an Italian wife.

'In that case we three musketeers with our families must have a grand reunion once this bloody war is over and the venue will be none other than the beautiful vale of Kashmir,' said Major Daler Singh as they parted company.

'May be we will bump into each another again somewhere later inside Burma,' said Gul Rehman as he boarded the Dakota and gave a farewell salute to his old friend.

On arrival at Dum Dum airport, Major Gul Rehman picked up a copy of the Calcutta Statesman and was shocked to read about the death of Field Marshall Rommel. Despite the fact that Rommel was a German, Gul Rehman was a great admirer of the Desert Fox and his capabilities as a great military commander. He even kept a photograph of the man dressed in his favourite Afrika Korps uniform and that had the Iron Cross prominently displayed around his neck. Moreover like him, Rommel too was from the infantry. The German propaganda machine had hidden the truth and reported that the Field Marshall had died of his wounds. As cadets in the Indian Military Academy it was drilled into each one of them that one should never under estimate the capabilities of the enemy commander. In fact his weak and strong points should always be kept in mind while deciding on a course of action. And General Monty too when fighting the Desert Fox in Africa had always kept this principle in mind and he too like Gul Rehman had kept his adversary's photograph prominently displayed in front of his desk. That day as he made his way from Dum Dum in a taxi, he remembered the great battle of El-Alamein and in which he too had taken an active part.

Gul Rehman's sudden arrival took everyone by surprise. As a good soldier he never even informed them of his coming. For all the soldiers fighting a war there may not be another tomorrow and moreover there was also heavy censorship of all letters. On seeing his father, the five year old Aslam ran and jumped into his father's arms. Two days later there was one more addition to Gul Rehman's family when his wife Zubeida delivered another boy and the happiest person was the grandfather Colonel Attiqur Rehman. He immediately named him Fazal Rehman Khan.

Despite the strict rationing of sugar, rice and other day to day essential food products, but for the next ten days it was one big reunion with parties galore as the Hussein family, with the Rehman's, the Ghose's and the Sen's celebrated Gul Rehman's home coming. A few days later while missing his old friend Major Ismail Sikandar Khan, Gul Rehman wrote a long letter to him. It was datelined 28th October, 1944—Calcutta.

My Dearest Friend and Brother Ismail,

I arrived here in Calcutta a few days ago on a spot of casual leave to look up my family. Incidentally I am now a father twice over as Zubeida has produced little Fazal. It is therefore one big round of parties ever since I landed here and we are all missing you. How I wish you were here too.

Before I give you any news from the Burmese Front, let me first update you with who is where and doing what.To begin with though presently my parents are here in Calcutta, but they have now moved back into my grandfather's old big haveli in Peshawar and both of them are enjoying the retired life. They are now very much a part of Peshawar's so called high society and one can see them regularly around the bridge tables in the Club. But Dad and Mum do not partner each other and neither do they play on the same table for obvious reasons. Dad's regular partner is his old friend Dr Khan Sahib who is now the Chief Minister of the Province and he is mad about bridge. The only thing Dad complains about everyday is the rationing and the spiralling prices of foodstuffs.

All of us are staying in Dr Ghulam uncle's new palatial bungalow, which also has a big garden around it. However, the only minus point about the house is its location. It is right in the middle of the hustle bustle of the city. The reason given for the selection of the site was purely business oriented. You see now that his son Nawaz has also qualified as a gynaecologist, the plan ultimately after the war is over is to construct a large nursing home adjacent to the bungalow. With India's biggest pastime being the quick production of more and more children, I am sure they will do roaring business all the year round.

My cousin Haseena, Ghulam Uncle's daughter who has just turned 18 will be completing her graduation next year. She is no longer all that skinny and in fact she now looks quite attractive. Therefore Aunty Suraiya has already started making enquires for a good match for her and if you have somebody in mind do let my aunt know. But he has to be a Mussulman and that too a Sunni.

Uncle Debu Ghosh's family has recently received some bad news. Their Sardarni daughter-in-law Yeshwant Kaur who was married to their second son Swarup died in an air raid over Rangoon. Since none of the members of the Ghosh family had ever met her, the news about the death of the poor girl was taken by the family somewhat matter of factly. Their eldest son Arup is married to a Russian girl. Presently he is covering the war as a correspondent with the advancing Russian Army on the Eastern Front. The third son Anup now 21 years old has joined the British Company of Balmer Lawrie in Calcutta as a junior clerk. And according to Aunty Hena it is better to work as a pen pushing 10 to 5 Babu (Clerk) than to have a few pips on ones shoulders. She feels that at least one son should remain at home with her in Calcutta rather than be serving in some Godforsaken place like El Alamein in North Africa or Kalewa in Burma which one cannot even find in a school atlas.Their daughter Mona Ghosh who is a very dear friend of my cousin Haseena has very confidentially conveyed to my sister Shenaz that she and Ronen Sen from the Sen family are madly in love with each other but the biggest hurdle for them to get married is that they are related and more so because they are also first cousins. I as a senior counsellor have however advised them that in case they are really serious about marriage then they should both take their parents into confidence as soon as possible. I agree that in the beginning there will be a few road blocks created by some of the senior distant relatives from both sides, but that should not matter if they really love each other and now that both are adults lawfully they cannot be stopped either. I have also advised Mona that she should quietly get both their horoscopes read by some Panditji, but without disclosing the family connection. And if it matches then they should boldly take the plunge and with the blessings of their respective parents get married. Let's see how it figures out in the days to come. To build up her morale I also told her that besides the Parsees and the Muslims who marry legally their own cousins or near relations, even in South India in traditional high caste Brahmin families this is quite common.

Now as far as Uncle Naren Sen's family is concerned, their eldest son Samir became a victim of Hitler's V-! Rocket attack on London and died a few months ago.Their second son Ronen Sen has turned out to be a bright spark. After joining the Bengal Civil Service in the officer cadre he is presently posted as an SDM, Sub Divisional Magistrate somewhere in North Eastern Assam and is actively involved in providing logistic support to the Chindit Groups who are now deep inside Burma. Incidently the word "Chindit" is the Burmese word for lion.The Sen family's only daughter, Purnima Sen with her round face, big eyes that look even bigger with kohl and with her knee length hair which is the hall mark of a typically feminine beauty from Bengal, she has decided to continue her studies after graduation next year. But her parents are desperately keen to get her married too. High level talks are already on with a rich Zamindar family from Dhaka for their eldest son. They too are Bengalees and Kayasts by caste and therefore it suits both the families. And though the boy is rumoured to be a good person at heart, but he takes great delight in wasting his time doing what the Bengalees call "Rock Bajee". Which means only gossiping and doing bugher all for a living?

As far as the Pugsley's are concerned, both the Sen and the Ghosh families were pleasantly surprised to get Durga Puja greeting cards from them. The hand made cards arrived only a few days ago and enclosed with the cards were two identical letters giving the whereabouts of their family members. Their eldest son Shaun now is in his early thirties and he with his family are presently posted at Mogulsarai. He is now a senior foreman. Debbie at 26 is now a mother of three children and she with her husband who is an engine driver are at Jhansi. They are however expecting a posting to Moghalsarai shortly and that should be good for them I guess.Their youngest son Richard Pugsley from the Indian Army Signal Corps after being declared missing believed killed during Operation Husky in Sicily is believed to have surfaced somewhere in France. The Pugsley family's youngest daughter Veronica, at 17 and before even completing her Senior Cambridge from Sanawar Military School has quietly run away and eloped with an elderly British Air force Sergeant who was nearly twice her age. The Air force Sergeant himself a product of the Sanawar school was invalided out of service after he lost his left hand while on a low level ration dropping mission to a "Chindit Group" that was well behind the enemy lines.After his discharge Sergeant Ervin Jones being an orphan had gone on a private visit to his old alma mater to make a small contribution to the school from his side. There he met and fell in love with Veronica Pugsley. According to Mr Edwin Pugsley, Sargeant and Mrs Ervin Jones have recently set up their new home at Perth in Western Australia. Aunty Leila celebrated her 54th birthday on D-Day and to celebrate the double occasion, Mr Pugsley wrote that he had alone polished off half a bottle of Beefeater Gin in the morning and another half bottle of "Something Special" Scotch whisky in the evening.

The old man though he is now in his late sixties seems to be still going strong.

And as far as my two younger brothers are concerned, Captain Aftab Rehman wrote and said that you celebrated his 26th birthday on 1st August with a get together of Indian Army officers of the 1/2nd Punjabees in your bunker somewhere in Central Italy and that the biryani cooked by you for the occasion was indeed very appetizing. Regarding my youngest brother Arif Rehman, he too like Ronen Sen at the age of 24 is one of the youngest, if not the youngest Sub Divisional Magistrate and is presently posted somewhere close to Chittagong.

Colonel Reggie who is presently settled at Kasauli is busy writing a book on the gallant Indian soldiers who fought in France during World War 1, and a good part of the book is also devoted to your late father Naik Curzon Sikandar Khan, VC. Colonel Reggie is also in regular correspondence with my father.

What is the news from your end? I hope the gallant Indian troops of the three Indian Divisions in Italy are giving the retreating Germans a licking of their lives, like we are doing the same to the Japs over here in Burma.Incidently on my way to Calcutta and at the Dimapur airfield I bumped into our old dear friend and third musketeer Captain Daler Singh Bajwa from the Jammu and Kashmir State Forces. He was delighted when I told him that you had finally tied the knot in Italy and he has extended his invitation to celebrate your wedding for the second time in the vale of Kashmir once you with our Italian Gina bhabi get back to India and soon after this bloody war is over.

May Allah the Almighty bless us with an early victory?
With fond love and regards from all of us,
Your loving friend and brother,
Gullu.

By the time Major Ismail received that long and informative letter it was already early December. With the seven armies of General Eisenhower now well into the guts of the German defences in Western Europe, and with the might Russian armoured and infantry columns playing hell into the Germans from the East and with the German defences in northern Italy slowly crumbling, it seemed that Germany's back had been finally broken. Similarly in the Far East, the ring was also closing in around the Japanese Forces both on the land and on the high seas. But then suddenly on 16th

December, 1944, the allies were in for a rude shock. On that day in blinding cold wintry weather at 5.30 in the morning the Germans launched a massive offensive on a fifty mile front through the densely forested Ardennes forest. The aim was to trap the allied armies that were west of the Meuse River and then drive on to Antwerp. It was Hitler's last desperate attempt to checkmate the Allies in order to gain some more time to work on the secret weapons and to build up more troops and defences in depth. Initially code named "Wacht am Rhein" (Watch on Rhine) it was now renamed "Operation Autumn Mist." Though the top German Army Commanders who were chosen to execute Hitler's daring plan and which included Field Marshall Rundstedt, Field Marshall Model, General Josef "Sepp " Dietrich and General Hoss Von Mantteuffel were sceptical about reaching Antwerp and had pleaded with the Fuhrer to go in for a limited objective that would weaken the Allied advance, but Hitler would have none of it.

It was in the first week of December 1944 that Richard Pugsley with his wife Simone had gone to visit one of their old friends Jacques Andre from the Belgian resistance movement who lived at Malmedy not far from the German border and who worked for the CDJ which was the Committee for the Defence of Jews. Though he himself was not a Jew, Jacques Andre was responsible in saving the lives of a number of Jewish children whose parents had been sent to concentration camps or were hiding in the many convents, monasteries and orphanages where the Catholic priests and nuns while risking their very own lives were providing them with shelter and food. Andre had managed to even smuggle a large number of such destitute children into the La Providence orphanage in the town of Verviers which was looked after by Sister Marie. Her real name was Mathilde Leruth, but she was like an angel among the Sisters of Charity of St Vincent de Paul. Richard with Simone had gone to celebrate a holiday and Christmas with Jacques Andre and his family. On 16th December early morning, while helping the family to cut wood from the near forest, Richard Pugsley noticed a group of soldiers in American army uniforms resting near a stream. They were drinking, smoking and talking loudly. But what surprised him was that all of them were speaking in German. Smelling something fishy he quietly withdrew with whatever wood he had chopped and went back to inform Jacques Andre. That morning Richard had also heard heavy artillery firing and presumed that it was an allied concentration for softening up the German defences on the German-Belgium border. However, to be on the safe side Andre decided to get out of the village and seek shelter in an isolated farm house in the nearby forest.

'Are you sure that they were wearing American uniforms and speaking only in German,' said Andre as he took out his small cache of arms and ammunition from the well camouflaged dug out inside the forest and handed them over to the small group.

But they could be Americans also. After all America is a country of migrants and this must be some special unit,' said Simone.

'Nevertheless we are not going to take any chances,' said Jacques Andre while distributing bundles of old newspapers to all of them.

'Just stuff them tightly inside your clothes to fight the cold and lets wait for tomorrow.'

Next morning they heard the rumble of tanks and decided to lie low. Soon thereafter a squadron of German Mark IV' tanks rumbled past them. It was sometime around 1 o'clock in the afternoon that they heard heavy firing of automatic weapons coming from the direction of a field, which was not very far from the village of Malmedy. The Bravo battery of the 285th Field Arttillery Observation Battalion of the US Army had been intercepted at the Baugnez crossroads by the 29 year old young Lieutenant Colonel Jochen Peiper who was commanding a tank regiment from the First SS Panzer Division.

Peiper had already earned the nickname of "Blow Torch" when he during the Russian campaign had burned to the ground two villages and had ruthlessly slaughtered all the civilians. He was once an ADC to Himmler and a holder of the Knights Cross with Oak Leaves That day on 17th December 1944, Peiper after opening fire with his leading two tanks he stopped the American convoy and took the whole lot of them as prisoners. After that he herded the unarmed American prisoners of war into a nearby field and massacred them with machine gun fire. There was little that Richard Pugsley or Jacques Andre could do except to remain in hiding inside the forest for some more time. It was around 4 o'clock in the evening that Andre decided that they should all get back to his old underground hiding place deep inside the forest. They had no clue till then that a major offensive operation by the Germans had already begun. While they were on their way they were spotted by a strong German armoured patrol. The coaxle machine gun on the armoured car without any warning simply opened up on the hapless four and riddled them with bullets. The men of that German armoured patrol it seemed were a heartless lot as they simply for fun pumped in a few more bullets from their automatics as they raced past the dead bodies. Richard and Simone who were looking forward to celebrate their first Christmas with friend Jacques Andre did not even get a proper burial and soon they were buried under the heavy snow.

Initially it was all honky dory for the Germans as the eight armoured divisions and thirteen German infantry divisions swept through the Ardennes. This bold move had caught the allies completely by surprise. But from the 17th of December, when the American 7th Armoured Division checked the advance of General Dietrich's 6th Panzer Army at St Vith, the tables began to turn. And when General Patton's Third Army by end December counter attacked and overran Bastogne and then headed north it was nearly all over for the Germans. On 8th January 1945, Hitler ordered his battered troops and tanks to withdraw from the tip of the bulge, and on the 28th of January, the Battle of the Bulge was finally over. Hitler's bold gamble had failed miserably.

And while the American forces in Europe regained the initiative, in Calcutta one day during that Christmas week, Debu Ghosh played a good samritan to a young American GI. The twenty four year old American soldier who had seen action at Guadacanal against the Japaneese on an appeal by President Roosevelt for dare devil American soldiers to join another special mission force that was being raised to fight behind the enemy lines in Burma had volunteered for it. Thinking that this would give him a chance to return to the United States for specialized training, the recently promoted Corporal David Randall from Pittsburg, Pennsylvania was surprised when he with other such volunteers landed instead in India. They were now under going extensive training in the dense jungles of Central India and were part of Brigadier General Frank D Merrill's elite Special Forces that would soon distinguish themselves as Merrill's Marauders.

During the Christmas week while under training a large number of them went absent without leave and popped up in several big Indian cities to blow away the wads of dollars that they had accumulated, but could not spend in the jungles of the Pacific and most of them therefore landed up in the city of Calcutta which had everyrhing to offer starting from wine, women and song.

It was 4.30 AM on the morning of Christmas Day that Debu Ghosh with his wife Hena while returning home in their baby Opel car from the Christmas Eve party at Dr Ghulam Hussein's house, were surprised to find Private David Randall drunk as a doodle and with blood oozing out from his upper lip lying unconscious outside the gates of their flat at 217, Lansdowne Road.It seemed that David together with a few of his friends after spending the better part of the evening with the whores at Karaya Road had come to the open air "Palm Grove" bar and restaurant that was located near the

Dhakhuria lakes. There they had a few more whiskies and then got into a fight with a group of four British Tommies who were sitting in a far secluded corner, drinking and smooching their babes for the evening. The four young well tanned Chineese girls in short skirts which revealed their shapely legs were in splits as Corporal David Randall with his buddy while doing the baby elephant walk went upto them with a wad of dollar notes and tried to lure them away from their own gracious British hosts. And that is what started the brawl and it soon became American GI's versus the British Tommies. The helpless manager together with his bouncers could do little except to close the bar and cancel the last cabaret. A liitle while later, when the Military Police arrived on the scene, the American GI's from Merrill's Marauders who had no out passes or leave certificates decided to make a run for it. In that melee, an injured and fairly drunk David had got separated from his buddies. Since he had no idea about the geography of the place he therefore decided to sleep it out till morning. Since it was very cold outside, and it was soon going to be Christmas morning, Debu Ghosh on noticing the young man in a American GI's uniform lying sprawled out infront of the gate, he with the help of his youngest son Anup literally carried the American soldier to his first floor flat. Then having laid him on the big sofa, they took off his shoes and socks and soon David Randall was once again snoring away to glory. And by the time David Randall surfaced, it was well passed noon.on that Christmas Day.

"Hey pal how the hell did I get here and where are all my buddies?' asked a bleary eyed David as Debu gave him a glass of cold lemon juice to get over the hangover.

'Well about your buddies I do not know and have no idea either because I only found you outside the gate, and if you so desire I could drive you to the Fort William Military Camp, or I can inform the military authorities at Ballygunge Camp to come and fetch you from here,'said Debu Ghosh as Anup laid a plate of omelette and toast and a cup of hot coffee for the guest on the centre table.

'No please don't and I beg of you not to inform the military police because they will put inside the Quarter Guard and I will probably be court martialled also,' pleaded David Randall as he took out a fistful of dollars from inside his back pocket and requested Debu if he could put him on a train to Ranchi. '

There is no need for that. You are our guest so do feel at home. And after breakfast have a good bath, and after a few quick gimlets and lunch I will definitely put you on the train to Ranchi,'said Debu Ghosh as David narrated to him about his escapade.

A fortnight later Debu received a New Year's card with a ten dollar bill inside it and with it was a small note which read. 'Thanks for the Christmas lunch and the car ride to the railway station and please do not mind buddy so just blow this tenner up in whatever manner you want to and give yourself and you charming family a little treat for the New Year from my side.' It was signed Private David Randall.'

'For his exploits the corporal of yesterday has been demoted it seems, but I am sure David would'nt care a damn,' said Debu Ghosh as he handed over the ten dollar bill to his wife Hena.

As another year dawned and signalled that the war may soon come to an end with victory for the allies, the Congress and the Muslim League once again flexed their muscles asking for Independence. But it was not all that easy or simple as the British were still heavily involved in the war. In the west Hitler was now fighting like a maniac and in the east the proud Japanese resorted to a do or die tactics as their Kamikazi dare devil pilots' targetted the U S naval ships.

In India too with most of the Congress leaders still in prison, tensions beween the Congress and the Muslim League leaders had reached a breaking point and the prospect of India getting her independence was hanging like an ominous dark cloud over the horizon. Gandhi wanted the Congress and the Muslim League to join hands so that a common agenda for the demand for full freedom could be made to the British Government. And therefore for this very purpose he even sent Mr Bhulabhai Desai to go and meet Mr Liaquat Ali Khan who was Mr Jinnah's number two man and hammer out an agreement with him and one that would be of advantage to both the sides.

Bhulabhai Desai who was the only child of his parents was born in Valsad, Gujrat. A product of Bharda High School and Elphinstone College Bombay, and a renowned advocate by profession who represented the rights of the poor farmers in the enquiry by the British Government on the Bardoli Satyagraha movement was now a full fledged senior member of the Congress Party. He was arrested on 10 December 1940 under the Defence of India Act and was released from the Yerwada Jail in September 1941 because of his poor health. Now 68 years old, Bhulabhai directed by Gandhiji went and met the Muslim League leaders, but there was no major headway made. After giving due consideration once again to Mr C. Rajgopalachari's formula for a Hindu-Muslim accord and having agreed to the idea that both the

Congress and the Muslim League would join the Interim Government with equal representation if and when it was formed within the frame work of the Government of India Act 1935, it looked that some compromise had been reached. But the talks soon broke down as unfortunately neither Gandhi nor Jinnah could reach a worthy agreement on the issue that the Congress should be barred from nominating even a single Muslim leader from its folds as a minister in the interim government. The failure of the Gandhi-Jinnah talks now spurred Viceroy Wavell to try and somehow break this political deadlock between the two leaders.

While Viceroy Wavell kept racking his brains to find a solution to keep India united, on both the war fronts, in the Far East and In Europe the Allies stepped up their tempo for a quick end to the conflict. The British also realised that if they still wanted the cooperation of Indians to quickly win the war, then they must promise to give India her freedom as soon as the war was over. The time for the British to finally quit India had arrived and it was now only a question of when and how.

In early January 1945, on the Burmese front after the capture of Kennedy Peak in which the Maharaja's 4th Jammu and Kashmir Infantry which was also known as the Fateh Shibji Battalion had also proved to the British Indian Army that they too were a force to reckon with. They were now a part of the 5th Indian Red Ball Division and the entire formation was given a much needed break. The Division after fighting the Japs for fourteen continous months in the dense leech infected jungles of India's North East and inside Burma had now moved to Jorhat in the plains of Assam. While General Frank Messervy's 4th Corps and General Stopford's 33rd Corps from General Slims 14th Army continued their relentless advance to rout the withdrawing Japanese forces, the officers and soldiers of the 5th Indian Division let their hair down by competing in inter-formation games, organizing pagal gymkhanas and which were followed invariably with Barakhanas. They were also shown Hindi movies that were screened by the Cinema Section of the army once a week. With flags and pennants fluttering above the tents it was now once again back to spit and polish for the Red Ball Division.

While the Red Ball Division was having its own ball in the plains of Assam, far away on the Black Sea coast at Yalta during the first week of February 1945, Marshall Stalin was playing host to President Roosevelt and Prime Minister Churchill. In anticipation of an early allied victory and the capitulation of Germany, the three Big Powers were now chalking out their plans for a four nation control of the conquered German territory and the realignment of the international borders with Poland to what it was prior to the First World War. The Russians was also now getting ready to declare war on the Japanese.

The command of the Red Ball Division had now fallen on the shoulders of Major General DFW Warren, the erstwhile commander of 161 Infantry Brigade and on his orders Major Gul Rehman Khan from the First Punjabees was now temporarily posted on his staff as GSO 2 operations. On the occasion to celebrate and honour the large number of gallantry awards that were won by the officers of the Mahrajas 4th Jammu and Kashmir Infantry and which included two Military Crosses won by the young Lieutenant Banaras Dev and Captain Mohammed Aslam Khan, and the mention in despatches of their own Commanding Officer Lieutenant Colonel Narain Singh Sambyal and Major Adalat Khan, General Warren also known popularly as "Daddy" Warren had organised a grand party in the Divisional Officers Mess in Jorhat.That evening with scotch and soda flowing like water, Major Gul Rehman from the First Punjabees together with Major Daler Singh Bajwa and Captain Mohammed Aslam Khan from the Maharaja of Kashmir's 4th Jammu and Kashmir Infantry with arms around one another's shoulders danced the Bhangra and the Khattak to the soothing music of the battalion's pipers. Nobody ever thought that soon the same friends would be fighting each other tooth and nail for the enchanting valley of Kashmir.

The respite from the war for the Red Ball Division was however shortived as Japanese having lost the strategic communication centre of Meiktila and its airfield to the 17th Indian Division, were now planning to recapture it with an attack by a full Corps.

In mid February, 1945 the GOC 5th Indian Div had been hurriedly summoned for a briefing at the higher headquaters at Kalemyo. Though initially Major Gul Rehman was to accompany "Daddy Warren" as his staff officer, but at the last moment Daddy Warren decided to take his GSO 1, Lieutenant Colonel PS Pryke along with him. On the 17th of February after the briefing was over and while they were on their return flight to Jorhat, the small aircraft vanished among the hills. It had crashed and though search parties were immediately despatched, no bodies were found. A gloom of sorrow and despair now descended on the 5th Indian Division camp. Ironically the much loved, admired and adored Major General Warren who was born in Japan the son of a missionary had to die fighting the very Japs. To all his officers and soldiers he was really their "Big Daddy.'Commissioned into the Royal Munster Fusilers in 1917, he was later transferred to the

Indian Army, when he joined the 34th Royal Sikh Pioneers and had even build roads inside the North West Frontier. After the Pioneers were disbanded, Warren was transferred to the 8th Punjab Regiment. He had a flair for Indian languages and was a qualified intrepeter too.

For Major Gul Rehman it was more of a personal loss. He admired the man because not only coud the man crack jokes in Urdu and Punjabi that were appreciated by the jawans, but he was always approachable at any time by his staff and it was irrespective of rank, colour, creed or religion. The man knew no fear and his bravery and enthusiasm was infectious to all around him. Ever cool in the face of adversity, his juniors loved to have him around which in most seniors is rather rare to find. Gul Rehman would now miss the tapping of his long staff, his wide brimmed hat, his big smile and the smoke from his pipe. A few days after the General's death, Major Gul Rehman was posted on the staff of 161 Infantry Brigade.

While the Red Ball Division was still mourning the death of their beloved GOC, far away in Europe, the 10th and 8th Indian Divisions were getting ready to set the pace for the British 8th Army's drive into Northern Italy.On 25th February, 1945 Turkey had also declared war on Germany, and a day earlier on 24th a haggard and aged looking Hitler on the occasion of the 25th anniversary of the proclamation of his Nazi party addressed his partymen secretly for the last and final time.

On 8th of March, secret negotiations between the representatives from the American Office of Strategic Services (OSS) led by Mr Allen Dulles and the German military high command in Italy had begun at Berne in Switzerland and Major Ismail Sikander Khan was aware of it. He was now confident that an early surrender of all German forces in Italy was imminent and he was now waiting patiently to be reunited with his wife Gina and his new born son Cassinoleni Ismail Khan.

By end March with the US Third Army across the River Rhine and with Monty's Army Group's launching "Operation Plunder', an angry and desperate Fuhrer replaced Field Marshall Rundstedt with Field Marshall Kesserling as the new C-in-C West and ordered a scorched earth policy of all industrial units and transport. With casualties mounting by the hour, the tottering German nation now started recruiting fourteen, fifteen and sixteen year old boys into the army. And while the Germans were being battered both by the Anglo American forces from the West and the Russians from the East, the Japanese and Netaji's Azad Hind Fouj, the INA, the Indian National Army too were getting there share of defeats inside Burma.

On 18th of February, 1945 Subhas Bose left Rangoon with a retinue of senior Japanese and Indian officers to tour the front and to raise the morale of his men. The Allies now had complete control of the sky and the air raids against Meiktila had now become a regular feature. On 26th February, Subhas Bose wanted to go to Mount Popa and if required to fight and die with his troops defending that place, but General Shah Nawaz Khan convinced Netaji that at this crucial juncture they could not risk the loss of their beloved leader. Next morning Shah Nawaz filled up Netaji's car with grenades and ammunition. After Netaji sat in the car with a loaded tommy gun on his lap, Doctor Raju accompanying him kept two hand grenades at the ready. Following behind in another escort vehicle was Swarup Ghosh with other members of Netaji's bodyguard.As they made their way to Yindaw during the hours of darkness, Swarup Ghosh felt a little homesick. Having lost his wife he was no doubt a bit demoralized. And on 2nd March, when Netaji received the shattering news that five staff officers from his 2nd INA Division at Mount Popa had deserted and that the surrender leaflets signed by them had been dropped on the INA positions, he was livid. It seemed that another flood of mass desertions now seemed eminent. And when a very worked up and angry Swarup Ghosh suggested that those coward officers should be shot in cold blood for betraying the solemn oath that had been take by them, everybody knew that there was now no time for undertaking such a reprisal.

And as far as the valour of the Indian officers of the Indian Army was concerned, they had set another another great example. On the 18th of March another brave twenty two year old young officer by the name of Lieutenant Karamjit Singh Judge from the 4/15th Punjab Regiment at Meiktila had made his unit, regiment and family proud by winning the Victoria Cross. But unfortunately it was once again a posthumous one. By the first week of April, Meiktila and Mount Popa was very much in the hands of the Allies and once again the Red Ball Division with its 161 Infantry Brigade to the fore began their hot pursuit of the retreating Japanese and the INA forces.

It was around this time and sometime in end March from his headquarters at Rheims in North Eastern France, General Eisenhower sent three important secret cables for the personal attention of Marshal Stalin the Supreme commander of the Soviet Forces, to General George C Marshall his senior in Washington and to General Montgomery the C-in-C 21st Army Group. This was the first time that the Supreme Ccommander of the Allied Expeditionary Force had communicated directly with the Soviet leader.

Since the final thrust to annihilate the Germans were about to commence, Ike thought it prudent to coordinate the thrust lines and the objectives of both the forces lest they clash with one another. In 1939, when the Germans and the Russians advanced into Poland to carve up the country between themselves and because no prearranged line of demarcation had been fixed or laid down by either of them, they had fought one another both for political as well as geographical advantage and which resulted in unnecessary heavy casualties on both the sides. This kind of a situation Ike wanted to avoid at all costs since he wanted to get the war over quckly and with as few casualties as possible.The mission given to Ike by the Combined Chiefs of Staff was crystal clear. And it had been spelt out in one simple sentence.'You will enter the continent of Europe and in conjunction with other United Nation forces undertake operations aimed at the heart of Germany and the destruction of her armed forces.' Thus Ike's aim and objective was purely military. But at Yalta in February 1945, when the map of post war Europe was being drawn, Prime Minister Winston Churchill had his own misgivings on Marshall Stalin's fast changing military and political aims at the strategic level. Churchill felt that if Monty could get to Berlin first and beat the Soviets to it then he would not only be in a solid bargaining position against the Russians, but it would also be a big propaganda victory for the Anglo American forces. But Ike was not keen to capture Berlin. Therefore, when Churchill was made aware that a similar telegram had also been sent by Ike to Stalin, he was furious and felt that this was a naïve and dangerous intervention by a man in military uniform into global political strategy.

But Ike had another reason why he did not want to capture Berlin right at the outset. He feared that the Germans would fight fanatically and desperately to save their capital and this would lead to bitter street to street and house to house fighting which would result in enormous casualties. Moreover, reliable intelligence reports now clearly indicated that the German High Command would give its last and decisive fight not at the gates of Berlin but on the mountains, forests and the lakeland region that lay south of Munich and in the region of Bavaria where incidently the Nazi party was born a quarter of a century ago. This was the 20,000 square miles of area known as the National Redoubt that included the Fuhrer's "Eagles Nest" at Berchtesgaden. The morning prior to sending the three secret telegrams, Ike had carefully studied the big intelligence map with the latest intelligence updates. Comparing to what the picture was a few weeks ago, the military conventional signs depicting the enemy in red on the map showed a very high increase in defence installations, fortified defences, food, fuel and ammunition dumps and radio communication centres in the area of the Redoubt. One report also indicated the presence of both Colonel Otto Skorzney and Brigadierr General Reinhard Gehlen from the Abhewr. Both these of officers were reported to be organizing and training their new type of do or die commando units that were known as the "Werewolves." Recruited mostly from the SS and the Nazi Party, the task of these fanatical Germans was to sneak out of the Redoubt in small parties and create mayhem on the advancing allied forces.

A week earlier on 21st March, General Omar Bradley's headquarters had also come out in writing with the "Re-orientation Strategy." This was a top secret intelligence appreciation which concluded that the initial allied objectives on entering German territory now required a decisive change and that the significance of Berlin as the final objective had been greatly diminished. To add to this, four days later when a report by the Chief of Intelligence of Lt General Alexander Patch's 7th US Army operating in Southern Germany reported that atleast 200,000 to 300,000 of the German elite SS Mountain troops with new type of weapons were believed to be deployed in the area of the Redoubt, the question of capturing Berlin became even more redundant at this stage. And to give this more authenticity, Goebells too chipped in with a national broadcast exhorting the German people and the German armed forces that like the wolves in the forests, they too should with stealth, noiselessly and mysteriously kill the advancing enemy.

With such like reports coming in, the allied high command was slowly being convinced that if and when Hitler was found it would not be in Berlin but most likely in the Redoubt in Southern Germany. But whether this was the final grand German plan or just an intelligently thought out German deception measure, it became clear only on 23rd April, 1945 when Lt General Kurt Dittmar with two other Germans crossed the River Elbe to surrender to the 30th US Infantry Division.The 57 year old German General Officer who was also known as the voice of the German High Command because of his regular broadcasting communiqués from the front was indeed a prized catch. So when he was interrogated about the "National Redoubt" defences and he gave the interrogators a blank and puzzled look and further added that it was nothing but a myth and a romantic dream that only existed in the imagination of a few fanatical Nazis, the Americans it seemed were convinced. And when the German General also confirmed and confidentially told his interrogators that the Fuhrer was very much in

Berlin and that he would either fight to the finish and be killed or he would commit suicide, the race for Berlin had now begun in right earnest.

But by now it was already too late for the Anglo American forces to reach Berlin first and capture Hitler. In fact Marshal Stalin on the very day he received Ike's secret telegram which suggested that Berlin was no longer a very important objective for them, he immediately ordered Marshal Sergie Zhukov to advance to the German capital at full speed and irrespective of the cost to his forces and claim the grand prize at the earliest.

In that month of April, while the war in Europe was coming to an end, and with the Bengali New Year fast approaching, Ronen Sen and Mona Ghosh decided to bare it all. Their secret romance could no longer remain a secret as they with the tacit support of the entire Ghulam Hussein family, Ronen's sister Purnima and Mona's brother Anup decided on that auspicious day to seek the blessings of their respective parents.Ronen and Mona were now both grown up adults and they could have if they so wanted eloped and got married, but that would have only led to a shameful disgrace of their respective families. The couple therefore wanted to tie the knot with the full blessings of their parents. It was during the Bengali New Year's Day party that was being hosted by the Sen family, when Ronen with Mona by his side boldly announced that they would like to get married. For a moment Debu Ghosh and his wife Hena together with Naren Sen and his wife Shobha were in a state of utter disbelief as both Ronen and Mona reverently touched their feet to seek their blessings.There was pin drop silence for a while till Dr Ghulam Hussein and his wife Suraiya took the two friends and their wives to the adjacent room for a frank and friendly tete-a-tete. There inside the room and in hushed tones after they had discussed and debated the delicate matter in great details and of what could be the likely repercussions and the fallout of such a marriage within the family, the issue was finally settled. Thanks to Dr Ghulam Hussein and his wife Suraiya both of them had managed to convince them that there was nothing wrong in marrying within the family because even within the orthodox Muslims, the Tamil Brahmins, the Maharashtrians and even the Parsees the marriage between first cousins and near relations was not entirely taboo. Moreover since the young couple had the decency to be frank and fortright to seek their blessings, the proposal should be agreed to. However it was decided that the marriage would be on three conditions. The first condition being that the horoscopes of the boy and the girl must match. Secondly the wedding would take place only once the war was over and preferably during the coming winter season. Lastly it would be a quiet traditional Bengali wedding that would be solemnized not in Calcutta but in Mona Ghosh's grandfather's ancestral house in Chittagong. And the reason for all this was that both Naren and Debu did not want too many tongues to wag.

A week later after the Brahmin Pandit who had been asked to compare the two horoscopes gave the green signal, the preparations for the wedding also began. To begin with there were only in house celebrations to bless the couple. Coincidently on the day Debu Ghosh and his wife Hena were playing host they were pleasantly surprised to receive another long letter from their eldest son Arup. It was dated 25th December 1944 and was written from some place inside Poland and not far from the old Polish-German border. But because of the long route that the letter had to travel, it was delivered by the postal department to them on 23rd April, and which was also William Shakespear's birthday.

Dear Baba and Ma,

'I do not know if at all this letter will ever reach you, but if it does then no matter what happens, you must please tell the world about the terrible pogrom that the Germans have so mercilessly unleashed on innocent and hapless Jews But before I do that let me wish you all including Hussein Chacha, Naren Kaka and all their family members festive greetings and a very very happy new year. And let us all pray that this terrible war which has brought so much sorrow and misery to this world should end soon.'

'While the Soviet Forces were routing the Germans on the Eastern Front, I came across a Polish Jew who had escaped from the biggest extermination death camp that had been especially built by the Nazis inside occupied Poland. Located some 60 kilometers west of the city of Krakow in a suburb of the Polish town of Ozweicim and from which it derived its new German name of Auschwitz, this was the main killing centre and zone for the elimination of all Jews and other non Teutotonic races inside German occupied Europe.'The man in his early thirties whom we found lying dazed near a railway track was all skin and bones. We would have given him up for dead had he not moved his little finger summoning us to come to his help. I have promised the man that I will never ever disclose his name and it is only on that assurance that he told me the terrible tragic story about that wicked and sinful place. He had escaped from a death train a month ago in early November. He was among the last few groups that were being taken in railway cattle cars from Auschwitz to Dachau concentration camp which is not far from the big German city of Munich. The Dachau camp was the first one constructed by the Nazis inside Germany to imprison and execute all those who opposed the Hitler regime, but it was now coverted to aid in the final solution of the ill-fated Jews.

On 27th April 1940, Heinrich Himmler, the head of the SS and German Police had ordered for the establishment of the Auschwitz death camp. And as more and more Jews were brought in, another larger camp was constructed at Auschwitz-Birkenau some three kilometres from the main camp. Then a third camp was built near the Buna synthetic rubber works at nearby Monowice. The biggest and the worst camp was the one at Birkenau which also had the gas chambers and the crematoria. This was to become the biggest killing centre of the poor and helpless Jews.The drill for carrying out the murders was simple and well taped out. Once the train arrived at the man camp, the people were made to leave all their belongings inside and were hurriedly formed into two lines. One line was for the men and the other for the women. Then the selection process started. The elderly and the infirm were separated and were taken to the gas chanbers for disposal on the same very day, while the able bodied were sent into quarantine and earmarked for forced labour. While the able bodied were under quarantine, and irrespective of their sex, the hair of all the inmates was shorn and they were given the stripped prisoners garb. Above the main gate of the camp was written in bold capital letters the words "Arbeit Macht Frei"—"Work Leads to Freedom." It actually led to death and freedom from this world. Those who were recruited for forced labour perhaps could hope to live for say a few more months after they were registered and received their numbers which was tattoed on their left arm.

In July 1942, Himmler instituted forced sterilization for the Jewish women and started their pseudo-scientific medical experiments on others. These were conducted by Dr Carl Clauberg and his team of German physicians. It was plain torture for those who were selected as guinea pigs. Progressively as the population of Jews started increasing in the camp, more gas chambers were constructed till it reached the figure of five and each gas chamber had the capacity and potential to kill 6000 people per day. Ultimately, when the Jews inside realised that death was inevitable they began secretly organizing their own small resistance groups. Though the largest camp at Birkenau was like a fortress with barbed wire fencing all around and SS guards with machine guns on watch towers, but some of the Jews inside were a clever lot. And it was only in early 1944, that one of the resistance leaders, Josef Cyrankiewicz held a secret conclave and boldly declared.

'Gentlemen some of us must escape to tell the world about our plight or else the world will never believe the inhuman atrocities that are being committed on us by the barbaric German SS officers and men and they must be brought to book once this war is over. We must also have some documentary evidence in the form of photograps and documents to substantiate our charges and these should be smuggled out by those who are willing to take the risk to escape. The escapees should also approach the Papal Nuncio and through him the Pope in Rome to tell them about our plight and misery."

Josef then gave someone who was also a Jew and who worked as a roofer a small camera to have the needful done. The man had been tasked to repair some of the leaking roofs and since he had more access to freedom, he managed to click three vital photographs. The first one was of a group of shorn half naked women who were already like skeletons being taken to the gas chamber and the other two were of gassed bodies being burnt in an open pit.

On the 5th of April 1944, with the connivance and help of an SS Corporal Viktor Pastek who was madly in love with his Jewish girlfriend, Siegfried Lederer who had successfully motivated and befriended the German got into his Nazi uniform and both together made their escape from Auschwitz. Siegfried Lederer managed to get into the Theresienstadt Ghetto inside Checkzovakia and from there he told the world in his detailed despatch to the International Red Cross about the inhuman methods of genocide that were being conducted on the Jews. Two days later on 7th April, two more Jews escaped from the same camp and Rudolp Vrba submitted his report to the Papal Nuncio in Slovakia. The Jews inside now grew even bolder, for it was better to die fighting rather than be gassed to death, thought the young girl Rosa Robota as she helped in smuggling in dynamite and explosives inside the camp. On 7th October, 1944 a huge massive explosion rocked Auschwitz and the crematorium number four was completely destroyed. Unfortunately Rosa Robota who had spent months crafting the plan was hanged a few weeks later. With the Russian Forces closing in from the east, on 30th October, 1944 the gas chambers at Auschwittz was used for the last and final time.

Well Baba and Ma this in short is the real story of the horrors suffered by the Jews and others in the hands of Hitler's dreaded SS officers and men from the brutal Totenkopf Battalion which is also known as the "Death's-Head Unit.' It is headed by Heinrich Himmler and executed by men like Rudolf Hoss, Richard Baer and Adolf Eichmann to name a few.

I am sorry if I have once again burdened both of you with worries about the whereabouts of this wayward son of yours, but do not worry I am still alive and kicking. Incidentally Galya and I have a young two year old daughter whom we lovingly call Lalima from the word Lal in Bengali meaning red colour and to go with my own nickname of Lalu which I guess was given to me when the Red Army of the Bolsheviks defeated the White Army to bring in the Russian revolution of 1918. But Galya's mother calls her "Mia Indiskaya Lubimaya" meaning My Indian loved one and according to Galya she really dotes on her. But that's besides the point.I only hope and pray that this terrible war soon comes to an end and that maniac called Hitler is got rid off at the earliest so that peace descends on this Earth and it is high time it did. Do convey my pronams to all the elders in the family and love to all the others

With pronams to both of you,
Your loving son,
Lalu.

On 30th April 1945, in order to celebrate and formalize the engagement of his daughter Mona with Ronen, Debu Ghosh threw a lavish party but the invitees were only the Hussein, the Rehman and the Sen Families. On that very evening at the party, Colonel Attiqur Rehman also announced in absentia the engagement of his second son Aftab Rehman Khan with Sakina. The nineteen year old convent educated Sakina had just completed her graduation from Delhi University. She was the only daughter of Mr and Mrs Iftiquar Ahmed and they were old family friends. Iftiquar Ahmed was also from Government College, Lahore. He was a heaven born and had joined the Indian Civil Service in 1925, but after serving for 15 years had resigned in 1940 to join the Muslim League, when Jinnah gave his clarion call at Lahore for all Muslims to unite and made his demand for an independent Pakistan.

'But tell me how you can announce my dear nephew's engagement without throwing a party. I agree this is a rare case of an engagement by proxy, but that does not absolve you my dear brother of getting away with it so very easily,' said Suraiya Hussein to Colonel Attiqur.

'I think she is very right. Captain Aftab Rehman Khan is still fighting a war in Italy Sir and I hope he is aware of all that is happening over here,' said Debu Ghosh as he helped himself to another scotch on the rocks.

'Don't you all worry about that my dear because I had already sounded him about this proposal confidentially two years ago. It was during Shenaz's marriage and in my letter I had also enclosed Sakina's photograph and now he has also given me his word. But this marriage too will be solemnized once this dirty war is over and it is going to be over very soon I can tell you,' said a proud Colonel Attiur Rehman while raising a toast to Ronen and Mona.

'In that case it is going to be a double grand celebration tonight,' said Debu Ghosh as he opened the big bottle of champagne with a bang. It was a gift from Major Gul Rehman and as he poured the bubbly contents and clinked glasses with the handsome Major, Debu very sportingly also raised a toast to Aftab and Sakina. Thanks to Dr Ghulam Hussein and his wife Suraiya, the Ghosh and the Sen families had finally reconciled to the idea of the marriage within the family.

But a fortnight later, when a telegram arrived conveying the tragic news about the death of Captain Aftab Rehman Khan of the Second Punjabees, a pall of gloom descended on the Rehman family. Aftab no doubt had died a hero with a Military Cross to his name, but that was no compensation for the big loss to the family. He was killed by a German sniper's bullet during the battle for the establishment of a bridgehead across the River Idice.This was the last river barrier before the River Po in Northern Italy and the Germans it seems were determined to make a stand there. On the afternoon of 20th April, 1945 after mopping up the scatterd enemy pockets of resistance, the leading section from Captain Aftab's Dogra Company had reached the River Idice. The near bank of the river was covered by a wide irrigation ditch, while the far side had flood banks that were nearly thirty feet high. Despite the heavy odds, the first Battalion of the Second Punjabees moved forward to storm the defences. With great effort and unprecedented gallantry a platoon of Dogras had finally managed to reach the far bank. Then began one of the bitterest hand to hand fighting with bayonets and the valiant Dogras fought to the last man. Their heroic effort helped the rest of the Battalion to cross the River Idice without any further opposition. Leading them from the front was the young Captain Aftab Rehman Khan whose last words were. 'Ya Ali and Jai Durge let's give the Germans hell and come what may but we will not give up.' He fell literally fighting at River Idice, but not before he had bayoneted the last few Germans on the far bank of the water obstacle. For Major Ismail Sikandar Khan it was a tragic double blow. Not only did his battalion loose a large number of young Dogra soldiers from the company that he once commanded, but he had also personally lost a dear friend and colleague in Captain Aftab Rehman Khan who was like a younger brother to him.

A fortnight earlier before the battle for the crossing of the River Idice began; Major Ismail Sikandar Khan had been attached for a fortnight with the Headquarters of the 8th Indian Division which was now being commanded by Major General Dudley Russel who was ever popularly known as "Pasha". Ismail had been tasked to interrogate a large number of senior German Officers who had surrenderd and who had been taken prisioners by the Division.

In the first week of April, the 8th Indian Division was tasked to cross the River Senio which the Germans had reinforced with strong machine gun nests on the far bank. The Germans were holding both the banks and General Russel had decided to capture both banks in one single phase of attack. It was indeed a very bold plan and Major Ismail Sikandar Khan who had a large number of friends and colleagues amongst the officer cadre of the 6th Battalion of the 13th Frontier Force was physically there to see the actual conduct of the operation as a frontline observer. The battalion had be tasked to lead the attack.

On 9th April at 1345 hours, under a clear blue sky, the allied heavy bombers and the entire Corps artillery pounded the German defences on both banks for nearly four hours. The 6/13 Frontier Force Rifles supported by tanks had made it to the near bank of the river, but the main batlle was yet to start. As the leading elements dashed into the river many fell dead and wounded as the enfilade fire from the German machine guns with vengeance opened up on them. The river at places was now turning red with the blood of the heroic Indian troops. Only one young Sepoy Ali Haider with just two more of his comrades from his platoon had managed to get to the far bank.

'If the attack is to succeed I must destroy the machine gun nest which was just 30 yards away,' thought Ali Haider as he under the covering fire of his two colleagues charged single handedly. Crawling forward he managed to lob a grenade. It was an accurate throw and the enemy machine gun had been silenced. Though wounded and without caring for his own life, Sepoy Ali Haider charged the next enemy weapon pit that was bringing murderous fire on to the river. Though he was himself struck twice, the brave and courageous Pathan once again crawled forward and having pulled the pin of a Mills bomb with his teeth he hurled it into the Spandau nest. Though weak with loss of blood he had silenced the second one too. Ail Haider's gallant action was the turning point of the operation as his comrades now crossed the river unopposed. Ali Haider with his single handed action had survived to honour his unit and himself with the coveted Victoria Cross.

Elsewhere on the leading19 Indian Brigade front, things were not going all that smoothly either. This time a young gallant Mahratta soldier took up the challenge. Sepoy Namdeo Jadhav from the 3rd Battalion of the 5th Mahratta Regiment had also made it to the far bank, but only with two wounded comrades. In the face of heavy machine gun fire, Namdeo had half dragged and half carried his two comrades back to the home bank. Having saved his friends he now took up the challenge single handedly. He swam back once again to the far side and then dashed forward to wipe out the nearest machine gun post. Having done that and even after an enemy bullet tore his hand, young Sepoy Namdeo Jadhav dropped his weapon and with just hand grenades closed in on the next two enemy nests and silenced them. He then shouted the Maratha war cry of "Bolo Chatrapathi Shivaji Maharaj Ki Jai' and waved out to his comrades on the home back to rush forward. Though three of their own Company Commanders had fallen, Sepoy Namdeo Jadhav with his inspiring leadership had made the day for his Battalion. He too had honoured his unit with a Victoria Cross.

The heroic actions of both Ali Haider and Namdeo Jadhav were practically identical. One was by a Muslim and the other by a Hindu, and both the gallant actions took place within a few hundred yards and a few minutes of each other. The valour and the guts of these two young Indian Sepoys had altered the fortunes of the entire 8th Indian Division that day. Early next morning Major Ismail Sikandar Khan visited the 6/13 FF on their objective to congratulate them. Sitting in the cold with the officers and men of the battalion he sipped the tasty Indian gunfire tea. It was a concoction of tea made with Nestle's condensed milk laced with a generous doze of rum. That drink as the saying went could put heart into any damn louse and it definitely did as far as the men of the Frontier Force was concerned. On that evening over a drink in the 8th Indian Division Headquarters field mess, Major Ismail Sikandar Khan was introduced to Lieutenant Colonel Ingall, the commanding officer of the 6th Indian Lancers by General Pasha.

"I think we have met before and if I am not mistaken and if my memory does'nt fail me, it was at a party thrown by the Maharaja of Kashmir when he took the pants off of his vassal from Poonch and you were very much there with Colonel Reggie Edwards. You were then preparing to join the new Indian Military Academy at Dehra Dun if I am not mistaken,"said Lt Col Ingall.

'My God and I must say that you do have a fantastic memory Sir and this certainly deserves a royal salute,' said Ismail as he clicked his heels to give Ingall an American salute and told the barman to pour another large peg of that expensive whisky into the handsome cavalryman's glass.

Tragically it was on the 12th of April, the great man who guided the American nation for a record four elected terms starting from the days of the Great Depression and through the traumatic years of the Second World War died in harness without tasting the fruits of the Allied final victory. Born on 30th January 1882, Franklin Delano Roosevelt or FDR as he was more popularly known had served in the US Navy during the First World War after completing his degree from Harward. Married to Eleanor, the neice of President Theodore Roosevelt, the man he most admired, young Franklin as a Democrat jumped into his political bandwagon and soon became a young Senator from New York State. Unfortunately at the age of 39 he suddenly fell ill with polio and though he became chair bound that did not deter his fighting spirit. In 1928, he was elected Governor of New York and in 1932 became President of the United States of America for the first time. On hearing about his death the entire free world had gone into mourning.

Three days later on the night of 15th and 16th of April, the Red Army unleashed a devastating barrage with all the artillery at their command including the dreaded multibarrelled Katyusha rockets on the German capital. The German defences west of the River Oder and on the Seelow heights held on doggedly. For the next three days under a permanent air umbrella the Russians unleashed their reserves. The induction of fresh Soviet troops in such large numbers was staggering. It was as if they were coming out of some conveyor belt as hordes of them came pouring into the roads, avenues, lanes and bylanes of the German capital closely supported by their armour.

On the 20th of April, Hitler celebrated his 56th birthday in his bunker. It was a quiet affair as he cut the cake while the German and the Russians were slugging it out on the outskirts of Berlin. On 25th April, the first contact between the Americans and the Russians troops were made when a patrol led by First Lieutenant Albert Kotzebue of the US Army took his team across the River Elbe and was warmly greeted by Lt Col Alexander Gardiev from the 58th Russian Guards Division. Finally at 1600 hrs local time on 27th April the link up was completed at Torgau, South of Berlin. The once mighty German army had now been sliced into two and only the final knock out punch now remained to be delivered.

By 28th April, 1945 the 8th and the 10th Indian Division had crossed River Adige, the last river in Northern Italy, and they too had now reached the end of the road. The senior German emissaries had arrived at the Allied 15th Army Group Headquarters at Casserta to arrange for a ceasefire and the Germans were now ready to throw in the towel. Meanwhile on reaching the town of Padua that was studded with old castles and monastries, the victorious Indian troops were greeted as heroes and saviours. As the Italian men, women and children of all ages felicitated them with flowers, pastas and wine, the joyous Indian sepoys loudly shouted in the little Italian that they knew "Guerra e finite"(The War is Over).Hearing those words from Indian soldiers, the Italians cheered, cried, kissed and embraced them. It was now the turn of the troops to be wined and dined by the poor but hospitable Italians. On the very next day Major Ismail Sikandar Khan, DSO and MC proceeded on a few days casual leave to be with his wife Gina and his two and a half month old son Cassinoleni Ismail Khan. At Padua he bought for Gina a golden chain with the sign of the holy cross and to his son he decided to give him the old medallion that Lord Curzon had blessed his father with. But that was not to be.

On reaching the devastated town of Cassino there was no sign of Gina and his son. He was told by the parish priest in the old burnt down church that after the death of the old man Rosselini, Gina's grandfather who had died of pneumonia in early March, Gina after a fortnight had with her one month old son left for some destination in North Eastern Italy. She had however left a letter for Ismail with the priest and in that letter she had conveyed that she was answering a call made by a Jewish Brigade who were in need of Italian speaking Jews from either sex for their clandestine operations against the Germans somewhere in Northern Italy.

The Jewish Brigade with their own flag was raised in Palestine in October 1944 and after doing duty at El Alamein had boarded the ships at Alexandria to fight the Germans in Italy. The Brigade, 5000 strong consisted of young and old dare devil Jews who wanted to take revenge on the Germans for the holocaust. They had arrived in Italy in early March and were part of the British 8th Army. Gina thought that by volunteering for this mission not only would she do her duty as a Jew to avenge her parents death, but she would probably be also a little closer to Ismail now that the war was slowly and steadily coming to its logical end.

Ismail was also aware of this newly formed Jewish Brigade which was under the command of Brigadier Ernest Benjamin, a Canadian Jew, but when he arrived at the Brigade headquarters to trace out Gina and his son, and was given the shocking news about the brutal double murder that the German SS had committed on his family, he refused to believe it.It was revealed to him that while Gina was on a secret mission to gather some vital intelligence about the whereabouts of the Duce from a nearby village, a two men German SS patrol with a handful of young and armed Italian Fascists who were from the Duce's outfit had spotted her in that small village. It was early in the morning and the temperature was well below zero and most of the people in the village were still fast asleep. The patrol had come to the village to pick up their weekly rations of free eggs and chickens. On seeing the pretty young Gina who had her little son Cassinoleni strapped on her back they at gun point arrested her since in that small village they had never seen her before. On the pretext of taking her to their Headquarters for interrogation, the two SS men in a lonely barn outside the village raped and tried to kill her while the Italian fascists kept guard. But before she died Gina with the small sharp pointed pocket scissors that she always carried with her for her self defence had stabbed one of them on the back. The German who was badly injured had started bleeding profusely and the others in order not to leave any evidence of the act first throttled the mother and then the infant child. Thereafter they hurriedly buried both the bodies under the snow and escaped. The village was not very far from Bologna and from where a reliable intelligence report from a partisan group had indicated that Mussolini was on the run and that there was every possibility of his escaping into neutral Switzerland or Austria. Gina had been given the task to contact the partisan group and to ascertain the veracity of the report about the likely presence of the Duce in that area. Two days later on 26th April, when Gina did not report back to the Brigade', a search party was sent to the village. Under the spring sun the snow had melted and the frozen bodies of the mother and son were found at a place that was well away from the village. The members of theJewish Brigade then gave Gina and her infant son a proper burial. A tearful Ismail Sikandar Khan while laying flowers at their graves wondered why God was so cruel to him. It was only a little over two years ago that he lost Sandra and now Gina and the son too.

Three days later on 29th April, 1945 another kind of gruesome executions took place in Northern Italy. It was that of the Duce himself, his mistress Clara Petacchi and 15 other Fascists. They were first shot and then brought to Milan to be hung upside down in public view from a gas station in the Piazalle Lorreto area of the city. Benito Mussolini was trying to escape in a German convoy to Austria. He was found hiding in one of the trucks wearing a soldier's overcoat over his stripped general's pants by a vigilant partisan group near the village of Dongo not far from Lake Como. The son of a blacksmith who was born on 29th July 1883 in the small village of Predappio near the city of Forli and whose father ironically named him after the great Mexican patriot, Benito Juarez had now become an object of ridicule by the same Italian masses who once adored him. On that May Day while people spat on Mussolini's dead corpse while it was being taken for burial in a pauper's grave in Milan, a heart broken Major Ismail Sikandar Khan once again visited the graves of his beloved Gina and his infant son Cassinoleni. He had only seen his son in a photograph that Gina had sent to him and he now cried and prayed for their souls to rest in peace. From that very moment as he knelt and prayed, Ismail Sikandar Khan also made a solemn vow that he would never ever marry again.

Soon after the Duce's coffin had being covered with fresh mud, at 9.30 PM on the 1st of May 1945, the radio announcer at the Hamburg radio station in a gruff voice asked all listeners to standbye for a very important announcement. The announcement was followed by music from one of Hitler.s favourite Wagner Operas. At 10.25 PM Grand Admiral Karl Doenitz the man who claimed to have been been annointed by Hitler as Germany's new Fuhrer announced in a sombre tone that the Fuhrer had fallen fighting the enemy at the head of his troops that afternoon in Berlin. He had not spoken the truth thoughfor fear that the Germans who were still fighting and resisting the enemy may simply give up if he mentioned that Hitler like a coward had taken his own life and that would be a real big shame on Germany.

On the afternoon of the 29th of April, a few hours before Hitler was to be married to his long time mistress Eva Braun, the Fuhrer was given the horrible news that his dear old friend Benito Mussolini together with his mistress Carla Petacchi had been executed by the Italian partisans.The gruesome death and the blatant exhibition of their half naked bodies that were hung upside down at Milan now convinced the Fuhrer that both he and and Eva should take their own lives rather than be made a public spectacle off. That very evening the final preparations also started. First he had his favourite Alsatian dog Blondie poisoned and then had the other two dogs shot dead. After that he called for his two faithful lady secretaries and told them to destroy all the papers and files that were in his bunker. Then he gave specific instructions for one and all that nobody should go to bed until further orders. At 2.30 AM of 30th April when it was well passed midnight, the Fuhrer emerged from his private quarters inside the bunker and appeared in the passage of the general dining area for the staff. Hitler then shook hands with some 20 of them mostly women and went back into his quarters.It was his last farewell and thank you gesture to all of them. Thereafter to ease the tension that had been building up for the past forty eight hours, the Fuhrer's entire household staff apprehensive of what would now be there own fate gathered inside the canteen to dance away the night. By now it was amply clear that Berlin was no longer defensible. The Russians had practically taken over the entire city and it was only a question of time for them to storm the Reichstag and the Chancellory.

At noon on the 30th of April 1945, Hitler held his last and final conference with his senior staff, while the Russians were just a block away looking for him. With his young bride Eva having no appetitie, Hitler sat with his two secretaries for the vegetarian lunch. The cook Miss Manzialy perhaps did not realize that she had that day prepared the Fuhrer's last meal. Like the last supper in the holy Bible, Hitler the once most powerful man in Europe was now waiting to call it a day. But it was with a difference. Whereas during his last supper, Jesus showed his disciples that he was about to become the Passover Lamb of God and that his blood would open the door to freedom, but in Hitler's death his blood would open the door to rising tensions between the Russians and the Americans and the dangers of a nuclear war. The hot bloody war that was fought for nearly six years to get rid off the German Fuhrer and the Italian Duce would soon become a cold war between the communists and the non-communists of the world.

That afternoon inside Hitler's bunker, the 33 year old Eva Braun, the daughter of a school teacher too was counting her final hours. She had first met Hitler in 1929, while working as an assistant in a photo studio that was run by Hitler's old friend Heinrich Hoffmann. In 1932 she had become his mistress, but that did not prevent Hitler in having a fling or two with some female movie stars from the German screen. One of them was Renate Mueller who eventually committed suicide by jumping out of a hotel window in Berlin. A jealous Eva too in a bid to commit suicide had once shot herself in the neck, but the doctors had managed to save her life. Thereafter, Hitler became more attached to her. After her suicide attempt, the blonde, slim and athelitic Eva, was moved into a villa and Hitler also gave her a chauffeur driven Mercedes for her comfort. The Fuhrer wisely kept her away from the limelight and the Nazi Party too helped in keeping their affair a well guarded secret. In 1936, Hitler had moved her to his Alpine retreat of "Eagles Nest" at Berchtesgarden. Even while in Berlin they rarely appeared in public together. The young newly married Eva was totally loyal to the man she loved and who was old enough to be her father. After

Hitler had survived the July 1944 plot she wrote and said "Darling from our first meeting I swore to follow you anywhere, even into death. I live only for your love." She was now waiting to keep her promise.

After his last meal at around 2.30 PM that afternoon, Hitler with his wife came out of his quarters to bid his final farewell to his close senior confidants who stood by him through thick and thin. Meanwhile Erich Kempka his devoted chaffeur with 200 litres of petrol in jerrycans prepared for the Viking funeral that Hitler had requested for. Hitler then shook hands with with Dr Goebells, Bormann, General Krebs and General Burgdorf and his two secretaries and with his wife retired back into his room inside the bunker. A few minutes later, while the six of Hitler's trusted lieutenants stood outside the bunker to hear the sound of the two bullets that were to be fired from a revolver by the Fuhrer, they only heard the sound of one shot and waited for the second. But the second one never came. After a decent interval all of them quietly entered the Fuhrer's private quarters and found Hitler's body dripping with blood from his mouth. He lay sprawled on the sofa and by his side was his young wife frothing from her mouth. The two revolvers were lying on the floor, but Eva had not used her's. She preferred the cyanide capsule instead. On that Monday of 30th April 1945 at 3.30 PM the man who created and ruled the German Third Reich and his newly wedded wife of hardly twenty four hours as instructed were soaked ln petrol and their dead bodies were set on fire. Adolf Hitler's promised one thousand years of the Reich had lasted for only 12 years and 3 months. But the fact that Hitler with his long time mistress Eva Braun had both committed suicide on 30th April was known only to a handful of Hitler's personal staff and to Admiral Doenitz. But as no bodies were physically found, therefore the possibility that Hitler with his newly wedded wife had escaped could not be ruled out by the allies.

On the 2nd of May 1945, the imposing and magnificent German Reichestag building in Berlin fell to the Russians. With the Red hammer and sickle banner held aloft from the roof top of the battle scarred building, the officers and soldiers of the Soviet heralded their military commander Marshall Zhukov as the conqueror and hero of Berlin.

On the 3rd of May, though sporadic fighting still continued in parts of Berlin, Arup Ghosh on that evening at sundown in his uniform of a Russian Captain sat on the steps of the Reichstag to write a long letter to his darling wife Galina informing her that the war was now practically over and that he would soon be back with her and his darling daughter Lalima. A few yards away from him a group of young Russian soldiers were celebrating their victory by singing and doing the acrobatic Cossack dance to the music of the accordion and the balalaika. Then suddenly there was a spurt of machine gun fire. A German Spandau nest manned by two teenagers from a nearby building had opened fire on the dancing Russians. Seeing the two young Russian soldiers fall, Arup Ghosh without caring for his own safety fell on top of their bodies, while the rest of the group picked up their weapons, took cover and engaged the German nest. A short burst of machine gun fire ripped threw Arup's body and then there was total silence. By sacrificing his life, Arup Ghosh though an Indian had saved the lives of the two young wounded Russian soldiers.

A day earlier far away in the East, Rangoon the capital city of Burma had also been liberated by the allied forces. In view of the threatening monsoon clouds that were gathering over the Burmeses capital and which could delay the operations, Mountbatten had launched a combined amphibious, air and land operation to capture the capital city.

During the early hours of the 1st of May, 1945 one battalion of Gurkha parachutists from the 3rd Gurkha Para Brigade was dropped at Elephant Point to knock out the small Japanese force holding it. This paved the way for the amphibian landing crafts and motor launches to come up the River Irrawaddy unhindered. Later that day Wing Commander Saunders while piloting his Mosquito twin fighter bomber over Rangoon found to his surprise the message "Japs gone extra digit". It was freshly painted in bold capital letters on the roof of the jail. It was a slang that only those with a sound grasp of the RAF, the Royal Airforce only knew. Promptly Saunders landed his aircraft at the deserted Rangoon airfield and immediately informed the Commander of the amphibious landing force that the Japs had left Rangoon. For the 26th Indian Division, Rangoon was now just a cake walk. By the end April 1945, the Japanese had begun to withdraw from Burma and Subhas Bose's Indian National Army also joined in the retreat. In that process some defected, some deserted and others surrendered, but there were a few like Subash Bose who decided that come what may they would stand their ground and never ever surrender.

It was sometime during the end of May, 1945 that Debu Ghosh and his wife Hena was surprised to receive a letter from their second son Swarup Ghosh. The postage stamp on the envelope was that of an Indian one anna and it had King and Emperor of India King George VIth's handsome face on it. The not too legible postmark on the envelope was that of the Madres General Post Office.

Dear Baba and Ma,

I am not sure whether this letter will ever reach you all, but incase it does then be rest assured that all is well with me. I am sending this letter from somewhere in the jungles of Burma through Naik Govindswamy an INA fighter who hails from Madras. Govindswamy is an ex Indian Army sapper from the Madras Engineers who had crossed over to us. Because of a mine injury in which he had lost a leg during the battle of Mount Popa, he has now been medically boarded out. We smuggled him out as a civilian stowaway in a fishing craft from the port of Akyab and I hope he reaches the shores of India safely and posts this letter to you.

Though we have suffered a few reverses in Burma, but on 23rd of April, 1945 Netaji for his own safety was persuaded to leave the country. This was done so that he as our revered leader while in Bangkok could reorganise his forces and keep fighting the British Imperialists. I am also in this party as part of his personal security staff and our task is to ensure his complete safety. For those of you at home who are unaware about the sincerety and honesty of Netaji's cause, I am quoting from his latest special order of the day. This was issued by him on that very day of 23rd April, 1945 when he had to leave Burma and it reads as follows-:

'Dear Comrades, it is with a very heavy heart that I am leaving Burma, the scene of many a heroic battle that you have fought since February 1944 and are still fighting. In Imphal and in Burma we have suffered a reverse in our first round for our fight for Independence. But it is only the first round. We still have many more rounds to fight. I am a born optimist and I shall not admit defeat under any circumstances. Your brave deeds in the battle against the enemy on the plains of Imphal, on the hills and jungles of the Arakans will live in the history of our struggle for all time. Comrades at this critical hour I have only one word of command to give you, and that is if you have to go down temporarily, go down fighting with the national tricolour held aloft: and go down upholding the highest code of military honour and discipline. So far as I am concerned I shall steadfastly adhere to the pledge that I took on 21st October 1943 to do all in my power to serve the interest of the 38 crores of my countrymen and fight for their liberation. I appeal to you to cherish the same optimism as myself and to believe like myself that the darkest hour precedes the dawn. India shall be free and before long. God bless you. Jai-Hind.

Now that you have read it, do please tell all the others and especially Naren Kaku and Ghulam Chacha and all your other friends in the Congress that Subhas Chandra Bose and our Netaji will never ever surrender to anyone and no matter what the cost. And that he will rather lay down his life for the motherland than remain a slave of the British.

The next few weeks will be indeed tough for all of us as we make our way through the dense jungles and head for our new destination. But please do not worry because the bullet that has my name on it is yet to be manufactured.

With Pranams to all of you and love to my juniors
Inquilab Zindabad, Azad Hind Fouj Zindabad and Jai Hind
Your loving son,
Swarup.

Hena's face was in tears and while sobbing inconsolably, she took the loving letter from her husband's hand and placed it at the feet of Goddess Durga in her prayer room.

'Oh oh please don't cry. Our brave son is only doing his duty and we should be proud of him,' said Debu to his wife as he tried to console her, but he too had tears in his eyes. But those were tears of joy and pride as he kissed his son's photograph and prayed for his long life.

On 2nd May, 1945, the Allied troops having entered Rangoon started their mopping up operations inside the city and in the pursuit of the Japanese who had also started withdrawing from Burma. On the 13th of May, the ex Indian army Captain and GOC of the 2nd INA Division, Captain and self styled "Major General" Shah Nawaz Khan together with Captain Gurbax Singh Dhillon and 50 others surrendered to the British at Pegu. They were aware that the war in Europe was finally over and now it was only a question of time for the Japanese to surrender. Hence they thought that it was pointless to keep fighting anymore.

Born in 1914, in the small village of Matar in Rawalpindi District, Captain Shah Nawaz Khan was commissioned in 1935 from the Indian Military Academy, Dehradun. The academy was now popularly known as the IMA, but on the day of his surrender the young General was from the INA, the Indian National Army. It was was also known as the Azad Hind Fouj, but with his surrender he had been once again demoted to the rank of a captain and would now be tried for, treason and sedition.

On their way to Bangkok, Subhas Bose with his group had to now move like fugitives and that too only by night because the sky over Burma was completely dominated by the allied Air Forces. The party had covered the last 10 miles to the River Sittang on foot and on the 3rd of May, they had reached Moulmein. From there they made it safely to Bangkok which they reached on the 15th of May, 1945. And while during that hot month of May, 1945, the close pursuit of the Japanese military machine by the allied forces in the Far East continued relentlessly, the war in Europe was also coming to an end.

It was during the Casablanca Conference in January 1943, that the Big Three, the USA, England and the USSR had made it amply clear to one another that only the unconditional surrender of Germany would be acceptable to all of them. So on the 7th of May 1945 at 0241 hours early morning the German Chief of General Staff, General Gustav Jodl in a cold and business like manner inside the school at Rheims in France which was the Headquarters of General Eisenhower the allied Supreme Commander he signed the historic surrender.The next day 8th of May from the same room in 10, Downing Street where on 3rd September 1939, Prime Minister Neville Chamberlain had declared war on Germany, Prime Minister Winston Churchill announced to the world that the war in Europe was over and declared the day as VE Day or Victory in Europe Day. No sooner was the announcement made by the Prime Minister, people in England, USA and in all the Commonwealth countries came out in thousands to dance on the streets. In London huge crowds dressed in red, white and blue of the union jack made a beeline for the Buckingham Palace. Standing on the balcony, the King, Queen with their two lovely young daughters, Elizabeth and Margeret waved out to them. It was a moment of glory as some burnt the effigies of Hitler and Mussolini, while others greeted Churchill with a loud chorus of "He is a jolly good fellow" as the Prime Minister's car made its way to Whitehall.

In Moscow, Stalin however refused to accept the surrender that was signed in Rheims and once again the ceremony of signing the surrender document on the 8th of May with Marshall Zhukov representing the Soviet Union was held in Berlin. Thus for the Russians the VE Day was celebrated twenty four hours later. As the streets of Moscow reverberated with fireworks and dancing to the music of the accordion and the balalaika, a despondent and sad Galina Ghosh with her little daughter Lalima in her small one dingy little room flat on Kropotinskaya Street placed two red roses below the framed photograph of her beloved husband. Her only consolation was that her brave husband had been awarded the Order of Lenin. It was the highest honour one could get, but that never ever could compensate Galya for the loss of her dear beloved Indian husband.

Though the Second World War in Europe had ended with the surrender of Germany, the Cold War between the Americans and the Russians had already commenced. Both the countries were now desperately looking for the Germans brains that had developed the devastating V-2 rocket and which were fired from Peenemunde, the small coastal village on the north-east coast of Germany. Allen Douglas the top American intelligence sleuth from the OSS operating from Berne in neutral Switzerland in December 1944 in a secret telegram had already mentioned the name of Werhner von Braun. He was the premier rocket scientist who had developed the V-2 rocket. In March 1945, a Polish laboratory assistant at Bonn University had found pieces of the Osenberg List that was stuffed in a toilet. This list contained the names of Germany's top scientists and engineers who earlier had been politically cleared by the Nazi regime and had been assigned to carry out secret scientific work in the field of military armament and rocketry. The list had been cleared by Werner Osenberg, the engineer scientist who was the head of the German Military Research Association. And when this list of names surfaced and reached MI6 and the US Intelligence headquarters, the hunt to capture and interrogate them had begun. With the list in his hand Major Robert. B. Staver, the Chief of the Jet Propulsion Section of the Research and Intelligence Branch of the U.S. Army Ordnance immediately got on with the job. Heading his list was Wernher von Braun, Nazi Germany's premier rocket scientist. Most of those on the Osenberg List were working at Peenemunde and the Americans soon captured them. To keep their capture a secret they were transported with their families to Landshut, a historical town in the Bavarian region of southern Germany and were kept in complete isolation over there. Thereafter on the plea that they would be better looked after and treated by the Americans, more German scientists and engineers were lured to surrender to the Americans.

After carrying out detailed interviews and interrogaton of Braun and other top scientists, when Major Staver realized the importance of these German brains which could thereafter be fruitfully used by America, he on 22nd May 1945 transmitted his findings to his boss at the Pentagon Colonel Joel Holmes and told him about the urgent need to evacuate all of them to the United States at the earliest. From 19th July 1945 the US Joint Chiefs of Staff launched 'Operation Overcast' and soon the German scientists were all secretly on their way to the United States. Beginning in late 1945, three rocket-scientist groups as 'War Department Special Employees' arrived for duty at Fort Bliss Texas and at White Sands Proving Grounds,

New Mexico. In March 1946, the operation was renamed as 'Operation Paperclip.' Organised by the OSS, the Office of Strategic Services it was a program to recruit the scientists of Nazi Germany for scientific employment in the United States. Conducted by the Joint Intelligence Objectives Agency (JIOA) it was with the primary aim to deny German scientific knowledge and expertise to the USSR, UK and to a divided Germany. On his arrival in America, Wernher von Braun was initially kept in a secret military-intelligence prison in Fort Hunt, Virginia, but soon thereafter he soon became the most sought after German scientist in America's progress towards short range and long range ballistic missile program. In order to circumvent President Truman's anti-Nazi order and the allied Potsdam and Yalta agreements, the JIOA therefore started working independently to create false employment and false political biographies for all these German scientists. Amongst them was Wernher Braun, Arthur Rudolph the two top German rocket scientists and physician Hubertus Strughold. All three of them were members of the Nazi Party, but the JIOA very cleverly had it expunged from public records so that their expertise could now be fully used by the Americans. The projects operational name was derived from the paperclips that were attached to the scientist's new political personae. And as per the JIOA's records all of them were now 'US Government Sientists.'

Soon after the war ended in Europe, the treasure hunt for German brains who were responsible for the might of the Nazi war machine had begun. This was also undertaken by the Russians, but the Americans had taken the cream of them. Arthur Rudolp was the operations director of the Mittelwerk factory at the Dora-Nordhausen concentration camps where more than 20,000 workers died from torture, hangings and starvation. He had been a member of the Nazi party since 1931and would be the man who would ultimately design the American Saturn 5 rocket, while Von Braun would become the director of NASA's George Marshall Space Fight Centre. Kurt Blome the high ranking Nazi scientist who experimented with plague vaccines on concentration camp prisoners and other experiments on human beings would be hired by the US Army Chemical Corps to work on chemical warfare.

And while the Americans and the Russians were targeting German engineers and scientists for technical know how of weapons, equipment, rockets, aircrafts, ships and submarines, a group of Jews from Europe who had escaped the holocaust were planning to take their revenge on the German population. One bizarre plan was to poison the drinking water in four major German cities that would kill six million Germans. This would be a tit for tat for the six million Jews that the Germans had so mercilessly exterminated. Another plan was to infiltrate into Stalag 13 which was near Nuremburg and where thousands of German prisoners of war were being kept and poison the bread that was to be served to them with arsenic.

CHAPTER-16

Marching Towards Judgement Day.

While America was busy rounding up the German scientists in Europe, and the Jews were seething with revenge to kill all Germans, in Asia the Second World War was also coming to an end. But as the war in the East entered its final lap, there was more trouble in store for India.and for the Indians. The political infighting between Jinnah's Muslim League and Gandhi's Congress Party kept widening the communal divide between the two major communities of Hindus and Muslims in the subcontinent. India was also saddled with shortages of food, clothing and unemployment. On 29th March, 1945 Viceroy Wavell in his long meeting with Prime Minister Winston Churchill in London had warned that the problems in India were indeed very serious and it therefore needed an urgent solution. But Churchill ordered that the problems of India could be kept on ice till such time the war was not finally over and till the unconditional surrender of Germany and Japan was not fully completed.

On the 14th of June, 1945 Viceroy Wavell made a very important broadcast over the All India Radio from New Delhi and stated that the British Government's new proposals to give India her much needed freedom was on the cards and he hoped that both the Muslim League and the Congress would agree in the settlement of the communal issue amicably. Thereafter, he announced his first Wavell Plan which would have the following three main functions. Firstly to prosecute the war against Japan with greater vigour and energy till her final capitulation. Secondly to carry on with the governance of British India for India's post war developement till such time a permanent constitution could be agreed upon. And lastly to achieve in having an agreement that would be beneficial to all between the Congress and the Muslim League. He then invited the leaders from both the sides for a free and frank meeting with him at Simla.

Next day at their weekly coffee house session, the three old friends Dr Ghulam Hussein, Debu Ghosh and Naren Sen over a cup of the special ground coffee discussed the future of India.

'I am very doubtful if Mr Jinnah will ever compromise on his demand for a separate Pakistan. I think he is hell bent to create history by carving out a country for the Muslims of India,' said Debu Ghosh as he lit his newly acquired Dunhill pipe.

'But what happens to the Muslims who are from South India or from say Bihar and the United Provinces, I am sure they wouldn't like to leave their ancestral homes and go to Pakistan and it will be stupid of them to do so. Why even I will not leave my loving Calcutta,' said Dr Ghulam Hussein.

'But my only fear is that in case the country is divided it could lead to a civil war between the Hindus and the Muslims and especially between those who will be caught innocently in the vortex of partition,' said Naren Sen.

'Anyway let us hope and pray that better sense prevails on our political pundits and they stick together for a unified, prosperous and a secular India,' concluded Debu Ghosh as he paid the bill.

On 25th June 1945, Wavell held his first Simla conference. A day prior he had interviewed Mr Gandhi, Mr Jinnah and Mr Abul Kalam Azad, the President of the Congress Party and also declared that in order to pave the way for peace he was immediately releasing all the members of the Congress Working Committee who were still under detention in jails. Gandhi however insisited that he would attend the conference, but only as an independent observer. He therefore did not attend the meeting on the 25th, but remained available for consultations in Simla. When the subject of setting up of the Executive Council came up for discussion, the Maulana as the Congress President accepted that equality in numbers of Hindus and Muslims in the formation of the proposed Viceroy's Executive Council was in order, but he would not compromise on the method of selection. He argued that since he himself was a Muslim and the President of the Congress party, the Congress therefore must have a voice in the method of selection of Non Hindus and Muslims from within their own party in the formation of the new Council. While the composition of the proposed executive council was being discussed, the Congress reiterated that only they as a political party represented all communities in India and therefore they had all the right to nominate Muslims to the council also. But Jinnah was adamant and he argued and insisited that the All India Muslim League of which he was the President, his Muslim League therefore represented all the Muslims of India and only they could nominate the Muslim members whom they wanted in the council. Thus on the very first day of the conference, the composition of the proposed executive council became the real core issue. On the 27th of June, Mr Jinnah proposed that the Executive Council should include both the Viceroy and the Commander-in-Chief of India and there should be five Hindus, five Muslims and one each from the scheduled castes and other minority communities, but this was not acceptable to the Congress.

On the 14th of July, 1945 Wavell held his Second Simla Conference. While he as the Viceroy envisaged a United India, the All India Muslim League kept insisting on a separate homeland for the Muslims. Since that was not acceptable to him as the Viceroy or to His Majesty's Government, he asked both the Congress and the Muslim League to submit to him the list of their members for inclusion into the Executive Council. The Congress immediately submitted their list which also included the names of two Muslims. The Muslim League objected to it and did not care to submit theirs at all. On that very day Italy also declared war on Japan. Meanwhile at Singapore a week earlier on 8th of July on the Singapore waterfront, Subhas Chandra Bose dressed in his smart military uniform and as Commander-in-Chief of the Indian National Army laid the foundation stone for a memorial to be built for all his dead heroes. That day as Swarup Ghosh read out the names for the roll of honour there were tears in Subash Bose's eyes as he saluted and laid the first wreath in tribute to his martyred gallant fighters of his Azad Hind Fouj.

On 15th of July, 1945, Viceroy Wavell announced the failure of the Simla talks and he very sportingly took the blame on himself. An angry Jinnah referred to Gandhi's presence in Simla as that of a spoiler and a wire puller. In a scathing attack on Gandhi during the press conference Jinnah said. "Having gone to Simla why did he, Mr Gandhi not attend the conference"?

But a much greater calamity for the entire world was now on the cards and the secret of which was known only to a few top people in the United States of America. A group of American scientists working on the Manhattan Project had beaten the Germans to it. On a hot summer day in July 1945, at the Alamogordo bombing range near the Los Alamos Scientific Laboratory in New Mexico, the first atomic bomb code named 'Trinity' which took four years to produce and that to at the mind boggling cost of two billion US dollars was successfully tested under the overall supervision of Lieutenant General Leslie Grove, an officer from US Army Corps of Engineers and Mr Robert Oppenheimer the leader of the atomic scientific team.

On the 5th of July and not even two months after VE Day and ten years after the last general elections were held in England, the British people once again went to the polls to elect a government. With the war over in Europe and Churchill riding on the crest of his individual popularity everyone thought that the Conservatives would be swept into power, but it resulted in a shock election defeat for them as the British Labour Party under Clement Attlee won by a thumping majority of 145 seats. It was in 1940, when the Germans were knocking at the gates of the British Isles, Winston Churchill became Prime Minister, and on that day and after the war had been won under his astute leadership he had been thrown out in a most humiliating manner by his own countrymen. Five days later on 20th July, 1945 the British Labour Party under Mr Clement Attlee was swept into power and on that very same day Debu Ghosh received the tragic news about the death of his eldest son Arup in Berlin. It was sent by the Russian Government not through the British Indian Government in New Delhi, but through the channels of the emerging Communist Party of India. The death of her eldest son came as a rude shock to his wife Hena who soon became a mental wreck. A heart broken Debu Ghosh too cried silently for his beloved Lalu, but without shedding any tears.

From the 17th of July till the 2nd of August the Big Three, Attlee, Truman and Stalin met at Potsdam to redraw the political map of post war Europe. The Americans who were still fighting the Japanese now had the secret atomic weapon in their hands and without revealing it to the world; they once again warned the Japanese of serious consequences if they did not surrender unconditionally and immediately. On 21st June after 82 days of bitter fighting, the Americans had captured the strategic island of Okinawa which was located 340 miles south of the Japaneese mainland, and on 28th June 1945 they had also liberated the Phillipines.On the morning of 6th August 1945, with the Japanese not willing to surrender, the nuclear bomb as a weapon of war was made public to the world, when Harry S Truman the President of the United States on board a US naval cruiser announced at 0815 hours local time that an American military aircraft had dropped the first ever atomic bomb on the Japanese city of Hiroshima.

The atomic bomb of 20,000 tons of TNT power code named "Liitle Boy" in reference to the late US President FDR was dropped by "Enola Gay", a B-29 Superfortress bomber that was piloted by the experienced Colonel Tibbets. Seconds after the bomb was released a grand ball of fire rose from the bowels of the Earth and shot up like a giant pillar towards the sky. 'My God what have we done,' said Colonel Tibbets to his co-pilot while evaluating from his cockpit the extensive damage that was caused by the bomb. With that deadly weapon of mass destruction "Little Boy" had devastated five square miles of the city and had killed and wounded nearly 150,000 innocent Japanese people. With just one bomb Hiroshima which was the Japanese Army's main supply depot had been raised to the ground. It was a heavy penalty that the Japanese Government had paid for not heeding to the unconditional surrender ultimatum that had been given by the Americans ten days earlier.

Despite the heavy casualties and practically the loss of an entire important city, the Japanese Government during the next forty eight hours and even after three million leaflets had been dropped over Japan to warn them that more destruction could be in store for them, they did not come up with the white flag. So on the 9th of August at 1102 hours in the morning, when the vital Japanese port city of Nagasaki was buzzing with activity another atomic bomb code named "Fat Man" in reference to Mr Churchill and which was even more powerful than "Little Boy" with vengeance flattened the city. Two days later on 11th August, Russia declared war on Japan and that was enough for the Japanese who now had no other option but to raise the flag of surrender uncondtionally.

On 13th August, 1945 Swarup Ghosh as part of Subash Bose's bodyguard and protection section accompanied his Commander-in-Chief to Seremban where a group of soldiers in the INA Training Centre had mutinied. That night having quelled the mutiny, Subhash Bose at around 2 am in the morning was informed by his staff officer that an unconditional surrender by the Japaneese was in the offing. The news was indeed very disturbing for him as he sat in his vest under a fan and while chain smoking thought about the possible consequences. But he was not a man who would give up so easily. For him the possible surrender by the Japanese Armed Forces had nothing to do with his own command. On that very night Swarup Ghosh was struck with the dreaded thypus fever. On the 14th of August Subash Bose with his party returned to Singapore. They had to leave Swarup Ghosh behind for treatment by the doctor in the training centre. Unfortunately the doctor too could do very little and at midnight of 14th and 15th August Swarup Ghosh breathed his last. On the morning of 15th August 1945 to the accompaniment of the last post on the bugle and a gun salute, the funeral pyre of young Naik Swarup Ghosh was lit by an Indian doctor.

While Swarup Ghose's comrades in the INA were mourning his loss, in India and all over the world the people were celebrating VJ Day for the Victory over Japan. Unaware of his second son's demise, Debu Ghosh on that very evening treated all his dear friends and their wives to a new hit Hindi movie.starring the beautiful Nur Jehan and the handsome Dilip Kumar.The film Anmol Ghadi was running to packed houses in all the three cinema halls in Calcutta and Debu had to buy tickets in the black market.

'I must say that this new young music director Naushad is a real genius,' said Dr Ghulam Hussein as he sang a few lines of the song "Aajaa Aajaa mere barbad mohabat ke sahare' from the same film while inviting all of them for pot luck to his house after the show.

'But what ever you my say, Naushad I am afraid cannot be compared to Anil Biswas and nobody can beat his music. Anil is a real genius and overnight he has made a singing hero of a young aspirant by the name of Mukesh whose very first song "Dil Jalta hai to Jalne de" from the film "Pehli Nazar" is already on top of the charts, and we will only accept your invitation Daktar Babu if you promise to sing it for us,' said Hena Ghosh.

'With pleasure, but provided you also sing my favourite song that was sung by Kananbala Devi and I am talking about "Diniya ye duniya toofan mail" replied the good doctor as Naren Sen imitated the long whistle of a steam engine. It was indeed an evening to remember as the sing song session to celebrate the end of the war carried on till the wee hours of the morning.

On his return to Singapore on 14th August, 1945 Subash Bose who was suffering from a tooth ache went to a dentist to have it extracted and on that very evening he also attended a motivational play that was enacted by the ladies of the Rani of Jhansi Regiment. The news of the Japanese surrender within the next twenty fours was now a dead certainty and the leader of the INA now contemplated the idea given by some of his colleagues that he should now try and get in touch with the Russian Government and if possible undertake to seek asylum there.

On 15th of August 1945, while Subhas Bose was holding his last cabinet meeting, the announcement came over the radio that the Japanese had finally surrendered unconditionally. The very next day with a skeleton staff consisting of Lt Col Habibur Rehman, his Chief of Staff and two others, Subash Bose arrived in Bangkok. Since no specific orders had been received by General Isoda regarding the surrender of the INA forces, the kind Japanese General Officer offered Subash Bose a seat on a military aircraft that was bound for Tokyo via Formosa, Darien and Manchuria on the next day. At Subash Bose's request General Isoda also allotted an additional seat for Lt Col Habibur Rehman.

On the evening of 17th August, 1945 at 5.15 PM, before boarding the twin engine Japanese military bomber, a sad Subhas Bose shook hands with the other members of his staff who had come to see him off at the airport. As he stood at the door of the aircraft he gave a smart salute and after a loud Jai Hind went and sat on his allotted seat. A few hours later the aircraft landed for a night halt at Tourane airfield in French Indo China. Next morning on 18th August, the aircraft took off for the Taihoku mlitary airfield in Formosa and at 2 PM landed there safely for refueling. There all the passengers and the crew were given a quick working lunch. Half an hour later at 2.30 PM the aircraft took off again, but a minute or so later as it got airborne it lost part of it's left propeller.And as a result of which the aircraft immediately caught fire and crashed nose down at the end of the runaway. As the passengers and the crew struggled to get out from the wreckage of the doomed aircraft, Lt Col Habibur Rehman who had a head injury seeing Netaji enveloped in flames rushed to put the flames off. A quarter of an hour later, 12 persons including Netaji with severe burns were wheeled into the Nanmom military hospital and where Captain T Yoshini the medical officer on duty assisted by Dr T. Tusuruta and half a dozen nurses tried their level best to save the life of the Indian freedom fighter. And though they tried their level best, but around midnight he was no more. His cause of death signed by Captain T.Yoshini was death by third degree burns. And on the 21st August when the tragic news of Netaji's death in a plane crash was made known to the people of India, the majority of the Indians refused to believe it.

'He must have escaped and may have gone into hiding to fight another day,' said Debu Ghosh who till then was still unaware of the death of his own son Swarup.

'Yes that is quite possible, but what will happen to those Indian army personnel who changed horses mid stream and fought against the Allies and their old comrades in arms. Will they be treated as prisoners of war or as traitiors,' asked Dr Ghulam Hussein.

'Well technically speaking all of them as per military law can be court martialled and charged with treason and for which the penalty could also mean death by a firing squad. But as of now since a large number of our counyrtmen consider them as patriots, and now that India is on the threshhold of getting her freedom, it may be quite a tricky problem for his majesty's government on how to deal with this sensitive problem. Nevertheless, if requested then both Debu and I have decided that we will defend them at their trial free of cost,' added Naren Sen.

On the morning of 2nd September on the deck of the battleship USS Missouri in Tokyo harbour the Japanese military high command led by

General Yoshijiru Umezu, Chief of the Army General Staff together with a large retinue of Japanese senior officers in the presence of General Douglas MacArthur and other senior representatives from the Allied Forces signed the Instument of Surrender. By the time the ink dried up on that historic document, the war planes from the US aircraft carriers to show their military might flew in close formation over the ship. The entire ceremony was over in just half an hour. It was a proud moment for General MacArthur and Fleet Admiral Chester Nimitz both of whom master minded the end of Japanese domination of the Far East. Finally the disaster and humiliation suffered by the Americans on 7th December 1941 at Pearl harbour had been finally avenged and vindicated. Speaking on the occasion General MacArthur urged the Japanese to comply with the terms of the surrender fully, promptly and faithfully. He also added that the nuclear bomb attacks on Hiroshima and Nagasaki had henceforth revised the traditional concept of warfare and the world already had its last chance and if it did not devise some greater and more equitable system, Armageddon would certainly be at its door step.

A few days later at Singapore, Major Gul Rehman was witness to another historic surrender meeting. This time it was on board the HMS Sussex and by late evening on completion of the surrender talks for the first time in three years the black out on the naval convoy in the Singapore harbour was lifted. On 12th September, in the Council Chamber of the Singapore Municipal Building, General Itagi signed the instrument of surrender in the presence of Admiral Mountbatten and General Slim. That evening in a party to celebrate the occasion, a young handsome Captain with the tag of an ADC on his well starched khaki unform shirt came up to Major Gul Rehman Khan and said.

"Sir may I introduce myself. My name is Gul Hasan Khan and I am the ADC to General Slim and like you I too am a Pathan and a product of the PWRIMC.'

'Alright then in that case let one Gul drink to the health of the other and I being senior it is therefore my privilege and honour as one Rimcollian to another to offer you the first one,' said Gul Rehman as he shook hands with the smart Captain and ordered for two large Black Dog whiskies on the rocks.

Born in Quetta in 1921, the 24 year old Captain Gul Hasan Khan was commissioned in February 1942 into the famed Frontier Force Regiment and his first posting was in Delhi with his unit. It was only in December 1944 that he was selected as an ADC to the 14th Army Commander General Slim. A keen sportsman, Gul Hasan had excelled in hockey and boxing at the Indian Military Academy and today in the company of his senior namesake he was absolutely at ease and at home. And when he realised that Gul Rehman's youngest brother was non other than Arif Rehman Khan, his buddy and classmate at PWRIMC, his joy knew no bounds.

.'Well in that case you must make it a point to definitely attend Arif's marriage which is scheduled during this coming winter and the reception will be at the Grand Hotel in Calcutta where you will meet another colleague of yours from the same institution and he is non other than the son of the hotel owner and the young handsome man is popularly known as Tikki, and I believe he had to quit the PWRIMC because he was caught driving the headmaster's car,' added Gul Rehman while ordering a plate of cherries on pineapple and cheese to go with the drinks.

'That is right Sir, but he only played a practical joke and he had no intention of stealing it. With his father Rai Bahadur Oberoi's wealth he could have had quite a few cars at his disposal, but that was not permitted in the College. All the same I will look forward to the wedding invitation and I will be there positively to congratulate my old friend and classmate Arif Rehman Khan,' said Captain Gul Hassan Khan as he ordered the bar tender for two more large whiskies with lots of ice.

In the middle of September 1945, the Working Committee of the Indian National Congress restated firmly its stand regarding the future constitution of India. Referring back to the historic declaration that was made at the Allahabad AICC session in May 1942, it reiterated that it cannot and will not agree to any proposal that would disintegrate India and that it stood wedded to India's freedom and unity. However, it also declared that it cannot think in terms of compelling the people in any territorial unit to remain in the union against the will of its own people.

Next day, when the three bosom friends met for their weekly coffee house session, they debated the pros and cons of that declaration.

'It seems that the Congress is now mellowing down. On the one hand they say that they want a unified India and on the other hand they are also talking about giving people an option to decide for themselves. This could be rather dangerous,' said Dr Ghulam Hussein as Debu Ghosh tapped the ash from his pipe into the alluminium ashtray and having put some more of the aromatic Irish tobacco into the pipe said in a somewhat agitated mood.

'Well on principle what the Congress is saying is that they cannot force the issue and on that matter I too am with them. But the aim should now be not to bicker and fight amongst ourselves and make it a communal problem. Both the Muslim League and the Congress should now endeavour and aspire to create conditions which would help in developing some kind of a national unity and cooperation for the economic advancement of the poor masses. As it is India has been bled profusely to support this ugly war and our so called political leaders who will soon be at the helm of affairs should realise it.'

'Undoubtedly so, but now that the war is finally over I think we as fathers should all seriously think about more serious issues and which to my mind is to set the ball rolling to find suitable partners not only for the other two girls, Haseena and Purnima but also for Anup who I guess now fully qualifies for that status since he too is a working hand, 'said Dr Ghulam Hussein somewhat seriously.

'But for taking such important decisions I guess we all have to first consult our better halves', said Naren Sen.

'Well in that case I would suggest that all of us with our dear wives meet up at my house tomorrow evening and there over some mutton biryani, raita and kebabs we will kill the issue once and for all,' said Dr Ghulam Hussein.

'Splendid idea and I will bring the dessert and Debu will organize his bar as usual,' said Naren Sen as they all went Dutch to pay the hefty breakfast bill.

The high level meeting of the three families at Dr Ghulam Hussein's sprawling bunglow in the heart of Calcutta was jointly presided over by Colonel Attiqur Rehman and his wife Nafisa. In anticipation of the arrival of their eldest son Major Gul Rehman who had received his posting orders to Barrackpur, the elderly couple had already arrived in Calcutta from Peshawar with their daughter-in-law Zubeida and their two grandsons, Aslam and Fazal who were now just five and one year old respectively.

"Ladies and Gentlemen let me first tell you that the "Nikka " ceremony of our youngest son Arif Rehman to Ruksana has been tentatively scheduled during the last week of December and it will be done here in Calcutta and no place else. This is however subject to two major conditions and these are, firstly that my eldest son must be physically present for the grand occasion and secondly my daughter Shenaz who is expecting her first child must bloody well produce a damn son like I did, and mind you I produced not one but three in a row and so did my friend Debu. And with that we had both scored hatricks,' said Colonel Attiqur with a smile while all the ladies blushed at the oldman's sense of humour.

'Now may I announce our dates for Ronen's marriage Sir,' said Naren Sen as Debu Ghosh handed over a large scotch and soda to Colonel Attiqur.

'Certainly be at ease and go ahead, but don't let it clash with ours,'said Colonel Attiqur as he went and sat next to his wife Nafisa.

'Well since my son Ronen can only get a spot of leave in early October, we have therefore decide to solemnize his wedding to Mona at my brother-in-law Debu's ancestral house in Chittagong, and needless to say everybody has to be there atleast a week in advance,' said Naren as Nawaz Hussein looked and smiled at Mona. She with her two dear friends Haseena and Purnima were standing in one far corner, and no sooner was the announcement made, the three young ladies left the room giggling away with happiness.

The wedding of Ronen Sen with Mona Ghosh on 5th October, 1945 at Chittagong was purposely kept at a very low key partly because of the rationing in the country and of the fact that they were cousins. Though it was quite a hush hush affair, however for the few selected friends and parents it was indeed a nice reunion far away from the hustle and bustle of Calcutta. But the very next day, Debu Ghosh who after the death of Netaji had been trying desparetly to trace the whereabouts of his second son Swarup was surprised to receive a young visitor. After doing the traditional ritual of touching the feet of the elderly Debu Ghosh, the young man who had only one hand said very humbly.

'Kaka Babu, do pardon me for interrupting the proceedings early in the morning, but can I talk to you for a minute on something very confidential and personal,' said the visitor somewhat apologetically.

"Of course my son,' said Debu looking somewhat confused as he with the young man quietly walked into the garden. And as soon they were well away from the hearing distance of all the others, the man in a very soft and pathetic tone said.

'Kaka Babu my name is Usman Ahmed and I also hail from a village not far away from Chittagong. To be frank and honest I am a deserter from the Indian Army. But at the beck and call of Netaji I had switched my allegiance and had joined the INA. And I am not ashamed but indeed very proud of that fact. And though I lost my right hand while fighting for my country, it would have been better if I had died. For my act of bravery at Imphal, when we actually had the British on the run, Netaji had promoted me from an ordinary sepoy directly to that of a havildar in the INA. But because of my physical handicap wherein I lost my left hand during the battle for Popa, Netaji had sent me on sedentary duty to work as a helper at the INA training camp at Seremban. I know today it is a day of joy and celebration for you and for all your friends and family and I have no intention of making it a day of sorrow and grief, but I just cannot help it. This is a mournful duty which I am duty bound to perform on a day like this.'

And having said those words when he touched Debu Ghosh's feet in reverence once again and took out a small copper urn that was covered with a newspaper and a few other articles from an old half torn army satchel, Debu's heart sank.

'I do not know how to put it across to you Kaka Babu and all I can say is that though your son Swarup is physically not present here today to bless his loving young sister, but his spirit is definitely going to be around,'said the man as he handed over the urn containing Swarup's ashes to his father.

Hearing those words, Debu wiped away the moistness in his eyes and having got the heartbreaking message, he put on his pair of dark glasses to hideaway the tears that had swelled under his eyes. Hiding the satchel under his dressing gown, Debu Ghosh thanked the visitor and saw him off at the gate. Then having sent word to his wife that he had some urgent payments to be made to the grocer, he went for a long lonely walk along the seaside. He simply wanted to be alone by himself for a while. Inside the satchel was a diary, a pen, a wrist watch and some photographs. On seeing the photagraph of his son and his wife with Netaji's arms around both of them he felt indeed very proud. But he did not know how to put across this tragic loss to his wife Hena. The catastrophic death of both their elders sons Arup and Swarup in a span of just three months and that too after the war was over was indeed too much for both of them to bear.

"Oh God please give my wife the strength to also bravely bear this enormous loss,' said Debu Ghosh to himself as he kissed the photograph and made his way back home. Having surveyed that he was not being watched by anybody, Debu Ghosh went inside the house and placed the urn containing his son's ashes in one far corner of the small family prayer room.

Touchy and finicky that she always was as far as the cleanlieness of the house and pooja rituals were concerned, Hena was furious when she while doing her morning puja noticed that small urn which Debu without her knowledge had kept slightly hidden away behind the big holy water jar that contained the sacred water of the River Ganges. Before the start of her pooja, the sacred Ganges water as a daily ritual was sprinkled on all the deities inside the pooja room by Hena and today was no exception.

'This must be the work of some illterate stupid idiot who probanly wants to bring bad luck to the family on an happy occasion like, said the lady of the house fuming with anger as she called out with her violent temper to all the domestic servants to present themselves outside the pooja room immediately.

"Who is the damn culprit who has done this act of sacrilege,' said Hena as the five servants with folded hands kept trembling before her.

'Either all of you are blind or you all are simply not interested in doing your duties,' added a visibly upset Hena while pointing to the urn.

'But do believe us Boro Ma, we are all innocent and we have no idea from where the urn suddenly has surfaced from,' said Maharaj the senior most old trusted cook who had been with the family now for over three decades.

'You mean to say it fell from the sky or some ghost placed it there,' said a worked up Hena as she got hold of the urn and threw it out of the window into the garden below. Inspite of all the tantrums that were being thrown by her, her grief stricken husband Debu Ghosh simply did not have the heart to tell her the truth at that moment of time. He thought it was better to plead ignorance.and keep it a secret and atleast till such time the rest of the marriage ceremonies were over with. Debu Ghosh then quietly went back to the garden and having made sure that nobody was watching, him, he picked up the small copper urn from the garden and put it inside his big dressing gown pocket.

A few days later, while the Ghosh family was mourning the loss of their second son Swarup, Viceroy Wavell with the Vicerene were enjoying a well deserved short holiday in Kashmir as the guest of the Maharaja. During the visit for the Viceroy luckily there was only one official function and that was the opening of a new hospital in the capital Srinager and the rest of the days were spent on shoots, fishing, and it finally ended with a round of golf at Gulmarg.

"I must say the Maharani is really very charming and attractive too,' said the Viceroy to his wife while both of them over a cup of hot tea at the nineteenth hole admired the scenic beauty of the Pir Panjal mountain ranges.

"Yes darling, but compared to her husband the Maharaja, she is rather young and he must be doting on her. And have you noticed the awesome sets of jewellery that she displays on her at every function both official and otherwise,' added Lady Wavell as Major Daler Singh Bajwa their Liasion Officer from the Kashmir State Forces introduced his wife Simran and their three year old son Montek Singh Bajwa to their excellencies.

"So you are a Military Cross winner too and where did you earn it,' said the Vicerene when she noticed young Montek trying to play with the medals on his father's chest.

'I earned it during the Battle of Meiktila in Burma,' said Major Daler Bajwa very proudly as Mrs Bajwa took her son from her husband on to her lap.

'In that case since Major Daler Singh is also a gallantry award winner, he too should be part of the victory parade contingent that we are planning to send to England in the summer of next year,'said the Viceroy to Mr RC Kak the newly appointed Prime Minister of the State.

'Oh that indeed will be lovely and I wish we could go too darling,' said Mrs Margaret Kak the English wife of the Prime Minister.

'That may be quite possible for you Mrs Kak, but with the present political situation prevailing in the State and with one faction of the Kashmiris being supported by the Muslim League, and the National Conference of Sheikh Abdulla being backed by the Congress, I very much doubt if Mr Kak will be able to make it,' said the Viceroy somewhat sarcastically as the liveried waiter brought a glass of lemonade for little Montek that the Vicerene had ordered for him.

By the end of the year 1945, the 25,000 prisoners of war from Netaji's INA had started arriving in India and they were totally surprised that the country was ignorant of their very own existence. The majority of the Indians till then had never even heard of the INA and their much touted slogans of "Jai Hind" and "Chalo Delhi". India was still under tight British censor control and as one INA officer rightly remarked.

"Dammit all not even a dog barked when we disembarked on home soil, and therefore it is not their fault and our I.N.A. propaganda I guess was not good enough.

The month of November saw uncertainty and despair in the faces of those who were charged with serious war crimes. On the 5th of November, inside the historical Red Fort in Delhi the General Court Martial of the three prime accused charged with treason, murder and waging war against the King began. Captain PK Saigal a Hindu, Captain Shah Nawaz a Muslim and Lieutenant Gurbaksh Singh Dhillion a Sikh were once all regular officers of the Indian Army. To his Majesty's Government they were now traitors, but to the Congress and the Muslim League and their supporters they were now overnight national heroes. During the war, the British had suppressed all news about Subash Bose and his INA, but when the news of Netaji's death was made public and acts of gallantry by some of the officers and soldiers from Netaji's ill equipped army started surfacing, the general public too was in full sympathy with them. It was thus after his death that Netaji's prediction about the physcological values of his Azad Hind Fouj on the general Indian population were now being fully vindicated.

'But how can a Muslim, a Sikh and a Hundu and who are all Indians be tried for fighting for the independence of their own motherland?' argued Debu Ghosh, when the three old friends met over the weekend for their coffee session.

'I agree but they were fighting with Japanese backing against their own kith and kin which today constitutes the real Indian Army that has Muslims, Sikhs and Hindus in much greater numbers and they all had stuck to their oath under fire. And pardon my saying so but quite a few of these sepoys, JCO's and officers who switched horses in mid-stream were to my mind rank opportunists, and they only changed their uniforms once they were captured by the Japanese so that they could avoid the torture and the hardships in the Japanese prisoner of war camps. Therefore I will not consider them heroes at all. In fact I think they were cowards.Yes on the contrary those Indian civilians settled in South East Asia who voluntarily contributed and donned the uniform of the INA like Netaji did, they I think should be honoured as the real heroes and that includes your own son Swarup and also his late wife Yeshwant,' said Dr Ghulam Hussein.

'Yes and come to think of it, this is the same Congress party which had once sidelined Netaji for his do or die attitude against the British and is today eulogising the same man because he is no more,.And ironically while the Muslim League under Mr Jinnah is hell bent in getting his Pakistan,'added Debu Ghosh somewhat angrily.

'And that is not all, even Mr Gandhi has been visiting these officers and conferring with them inside the confines of the Red Fort. The Congress has even formed an exclusive Defence Committee of not two or three, but of 17 renowned advocates and barristers including Tej Bahadur Sapru, Vallabhai Patel, Pandit Nehru, Asaf Ali and the defence will be led by non other than Mr Bhulabhai Desai,' said Naren Sen with a mild doze of sarcasm in his voice.

Fearing that Subash Bose may still be alive and in hiding somewhere, the British now were apprehensive that the fiery Bengali could still engineer a revolt inside India. Even Viceroy Wavell expressed his doubts over the Japanese announcement of Bose's death in an aircrash. The British also realised that Mr Bose was never a puppet of the Japanese either. Infact he was now a great national hero who had successfully created India's first national army and that was no mean achievement.Thus with the return of the 25,000 Indian prisonersof war and their trials even without their Netaji had created a potential revolutionary situation which both the political parties were now waiting to cash on, and leading them were the Congress. The same Congress party once dedicated to Gandhiji's non violence had started realising the usefulness of violence as they led the protests against the trials being conducted. Jinnah too urged the British too treat the Muslim INA prisoners with leniency. As far as negotiations for independence with the British was concerned it was making no headway. The saying went that when the Congress proposes, the Muslim League disposes and vice versa. And how true that was as the political divide between the Congress and the Muslim League kept widening. However, now that the war censorship had been fully lifted, the Indian press and notably the popular vernacular ones were full of heroic stories and legends about the leaders of the Indian National Army. Netaji's "Jai Hind" now became the popular form of greeting and in millions of Indian shops starting from the paanbidi wallas to the barbers and the roadside tea vendors and dhabhas it was the photo of Netaji looking smart in his military uniform and sidecap that greeted the customers

Realising that it would be not only foolish, but also ridiculous to put on trial all 25000 INA prisoners for waging war against the King Emperor, the government decided to first categorize them into "Whites", "Greys" and "Blacks" There were nearly 4000 "Whites" who had joined the INA under compulsion and they were cleared and sent back to their respective regimental depots. The majority of over 13,000 'Greys" who had joined the INA voluntarily, but they did not take active part in the operations were discharged from service and were sent home. The "Blacks" numbering 6177 that were categorised as ring leaders, active members who not only waged war against the King, but were also involved in brutal killings and war crimes were the ones who were now being tried. For them the punishment could be not only cashiering and dismissal, but could also be facing the firing squad, long terms of rigourous imprisionment and also "Kala Pani," transportation for life to the dreaded Andaman Islands.

The Congress now took up the defence of the key INA personell in right earnest. To help their families, they even set up a relief and enquiry committee who provided small sums of money, food and employment to them. Bhulabhai Desai the one time strong critic of Subash Bose now became a great champion of Netaji as he led the defence in the historic trial. For the Indians, the INA had now become the true national army and for them it was Netaji who had totally succeeded in integrating and uniting the Hindus, Muslims, Sikhs and other communities to fight for the common cause of independence.

As the General Court Martial of the three main accused, Shah Nawaz Khan, PK Saigal and GS Dhillon progressed inside the precints of the Red Fort which was put out of bounds for the press and photographers while it was in session, the surging crowds outside the fort daily grew larger in numbers as they hurled abuses and insults on the British and hailed the under trials as heroes. One day they even besieged the fort. This led to a police firing in which many were killed and a large number wounded. The anti British stance therefore now started surfacing in other major Indian town and cities and. In Calcutta an INA week was hailed and celebrated from 5th to 11th November, 1945 and the 12th of November was declared. as INA Day all over India. The largest public meeting for the INA cause was held at Calcutta's Deshopriya Park. It was organised by the INA Relief Committee and was attended by Sarat Bose, Jawaharlal Nehru and Vallabhai Patel. From 21st November to 26th November, 1945 the city of Calcutta was completely paralysed. In a rare gesture of communal unity and harmony that were unseen since the Jailanwala Bagh massacre and that were witnessed by the Brtish, hordes of Hindus, Muslims, and Sikhs in truckloads with the Congress and the Muslim League flags flying high practically took over the city. And when they also started attacking the American military bases and the British Military establishments inside the city, the situation became rather serious. And when they kept shouting slogans of freedom and independence, and the handouts and posters with captions like "Patriots not traitors", "Death to 20 English for every INA man convicted", "Quit India" and "Jai Hind" also started surfacing on the walls of government buildings and at public places, the Britisn were now really worried.

For the Viceroy and his Commander-in-Chief, both of whom knew the Indian Army very well, this was a matter of very serious concern indeed. They now feared that the loyalty and allegiance of the Indian soldier who had dutifully and loyally served and who were still serving the British Crown could get affected. The Director of Intelligence whose agents had been attending such meetings all over India gave his final assessment by stating in writing that there has seldom been a matter which has attracted so much Indian public interest and that he would not hesitate to say that it was genuine sympathy. With the Red Fort trials now nearing for its final verdict, the Viceroy empowered his Commander-in-Chief, General Claude Auchinleck to commute sentences of death or transportation for life as per his discretion.

On 31st December, inspite of Bhulabhai Desai's heroic defence of the three main accused, the members of the General Court Martial having found them guilty sentenced them to transportation for life, cashiering and forfeiture of all arrears of pay and allowances. Though his conscience did not allow him, but a few days later, when the matter was put upto him for confirmation of the sentence, the Auk in the longer interest of India and the Indian Army in particular and which he dearly loved confirmed only the cashiering and forfeiture of pay and allowances.

When the three accused were now set free, they were profusely garlanded and welcomed as heroes. Now Gandhiji also started believing that Subhas Bose may still be alive and he therefore in his weekly column in the paper "Harijan" not only started praising him and the INA, but also hailed Netaji as a true patriot and a valiant freedom fighter.This however did not stop the British for the sake of Indian army discipline to let everyone go scot free. They carried on with the selective trials of a few who had been charged with serious war crimes. One such person was Captain Abdul Rashid who on the 4th of February 1946 was sentenced to seven years rigorous inprisionment for acts of brutality. Now it was the turn of Mr Jinnah and his Muslim League to show their sympathy and they too came out openly against the harsh verdict. Once again from 11th to 14th February, the streets of Calcutta, Bombay, Delhi and Lahore witnessed unique and unprecedented political demonstrations wherein the Muslims and the Hindus once again joined hands to protest against such trials. In the police firing in Calcutta after the mob had turned violent it resulted in 50 deaths and with over 500 wounded. A month earlier in January, some 5000 Indian airman from the Royal Indan Air Force had gone on strike complaining against the terrible living condtions and the quality of food that was being served to them vis a vis to the 'Goras' in the Royal British Air Force. In the Royal Indian Navy too bickerings against discriminations had started surfacing.

To the British, the men of the Indian National Army who had fought hand in glove with the Japanese or with the Germans and whom they were termed as JIFS and HIFS were no longer Japanese inspired Fifth Columnists, or Hitler Inspired Fifth Columnists as far as the Indians were concerned. They were now being hailed as patriots and freedom fighters. It was under these circumstances on 16th February, 1946, that Mr Frederick Burrows with his wife Dorah arrived in Calcutta to take over from Mr RG Casey as the new Governor of Bengal. Once a proud Sergeant Major from the elite Grenadier Guards Regiment, and an ex President of the National Union of Railwaymen, Frederick Burrows an honest and straight forward man was soon to witness something yet more terrible than the Calcutta riots of February. On arrival at Government House and true to Indian tradition, he and Mrs Burrows were greeted with huge giant size garlands made of marigold flowers.They had never experienced this kind of welcome ever before. As the water from the garland dripped down their necks, they stood smiling at their many well wishers, while a dozen photographers clicked away.

Lord Wavell, the Viceroy had correctly predicted that the end of the war would be a testing time for him in India and how right he was. The left wing elements in the Congress party who had only been recently released from jail were itching to launch a fresh "Quit India" rebellion by employing some of the INA officers and men to spearhead it. But some of the moderates in the Congress concluded that it would be foolish to stir up trouble and create disorder which would economically weaken India further and they therefore thought that it would be safer and wiser to gain freedom by peaceful means since it had been agreed to by the British in principle to give India her freedom. The weekly intelligence briefing to the Viceroy by Mr Norman Smith, the Director of the Intelligence Bureau, Government of India projected a gloomy picture. According to him Nehru in his speeches had also now started preaching violence on the plea that through dialogues nothing was being achieved. Even Gandhi said that if the process of gaining freedom was not expedited, things could get hotter.

The disturbances eversince the INA trials began and the intelligence reports that were now coming in from India convinced the British Prime Minister Mr Clement Attlee that the Imperial tide in India had finally ebbed and that India could not be held by force of arms any longer. If they did that it would be too costly for Britain which had already been devastated by the ghastly war. Mr Attlee therefore decided that it was time to give India her promised freedom and that too in the not too distant a future.

Meanwhile in Nuremberg in Germany the trials of the German leaders that had begun on 20th November, 1945 were still in session. The war crime trials conducted by a joint United States, British, French and Soviet military tribunal with each victorious nation being represented by two eminent judges were now hearing the charges against the German Nazi leaders and senior service officers. The charges were on four major counts which besides starting an aggressive war against peaceful nations, also included crimes against humanity as well as that of murder, extermination, genocide and enslavement. While the 21 under trials that included Hermann Goring, Rudolf Hess, Joachim Van Ribbenthrop, Field Marshall Wilhem Keitel, Grand Admiral Karl Doenitz, General Alfred Jodl, Albert Speer and others sat in the two rows flanked by armed guards with automatic weapons, there was a cry of horror and shame as films and photographs of the inhuman atrocities committed by the Germans on innocent men women and children were displayed on the large screen. When the same was also shown in cinemas all over the world, for some like Shobha Sen, Hena Ghosh and Suraiya Hussein it was beyond their comprehension that in a so called civilised European country, people could commit such terrible carnage and mayhem against human beings simply because they were Jews.The three ladies with their husbands had gone to see the movie "For Whom the Bell Tolls,' at Metro which was Calcutta's best movie theatre hall. The film was based on the best seller written by Ernest Hemingway on the Spanish Civil War which the author himself had covered as a war correspondent. With both her favrourite actors Gregory Peck as Robert Jordan and Ingrid Bergman playing the role of Maria the guerrilla fighter who falls in love with the hero, it was Hena's idea that all of them must see the film, but none of them actually saw it that day. Prior to the main movie, the British Movietone News had showed a long newsreel about the atrocities committed on the Jews by the Germans at the notorious concentration camp at Auschwitz. The visuals were so sickening that Hena, Shobha and Suraiya nearly threw up inside the hall itself. All of them had to be escorted out by their husbands and that was the end of the movie for them that day.

That winter in the cold weather the elections as promised to the Central Legislative Assembly and to the various Provincial Assemblies took place peacefully. In the Central Legislature, the All India Muslim League won all the Muslim seats and the Congress practically walked away with the rest. The same trend also showed in the Provincial elections except in the North West Frontier Province where the Congress party led by Abdul Ghaffar Khan and his elder brother Dr Khan Sahib had won and the party had been asked to form the Government there. The Muslim League formed the government in Bengal and Sind, but in Punjab despite winning the largest number of seats, the Muslim League were made to sit in the opposition as the small Unionist Party with a handful of seats led by Mr Khizar Hyatt Tiwana the Chief Minister with the backing of the Congress and the Sikh Akali Dal formed the government. After the election results were announced and when the three old friends met at their usual weekly coffee session, Dr Ghulam Hussein said.

'But don't you think that they have been unfair to the Muslim League in Punjab?'

'But this is what politics is all about. Today's friend is tomorrow's enemy and yesterday's enemy is today your friend. It is the question of how to remain in power,' said Debu Ghosh.

'That is alright, but I am sure Mr Jinnah will not take it lying down, and believe you me this has caused a lot of resentment and heart burning in the rank and file of the Muslim League,' said Dr Ghulam Hussein.

'I agree and this will not only widen the rift between the Muslims and the Hindus but it will also create more bad blood between Mr Jinnah and Mr Nehru too,' said Naren Sen while settling the bill.

In late January of 1946, Sheikh Abdulla commenting on the speech made by the Viceroy in the Chamber of Princes which was followed by a declaration made by the Chancellor of the Chamber, the firebrand Kashmiri leader made no bones of what he had to say to the Working Council of his own Jammu and Kashmir National Conference.

"Gentlemen these so called treaties were made in times and under circumstances which do not obtain now, and these were framed without the consent of the people of these Princely States. Therefore, under such circumstances no treaty, which acts as a dividing line between their progress and the progress of their brothers in British India, can be binding on them. These treaties I am afraid are now completely outdated. They are in fact reactionary and questionable. To think that the present Princely Rulers will give up their privileged positions that they always enjoyed is nothing but wishfull thinking."

The Sheikh it seems had now decided to openly challenge the authority of Maharaja Hari Singh and the members of his government. He criticised the Maharaja's so called experiment with Dyarchy and called it a fraud to hoodwink the general illiterate public and to please his British masters. He therefore asked the two members from his National Conference who had been inducted into the Maharaja's government as ministers to put in their resignations.

With Independence for India on the cards, yet a third of the British Indian Empire and more than a quarter of its huge population were not under direct British rule and Sheikh Abdulla's outburst against the Princely States and more particularly against his own Maharaja was therefore not to be taken lightly. For the 563 Princely States, big and small their treaties were only with the British Crown and the Governor General of India was also the Viceroy.

That January of 1946, the Viceroy decided to have a grand victory parade in Delhi to honour the Indian Officers and soldiers who had so gallantly fought for the British Indian Army and the Empire. It also included contingents from the Princely State Forces. Major Daler Singh Bajwa with his contingent from the Jammu and Kashmir State Forces arrived in Delhi and during the final dress rehearsal he was surprised to find Major Ismail Sikandar Khan supervising the seating arrangements with Mr Charles Chenevix Trench from the Indian Political Service. While Major Ismail was responsible for the seating of the VIP invitees, Charles Chevnix Trench was responsible for the seating of the Maharajas, Rajas from the many Princely States both big and small.

'But damn it all with so many of these Princes coming for the parade and some with large family's too, it is becoming very difficult for me to work out the seating plan as per protocol and gun salutes,' said a confused Charles Chevnix Trench as he retreated to a far corner to light his cigarette

'Just take it easy youngman and I am sure it is not such a major problem,' said Colonel Reginald Edwards as he also lit his pipe and took the list away from Charles to work out a quick and pactical seating plan.

'I"ll tell you what. We will simplify the whole exercise and have the seating arrangements made, provided you can tell me who among the invitees are entitled to how many gun salutes,' said Colonel Reginald Edwards.

'That's all very fine Sir, but the problem is what do I for those who have an equal number of gun salutes,' said Charles Trench.

'All the more that makes it even more simpler and all that is required to be done is to put all those names in that big solar toppee of yours, give it a big shake and then simply draw lots. And to you it should matter little whether the heir to the throne or the present ruler was a legitimate offspring or otherwise, and in anycase with India's freedom around the corner there is little likelihood that they will make an issue of it,' said Reggie as Major Gul Rehman clicked his heels and saluted. He had been given the honour to command the contingent from the First Punjab Regiment. And when Gul Rehman also told Trench to sincerely take the experienced Colonel Edward's advice, Chevnix Trench immediately got on with the job and did exactly as he was told.

That very evening, Reggie held a candle night dinner party for the three musketeers at his suite in the Imperial Hotel in New Delhi. Built in 1933, the luxury hotel with its Victorian and old colonial style architecture was Sir Edwin Lutyen's brainchild and it was now the place for the rich and the famous in India. Though the dinner that evening was a stag affair, but it was a very memorable one as each one of the three musketeers nostalgically recalled their days at the PWRIMC, the IMA, and their own personal experiences during the war and pulled each others legs in good humour. However, when it came to the topic of their wives, children and parents, Ismail diplomatically commented.

'Gentlemen here I must that add that had it not been for Colonel Reggie, we probably would have never met. But Inshallah, now that we are all still alive and kicking after having survived the war, which in itself is a big blessing from the Almighty, let me in all humility declare that I have decided to remain a confirmed bachelor like my mentor the good Colonel Reggie and therefore when. I die I would like all my assets whatever little that I have or will have should be donated to the Poppy Day Fund.

'But why are you being so damn pessimistic. Let us all enjoy the evening and let me tell you that you still have a long life ahead of you,' said Colonel Reggie as he gave the honour to Ismail to open the first bottle of Champagne.That evening as the champagne cork at Delhi's Imperial Hotel went off with a big bang and after Ismail had poured the bubbly contents into the four tall fluted champagne glasses, Gul Rehman immediately drank a toast to the health and happiness of Colonel Edwards.Reciprocating the good gesture when Reggie raised a toast to all the three musketeers and also to a soon to be free India, Daler Singh Bajwa's only comment was that it should be a united India and not a Balkanized or fractured one.

'Well let us sincerely hope not,' said Reggie as the all of then drank to a free and united India.

On 19th February, 1946, the day Lord Pethick Lawrence the Secretary of State for India made the announcement in the British Parliament that a high level delegation consisting of three senior British cabinet ministers would soon be on their way to India as part of a Cabinet Mission to work out the modalities of granting India her freedom, Colonel Reggie in the company of Major Ismail Sikandar Khan arrived in Bombay.Major Ismail who had returned to India with the Fourth Indian Division's advance party had been detailed to receive the main body at Bombay's Ballard Pier. The Red Eagles who were the first to leave India were also the last Indian contingent to get back home. While waiting for the arrival of the ships at Bombay harbour when he heard some rumours about discontentment among the ratings of the Royal Indian Navy on board the HMIS Talwar, which was the Naval Signal School, he did not pay much heed to it. But the matter was indeed very serious.

The trouble it seems began on 2nd February 1946, the day when Vice Admiral John Godfrey, the C-in-C Navy was scheduled to inspect the establishment. With the strong anti British feelings that were being propagated by the Congress leftists which included Aruna Asaf Ali who also happened to be in Bombay at that time, and fired by the idea of freedom, some ratings very early that morning had cut the halyard, the rope of the main mast where the C-in-C's flag and the naval ensign were to be hoisted. They had also painted 'Quit India' slogans in bold letters on the walls facing the parade ground. Sometime later that morning though the senior staff had tried to repair the damage, but it was a bit too late. When the matter was brought to the notice of the C-in-C, he was livid and he asked for a court of inquiry to be conducted immediately. He also had the commanding officer of the ship, Commander Cole posted out and had him replaced with Commander King, a gunnery officer and who immediately with a big stick in his hand decided to clean up the mess and reinstill discipline in the school. A few days later after having taken over command of the Naval establishment, Commander King while on a routine visit to the rating's mess during lunch time, became rather furious when the Indian ratings who were sitting and having their lunch did not stand up to greet him.

"Sooer ke bache.' You sons of pigs is this how you show respect to your own commanding officer? and I will have the whole lot of you severely punished for this disrespect and insult,' shouted Commander King while instructing his Executive Officer to have all of them charge sheeted immediately.

Though the orders on the subject were very clear that during meals there was no need for anybody to stand up, but Commander King could'nt care less and directed that the offending sailors must be punished. When the sailors filed a written petition against the unfair punishment, it was dismissed by the higher authorities. The Indian ratings then decided to take law into their own hands. They went on hunger strike and shouted anti British slogans. Seeing the situation getting out of control, Commander King deputed Lieutenant SM Nanda and Lieutenant SN Kohli the two young Indian officers on his staff to try and speak to the agitated sailors. The adamant sailors first demanded an apology from their Commanding Officer for his abusive language and the withdrawal of all charges against them. But for Commander King and his staff it had now become a prestige issue and they were not willing to compromise to such gross indiscipline. Half an hour later around midday the angry sailors put out a message on tape without the knowledge of the officers to all ships and establishments of the Royal Indian Navy in India stating that the Signal School was on strike because of unfair punishments and discrimination that they were being subjected to and asked the others to also follow suit.

This soon had a snowballing effect and the strike spread like wild fire as the Indian sailors on board the ships and shore establishments congregated to hold meetings and to force a showdown with the authorities. Some even flew the Congress flag on their ships and shouted anti British and pro INA slogans. The government was now forced to call in armed troops to quell the rebellion which the naval authorities had termed as mutiny. An angry C-in-C Navy declared that he will destroy the Royal Indian Navy if need be and ordered the move forthwith of the British East Indian Fleet of the Royal Navy from Ceylon to the Bombay harbour. Besides the army, the Royal Air Force was also put on standbye to bomb and sink the ships if necessary. Since Indian troops were not prepared to fire on their own countrymen, British Tommies under their British officers had to be called to conduct this operation. To make matters worse the people of Bombay and those especially from the labour class, trade unions and leftist organizations including those within the Congress party in sympathy with the Indian sailors joined the strike. Soon Bombay too was in flames.

On 21st February, 1946 on the small little island of Manora off the coast of Karachi there were no visitors to the small Jhule Lal temple from across the harbour that day. The temple in the centre of the island was that of the revered patron saint of the Sindhi community. On that very morning, the Indian sailors had taken over HMIS Hindustan and gave an ultimatum that they would not hesitate to fire its four inch guns incase any attempt was made to storm the ship. They had also successfully taken over HMIS Bahadur, Chamak, Himalaya and even the Royal Navy Anti Aircraft School. These were all static naval training establishments on the island.

At midnight the British 2nd Blackwatch Regiment based at Karachi went into action as the fully armed Tommies with their supporting weapons and mortars were silently ferried across the harbour. By dawn they had successfully secured the island and the small civilian population was surprised to see so many “Gora Sahibs” with their faces blackened with polish on their sacred territory. And as their camouflaged faces broke into a sweat, the British Commanding officer now gave an ultimatum and set a deadline for the Indian sailors to put down their weapons and to surrender peacefully. The deadline came and went. At 10.30 that morning the Commanding Officer once again focussed his binoculars on HMIS Hindustan and finding no white flag or movement on board the ship, he ordered the three gun artillery field battery that had been deployed to fire point blank on the ship.Then at 10.33 that morning, when the first shell with a big bang landed right on target, the Indian crew on board HMIS Hindustan retaliated by opening up with their four inch guns. But all the shells simply whistled harmlessly over the royal artillery gun positions and landed in Karachi instead. At 10.51 it was all over as a white flag appeared from the hatch of the HMIS Hindustan. The ship had been extensively damaged and the Indian sailors had paid a heavy price with the many casualties that they had suffered. By early evening all the naval ships and establishments on Manora Island were once more in the hands of the British.

Meanwhile on the morning of 22nd February, 1946 at the Salbani airfield West of Calcutta, Major Gul Rehman who was now posted at Barrackpore was enjoying a hot cup of tea with his old friend Squadron Leader R Y Williams who had only ten days ago taken over command of the 159 Liberator Squadron that was based there.During the war in Burma and while the squadron was based in Assam and the Fifth Red Ball Division were enjoying a well deserved break at Jorhat, Major Gul Rehman just for the sake of adventure and the thrill of seeing the Air Force in action had as a guest of Williams flown with him on a few missions and one of which could have spelt disaster for all of them. This was sometime during the first week of March 1944 after the successful launch of "Operation Thursday" by Major General Orde Wingate's Chindit columns behind the Japanese lines and the setting up of "Broadway", an airstrip for supplies and for evacuation of casualties from the heart of enemy territory.The Chindit long range patrol columns had already effectively secured "Broadway," which was nearly 200 miles deep inside enemy territory. On that day Flight Lieutenant RY Williams while on a sortie to "Broadway" had met with unexpected rough weather. Despite the bad weather he had landed at 'Broadway' with the much awaited fresh rations and the private mail. But on the return flight with the casualties on board and due to very low clouds and bad visibility, the left wing tip of his aircraft had brushed against a tree top while taking off from Broadway. This had badly affected the balance and the centre of gravity of the aircraft as it kept banking sideways. But an experienced pilot that he was, Williams manouvered the aircraft skilfully and having sent a May Day signal managed to successfully land at Dimapur airfield with a badly damaged wing. That day they were all lucky to have survived. But the same luck did not hold good for the very man whose brainchild the Chindits were. The son of an army officer, Major General Orde Wingate was born in Nainital in India. In 1923 he graduated from the prestigious Woolwich Academy and was commissioned into the Royal Artillery. In 1936, he had joined the British Intelligence staff in Palestine and had organised training and raids against the terrorist bases where he was subsequently wounded. In Sudan he had formed the Gideon Force which time and again conducted raids on the Italians on the Eithopian border. It was in February 1943, that Wingate with 3000 of his spirited Chindits in 'Operation Longcloth' first entered Burma to disrupt and destroy Japaneese communication centres, outposts and bridges. In March 1944, with the launch of 'Operation Thursday' it became the largest Allied Special Forces operations behind enemy lines and which also in a big way assisted not only General Slim's operations in South Burma, but also General Joseph Stilwell's operations against the Japanese in the North. But on 14th March 1944, just 11 days after launching 'Operation Thursday', the gallant General Wingate died in an aircrash when his aircraft crashed on a hillside near Imphal.

'I wish we could have had some beer and lunch to celebrate my promotion, but that will have to wait for some other time I guess because there seems to be a war on in Bombay now,' said Squadron Leader Williams while studying the navigation chart. Gul Rehman who still had no clue about the happenings in the Navy was quite surprised when Williams added that he was off on a delicate mission with three of his bombers who would after refuelling and arming each aircraft with a 500 lb bomb at Nagpur would then proceed to attack and sink Indian Naval ships in the Bombay harbour.

'Are you really serious or joking,' said Major Gul Rehman as Williams showed him the order that had come to him in writing.

'My God what are we upto. First it was the INA, then the airmen and now the damn navy too is up in arms it seems. But this will get us nowhere and will only give the armed forces a bloody bad name,' added Gul Rehman as the first bomber taxied off the runaway for the take off.Luckily by the time the aircrafts landed at Nagpur the uprising by the naval ratings was over. For once both Mr Vallhabhai Patel and Mr Jinnah working on the same wave length had managed to convince the ring leaders to give up and surrender to the authorities concerned. They argued that the actions to continue with the stir would not only precipitate matters and result in more bloodshed, but it would inordinately also delay in getting India her freedom now that the war was finally over. The leaders of the agitation had got the message loud and clear as they were rounded up and taken to the jail at Thane.

One afternoon a few days after the naval uprising, Major Ismail Sikandar Khan while on his way to the Embarkation Headquarters on Ballad Estate to enquire about the likely date of the arrival of the Red Eagles main body stopped by for a quick beer and a bite at the Sea Lounge, the coffee shop on the first floor of the luxurious Taj Mahal Hotel facing the beautiful Bombay harbour.Having placed his order for a chilled beer and a plate of club sandwiches with the smartly dressed steward, Ismail picked up a copy of the Times of India and went and sat at a table that was far away from the others. After a while, when he did a quick casual survey of the customers and most of whom were British or Americans, he suddenly noticed someone who looked very much like Sandra. From where he was sitting he could only see her side face profile. She was sitting at the last table at the end of the long verandah and was in the company of a handsome naval officer who did not look very British though. Ismail then on the pretext of having a closer look at the lady casually made his way to the toilet. And when he did see her from close quarters, he just could'nt believe his eyes.

'No it simply cannot be her and it must be a question of mistaken identity' thought Ismail as he entered the wash room and splased some water into his eyes. Sandra had died some years ago but then did she really die or maybe she had ditched him for the naval officer? And did the Pugsley family make a fool of him by returning the diamond ring? As all such wild thoughts and memories whizzed past his mind, he returned to his table and took a long sip of the chilled beer.'Maybe it is her twin sister Debbie, but then she had married a railwayman who was a dear friend and colleague of her brother Shaun and they had quite a few kids too. So it could'nt be her either. Then who the hell could she be but Sandra,' thought Ismail till he realized that it was pointless keeping himself under suspense any longer. Finally picking up courage, he simply walked up to the table with his glass of beer and said.

"Please do excuse the interruption and may be I am mistaken, but are you by any chance Sandra Pugsley?' And before he could even complete his sentence, the lady stood up stared into his face and said.

'My God I just cannot believe it. Don't tell me it is you Smiley?" Hearing the name Smiley Ismail was further taken aback because only Sandra addressed him by that name. Nevertheless he politely nodded his head but said rather tersely.

'Yes maam, it is me Smiley alright but my full name is Major Ismail Sikandar Khan.'

'But by Jove you are as dashing and handsome as ever when I last met you and by the way I would like you to meet my husband Lieutenant

Michael D'Cunha from the Royal Indian Navy,' said the lady as the two men shook hands.

'But when did you two get married?' Asked Ismail feeling somewhat cut up with the casualness with which he was introduced to the naval officer.

'Oh that was only a year and three months ago on Boxing Day to be precise and during the Christmas week of 1944,' said Michael as he ordered one more beer for his guest.

'No please that will not be necessary,'said Ismail while refusing the offer somewhat curtly and having lit a cigarette added somewhat rudely.

'But I simply don't understand as to why did you have to do this to me and fake you own death. You could have told me the truth and I would have walked away from your life forever.'

Now there was an uncanny silence for a few seconds and it could have even led to a nasty situation as the angry naval officer got up from his chair to confront Ismail. But when the lady burst out laughing and said to her husband that it was only a question of mistaken identity and that the gentleman was not to be blamed because even now people at times mistake her for her dead sister, that the misunderstanding was resolved amicably.

'Well now I know for sure you must have been terribly in love with my late twin sister and incidently I am not Sandra, I am Debbie.'

Ismail now looked like a stupid fool as Debbie hugged and kissed Ismail on his cheeks and then invited him over for dinner that evening to their war time requisitioned apartment on Bombay's fashionable Marine Drive.

'Do please come. We are on the top floor of the corner building facing the sea and it is called the "Riviera' said Michael as he renewed his offer for a beer for Ismail.

'Yes most certainly I will and I must say it is indeed a small world,'said Ismail while apologizing to the Naval officer.

After having produced three children in quick succession, Debbie's first husband a railway engine driver had lost interest in her and the family and he took too drinking and had turned an alcoholic. He would often come home even from duty half drunk during the daytime and if Debbie objected he would turn violent. At the railway club in Moghulsarai he would regularly make a nuisance of himself by getting drunk on cheap country liquor that he always carried in pint size skotch whisky bottles in both his pant pockets and he would iInvariably pick up a fight with anyone who even looked at Debbie. For drinking on duty he had already been suspended twice and then finally one day while under suspension when he walked into the office of his foreman fully drunk and knocked him out cold with an empty Teacher's skotch whisky bottle, his fate was sealed. That evening after he was released on bail by the police authorities he did not go home, he was so ashamed of himself that he killed himself by jumping in front of the very steam engine on which he had done most of his duties as an engine driver on the biweekly runs to Howrah. Strangely his death also coincided with the Anglo American landings on the beaches of Normandy. It was D-Day for him too that day. That evening while the anglo allied forces under General Eisenhower were battling it out with the Germans on the Cotentin peninsula and on the many beaches of Normandy, the mutilated body of the engine driver inside a wooden coffin was being carried for a final burial at Moghulsarai.

Debbie's parents, Edwin and Laila Pugsley both of them were no more either. They had died a year earlier and out of sheer pity the railway authorities gave Debbie a job as a teacher in their primary school at Moghulsarai. Then in December of that year the handsome naval officer, Lieutenant Michael D'Cunha came to visit his parents during Christmas. Michael's father was also in the railways and he was the assistant station master of Moghulsarai, which was one of the busiest railway junctions in India. A day after his arrival, there was a whist drive competition at the railway club and that was where Michael met Debbie for the first time. At twenty eight, Debbie was a year senior to Michael and a mother of three lovely daughters. But that did not matter as far as Michael was concerned. For soon he was madly in love with her. On Boxing Day with the blessings of his parents they were married. It was a traditional church wedding and Michael with his readymade family returned to Bombay to celebrate the New Year before returning to his ship HMIS Bengal that had been credited with the sinking of a Japanese raider.

While Michael was at sea on war time duties, Debbie like the wives and senior daughters of other naval officers had joined the WRINS, the Women's Royal India Marine Service. This Service had been created to handle the huge increase in the naval signal traffic during the war. The ladies wore a distinctive uniform and were also subject to strict naval discipline. They were not only employed in sensitive posts in the operation rooms and signal centres where they were required to encode and decode classified secret messages, but they also worked as telephone operators. That evening at the party in Michael and Debbie's flat, Major Ismail Sikandar Khan was introduced to Lieutenant SM Ahsan and Lieutenant AR Khan both young and handsome Muslim bachelor officers from the Royal Indian Navy. Both the officers after partition would join the Pakistan Navy and rise to dizzy heights.

On 23rd March 1946, the high powered Cabinet Mission led by Sir Pethick Lawrence and with Sir Stafford Cripps and Mr AV Alexandar as members landed at Karachi. Speaking to the press they said that their mission was to get the machinary set up for framing the constitutional structure in which the Indians will have full control of their own destiny, and in the formation of a new Interim Government.

During the hot summer of 1946 though the negotiations carried on for a full three months but they could not arrive at any workable solution. Whereas the Congress wanted an undivided India, the Muslim League kept on insisiting on their demand for a separate Pakistan. Meanwhile Viceroy Wavell apprehensive that there could be trouble within the Indian armd forces, he reviewed the plans for "Operation Bedlam" and "Operation Madhouse." Both were contingency plans that were aptly named and they spelt out in detail the actions that were to be taken by the army and the civilian authorities incase the Indian Army became unreliable and hostile. It also included the procedures and drills for the evacuation of the British families in India to central safer areas.

In April, 1946, while the Cabinet Mission was in India, Sheikh Abdulla in Srinagar once again lashed out at the Maharaja and what he termed as the Maharaja's coterie of Dogra and Kashmiri Pundit henchmen ruling the State. He reiterated that no sale deed however sacroscant can condemn four million men, women and children of Kashmir to servitude of an autocrat where there very own will to live under his rule was no longer there. The people of Kashmir are therefore determined to mould there own destiny added the Sheikh and made a fervent appeal to the Cabinet Mission to recognize the justice and the cause for such a demand.

On learning about Sheik Abdulla's appeal to his own Kashmiris and to the Cabinet Mission, Mr Jinnah decided to visit the State. On arrival at Jammu, the leader of the Muslim League clarified that it was not the policy of his party to interefere with the internal administration of the Princely State or on the grave issues that had surfaced between the ruler and his people. But Jinnah also added that the members of the Muslim League were certainly very deeply concerned about the welfare of the Mussalmans who constitute the majority in the State. He also declared that he had met Sheikh Abdulla and other senior members of the Sheikh's party only recently at Delhi and Lahore, but regretted the fact that not only did the Sheikh not take his advice to first organise the Mussulmans under one flag and on one platform, but instead the Sheikh indulged in attacking him in a language that was most insulting and vituperative in character.

A few days later the Sheikh gave it back to Mr Jinnah, when he said that the Muslim League's cry for an independent Pakistan was born out of distress and now it was even stripped of all reason. He argued that the realization of Pakistan for the Muslims would not help the Muslim masses, but it would instead hinder them in their struggle for political and economic emancipation. He also added that in his own State of Jammu and Kashmir this question did not even arise because the majority of the people were overwhelmingly Muslims and there was no need to fear any Hindu domination.And soon after Mr Ram Chandra Kak was sworn in as the new Prime Minister of Jammu and Kashmir, Sheikh Abdulla had made another very vital statement and in which he said.

"It augurs ill for the future that we are entering the tumultuous time that lie ahead with a discredited constitutional experiment of so called dyarchy at our back. In the name of the the National Conference I appeal to the Maharaja once again to end this bloody farce and grant truly a responsible government to the people of Kashmir. To the members of the British Cabinet Mission, I say please judge the constructive strength of the people of Kashmir and their urge to also become free. Because with your commitment to give India her freedom is linked our own destiny and our freedom and that is the ultimate guarantee of the stability of Independent."

When the Cabinet Mission was to visit Kashmir for a little sight seeing and a much needed break, Sheikh Abdullah in his telegram welcomed them and sincerely hoped that it would usher in a new era of both political and economic freedom for the four million people of the state. He also stated the need of re-examining the century old Treaty of Amritsar in which the land and the people of Kashmir were sold to the Dogra rulers for a paltry sum of just Rupees seventy five lacs. He called the old sale deed a misnomer as it conferred no privileges to those claimed by other States that were governed by the very same treaty.In the Kashmir valley the majority were Sunni Muslims, the followers of the Prophet. But it also had small communities of Shias, Sikhs and Kashmiri Hindu Pandits. Along the western boundary with British India from Muzzafarpur to Mirpur the population was mostly Punjabi Mussulmans with a sprinkling of Sikhs in the Poonch and Rajouri regions. While the Jammu Province and the plains and hills to its east were predominantly Hindu Rajput Dogras. Whereas in the areas to the north like Gilgit. Skardu and Kargil it was mostly the Khoja and the Shia Muslims, while the sparsely populated Ladakh Region were largely Buddhists.

The contents of the Sheikh's telegram to the Cabinet Mission did upset Maharaja Hari Singh, but since he was playing the gracious host to them he decided to play it cool and waited for Sheikh Abdullah to make his next move.

On the 5th of May, 1946 the Cabinet Mission started negotiations with Mr Jinnah and Mr Abul Kalam Azad, the two leaders and the heads of their respective political party's. That day also happened to be the Viceroy's 63rd birthday. But the negotiations started off on a very bad note when Mr Jinnah even refused to shake hands with Mr Azad, the President of the Indian National Congress though both were Muslims, but unfortunately they were from opposite camps. To Mr Wavell this was indeed a bad omen.

On the 16th of May, the Cabinet Mission gave their final plan. It rejected decisively for a wholly sovereign Pakistan be it of the larger or the smaller truncated variety that Mr Jinnah had been asking for.They proposed a plan for an all Indian Union based on a three tier constitution with three major groupings.

Group A would consist of the representatives of the six Hindu majority provinces of British India. Group B would consist of the representatives of the Muslim majority provinces which would include Punjab, Sind, and the North West Frontier including Baluchistan. Finally Group C would comprise of the representatives of Bengal and Assam which had a sizeable equal mix of population of both Hindus and Muslims. As far as the Princely States were concerned they were advised to enter into a federal relationship with the Government of India as units in the proposed Union thereby retaining their internal sovereignty and powers in all other disciplines except foreign affairs, defence and communications which were to be dealt with centrally.

Initially the Congress, the Muslim League and the Sikhs were quite happy and content with the plan and therefore the Viceroy now mooted the formation of an Interim Council where all the members except the Viceroy would be Indians. Viceroy Wavell also wrote to all the Princely rulers and warned them that once the British were out of India it would automatically cease their powers or shoulder their obligations of paramountcy. However, the British would not under any circumstances transfer the paramountcy to the new Indian government. He also cautioned the Princely State that once the British left this would create a big void and as suggested by the Cabinet Mission it would therefore be in their own interest that they should enter into a federal relationship with the new Government of India. Now the Rajas and Maharajas too seemed fairly satisfied with the deal.

While Wavell was busy with the Cabinet Mission, the Commnader-in-Chief India, General Claude Auckinleck on 22nd May,

1946 visited Shinkiari in order to attend “Exercise Embrace” that was being conducted by the Army Headquarters.This was an internal defence exercise to cater for a situation in case of another uprising like that of Quit India in 1942 by the people of India. The exercise was primarily to test all signal communications, and the contingency plans for the protection of important airfields, railway junctions and other such vital government targets. During the exercise, Major Ismail Sikandar Khan was pleasantly surprised when he was introduced to Lieutenant Colonel Shaheed Hamid.

A product of Sandhurst, Lt Col Hameed had only recently taken over as the PS or Private Secretary to the C-in-C. It was a very prestigious appointment and Hameed was the first ever Indian officer to occupy that coveted appointment and office.

“Oh you must visit me and my family while I am still in that chair and whenever you get an opportunity to do so,” said Lt Col Shahid Hameed who was very impressed with Major Ismail Sikandar Khan’s credentials and his war record.

“Most certainly Sir and it would be a pleasure to meet your charming wife Tahira and the three beautiful little children, Hasan, Shenaz and Chotoo or rather Hassu, Gudiya and Chotoo as you call them and I have also been told that all your children also lovelingly address the the oldman as “Chiefy.” And not only that, the great Auk too I am told also dotes on them and he often takes them out for drives in big Cadillac car and he even lets them play with his two big pet crames, George and Mary,’said Ismail.

‘Well I must confess that you are fairly well imformed and there is no doubt that I am indeed very lucky to be working directly under the Chief who is not only a thorough gentleman but a good human being too. Moreover, he is very concerned about the future of the Indian Army and last month on the 28th of April, he not only visited Landhikotal and Peshawar to witness the re-raising of the legendary Khyber Rifles, but on the 24th of June he also plans to visit the small village of Kharakvasla near Poona to approve the site for the proposed National Defence Academy, a unique tri-service institution which will be the only one of its kind in the world,’ said Lt Col Shaheed Hameed very proudly.

On the morning of the 31st of May, a very happy looking Lt Col Shaheed Hameed with an important signal in a file walked into the C-in-C’s office and said very seriously.

“Sir on your promotion to Field Marshall we all want a big party tonight.”

Stop kidding and don't be funny,' said the Chief with a smile as Hameed opened the file and placed it on the C-in-C's table. The Chief could'nt believe that he had been promoted to a Field Marshall and that His Majesty himself would present him with the Field Marshall's baton at the Victory Parade that was scheduled to be held in London on the 8th of June.

Sometime during the third week of May, 1946 at their weekly coffee house session, Debu Ghosh walked in with a copy of the Calcutta Statesman and said.

'Gentlemen it seems that the Maharaja of Kashmir and the other powerful princes of India are going to get after this man called Sheikh Abdullah for speaking out so bloody openly against them and for criticizing them on their lifestyles and their misrule.'

'But come to think of it what the Sheikh said in a public speech at Srinagar recently, it definitely had some element of truth in it and that man has been asking for trouble eversince 1931, and for him getting behind the bars has become quite a habit it seems,' said Naren Sen.

'But what did he say this time,' asked Dr Ghulam Hussein.'

'Alright then in that case let me read it out to you,' said Debu Ghosh as he lit his pipe and got ready to read out the speech verbatim. Well gentlemen while lashing out at his own Maharaja in particular and at the other 500 odd princely states in general, this is what the Sheikh had to say and I quote.

'The tyranny of the Dogra rulers has lacerated our souls. The Kashmiris are the most handsome people yet they are the most wretched looking. It was therefore now time for action.To end your poverty you must now fight slavery and enter the field of jihad as a soldier. India today is fighting against Imperialism and therefore the fight for the rights of our people is not only for our State but for the whole of India too. The princely rulers of India possess one fourth of India but they have always played traitors to the cause of Inda's freedom. The demand therefore that the princely order should quit is a logical extension of the policy of "Quit India" since the Indian freedom movement demands the complete withdrawal of British power. Logically therefore these so called Princes and Rajas, the stooges of British imperialism should also go and restore sovreignity to its real owners, the people of their State. The Hindus who think alongwith the Prime Minister Mr Ram Chander Kak that the Dogra rule should remain must never forget that we are treated in Kashmir as a bought off race without distinction of religion. The voice of truth will prevail. Prophets have spoken for the truth which has always triumphed. Sovreignty is not the birthright of a ruler. Everyman, woman and child will now shout "Quit Kashmir". The Kashmiris have expressed their will and we will ask for plebiscite on this very question.'

'By God this firebrand Kashmiri it seems means business, but I only hope this does not precipitate into a major law and order situation, because it is the tourist season now and it will only bring more misery to the people of the valley who depend a great deal on it for some sizeable extra income,' said Dr Ghulam Hussein.

A few days later the fiery Sheikh Abdulla in another hard hitting speech entreated the people to contribute just one rupee per family so that the Rs 75 lacs could be paid back to the Maharaja to buy back the Independence of Kashmir.A few days after his call of "Quit Kashmir" to the Maharaja, Sheikh Abdulla while on his way to India to visit Pandit Nehru was arrested at Garhi Habibullah near the border town of Muzzafarabad and was brought back to Srinager to face trial for treason.

On getting the news about his arrest, Pandit Nehru decided to visit the valley. The Maharaja however considered Nehru's visit as an unwanted interference in the affairs of his State and he therefore ordered the State Force unit that was deployed in the Muzzafarabad area to prevent him from crossing the border. Halfway across the bridge over the River Jhelum at Kohala, a full section strength of sepoys from Major Daler Singh Bajwa's company with fixed bayonets now awaited the arrival of the unwanted visitor.

'But what do we do Sir if he gets out from the car and starts walking across the bridge on to our side,' said Major Daler Singh Bajwa to his senior Major Bhagwan Singh who had been made incharge of this very delicate operation.

'Well we have to follow the Maharaja's orders and place him under arrest,' said Major Bhagwan Singh very confidently.

'But won't that create a crisis for the future. After all Pandit Nehru is most likely to become free India's first Prime Minister,'said Major Bajwa.

'Well we are after all soldiers of the Maharaja and these are his orders and we have to comply with it implicitly,' replied Major Bhagwan Singh.

Half an hour later the car carrying the VIP's from India was stopped at the Kohala Bridge. A visbly angry Pandit Nehru himself a Kashmiri simply walked through the barricade pushing aside the bayonet fixed rifles of the soldiers. But as soon as he crossed into Kashmir territory, Major Bhagwan Singh very politely told him that he was now under arrest. From Kohala he was driven to Uri where he rested for the night at the dak bungalow and was forced to return back to India the next day. This was Major Bajwa's first ever meeting with the man who was soon destined to rule over India and he was highly impressed by the man's demeanour, bearing and conduct.

While the Sheikh was facing trial at Srinagar assisted by a battery of top Congress leaders that included Asaf Ali and even Pandit Nehru who had once again donned the black robe of a lawyer, a big contingent from the Indian Army were on the high seas to London. They were on board "The Mauretania" It was the biggest ship ever to pass through the Suez Canal.The officers and men on board were all winners of gallantry awards and decorations that they had earned during the recently concluded Second World War and were on their way to take part in a historic parade that was to be held in London on the 8th of June. 1946. Colonel SJH Greene from the famed Frontier Force Rifles had drilled the contingent extensively at Bareilly and to make sure that the men would not miss there home food he had also very thoughtfully carried on board enough dry rations and condiments for the entire duration of their stay in England.

'Welcome to London,'read the huge banner as the Indian contingent arrived at the Kensington Gardens behind the Albert Memorial to set up their camp. To keep the general public away and for the sake of security, the outer perimeter of the camp had been fenced all around with barbed wire. That very first evening at the camp, Major Gul Rehman and Major Ismail Sikandar both of whom as holders of the Military Cross were part of the contingent were pleasantly surprised by the presence of Colonel Reginald Edwards, Colonel Attiqur Rehman and Major Daler Singh Bajwa inside the big tented officer's mess. The three of them were also winners of the Military Cross and they had taken a flight from Karachi to take part in the Victory Day celebrations voluntarily. Though Colonel Reginald Edwards and Colonel Attiqur Rehman were not there as official invitees, but both of them just wanted to be there to cheer the Indian Contingent.

England and London in particular was still reeling under the devastations of the war. There was strict rationing, but that did not deter Colonel Reginald Edwards who was now nearing seventy. He was there to prove a point that the Indian soldier was second to none in the world. The Indian Army during the war had produced the largest number of Victoria Cross winners, and Reggie felt that the largely ignorant British politicians and the general public in England and the world must be made aware of this very important fact.

"Maybe this could also help the Cabinet Mission now in India to expedite the issue and give the Indian people their freedom,' said Reggie as he ordered a round of drinks for the three musketeers.

'But Sir I hope it will be a united India and not a fragmented one,' said Major Gul Rehman.

'That is entirely upto you all, the people of India and your political leaders,' said Reggie as he raised a toast to the Indian Army and diplomatically avoided a discussion on the subject.

A fortnight later and early one the morning and after quite a few drill rehearsals for the parade, while the Indian contingent was looking forward to the event, they were distracted by a bevy of good looking females in P.T.uniform.

'We have proved ourselves on the battlefield but now we have to prove ourselves on the Victory Parade,' said Colonel Greene while addressing the large Indian contingent during the final dress rehearsal. Just then and while he was still speaking, there passed by in full view Prunella Stack the Commanding Officer of the women's League of Health and Beauty with her squad of well proportioned young ladies dressed in their brief physical training kit. An Indian soldier on seeing those shapely legs said.

"Colonel Sahib hum ko bhi thodasa mauka milna chahie aur phir dekho hum unko bhi hum jeet lenge. ("Sir all you have to do is to just give us a chance and you will see that we will win those ladies over too)' On hearng that remark, Colonel Greene sportingly smiled at the young Indian soldier and carried on with his next word of command. But the soldier was damn well right it seems. For after a day or two at around lunch time arrived at the sentry gate a young and shapely blonde looking for one Mr Piroo. On being imformed about the lady's presence near the gate, Colonel Green who was sharing a bottle of beer with Major Ismail Sikandar Khan asked the sentry on duty to show her in. Both of them were quite surprised when the young lady very confidently said.

"Please do not mind my disturbing you all at lunch time, but could you please inform Mr Piroo that I am waiting outside for him."

'Ofcourse young lady, but do first sit down till we trace out who this lucky Mr Piroo is,' said Colonel Greene very chivalrously.

'There is no need for that Sir because Mr Piroo is none other than my company cook and I will call for him right away,' said Ismail.

A few minutes later as Major Gul Rehman and Major Bajwa also walked into the officer's mess which was under a tent and when they all saw Cook Piroo walking out with his beautiful date, Major Gul Rehman could not help but comment.

'Well that is not bad at all and even the damn cook has all the luck.'

'That's damn well right and so what if he does not know a word of English but I am quite sure Mr Piroo will do justice and come back safely with his sword of honour under his trousers fully intact,' said Colonel Greene as everyone joined in the laughter.

A few days later even sweeper Meher Din from the 59th Frontier Force Rifles who had won the IDSM, the Indian Distinguised Service Medal in Italy for carrying ammunition to the forward troops while under heavy enemy fire was seen in the company of a buxom English lady. And it was indeed very creditable that during their entire stay in London and elsewhere there was not one single case of ill discipline among the officers, JCO's and Jawans of the Indian contingent. The Londoners took them not only to to their hearts but often even to their houses. Even the King and the Queen with their two pretty young daughters Elizabeth and Margaret visited and talked to the Indian soldiers in the camp.

At a camp fire the Indian soldiers and officers besides singing popular Hindi film songs of the forties like' Chal Chal re Naujawan' and 'Diya jalao jag mag, jagamag' which even a large number of the British Officers from Indianised units were familiar with, the Indian jawans also sang Lily Marlene, Oh My Darling Clementine and' She will be coming down the Mountain when she comes', much to the delight of the general British public who watched the performance with pleasure from outside the barbed wire fencing. They were even more surprised when the Indian Military Brass Band played the Blue Danube and the Glenn Miller super hit "In the Mood". And finally when the Pipe Bands played Scottish numbers like 100 Pipers and Highland Laddie, the crowd was in ecstasy. They could never imagine that the Indian soldier were so versatile not only on the battlefield but also in the field of music and histrionics.

At the final parade, the eight hundred strong Indian contingent commanded by Brigadier J N Chaudhuri who was popularly also known as "Moochu Chaudhuri" because of his moustache gave a sterling performance of military drill. He was ofcourse ably supported by Colonel Greene, Major Jangu Satarawala and Major Gobinder Singh. The Indians were repeatedly cheered by the vast crowd as they smartly marched in perfect step to the beat of the drums and the haunting music of the brass bands. For the three musketeers, Gul, Daler and Ismail who were leading their respective company's it was indeed a day of great honour for all three of them.

While the Londoners enjoyed the company of the Indian soldiers, at home in India a major crisis of political wrangling was brewing. It all revolved around the composition of the Interim Government. The Cabinet

Mission had proposed to include a total of 14 people, all Indians for its formation. Besides the Viceroy, the Interim Government would comprise of six Hindus from the Congress Party including one from the scheduled class, five Muslims from the Muslim League and one Sikh, a Parsi and a Christian who would represent the minority community respectively. To this the Viceroy also added that if any major party was unwilling to join such an interim coalition government then regardless what others had to say he would still go ahead with its formation and make it as representative as possible.

Initially both the Congress and the Muslim League were quite content with the offer, but Gandhi objected by saying that the Congress was a secular party which had Hindus, Muslims and others also as active members. He also added that the present elected President of the Congress Maulana Abul Kalam Azad was himself a Muslim, therefore the non inclusion of a Nationalist Muslim from the Congress in the interim government would not be correct and more so because the Congress which always maintained and professed that it was a national party would be going against their very own principle of a secular India. Now this came as a bombshell to Mr Jinnah and when the Congress on the advice of Gandhiji rejected the proposal and insisted that the Congress reserved the right to nominate not only Hindus, but also the Muslims who were capable of running the country, the daggers were drawn. An infuriated and an angry Mr Jinnah felt that he had been outwitted by Mr Gandhi and the Congress and he even charged the Cabinet Mission and Viceroy Wavell with breach of faith. He therefore decided to boycott the Interim Council and refused to send his list of names to the Viceroy. Regardless of that, when Jinnah was told that by not joining the interim government he would only be harming his own interest and that of the Muslim League, Jinnah for a while remained non committal. He even rejected Mr Gandhi's offer of becoming India's first Prime Minister.

On the 7th of June, Viceroy Wavell spent an hour alone with Mr Jinnah in his office regarding the composition of the proposed Interim Government. Mr Jinnah however kept insisiting that the Muslim League would only join provided they got equal representation.

'If it is five Hindus, five Muslims and two from the minority committee then your Excellency we would willingly join, and in that case I would like to have the Defence portfolio to myself and the Foreign Affairs and Planning should also be with the Muslim League,' said Mr Jinnah as the tall liveried waiter rolled in the tea trolley. The meeting however ended with no firm commitments from either side.

Four days later on 11th June, 1946 at around midday, Mr Gandhi turned up unexpectedly for a meeting with the Viceroy. He was very anxious for an amicable settlement and declared that a coalition was the need of the hour and parity should not be a bottleneck.

'Your excellency regardless of the numbers and whether they belong to the Congress or the Muslim League, the best men available must be inducted into the government,' said the Mahatma. He insisited that the Viceroy must convene a meeting with Mr Jinnah and Mr Nehru at the earliest and pin them down to form a government and only allow them to leave his office once they have done so.

Two days later on the 13th and with the one to one meeting of Jinnah and Nehru with the Viceroy not yet in sight, Mr Gandhi in his own hand wrote to the Viceroy and in which he said very plainly of what he expected of the Viceroy.

'You are a great soldier-a daring soldier. Dare to do the right. You must make your choice of one horse or the other. So far as I can see you will never succeed in riding two at the same time. Please choose the names submitted either by the Congress or the Muslim League. For God's sake do not make it an incompatible mixture and in trying to do so produce a fearful explosion.'

On the day the Cabinet Mission with failure in their pockets flew back to London, the three old friends at the coffee house debated the possibility of whether India would remain as one entity or will she be balkanised.

'Well if you ask me, come hell or high water Mr Jinnah will have his Pakistan someday whether we like it or not. He too has his own principles and if he compromises now then the Muslims of India and specially those in the Muslim dominated provinces and the members of his own Muslim League will lose faith in him. There is no doubt that he is their undisputed leader, their Quaid-e-Azam and he is not the type who will bend easily. My reading is that he will give the Congress a run for their money,'said Debu Ghosh.

'But what do you think he will do,' asked Dr Ghulam Hussein.

'To my mind he will now do nothing else but keep demanding for an independent homeland and I do not find there is any other option left for him. The very fact that he himself has thrown away Mr Gandhi's offer to become the Prime Minister of India itself shows that he is probably aiming for something bigger,' said Naren Sen.

'And what do you think will happen to all those Princely States,' asked Dr Ghulam Hussein.

'Well those who are big in size and have their own armies will probably agitate to keep themselves in power as they have been doing hithertofore, while the smaller ones will either be eaten up or will join the federation that suits them best,'said Debu Ghosh.

'But do you think that people like Sheikh Abdulla and his National Conference who have been demanding the overthrow of their Maharaja will ever succeed in doing so,' asked Naren Sen.

'Definitely not under the present circumstances and atleast not while he is being tried for sedition and high treason,' said Debu Ghosh.

On 20th of June, 1946 the Provincial Committee of the National Conference in Jammu had sent a telegram to the Viceroy stating that the solution of the Kashmir problem is an acid test for the honesty of the British Government and demanded for the immediate release of Sheikh Abdulla and other leaders. It also said that the idea of an independent Kashmir was ridiculous and the wisest course of action would be for the State to join the Indian Union under the leadership of the Sheikh. It seems that the Maharaja too was toying with the Idea of remaining independent and he would be the last one to release the National Conference leaders lest they play more mischief.

The conviction of Sheikh Abdulla now seemed to be a foregone conclusion, when he was permitted to address the court. The Sheikh it seemed had done his home work well when he said.

"Milord I am not interested in my personal defence and I would not have undertaken this Quit Kashmir campaign if I had not felt that my trial for sedition is far more than a personal charge against me. This is in fact a trial of the entire population of Jammu and Kashmir. Oppressed by the extreme poverty and lack of freedom and opportunity of my people, I with my National Conference colleagues now behind bars only tried to give to the people of Kashmir the courage to fight for their rights, aspirations and desire for freedom. This I have been doing relentlessly for the last sixteen years and have attracted the penal and preventive provisions of the law. But where the law is not based on the will of its people, it can and will lead to the suppression of their aspirations. But such law has no validity though it may be enforced for a while.There is a law however higher than that. The law that represents the peoples will and secures their well being. I, therefore will face with confidence and without fear and I will leave it to history and to posterity to pronounce their verdict on the claims that I and my colleagues have made not merely on behalf of the four million people of my State but also of the other ninety three millon people of all other such States who are under the subjugation of the Rajas and the Maharajas. The cry of Quit Kashmir had nothing personal about it, but is now being projected by the prosecution that it had communal and even communist undertones. This is a travesty of fact and I deny and repudiate these baseless allegations and trumped up charges. The National Conference is essentially a National Organization which includes in its fold all people who agree and stand up for India's objective of Independence and freedom."

'I must say that the Sheikh spoke very well indeed,' said Debu Ghosh as he read out the address to his two friends, Ghulam and Naren.

'Well with the Sheikh now behind bars, I guess both Mr Jinnah and Pandit Nehru will now have to realign their focus on that strategically located State of Jammu and Kashmir,' said Naren Sen.

'Yes and I also feel that the race for Kashmir has now already begun in right earnest for both of them,' said Debu Ghosh.

CHAPTER-17

The Great Cacutta Killings

In late July,1946 Mr Mohammed Ali Jinnah, the cool and calculating England returned Barrister and the supremo of the All India Muslim League held a press conference at his sprawling bungalow on Bombay's fashionable Malabar Hills. He was dresssed very soberly in a well pressed double breasted Saville Row suit with a matching tie and handkerchief on his top coat pocket. Before coming out to meet the Press, Mr Jinnah once again adjusted the Windsor knot on his tie and having had one last look at himself in the mirror, he walked out boldly into the big verandah to meet the waiting press. On that wet monsoon morning as he approached the steps of his spacious verandah, the flash bulbs and the cameras clicked away. He was about to make a statement that would not only send the Congress on a tailspin, but it would split India and hasten the partition of the country also. The date was 29th July, 1946, as the clean shaven tall lean man with a mind as sharp as a razor slowly fitted his monocle to his eye and in an icy cold tone declared that the "Direct Action Day" for the Muslims in India was not far away and then having lit his cigarette added.

"Gentlemen we are preparing to launch a struggle and for this we have chalked out a well thought out plan. We the Muslim League have decided to boycott the constituent assembly and also to reject the latest British plan in its entirety for the British transfer of power to an interim government. Let me tell you Gentlemen this is not of our doing, but we are being forced in our own self protection to abandon the constitutional method. I know that the decision we have taken is a very grave one and if the Muslims were not granted their separate Pakistan,' Direct Action' will be launched. You don't expect me to sit with folded hands for I am also going to make trouble,' concluded the man who come what may was now determined to get his Pakistan.

On the very next day dressed in a traditional Muslim dress of a sherwani and a fez cap over his head, Jinnah stood on a public platform to address the Muslims of Bombay. With red fez caps on their heads as a symbol of unity, the mammoth crowd of Muslims greeted their leader with thunderous cheers as he walked up to the podium to address them. Standing in front of his own huge portrait that was in the backdrop Jinnah said.

'Gentlemen two and a half weeks from today, the 16th of August will be observed religiously by all Mussulmans as' Direct Action Day.' Then he continued in a fiery and defiant tone to remind the Congress that if they wanted peace, the Muslims did not want war. But if the Congress wanted war than the Muslims would accept that offer unhesitatingly.

'Gentlemen, we will either have a divided India or a destroyed India and are you all with me.' There was a hushed silence for a few seconds and then the clapping and the cheering began. As the shouts of "Mohammed Ali Jnnah Zindabad and Pakistan Zindabad" rented the air, the joyous crowd tossed their fez caps high into the sky and warmly embraced one another.

That evening the 69 year old Karachi born lawyer lighted probably his fortieth Craven A cigarette of the day. He then poured himself a stiff Black Label skotch and with his dearest sister Fatima for company, sat on the long rattan chair on his verandah to enjoy his well deserved drink. He was now fairly confident that he would one day get his Pakistan and wished that it should be during his lifetime. He was getting old and was not in good health either.

'The dye has now been cast for good it seems,' said Dr Ghulam Hussein as he read out the Urdu version of Mr Jinnah's speech from the Muslim League mouthpiece "The Star Of India" to both his friends at the coffee house on the next day.

'I think "The Star of India" is soon going to become a misnomer and as far as the Muslim League is concerned they probably will have to rename it in the near future as "The Star of Pakistan" said Naren Sen very matter of factly.

'Well unfortunately neither Naren nor I will be present in Calcutta on Direct Action Day, but I guess we will see its effect in East Bengal since both our families are going to be in Dhaka to kill two birds with one stone. In other words we have finally found the right match for both my son Anup and Naren's daughter Purnima in the same family and we are off to finalize the dates for their marriage during this coming winter,' added Debu as he lit his precious Dunhill pipe.

'And when do you all intend getting back to Calcutta,' asked Dr Ghulam Hussein.

'Definitely not before the the first week of September because we intend leaving on the 14th of August and we will spend atleast a week in Dhaka to finalise the dates and then go to Chittagong and spend atleast another fortnight with my son Ronen and daughter-in-law Mona, since they have recently been posted there, and moreover Mona is in her sixth month of her first pregnancy and if all goes well and as per schedule, we will all should be back on the 3rd of September,'said Naren Sen

'Well that is indeed really good news and both you and Debu will be grandfathers soon I guess. But I must also inform you that my brother-in-law Colonel Attiqur Rehman with his wife Nafisa have also arrived from Peshawar last night and presently they are both staying with their son Major Gul Rehman at Barrackpur. And the reason is that their daughter-in-law Zubeida is expecting her third child. And while you are all on your way to Dhaka, my wife and I will also make a trip on the 14th of August to Murshidabad to finalize my daughter Haseena's wedding', said Dr Ghulam Hussein very proudly.

But who is the lucky boy?' asked Debu Ghosh as he called for the bill.

'He is the eldest son of an old family friend of ours, but he is not a doctor but a briefless lawyer like you,' said Dr Ghulam Hussein while having a friendly dig at Debu.

'In that case I also give my word that if you get him here as your "ghar jamai" that is as your live in son-in-law, I will make him my junior partner immediately and that is a gentleman's promise,' said Debu Ghosh with his typical sense of humour.

'Well in that case before we all go in our respective directions looking for grooms and brides, let us all meet for a good family get together, said Debu as he took out a deck of cards from his pocket to decide who should play the host.

'Gentlemen the lowest card will have the honour,' said Debu Ghosh as he took out the pack of Bonus cards from his pocket, and having expertly shuffled it put it on the table and asked for the cut. As soon as Dr Ghulam Hussein had done the needful, Debu kissed the deck and dealt. Surprisingly it was the two of clubs for him, the lowest card in the pack. "What bloody shit luck,' said Debu Ghosh as he paid for the coffee and snacks too.

The date for the get together was therefore fixed for the evening of 13th of August after sunset. Firstly because it was the month of the Ramzan and secondly the very next day all of them were scheduled to leave for Dhaka and Murshidabad as planned.

'My God I do not know what Mr Jinnah and his Muslim League is upto,' said Dr Ghulam Hussein as he walked in with his new born grandson Imran Hussein in his arms and a copy of that day's edition of the "Star of India".

Imran Hussein was born on 29th July, 1946 in Calcutta to Nawaz and Shenaz on the day Jinnah gave his ultimatum for the Direct Action day. Noticing the big half circular black patch that resembled a prominent waxing crescent moon which was a birthmark on the little boy's backside, the grandfather in all seriousness remarked.

'I only hope and pray that the 16th of August should pass off peacefully and it should not leave a black mark like the one the doctor has left on my poor little grandson's right bum and with which he will have to now live forever I guess.'

'Yes in medical parlance it is commonly known as a port wine stain and though such shaped birthmarks are very rare, but I am afraid he may have to live with, but it wont do him any harm,' said Dr Ghulam Hussein.

'Well whatever it is, thank God it is on his right bum and nowhere else and since Dr Ghulam has said that such kind of a birthmarks are very rare, maybe it will prove lucky for the boy,' said Arif Rehman who had come on a spot of leave to be with his only sister Shenaz.

The Muslim League had printed the programme for the Direct Action day in the "Star of India" and exorted all the Muslims of Calcutta and those from the nearby villages to make it a resounding success. The last para was very significant and it read.'Muslims must remember that it was in Ramzan that the Holy Quran was revealed. It was in Ramzan that the permission for Jihad was granted by Allah. It was during Ramzan that the great Battle of Badr was fought way back in 624 AD, when just three hundred of the Prophet's (Peace Be Upon Him) loyal and devoted followers defeated 900 Meccans. This was also the first open conflict between Islam and the heathens. Once again it was during Ramzan in 631 AD that 10,000 Muslims under our holy Prophet captured Mecca and established the Kingdom of Heaven and the Commonwealth of Islam in Arabia. Our Muslim League is therefore fortunate that it is starting its 'Direct Action' in this holy month of Ramzan. So as a sacred duty all Muslims must come in large numbers for the meeting on the Maidan on 16th August.'

Everyone that evening at Debu Ghosh's house was in a somber mood. And to make matters worse the Muslim League government in Bengal under the leadership of Mr HS Suhrawardy, the very Chief Minister who in April had moved the resolution for an Independent Pakistan during the Muslim League convention and had even advocated that Calcutta should become the capital of East Pakistan therefore very conveniently decided to declare 16th of August as a public holiday in Bengal. It was now evident that Mr Jinnah and his Muslim League were now determined to keep their promise for a divided India or a destroyed India. The battle lines were now getting primed to prove that very point, and what better place than Bengal and Calcutta, which was still the second city of the British Empire and the commercial capital of India.

The sparring and shadow boxing to test each other had already begun after Jinnah gave his call for Direct Action on 29th July. It was now getting time for the Hindus and Muslims to have it out with one another and with a free for all, with no rules barred and with no referees to judge.

'I think this sort of propaganda and unreasonable demands from both the Muslim League and the Congress will only add to more miseries and delays in getting us our freedom,' said Colonel Attiqur Rehman as Debu Ghosh poured him another stiff scotch, and for good company poured himself a large one too, while his wife Hena gave him a dirty look and announced that dinner was ready.

'Now that 16th of August has been declared a holiday and my wife Nafisa who has never been to Murshidabad is desirous of seeing the old Muslim capital of Bengal, I hereby grant her permission to accompany my brother-in-law's family while I till they return will do the baby sitting and look after little Imran Hussein,' said Colonel Attiqur Rehman as the men folk sat down for the delicious Bengali food that had half a dozen varieties of fish preparations selectively cooked by the hostess and their only daughter Purnima.

That very evening Major Ismail Sikandar Khan the GSO2 Intelligence of the 4th Indian Division which was now part of Eastern Command suddenly landed up at Debu Ghosh's house with a huge cake from Flury's on Park Street.The Red Eagles under Major General TW Rees were now in the area of Ranchi and Major Ismail had come to Fort Whilliam that very morning on some important liasion work with the Area headquarter that was located there. It was directly related to the requrement of additional troops if necessary for the Calcutta garrison in case of a major law and order problem on Direct Action Day. He had also been tasked to find out about the security arrangements at Kanchrapara where the Americans had dumped a huge cache of arms and ammunition that had been declared surplus after the war.

There was very reliable information that goondas and unlawful elements in the city were involved in large scale thefts of such arms and ammunition and in case of a showdown this could prove very costly.

Immediately on his arrival at Fort Whilliam, Ismail tried to get in touch with his old bum chum Major Gul Rehman Khan at Barrackpore, but on being told by his orderly that Sahib with Burrasahib and family had gone to Calcutta to Mr Ghosh's house, Ismail decided to give all of them a big surprise.

'Welcome home and what a pleasant surprise this is indeed,' said Colonel Attiqur Rehman as he hugged Ismail and kissed him on both his cheeks.'

'My God he is really as handsome as ever,' said Debu Ghosh as he handed over a large peg of "Something Special" scotch whiskey with soda to the dashing infantry officer from the Second Punjabees.

'Yes and we must now also look for a pretty bride for him too,' said Hena Ghosh as Purnima Sen, the 20 year old charming daughter of Naren Sen dressed in a saree offered Ismail a Bengali shodesh for good luck.

'My my you have become quite a young lady since I last saw you as a frock clad toddler and that was quite very many years ago I guess,' said Ismail as he picked up one piece of that mouth watering shondesh and smiled at the girl. Poor Purnima overwhelmed by the complement blushed and quickly retreated from the drawing room.

'Now first let me get my bearings right,' said Ismail as he gave a bar of Mars chocolate each to Aslam and Fazal, the two sons of his dear friend Gul Rehman who were now five and two years old respectively. Then he very carefully took the little new born Imran Hussein from the arms of his mother Shenaz and having pecked him on both his rosy ckeek, said somewhat nostalgically.

'Today I too would have also had a family of my own and my little Cassinolenni would have been a few months younger to Faizal I guess. But Allah it seems did not will it that way and I have therefore decided not to ever marry again. And as far as these three little boys are concerned I will always be their Godfather.' Thereafter Ismail walked up to Gul's wife Zubeida and knowing that she was pregnant and expecting her third child soon said.

'Bhabhi Jaan we all seem to be specializing in producing sons only, but this time you must produce a daughter and if you do that I promise all of you a grand holiday in Kashmir.'Today Inshallah I have with whatever little money that I managed to save during the war a well furnished personal houseboat under construction in Srinagar and It will be moored on the picturesque Nagin Lake by the autumn of next year and all of you will be my honoured guests at its inauguration', added Ismail.

'That will be simply wonderful and you must also take us to Gilgit,' said Debu Ghosh.

'But by the way Bhaiya what name have you thought of for the beautiful houseboat of yours', asked Shenaz Hussein.

'I propose to name it "Cassino Royale" in memory of my late wife Gina and my son Cassinoleni,' said Ismail very proudly.

It was indeed an evening to remember. That day Debu Ghosh's house on 217 Lansdowne Road in Ballygunge had a very festive look and everyone sportingly joined in the merriment. Dr Ghulam Hussein with his Begum Sahiba regaled everyone with their favourite numbers like "Toofan Mail" and "Diya Jalao." Naren and Shobha sang a couple of Rabindrasangeets and Debu and Hena Ghosh too for a change also chipped in with a song by Kazi Nazrul. The younger lot with Anup and Purnima in the lead and with Nawaz and Shenaz in chorus sang "Chal Chal re Naujawan" and "Dhoor hato ye duniya walon Hindustan hamara hai." Colonel Attiqur Rehman with his wife Nafisa also sang the popular KL Saigal number "Chupona Chupona O Pyari Saajaniya" from the film "My Sister". Not to be out done even Gul Rehman and Ismail joined in with a duet. They first sang "Lili Marlene" the war time hot favourite and followed it up with a fast Punjabi folk song on the typical bhangra beat and that got everybody on to their feet. Colonel Attiqur Rehman was very touched. It was the same Punjabi song that was sung in his honour at the first Barakhana that he attended as the Regimental Medical Officer of the Punjabees. The men only knew him as the RMO, but he was also the only one who could make your day for you by giving you 24 hours of bliss and happiness by just signing a small little chit to say that you were confined to the barracks and with food in bed. To the sepoys, the Regimental Medical Officer was a very important person who not only looked after your health, but the health of all the families in the Station too and an 'Attend C' in the army medical parlance ensured food in bed also.

Early on the morning of the next day, which happened to be the 14th of August in the month of Ramzan, Debu Ghosh and Naren Sen with their families left for Dhaka. The same very afternoon on the advice of Colonel Attiqur Rehman not to go to Murshidabad by car because of the Monsoon weather, Dr Ghulam Hussein with Suraiya his Begum Sahiba, his sister-in-law Nafisa and daughter Hasina caught the Darjeeling Express train from Sealdah. While Colonel Attiqur Rehman stayed back at Dr Ghulam Hussein's house to keep company with his new born grandson Imran Hussein, Major Gul Rehman with his family after dropping Major Ismail Khan at the officer's mess in Fort Whilliam left for Barrackpore.

Eversince the day Mr Jinnah gave his call for Direct Action, the Muslim League Government in Bengal under the Chief Ministership of Mr H.S Suhrawardy started getting ready to make the day a grand success for the Muslims of Calcutta and the villages nearby. The Congress too who were in the opposition also started flexing their muscles. Mr Jinnah's call had only further widened the chasm between the Hindus and Muslims of Calcutta, but now with every passing day it grew wider and wider.

Born on 8th September 1892, the fifty four year Hussein Shaheed Suhrawardy from an illustrious Muslim family of Midnapore in West Bengal and with a degree from Oxford had now become a Muslim League hard liner. It was he who during the convention of all elected Muslim League legislators at Delhi on 8th and 9th of April 1946, with Mr Jinnah in the chair had said that the Muslim League will only be satisfied with an Independent Pakistan and nothing more and nothing less. He even suggested that Calcutta should be the second capital of East Pakistan.During the visit of the Cabinet Mission to India, Mr Suhrawardy thought, argued and talked nothing but about the Muslim League's commitments and their just demands. Soon after 22nd July, when Viceroy Wavell had declared his proposal for the formation of an Interim Government, Mr Suhrawardy in Bengal proclaimed that the Muslims would never participate in it unless it was on equal terms and on full parity with the Congress. On the 4th of August, both Mr Suhrawardy and Kwaja Nazimuddin spoke violently against the Cabinet Mission and compared it to Hitler's Nazi Party which they said would be crushed the way Hitler was. Simultaneously to show more teeth, the Muslim League National Guard commonly known as the MLNG officially opened its office on 5, Wellesly Street in Calcutta. To make matters worse on the night of 8th and 9th August far away at Narayanganj near Dhaka communal violence broke out, when a group of Hindus insisted on erecting a pandal for the Hindu religious festival of "Jalan Puja".

On 9th August, the Congress celebrated "Remembrance Day" to honour all those who died during the Quit India movement of 1942. Then as 16th August neared, the speeches and body language of the political leaders from both the factions became more and more volatile, acerbic and inflammatory.

On 11th August, Kwaja Nazimuddin who was born on 19th July, 1894 at Dhaka and who was a product of Aligarh College and Trinity Hall

Cambridge and who had earlier held the post of the Chief Minister of Bengal let off another inflammatory salvo, when he said that the Hindu Interim Government without the support of the Muslim League would only precipitate matters. He also reminded the Hindus that there were scores of ways by which the Calcutta Muslims of the Muslim League could make a thorough nuisance of themselves since they were not bound by Mr Gandhi's and the Congress policy of non violence.

On the 14th of August, Mr K Roy the leader of the Congress in Bengal while addressing a meeting at Ballygunge condemned the Muslim League Government's decision to declare 16th August a public holiday and their diktat for all shops and business to be closed that day. He therefore called upon on all Hindus and Sikhs to ensure that their shops and businesses were kept open. To add more fuel to the fire a local Sikh leader added that if they were obstructed then they too would teach the Muslim Leaguers of Calcutta a lesson like they did during the communal riots of 1926.

On the very next day on 15th August, 1946, the die was cast. During an acid debate in the Bengal Legislative Assembly the Muslim League Government not only did it officially declare 16th August as a public holiday, but they also proclaimed that they would also enter into that coveted field of declaring a total strike and hartal which was once the sole prerogative of the Congress.

On the evening of the 15th of August, and with the 16th being declared a holiday, Governor Fred Burrows hosted a party at the Government House for a few selective guests. Colonel Attiqur Rehman and his wife Nafisa were also special invitees. When Colonel Attiqur dressed in the formal evening wear of a black jacket with a white trouser and a black tie and Nafisa in a peacock blue silk saree walked in, they were received by Colonel Jerry Hugo, the military secretary to the Governor.As was customary all the guests first met in the ADC'c room for a snifter which automatically gave all the invitees a chance to meet one another informally. With the drink they were also handed over a copy of the seating plan and a thumbnail sketch of all the guests who were invited for the formal sit down candle light dinner. This automatically gave everyone an opportunity to begin a conversation at the dinner table with the persons sitting to ones right or left. The seating plan on all such sit down dinners had to be worked out very meticulously by the concerned ADC. It had to be as per correct protocol and seniority. For example it would be foolish to have the wife of Mr A seated next to Mr B when it was well known that both the the wives were not even on talking terms. Or it would be criminal to make a Mrs X sit next to a much married Mr Y when it was the talk of the town that they were having an affair.

Dora Burrows the first lady of Bengal with a quiet demeanor being relatively new to Calcutta was not aware of one such affair between a Maharaja of a small Princely state in Bengal and the young wife of a senior British Political Officer who with their respective spouses had also been invited for the sit down dinner that evening. The young ADC who was also new to his job but who had no knowledge of the affair had as per correct protocol seated the couple next to each other. Suddenly the Military Secretary who was very much in the know of what was going on between the two very diplomatically changed the seating plan at the very last minute. Mrs Nafisa Attiqur Rehman now had the privilege of sitting next to the Maharaja while Colonel Attiqur had the pleasure of both, the Maharani on one side and the Political Officer's wife on the other. As soon the dinner was over, Governor Fred Burrows with his wife Dorah dressed in a simple but elegant cotton dress by his side invited the guests for some French Napoleon Cognac and Drambuie into their spacious living room. There over a drink, the friendly Governor very humourously remarked that while his predecessors as Governors had been hunting and shooting big game, he merely being a shunting and tooting man from the railways would not get time to indulge in such luxuries.

'Yes Sir I fully agree with you and now especially since Mr Jinnah has given his clarion call for Direct Action tomorrow there will be I guess some real action from now on, and more so in Bengal where the Hindus and the Muslims are at par,' said Colonel Attiqur Rehman as the cigarettes and the cigars in a silver case was shown to all the guests.

'That evening, while the dinner was in progress in the Government House, the Army Intelligence Centre in Fort Whilliam, Calcutta and also at the Eastern Army Headquarters at Ranchi had started receiving reports of ever mounting tension inside the second city. Though such reports kept pouring in, but neither the civil nor the military authorities thought that it would lead to such a catastrophe. Such like tensions particulary in a place like Calcutta was not very uncommon. They were there earlier too and it only resulted in limited riots and arson which the civil authorities confidently and effectively handled with their own police force. But they were soon to be proved wrong.

On that very same day Mr Nehru too called on Mr Jinnah at his Malabar Hill residence in Bombay and inspite of his best efforts he could not persuade him to join the Interim Government and to call off the

Direct Action. For Mr Jinnah had already made up his mind and now there was now no going back from it. However, keeping in view the riots that had erupted in February against the INA trials, the GOC-in-C Eastern Command, Lt General Tuker had very wisely ordered the move of three more Infantry Battalions to Calcutta.

On 12th August, 1946 Brigadier Mackinlay had ordered all troops under his command inside Fort Whilliam to remain confined to barracks, but at the same time to be in readiness also for Internal Security duties in aid of the civil authorities if required, and as and when called for. He also restricted military movement of vehicles and troops to the barest minimum inside the city.

16th of August happened to be the day of prayers and namaz for the Muslims and especially since it was a Friday of the holy month of Ramzan it had an added significance to it. Early morning of that warm sticky monsoon day and with the sky overcast, the mobile military patrols out on duty reported through their caterpillar broadcasts over the wireless net about the general situation inside the city. The buses, taxies and rickshaws were as usual on the roads, but the trams which were the pride of Calcutta were missing. They had gone on strike demanding more wages.The city was generally peaceful till about 7 am in the morning. But soon thereafter Major LA Livermore the officer on duty at Fort Whilliam received information about large groups of Muslims from the area of Howrah and North Calcutta moving towards the Maidan and he immediately went up to the roof of the Dalhousie block to observe for himself. When he focussed his binoculars on the majestic silver coloured Howrah Bridge he was horrified to see that a very large number of them were armed with clubs, iron bars, spades, shovels, lathis, hockey sticks and other such like intimidating weapons. The cantilever double deck bridge constructed by Cleveland Bridge and Construction Company over the River Hoogly which to the Hindus was also known as the sacred Ganga was commisssioned in 1943 and was hardly three years old. It was the pride of the city that would soon become a horrific battleground.

"I think the city is once again in for big trouble,' said Major Ismail Sikandar Khan as he joined the duty officer on the terrace. When both of them heard those loud cries of "We want Pakistan" "Pakistan Zindabad, and Quaid-e-Azam Zindabad', Major Livermore simply said.

'I think you people are bloody mad' and went back to his duty officer's desk to inform Brigadier Sixsmith the officiating Area Commnader about the prevailing situation in the city. A few minutes later another report arrived that stated that the Hindus had erected barricades at the Tala and Belgachia bridges and were preventing the Muslims from entering the city.

The Muslims in the city and the villages around were faithfully answering Mr Jinnah's call and all of them were making a beeline for the tall Octerlony monument on the great Calcutta Maidan and in the centre of city and from where Mr HS Suhrawardy, the Chief Minister of Bengal and other Muslim League leaders were scheduled to address the crowd at 3.PM that afternoon.

The 300 feet tall monument with its 218 steps near Chowringee was built in honour of Sir David Octerlony who had brought the Napalese War of 1812-1814 to a successful end. Today it would be used to trigger a war between the Hindus and Muslims of Calcutta in particular and in Bengal in general. Early that morning at Manicktolla not very far from the old "Bomma Bari", looting and arson by the goondas of Calcutta had also been reported.

At 9 AM that morning, Brigadier Mackinlay visited the Calcutta Police Headquarters at Lal Bagh and despite the fact that they too had received reports of Hindus erecting barricades and the Muslims compelling Hindus to close their shops, they as a police force were taking things rather lightly it seemed. Soon after midday, when reports of sporadic clashes between the two communities started coming in from the various intelligence channels, Major Ismail Sikandar Khan decided to accompany a staff officer who had been detailed to position himself at the Governor's House. As the American Willy's jeep made its way through the Red Road and along the Maidan, Major Ismail Sikandar Khan was surprised to see groups of young children playing football, the favourite game of the Bengalees.They seem to be enjoying the special holiday and were oblivious of the fact that the city would soon become a battleground between the Hindus and the Muslims.

At the Government House, Sir Frederick Burrows who had taken over charge from Mr RG Casey after the mid February riots only a few months ago was a person who could keep his cool under the most difficult of circumstances. The man who was once a sergeant in the famous British Grenadier Guards Regiment and who had relinquished his post as the leader of the strong British railway union was now the Governor of the most volatile province of British India.

'Tell me as a man in uniform do you think that an army unit or subunit with a mix of Hindus and Muslim troops will get carried away if deployed for internal security duties here,' asked the Governor as he quickly went through the latest situation reports that were indicated by red dots marked on a tourist road and rail map of Calcutta.

'To my mind I don't think so Sir. The Indian army soldiers are a disciplined lot and they will not take sides provided they do not function in small penny packets and are kept fully mobile under their own responsible officers to rush to the troubled spots when ordered to do so,' said the British Staff officer.'

'But Sir under the present circumstances I feel that the British Regiments would be more effective since they would remain completely neutral,' said Major Ismail Sikandar Khan.

'Well then let us see how it goes and be prepared for the worst,' said the Governor very confidently.

It was around 3 PM, when the police and the civil authorities sent an application for aid to civil authorities to Brigadier Sixsmith the acting Bengal Area Commander at Fort Whilliam. The Brigadier immediately ordered the Lancasters and Yorks to standbye and to be ready to move to the area of the Sealdah railway station and Burra Bazaar where rioting and police firing had been reported from. Thereafter Brigadier Sixsmith on an urgent call from the Government House rushed in his staff car only to find that the Police Commissioner of Calcutta and the Chief Secretary had already raised their hands. He immediately despatched both the York and Lancaster Regiments to the Sealdah railway station military war time transit camp.

Meanwhile the mass meeting of the Muslims at the Octerlony monument was in full swing. And while the Governor with the acting Area Commander and the Commissioner of Police with an armed escort went on a tour of the tension filled areas of the city, Major Ismail Sikandar Khan walked over to the Maidan to listen to what Mr Suhrawardy had to say.

'Let me tell you my dear Muslim brothers that the so called Cabinet Mission was a big bluff and we shall see how the British can make Nehru rule Bengal,' roared the man through the array of microphones that had been placed in front of him. When that concluding remark by the Chief Minister was greeted by a deafening roar from the massive crowd, Ismail walked a few paces ahead to listen to what the next speaker had to say.

My God what is this country coming to thought Ismail when he noticed groups of armed Muslims in lungis and vests who looked like hired goondas and who were well armed quietly slipping away from the meeting while it was still in session. Finding it to be rather strange, Major Ismail immediately went back to the Area Headquarters and reported the matter.

At 4.15 PM in the evening, Fortress headquarters Fort Whilliam sent out the codeword “Red”.They were now convinced that the city founded by Job Charnock on the banks of the River Hoogly was in for a bloodbath. At 6 PM the Governor ordered the Chief Minister to clamp curfew throughout the city. Major Ismail Sikandar Khan who had returned to Fort Whilliam and who was scheduled to go back to Ranchi that night was told that all trains had been cancelled. He therefore ordered a large Black Label whisky with soda and plonked himself on the leather sofa in the Officer's Mess to read Circle 7 of Dante's Divine Comedy. The book written by the Italian poet from Florence in the early part of the 14th Century was of special value to him since it was the first gift that Gina presented him with after the fall of Mount Cassino. The Divine Comedy was written in three sections and the first section was titled the Inferno and Circle 7 dealt with the subject of violence which was divided into three parts that included violence against others, violence against self and violence against God, Nature and Art.That evening by the time Ismail downed his second Black Label, the second city of the British Empire was already heading towards an inferno as acts of violence, savagery, brutality, arson, murder, slaughter, massacre and looting was reported from various parts of the city. The battle lines were now being drawn up for the great Calcutta killings. Two decades ago in 1926, Calcutta had reeled under a big communal riot between the Hindus and the Muslims of the city, but this time it would be much worse.

On the morning of 16th Aiugust, 1946 as was his regular routine and habit, Nawaz Hussein while retuning from his morning jog walked into the 'East Bengal Cabin' for a cup of tea. It was one of the popular tea shops at the junction of Harrison Street and Mirzapur Street and a few hundred yards away from his father's palatial house. As usual on that morning there was the usual group of elderly Bengalees both Hindus and Muslims who regularly patronised that place. Some of them were discussing the probable fall out from Direct Action Day, while others were busy reading the morning papers. It was nearing 8 AM when suddenly from nowhere came tearing down Harrison Street seven civil trucks. They were all packed with young and middle aged Muslims who were dressed in their traditional lungis and vests and they now started throwing brickbats and soda bottles at all the Hindu shops that had dared to open their premises and establishments that morning. This was against the Muslim League diktat for a total shut down and though some of the elders from both communities pleaded to them to refrain from such unlawful activities, but they just could'nt care less and continued with the rampage. Hired by their mentors, these hired goonda gangs were now getting ready for their subsequent action of looting these shops and establishments.When a couple of more bottles and stones landed in the nearby offices of the "Happy Home Boarding House" and the Minerva Banking Corporation, and as tempers kept mounting, Nawaz Hussein decided to make his way home. Resuming his jogging at a much faster pace, he immediately on reaching home told his old faithful servant Dhoni Ram to close all doors and windows and to lock them firmly from the inside also.

Dhoni Ram, the poor aged and illiterate peasant from Orissa had been serving the family as a domestic servant eversince Nawaz Hussein was born. He was witness to the riots of 1926, when Nawaz Hussein was only eight years old and on hearing about the incident from his Choto Babu said.

'Chotto Babu I am not a politician but if what you witnessed and said is true then I would suggest that all of us should get out of Calcutta and go to our Bagan Bari, the country house at Modhomgram near Dum Dum.'

'Don't be bloddy silly nothing will happen. This is only a passing phase and we are only taking precautions, and once the riot police arrives and they fire a few rounds of tear gas shells it will all be over,' said Nawaz Hussein very confidently.

'But Choto Sahib you do not know the psyche of these hired goonda gangs. They have no religion when it comes to greed and looting. The Hindu Goonda will loot even a Hindu and so will the Muslim a Muslim. He will not spare anybody when it comes to getting rich fast. For them this is the ideal opportunity under the garb of so called loyalty to the political partys to make hay while the sun shines,' said Dhoni Ram as Colonel Attiqur Rehman with little Imran Hussein in the pram walked in for his breakfast.

'Well when are my dear wife Nafisa and your parents with Haseena expected back from Murshidabad today,' said the Colonel while requesting Dhoni Ram to instruct the cook not to put green chillies in the stuffed omelette that he had ordered.

'The correct arrival time of the train is 5.30 in the evening and therefore hopefully they should be back home latest by six I guess, and provided the train is not late,' said Nawaz Hussein as Shenaz put a bowlful of delicious Malayabadi Dusherri mangoes in front of her loving father. This was the Colonel's favourite fruit and as he attacked the bowl single handedly, he pecked Shenaz on her cheek and said that it was indeed a pity that such a delicious variety of mango is not grown in the North West Frontier.

For the next few hours and till lunch was served everything seemed very peaceful and quiet. Then at around 4 o'clock that afternoon, Colonel Attiqur Rehman who was reading Leo Tolstoy's War and Peace while relaxing in bed with Imran Hussein by his side was suddenly disturbed by the loud shouts of "Pakistan Zindabad" and "Jinnah Zindabad." Fearing that this could mean real trouble and that the noise may wake up the little boy, Colonel Attiqur called out to his daughter Shenaz to take the child away and he with his son-in-law Nawaz Hussein went up to the terrace to see what was happening on the streets below.And when they saw what was happening they were simply horrified. Groups of young men and boys wearing the green arm band of the Muslim League volunteers and shouting Allah ho Akbar and Pakistan Zindabad at the top of their voices while returning from the meeting in the Maidan were trying to intimidate the Hindus to challenge them.The young Congress volunteers flying the Congress flag therefore decided to take up the challenge as they too started shouting "Jai Hind" "Hindustan Zindabad "Congress Zindabad" and Pakistan Murdabad" (Victory to India—Long Live Hindustan—Long Live Congress—and Death to Pakistan) on the top of their voices. Soon there was an argument with unprintable expletives flying from both the sides. For the Goondas of Calcutta whether they were Hindus or Muslims that did not matter in the least. They were now fully ready to unleash their power to make the best of the situation. The Great Calcutta killings had now begun. And by late evening of 16th August, Calcutta would not only become a battlefield between the two communities, but by daybreak the next day the Province of Bengal too would be engulfed in a communal war that would spell disaster for the three old friends and their families.

At five o'clock that evening Ajmal Khan, Dr Ghulam Hussein's personal driver drove the Baby Austin to the Sealdah railway station to pick up Dr Hussein and party. But when It was nearing half past six and there was still no sign of the car, Nawaz Hussein got a bit worried.

'Maybe they are caught in a traffic jam,' said Colonel Attiqur Rehman as he wheeled in Imran Hussein's pram into the drawing room with little Imran fast asleep inside it.

'But Abbajaan, the railway station is not even 10 minutes drive from here,' said Shenaz as a panting and terrified Dhoniram with a lost look on his wrinkled face came back with the horrifying news that Hindus and Muslims were now burning buses, trams, cars on the roads and killing each other on the streets, lanes and bylanes in the vicinity of Sealdah, Burra Bazaar and other areas of North Calcutta. Dhoniram had gone to the nearby market to buy fresh mutton for the Dum Biryani and kebabs that Shenaz was planning to cook for dinner that evening.

'In that case I think I will go and see for myself what is happening,' said Colonel Attiqur Rehman as he got up from the sofa to go to his room and change from his pyjamas into something more respectable and decent.

'No Abbajaan this is Calcutta and you do not even know the roads well. Moreover, it is already getting dark and you are getting old too. And therefore while you take care of your grandson and Shenaz gets busy preparing the dinner, I will go and find out. Maybe the train is late and which is nothing unusual,' said Nawaz Hussein while requesting Dhoniram to get hold of an umbrella and to accompany him.

'But Choto Huzur it is not safe at all to venture outside now. These hired goondas irrespective of whether they are Muslims or Hindus will now be on a looting spree and they will spare nobody. Moreover, there are very strong rumours that curfew is being imposed and that the police and the military are being brought in to shoot at sight those violating the order,' said Dhoniram as he fell on his master's feet and requested him not to take such a great risk.

'But surely we cant just sit at home and do nothing,' said Colonel Attiqur Rehman as he got up, took out his pocket diary and walked to the telephone to ring up his son Gul Rehman at Barrackpur. Luckily the military phone lines were working and the exchange at Fort Whilliam got the call through immediately.

'Yes Abbajaan a strict curfew has been imposed but I will request my friend Ismail who luckily is still in Fort Whilliam to take out a mobile armed patrol and go looking for them. I will also try and speak to the military movement control headquarters in Calcutta and find out if the train from Murshidabad has arrived or not. In the meantime let us all pray to Allah that all is well,' said Gul Rehman as he hung up the phone.

Five minutes later the phone rang and Nawaz ran to pick it up. It was from Major Ismail Sikandar Khan.'Just get ready to accompany me to the Sealdah railway station. I am coming with an armed escort to your house and Inshallah I will be there in the next twenty minutes,' said Major Ismail.

Now there was a smile on everyones face as they anxiously kept looking at the clock and for Ismail's arrival. But by nightfall a terrible tragedy had completely shattered both the Hussein and the Rehman families and it was only around 10 PM that night when Ismail and Nawaz Hussein finally did manage to locate and trace out the dead bodies of their nearest and dearest ones. Their charred remains with innumerable stab wounds on their bodies were found piled up one on top of the other in a small narrow lane that led to a nearby big bustee(shantytown) and which was not very far from the Sealdah railway station. Till a few hours ago both the Hindus and the Muslims from the same slum lived there peacefully, but now there was nothing much left of the bustee anymore. It was now a heap of rubble with some of the thatched houses still emitting smoke. Dead bodies of men, women and children were all over the place. Even the poor driver Ajmal Khan had not been spared.

It seems that the train from Murshidabad was late by half an hour, when a gang of goondas stopped it at the outer signal for the purpose of looting it. But seeing the presence of Tommies who were on their way to the Sealdah Station Military transit camp they abandoned the idea. When the Baby Austin with all the occupants inside came to an important cross road, which was not very far from Dr Ghulam Hussein's bungalow, they found it was barricaded by a gang of goondas. Earlier two buses and two private cars had been set on fire and the passengers looted. It was also getting dark, when the Hindu Goonda leader with his gang and with mashals in their hand surrounded the car. On noticing that all the occupants were wealthy Muslims, the leader of the gang with a long knife in his hand shouted to them in Bengali.

'Aapnader kache ja kichu ache she shob age amader din tar pure onno kotha hobe." (First hand over all your belongings and only after that we shall talk.") When Dr Ghulam Hussein pleaded with them that there were ladies inside and some respect should be shown to them, someone else from the gang now shouted "Maar shalader, shobkota sala mushulman." (Let us kill all of since they are all bloody Muslims.") Immediately the gang attacked the car and mercilessly set fire to it. When the occupants tried to get out of the flaming car, one by one they were stabbed to death. As they fell by the roadside, the gang looted all their belongings that were inside the car and in the dicky. Then as soon as somebody raised the alarm and shouted run run the police are coming, the gang of goondas picked up all the dead bodies and ran inside the smalll lane to rob each one of them of all their personal belongings. Thereafter they dumped one dead body on top of the other and stealthily faded away into the maze of the dirty stinking lanes of the city.

That very night there was a big thunderstorm and it was nearing midnight when all the dead bodies were taken to Fort Whilliam for burial the next day. A visibly shaken and grief stricken Shenaz fainted, when she heard about the tragic deaths of both her in-laws, her dear mother Nafisa and his sister-in-law Haseena and the old faithful driver Ajmal Khan. That very night they all stayed huddled together in Major Ismail's suite inside the Fort Whilliam Officer's Mess, while Calcutta burnt. And with very many others too griefing the loss of their near and dear ones, Governor Burrows dispatched urgent telegrams both to Lord Pethick Lawrence, the Secretary of State for India in London and to the Viceroy in Delhi describing the terrible state of affairs in the city and the actions that were being taken by him.

'Reference the situation in Calcutta, arson, looting, rioting and killings on the increase. Goonda gangs taking full advantage of the situation. Communal tension prevails. Action is in hand to restore normalcy at the earliest.' This telegram was sent by the Governor at around midnight.

On the very same evening at Dhaka, unaware about the tragedy that had befallen Dr Ghulam Hussein and his family in Calcutta, Debu Ghosh with his wife Hena and son Anup together with Naren Sen, Shobha Sen and their daughter Purnima were returning to Hena's parents house at Wari after a dinner party at Mr Subimal Dutt's place.

The Dutt family that evening had approved of Anup Ghosh for their daughter Kalpana and Naren Sen too had reciprocated by approving their son Siddhartha for his own daughter Purnima. The wedding dates for the two couples was tentatively fixed for the 21st and 28th of December. Both the dates according to the Brahmin Pandits who had studied the horoscopes of the prospective grooms and the brides were found to be very auspicious and the match making that evening therefore was immediately finalized by both the sides.

It was well past midnight, when the Sen and the Ghosh family after a wonderful evening with the hospitable Dutt family also became victims of communal violence at Dhaka. This was also a fall out of the Direct Action Day that was called by the Muslim League and the goondas of Dhaka had taken full advantage of it. They were all returning home to Debu's in-laws house and were in a very happy mood when suddenly from nowhere appeared a group of young uncouth Muslims dressed in their traditional lungis and vests. The news about the communal riots and killings in Calcutta had already spread like wild fire and it was now the turn of Dhaka, Chittagong and other important towns in East Bengal which were predominantly Muslim to take on the Hindus.

Seeing the entire group dressed fashionably in typical Bengali style and with the loads of precious jewellery on all the women folk who were attired in heavy gold brocaded Benarasi silk sarees, the gang stopped the three cycle rickshaws that they were all travelling in. Seeing the apparent danger the cycle rickshaw drivers with folded hands fell at the feet of the gang leader.

And on being questioned when the rickshaw drivers disclosed that they were Bihari Muslims while all the passengers were Bengali Hindus from Calcutta, their was a big smile on the gang leaders face. And while the rickshaw drivers were told to get lost, the gang leader feeling very happy said.

"Arre erra shob shala Kolkatar Hindu. Allah kasam aaj edder amra kichuteye chardbo na. Jarra Kolkatete atto bochor ottechar koreche ammader opore, aaj aamra badla nishchoi nebo. (They are all bloody Hindus from Calcutta and in the name of Allah today we will not spare them. The atrocities that they have committed on us the Muslims for so many years in Calcutta must be avenged and we will not spare a single one of them.). When Debu, Naren and Anup the three men folk tried to confront them and dared to put up some resistance, the goondas simply whipped out their long Mainpuri knives and repeatedly stabbed them. The ladies became hysterical and when they started running and screaming for help they too were brutally killed. And by the time any help could comeby, the goondas had vanished with all their jewellery and other valuable personal belongings that belonged to all the victims.Thus in a span of not even 24 hours Mr Jinnah's call for Direct Action had eliminated from this world a bond of friendship, love and happiness that existed for nearly a century between the Sen, Hussein and the Ghose families.

By the early hours of the morning of 17th of August, Calcutta was virtually under mob rule and it was now very much evident that the underworld of Calcutta had taken charge of the city. Leading the attacks were the goonda gangs as they not only went on a mad killing spree, but also on a treasure hunt ransacking and looting the shops and establishments at will. The dark clouds above were now full of hungry vultures that kept diving in large numbers to feast on the blood clotted and blood stained victims lying on the streets and lanes of Calcutta. To the vultures it didn't matter wether they were Hindus or Muslims. They were simply having a grand feast.

Being the holy month of Ramzan, the Muslim Goondas too feasted before the sun came up in the morning and soon after sunset in the evening they were back in action again. Not to be left behind gangs from other communities too joined in the fray. By afternoon scores of mutilated dead bodies bloated and stinking were seen floating down the narrow Hoogly River channels that passed through the areas of Alipore, Kalighat and Tollygunge. By midnight the killings had reached maniacal proportions as the goondas maimed, burned and stabbed people to death with unbridled savagery. The riots and looting had been fierce, but the bloodiest butchery had taken place during the hours of darkness.

On the 17th of August, while Calcutta was reeling under the terrible communal riots, Pandit Nehru in Delhi while on his way in his car to discuss the modalities on the formation of the proposed Interim Government with the Viceroy accidentally ran over and killed a small child. He was no doubt visbly very much upset after the tragic accident, but there was little that he could do. For the Congress this too was a bad omen it seemed to keep India unified.

On the 18th of August, army tanks with searchlights were now brought into action to engage those who broke the curfew. That day happened to be a Sunday and while Governor Burrows with Mr HS Shurawardy the Chief Minister of the province together with Lt Gen Tuker the Eastern Army Commander, and the Chief Secretary of Bengal escorted by a combined police and military armed patrol toured the battered city, Major Littleboy the Assistant Provost Marshall started organising relief and rescue operations for those who had been displaced and badly affected by the riots. But Sunday or no Sunday, the Hindus and Muslims were still at each others throats. At the Gray Street-Chitpur Road crossing the place was littered with dead bodies. This was as a result of a pitched battle and hand to hand fighting between the two communities. In the Shobha Bazaar area too there was wholesale slaughter.

On that terrible afternoon of 18th August, while Calcutta was reeling under the communal onslaught of looting and killing, Major Ismail Sikandar Khan accompanied by an armed escort from the 8th Gurkha Rifles was on his way to the late Dr Ghulam Hussein's bunglow. He was gong there at the request of Nawaz and his wife Shenaz to pick up for them some clothes, the box of jewellery and a few other small knick knacks for the family. When the jeep he was travelling in reached somewhere near the junction of Park Street and Lower Circular Road, Ismail was strangely surprised to spot a short statured middle aged nun with a couple of jute bags in her hand crossing the lonely deserted street. She was on a mission to get some food and rations for the 300 hundred odd poor young girls who were under her care in the nearby hostel that was being run by her. The girls were starving and the Nun had very bravely ventured out even while the curfew was still on. Realizing that her life could be in danger, Ismail immediately halted his jeep, got out and having smartly saluted the lady said.

'Do pardon me Reverend Mother but this is no time for you to go shopping on the streets. Moreover all the shops are closed and it could prove fatal.'

'I know that officer but what am I to do. I cannot let my poor children die of hunger. I am the Head Mistress of Saint Mary's School and because of the sudden riots the school has not received any supplies because for the last couple of days all deliveries have been stopped,' said the Nun expressing her helplessness and requesting Ismail to help her out somehow. Ismail could make out that though she was in her early thirties and fairly young to be a headmistress of a school, but she seemed determined to fulfil her mission that day.

'Right Reverened Mother for the sake of your children I will get one of the shops opened for you and then with your rations we will escort you back to your school,' said Reggie. The Mother was delighted and.when Ismail saw her off at the school gate, she blessed him by doing the sign of the cross.

The young Nun Agnes Gonxha Bojaxhuu was born in the small town of Skopje in Macedonia in 1910. At the age of 18 she had left her home and family to join the sisters of Loretto. On 6th June 1929, soon after her initiation in Ireland, she arrived in Calcutta. A year later in 1930 she took the name Sister Teresa of St Teresa of Lesiux, the patroness of the missionaries and thereafter started teaching at the Loretto House. In 1942, when the Japanese were at the gates of India, the Loretto College and the compound was converted into a military hospital and Sister Theresa with her students had moved to the new premises on the Lower Circular Road. That afternoon the sight of the innocent dead lying on the streets, in the lanes and by lanes and in the sewers and ponds of her beloved city had affected her tremendously. She could never imagine that human beings could turn into such ruthless and merciless savages and that to in the name of religion.

On the 19th of August, with the induction of additional military units and the presence of more armed troops on the streets, the shopkeepers now started opening their shops and public transport in small numbers could also be seen on the roads. By evening the fanatic fury that had gripped the Hindus and Muslims of Kolkatta as the Bengalis call the city seemed to have ebbed, and things were looking a bit more peaceful again, but the damage had been done. For those four dreadful days and till the morning of the 20th of August, the city of Calcutta had become a killing field and most of the victims were either the poor people from the bustees and shanty towns and those from the lower and lower middle class families. They were the same unfortunate residents who had been living together as good neighbours for years together, but for those four days they had all gone mad and had become sworn enemies.

At 9 PM on the evening of the 19th August, orders were received that next morning the curfew would be lifted and all dead bodies lying on the main streets of Calcutta must be removed, cleared, buried and cremated as per their religious beliefs of the dead. And all this was required to be completed by first light the next dayby the army.On receiving those orders, all the commanding officers of the British Battalions therefore immediately held a conference with their own company commanders and officers.

'But do please tell me Sir how the hell do we distinguish between a poor dead Hindu and a dead Muslim when they have all been dead for the past three days,' said acting Major Dooland who had just returned from his annual leave and whose wife only a month ago had delivered their first child whom they named Penny.

"Well in that case it is penny for your damn lousy doubts and thoughts and that I am afraid is your bloody headache George and not mine,' replied the Colonel as others appreciated the oldman's witty remark. But the subsequent remark by the Battalion Second in Command though a little vulgar added even more humour to the proceedings when he said rather crudely.

'Well dear George to get over the problem I suggest you inspect their bloody cocks first and if you find that it is a circumcised one, then send it for a bloody burial and if not than despatch it to the burning ghats and that's about all.'

'But Sir that solution may be alright for the cocks, what about the women folk and the girls. How do we distinguish them unless they too have circumcised cunts,' asked young Lieutenant Mitchell.

'Just use your bloody common sense and discretion son,' said Colonel Bonny while directing the Adjutant to familiarize the company commanders with the various cremation and burial grounds in the city.Thereafter there being no more questions, the company commanders were now huddled together as the Adjutant of the Battalion indicated the known cremation and burial grounds on a survey of India map of the city.

"Gentlemen the places marked in green on the map by me are the Muslim burial grounds, while those in red are the burning ghats of the Hindus. Half an hour later having briefed all the platoon commanders, the Battalion was now ready to launch "Operation Grissly". Since Major Ismail Sikandar Khan had nothing useful to do he also volunteered to act as a guide and accompanied one of the company columns.

By the morning of the 20th of August, the second city of the Empire was slowly limping back to normalcy. For the good work done by a platoon of British Tommies, one affluent Bengali gentleman as a gesture of appreciation presented two bottles of French champagne to the British sergeant incharge. It however didn't take much time for that platoon from Major Livermore's outfit to finish of the contents in a jiffy and to get back to collecting the stinking dead bodies that were lying on the streets, in the lanes and the bylanes of that big sprawling city.

Later that day the company mobile columns of the Indian army were reinforced with the garbage and refuse trucks of the Calcutta Municipal Corporation. And they together with their team of "Domes,' the lower caste who handle dead bodies for cremation and a local police officer for liaision made their way to the appointed areas. "Operation Clean Up" had now begun in real earnest.

The military sub units were divided into teams and each team with a Police Sergeant and with four Domes now drove to the assigned body collection points. Though everyone was provided with a stench mask, the Domes not being used to it discarded them. The British Tommies and others using the masks looked like members of the Klu Klux Klan. The only difference being that whereas the KKK was started as an underground terrorist group against the Civil Rights Movement that abolished the slavery of the coloured people after the American Civil War, these men in masks were on a humanitarian mission to do an overground operation after the Calcutta civil war was finally over.

'Alright place all the lungiwallass to my right and all the dhotiwallas to my left,'ordered the British Police Sergeant as the Domes got busy with their task.

'That is understable, but what about those in pants, shorts, frocks and sarees, how do we segregate them,' asked one of the Domes.

'Use your bloody head and don't ask anymore silly questions,'shouted the British Police Sergeant while give the cheeky Dome a dirty look. Once the garbage and refuse lorries were full of dead bodies, they were driven to the burial grounds and burning ghats for final disposal.

In a gesture of strange ironic magnanimity, the Muslim League Government in Bengal who were primarily responsible for the catastrophy that had engulfed the city had decided to pay a sum of Rupees Five for every dead corpse on condition that they were cleared within the deadline which was set for 8 o'clock on the morning of the 20th of August.Thus for the British army units Operation Grizzly soon became a prestige issue as they competed with one another for the highest tally. And while the Green Howards, the Yorks and the Lancasters went all out to get the highest score in the collection of dead bodies, a dejected and crestfallen Mahatma Gandhi wondered whether his preaching of non violence was also now a dead issue. As the word spread that the mad English soldiers were competing with one another in the collection of the dead bodies, more copses from the hovels, lanes, sewers, gutters and labyrinths started surfacing on the roadsides. In order to motivate the Domes and to keep them happy, the Army team leader also rewarded them with the clothes that the dead men, women and children were wearing. Though the time limit for the rupees five per corpse was set at 8 AM next morning, the Domes now worked overtime to claim a monetary commission for each extra corpse delivered, and they therefore kept searching high and low and throughout the night to make that extra buck.

By the given deadline the British Tommies had made the dead city of Calcutta to breathe life again. The vultures now hovered mostly over the burning ghats and the burial grounds to enjoy a second feast, while picking the human stinking bones clean.By sunset everbody in the Battalion seemed to have had their fill of stinking bodies. At the entrance to the Green Howards Officer's Mess, Major Ismail Sikandar Khan read the notice that had been written in big bold capitals.

'Anyone talking or mentioning about bodies and corpses or anything even remotely related to it will stand drinks all around.' For the Tommies and for the civilian drivers of the general transport company a grand feast and Barakhana had been arranged and that too with an additional two extra issues of free rum. But that evening at the Barakhana there were hardly any takers as far as the non vegetarian food was concerned.

The Indian soldiers both Hindus and Muslims patrolling the streets and while establishing picquets and posts in the riot affected areas were a true example of compassion and brotherhood. They did not take sides and on the contrary helped out the people and it was irrespective of the religion to which they belonged. A few days later the three adjutants of the three famous British Regiments signed the required receipts for "Operation Grizzlly." One of the receipts read as follows.

'Received with thanks the sum of Rupees one thousand five hundred and forty five for corpse collecting on the night 19/20 August 1946'.The money thus received was promptly deposited into the regimental fund to be used for the welfare of the British Tommy who had saved the second city of the British Empire from epidemic and widespread desease.

While Operation Grissly was in progress, the news about the tragic end of the Sen and Ghosh familes at Dhaka reached Calcutta. It was sent over the telephone by Ronen Sen to Nawaz Hussein. On learning about the tragedy, Ronen with his pregnant wife Mona immediately rushed to Dhaka from Chittagong. And when Nawaz also conveyed to him about what had happened to his own family in Calcutta, Ronen and Mona simply could'nt believe it. It was a tragedy beyond their comprehension and which also resulted in a miscarriage for pregnant Mona that very night.

As Calcutta slowly limped back to normalcy, the Bengali Babus in their dhotis and the Bengali Muslims in their lungis were once again out in the streets, but both were still walking with one end of their dhotis and lungis covering their noses. The lousy stink of burnt human flesh and blood was still very much in the air.

As Ismail made a quick survey of the city he found whole big bazaars were a mass of ashes. Some of the covered markets that were bult by the British were nothing more than twisted and blackened corrugated iron. When Ismail asked a few members from both the communities as to what did they gain from this man made mayhem, the Muslims who suffered the most said that Allah had deserted them, while the Hindus claimed that the Kalyug or the dark ages had now really set in. And during those four shocking days the Allah of the Muslims and the Gods of the Hindus seemed to have forsaken them. But more was to come as communal trouble now started raisng its ugly head not only in Bengal, but also at other places and provinces. The Hindus who had for ages settled in Muslim majority Provinces and the Muslims who had so far lived peacefully and in harmony in the Provinces that had a majority of Hindu population were in a quandary. Some of them who had close relatives on either side migrated to safer havens, while others waited in the hope that their lives will not be disrupted further.

Colonel Attiqur Rehman with Shenaz, Nawaz Hussein and little Imran Hussein were now staying with Gul Rehman and his family at Barrackpore. Calcutta was still not safe and more so because since they were quite a few fairly well to do Muslims like them who could be targeted for money by the local goondas, and they were only waiting for another opportunity to strike.

Luckily the big Hussein family bunglow at the junction of Mirzapur Street and Harrison Street had not been targeted. And this was thanks to Major Ismail who had timely deployed a picquet from the 3/8 Gorkha Rifles outside the gate. With Cacutta under control, Ismail took ten days casual leave to be with his dear old pal Gulu and his father who had suffered so much. The loss of his wife Nafisa, his brother-in-law Dr Ghulam Hussein, his sister Suraiya and young Haseena was too much for Colonel Attiqur Rehman to bear. It had come as a rude shock to the oldman who now seriously advocated that Nawaz Hussein should sell off all their property in Calcutta and with the family migrate to Peshawar where he could with that money open a bigger hospital and serve the poor too.

On 22nd August, 1946 Governor Burrows sent his secret report about the causes for the bloody Calcutta killings to the Viceroy and the main cause listed by him was the call given by Mr Jinnah for the Direct Action by the Muslims and the demand for a separate Pakistan by the Muslim League.

Three days later on the 25th of August, the Viceroy himself arrived in Calcutta to survey the damage caused by the communal madness. Having interviewed Mr Hardwick, the Commissioner of Police, Major General Boucher the acting Eastern Army Commander, Major General Sixsmith the acting Area Commander and a few others including Mr Walker the Chief Secretary of Bengal and his number two Mr Martin, the Viceroy was convinced that the main cause of this short lived holocaust was non other than the communal bias as was advocated and instigated by Mr Shurawardy the Chief Minister of Bengal and his Muslim League henchmen. Having visited the two main relief centres, one for the Hindus at Ashutosh College, and the other one for the Muslms at Lady Brabourne College near Park Circus, Viceroy Wavell returned to Delhi a very sad man. The carnage that he saw convinced him that unless some early settlement was reached between the Congress and the Muslim League such outbreaks of communal violence were bound to break out in other parts of the country also.

Chapter-18

Agreeing to Disagree

On the 27th of August, 1946 after hIs return from Calcutta, Viceroy Wavell held a joint meeting with both Mr Gandhi and Pandit Nehru. That day both the Indian leaders were in a belligerent, legalistic and malevolent mood. When the question about the grouping of the proposed Constituent Assembly came up for discussion, which was the main point of contention and the only obstacle for full cooperation by the Muslim League, the otherwise non violent and peaceful Mahatma thumped the table and said.

'If India wants her bloodbath she shall have it.' Such strong words coming from the lips of the man who always preached non violence took the Viceroy by complete surprise.The Viceroy therefore once again appealed to Mr Jinnah and the other Muslim League top leaders to join the Interim Government, which was scheduled to take office from the 2nd of September, but Jinnah remained adamant.

That very evening Major Ismail was invited for cocktails by Major Dooland at his ground floor apartment at 52/2 Ballygunge Circular Road. Major Dooland had finally found time to celebrate the arrival of his pretty little daughter Penny with his friends. The only other Indian in that selective small crowd was Mr and Mrs Bhattacharya, a couple who with their three young children, two girls and a small boy lived on the floor above. The two storey house with a wooden staircase had a total of only four apartments, two on the ground floor and two above it. It was located in one of the most fashionable areas of South Calcutta and these apartments and flats were normally allotted to senior British officers only.

Mr Bhattacharya was a chartered accountant from the Military Accounts Department of the government. This was the department that looked after the pay and allowances of all service officers and he felt very privileged to have all his neigbours as British Army Officers. That evening he too with his wife had been invited for the cocktails at Major Dooland's residence.

Mrs Bhattacharya a good looking lady in her early forty's dressed in a silk saree that she had worn for the first time in the traditional Parsee style was feeling a bit out of place in that crowd. More so because she could not speak a word of English except for saying thank you. But her Hindi was excellent and her Urdu was fairly good too. The reason for this was that she had spent her early years before marriage at Benaras and Allahabad and later after her marriage at Lucknow, Meerut in the United Provinces. On being introduced to Major Ismail Sikandar Khan, Mrs Bhattacharya felt somewhat at ease. Atleast she had someone now to converse with. A little while later when he accompanied Mr Bhattacharya for a reflll at the bar, Ismail took the opportunity and said.

'Sir, now that I know you are from the office of the Field Controller of Military Accounts Eastern Command maybe you will be able to help me out with my pay and allowance problem.'

'Well if it is withn the rules why not and that's my job,' said a delighted Mr Narendra Nath Bhattacharya while enjoyng his second large peg of the Black Label Skotch whisky with soda and ice.It seems that Ismail during his war service in Italy had not received some of the acting allowances that were due to him, while all the other Indian officers of his seniority who had also fought in that same theatre of operations had already received theirs.

"Don't you worry and since you are a Military Cross winner and you also have the coveted DSO to go with it, I will sought it all out within the next one week and you will given the answer in writing,' said Mr Bhattacharya very confidently.

'Thank you very much indeed,' said Ismail as he smiled at Mrs Bhattacharya whose first name was also Shobha and narrated to her in Urdu some of the humorous stories of the war. A week or so later, when Ismail returned to Ranchi from his temporary duty in Calcutta, he was delighted to find a letter in his pigeon hole at the officer's mess and inside it was an Imperial Bank of India cheque for a handsome sum of Rupees two thousand five hundred and ten only.Mr Bhattacharya it seems had taken up the case directly with his boss, the Military Accountant General in Delhi and who promptly cleared the amount under his own financial powers.

On the 2nd of Sptember 1946, despite the refusal by Mr Jinnah and his Muslim League to join the Interim Government, the Viceroy swore in the seven members of the New Government. And Pandit Nehru having taken his oath added a soft Jai Hind to it. On that very evening Mr Jinnah from his posh residence on Malabar Hills announced that India was now on the brink of a civil war and his demand for Pakistan or nothing once again sent shock waves of hate and terror across the length and breadth of the country. Seeing Mr Jinnah's belligerent mood and the threat of a possible civil war looming over India, Viceroy Wavell gave the warning order for the British administration and troops to be ready for "Operation Ebbtide". This was a top secret plan for the evacuation of all British personel in phases from India if the situation so demanded.

On the 10th of September, 1946 Mrs Sarojini Naidu the Nightingale of India and a lady with a subtle sense of humour on being invited by the Viceroy to dinner while discussing the character traits of the big two Indian leaders with the Viceroy remarked very aptly that whereas Mr Jinnah who had once promised to be a great leader of Indian freedom was now portraying himself as Lucifer, to the Indian National Congress it was costing a great deal more to keep the Mahatma in poverty.

'Your Excellency if only that oldman knew how much it costs to keep him in poverty, maybe things could be a little different,' said Mrs Naidu in her usual witty style as one of the Viceroy's ADC's gave a signal to the band to get ready. A little while later when the band started playing God Save the King, everyone on the table stood to attention and drank to the health of the King of England and the Emperor of India.

Meanwhile having learnt from Major Ismail about the tragedy in the Rehman family, Colonel Reginald Edwards arrived in Calcutta to pay his condolences to Colonel Attiqur Rehman. That day happened to be the 2nd of September, the day the new Interim Government with Pandit Nehru as the Prime Minister was sworn in. That day Viceroy Wavell made another broadcast over the radio from Delhi. After giving his best wishes to all those who had taken office that day, he once again appealed to Mr Jinnah to reconsider his decision and requested him and his party to cooperate and join the Government. On that evening over a drink at Major Gul Rehman's house, when Reggie heard the macabre stories as to how the families of Dr Ghulam Hussein, Naren Sen and Debu Ghosh had been brutally massacred, he was simply stunned.

'My God what is this country coming to? The people who perpetuated such dastardly acts are not human beings at all. They are bloody devils and worse than animals too. Even the thought that India would soon be free does not seem to strike a cord of friendship between the two main rival political groups and I wonder where will it all end,' said Reggie in utter disgust A week later, when Reggie suggested to Colonel Attiqur that a change of place for a few days could probably do him a world of good, Major Gul Rehman butted in to say that Darjeeling or maybe Kalimpong could be the right choice.

'Yes I guess you are right son and may be the two of us can offer our voluntarily services to Dr Graham's Home in Kalimpong and do some useful work for those unfortunate children,' said Colonel Reggie.

The Grahams Home and School was founded by the Reverend John Anderson Graham, a zealous Church of Scotland Missionary in 1900, and it was primarily for the education of the neglected and poor Anglo Indian children of the Tea gardens in the Darjeeling District of Bengal. The school with only six children was started in a rented cottage.Both Dr Graham and his devoted wife Katherine were close friends of the Edward family and Reggie had known them from his subaltern days. Starting with a humble beginning the Home was now a full fledged school that also catered for the children of mixed parentages from the Army, Railways and other Government Civil Services.

On the 16th of September and exacrly a month after the great Calcutta killings began, while Attiqur and Reggie were waiting on the platform at the Sealdah railway station to board the train to Siliguri, they were both surprised to see an European Nun in fluent Bengali commiserating and sympathising with groups of poor desitutes both Hindus and Muslims who had lost their homes and hearths during the riots and had now occupied the railway platforms for shelter.

'You must have faith in God and live in harmony with one another. We are all his children irrespective of our colour, creed and religion and we must always love our neigbours and live to give and share whatever little we possess,' said the young Nun as she took out the small packet of plain sandwiches that she was carrying in a small cardboard box for her journey and gave it to the little hungry children who had crowded around her.

'If only I had more to give,' said the Nun as she made her way with the empty tiffin box, a small bedding and an attaché case to the ladies second class compartment. When Colonel Attiqur Rehman noticed that because of her small height the dimunitive Nun was having difficulty in boarding her railway compartment with her luggage, he promptly offered his help.' That was indeed very kind and thoughtful of you,' said the humble Nun as she thanked Colonel Attiqur with folded hands. The young Mother Teresa was on her way to Darjeeling for her annual retreat. For her too this was not a pleasure trip, but a journey for more prayers to help the poor. Unknown to Reggie and Attiqur it was on this very train journey that she had received the call from her Lord to give up everything and follow God into the dirty slums, shanty towns and bustees of Calcutta and from there to serve the poorest of the poor. She therefore knew from that very moment that it was the Lord's will and she decided to follow him both in mind and spirit.

While Colonel Attiqur and Reggie carried on with their humanitarian work at Dr Graham's Home, on the 13th of October, Mr Jinnah finally agreed to let the members of his Muslm League join the coalition government, though he himself decided to keep out of it. Even while doing so he made it plain to the Viceroy and to the British Government that the Muslim League was joining it with a lot of misgivings. In his letter to the Viceroy, Jinnah reiterated that the Muslim League did not approve of the basis and the scheme of setting up the Interim Government, and that they considered the imposition of this decision contrary to the declaration of 8th August 1940. He finally added that the Muslim League was joining it with its five members not because they were very keen, but because by staying away it could prove fatal for them as they dd not want to leave the entire field of civil adminsraion in the hands of the Congress.

Late that night, when the Viceroy received the list of the Muslim League nominees there was a smile on hs face. But what surprised him was the inclusion of Mr Jogindra Nath Mondal an erstwhile minister of Bengal and who was from the Hindu Scheduled Caste. It was a tit for tat to the Congress. However on the very next day, when matters took a serious turn, the smile on the Viceroy's simply vanished as more trouble broke out in East Bengal with Muslims at will targeting and killing isolated Hindu communities.

And while sporadic incidents of communal killings in East Bengal kept surfacing, on 26th October1946 and after much haggling for portfolios, the Coalition Government with the Muslim League members was finally sworn in. After the five nominated Muslim League members took their oath and seats in the council hall, the Viceroy in order to welcome them and their leader raised a toast.

'Gentlemen let us all drink a toast to a free and unified India.' On hearing that there was angry scowl on Mr Jinnah's face and he did not even care to reply.While the Congress managed to keep External Affairs and Home, the Sikhs were given Defence, and both the Finance and Commerce Ministries went to the Muslim League.

With the communal riots in East Bengal and in the Noakhali District in particular showing no signs of abating, GovernorBurrows while reviewing the situation very aptly remarked that the total loss of lives during the four days of Calcutta riots was far greater than what the two warring sides had lost during the Great Battle of Plassey. And therefore it was now costing more in casualties to hand over Bengal to a local government than it did for the British to conquer it.

During the month of November 1946, the small impoverished Muslim dominated coastal district of Noahkali in the Sunderban area of East Bengal exploded with unprecedented violence with the Hindus being massacred mercilessly by the Muslims. And It was only a fortnight ago that both Arif Rehman Khan and Ronen Sen had taken over their new appointments as Sub Divisional Magistrates in those trouble affected areas. And while Arif Rehman Khan was stationed at Chandpur, Ronen Sen was based at Noakhali which was also the district headquarters.When the situation deteriorated further, the services of the army was requisitioned. It was once again the 161 Bde with its troops from the 1st Punjabees, 8th Gorkha Rifles, 4th Rajputs and 3rd Gorkha Rifles under Colonel PN Thapar the Officiating Brigade Commander that was sent to their rescue. With the many villages in that coastal belt, the troops perforce had to be therefore deployed in penny packets for the task. As they watched in disbelief the thousands of poor Hindus with their women, children and the meagre belongings that they could salvage from the holocaust leaving the villages that were once their homes and making their way into safer areas of Bihar and West Bengal, Major Gul Rehman Khan who was now the Second in Command of the 1st Punjabees during a special parade reiterated to his mixed troops of Hindus and Muslims that the uniform of the soldier was his true religion and therefore there should be complete impartiality in dealing with the culprits.

By now Gandhi also had arrived at Noakhali. Dressed in his half dhoti and the stick for support in his hand, the Mahatma in his barefeet walked through the blood soaked mud of the stricken villages. He was now in a dilemma on how to stop this madness. The value of human lives had reached its nadir as the young Hindu women who till a month ago were living peacefully with their Muslim neighbours had now become widows. They had watched with horror as their husbands were butchered before their very own eyes, and even before their dead bodies were cremated these young women were forcefully dragged away to be converted and married to the same killers. For them it was either convert or die. Some of them to save their honour did follow their husbands to the grave by taking their own lives, but there were quite a few others with young children who had no other option. One afternoon, while speaking to the poor villagers both Hindus and Muslims who had come to meet and share a frugal meal with him, the Mahatma said.

'I am not only a Hindu I am also a Muslim, a Sikh, a Christian, a Jew, a Buddhist and a Parsee too. We are all human beings irrespective of the religion that we belong to and God belongs to everyone. So why not live like brothers and in peace.' On hearing those words the congregation of Hindus and Muslims were stunned into silence. The great Mahatma was only trying his level best to keep India united.

With the riots in Bengal showing little or no signs of abetting, a large number of Hindu refugees now made their way to neighbouring Bihar. Their tales of woe and misery had now got the Hindus of Bihar in a mad frenzy as they also now went on a murderous mission to eliminate their Muslim neightbours. The retaliation was now ready to snowball and not only engulf Bihar and Bengal but also all the other northern States of India that had mixed populations of both Hindus and Muslims.

On the 7th of November, the Viceroy together with his Military Commanders General Boucher, General Russel Pasha, accompanied by Pandit Nehru and Dr Rajendra Prasad who himself hailed from Bihar visited Patna. After interviewing Mr Bowsteed the Secretary to the Government of Bihar and Mr Creed the Inspector General of Police, the Viceroy was horrified to hear the tales of slaughter that had taken place on the poor and the innocent in the many districts of the once peaceful State.

On 19th November, Viceroy Wavell after having held long talks both with Mr Jinnah and Pandit Nehru was finally convinced that a settlement between the two communities with peace and honour was now simply out of question as both the leaders went back to the history of the Moghuls and of Aurangzeb in particular to prove the point. Now the only solution Mr Jinnah sought was to have his own country for the Muslims of India and it was irrespective of its size. But it must be their own motherland and to achieve it Jinnah reiterated that the Muslims were prepared to even live on one meal a day.

After the killings and riots had subsided in the district, Ronen Sen and his wife threw a small family party at their residence in Noakhali for Major Gul Rehman and his brother Arif who was accompanied by his wife Ruksana. While the dinner was being laid, Ronen asked Major Gul Rehman.

'Bhaijan with the Muslim League now being very much in the chair as a part of the Interim Government, do you think Mr Jinnah will change is mind so that India could remain united? To that query, Gul Rehman having called for one more drink very candidly said.

'If the Army, the Navy and the Airforce of India can remain united as one composite force and even if we get divided as two different nations, one for the Hindus and the other for the Muslims, then there will be nothng to fear. But if we also get the three military services divided then everything will be lost and there will be hell to pay.'

As the debate on whether the Muslims of India should have their own country started getting a little heated, Arif' Rehman's wife Ruksana very diplomatically announced.

'I think we should change the topic and do justice to the food first,' And while Ruksana helped Mona to lay the food on the table, Ronen complimented her for the timely intervention.

Back in Calcutta and with the Muslim League having joined the Interim Government, Colonel Attiqur Rehman felt that probably better sense had prevailed on the politicians and that India may still remain united. With that in mind he felt that that there was no immediate need to pressure his son-in-law Nawaz Hussein to sell of all the property that the family owned in Calcutta and go back with him to his palatial house in Peshawar.Therefore in mid November, 1946 with Colonel Reggie for company when Colonel Attiqur Rehman boarded the Kalka Mail from Howrah for their journey back to their respective homes, and the guard blew his final whistle, Colonel Attiqur who had little Imran Hussein in his arms broke down. And as he kissed his little grandson for the last and final time and handed him back to his mother, Shenaz with tears streaming down from her eyes said.

'Please do not worry Abbajan we will all be soon with you.'

At around 8.30 pm after having had their two small regular scotch and sodas in their reserved coupe, when Reggie and Attiqur went to the dining car of the train for their four course continental dinner, they were surprised to see only one elderly English couple there. All the the table as usual were well laid out with bone china crockery and silver cutlery but there were hardly any takers. When the two waiters from Brandon's catering department in their spotless white uniforms and big red turbans covering their heads served them the steaming hot tomato soup with cream, Reggie was reminded of his days in boarding school where this was standard fare everyday except on weekends. That evening while enjoying the delicious meal, Colonel Attiqur Rehman and Colonel Reginald Edwards once again went back to the topic of the future of India.

'But tell me Sir honestly what you frankly feel. Do you think that the Hindus and Muslims after what has happened in these last few months in the Provinces of Punjab, Bengal, Bihar and in the United Provinces, will they be ever able to live like friends and brothers together again? And irrespective of the fact whether India remains united or gets divided communally, do you think that Mr Jinnah will still have his way?' asked Colonel Attiqur.

'It is indeed a good question and since you have asked me I will say that they certainly can remain as brothers and good friends provided the political leaders from both sides stop playing communal and partisan politics with them. Haven't the two communities lived as good friends and neighbours for the past so many centuries, so why can't they do so now? I agree that now and then such communal flare ups do occur, but that does not mean that we break away from each other for good. Why even in Great Britain we have similar problems and it is especially so in Northern Ireland between the Protestants and the Catholics, but it is the political greed and power that is dividing us. The problem today is not with the poor Muslims or Hindus or the badly exploited many scheduled castes and tribes that this country has, but with the political parties and their selfish leaders who simply want power and authority at any cost to rule over the illiterate masses in this subcontinent. Truly speaking except for Mr Gandhi who genuinely feels for the poor people of India irrespective of their caste, creed or religion and who with his mantra of Ahimsa and non violence genuinely desires that come what may the country should remain united, all the others simply want to carve their own fiefdoms and this includes some of the Rajas and Mahrajas too who want to remain independent', added Reggie while requesting the waiter to hurry up a bit with the main course.

'Perhaps you do have a valid point in what you just stated, but why cant you the Englishmen who have been ruling this country for nearly three centuries be more firm with these political parties and their leaders and of which there are presently only two major ones, the Congress and the Muslim League. In fact it should be the British Government who should be dictating the terms and conditions under which they propose to give India her freedom and they should be firm and candid about it And it is time Mr Attlee told them that power will not not handed over till such time all those terms and conditions were fully met,' said Attiqur as the waiter got ready to serve themthe main course.

'But my dear friend what according to you are these so called terms and conditions,' said Reggie as he helped himself to another piece of his favourite fried Beckti fish with tartare sauce.

'Well to begin with His Majesty's government should simply put its foot down and bluntly tell the Indian leaders that freedom will only be given provided the leaders and members of all the political parties irrespective of their party affliations, caste, creed and religion agree for a secular, democratic and a united India. It should also be made plainly clear to them that the Hindu-Muslim divide must be bridged and there should be no more killings of the hapless innocent people. They should also make it clear and in no uncertain terms that there will be no more discrimination or exploitation of the under privileged schedule castes, the schedule tribes and other such minority religious groups who are in fairly large numbers and who as citizens will also have equal rights. Finally it must be drummed into their heads that every individual whether he be a Muslim, a Hindu, a Sikh, a Parsee or a Christian is first and foremost an Indian. And as far religion is concerned, everybody must individually and collectively respect one another's time honoured customs, culture and heritage,' concluded Attiqur as the waiter cleared the table for the dessert to be served. Reggie who was listening very attentively to Attiqur's discourse appreciated his views and said somewhat candidly.

'You have spoken like a true soldier and I wish more educated Indians like you were in politics today rather than the ones who with their high flaunting law and other degrees from England and elsewhere are now making a real mess of it, and I only hope and pray that their leadership should not push India into a bloody civil war,' added Reggie as the big bowl of caramel custard was placed in front of him.This was also one of Reggie's favourite and Attiqur had especially ordered it for him. The pudding brought back memories of the days when Reggie was a regular guest of the Rehman family in Peshawar and Attiqur's charmimg wife the late Nafisa Begum who had become an expert in preparing this particular pudding would religiously serve to to Reggie at supper every night.

After the sumptuous dinner was over, and the two of them had returned to their first class coupe, Reggie in order to reciprocate Attiqur's thoughtful gesture opened the bottle of Napoleon cognac that Nawaz Hussein had presented him with. Then having poured a large peg each into the two cognac glasses that Shenaz had so thoughtfully packed for them, both Reggie and Attiqur clinked glasses and drank to an united and free India.

A few days later on 21st November 1946, while the members of the Interim Coalition Government were still finding their feet, the CWC, Central Working Committee of the Congress Party came out with a bombshell on Kashmir. Highly explosive in its content it would now severely rock the princely state. The CWC had passed a resolution on Kashmir expressing their utter disapproval of the activities of the Maharaja of Kashmir's Government and accused them of repressing the Kashmiris and of denying them their normal basic civil liberties. The CWC also alleged that the Kashmir authorities were now not only trying to prevent fair and free elections to the state assembly, but with Sheikh Abdulla who was the leader of the National Conference in jail, they were now also trying to arrest the acting President and other members of the election committee of the party. To rub more salt into the allegations made by the Congress Party, the CWC even suggested that they would send their own delegation to enquire into the matter and for this they sought the cooperation of the state authorities. Besides the Maharaja and his cabinet feeling highly offended and annoyed, it was Yusuf Shah, the Mirwaiz Maulvi of the Kashmir Valley who lashed out at the Congress party.'

'What damn cheek and this is utter nonsense. How can the CWC of the Congress Party which has no authority whatsoever to interfere in the affairs of our State make such a stupid request,' said the Head priest of the Srinagar Jumma Mazjid as he hit back at Nehru and at the Indian National Congress.Besides calling them Fascists, the Mirwaiz also accused the National Conference of being the stooges of the Indian National Congress. Four days later on the 25th of November, the Maulvi also made the matter highly public when he said.

'Dear Kashmiri brothers and sisters I regret to say that the decision of the CWC to send a delegation to Kashmir to enquire into the political conditions prevailing in our State amounts to nothing else but gross interference into the domestic policies and affairs of Kashmir.' He then further added that such interference was a positive proof of the fact that the Congress leaders who now cherished the dream of turning Kashmir into an ante Pakistan base and of getting the State under their grip were bound to fail and the idea of sending a delegation to Kashmir was part of their sinister game to enslave the whole of Muslim India. He therefore now called upon all Kashmiri Muslims to smash this uncalled for and brazen onslaught.

With the Mirwaiz Maulvi Yusuf Shah backed by Mr Jinnah and his Muslim League advocating that the State of Kashmir with its Muslim majority should form part of Pakistan, and Sheikh Abdulla's National Conference with the backing of Nehru and the Congress Party favouring a tie up with India, the battle lines for the future of Kashmir were now clearly being drawn up. Caught in the middle was Maharaja Hari Singh the princely Hindu Dogra ruler of the State. And tThough Sheikh Abdulla was still in jail, but his call to the Maharaja and his Government to quit Kashmir had not died down. And with the Mirwaiz Maulvi also being a very influential religious leader in the valley, his call to the people to join Pakistan could not be taken lightly either. The Maharaja it seems now decided to play one faction against the other and started toying with the idea of retaining an independent kingdom of his own after the paramountcy of the British was legally over.

With the Congress Party and the Muslim League pulling in different directions, the British Labour Government of Prime minister Clement Attlee invited the leaders of both parties and that of the Sikh community for a summit conference at London and with the hope that sitting together they may be able to arrive at some reasonable consensus. On 1st December 1946 at 7 AM, the aircraft carrying the Viceroy, Pandit Nehru, Mr Jinnah, Mr Liaquat Ali Khan, Sardar Baldev Singh and a few other leaders with their small staff of secretaries took off from Karachi and on the 3rd of December after stop overs at Cairo and Malta they arrived in London.

They were all there to discuss what would be the fate of India. The second city of the British Empire was still reeling from the devastations of the war and the communal riots and as the talks progressed it became amply clear that there was no chance whatsoever of any reconciliation between the Congress and the Muslim League as far as having a united India was concerned. The summit conference held from the 3rd to the 6th of December produced no results as Mr Jinnah was hell bent in getting his own Pakistan. For the British Prime Minister Clement Attlee and his Labour Party Ministers the stage was now set to look for some other viable alternative for the subcontinent. Unhappy and disillusioned with Viceroy Wavell's handling of the situation, the British Prime Minister now started looking for a suitable replacement for him.And it was sometime in mid December of1946 that the tall and handsome grandson of the late Queen Victoria was summoned by Mr Attlee at the British Prime Ministers residence at number 10 Downing Street.

Rear Admiral Louis Mountbatten the son of Princess Alice the third daughter of the good Queen Victoria was also the nephew of the last Tsar of Russia. Elegantly dressed in his naval uniform the charming and young Admiral from the British Navy with royal blood had no clue whatsoever as to why he had been summoned by the Prime Minister till he was ushered into his office.

'Please do come in Admiral and be seated,' said the 63 year old Prime Ministter as he lit his pipe and ran his right hand over his bald head. And after the handshakes were over, when Mr Attlee addressed theAdmiral by his popular nickname Dicky and said that the cabinet had decided to send him to India as His Majesty's last Viceroy and since that decision was final and he would not take no for an answer, Dickie for a moment remained speechless.

And it was only after the Prime Minister had given out the reasons for the choice that Dicky knew that there was no point in arguing with him.

'We have chosen you Dickie after a lot of thought and deliberations. Firstly because both you and your charming wife know India well and it started from the year 1922, when you accompanied the Prince of Wales as his ADC to that country and soon thereafter Edwina too followed you. And if I am not mistaken the declaration of the engagement too was made from Delhi. And till recently during the war you as the Supreme Commander also did a commendable job in India and in South East Asia. His Majesty therefore feels that since you and your charismatic wife both love India, you will be the ideal choice to guide our jewel in the crown to her final destiny of getting her freedom, while remaining as a member of the British Commonwealth ofcourse.'

There was no doubt that Admiral Mountbatten was stumped by that prestigious offer, but he also knew that it was being thrusted upon him. But since it had the blessings of the King himself, he was atleast bold enough to state his own terms of taking on the assignmentand before signing on the dotted line.

'Honourable Mr Prime Mnister Sir, I no doubt feel highly honoured with the offer, but with the deadline being set for June 1948, I feel that the time is rather too short and therefore I will only agree to take on the offer provided you and your Government give me full plenipotentiary powers so that I as the Viceroy can take quick on the spot decisions.'

Hearing the demand made by Dickie there was big smile on Mr Attlee's face as he tapped his pipe into the big brass ashtray and said. "Alright and granted.'

That day when Dickie conveyed the news to his wife Edwina she was simply thrilled. And while hugging and congratulating her husband when she said that they would not only be creating history, but they would also be closing the lid finally and for the last time on Britain's precious jewel in the crown, for Dicky it was just the kind of moral support that he wanted from his wife.

"That is udoubtedly so my dear and no greater country and its people deserve the freedom more than India does today. Had it not been for their supreme sacrifices both in men and material during both the world wars, we would today not be what we are," added the Viceroy designate to India.

On that cold December evening of 14th December 1946 in London, while the Mounbattens were celebrating the announcement with champagne, in New Delhi at around midnight at India's Interim Prime

Minister's York Road bungalow, Indira Gandhi the one and only daughter of Pandit Nehru was complaining of severe labour pains. She was expecting her second child, but according to her doctor the child wasn't due for a few more weeks. Not willing to take any chance and unable to bear the severe pain, and seeing the terrible agony that his wife was in, her husband Feroze Gandhi with her aunt Mrs Krishna Hutthesingh popularly known as Aunty Betty decided to take her to the nursing home and hospital. Not wishing to disturb his father-in-law who after a gruelling day's work in office had already gone off to sleep, the three of them quietly drove off in the baby Austin car that was parked in the porch. On arrival at the hospital, when the concerned English doctor was summoned from his residence at that unearthly hour, he wasn't the least pleased to leave his warm bed on that cold December night. But he had no choice. Afterall the young pregnant lady was none other than the Prime Minster of India's daughter.

Having inspected the patient, the English doctor summoned the nurse on duty. though it was very late in the night, luckily Indira had made it in the nick of time and a few hours later she gave birth to another son. Early next morning, when Pandit Nehru was informed, he rushed to the hospital. On reaching there, he could make out that his daughter had lost a lot of blood because she was completely white in the face as she lay semi-conscious on the hospital bed. For the next two hours Nehru with his son-in-law Feroze Gandhi and with his sister Betty they prayed and stood vigil around her bed. Finally when Indira opened her eyes and was told that she had produced another son, she gave a feeble smile, while her husband tenderly stroked her hand. They named him Sanjay after the great Indian philosopher in the Bhagwad Gita, the holy book of the Hindus in which the philosopher relates the great epic story of Arjuna and his battle with his own cousin brothers. However they probably did not realize that day that Sanjay who was born prematurely was destined to also go down in history, but with a different kind of Mahabharat that would take place with the imposition of the emergency in the country twenty nine years later. And what would follow thereafter would be even more tragic for the Nehru-Gandhi family. Not only would Indira lose her young Sanjay in an air accident, but she and her elder son Rajiv too would be killed in a brutal manner by assasins and the two Gandhi Bahus and their grandchildren would become political rivals in two vastly different political camps.

And while the Nehru-Gandhi celebrated the birth of little Sanjay, at Dehradun preparations were on for the passing out parade of the gentlemen cadets of the IMA. On 20th Dec 1946, the Commander-in-Chief of India,

Field Marshall Claude Auchinleck took the salute at that historic passing out parade. Also present on that occasion were Colonel Reginald Edwards, Colonel Attiqur Rehman, Major Gul Rehman Khan and Major Ismail Sikandar Khan. All of them winners of the Military Cross were there as special invitees of the Government. During the formal sit down dinner at the Commandant's House on the previous evening and for which Colonel Attiqur Rehman and Colonel Reggie were especially invited, a very funny incident took place. One of the Gentleman Cadet's holding the appointment of a Senior Under Officer and who was to get his commission the next day while sitting next to an attractive middle aged English lady who incidently also happened to be the wife of a senior directing staff of the academy accidently dropped his napkin. But while trying to pick it up quietly and without being noticed by the others, he by mistake and to Colonel Attiqur's horror who was seated on his left picked up the end of the lady's evening dress instead On noticing the unintentional misdemeanour, Colonel Attiqur Rehman with his superior sense of humour saved the day, when he wittingly remarked that the Under Officer being young and nervous while sitting on the main table was probably trying to hold on to the lady's skirt for moral support.

Next morning during the traditional coffee break and after the passing out parade was over, Colonel Attiqur Rehman noticing the same Under Officer now with a pip on each shoulder standing with his proud parents, walked upto them to offer his congratulations. When he observed that he had been commissioned as a Second Lieutenant in the famed cavalry regiment of the Skinners Horse, Colonel Attiqur as usual with his subtle sense of humour remarked.

'Well son thank God that the amiable English lady sitting next to you last evening during dinner was not thick skinned, for had she complained about your impropriety to her husband who is from the Royal 5th Gurkhas and who is also a Piffer,. he would have probably skinned you alive with his khukri'

Noticing the blank look on the face of the young officer's parents who had come for the passing out parade, Attiqur quickly took the young man to a side and whispered into his ears.

'I hope you only lifted her skirt and did'nt go any further, my boy. Nevertheless the smoothness of her skin must have thrilled you alright. And no wonder you joined the Skinner's Horse,' added Attiqur with a smile as he patted the subaltern and joined Reggie and the other VIP's for a hot cup of coffee.

Major Ismail Sikandar Khan on his return from Dehradun joined duty in Delhi He was now posted as General Officer Grade Two with the Military Intelligence Directorate at the Indian Army Headquarters. That very evening Ismail decided to officially call on Lt Col Shahid Hameed whose bunglow on 12, Wellingdon Crescent was located close to that of the C-in-C's palatial house.

Col Shahid a product of Colvin College Lucknow and Military Academy Sandhurst with his suave manners and Tahira his beautiful and charming wife was a made for each other couple and they were great hosts too. No sooner had Ismail knocked on the door, when the C-in-C's shining Cadillac car without the star plates and the flag entered through the big irongate. But when it stopped under the portico both Hassu and Guriya, the two sweet little children of the Hameed couple who were being escorted by one of the Chief's Indian ADC's simply refused to get out of the car. They were demanding one more opportunity to press the window buttons that would automatically roll down and roll up the windows of their Chiefy's big car.

'OK one last time,' said the ADC as the two kids pressed the buttons to get their thrill from it. Both of them were returning home from their dear Chiefi's house with their little gifts that the C-in-C invariably presented them with on his return from every tour of the many military stations and establishments in the subcontinent.

'Well I too have got a small gift for both of you and a slightly bigger one for your parents,' said Major Ismail Sikandar Khan as he gave the two little children a slab of Cadbury chocolates each and then handed over a 78 RPM record to Mrs Hameed the charming hostess. It was the the most popular song of the year sung by none other than the most popular singer of India, Mr Kundan Lal Saigal. The song was from the film "Shahjehan" the Moghul emperor who not only built the famous Red Fort in Delhi but also the beautiful Taj Mahal at Agra in memory of his beloved wife Mumtaz Mahal. When Tahira played it on their HMV gramophone everyone listened with pin drop silence as the golden voice of the man with all sadness rendered those touching words. "Hum jeeke kiya karenge, jab dil hi toot gaya." (What is there to live for now that my heart is already broken)' Ironically this was also the great singer's last song to be ever recorded. By now Mahatma Gandhi's heart too was broken as he kept desperately trying for a united Indias. A month later on the 18th of January 1947 as another year dawned, Kundan Lal Saigal was no more. The whisky that he loved had got the better of him it seems and he was only 41 years old.

Kundan Lal Saigal who was born in Jullunder had started life as a timekeeper in the Punjab Railways. For a while he even sold typewriters for a living. He was spotted as a singing star by the Hindustan Recording Company in Calcutta, while he was singing in some friends circle. In 1932, with the release of his first film aptly titled "Subah Ka Tara", (The Morning Star) which was directed by Nitin Bose and had music by RC Boral, the handsome Punjabi really became a star overnight. A natural singer, he was honoured by none other than the legendary Rabindranath Tagore, when he became the first non Bengali to be given permission by the poet to sing his melodious Rabindrasangeets. In 1935, with the release of the film "Devdas" by New Theatres, followed by other super hits like 'Zindagi', 'My Sister' and 'Tansen' that had music by Khemchand Prakash, Saigal by the early forties had become a super star. His rendering of the song 'Diya Jalao" in the Deepak Raag in the film 'Tansen' that was released in 1943 during the war had already made him a legend. On his passing away so very early in life there were tears in the eyes of many, including Ismail Sikandar Khan and his dear friend Gul Rehman Khan.

Though Kundan Lal Saigal was no more, but his melodious voice had created a true national spirit of integration among all Indians irrespective of their caste creed or religion. Through him the Hindi film music had come of age and which more than anything else gave the masses of the country the power to be tolerant and patient. With the partitioning of the country looming large on the horizon, Hindi film songs would now become a great healing factor in times of crisis and act as a tonic to soothe the nerves of the people of India. For the Indian soldiers during the recently concluded Second World War it was the voice of Saigal, Pankaj Mullick, Noor Jehan, Kannanbala, Suraiya, Zohrabai and such like other singing stars that kept their morale high while fighting the enemy. Songs like "Aankhiyan Milake, Jiya Bharma Ke, Chale Nahin Jaana from the film "Rattan" that had music by the young Naushad and "Chupona Chupona O Pyari Sajaniya' sung by the great KL Saigal was still on everybody's lips.

With the war finally over, not only the Indian Army, but also the others too from the Allied Forces were now in the process of demobilization. But strong rumours were still afloat that both Hitler and Subhash Bose were still very much alive. During the middle of 1945 and even during 1946 the sighting of the late Fuhrer in various disguises was reported not only from remote areas of Germany, but also from Italy, Spain, Scandanavia and even Argentina.And it was only during the Christmas week of 1946 that the truth about Hitler's last hours and death was finally revealed. And that was when

Wilhelm Zander, the Adjutant to Martin Bormann under his new psuedo name of Paustin while working as a gardner in the quiet village of Tiergnsee in Germany was captured by the British and American sleuths from the MI5 and OSS respectively, and a suitcase with a secret compartment was found in his possession.The suitcase contained very important documents. These documents had been brought out by Zander from the Fuhrer's bunker forty eight hours before Berlin finally fell. It contained Adolf Hitler's will, his political testament and the marriage contract with the late Eva Braun. With that the hunt for Hitler was now finally over, but the hunt for Subhash continued. There were rumours that he had become a monk and was now somewhere in Tibet or the Himalayas. Someone else reported his presence in Kabul, whle others said that he could well be in the Soviet Union or even in Austria. As the year 1946 ended there was still no sign of Subash Bose resurfacing again and the start of 1947 did not augur well for the subcontinent either, as the divide between the Hindus and the Muslims grew wider and wider.

After the failure of the talks in London during December 1946, the dawn of another year for India which was eagerly looking forward to be free from British colonial rule seemed destined to be a year of torment, misery, gloom, despair and of inhuman killings of the innocent. The rest of the world had now slowly started recovering from the ravages of the war, but India was on the verge of collapse and disaster. The year 1947 for the subcontinent would now be a year of inmitigated calamity that would be unprecedented in the annals of world history. It would also be a tragedy that would leave millions homeless, and a catastrophe that would break the hearts of people who were once good friends and good neighbours. In spite of the country inching forward towards freedom and freeing the shackles of colonial rule and bondage, the cancer of communal discord was now once again raising its ugly head. With the Hindus and Sikhs on one side, and the Muslims on the other, the road to freedom was now about to take a more vicious, violent and ugly turn.

On that cold afternoon of New Year's day of 1947, as the frail old Mahatma Gandhi, the apostle of peace lay stretched on the grimy and mucky floor of a poor Hindu peasant's burnt and blackened dilapidated hut in the small little village of Srirampur in the Noakhali District of East Bengal, he was surprised to be greeted by a group of government district officials that was led by none other than the District Commissioner himself. The exponent of Indian unity having put on his steel rimmed glasses checked the time on his one and only favorite Ingersol watch that was tied to his bony and skinny waist. It was nearing midday as he folded his hands to reciprocate the greeting and both Ronen Sen and Arif Rehman were shocked to see the great Mahatma in that state. Both of them with a few other district officials had been seconded to assist the British District Commissioner of Noakhali to survey the destruction caused by the Bengali Muslims on the minority Hindu Bengali community in the areas around. The destruction of the Hindu huts in the village of Srirampur that ironically bore the name of Rama the great Hindu God had been carried out remorselessly and mercilessly by their own Muslim brothers who till a few weeks ago were good neighbours and friends. All the Hindu villages in the District of Noakhali had become prime targets of slaughter, rape and loot, and the Mahatma had especially arrived there to restore peace and harmony.

The weak and feeble Mahatma for days together on his bare feet had walked through dirt, slush, filth and muck from village to village trying to pacify both the communities to remain as friends and brothers. With his wooden lathi for support and the message of peace and harmony on his lips, the poor peasants from both the communities now followed their messenger of God, as they sang along with him Rabindra Nath Tagore's famous song. "Jodhi tor dak shune keyu na ashe tobe akela cholo ray." (If they answer not your call, walk alone, walk alone.) That afternoon, when the District Commissioner an Englishman raised doubts about India remaining united, the Mahatma looked him straight into the eye and very candidly and firmly said.

'Let me tell you my dear friend that you will have to divide my body before you divide India.'Hearing those words coming from the lips of the Mahatma, both Ronen Sen and Arif Rehman said.

'Gandhiji let us all pray and hope that these golden words from you puts a little more sense into our political leaders so that we all remain united as one great nation.

'Yes, and I too will pray for that Mr Gandhi,' said the Englishman as he once again doffed his hat in respect to the old man. Soon thereafter, the 77-year-old man, the great soul in a beggars garb got ready with his bamboo stave to visit the next affected village.

On 20th February 1947, while Viceroy Wavell in Delhi was celebrating his daughter Felicity's marriage with Captain Peter Longmore, a decorated soldier with a Military Cross, in the British Parliament house in London, the 63 year old balding British Prime Minister Richard Clement Attlee who was once a lawyer by profession and who was born in Putney was making his historic statement.In the summer of 1945 and soon after taking over as the Prime Minister and with the war just over, he had realized that there was now no other alternative, but to give India her much deserved freedom as promised. On 27th December 1945, in order to safe guard the world from a another major financial depression and collapse, the World Bank and the International Monetary Fund had been created, but England in spite of her vast Empire was still in the process of recovering from her war ravaged economy.

Speaking to the Parliamentarians in the British House of Commons Attlee said. 'Gentlemen the present state of uncertainty in India is fraught with danger and cannot be indefinitely prolonged. His Majesty's Government therefore wishes to make it clear that it is their definite intention to take necessary steps to affect the transference of power to reasonable Indian hands by June 1948. If the Muslim League continued to boycott the constituent assembly, the British Government would then have to consider to whom the powers of the Central Government should be handed over to on that due date. Whether it should be handed over as a whole to some form of Central Government, or in some areas to the existing Provincial Government or in such other way as may seem most reasonable and in the best interest of the Indian people.'

The statement by the British Prime Minister did bring a smile on the faces of the Hindus and Sikhs, but to the Muslims specially those in the Punjab and Bengal and to the members of the Muslim League this only created more bad blood of hatred, revenge and vengeance. Infuriated by the British resolve to keep India United, an angry and fuming Mr Jinnah and his Muslim League now started a raging campaign to bring about the partition of the country at any damn cost. The backlash led to more riots and killings as the Muslim League with their Muslim National Guards resorted to unleash violence and terror among the Hindus and the Sikhs in the Muslim majority provinces of Punjab and Bengal in particular. Not to be left behind the Hindus and Sikhs too geared up their own own militant cadres like the RSS, the Rashtriya Sevak Sangh and others to sought the Muslims out in the Hindu dominated provinces of India.

And while communal tension in India was on the rise, on the morning of 20th March, 1947, Charles Smith the faithful and loyal valet of the Viceroy designate at the Northolt airport in England got busy loading the personal baggage of the Mountbatten's into the Lancaster bomber. It was the same aircraft that Admiral Mountbatten had used during the war, when he was Supreme Commander South East Asia. These were two wartime aircrafts, the MW 101 and MW 102 that had been now specially converted for use by the King and other VIP's. A day prior, the MW 101 with Lord Ismay, Eric Melville and with some other personal staff of the last Viceroy designate had already taken off on their long flight to India.

On that day of 20th March, 1947 after Captain Ronald Brockman the head of the Viceroy's personal staff and Lieutenant Commander Peter Howes the Viceroy's senior ADC had checked the Viceroy's personal luggage that was already inside the aircraft and had given the green signal, the Captain of the aircraft was now ready to welcome the VIP's on board. On receiving the word from the Captain of the aircraft that the MW 102 was now ready for take off, Louis Francis Albert Victor Nicholas Mountbatten with his charming wife Edwina and their pretty young daughter Pamela walked across the tarmac to board the York. As the amiable Edwina with her new magnificent tiara in an old battered shoe box held firmly under her arm and Pamela with their pet dog Mizzen safely in her hands went up the gangway and they were followed by the young Viceroy designate, a round of cheers and clapping greeted them. When the handsome 46 year old Naval officer in his naval uniform gave a final salute to all those well wishers who had come to see him off, another round of loud cheers, clapping and waving of hands followed.

Forty eight hours later on 22nd March, when the MW 102 taxied to a halt at the airport in Delhi, once again the new Viceroy immaculately dressed in his naval admiral's spotless white uniform and with his chest covered with rows of medals stood silently at the door of the York and with the Vicerene by his side he gratefully acknowledged the warm welcome that was being given to them. And as they came down the ramp the cheering only grew louder and louder.Later as they rode along the Kingsway in the same landau that his own cousin, the late king George the Fifth used half a century ago, there were not very many people on the road to greet them. As the landau approached the magnificent Viceroy's Imperial Palace built by Lutyens on Raisina Hill, Viceroy Wavell with his devoted wife waited patiently to welcome them. It was nearing 4 o'clock in the evening and only after they had climbed the red carpetted broad flight of sandstone steps that the outgoing Viceroy and his wife officially greeted the new incumbents. As the handsome couple reached the last and final step of the magnificent edifice, the Mountbatten's bowed in respect, while the battery of cameras recorded the event for posterity. Within less than twenty fours hours the Viceroyalty of British India would change for the last and final time in the jewel of the Empire's crown.

From the very minute after they had exchanged the customary pleasantries, both the out going and the incoming Viceroys with their senior staff members got busy to understand the complexities that would eventually give India her freedom and they had just 24 hours to do it in.

While the young Viceroy was being briefed, his wife feeling dead tired after the long flight with her dog Mizzen by her side on the bed waited for some food that she had ordered for the hungry dog. As Faiz Mohammed the head butler with two liveried waiters knocked on the door and walked in with the silver salver that was covered with a spotless white damask napkin, Mizzen jumped out of the bed wagging his tail. The whiff of the cold roast chicken was enough for the dog to know that he was in for a treat, but he felt disappointed, when Edwina after having dismissed the butler and the waiters walked into the bathroom with the contents. She was hungry too and in war torn England this was a delicacy. However, after relishing the one course meal inside the bathroom when she came out with whatever was left for her dear Mizzen and the cat was more than delighted with the chicken bones.

That very evening at a formal ceremony, Viceroy Wavell whose famous remark that he had been dismissed as if he was a cook handed over to Louis Mountbatten the Viceroy's diamond crusted badge of office as the Grand Master of the Star of India. Soon thereafter he took out a top-secret file from the iron safe that was marked with a big red cross. The heading on it read "Operation Madhouse."

'Do not worry, this country is not such a Madhouse as the name suggests but it could become one soon,' said Wavell as he explained the contents.'Operation Madhouse' was a secret plan for the evacuation of all British nationals city by city, province by province to safer places in India incase their was a general uprising or communal riots. The priority to be given was first to the British women and children followed by the civilian men folk and lastly the men in military uniform. Little did Louis Mountbatten and his wife realize then that a few days and months from that date India would literally become a madhouse with Hindus, Sikhs and Muslims slitting each other's throats, but with the consolation that the British subjects would be left completely unharmed and unscathed in that macabre dance of death that had already begun.

On 23rd March 1947, after the young Mountbatten bid a final farewell to the Wavells, he knew fully well that as the last Viceroy of India his task was not going to be an easy one at all. He was now pitted against a battery of lawyers who had turned politicians and leaders in both camps. Most of them had got their lawyer's degrees and credentials from England and he would now have to deal with them day in and day out, with firmness, kindness and shrewdness. Though most of them had practically left wearing their black gowns, some of them did put them on occassionaly since it gave them a good source of income too. But most of them were now in active politics and they were no longer novices in the law courts or in the political arena. Confronting him now were senior and seasoned politicians like Gandhi, Nehru, Patel, Sapru and Asaf Ali on one side and Jinnah, Liaquat Ali Khan, Nizamuddin and Shaheed Suhraardy on the other. The new Viceroy was also now aware that the coalition government that he was required to deal with was an assembly of bitterly divided adversaries who now even avoided wishing and talking to each other.On that day of 23rd March, 1947 at Delhi as the Mountbattens while breaking all protocol saw off the Wavells at the airport, Mr Jinnah with Liaquat Ali Khan held a mass rally of their followers in Delhi and reiterated once again that the time had come for all Muslims of India to shed their last drop of blood for the struggle to have their own homeland, their own land of the pure, their very own and precious Pakistan.

Early morning next day as MB and Edwina started getting ready for the swearing in ceremony of the last Viceroy of India, MB could not but help recall to his wife the words of Lady Reading. The Vicerene had very seriously in 1921 on the day of their engagement in India which was a good twenty six years ago had said to Edwina.'But dear Edwina you must be a fool to marry a young Lieutenant from the Royal Navy who hardly has any worthwhile career ahead of him.'So when Dicky repeated those very words to her, Edwina simply smiled. Thereafter having softly placed the diamond tiara at the correct spot she very gracefully adjusted the Order of the Crown of India on her head and said.

'But now Darling since Lady Reading has been proved absolutely wrong in her judgment, the time has come when you will now be judged by the people of this very land where we were engaged.Then as she in her long ivory brocade gown looking beautiful and elegant as ever took her husband's hand for the historic walk to the red and gold thrones inside the durbar hall, MB affectionately pecked her on her cheek.

Under the white marble dome of the durbar hall inside the Viceroy's palace, the elite of India waited anxiously for their arrival. Starting with the Governors of the Provinces, the High Court Judges, the top military brass, the senior ICS staff, the Rajas and the Maharajas and the Indian political bigwigs, anybody who was somebody in the blue book, they were all there. Pandit Nehru dressed in his homespun Khadi and with the red rose fastened to the third button and which would soon become his trademark broke into a big smile. Then as the fanfare by the buglers was sounded and the 31 guns boomed in salute to the last Viceroy of India, Dicky with his charming and attractive wife majestically walked into the magnificent durbar hall.

The Viceroy wearing the uniform of an Admiral of the royal navy and with the pale blue velvet mantle of the Grand Master of the Star of India over his lean shoulders indeed looked very majestic in his ceremonial outfit. While clasping the historic scepter that had been passed down for two centuries from one Viceroy to the other, he also kept surveying the faces of those with whom he would now have to work so very closely with. Flanked by two of his ADC's he looked as handsome as ever as he as the last representative of the Raj stood up to take the solemn oath.

When Sir Patrick Spens the Lord Chief Justice of India in his own dignified manner administered the oath of office to the last Viceroy of India, and as the solemn words echoed through the great durbar hall, for the first time in the history of Lutyen's magnificent creation on Raisina Hill, the cine cameras of the world press whirred to record the event for posterity. Once the swearing in was finally over, the new Viceroy broke another protocol. He simply stood up to address the Assembly. This was something that no other Viceroy had ever done before, but to MB it warranted a necessity. While MB cleared his throat, Pandit Nehru smiled at the Vicerene and waited patiently for the Viceroy to begin.

'Ladies and Gentlemen although I know I am breaking protocol, but I would very much like to take this opportunity to say a few words to all of you and to the people of India. You will agree that this is not a normal Viceroyalty, at least not for me, because I am now embarking on a task to give India her much awaited freedom. His Majesty's government as you are all aware has resolved to transfer power by June 1948. This is not going to be an easy task, because as of now constitution arrangements have to be made, and many diverse and complicated questions of administration have to be resolved. Consequently all this will take time to be put into effect. Hence a proper and a justifiable solution must be reached within the next few months. Likewise every Indian political leader who also feels the urgency of this task like I do, and with whom I will soon be in consultations, it will be my earnest endeavour to give all of them all the help I can. In the meantime it is imperative for each and every one of us to do what we can to avoid any word or action that might lead to further bitterness and add to the toll of innocent victims of hatred to say the least. I know I have a very difficult task and therefore I shall need the greatest goodwill of the greatest possible number of Indians and all that I am asking India today is for that goodwill of yours.'

As the new Viceroy closed his address with the appeal to every Indian to offer him the help that he earnestly desired, the majority in the Durbar Hall were now confident that the man was truthful, honest and he meant business. That evening after the garden party which was thrown in honour of the new Viceroy and Vicerene by Pandit Nehru in his York Road bungalow, the future Prime Minister of India after all his guests had departed could not but help remark in a lighter vein to his charismatic and attractive sister Vijaylaxmi Pandit.

'Thank God India has finally got a human being for a Viceroy and not a stuffed shirt.'

That evening the Mahatma too felt happy on MB's appointment as the last Viceroy of India, and at his prayer meeting he urged all Indians to unite and as per the wishes of the Viceroy give him the helping hand of goodwill that he had so humbly requested for. He concluded with the words that the tree has many leaves but only one trunk and so was it with all religions and the one God that we all pray to. In order to spread the message of brotherhood and love amongst the various religious communities of India and to keep the country united, he once again reiterated to the congregation that he was not only a Hindu, but also a pious Mussulman, a good Sikh, a devoted Christian, a faithful Jew, a humble Buddhist and a virtuous Parsee. But above all he was a proud Indian.

While Gandhi was trying his level best to bring all the communities together, Mr Jinnah sitting in his study at his residence on 10, Aurangzeb Road in New Delhi was thinking and planning his next course of action. After neatly rearranging the files, pens, pencils, the ink pots and other writing material in perfect alignment on his big study tabl as was his habit, the meticulous man with a large scotch and soda in his hand and a Craven A cigarette on his lips walked slowly up to the marble fire place on the top of which hung a large political map of India. Facing the map he deliberated over the Provinces and the Princely States that would form his own great country. Next day he had them highlighted in enameled green colour, the colour of the Great Prophet Mohammed and felt proud, for he knew he would in time to come be the architect of a new country, a new nation for the Muslims of India and he would thus create history.

In that very month of March 1947, when Khizr Hayat Khan the leader of the small Union Party who was also the Chief Minister of Punjab and was ruling the State with the help of a coalition resigned, the Muslim League staked its claim, but they could not muster the necessary majority support. The Governor Sir Evan Jenkins therefore invoked section 93 and declared Governor's rule in the State. The granary and the buckler of the country and the land of the five rivers was now without an elected government. The Province which was half the size of France and to the British, the crown jewel of India and through which the River Indus, the longest of the five rivers of the Punjab ran and which gave India her name was now getting primed to explode.

Not far away in the North West Frontier Province there was trouble brewing too. The Province had a Congress Government with Dr Khan Sahib, the elder brother of the Frontier Gandhi as its Chief Minister, but the Pathans were not at all happy about it. When various reports by Mr Olaf Caroe, the Governor of the Province consistently indicated that the Pathans were more inclined to side with Mr Jinnah and be part of Pakistam, the Viceroy decided to visit the Province in order to get a first hand account of what was happening there.

In the summer heat of April 1947, when the Viceroy's York landed at Peshawar, Governor Olaf Caroe looked a very worried man. When the Viceroy with the Vicerene came down the ramp and after the God save the King had been played, the Governor confided to the Viceroy about the hordes of angry and agitated tribesmen under their Maliks and leaders, numbering a few thousands, and some of them with guns and rifles had congregated in the city's biggest park. Then as they drove along the railway embankment to the Governor's House and when he was further told by the Governor that the wily Pathans had gathered at the Cunningham Park which was just across the railway embankment with the purpose of presenting the Viceroy with a long list of their complaints and grievances, the Viceroy immediately halted the vehicle and got out of the car. After dismissing the military and police escort that was accompanying the long cavalcade, he firmly held on to his wife's hand, and with the Governor following behind, they all started climbing the embankment.Everybody else was shocked as the Viceroy with his long strides and with his wife by his side quickly got on to top of the embankment. Luckily and coincidently both of them were dressed in their light summer olive green army uniforms. On being recognized, the crafty Pathans with antagonism written all over their unkempt faces and in angry tones kept shouting in a continuous loud crescendo "Pakistan Zindabad, Pakistan Zindabad" (Long Live Pakistan. Long live Pakistan). Some of them were also seen waving their guns and rifles in desperation, while a few others were even firing into the air. It was indeed a very tense and volatile situation because one wrong move by some lunatic Pathan could have lead to the Viceroy, the Vicerene and the Governor being killed like sitting ducks. On seeing the desperate mad mood of the fuming Pathans, the Viceroy confidently whispered something into his wife's ears and a second or two later the two of them with a big smile on their faces started waving back at the crowd. With that friendly gesture there was a sudden transformation in the mood of the angry bearded Pathans. Now the slogan shouting and the hooting progressively subsided, and when the Viceroy with the Vicerene and with their big smiling faces came down the embankment to greet the tribesmen, only the shouts of "Mountbatten Zindabad. Mountbatten Zindabad' (Long Live Mountbatten) could be heard. Then as they walked hand in hand through the crowd and some of them affectionately patted the Viceroy on his back, while a few others tried to shake his hand, the defiant mood of the Pathans miraculously had been transformed to one of friendship and goodwill. Maybe it was providence that had come to their rescue or may be it was the olive green colour of their uniform that had saved the day for them. For the green colour was the sacred colour of Islam and of the Holy Prophet.

Whatever it was, but those few minutes while they stood on top of the embankment it was all touch and go thought Colonel Attiqur Rehman as he in his navy blue blazer over his light blue shirt, grey flannels and a silk scarf around his neck walked up smartly towards the dais to be formally introduced by the Governor to the Viceroy and his wife.

'Your Excellency may you bring peace, happiness, joy and prosperity to India in general and to our land of the Pathans in particular,' said Colonel Attiqur as he smartly saluted the Viceroy. And when it came to shaking hands with the Vicerene, the old suave and witty medico colonel very gallantly and chivalrously said.

'Your Excellency I was only 15 years old, when one day by chance I met Lord Curzon and his beautiful wife Lady Curzon. They too were on an official visit to our land. And though they as a couple were also very handsome and charming, but today I think both of you with your humble and friendly approach have beaten them to it.'

'Well that was indeed very kind of you to say so Colonel and I only hope that the ghost and spirit of the Curzon's are not anywhere around to hear that compliment. Because whereas Lord Curzon as the Viceroy divided only Bengal, I have been given this hopeless task of dividing the whole of India, and which is indeed very sad,' said the Viceroy in a somewhat serious tone.

Soon as the visit to Peshawar was over and when the Viceroy was told that there had been widespread looting and killing of Hindus in the small village of Kahuta in the Rawalpindi District of the Punjab, the Viceroy immediately decided to visit the place.The village of Kahuta which till a week ago with its mixed population of 3000 odd Hindus, Sikhs and Muslims was a beehive of activity was now a devastated one with the Hindus and Sikhs being the prime targets. On the previous night and during the hours of darkness while the inhabitants of the village slept peacefully, a horde of Muslim marauders with buckets of gasoline had set fire to the houses of the Hindus and the Sikhs. And as soon as they came out of the raging fire to escape into the open fields, they were caught and mercilessly slaughtered in cold blood. Some were even burnt alive like flaming torches.

When the Viceroy with his wife arrived on the scene, they were simply horrified. The dead and badly charred bodies of men, women and children from the Hindu and Sikh families were lying on the only narrow street of the village. Their bodies were still in the process of being lifted by a team of Red Cross volunteers for final disposal. As the dead stinking bodies lay on the ground with no one to stand guard over them, the vultures in packs dived periodically to feast on them. While all the houses of the Muslims were left untouched, the houses of the Hindus and the Sikhs had been reduced to ashes.

'This I am afraid is only the beginning of the end your Excellency and we shouldn't be surprised if things get worse in the days to come,' said Evan Jenkins the Governor to the Viceroy, while the Vicerene expressed her genuine sympathy and offered her heartfelt condolences to those few who had managed to escape from the premeditated and horrible carnage.

For the Viceroy and the Vicerene it was the first ever such visit to a riot affected area of India. That evening as they drove back to Rawalpindi, the Viceroy had come to one single very important conclusion. Over a drink with Evan Jenkins, the Governor of Punjab he said.

'Well Governor I am afraid if we the British have to wait as long as June 1948 to give India her freedom then it may well be a bit too late. Because such ghastly incidents of massacre, killings and looting may lead to more such occurrences in the days to come, and that may escalate into a grizzly civil war which will be damn difficult to control.'

'I think you have hit the nail right on the head your Excellency,' said the Governor as the liveried waiter wheeled in the drinks trolley. That very night the Viceroy had firmly made up his mind that the sooner the country was divided and its people the Hindus, Sikhs and Muslims were given their freedom, the less would be the loss of innocent lives and property. He therefore decided to inform His Majesty's Government and seek the consensus of the political leaders back home to advance the date of transfer and give the Indian people their much-desired freedom as soon as possible and one that would be based on the two-nation theory.

As was the custom during summer, the Raj by mid April, 1947 had moved to Simla and in early May, MB had drafted and dispatched for the final approval of his majesty's government his initial partition plan. The plan had a clause that would allow any Indian province to become independent if a majority of both its communities, Hindus and Muslims desired so. Keeping the province of Bengal in mind which was not only very large but also had a mixed population of nearly 65 million people and who spoke the same language, MB had decided that the large subcontinent should not be divided into two but into three independent nations with Bengal being the third and with its capital at Calcutta. The idea had been earlier sounded to him by non other than the fun loving Don Juan of Bengal, Mr Suhrawardy, the same man who as the ex Chief Minister of the Province not even a year ago had unleashed the horrors of the Direct Action Day on the city.

Having sent feelers earlier to the Hindu Congress leaders of Bengal and to Mr Jinnah, the Viceroy was now confident that the plan maybe acceptable to them. But till then somehow through oversight or omission he had not exposed the feasibility of such a three-nation plan to the two top congress leaders, Nehru and Patel. With his guilty conscience pricking him and conscious of the fact that he would look a bloody idiot if the plan was unacceptable to the Congress later, MB much to the discomfort and advice of his staff decided to show the plan unofficially to Mr Nehru who was his guest at Simla. All that MB desired was to find out what reaction the plan was likely to have on the Congress.

That evening nursing a glass of port wine as Nehru in the confines of his bedroom in Simla went through the text page by page, he was simply horrified. On the very next morning in his confidential reply to the Viceroy, Mr Nehru candidly told the Viceroy that the plan was one of fragmenting India as some of the large Princely States would only be too happy and it would only lead to more bitter conflict and greater disorder.

Realizing that the plan needed immediate post mortem, rethinking and redrafting, MB turned to his most trusted Indian civil servant, the hard working, trustworthy and intelligent Mr VP Menon. The man from South India who had started life as a coal miner and a construction worker had now diligently worked his way up from that of a junior clerk in 1929 to the highest-ranking Indian bureaucrat in the Viceregal establishment. The man who had neither been to Oxford or to Cambridge and who was not from the heaven born ICS either was a very hardworking bureaucrat. Sitting in his office the man single handedly using the two fingers on the Remington typewriter and before it was time for the others to have their first sundowner had redrafted the plan that would soon change the geography of the subcontinent and the map of British India forever.

Meanwhile unaware to the Viceroy, Sir Conrad Corfield the son of a missionary and the Viceroy's Political Secretary had arrived in London to fervently plead the case of the Princely rulers of India. Having worked with them for very long, Corfield wanted to give all of them a better deal. Giving the argument to the Earl of Listowel, the Secretary of State for India, that the Princes had surrendered their powers only to the British Crown and to no one else, and therefore it would only be correct and proper to give them back those powers so that they could decide for themselves which country they would be willing to join, or remain independent if they so desired. Sir Conrad was therefore confident that he would have his way and accordingly help out the Princely states. However Corfield's impassioned plea luckily did not get the desired impetus from the powers that be, or else India would have been a fractured and Balkanized in a manner that would have spelt complete disaster for the whole of the subcontinent.

In the month of May 1947, the Viceroy returned to London to project his case for the early partitioning of the country. However, to do this he had to first take into full confidence the leader of the opposition, the one and only Sir Winston Churchill. The Viceroy knew that if the Indian Independence Bill had to be expeditiously tabled and passed by the British Parliament then the go ahead signal was very much required from Mr. Churchill, the very man who once called the Mahatma the naked Indian fakir and he knew that wouldn't be easy. One fine morning and having taken a prior appointment, the Viceroy of India smartly dressed in a three piece pin striped light coloured suit arrived at the appointed time at Mr Churchill's residence at Chartwell. The round faced gentleman and former Prime Minister of the country who had saved England and her Empire during the war was now the leader of the opposition Conservative Party in parliament, He had only surfaced an hour or so earlier and was still in his dressing gown with his head propped up in bed reading the morning papers, when the Viceroy was ushered into his bedroom. With his half moon spectacles low down on his nose and a fat cigar in his mouth, Mr Churchill was busy reading the Daily Telegraph and he did not even look up as the Viceroy wished him a very good morning.

'Well Dickie I do not know how good the morning is going to be for you but nevertheless just shoot whatever you have to say,' said Mr Churchill while ordering a cup of tea for his guest. As the Viceroy with full statistics started narrating the horrible macabre facts of the riots, looting and killings that was slowly engulfing the Indian subcontinent, Mr Churchill with whiffs of smoke emanating from his cigar patiently listened to the narrator. He did not even stir, but occasionally kept staring at the ceiling. He was now feeling perturbed and seemed very concerned about the loss of innocent lives and the destruction of property of the very people who had contributed and sacrificed so much for the well being of the once mighty British Empire. After the Viceroy had concluded with whatever he had to say, Mr. Churchill smoothed his wispy ruffled hair of whatever that was left on his bald head, took another long drag from his cigar and asked for a second cup of his favourite Darjeeling tea both for his guest and for himself. With the first sip as he took another long drag from his cigar, he looked at MB with compassion. Then as the smoke started drifting towards the ceiling, Mr Churchill looked straight into the eyes of the Viceroy and with all seriousness and sadness said.

'Well Dickie so you want me to destroy over two hundred years of precious British History of the Jewel in Our Crown. But then if what you have just stated is really true then India can have her damned independence sooner than she expected.'Having said that sentence, Mr Churchill flicked the ash from his cigar into the big crystal ashtray, got out of his bed and shook hands with the last Viceroy of the British Raj in India. The man who had kept religously sending two pounds sterling to his Indian bearer even after his return from that country as a young British Army officer some four decades ago, and who during those dark days of the war in 1941 had said to his own people "Never give in, never, never, never." on this very important and sensitive issue had finally given in.

For Dickie it was a moment of triumph, joy and of victory. He was now confident that the first big hurdle in the race for India's freedom had been successfully crossed, but there was yet another big hurdle awaiting him when he returned to Delhi. And that was when the Mahatma called on him and reiterated.

'But Your Excellency come what may there must be no partitioning of the country. For if that happenes then it would only make a complete mockery of me and my principles and all that I stood for, when on my return from South Africa in January 1915, I took up the challenge and the struggle to give India her freedom. If we are going to be free then India must remain undivided, secular and democratic,' added the Mahatma.

Realizing that there was no point in arguing with the apostle of peace, the Viceroy simply said that he would strive all out and try his level best to keep the country in one piece. That evening at his prayer meeting a belligerent Mahatma told the gathering.

'Let the whole country be in flames but we will not allow the country to be divided.'

On the morning of 2nd June, 1947 and soon after his return from London, the Viceroy while going through the agenda points for the historic meeting that was scheduled for the next day asked his staff to arrange for a large round mahogany table so that the protocol difficulties in the seating plan could be avoided and eliminated. One of the British staff officer who was in charge of the seating however did not find it funny as he kept looking for a decent table and finally having found one worked out the seating plan. Next day, when all the participants arrived, the Viceroy sat in the centre with all the Congress and the only Sikh leader to his right and the Muslim League leaders to his left. After Mr Jinnah who arrived late took his seat to the immediate left of the Viceroy, MB began the meeting with the words.

'Gentlemen I must thank all of you for accepting the invitation for this conference at such short notice, and today we have all gathered here for no less a reason than to settle the future of India.'Having completed that sentence which took all the delegates completely by surprise, the Viceroy first surveyed all the faces and then looked appealingly at Mr Jinnah who looking dapper as usual in his well cut Saville Row suit took out a Craven A cigarette from his sleek pure silver cigarette case and lit it, while all the others with the blank new note books in front of them and pencils in their hands waited for the Viceroy to continue.

'Well Gentlemen what I have just stated is not my own firm view, but it is also the view of His Majesty's Government.' The tone and manner in which he said those words caught everyone completely off guard, but the Viceroy meant each and every word of what he had just uttered as he looked for vibes and reactions from al the participants.Pandit Nehru then broke the silence by saying. 'Your Excellency I am sure on that issue of the future of India all of us totally agree with you.' And when that remark brought a smile on the faces of everybody, the Viceroy turning his face towards Mr Jinnah looked expectantly at him and directed his next question to the undisputed leader of the Muslim League.

'Mr Jinnah it is now my solemn duty to ask if you and your party will accept the Cabinet missions plan for a United India.' All eyes were now focused on the man who would soon create history. Mr Jinnah then took one more puff and as the smoke drifted across the table said.

'Your Excellency the Cabinet Mission Plan is totally unacceptable not only to me but also to the Muslim League of which I am their undisputed leader.'

Without waiting for Mr Jinnah to elaborate and give reasons for his stand, the Viceroy butted in to say.'Alright in that case Independence it shall be, but with the partitioning of the country.'Now there was stunned silence as General Ismay popularly known as Pug directed his staff to hand over all the files with the agenda points for the next day's crucial conference to all the participants. Once the files were handed over, the Viceroy very firmly and candidly said.

'Gentlemen I would like and expect all of you to thoroughly go over all the agenda points very carefully and by midnight tonight I would like to have the firm views from both the parties and that to in writing to all the clauses that have been clearly spelt out and placed inside the file that is in front of you now.'And having said that last sentence, the Viceroy very confidently left the conference room.

As Mr Jinnah, Pandit Nehru, Liaquat Ali Khan, Vallabhai Patel and others browsed through the points, the heading at para 20 read. 'Immediate Transfer of Power to India.

Soon after the conference was over and on that very hot and humid day when the Viceroy called on the Mahatma to give him the terrible news, there were only tears and sadness in the man's face. The day happened to be a Monday, the day of the great man's total silence and as he patiently listened to the Viceroy and took notes with a pencil stub in his hand and on a bunch of old envelopes that were stapled together to serve as a writing pad, the great Mahatma knew that he had lost the battle to keep India united. That evening the soon to be father of the nation felt that he had been totally betrayed.

It was well before midnight that the Congress and the Sikhs having accepted the partition plan conveyed the same to the Viceroy, but there was no news from Mr Jinnah and his Muslim League.

'I think we should ask Mr Jinnah to come and have a drink with us,' suggested Pug and the suggestion was immediately accepted. It was now nearing midnight, when Mr Jinnah arrived at the Viceroy's Palace and very apologetically stated that he needed some more time to give his reply.

'But Mr Jinnah time is running out and the Congress and the Sikhs have already accepted the partition plan and now if we do not have a positive answer from you, the historic conference scheduled for tomorrow will become a complete non starter. Therefore I need the answer tonight and right now,' said the Viceroy as Mr Jinnah with a frown on his face took one large sip of the Black Label whisky that had been offered to him. Though he felt that he had been badly stumped by the Viceroy's ultimatum, Mr Jinnah still pleaded for some more time and added.

'But Your Excellency I regret that I cannot as an individual make such a major commitment without consulting the other members of my party and to do that I need at least another seventy two hours minimum."

Now there was anger in the eyes of the Viceroy as he confronted the ailing Mr Jinnah and in a very stern and commanding voice said.

'Well in that case Mr Jinnah you must realize that having struggled and worked for years together you will now be ruining your very own dreams. I might as well make it clear to you that the Congress are now insisting that the adoption of the partition plan as envisaged must be accepted by all the parties simultaneously, and if you do not accept it now, then the Congress and the Sikh leaders will suspect you and the Muslim League with some sinister motive, and they will also withdraw their own acceptance. This will in other words mean wrecking the whole damn plan which my loyal and dedicated staff and I have so meticulously drafted by burning the midnight oil for nights together. Therefore, I regret to say that I am sorry and I just cannot possibly grant you any more time,' added the Viceroy in an even more angry tone.

There was now a dazed look in Mr Jinnah's face. The Viceroy and his team now knew that the great Muslim League leader was now in a fix, but in order to diplomatically get over the problem the Viceroy suggested a clever way out for him to get out of it.

'Well Mr Jinnah I think there is one way to get over the impasse and that is by you giving a simple nod of your head at tomorrow morning's conference.when I will open the proceedings by stating to all the participants that last night having discussed the plan with Mr Jinnah, he too has given me his assuarance to it. And having said that, I will look at you and all you have to do is to give me that precious nod of yours and without you uttering a single word. Now is that understood? But if you fail to give me that nod then I am afraid that it will be a very sad and tragic day for you, because in that case you will lose your precious Pakistan and as far as I am concerned you can then go to hell.' The tone of the Viceroy's last sentence and the body language that he used probably left Mr Jinnah with no other alternative.

Next morning as soon as the historic conference was in session, the Viceroy opened the proceedings by stating.

'Gentlemen last night Mr Jinnah and I had a nice long informative discussion and in the course of which he gave me an assurance on behalf of the Muslim League vis a vis the partition plan and which satisfy me and which I have accepted.' Having said that well rehearsed sentence, the Viceroy looked expectantly at Mr Jinnah for his precious nod. But when for a few seconds there was no response from the man, for the Viceroy and for Pug Ismay and his staff it seemed that all their hard work would now simply crumble like a pack of cards. General Ismay, a veteran of the Indian Army and who was now the Viceroy's handpicked Chief of Staff was in utter disbelief as he kept looking at the Muslim League leader. Then at last when Mr Jinnah very reluctantly and curtly gave that nod of his, there was a big sigh of relief as a silent but jubilant Pug Ismay directed his staff to bring in the big bunch of the buff coloured folders.

As soon as the big heap of folders with the thirty neatly typed pages inside each one of them was placed in front of the Viceroy, a smiling MB took the top most one and thumped it hard on the table. The noise no doubt startled some of the participants, but it also soon brought a smile on the faces of all of them, when the Viceroy suggested that each and every point must be thoroughly, scrupulously and carefully considered one by one. The heading on top of the folder read. 'The Administrative Consequences of Partition.'

Once all the points were discussed and the conference came to a close, the Viceroy got up and concluded by saying.

'Gentlemen this very evening an official announcement on the acceptance of the partition plan to the people of India over the All India Radio will be made first by me and thereafter by Mr Nehru and Mr Jinnah, so that the message is passed on to the millions of Indians not only all in India, but also all around the whole world.'

On that evening of the 3rd of June, 1947 while the Viceroy with poise and dignity spoke to the millions of Indians on the impending liquidation of the mighty British Empire in India, at the residence of Major Gul Rehman in the Princes Park Officers hostel near the India Gate at Delhi, the two old bosom friends were getting ready to host a combined party for all their dear friends and colleagues.

After the demobilization of a large number of the wartime emergency commissioned officers, a lot vacancies had been created. And since both Gul Rehman and Ismail were holding permanent commissions they had been cleared for their next promotion to the rank of acting Lieutenant Colonel and both of them therefore had decided to celebrate it in real style. It was in fact a double celebration since Gul Rehman had been earmarked to go as an instructor to the prestigious Defense Services Staff College at Quetta, while Ismail was tipped to go as a General Staff Officer Grade One in the Military Intelligence Directorate of the Army Headquarters at New Delhi. In order to congratulate and felicitate the two of them personally, both Colonel Attiqur Rehman and Colonel Reginald Edwards had landed up from Peshawar and Kasauli respectively.

As the guests arrived for the party, the only topic under discussion that evening was the pros and cons of a divided India.

'First of all I personally do not agree at all to this idea of partition, and even if it does take place it will be a curse on both the young nations,' said Colonel Reggie very forthrightly.

'Well even if one accepts that the country can be divided into a Hindu and Muslim State on communal basis, but how does one divide the Indian Army, which after the great uprising of 1857 have lived, fought and have died together as brothers in arms while holding the flag of the regiment and the unit high, and for whom the only religion is their damn uniform,' added Colonel Attiqur Rehman somewhat gruffly. Attiqur was not at all pleased with the partition plan that the Viceroy had announced, and which was seconded both by Mr Nehru and Mr Jinnah. A British officer who had heard Mr Jinnah's speech that was delivered by him in English could not also help but remark.

'But tell me was Mr Jinnah going on a chakor or rabbit shoot when he concluded his address by saying 'Pakistan in the Bag.' Hearing that, the alert an attentive seven year old Aslam Rehman, the eldest son of Gul Rehman burst out laughing. He was helping his favourite Uncle Ismail Sikandar Khan and was behind the makeshift improvised bar. The bar counter in the verandah was made by putting a couple of old big empty steel trunks that had been piled one on top of the other and was covered with a big white bed sheet.

'But Uncle Jack you heard it all wrong. What the Quaid-e-Azam said was not Pakistan in the Bag, but Pakistan Paindabad,' which means long live Pakistan said the young boy with a big smile on his chubby face as he handed over a bottle of chilled soda and the bottle opener to the Englishman

'I must say that was rather smart of you Aslam,' said Ismail as he poured Reggie another small peg of scotch.

That evening in his address to the people of India, the Viceroy had stated categorically that it was not the intention of His Majesty's Government to interrupt the working of the existing constituent assembly and he also clarified that any constitution likely to be framed by this assembly could not apply to those parts of the country which were unwilling to accept it. The plan also spelt out that the Provinces of Punjab and Bengal may be partitioned provided the respective members of both Hindus and Muslims in the respective legislative assemblies agree to it. In that case a boundary commission would be set up to demarcate the boundaries. As regards Sind was concerned, it would be left to its legislative assembly to take its own decision, but in the North West Frontier Province a referendum would be held to ascertain the wishes of its people whether they would like to join Pakistan or India. Likewise the people of the Sylet District in East Bengal could also decide through a referendum whether they would like to join Pakistan or remain as part of Assam in India. Concluding his address with the message that power would now directly be transferred by the British to the successive sovereign states, the Viceroy added that he had full faith in the future of the subcontinent and of India though it was now going to be divided.

After Pandit Nehru in his address solemnly announced that the Congress had accepted the plan for Independence as envisaged by the Viceroy, Mr Jinnah in his address exhorted all the Muslims of India to gracefully accept the momentous decision and appealed to all to ensure that the transfer of power is affected in a peaceful and orderly manner. He concluded by expressing his appreciation of the sufferings and sacrifices made by all the Muslims of India for this great cause.

The members of the Muslim League were now jubilant. They were now definite that they would get their own homeland, though they knew it would only be a truncated and a moth eaten one that would be located in the two distant far corners of the subcontinent and would be separated by the huge land mass of India. But that it seemed did not matter at least not for the time being. However, not all Muslims of India were happy with the partitioning of the country. Some of them for generations together had settled in East Punjab and West Bengal and they would now with one stroke of the pen lose everything that they possessed and cherished. For the Hindus and Sikhs of West Punjab, Sind, the North West Frontier, Baluchistan and East Bengal they also now knew that their fate too would be the same. The

Congress had accepted the plan because there was no other option and the Sikh leaders too gave their nod though somewhat bitterly and grudgingly.

After his address and on his return to the Viceroy's House, when MB was told that the Mahatma was intending to speak out against the partition plan at his daily evening prayer meeting, he was now very worried. Fearing that this could pose as a major hurdle, he immediately invited the Great Soul for an urgent meeting with him at his residence. Half an hour or so later, when a dejected, crestfallen and a sad Mahatma in his half dhoti and with the stick in his hand was ushered into the Viceroy's private study, a very apologetic and remorseful Viceroy having greeted his guest said.

'Mr Gandhi let me tell you that I never wanted to do it, but I had no choice. It was the will of the people and their leaders and it was you who said when I arrived in India that let the people decide and I have only done that.'

After checking the time on his Ingersoll watch, so as not to get late for the prayer meeting, a heartbroken, forlorn, despondent and ageing Mohandas Karamchand Gandhi with sadness written all over his wrinkled face said.

'Yes and time is running out for all of us and we must trust the people. In any case it is now too late for me to intervene for if I do I will only make things worse and now I must be back for the prayer meeting because people must be waiting for me. But I will tell them that you are not to blame for the partition of the country, because it is we ourselves who have asked for it. For I know either way many in this country will be angry with me for this, but at this late stage I guess there is no other option.'

On the morning of the very next day 4th of June, when the Viceroy while holding. an impromptu press conference was asked by one of the more enthusiastic American reporters about the likely date for the transfer of power, and he very confidently said 'I think 15th of August should be fine,'there was look of bewilderment on everyones face.That statement by him not only took the press by complete surprise, but also his entire senior staff members, because they too till that moment had no clue of the date that the Viceroy had in his mind and the Viceroy had not even discussed the date with them.

For MB the date of 15th of August had some special historical significance too, for it was on that very date two years ago that the Japanese had unconditionally surrendered and the Second World War had finally ended with victory to the Allies. Moreover, he was personally of the view that the earlier the partition, the lesser would be the loss of innocent lives and property.

No sooner the date of partition was made public, political leaders from the Congress consulted the astrologers to ascertain whether it was an auspicious day or not for India to unfurl her tricolour. The 15th of August happened to be a Friday and India on that date according to the Pundits would not only lie under the Zodiacal sign of Makara, (Capricorn) which was not at all propitious, but would also be on that particular day under the strong influence of Saturn.

'But Your Excellency, we cannot have our freedom cursed by the stars'said the Congress political bigwigs while requesting the Viceroy to prepone it to the midnight of the 14th and the 15th. o August and to which the Viceroy readily agreed. However, now with only 73 days left to carve up the two nations, the countdown to the disaster, tragedy and catastrophe had already begun.

During those fateful days that would finally decide the future of the subcontinent, the tensions within the country too progressively increased, not only between the Hindus, Sikhs and Muslims but also within the Muslims and the Hindus of India itself. On 9th of June,1947 a fanatical Muslim Group called 'Khaksars' in the guise of gardeners and with shovels and spades in their hands were lurking behind the hedges and bushes of New Delhi's elite Imperial Hotel near Connaught Place. They were waiting to strike at Jinnah.

The dissident Khaksars who called themselves as servants of the dust was a movement that was founded by Mr Inayatullah Mashriki, a highly educated man who was born on 25th August 1888 and who had completed his eduation from Cambridge University. He founded the Khaksar movement in 1930 to bridge the ever-expanding gap between the 'Haves' and the 'Have Nots' among the Muslims of not only India but also of the world. The Khaksars were dissatisified with Mr Jinnah's acceptance of the partion plan and for agreeing to a truncated Pakistan. They thought that a united India would have been a better option and they now felt that Jinnah and the Muslim League had sold them out. Therefore, they were now waiting to seek revenge against him and his Muslim League members.

On that day, the magnificent ornate splendour of the hotel's ballroom on the first floor had been chosen as the venue for the all India conclave of the Muslim League leaders. It was scheduled to be held that afternoon and over which the Quaid-e-Azam was expected to preside. Unaware of what was in store for the hotel, Reggie and Attiqur after shopping for a few give away small gifts at the nearby Connaught Circus market place had dropped in at the hotel for a cup of tea with a piece of the black forest cake and almond biscuits. These were some of the bakery items for which the hotel was known and it was also a popular sojourn for those who liked their evening tea in the comfort of the coffee shop. That day besides the two of them, there were also a few elderly English couples and some foreign tourists including a few foreign correspondents who were also enjoying their afternoon tea, when all of a sudden all pandemonium broke loose.

As soon as the big American Sedan carrying Jinnah stopped at the foyer of the Hotel, the leader of the Khaksar group gave the signal for the attack. But it seems his time and space calculation went a little awry, because by the time his spade and shovel wielding attackers could reach the foyer of the hotel, Mr Jinnah was safely inside and half way up the staircase that led to the ballroom.Meanwhile volunteers from the Muslim League National Guard with bamboo staves in their hands and who were escorting Mr Jinnah immediately rushed out to take on their adversaries. Frustrated with their abortive attempt, the group now went on a rampage destroying anything and everything that came in its way, as they smashed the big glasswindows, the cutlery, crockery and even a few chandeliers. Except for some minor injuries to an odd customer who unfortunately had arrived around that very time at the Hotel, all the rest of them who were inside including Reggie and Attiqur were whisked away by the alert staff to safer areas.Seeing the commotion, the security officer of the hotel had immediately alerted the nearest police station and the police luckily arrived in the nick of time. They not only lathi charged the group, but also used tear gas to disburse the intruders. A few minutes later while a group of Khaksars were bundled into the Black Maria and were taken away by the police, most of the others however had managed to run away. The incident that afternoon had visibly shaken the man who was now destined to rule Pakistan.

A few days later, and soon after the incident at the Hotel Imperial, the Great Mahatma seated on a make shift rostrum in the middle of a dusty square inside the sweepers colony in Delhi addressed a large group of Hindus, Sikhs, Muslims and others from the low caste communities. He was explaining to them that the colour, caste, creed and religion had no meaning in life and if only people embraced one another as brothers and sisters and respected each other's customs and religious beliefs, only then would this country prosper and be worth living in. Having said that, the Mahatma surveyed the crowd and on noticing that the attendance by the Muslims that evening for the daily prayer meeting had dwindled considerably, he in order to placate them and to raise their morale therefore decided to begin the meeting with a quotation from the Holy Koran.

But as soon as he began, he was greeted with an angry and loud 'No No' by the Hindus and the Sikhs who told the Mahatma that the Koran no longer had a place for them. When the small crowd of Muslims sensing trouble started walking away, a hapless, depressed and dejected Mahatma Gandhi was in a quandary. He got up from the rostrum and with tears swelling in his eyes and with young Manu for support he slowly walked back to his hut in the sweeper's colony. That evening sitting in the darkness of his hut, a lonely Mr Gandhi felt totally isolated and powerless.

On the 15th of June, when the All India Congress Party passed the resolution accepting the partition plan and expressed the hope that India would one day again be united, the Mahatma's dream to keep India united had been shattered once and for all.A few days before he announced the partition plan, the Viceroy sensing correctly that the strategically located Princely State of Jammu and Kashmir with its large Muslim population under a Hindu ruler could prove a major obstacle at a later date, he therefore deputed his number two man, General Pug Ismay to visit the State and give him a correct feedback on his return. The Viceroy had already received some feelers about the Maharaja's intentions of retaining his throne, and with Sheikh Abdullah still behind bars, he had correctly appreciated that there could be trouble in the near future. He therefore briefed his close confidante Pug Ismay to call on the Maharajah and get a first hand account of the situation there. Pug was also asked to try his best to get the Maharajah to make up his mind to accede to whichever country he and his people desired. On the 29th and 30th of May 1947, Pug Ismay visited the valley but he came back empty handed. Inspite of trying his best he could not get a firm commitment from the Maharajah about his future plans.

Now the Viceroy therefore decided to try his luck with Maharaja Hari Singh and he planned to visit the valley with his wife from the 18th to the 23rd of June. In order to get some more inputs about the history of the present dynasty and the political climate prevalent in the state, he asked Pandit Nehru to send him a short brief about the land and its people. A day before the Viceroy was to depart for the valley, Pandit Nehru had sent him the required brief and in the last paragraph he wrote. 'If any attempt is made to push Kashmir into the Pakistan Constituent Assembly, then there is likely to be much trouble because the National Conference is not in favour of it and the Maharajah's position would also become difficult. The normal and obvious course would be for Kashmir to joln the Constituent Assembly of India. This will satisfy both the popular demand and the Maharaja's wishes. It is absurd to think that Pakistan would create trouble if that happens.'Maybe when he wrote that last sentence, Pandit Nehru himself being a Kashmiri never realized the mindset of Mr Jinnah and the leaders of the Muslim League on what would soon become the biggest bone of contention between the two sides.

On the 18th of June 1947, the Viceroy accompanied by his wife began their short sojourn in the beautiful valley as the honoured guests of the Maharajah whose magnanimity in looking after such important dignitaries knew no bounds. From duck shooting to angling, from croquet to riding and golf there was some activity or the other that was laid out for them in style everyday. In addition there was the usual sightseeing to the famous Moghul gardens of Shalimar and Nishat, boating on the Dal Lake and the Jhelum followed by picnic lunches and banquets.

But no matter how diplomatically the Viceroy tried to get the Maharajah to firmly commit himself either to join India or Pakistan, the clever and shrewd Maharajah kept evading the issue on some pretext or the other. Sometimes he gave the excuse that he needed more time for consultations with his ministers and staff, and on occasions when he felt that he was being cornered, he would conveniently also feign illness, and the most common of which was his stomach ache. Little did the Viceroy realize then that very soon the same Maharajah would not only be a pain in the neck for himself but also a big headache for the two emerging nations and the world.

However, during the last formal banquet for the Viceroy and Vicerene that was hosted by the Maharajah in his opulent palace, a hilarious and funny incident marked the grand finale to the visit. An hour or so before the state banquet was to begin, Major Daler Singh Bajwa who had been appointed as the officer on special duty for the banquet checked all the arrangements, which also included the seating plan as per protocol, the lay out of the tables and the trophies, the menu card and the music score that was to be played by the State's Military Brass band.

On fully satisfied that everything was perfectly in order, he together with one of the Maharajah's many ADC's waited to receive the Maharajah and his honoured guests. A few minutes later after all the other invitees were ushered in and as they stood behind their respective chairs, the fanfare by the buglers was sounded. This heralded the arrival of the VVIP's. A stickler for military protocol, the formal banquets at the Maharajah's palace were like the regimental guest nights with the band playing with every course that was served in royal style. Then all of a sudden, when everyone was busy enjoying the delicious chicken curry cooked in traditional Kashmiri style with the fragrant Basmati rice pulao that had dry fruits thrown in for good measure, the State Military band suddenly and from out of the blues started playing 'God save the King.' Leaving their half finished meal on the table, everyone immediately got up and stood to attention. A stunned Maharajah first looked at his ADC and then at Major Daler Singh Bajwa the Officer on Special duty. Both of them together with a few other senior officers from the Mahraja's personal staff were seated on the adjacent table in the company of the young and handsome 16-year-old Yuvraj Karan Singh, the only issue of the Maharajah and the heir to the Kashmir throne. But like the Maharaja, they too had no idea as to how such a stupid blunder had occurred. And it only dawned a little later that the culprit was none other than the Viceroy himself who was seated next to the Maharaja on the main table. The Viceroy with his long lanky legs while trying to make himself a little more comfortable on the big ornate dining chair had inadvertently pressed the bell button that was under the table with his left knee. Normally the Maharaja who was seated to his left would have done that drill by pressing the bell with right hand and that would have been the signal for the State Military Brass band to play the British national anthem. But unfortunately the bell had now gone off prematurely and the band simply did their duty. Initially the Maharaja was livid, but when he tried to explain to His Excellency that probably the bell that was under the table had gone off by mistake and that he was sorry for the terrible faux pas, it had both MB and his wife in splits of laughter and even young Karan Singh too was seen giggling away.

Next morning prior to his leaving for Delhi, the Viceroy once again tried to arrange for a one to one meeting with the Maharaja. He had also earlier conveyed to him Sardar Vallabhai Patel's message that incase the Maharaja decided to accede to Pakistan, then India would not consider it as an unfriendly act. But that morning also the Maharaja chickened out at the last minute feigning sickness. The indecisiveness of the Maharaja would not only later cost him his throne, but it would also lead to a never ending war between the two new nations who were yet to be born. The Princely State of Kashmir which was popularly known as a Paradise on Earth would now soon become the gateway to hell for the men in military uniform.

A week or so later after the formal decision to split the valiant Indian Army was given the go ahead signal, a large number of senior Muslim officers now started calling on Mr. Mohammed Ali Jinnah their Governor General designate at his number 10 Aurangzeb Road residence in New Delhi. However, the very idea of splitting the Indian Army did not appeal at all to the Commander-in-Chief, Field Marshall Auckinleck who in no uncertain terms asked the Viceroy to reconsider this decision. During his interview with the Viceroy on the subject Auk said rather candidly.

'Your Excellency by splitting the armed forces you will only ruin the brave and gallant Indian Army which in each and every battle against our enemies had been the corner stone of our success. You must realize that ever since the sepoy mutiny of 1857 we worked hard to structure most of the regiments on a mixed class basis and with each one of them having its own compliment of Hindus, Muslims and Sikhs. This was primarily done to balance one community with the other. The only exception was the Gurkha Regiments since they hailed from Nepal and only our own British Officers always commanded them. And now you suddenly want to split this brave army, which is going to be a very complicated affair. It will be like unscrambling a good omelette, because it won't be easy to separate the tomatoes and the onions fom the yellow and white of the egg and that to in the limited time at our disposal.'added Auk with a bit of sarcasm in his voice.

After the C-in-C had given his valid reasons, the Viceroy simply looked at him and summed up the issue by saying.

'But my dear Auk all that is required to be done is to simply give all the Muslim sub-units to Pakistan and be done with it once and for all.'But the Auk was not convinced at all and this time addressing the Viceroy by his popular name he said.

'But Dickie it is not all that simple as you think. You don't realize that by doing a thing like that we will only be creating shambles in the command and control set up of the units and sub units and in the entire armed forces of India as hundreds of disconnected units and sub units will make their way from one side to the other.'

Though there was a look of sympathy in the face of the Viceroy for his able and hardworking Commander-in-Chief, but he did not relent at all. With all firmness he simply said.

'But dear Chief on this score we have no choice at all. I too had pleaded with Mr Jinnah to leave the Indian Army intact at least for a minimum of one year under your Supreme Command since I personally considered that option to be a sure guarantor of peace in this country, but Mr Jinnah would have none of it. Therefore this is not my or your requirement, but those of the Indian and Pakistani leaders themselves and Mr Jinnah in particular, because he is adamant to have his own armed forces at the earliest and therefore we have to simply get on with the job and have it done as quickly as possible and that's it.'

On the 4th of July 1947, a date that coincided with America's day of Independence, the Indian Independence Bill was introduced in the British Parliament and a fortnight later on the 18th of July it was enacted as law. The Act was the swan song of the British Power as far as India was concerned and was acclaimed as the noblest and greatest law ever enacted by the British Parliament. The Act would now enable the two emerging nations to frame their own constitutions and provide for the exceeding difficult period of transition that they were soon going to be faced with. The Act would also ratify the establishment of the two Dominions from the 15th of August and give them their own legislative supremacy. The Act also declared that the British paramountcy over the Princely States would lapse on the 15th of August and they will be given the option to choose and join either of the two Dominions. From the 15th of August, 1947 therefore His Majesty's Government would be divested of all its powers and control over the affairs of India and Pakistan.

No sooner had the Punjab and Bengal legislative assemblies given their verdict to partition their respective Provinces, and the people of Sylet and those of the North West Frontier Province voted to be part of Pakistan, and the legislative assemblies of Baluchistan and Sind too threw in their lot with the Muslim League, once again all hell broke loose as the killings of the innocents, destruction of properties and the exodus of the refugees from one side to the other started assuming gigantic proportions. It was under these circumstances that Colonel Attiqur Rehman decided to make his last final visit to Calcutta in order to coax and convince his only son-in-law Nawaz Hussein to wind up his establishment in Calcutta for good and to return to the North West Frontier and settle with him at Peshawar, or at any other place of his choice in Pakistan.

While Colonel Attiqur was on his way to Calcutta, on the 8th of July arrived in Delhi the man who with a stroke of his pen would now decide which territory will be part of India and which territory should go to Pakistan. The same man would also decide the fate of millions of Hindus, Muslims and Sikhs who still did not know which side and which country they would finally belong to.

Sir Cyril Radcliff, a distinguished Barrister whose name had been suggested by Mr Jinnah himself had never been to India ever and here he was now in the midst of chaos sitting with census records and Survey of India maps trying to demarcate the International border between the two new emerging nations. One of the main reasons of assigning this thankless task to this brilliant barrister by his majesty's government was primarily his ignorance of the country so that he without any prejudice could do his duty to divide India freely and fairly.

On that very day, while Cyril Radcliff was trying to figure out as to how to divide the homelands of the 80 million people of Punjab and Bengal, the Hindu and Sikh shopkeepers at Delhi downed their shutters to show their dissent. And when the Sikhs and the Hindus with black arm bands were out in the streets protesting vehemently against the partition of the country, the fuze was lit for the holocaust to begin.

While Mr Radcliffe with his team of two eminent Hindu and two eminent Muslim Judges got busy to demarcate the future boundary of the two nations, Mahatma Gandhi who had expressed his desire in writing to the Viceroy to use his good offices with the Maharaja and permit him to visit Kashmir was thoroughly disappointed when the Viceroy forwarded to him a copy of his own letter of 12th July, which was in reply to the letter that the Maharaja had written to him on the same subject.According to the Maharaja it was a clear no and that was because the Majaraja felt that even a tiny spark in spite of the Mahatma's best intentions in the world may well set alight a conflagration which it would be impossible to control, and he therefore was not at all in favour of the Mahatma or any other political leader be it a Hindu or a Muslim visiting the valley now.

On the 18th of July 1947, while the Mountbattens were celebrating their silver wedding anniversary by hosting a banquet at the Viceroy's Palace on Raisina Hill, Colonel Attiqur Rehman with his son-in-law Nawaz Hussein, his daughter Shenaz and little Imran Hussein were getting ready to board the train at Calcutta for their long journey to Peshawar. It did take a lot of convincing by Colonel Attiqur Rehman to get his son-in-law to agree to his request to migrate to Pakistan, but it was with the option that incase it did not suit him, then he could with his family always come back to Calcutta, the city where he was born and which he so dearly loved. Ofourse it was on condition that peace prevailed and there was no repeitition of the August 1946 massacres. Attiqur even promised them a holiday in the vale of Kashmir during the coming Dusshera and Eid Festival that coincidently was scheduled to fall sometime at the end of the month of October that year.

'The holiday in Kashmir together with a new Studebaker car for your travels will beyyour wedding anniversary gift in advance from me and you could celebrate it as a second honeymoon too in Srinagar,' said Colonel Attiqur as he warmly hugged his son-in-law.

'This is sheer downright bribery and what about us,'said Ruksana as she helped her father-in-law to get into the big reserved first class compartment.

'Yes ofcourse you and Arif too will also get you dues too, but a little later after I have one more grandson in the family from your side,' said Colonel Attiqur as a blushing Ruksana got into the compartment to check that all the ten pieces of luggage were safely inside.

Arif Rehman Khan, the youngest son of Colonel Attiqur Rehman had opted for the Pakistan civil service and with reports of rioting and killings coming in from the Punjab and the North West Frontier everyday he had taken a fortnight's leave so that he could safely escort all of them right upto Peshawar. The only people to see them off at the Howrah railway station that evening was Ronen Sen and his wife Mona.

'Please Sir do keep in touch with us,' said Ronen Sen while presenting Colonel Attiqur Rehman with a bottle of Black Label Scotch whisky. Then putting his arms around Nawaz Hussein, Ronen presented him and his wife Shenaz a huge pure silver salver with the names of all the Ghosh and Sen family members past and present neatly engraved on it.

'Don't you all ever forget us, and we promise that we will also never forget you,' said Ronen as he warmly embraced Nawaz and touched Colonel Attiqur's feet. Cuddling and kissing the infant Imran Hussein, who was in her arms, Mona Ghosh with moistness in her pretty black eyes presented a tall silver glass for the child to have his milk in.The engraving on the glass read.'To our dearest darling Imran. May you grow up to be tall, handsome and kind, and may the Almighty grant you all your wishes.'

That evening as the train steamed out of the crowded Howrah railway station platform, everyone was in tears. They all prayed that the strong bond of love, brotherhood and friendship that had existed between the families for nearly seventy five years and more should always remain forever, but fate it seemed would decide otherwise.

On arrival at the Delhi Railway station, they were met by acting Lieutenant Colonel Ismail Sikandar Khan. He was now on the staff of the 4th Indian Division, the same Red Eagle outfit which was now earmarked for duty with additional troops for the safe conduct of the beleaguered refugee foot columns and also for those moving by road and by rail from one side to the other. On being told by Shenaz that they were planning to holiday in the valley during early autumn of that year, Ismail Sikandar Khan promptly offered them his own houseboat.

'Yes I guess hopefully by early October my houseboat 'The Cassino Royale' with all the required cutlery, crockery and the linen will be moored on the picturesque Nagin Lake and will be fully ready for occupation and use. It will also be equipped with a radio, a phonogram with a complete set of all Kundan Lal Saigal's hit songs that I know are also Nawaz's favourite. And as for you dear Shenaz there will a complete set of Sherlock Holmes and Agatha Cristie's who done it and other books of suspense that both you and I love.'

'That is indeed very thoughtful and kind of you Bhaijan, but we will only consider your generous offer provided you also keep us company for a few days if not more,' said a beaming Shenaz.

'That will be simply fantastic and if time permits all of us will visit Gilgit too and I will show you the hut where I was born,' said Ismail Sikandar Khan very proudly as he took the chubby little Imran Hussein in his arms and kissed him on both his chubby pink cheeks.

As the guard blew his whistle and the train was about to depart, Ismail quickly took out the big neatly covered presentation pack that had a red ribbon with a red rose nicely tied to it from his big leather office briefcase and gave it to Colonel Attiqur Rehman.

'Sir the two bottles of Channel No 5 inside is for the two lovely ladies, Shenaz and Ruksana, the two bottles of the French red wine is for Nawaz and Arif, while the bottle of the French Champagne with a box of Black Magic chocolates are for you and darling Imran respectively,' said Colonel Ismail as he kept running along the platform waving out to them.

'Inshallah we shall meet again soon for a lovely holiday in Srinagar,' shouted Nawaz Hussein as he stood at the door and extended his hand for the final time to thank Ismail.

That evening while on his way back to the officer's mess, acting Lieutenant Colonel and substantive Major Ismail Sikandar Khan was in a dilemma. For him it was a difficult question and for which an answer had to be given by him soon. Being a Muslim, he had to in a day or two take the most difficult decision of his life. He had to decide and specify in writing on a small mimeographed piece of paper that was handed over to him by the army authorities that afternoon whether he wished to serve in the Indian or in the Pakistan Army. As he walked along the Kingsway he stopped for a while to admire the India Gate. It was a historic monument that was built to commemorate and honour those who had so gallantly laid down their lives for the Empire during the First World War. On reading his father Naik Curzon Sikandar's name that was inscribed in golden letters under the list of the 2nd Punjabees, he got the answer immediately. The 2nd Punjabees was his regiment too and that is where he belonged. Therefore irrespective of which country the regiment was going to be allotted to, he would forever remain faithful to them.

Once the final decision was given to split the valiant Indian Army, GHQ (I), the General Headquarters India was designated Supreme Headquarters and they kept operating from the South Block. The AHQ (I), the Army Headquarters of the Indian Army were now shifted to the Red Fort, while the. AHQ (P), the Army Headquarters Pakistan Army was superimposed on the British Northern Command Headquarters at Rawalpindi. A few days later, when Colonel Ismail met Lt Col Enaith Habibullah a veteran of El Alamein and a product of Sandhurst and whose family hailed from Lucknow and whose father was the Vice Chancellor of the Lucknow University, he was surprised to learn that though his brothers, his sister and brother-in-law had decided to go to Pakistan, but he himself with his mother had decided to remain in India. In the case of Major Yakub Khan from the Viceroy's Bodyguard who hailed from the Princely State of Rampur in the United Provinces for him it would also be Pakistan, while his younger brother Younis Khan from the Garhwal Regiment opted to remain in India. Strange were the ways of deciding ones future thought Ismail whose roots were neither in India nor in Pakistan but at Gilgit, a far flung frontier post in the Princely State of Kashmir and which would soon become a battle ground for both the armed forces of the yet to be born new nations of the subcontinent.

It was on 22nd July, 1947, that the Red Eagles under the command of Major General TW Rees was given the go ahead signal to deploy its many formations, units and sub-units of the mixed troops of Hindus, Sikhs and Muslims on the already volatile and explosive Punjab border. They were to act as a peace keeping force and according to the directive they were to remain there till the verdict and the implementation of the Radcliff Awards were announced and implemented.

However, before Mr Radcliffe and his team of Judges could even determine where the boundary in the West should start from, the great migration of Hindus, Muslims and Sikhs from across the Indian Subcontinent had already begun. To add to the miseries, sufferings, and hardships of these poor people, the worst ever floods in the land of the five rivers for nearly half a century only added to their problems. Combined with that was the ever present threat of attack by hostile religious fanatic hordes and gangsters from both sides. It seemed that the migration of the Jews as given in the book of Exodus in the Old Testament was like a trickle as compared to what was happening in India and especially so in the Provinces of Punjab and Bengal as the Hindus, Muslims and the Sikhs went for each others throats. It was nothing but sheer vengeance killing and none were being spared, not even the women and children.

To expedite the splitting of the old Army Headquarter Records, young Major SK Sinha representing the Indian Army and Major Bashir Ahmed representing the Pakistan Army were sent to Simla where all the old files were kept. Immediately on reaching there the two of them got busy as only one week was given to them to complete the task. Both of them therefore decided to resort to the rough and ready method. They simply marked all the files dealing with the territorial area, which would form Pakistan as Pak and the rest as India. And the files that did not fit into either category were simply destroyed.

Meanwhile in Delhi, Mr Justice Din Mohammed and Mr Justice Mohammed Munir representing Pakistan and Mr Justice Mehr Chand Mahajan and Mr Justice Teja Singh representing India under the stewardship of Mr Cyril Radcliff pondered through the old census record and the Imperial gazetteer of India to determine the population mix of those border districts in Punjab and Bengal that would finally be part of the either Pakistan or.

A few weeks ago and after days of haggling and arguments, the two senior civil servants one representing India and the other representing Pakistan under the watchful eyes of Sardar Patel finally agreed that all moveable assets should be divided with 80 % going to India and 20% going to Pakistan. The day after Mr HM Patel and Mr Mohammed Ali shook hands over the deal, the numbers game for the division of assets also began.

'Alright out of the total of 12 typewriters, 9 to go to India and 3 to Pakistan, Next item 48 writing tables, 36 to India and 12 to Pakistan. Next item blotting pads total 24, 18 to India and 6 to Pakistan.' But when it came to even a minor item like those of the 53 pin cushions, out of which 13 were to go to Pakistan and 40 to India there was serious objections by some of the Muslim clerical staff in that department who wanted 14 should be allotted to them. In order to compensate them it was decided that out of the 69 ink pots, 18 should go to Pakistan and the remaining to India. Dividing the booze in the wine cellars would have been even more problematic had it not been decided in a friendly manner. It was unanimously agreed by both the sides that India could keep the lot that was already in their stocks in India provided Pakistan was compensated for their share with a credit note. When it came to the validity of the Indian currency notes and postage stamps it was mutually decided that those lying in the treasuries and post offices inside Pakistan would simply be rubber stamped with the word Pakistan on them. There was no other alternative to this arrangement because the press printing the two items fell to India's lot and India refused to share it with her future neighbour.

While the officials and clerks in the various government offices were busy dividing the moveable assets, inside the Viceroy's stable yard on Raisina Hill another haggling match was in progress with Lt Commander Peter Howes, the senior most ADC to the Viceroy acting as the match referee and arbitrator.After the mess silver and the mess property had been settled amicably, it was now the turn to divide the two viceregal carriages, one of silver and the other of gold. Both the contenders represented by Major Yakub Khan for Pakistan and Major Gobind Singh for India wanted that the gold carriage should go to them and soon they got into a dispute over it. Basing his argument that India's share was 80%, Major Govind Singh claimed rightfully that the gold carriage should go to India. But when Major Sahebzada Yakub contended that it would be criminal to break up such valuable assets on an 80:20 ratio, the match referee Peter Howes diplomatically stepped in and suggested that the matter should be settled amicably with the toss of the coin and to that both the parties immediately agreed.Taking a silver one rupee coin out from his wallet that had King George the Vth's bearded face shining from it; Lt Commander Howes tossed it up high in the air and asked Govind Singh to call.

'Heads' said Major Govind Singh very loudly and when the flipped coin returned to earth it was gold for India. When a delighted Major Govind Singh shouted with joy to his Hindu troops from the Viceroy's Bodyguard that the gold carriage was theirs, it was as if India had won an Olympic gold medal that day.

A dejected Major Yakub gracefully accepted the verdict and settled for the silver carriage for Pakistan's first Governor General to be. Finally when it came as to who should get the Viceroy's long ceremonial post horn, and when another argument between the two contenders ensued, Commander Howes solved it instantly. Since it was the only one of its kind, Lt Commander Howes without much ado simply walked away with it as his prized memento.

And while other movable assets in that month of July were being divided inside the Viceroy's palace in New Delhi, Imran Hussein's first birthday on 29th July was being celebrated in style in the old Rehman Haveli at Peshawar. That evening while Shenaz was dressing up her little son in a white traditional Pathani dress that was made of pure Dhaka silk, her brother Arif Rehman on noticing the big birth mark on his nephew's buttocks which was in the shape of a minature rugby ball he quickly nicknamed him the rugger boy.

'Yes I hope my rugger boy will be as rugged and brave like your Afridi ancestors,' said Nawaz Hussein the little boy's proud father as he clicked a photograph of Imran in his Uncle's arm.

It was from 1st August, 1947 that the Punjab Boundary Force with its compliment of eleven mixed infantry battalions comprising of Hindus, Sikhs and Muslims with other mixed subunits of supporting arms and services started functioning from its headquarters at Lahore. And with only another 15 days left for the partition of the country, it was a back breaking, burdensome and a thankless job. With Brigadier Mohammed Ayub Khan and Brigadier Nasir Ahmed as advisers from the Pakistan side and Brigadier Digambar Brar and Brigadier Thimmaya representing India, the strength of the 50,000 troops was still grossly inadequate for the gigantic and sensitive task that was to be undertaken by them.They were there to protect the lives and property of those who were soon to loose their homes and hearths. But despite all the handicaps, the men in military uniform did it to the best of their ability irrespective of the fact whether they were Hindus, Muslim or Sikhs. They were the gallant Indian soldiers of an already half divided Army but they were still in the uniform of the regiment and the unit that they cherished and loved, and to them the uniform was the only religion they knew.

While the Punjab Boundary Force was diligently and dutifully carrying out their painful tasks of saving human lives and property, Maharaja Hari Singh of Kashmir was celebrating the reunion of the Gilgit Agency to his state. A day earlier on the 31st of July, the lease of the area to the British had been officially terminated and the Union Jack that flew from the Agency bungalow that evening had been lowered for the last and final time. But the lowering of the Union Jack and the appointment of Brigadier Ghansara Singh from the Maharaja's State Forces as the new Governor of Gilgit was not taken very well by the handful of British middle rung officers who till that date had been commanding the Gilgit Scouts and were an authority by themselves. To maintain their hold over the strategic area, they had already started conspiring and plotting to join the yet to be born nation of Pakistan.

Meanwhile in Delhi before the all important lunch that was being hosted by the Viceroy on that day for the leading rulers of the Princely States to determine their willingness to join India or Pakistan, the retinue of the Viceroy's ADC's and staff were getting ready to chalk out the teams of the Ayes and the Nays. The Ayes were those who were willing to join either of the two dominions while the Nays were those who either wanted to retain their own independence or were yet to make up their minds and were inclined to execute a standstill agreement to gain more time. Amongst the few nays who were yet to decide their own fate was Maharaja Hari Singh's state of Jammu and Kashmir However, to get over this anomaly it had been decided earlier at the conference of all the rulers that the Government would enter into a standstill agreement with only those rulers who were prepared to execute the Instrument of Accession in principle at a later date.

To add a little more colour and humour to the proceedings, and while the two teams of the Ayes on the right and the Nays on the left were being formed, the Maharaja of Patiala and the Maharaja of Bikaner with all seriousness written on their faces first walked over to the Nay's lobby which was much to the surprise of the Viceroy and his staff, and then came back laughing to the Ayes. Despite knowing fully well that the princely era as rulersof their prosperous princely states were slowly ebbing away from them, they still maintained a very dignified royal touch to the proceedings. But when it came to actually signing on the dotted line, some of the rulers from the bigger Princely States were so emotionally charged up that they literally wept, while others took it quite sportingly and some even showed arrogance. But some like the Maharaja of Kashmir and the Nizam of Hyderabad were reluctant to do so. They wanted to remain their own masters. The two big states of Jodhpur and Jaisalmer with its large population of Hindus had even contemplated the idea of joining Pakistan since Mr Jinnah had promised both the rulers with a carte blanche of getting whatever they wanted in return. But at the last moment and with some pressure being brought upon them by the Viceroy and his staff, it seemed that better sense had prevailed on the duo.

On that very day of 1st August, to rejoice over the return of Gilgit to the State, the Mahraja had ordered all public buildings and the palaces to be lavishly lit and while the preparations were on, there arrived on the scene at Srinagar the ageing Mahatma Gandhi.Pandit Nehru initially wanted to come, but the Mahraja had opposed it and his Prime Minister Mr Ram Chander Kak was deadly against it too. When instead of Nehru, the Mahatma's name was proposed by the Viceroy and was accepted by the Maharaja, an angry Nehru wrote to his mentor.

'I have seen the letter of the Viceroy. I am sick of hearing what Kak thinks or feels. For many months this decision of yours or mine to visit Kashmir has been hanging fire. I am fed up. This is not my way of doing things. If I had to choose becoming PM of India and staying among the people of Kashmir, I would go for the latter.' Having been rebuked by the ruler of the State to which he and his ancestors once belonged, Pandit Nehru was naturally very upset.

It was 5 PM on that evening of 1st August, when Mahraja Hari Singh with his wife Tara Devi and their only son Karan Singh met the old sage under a big chinar tree in the front lawn of their majestic Gulab Bhavan Palace in Srinagar. As the Maharani approached with a glass of milk held daintily on a plate of gold in her slender hands, Major Daler Singh Bajwa standing with his wife and six year old son Montek Singh Bajwa bowed in reverence and did a namaste to the man whom some now considered to be God. When the Maharani very humbly offered the glass of milk and said.

'Mahatmaji when a great seer graces our land it is our custom to offer him a glass of milk.' the Mahatma with a very sad face that seemed to be full of pity simply looked at her first and then at the Maharaja and said very candidly.

'I cannot accept the offer of milk from a Maharaja whose subjects are distressed. I regret to say that your subjects are unhappy and this is not a good sign at all. I therefore cannot accept the milk and will have to refuse all meal invitations in the Palace.'

Hearing those words, both the Maharaja and the Maharani were stunned. Daler Singh too was shocked and felt ashamed with the rebuff that was given so bluntly by the saintly man to His Highness. Later that evening at a prayer meeting after Akbar Jahan, the devoted wife of Sheikh Abdulla who was still serving his sentence in prison recited a few verses from the Holy Quran, the Mahatma while addressing the people said in no uncertain terms that only the people of Kashmir and the State have the right to decide about their own future and nobody else.

With only a fortnight to go for India and Pakistan to get their freedom, the Maharaja was still dilly dallying and remained undecided. His vacillation and indecisiveness would now not only cost him his kingdom, but it would also soon bring to his own people and that of the people of India and Pakistan untold misery, a deep wound that would never heal, and a curse that would spell disaster for both the nations. The Maharaja it seems was still hoping and dreaming to keep his beautiful Kashmir to himself.

On 11th August, while the Maharaja's Prime Minister was sitting in his office, a sealed letter from the Maharaja arrived dismissing him from the post. It was believed that Kak had been secretly conniving with the Muslim League leaders and with those in the State who had been advocating that the State should join Pakistan. A few days earlier a special emissary from Mr

Jinnah had arrived to persuade the Maharaja to accede to Pakistan with the proviso that he the Maharaja could in return get whatever he desired both protocol and status wise. But the emissary went back dejected and empty handed and this was despite Mr Kak's assurance to Mr Liaquat Ali Khan, the Prime Minister designate that Kashmir was all for Pakistan. When Mr Kak tried to flee he was arrested and thrown into prison. Insulted by the rebuff from the Maharaja, Mr Jinnah was now all set to work out a plan to get Kashmir under his own fold by hook or by crook.

And while the Maharaja kept dilly dallying, at dawn on 1st August, Lt General Francis Tuker the Eastern Army Commander on the orders of the GHQ also took over the new districts of Delhi and East Punjab under his command and Gdispatched 161 Infantry Bde to augment the Punjab Boundary Force which was now two and a half Divisions strong and under the command of Major General Rees. But that was still not strong enough to prevent the mayhem and anarchy that had already started with full fury.

Since early August, ever since Pakistan Army Headquarters started functioning from Rawalpindi there was a tremendous demand by them for maps of Jammu and Kashmir from the office of the Surveyor General of India in Dehra Dun, but nobody took any serious notice of it. By now a large number of Pakistani Service Officers in the rank of Colonels and Brigadiers, which was the senior most rank in the hierarchy had become regular visitors to Mr Jinnah's Aurangzeb Road residence in Delhi. On the 3rd of August, Lt Col Shaheed Hamid and his charming wife Tahira hosted a farewell party for Mr Jinnah at their bungalow on 12, Willingdon Crescent. It was a gathering of all the military bigwigs including the three C-in-Cs from the army, navy and the airforce, and other senior officers both Hindus and Muslims who would soon bid goodbye to one another. Lt Colonel Ismail Sikandar Khan was also one of the distinguished invitees that evening.

On being formally introduced to the chief guest, Ismail was very impressed by the now ageing Mr Jinnah, who though he looked emaciated, was in pretty good form as he mingled freely with all the guests. When Mr Jinnah was told that Lt Col Ismail was a Kashmiri and that had he opted to join the Indian Army, Jinnah wittingly commented.

'Well I only hope it is you and only you who has opted to join the Indian army and not the rest of the Maharaja's State Forces, or else their could be trouble since Kashmir with its large Muslim majority and with its ethnic, cultural, religious and geographical location logically should be part of Pakistan. Don't you think so Colonel?'The question being a highly sensitive one, Ismail very diplomatically said.

'Yes of course, but provided the majority of the Muslims in the State also feel the same way as you do Sir.' And when Colonel Ismail further added by saying that after all Kashmir is still a princely state and it may well nigh be possible that Sheikh Abdulla who is still languishing in prison with the support of his National Conference and who still has big hold on the Muslims of the valley may opt for India, there was now a scowl on Mr Jinnah's face as he closed the topic by helping himself to another large scotch and soda.

The 6th of August, 1947 was a day of final farewell to the Muslim Officers by their Indian counterparts and the venue was none other than the Imperial Delhi Gymkhana Club. For many of them Hindus, Muslims, Sikhs and others it was an evening of nostalgia, brotherhood and promises. When it was time to say au revoir to those brother officers who had opted to join the Pakistan army, Brigadier KM Cariappa, the senior most Indian officer in his speech said.

'Comrade in arms, during all our life in the various services we have lived together, played together and fought together in the various battle fields and in which our magnificent armed forces fought with the highest degree of fellowship and comradeship. Now may this spirit continue even after we are separated?'

As he concluded his address and presented to Brigadier Raza, the senior most officer from the Pakistan Army the beautiful silver trophy of a Hindu and a Muslim soldier standing side by side armed with their rifles, everyone felt that this truly was the best representation of communal harmony that had withstood from time immemorial the vagaries of political interference and the policy of divide and rule of the British Raj. For Brigadier Raza and his Muslim officers it would always be an evening to remember as they reached out for each others arms and to the massed bands of the pipers and the drummers playing the old Scottish dirge 'Auld Lang Syne" they swayed and danced for the last and final time. The party finally ended with the last toast for the Pakistan army and to the loud boisterous singing by the Indian officers of the all time favourite 'They are all jolly good fellows.'

That camaraderie and gaeity would however be rather short lived because that evening none of them knew that a few months hence they would be doing the dance of death in the beautiful valley of Kashmir. Strangely some of them that evening also sang in chorus the patriotic song," Sare Jahan Se Accha, Hindustan Hamara". (In the whole wide world, our Hindustan is the best). It was a song that was written by the great poet Mohammed Iqbal who himself was a Muslim.

The very next day, on the 7th of August, the man who loved his Saville Row suits had got into a knee length silk Sherwani coat and tight fitting churidar pyjamas that amply highlighted his thin and bamboo shaped legs. And as he waited to get into the special Dakota aircraft that would take him to the land of his dreams, he never realized that the country of the pure as visualized by him as a secular nationa would soon become a nation of diehard self seeking Muslim politicians, power hungry army Generals and diehard Muslim fanatics. The founder of Pakistan whose outward appearance was one of steel was clinically a very sick man. According to his faithful physician and doctor, the feeble man for the past three years had been living only on his will power, hope, Scotch whisky, his favourite Craven A cigarettes and his imported Cuban cigars.In June 1946, the two X-rays of his affected lungs had clearly indicated to Dr Patel that Mr Jinnah was suffering from the dreaded deasease of tuberclosis and that the end for him was not very far. But Mr Jinnah was not a man to give up anything without a fight. He was not prepared to park himself in a sanatorium as advised by his experienced doctor while leaving his dream and desire to create a new nation unfulfilled. Fearing that the Hindus and even the Muslims who had for ages together settled in the heart of India with the help of the Congress could change the political equation of the subcontinent, Mr Jinnah very wisely swore his Doctor into secrecy and forbade him to ever disclose the enormity of his own suffering. Since the Viceroy had decided that speed and only speed could save India from more bloodshed and devastation, Mr Jinnah also realized that the tempo of his task to create his own Pakistan had now to be further accelerated and for that every sacrifice was worth the effort. It now mattered little to him as to how many died or lived for that great cause. Escorted by Lieutenant Ahsan his young and handsome naval ADC and with his faithful sister Fatima by his side, as Mr Jinnah walked up the steps of the DC-3 for his historic flight to Karachi, he stopped for a brief moment to have one last look at Delhi from where he had led his Muslim League to victory.

As the aircraft approached the Mauripur airfield at Karachi, Mr Jinnah seemed to be a happy man as he looked out of the port hole to identify the many landmarks of the city where he had spent his childhood and from where he would now rule his newly crafted nation of Pakistan. When he saw the vast crowds with flags and banners that had congregated at the airport to receive him, he was overwhelmed with emotion. When the aircraft taxied to a halt he confided to his sister and to his young ADC that personally he had never expected to see Pakistan in his own lifetime and they should therefore all be thankful to Allah.

As soon as the ramp was placed and the door of the aircraft was opened for the first Governor General of Pakistan to alight, a virtual stampede followed, as the unruly mob shouting 'Jinnah Zindabad", Qaid-e-Azam Zindabad" and "Pakistan Zindabad broke the police and security cordon and rushed towards the aircraft.

For a man who believed in strict discipline this was tantamount to gross indiscipline and hooliganism and he showed his displeasure in no uncertain manner when he like a school master waved his walking stick at the crowd and refused to deplane till such time the crowd was not brought under total control. From that very moment when he set foot in Pakistan, Jinnah knew that ruling a country that was of his own making would not be a cakewalk at all. In fact it would be a challenge that despite his poor health he would have to face upto and all he now desired was a few more years of good health so that he could guide the new nation on the road to prosperity and greatness that he had always been dreaming of. A few days later on his being elected formally, Mr Jinnah in his first Presidential address to the Pakistan Constitutional Assembly and to his people told them that he only wanted a secular Pakistan and added that the first duty of every citizen of this new land would be to maintain law and order so that life, property and religious beliefs of all its subjects are well protected. He reiterated to all the people of Pakistan irrespective of their caste, creed or religion his great faith and hope when he said.

'You are free; you are free to go to your temples, you are free to go your mosques or any other place of worship in this State of Pakistan. You may belong to any religion or caste or creed, but that has nothing to do with the business of the State. We are starting in the days when there is no discrimination between one caste or creed or another. We are starting with the fundamental principles that we are all citizens and equal citizens of one State. My governing principle will be justice and complete impartiality and I am sure that with your support and cooperation, I can look forward to Pakistan becoming one of the greatest nations of the world.'

While Mr Jinnah was galvanizing and gearing the citizens of his new country towards a better and prosperous Pakistan, the greatest migration of Muslims from the provinces and districts of Bengal, Bihar, Assam and the United Provinces in India where the Muslims were in minority had already begun. Most of them having lost their homes and for a better future were now migrating either to East Bengal, or to East Punjab, Sind, Baluchistan and to the North West Frontier the geographical configuration that would now constitute their own Pakistan. All these people would now be given a new identity and most of them henceforth would be simply known as 'Mohajirs', meaning immigrants from India. As the migration of the 'Mohajirs' started gaining momentum, inside the old Moghul City of Lahore, which was the centre of trade and a perfect blend of both Hindu and Muslim culture and unity, a bearded Sikh, a small time school master who by now had attained political respectability amongst the Sikhs for opposing the partition of the country, and who was popularly known by the name of Master Tara Singh had already got into his act. Known as the Paris of the East with its many bars, restaurants, clubs, cinema halls and whore houses, Lahore would soon become a killing ground for the many innocent men, women and children of all communities who had no idea what the partition had in store for them. Population wise the numbers of Hindus, Muslims and Sikhs within the city were evenly matched and one wrong move by either side could only lead to disaster. And that disaster was triggered off in early March, when one of the Sikh leaders challenged the Muslims when he tore down a Muslim League flag and thereafter all hell broke loose as the Muslim community with vengeance came down very heavily on the Sikhs. For John Bannet the Inspector General of Police, Punjab and his limited mixed police force the stage was now set for revenge by the Sikhs. At a secret meeting in Lahore, which was presided over by the small time school master who had lost many of his own kith and kin in the communal violence, Tara Singh aided and abetted by the RSS, the Rashtriya Sevak Sangh, the militant arm of the fanatical Hindus in the city and in the Punjab, were now ready to settle scores with the Muslims. It would be a mission of seek and destroy the special trains that had been earmarked for the carriage of the Muslim refugees from India into Pakistan.

On the night of 11th and 12th August, 1947 near the small village of Giddharba in the Ferozepur district of the Province, Tara Singh's men derailed a heavily packed special train by using explosives and then slaughtered the Muslims who were travelling in it. With that act, the communal war in the Punjab would now reach its peak and one that would be impossible to control.

As the deadline of 15th August neared, the astrologers fearing that the date was simply inauspicious for India to get her freedom had now reluctantly agreed for the midnight of the 14th and the 15th for the bells to ring and for the conch shells to herald the new era. Pakistan however chose the 14th as their day of reckoning.

For Major General TW Rees who had taken over command of the 4th Indian Division from General CH Boucher in December 1945, and who was now the Punjab Boundary Force Commander, for him and his trustworthy disciplined force of Hindus, Muslims and Sikh soldiers every minute, every hour was an ordeal as they without taking sides escorted the long line of refugee columns and tried to safeguard whatever little household stuff that they and their families were able to carry with them.

The soldiers whether they were Hindus, Muslims or Sikhs were the sole restraining influence, but they could not be everywhere. While dealing with violent mobs, marauding armed bands and religious fanatics from both sides, they showed remarkable fortitude, discipline, and loyalty while acting with commendable impartiality. Though no conflict so far was reported between the non Muslims and Muslim troops from the mixed units and regiments, but as the news of horror killings, loot and rape of their own community people, including their near relations and friends started trickling in from various parts of the country, it started affecting them psychologically. But even despite that, they never lost their cool and carried out their tasks in the most honourable manner. Lot of credit for this could be attributed to the young and aspiring Hindu, Sikh and Muslim Officers under whose command these troops functioned. Whatever be their community, they did their duty most gallantly. They showed to the people and to the world what an Indian soldier's discipline and faith was all about. Officers like Major Baktiar Rana of the 2/18 Garhwal Rifles who had opted for Pakistan and many others like him ensured day in and day out that the long refugee caravans from either side and within their area of their own jurisdiction moved harmlessly and safely to their final destination.

It was during this period that Lt Col Ismail Sikandar Khan who was now on the staff of the 4th Indian Division in order to see the ground reality visited the 3/1st Punjabees who were deployed for refugee escort duties in strife torn Punjab. The Third First Punjabees was part of the gallant 1st Punjab Regiment that had been allotted to Pakistan and whose Colonel of the Regiment was none other than Field Marshal Auk, the Supreme Commander himself.

One day Ismail accompanied a young Muslim officer who with his company of Muslim troops had been tasked to escort a road convoy of over 5000 refugees of Hindus and Sikhs between Arifwalla and Pak Pattan. As they neared a railway embankment, the young Muslim officer noticed some 30 fully armed Muslims waiting to pounce on the hapless refugees. Throwing caution to the wind, the Muslim officer came out of his vehicle and warned them of severe consequences if they did not clear the road immediately. But despite the warning, when they fired and killed an unarmed and innocent Hindu, the young Muslim officer without wavering ordered his own Muslim troops to open fire with their automatics. Soon seven of them from the Muslim gang lay dead and another eight were severely wounded while the others fled. When an elderly Sikh and a middle aged Hindu gentleman came forward and hugged the young Muslim officer and all the others in that wretched column of refugees also thanked the Muslim troops for saving their lives, Ismail wondered why the Hindus and the Muslims cannot remain as friends for ever.

'May the Wahe Guru bless you, your men and their families son,' said another elderly Sikh lady to the young Muslim as she took out the tin full of ladoos that she had prepared for the journey for her big family and gave it all to them.

On that day Ismail Sikandar Khan recalled what the out going Viceroy Wavell before leaving the shores of India had remarked. That day he had said in all seriousness that the suitability of the gallant Indian Army may perhaps be the deciding factor for the future of India. It was an example for all. For only they have proved as to how all communities in uniform can work and live together to meet a common danger with courage, compassion, comradeship and fortitude.Ismail felt indeed very proud of the young Muslim officer's sense of duty and purpose, but his heart went out to all those unfortunate people from both sides of the border and especially to those who had to fend for themselves in getting across safely and in one peice to their new promised land.

And while India was still in the throes of partition, the hit Hindi film "Kismet" meaning "Luck" starring the debonair Ashok Kumar was still running to packed houses in all the cinema halls in the yet to be divided India. From the chaiwallas and panwallas to the sophisticated zamindars and feudal lords and from the clerks to the soldiers and the Indian elite everyone ironically were either singing or humming the tune. 'Door hato ye duniya walon hindustam hamara hai" or "Aana meri jaan meri jaan Sunday ke Sunday" from the film "Shenai" that had only been released in that very year to the music of Chitalkar Ramchander.

But despite the popularity of those two songs, the elders still missed their dear old Kundan Lal Saigal who unfortunately had died a few months earlier at an young age and before he could see India free. The bottle and the hot pickle that he loved had got the better of him, but he was fortunate not to witness the horrors of the partition.For the people of the subcontinent and irrespective of their caste, creed or religion Hindi film music was the corner stone of communal harmony, patriotism, love and unity. It was like a silent soothing balm that could transform even a devil into a good human being. Luckily with all the leading composers, lyricists, and music directors and irrespective of whether he was a Hindu, Muslim or a Sikh holding on to each other's hand to maintain communal harmony, they did manage at times to bring some sense of sanity to some of those who had temporarily become insane and were responsible for the rape, killing devastation and destruction that the partition of the country was now witnessing.

It was around this traumatic period that a frail young girl in a sari and in an old pair of old Kolhapuri chappals on her tiny feet, with her oily hair in two pleats walked into a recording studio in Bombay to give her first audition in Hindi of a song in a film that was aptly titled 'Aap ki Seva Mein,' and which when translated into English literally meant ' At your Service.'It seemed that the young girl with a golden voice had been ordained to serve and soothe the nerves of those who unfortunately were either witness to, or had the harrowing experience of having gone through the pangs of partition from both sides of the border. Her heart rendering melodies would soon provide the much-needed healing touch to the millions who had lost both their homes and their hearths. The young Maharashtrian girl having arrived at tinsel town together with the director Vasant Joglekar, the composer and the musicians of the film 'Aap Ki Seva Mein.' heard with awe and disbelief on that day the first ever recording of her own melodious voice as a playback singer. After she had sung her first song 'Paa Lagu Kar Jori Re' there was a big smile on her innocent face.

The young and shy girl however did not know that she was soon destined to create history. Lata Mangeshkar, who was born at Indore on 28th September 1929, had finally arrived. The eldest child of a Gujrathi mother and a Maharashtrian father who was a stage actor and a singer, Dinanath Mangeshkar had imbibed in her right from her childhood the knowledge of music. The couple had given to India and the world a rare gift that could never ever be replaced. It was the gift of a voice that for decades together would remain a symbol of communal harmony and national integration. Unfortunately her father did not live for very long to hear her golden voice and those of his many other children, who were all very very talented in the realm of music.

Strangely it was also around this time of mid August 1947, that the saintly old man realized that his own tryst with destiny was finally over and he therefore decided to leave Delhi and once again go on his pilgrimage of prayer and peace to Bengal and to Calcutta where only a year ago the people from that region had witnessed the worst ever killings, rape, massacre and plunder in the history of the Great British Empire. The man who returned to India some three decades ago with Christ's teaching of turning the other cheek to his white aggressors, and who had declared that to be right was more honourable than simply to be law abiding was now in a no win situation. He was now aware that nothing would now stop his beloved India to be sliced into two. The great soul who was always dressed in the attire of a drifter was now drifting away from the mainstream of national politics. The very man who always dreamt of an United India and who was even prepared to place all the Hindus under Mr Jinnah's rule as free India's first Prime Minister was now horrified about the country's future.

After the deal for the partition of the country was accepted by the Congress, the 77 year old "Bapu" had become a shattered man, and no amount of coaxing by his own disciple Pandit Nehru and other Congress leaders would make him change his mind to remain in Delhi and witness the celebrations for the birth of a new India. Speaking to those who had come to see him off at the railway station the Mahatma said.

'But what is there to celebrate. This is the vivisection of our own Mother and we should be mourning and praying and not giving proud speeches, singing songs and exploding fire works.'

While he now indirectly blamed the Congress and the Muslim League for the death of Mother India, Gandhi knew that he had failed to save India from her sad fate. He now also realized that his own vision had been clouded by the decision that he had taken to lead India to her freedom nonviolently had now become a total myth. India was now fully primed to erupt and explode in a most violent manner not against her British masters, but against one another. It was now going to be a battle royale between the Hindus and Sikhs on one side and the Muslims on the other.

On the eve of independence as the savage Hindu-Muslim riots spread like wild fire from the North West Frontier to the Punjab in the West and to Bengal, Bihar, United Provinces and Assam in the East, the Father of the Nation to be, fell into his darkest despair. On the train to Calcutta while 'Bapu' sat in his third class compartment lamenting on the tragic fate of India, at Karachi, the man who only 11 years ago in 1936 had revived the moribund Muslim League by giving it the religious spark that had ignited and united the Muslims of the subcontinent so that they could find their own independent identity was in a jubilant mood as he wore the triple crown on his head. Mr Mohammed Ali Jinnah the architect of the new nation was not only its Governor General, but he was also the President of Pakistan's only political party, the Muslim League and the President of the Pakistan Constituent Assembly, the country's sole law making body. But Mr Jinnah's wearing of the Triple Crown was not without its usual quota of thorns and risks. A few weeks earlier Mr Gerald Savage a very capable police officer from the Punjab Criminal Investigation Department had uncovered a secret plot to assassinate the very man who was now being referred to and revered as the father of Pakistan. Mr Savage with his experience together with his intelligence sleuths had successfully penetrated onto the labyrinths of communal intrigue and violence in the state. According to his reliable informer, the assassination of the Quaid-e-Azam would take place on the streets of Karachi and it would be executed by a group of Hindu fanatics on the 14th of August. They with their weapons would pose as spectators, while Mr Jinnah in an open car would be triumphantly returning to the Government house after his formal inauguration as Pakistan's first Governor General.

On the 13th of August, as the Viceroy's York aircraft approached Karachi for the touch down, both MB and his wife Edwina were delighted to see the huge crowds on the streets with small green flags in their hands waiting to greet them. From practically every building in the city fluttered the flag of the new nation in all its glory and spendour. In another couple of hours and on the dawn of the 14th a new nation in the big continent of Asia would be born. As the Viceroy with his wife came down the ramp, the ceremonial military band played "God save the King" for the last and final time to welcome and to say farewell to the last representative of the British Raj. Thereafter as the roar of 'Pakistan Paindabad' and 'Pakistan Zindabad' by the massive crowd echoed in the distance, and the formal handshakes and introduction had been completed, Lt Colonel Burney the Military Secretary to Mr Jinnah whispered to the Viceroy the news about the sinister plot that had been uncovered. The Colonel also stated that the information was from a very reliable source, but regretted that the police had not been able to round up the suspects who were expected to be eight in number.

'Well we shall see to that when it comes, and I only hope that it will not be a replay of the assassination that took place some 33 years ago at Sajaveo. A killing that sparked off the First World War and if this happens here in Karachi it would lead to a civil war of even greater proportions,'added the Viceroy as he confidently with his wife got into the car for their journey to the Governor General's House.

On arrival, a warm-hearted Mr Jinnah having welcomed his guest of honour suggested a slight deviation to the original plan. Realizing that the Viceroy's life was also in real danger he therefore said very honestly and courageously.

'Your Excellency since the threat posed to both our lives cannot be discounted, may I with all due regard to you as a soldier and statesman suggest that after the inauguration ceremony is over tomorrow, you and your charming wife should drive back to the Government house by a different route that has been proposed by my staff. Although I believe that Mr Gerald Savage in his briefing to you has strongly recommended that in order to avoid the possible catastrophe, the entire procession should be cancelled, but I am totally against it. You will agree that if we as a nation right from day one get cowed down by such threats, then we do not qualify to call ourselves as citizens of a self respecting country.'

It seemed that Mr Jinnah was prepared to die a martyrs death if need be and that to at the hands of Hindu fanatics because his death would then vindicate his stand that the Muslims of India needed a country of their own. And if India had remained united, the Hindu majority would never let the minority Muslims ever live in peace and that was his firm belief and perception.

'Well then that's it and I am with you. Both of us will therefore travel together, and the ladies could follow in another car while keeping a fairly good safety distance and I very much doubt if those so called Hindu fanatics will have the guts to fulfill their evil design,' said the Viceroy.

'That is indeed very kind and chivalrous of you your Excellency and I am sure my brother and I would hate to miss out on the festivities on this joyous and historic occasion,' said Fatima Jinnah as Edwina opted to be next to her husband in his hour of peril. But her handsome husband simply vetoed the idea.

'No honey you and Miss Jinnah will follow behind in the Packard car with one of the handsome ADC's to keep you all company,' said the smiling Viceroy as he helped himself with a biscuit to go with the tea.

At 0900 hours next morning, Mr Jinnah with the Viceroy by his side got into the black Rolls Royce convertible for their journey to the assembly hall to witness the birth of the new nation. While the open car with its motor cycle outriders of the military police in their ceremonial uniforms as escorts drove through the streets of Karachi, the sleuths from Mr Gerald's outfit, some in the guise of beggars, while others as hawkers, faith healers, fortune tellers and some as normal spectators lined the route that the returning cavalcade was scheduled to follow. Some of them posing as press people and photographers had taken vantage positions on trees, roof tops and balconies along the likely choke points. They could not afford a disaster of such magnitude to take place, because if it did happen there would be hell to pay. It would trigger off a holocaust and the worst sufferers would be none other than the large Hindu and Sikh population who were still inside Pakistan and conversely the Muslims within India.

After the formalities for the swearing in ceremony were over and as the two of them got back into the open Rolls Royce for their triumphant return journey through the streets of the country's new capital, the 31 gun viceregal salute was fired for the last and final time from the soil of Pakistan. As the cavalcade of cars moved in a slow procession through the crowded streets of Karachi to the tumultuous cries of joy and exultation by its people, the plainclothesmen keeping the eternal vigil had their fingers crossed. Every minute and every second was like a time bomb that could blow up any moment. As the cavalcade slowly made its way through Elphinstone Street which was Karachi's main and crowded market place and a hub of all the Hindu traders and shopkeepers of the city, the men from the CID department now doubled their vigilance and prayed that nothing untoward should happen to mar the festivities of that historic day. As the shouts and cries of 'Pakistan Zindabad', 'Jinnah Zindabad 'and 'Mountbatten Zindabad' echoed through the lanes and bye lanes, Gerald savage kept his fingers crossed as he and his men with powerful binoculars from rooftops kept the route under total surveillance. But it seems that the plotters at the last minute had lost courage to attack the cavalcade. They had planned to attack it with a barrage of hand grenades and home made bombs that they had with them, and it was probably seeing the presence of the Englishman the Governor General designate of India seated next to the man whom they wanted to eliminate, the leader of the heinous plot at the last moment developed cold feet. Thus after that agonizing journey, when the Rolls Royce entered safely through the gates of the Government house, a smiling and delighted Mr Jinnah told the Viceroy.'Thank God I brought you back alive.'

While the Viceroy with the Vicerene having breathed a sigh of relief for still being alive boarded the York for their return flight to Delhi, the handsome British Lieutenant Colonel from the 6th Lancers who had been selected personally by Mr Liaquat Ali Khan the Prime Minister of Pakistan to command the proposed Pakistan Military Academy with his two Australian terriers on the back seat of his blue Vauxhall car and a revolver by his side and the baggage in the dicky was on his way from Delhi to

Rawalpindi via Jullunder and Amritsar. Looking smart and elegant in his uniform and with the black cavalry beret stylishly perched on his head, Lt Col Francis Ingall who was one of the three General Staff Offficers Grade 1 from the prestigious Military Operations department of the Indian Army looked helplessly at the stream of refugees along the Grant Trunk Road as he kept honking his way through the never ending crowd. He was on his way to take up his new appointment as the Commandant designate of the PMA, the Pakistan Military Academy and that too on promotion to the rank of a Brigadier.

Synopsis

"NOTHING BUT!" is a saga of the 20th Century history of India and the Indian Subcontinent in particular and the world in general covering the period 1890-2002 It is a story of eight Indian families and one British family and their five generations. Though they were from different religions they were all once very close friends and comrades and how circumstances beyond their control separated them and some even became each other's sworn enemy

The complete book is in 6 parts and its main focus is on the disputed Indian Territory of Jammu and Kashmir—a volatile region that has been in the eye of the storm ever since the Great Game began in the late 19th century and remains the main bone of contention between India and Pakistan ever since the two countries became independent in 1947.

Book-1—'The Awakening' covers the period 1890-1919 and tells the story of the advent and rise of Indian nationalism through the eyes of these fictional characters and how the Great Game was played and how and the Great War (1914-1918) effected the lives of these people.

Book-2—'The Long Road to Freedom' covers the period 1920-1947 and tells the story about the sacrifices made to attain freedom and how partition came about.

Book-3—'What Price Freedom' covers the period 1947-1971 and tells the story of the horrors of partition and the 3 major wars that took place between India and Pakistan and which also gave birth to a new nation called Bangladesh.

Book-4—'Love has no Religion' covers the period 1971-1984. It is a tragic love story of two couples from the fourth generation with different religious and cultural backgrounds and how it affected their lives and those of their countrymen.

Book-5—'All is Fair In Love and War' covers the period 1984-1994 and tells us about the rise of communal, religious and regional politics in the subcontinent and corruption in politics together with the rise of fanatical religious organizations throughout the world in general and the subcontinent in particular.

Book-6—'Farewell My Love' covers the period 1994-2002 tells the story of the people from the 4th and 5th generation of these families and how the rise of militancy, terrorism and selfish coalition politics affected their lives and those of the people on the streets.